W9-BZA-729

THE ENCYCLOPEDIA OF
REALITY TELEVISION

THE ULTIMATE GUIDE *TO* OVER TWENTY YEARS *OF* REALITY TV *FROM* *THE REAL WORLD* *TO* *DANCING WITH THE STARS*

POCKET BOOKS

New York   London   Toronto   Sydney

Pocket Books
A Division of Simon & Schuster, Inc.
1230 Avenue of the Americas
New York, NY 10020

Original edition copyright © 2005 by Fox Reality Channel, Inc.
Revised edition: Fox Reality Channel™ and © 2008 by Twentieth Century Fox Film Corporation.
All rights reserved.

All rights reserved, including the right to reproduce this book or portions thereof in any form whatsoever.
For information address Pocket Books Subsidiary Rights Department, 1230 Avenue of the Americas, New York, NY 10020

First Pocket Books trade paperback edition September 2008

POCKET and colophon are registered trademarks of Simon & Schuster, Inc.

For information about special discounts for bulk purchases,
please contact Simon & Schuster Special Sales at
1-800-456-6798 or business@simonandschuster.com

Designed by Ruth Lee-Mui

Manufactured in the United States of America

1   3   5   7   9   10   8   6   4   2

Library of Congress Cataloging-in-Publication Data is available.

ISBN-13: 978-1-4165-7055-4
ISBN-10:   1-4165-7055-1

A previous edition of this work was published as *Fox Reality Presents the Encyclopedia of Reality Television* in 2005.

CONTENTS

An Introduction to Reality 1

Foreword 5

REALITY SHOWS 9

The Ultimate Reality TV Quiz 809

The Reality Catchphrase Quiz 815

Answers 816

Top Ten Network Primetime Reality Shows, by Season 818

Emmy Awards for Achievements in Reality, 2001–2007 821

The Reality Time Line 825

AN INTRODUCTION TO REALITY

The staff of Fox Reality Channel proudly presents the second edition of this labor of love, *The Encyclopedia of Reality Television*. With the enormous growth of this form of entertainment in the last few years, we felt it was long overdue to document what has become one of the most popular genres in television history. As the central source for reality television in the United States, we at Fox Reality Channel, which launched on May 24, 2005, feel we were best equipped to take on this enormous task.

What, exactly, is a "reality show"? We have had numerous meetings to try to define this ever-evolving part of the television landscape. The genre has grown so rapidly and broadly in the last decade that it has spawned many sub-classifications and nicknames, including "unscripted drama," "alternative television," "docusoap," "docu-game," "celeb-reality," "light entertainment," "factual television," "observational documentary" ("ob doc"), "emotainment," "infotainment," "lifestyle television," "nonfiction television," and "train wreck television." We've tried to be as inclusive as possible, counting as many shows as we could find that involved civilians (and occasionally celebrities in the course of their "real" lives) in "real" (though sometimes contrived and almost always edited) situations, theoretically reacting as they might if they weren't on TV. Many of these series cross genre lines and could also be labeled as game shows, dating shows, serialized dramas, variety shows, and quasi-documentaries.

The roots of reality television and its development, as well as the influences of the global reality marketplace, are covered in the foreword, written by Fox Reality Channel's president, David Lyle, who has created, produced, bought, and sold reality television all over the world for more than two decades.

For the purposes of this book, we were defining the "modern reality era" as beginning with the premiere of *Cops* in 1989. This is, of course, subject to extensive debate, but we felt that this particular series, more than any other, signified the broad acceptance of unscripted programs produced in a contemporary style on a broadcast network in prime time. At the time of this printing, *Cops* can still be seen worldwide on broadcast, cable, and satellite multiple times per day. We believe that this show and the formats it inspired have had a significant impact on the reality genre. Reality programs preceding *Cops* are discussed in the foreword.

We are particularly pleased to include some of our Fox Reality Channel originals in this edition, including *Solitary* and *Solitary 2.0, The Academy, My Bare Lady, Rob & Amber: Against the Odds, Corkscrewed: The Wrath of Grapes,* and *Camp Reality.* For the latest and greatest about all your favorite reality shows, and the entire world of reality TV, check out our website, www.FoxReality.com. And every fall, look for our raucous parade of reality superstars on the annual *Fox Reality Channel Really Awards,* which honors the highs and lows of the previous year in reality TV.

When we first decided to compile data on reality television, we quickly realized how overwhelming such a task would be. It has been quite a challenge to track down all the various pieces of information we wanted to include in this volume, and the book is far from complete. We have spent endless hours categorizing, researching, writing, and editing this collection of facts and figures tracing the history of reality series aired on national television, encompassing broadcast, cable/satellite, and syndication. We have included as much relevant information as we could, including broadcast dates, talent (celebrity and civilian), production credits, and a description of each series. For a few of the more prominent series, we also provide episode or season summaries. At the end of this book are a variety of lists and indexes, including talent, cast, and Emmy winners, as well as a time line of reality show premieres. And be sure to take our quiz on reality TV to see how much you know about the history of this ever-changing phenomenon.

Although we have endeavored in this book to be as thorough as possible, we have undoubtedly missed an occasional show or made a handful of errors. We apologize for these mistakes, and promise that in future editions we will correct them. Please let us hear from you with your comments and suggestions. Send your comments to encyclopedia@foxreality.com.

We'd like to thank the following people, for without their work and contributions this encyclopedia would not have been possible: Marc Berman, Tim Brooks, Jeremy Diller, Paul Goebel, Bob Henry, Shelley Herman, Joe Kaufmann, Albert Lawrence, Jennifer Lostrom, Earle Marsh, Hilary Schacter, Kyle Schmitz, and Aaron Solomon. We also acknowledge the tremendous support for this volume from our Fox Reality Channel marketing team, including Lorey Zlotnick and Charissa Chu. And last but far from least, we owe a debt of gratitude to the amazing Mandel Ilagan, whose tireless dedication to this project has already earned him permanent immunity from being voted off any reality island he ever visits.

Happy reading!

Bob Boden
Sr. VP, Programming, Production and Development
Fox Reality Channel

FOREWORD

Two years ago the first edition of this encyclopedia of reality television was compiled because at the new cable and satellite outlet Fox Reality Channel, we were trying to figure out which reality shows were out there. We all had our lists, but we realized we needed a master list that covered the lot—and what a lot there were.

Back then, Fox Reality Channel, which was devoted to 100 percent reality programming (all reality, all the time), had to argue with pundits that reality was *not* dead. *Desperate Housewives* and *Lost* had been big hits, so it was popular to say that drama was back and reality was a goner. Not so fast. In 2006 and 2007, reality TV thrived. And there are now more reality shows on more networks than in previous years.

It is not surprising that reality TV hasn't gone away. As I point out in the foreword to the first edition, reality TV (under different names) has been a staple of U.S. and foreign TV since the beginning. In fact, reality TV is as old as television itself. Its antecedents were panel, quiz, and game shows; documentaries; and variety shows. At the dawn of television, out leapt *Candid Camera* and *Truth or Consequences*. These programs were raw, immediate, popular, and cheap to produce. Reality television was on its way. American television pioneered the genre, creating early reality shows and then exporting them as *formats*—that is, recipes, or blueprints, that outline the making of shows so that foreign versions, following the recipe, can be made under license to the original show creator. *Who Wants to Be a Millionaire, Big Brother,* and *Survivor* are all fairly recent examples of foreign formats that were imported to the United States. In previous times, *That's Incredible, This Is Your Life, Queen for a Day,* and *The Price Is Right* were formats exported from the United States to the rest of the world.

As TV grew up in the sixties and seventies, the business models of television production became more sophisticated. Scripted programming such as dramas and sitcoms occupied the lion's share of the television schedule. Film and tape of scripted shows such as *Get Smart, M*A*S*H, Ben Casey,* and *Charlie's Angels* swept the world.

While the United States basked in its scripted television dominance, other parts of the world continued to devote a significant part of their TV schedules to local, unscripted entertainment. Often, because they couldn't compete with U.S. scripted production values, foreign television markets turned to unscripted entertainment as the most effective way to allow the public to see and hear on their television screens their own cultures and their own stars in their own languages. Because local shows tend to do better than imports, this meant that in markets outside the United States, some of the most successful programs tended to be local, unscripted entertainment.

Meanwhile, in the United States, the dormant unscripted entertainment of reality television had a few spurts of success in the eighties, with *Star Search* and, as a result of a television writers' strike, *Cops.* Of course there was MTV's *The Real World,* which debuted in 1992, is the model for so many of today's shows, and serves as a training ground for so many of today's producers.

In Europe during the nineties, technological advancement in mobile cameras and nonlinear editing resulted in a rash of large outdoor productions such as *Fort Boyard* (France), *Anika's Challenge* (UK), and *Treasure Hunt* (France); and at the same time, the documentary had morphed into docusoaps with *The Family* (UK), *An American Family* (USA), and *Sylvania Waters* (Australia). The trickle became a flood in the UK with more docusoaps such as *Jimmy's Driving School, The Cruise,* and *Airline.* Holland was punching above its weight with local shows such as *All You Need Is Love* and *Big Brother.* Belgium had *The Mole,* and in Scandinavia, *Expedition Robinson* (*Survivor*), *Villa Medusa,* and *The Bar* were all hits. Australia had an obsession with house makeover shows such as *Our House, Renovation Rescue* (a precursor to *Extreme Makeover: Home Edition*), and *Burke's Backyard.* It took a UK producer to blend house renovation with some game elements and come up with *Changing Rooms* (called *Trading Spaces* in the United States). Even New Zealand got into the act with *Popstars*, which was exported to Australia and the UK. Later, from the UK, *Pop Idol* (*American Idol*) followed.

The door to the modern era of reality television in the United States was kicked open by *Who Wants to Be a Millionaire*. True, it was more a traditional studio quiz show (a descendant of *The $64,000 Question*) than a reality show. Those differences could be argued for a long time. Regardless of the finer distinctions, *Millionaire* and the following modern reality shows had a number of things in common:

- they were not scripted dramas or sitcoms;
- their uniqueness allowed them to be promoted as events; and
- they featured "real people"—the *Millionaire* contestants seemed far more ordinary (and relatable) than the fictional detectives or even sitcom moms and dads in other prime-time shows.

As this encyclopedia will show, from these humble beginnings came a rush of reality programming. *Survivor* and *Big Brother* were cheaper to produce than prime-time dramas and more successful—it was a compelling combination. In just four years, television networks went from making excuses for their few reality aberrations to planning them as part of their strategy. The recent turnaround success for ABC was certainly due to *Desperate Housewives* and *Lost*, but also to *Dancing with the Stars*, *Extreme Makeover: Home Edition*, *Supernanny*, and *Wife Swap*.

While the modern era of reality television started in the United States with imported formats (partly because the buyers of alternative programming couldn't persuade their bosses to take risks on shows that hadn't worked elsewhere), the homegrown formats such as *The Bachelor*, *Temptation Island*, and *The Apprentice* were taking over and being exported. The one thing the U.S. market added to all its formats (imported or local) was incredible scale. The helicopter shots, the hundreds of cameras, and the stirring musical scores were very much a U.S. addition to reality television.

When unscripted entertainment was pushed out of the networks in the sixties, seventies, and eighties, some of its scattered descendants made their way to cable channels such as Food Network, HGTV, Discovery, TLC, and MTV. On the surface, it seemed that most of the modern reality action was happening at the networks, but in actuality the success of TLC's *Trading Spaces,* Bravo's *Queer Eye for the Straight Guy,* and MTV's *The Osbournes* showed that cost-efficient cable reality could transform the fortunes of cable channels struggling to be noticed overnight. The race for stand-out reality programming in cable has become a stampede in the last couple of years, and that is one of the exciting things about reality television. Amazing ideas with relatively short production periods can get on the air in weeks, not years. However, reality television changes very rapidly. In five years we've seen the vogue shift from outdoor competition to romance competition, to singing competition, to weekly bug eating, to business competition, to tricking contestants, to hidden cameras (with celebrities added to all of the above), to plastic surgery shows, to nice house makeovers, to nice family makeovers, to nice kid makeovers and then—who'd have guessed (even though the format had been a huge success in three markets before the United States)—to a dancing competition featuring stars. And get ready—as I write, all of the above might come around again but this time on ice!

Well, the ice age hasn't arrived, but Flavor Flav and his girls have. And even the History Channel got into the reality TV business with *Ice Road Truckers*. The discussion today is not "Is reality dead?" but "Where is reality going next?" No one knows. We at Fox Reality Channel *love* this type of TV because it is so often exciting and unpredictable, while at the same time, having familiar characters who never seem to change. If you want to predict where reality television is going, there is no better way than see where it has been: "Those who cannot learn from history are doomed to create their own formats."

So delve into this second edition of our labor of love and see how wonderful (and sometimes less than wonderful) the shows have been, and salute the inspired people, on both sides of the camera, who made them.

David Lyle
President
Fox Reality Channel

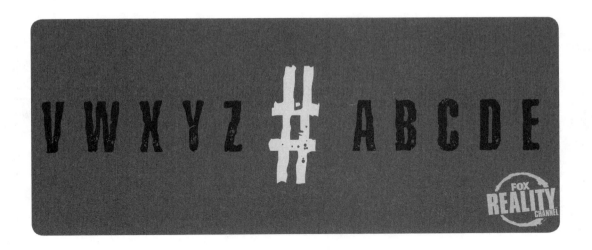

THE 5TH WHEEL

GENRE	Competition (Dating)
FIRST TELECAST	10/2001
LAST TELECAST	9/2004
NETWORK	Syndicated
EPISODE STYLE	Self-contained
CAST	Aisha Tyler (Host); Tom Gottlieb (Announcer)
PRODUCTION COMPANIES	Bobwell Productions; Renegade 83.6; Studios USA
EXECUTIVE PRODUCERS	David Garfinkle; Thomas Klein; Jay Renfroe
SENIOR PRODUCERS	James DuBose; Stan Evans
CO-EXECUTIVE PRODUCER	Harley Tat
PRODUCER	Dan Riley
CO-PRODUCERS	Archie Gips; M. J. Loheed; Greg Longstreet; Dave Pullano; Chris Ragazzo; Todd Sachs; Bradford Shultz; Adam Vetri
DIRECTORS	Keirda Bahruth; Zac Hartog; Sean Olsen; Dan Riley; Dixon Troyer; Joe Dea; Tom Greenhut; Cynthia Matzger

Each episode of *The 5th Wheel* featured two men and two women who met and got to know one another on a bus. The foursome then went on a group date, which was peppered with onscreen pop-up commentaries and graphics for the viewers. Halfway through the evening, the foursome was introduced to "the fifth wheel," a man or woman who attempted to shake things up and thwart the relations that had been brewing earlier in the evening. At the end of the episode, the four singles voted on whom they'd like to see again, with the option to choose no one.

8TH & OCEAN

GENRE	Docusoap
FIRST TELECAST	3/7/2006
NETWORK	MTV
EPISODE STYLE	Story Arc
CAST	Kelly Aldridge; Sabrina Aldridge; Vinci Alonso; Talesha Byrd; Briana Hicks; Teddy John; Britt Koth; Sean Poolman; Adrian Rozas; Tracie Wright
PRODUCTION COMPANY	MTV Productions
EXECUTIVE PRODUCERS	Tony DiSanto; Liz Gateley; Andrew Hoegl
PRODUCER	Vinnie Potestivo
DIRECTORS	Kabir Akhtar; Kasey Barrett; Jaymee Johnson; Jason Sklaver

The glamorous *8th & Ocean* follows the lives of ten professional, male and female Irene Marie models who live together in an apartment complex in the heart of Miami's South Beach. The show's title is derived from the intersection of 8th Street and Ocean Drive, where the Irene Marie Models office is located.

#1 SINGLE

GENRE	Docudrama
FIRST TELECAST	1/22/2006
LAST TELECAST	3/19/2006
NETWORK	E!
EPISODE STYLE	Story Arc
CAST	Lisa Loeb, Debbie Loeb, Gail Loeb, Illeana Douglas, Stephanie Ittleson, Michael Panes, Juan Patino
PRODUCTION COMPANY	Stick Figure Productions
EXECUTIVE PRODUCERS	Steven Cantor, Daniel Laikind

This celebrity series followed singer-songwriter Lisa Loeb as she tried to find romance as a thirty-something single woman in New York City. Before the series, Loeb had two long-term relationships, including one with musician Dweezil Zappa. Supporting her in her quest to find true love were her sister Debbie, her ex-boyfriend Juan, and actress Illeana Douglas.

30 DAYS

GENRE	Docudrama
FIRST TELECAST	6/15/2005
NETWORK	FX
EPISODE STYLE	Self-contained
CAST	Morgan Spurlock (Host)
PRODUCTION COMPANIES	Borderline; Reveille Productions
EXECUTIVE PRODUCERS	John Landgraf; Morgan Spurlock; R. J. Cutler; Ben Silverman; H. T. Owens; Mala Chapple; Nick McKinney
CO-EXECUTIVE PRODUCERS	Jonathan Chinn; Mark Koops

PRODUCERS	Sebastian Doggart; Patrick McManamee; Chris Nee
DIRECTORS	Sarah Levy; John Mans; Bob Maraist; Amanda Micheli

Expanding on the premise Morgan Spurlock established in his Academy Award–nominated documentary film *Super Size Me, 30 Days* ponders what it would be like to live for thirty days in someone else's shoes. The subject is often taken out of his or her comfort zone, while Spurlock discusses the social issues involved with the thirty-day exercise. Topics explored have included minimum wage (in which Spurlock and his fiancée struggled to live on minimum wage for one month), anti-aging strategies, and Muslims in America.

THE $25 MILLION HOAX

GENRE	Docucomedy (Hoax)
FIRST TELECAST	11/8/2004
LAST TELECAST	11/22/2004
NETWORK	NBC
EPISODE STYLE	Story Arc
TALENT	George Gray (Host); Ed McMahon ("Lottery show" host)
CAST	Chrissy Sanford
PRODUCTION COMPANIES	Hallock Healey Entertainment; Reveille Productions
EXECUTIVE PRODUCERS	Scott Hallock; Kevin Healy; Stuart Krasnow; Ben Silverman

A phony contest was the premise for *The $25 Million Hoax*. The series documented the reaction of a family who watched helplessly from the sidelines as the accomplice, Chrissy Sanford, spent her $5 million "fortune" from a fake lottery, thebigwin.net, on only herself. Ed McMahon, who delivered the "winnings," lent an air of credibility to the con game. Sweet small-town girl turned shopaholic Chrissy couldn't reveal she was playing a joke on her family, and her "purchases" were prearranged with actors posing as store clerks. After spending outrageous amounts of money, Chrissy's challenge was to have her entire family show up for the real payoff in order for her to win a genuine prize when the hoax was revealed.

30 SECONDS TO FAME

GENRE	Competition (Talent)
FIRST TELECAST	7/17/2002
LAST TELECAST	7/17/2003
NETWORK	Fox
AIR TIMES	Wednesday, 8:00 p.m. (7/02–8/02); Thursday, 8:00 p.m. (10/02–11/02); Thursday, 8:30 p.m. (5/03–7/03)
EPISODE STYLE	Self-contained
CAST	Craig Jackson (Host); Jonathan Brandmeier (Announcer)
PRODUCTION COMPANIES	20th Century Fox; Fox Television Network; Wild Jams Productions
EXECUTIVE PRODUCER	Michael Binkow
PRODUCER	J. P. Buck; Ellen Kennedy; Joe Revello; Jan Maxwell Smith
DIRECTOR	Don Weiner

A weekly prize of $25,000 was up for grabs when twenty-four acts with varying degrees of talent had thirty seconds each to showcase their skills to the judges on *30 Seconds to Fame*. The audience could eliminate an act if their booing reached a predetermined level on the "eliminator meter." After two preliminary rounds, the top three acts earned another thirty seconds to perform, and the audience voted on which act would receive the $25,000 weekly prize.

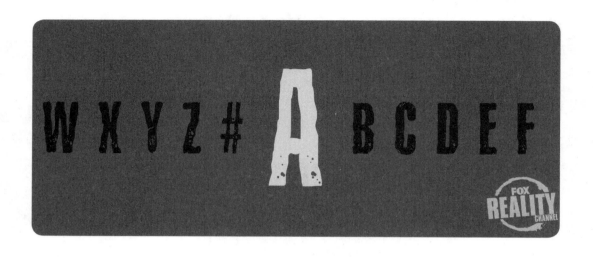

THE ACADEMY

GENRE	Docusoap
FIRST TELECAST	5/24/2007
NETWORK	Fox Reality Channel
EPISODE STYLE	Story Arc
CAST	Dep. Pete Enciso; Dep. René Garcia; Ofc. Jeremiah Hart; Dep. Ray Jones; Dep. Dwight Miley ("the Ramrod"); Dep. Sidra Sherrod; Sgt. Mark Wilkins
PRODUCTION COMPANY	Scott Sternberg Productions
EXECUTIVE PRODUCERS	Scott Sternberg; Scott Weinberger; Bob Boden
CO-EXECUTIVE PRODUCER	Jerome Beck
SUPERVISING PRODUCER	Tracy A. Whittaker
PRODUCERS	Brenda Coston; John Salcido

The Academy provided a gripping, behind-the-scenes look at Class 355 of the Los Angeles Sheriff's Department Training Academy. The season documented the grueling, intense, eighteen-week process of breaking down and building up raw recruits and turning them into ready-for-duty sheriffs and officers.

The series provided unprecedented access to the training process, as it was produced with the cooperation of the Los Angeles County Sheriff's Department, which oversees more than three thousand square miles of Southern California, and deals with some of the country's most dangerous criminals and the world's largest jail system.

The inaugural season began with "Black Monday," the 111 recruits' first full day at the academy. The intense first day thrust the recruits into a training program that challenged them physically, mentally, and emotionally. During training, they were put through exercises that taught them various aspects of law enforcement, including self-defense, weapons training, dealing with mentally ill and drug-addicted assailants, and learning the intricacies of gang warfare.

Viewers saw how difficult the process was to become a member of the Sheriff's Department, and the commitment it took to become one of Los Angeles's elite. Week after week, viewers saw recruits leave because of dismissal, injury, or simply because they couldn't handle it. Viewers also got a glimpse into the home lives of the recruits, learning about their dedication, passion, and how the rigors of the course affected their families.

Everyone in the class was vulnerable until graduation. In the season finale, the final exams proved to be the breaking point for some recruits, as failure cost them the opportunity to become a sheriff's deputy. The season concluded with the emotional graduation ceremony, at which the remaining recruits were made members of the Los Angeles police force.

ACE OF CAKES

GENRE	Docudrama
FIRST TELECAST	8/17/2006
NETWORK	Food Network
EPISODE STYLE	Self-contained
CAST	Duff Goldman; Sherri Chambers; Anna Ellison; Elena Fox; Adam Goldstein; Katherine Hill;

	Richard Todd Karoll; Geof Manthorne; Mary Smith; Ben Turner; Mary Alice Fallon Yeskey
PRODUCTION COMPANY	Authentic Entertainment
EXECUTIVE PRODUCERS	Lauren Lexton; Tom Rogan
CO-EXECUTIVE PRODUCERS	Willie Goldman; Dana Leiken; Kelly McPherson
DIRECTOR	Jeffrey R. Daniels

Baltimore's Duff Goldman and his eclectic group of friends were cake decorators who used power tools, welding equipment, blow torches, and whatever else it took to create edible art. Charm City Cakes creations included abstract wedding cakes; cakes shaped like a Jeep, an Xbox, Wrigley Field, and a Thai pagoda; and a King Kong bar mitzvah cake.

ADVENTURES IN HOLLYHOOD

GENRE	Docusoap
FIRST TELECAST	4/5/2007
LAST TELECAST	5/24/2007
NETWORK	MTV
EPISODE STYLE	Self-contained
CAST	Big Triece; Computer; DJ Paul; Juicy J; Project Pat
PRODUCTION COMPANY	Katalyst Films
EXECUTIVE PRODUCERS	Rod Aissa; Karey Burke; Jason Goldberg; Melanie Graham; Ashton Kutcher; Kevin Lee
PRODUCER	Paul Vaillancourt
DIRECTORS	Charles Davis, Anna Dokoza

The comedic *Adventures in Hollyhood* followed rap group Three 6 Mafia and their entourage on a mission to become Hollywood players. Along with their friends, Academy Award winners Juicy J and DJ Paul tried to stay true to their southern Memphis roots while capitalizing on LA's many opportunities.

AGE OF LOVE

GENRE	Competition (Dating)
FIRST TELECAST	6/18/2007
LAST TELECAST	8/6/2007
NETWORK	NBC
AIR TIME	Monday, 9:00 p.m.
EPISODE STYLE	Story Arc
TALENT	Mark Consuelos (Host), Mark Philippoussis
CAST	Amanda Salinas (Winner—Kitten); Jennifer Braff (Runner-up—Cougar); Kelli Brook (Cougar); Jodie Fisher (Cougar); Jayanna Howeton (Cougar); Megan Klehr (Kitten); Maria Rangel (Cougar); Mary Sanks (Kitten); Tessa Walker (Kitten); Adelaide Dawson (Kitten); Lauren Bryant (Kitten); Lynn Borges (Cougar); Angela Harrington (Cougar)
PRODUCTION COMPANY	3 Ball Productions
EXECUTIVE PRODUCERS	Craig Armstrong; Adam Greener; Todd A. Nelson; J. D. Roth
CO-EXECUTIVE PRODUCER	Sandi Johnson
PRODUCERS	Angela Molloy; Brian Tanke
DIRECTOR	Brian Smith

On *Age of Love,* single Australian tennis star Mark Philippoussis, thirty, was wooed by a group of thirteen women ranging in age from twenty-one to forty-eight. The twentysomethings, also known as the "kittens," competed against the older group of "cougars," as Philippoussis was constantly reminded of the question "Does age really matter?" After a trip to Mark's home country of Australia with the two finalists, twenty-five-year-old Amanda Salinas, and forty-eight-year-old Jennifer Braff, Philippoussis selected Salinas as the winner.

THE AGENCY

GENRE	Docusoap
FIRST TELECAST	2/20/2007
NETWORK	VH1
EPISODE STYLE	Self-contained
CAST	Anita Norris; Becky Southwick; Carlos Paz; Greg Chan; Sean Patterson
PRODUCTION COMPANY	Left/Right Films
EXECUTIVE PRODUCERS	Ken Druckerman; Banks Tarver
PRODUCER	Anneli Gericke

The Agency took a stark look at the modeling industry, from the perspective of the models, agents, clients, and the business as a whole. The series focused on Wilhelmina Models and the complex, high-stress business of marketing beauty.

AIRLINE

GENRE	Docudrama
FIRST TELECAST	1/5/2004
NETWORK	A&E
EPISODE STYLE	Self-contained
TALENT	Tim Flavin (Narrator)
CAST	Susie Boersma (Customer Service Supervisor, LAX); Colleen Bragiel (Customer Service Manager, Midway); Denise Brown-Bess (Customer Service Supervisor, Midway); Val Brown (Customer Service Supervisor, Midway); Michael Carr (Customer Service Supervisor, LAX); Anita Herbert (Customer Service Supervisor, Midway); Veolia Hewitt-Norris (Customer Service Manager,

Midway); Yolanda Martin (Customer Service Supervisor, LAX); Steve Ramierz (Customer Service Supervisor, LAX)

PRODUCTION COMPANY Granada Entertainment USA Distributors

EXECUTIVE PRODUCERS Charles Tremayne; Joe Houlihan

PRODUCERS Jo Inglott; Scott Mislan; John Mounier; Kelly Nathe; Lee Servis; Anita Shah

DIRECTORS Matthew Barbato; Jo Inglott; Scott Mislan; John Mounier; Lee Servis; Jim Warren

Based on the U.K. show *Airport,* and shot at various airports throughout the United States, *Airline* focused on the passengers, ground workers, and on-board employees of Southwest Airlines. Moments of frustration and humor were highlighted in the day-to-day adventures at America's fourth largest airline.

ALL-AMERICAN GIRL

GENRE Competition (Talent)

FIRST TELECAST 3/12/2003

LAST TELECAST 5/24/2003

NETWORK ABC (3/12/2003–4/24/2003); ABC Family (5/8/2003–5/24/2003)

EPISODE STYLE Story Arc

TALENT Mitch Mullany (Host); John Salley (Coach); Geri Halliwell (Coach); Suzanne De Passe (Coach)

CAST Jessica Felice (Winner); Kristi Foster (Runner-up); Natalie White (top-six finalist); Andrea Lynem (top-six finalist); Monica Palumbo (top-six finalist); Kira Pozehl (top-six finalist); Ashley Esqueda (top-ten finalist); Shannon McConnell (top-ten finalist); Tarah Paige (top-ten finalist)

PRODUCTION COMPANIES 19 Entertainment; Buena Vista Pictures
CREATED BY Simon Fuller
EXECUTIVE PRODUCERS Simon Fuller; Conrad Green; Nigel Lythgoe;
Marilyn Wilson
DIRECTORS Don Weiner

A group of forty-five talented young women was winnowed down to find the "All-American Girl." The women were put through a "training camp," and were coached by celebrities, who taught them how to stand out from a crowd. The winner, Jessica Felice, was chosen by viewer votes. Felice received an exclusive talent deal with Simon Fuller's (*American Idol*) 19 Management and a $100,000 talent contract with ABC.

RATINGS: The series averaged 5.4 million viewers during its spring 2003 run on ABC.

THE AMAZING RACE
(Season 1)

GENRE Competition
FIRST TELECAST 9/5/2001
LAST TELECAST 12/13/2001
NETWORK CBS
AIR TIME Wednesday, 9:00 p.m.
EPISODE STYLE Story Arc
TALENT Phil Keoghan (Host)
CAST Rob Frisbee and Brennan Swain (Winners—
best friends); Frank Mesa and Margarita Mesa
(2nd place—separated parents); Joe Baldassare
and Bill Bartek (3rd place—life partners);
Kevin O'Connor and Drew Feinberg (4th place—
frat brothers); Nancy Hoyt and Emily Hoyt
(5th place—mother and daughter); Lenny Hudson
and Karyn Jefferson (6th place—dating couple);

Paul J. Alessi and Amie Barsky
(7th place—engaged couple); David Groark
and Margaretta Groark (8th place—married
couple); Patricia Pierce and Brenda Mehta
(9th place—friends); Kim Smith and
Leslie Kellner (10th place—friends); Matt Robar
and Ana Robar (11th place—married)

PRODUCTION COMPANIES	Bruckheimer Films and Earthview Inc., in association with Touchstone Television and Amazing Race Productions
CREATED BY	Jerry Bruckheimer; Bertram van Munster; Elise Doganieri
EXECUTIVE PRODUCERS	Jerry Bruckheimer; Bertram van Munster; Jonathan Littman; Hayma Screech Washington
CO-EXECUTIVE PRODUCERS	Amy Chacon; Evan Weinstein

Eleven teams of two competed in a thirteen-leg race around the world for $1 million on *The Amazing Race.* Each leg finished at a Pit Stop, where the last team to arrive might be eliminated from the race. Each leg featured one "Fast Forward," which enabled the team that found it to advance directly to the next Pit Stop. Each team could use only one Fast Forward throughout the race. The teams also periodically encountered a "Detour," which offered two different ways to reach a destination or complete a task, and a "Roadblock," a task in which only one of each team's members could participate. Yellow and white "Route Markers" indicated the sites of further instructions.

Season 1's teams featured best friends Rob and Brennan, married couple Matt and Ana, separated parents Frank and Margarita, friends Kim and Leslie, mother and daughter Nancy and Emily, engaged couple Paul and Amie, married couple David and Margaretta, dating couple Lenny and Karyn, life partners Joe and Bill, friends Pat and Brenda, and fraternity brothers Kevin and Drew.

In the inaugural episode, the teams traveled from New York to South Africa to Zambia. The contestants visited Victoria Falls, rode a zipline, bungee-jumped off a cliff, and arrived at the first Pit Stop, Zambia's Songwe Village. Rob and Brennan took the Fast Forward and advanced directly to the village, while Matt and Ana were the last team to arrive and were eliminated from the race.

In Episode 2, the teams attempted to communicate with the villagers to locate the Songwe Museum. Rob and Brennan formed an alliance with Frank and Margarita, and Joe and Bill. Each team completed a photography task, except Pat and Brenda, who managed to secure the Fast Forward to advance to the Pit Stop—the Arc de Triomphe in Paris. Once in Paris, the other teams had to locate a monument through a telescope. Kim and Leslie were the last to arrive and were eliminated.

In Episode 3, the teams tracked down the Roue de Paris—a giant Ferris wheel—and obtained a Route Marker. The Detour challenged the teams to find Foucault's pendulum, then climb to the top of Notre Dame and ring Quasimodo's bell. Kevin and Drew earned the Fast Forward and advanced to the Pit Stop, at Château des Baux. Pat and Brenda fell behind early on by going to the wrong location, and wound up getting eliminated.

In Episode 4, the teams found a picture of a man in a red hat holding a flag, which they realized was from Tunisia—the next destination in the race. The teams traveled by plane and boat to Tunisia to locate the man, who offered them a Detour to either "Full Body Massage" or "Full Body Brew." From there, they went to El Djem amphitheater and tracked down a sword in the "Pit of Death." Dave and Margaretta were the last team to finish, and were eliminated.

In Episode 5, the teams traveled three hundred miles to a globe monument in the Tunisian city of Tataouine. Upon arriving, they received a Detour with the option of "Puzzling" or "Listening." All teams chose "Listening," and participated in a clue-finding task using walkie-talkies. They then had to find a Route Marker flag in the Sahara desert. Once they found the flag, a Roadblock required one member from each team to ride a camel. Paul and Arnie arrived last and were eliminated.

In Episode 6, the teams traveled to the Palace Hotel Tunis, then to the Colosseum in Rome, which was difficult due to an air strike. While at the airport, Joe and Bill (aka Team Guido) made enemies after cutting off the other teams at the boarding gate. The teams were given a Detour to find either a statue of a foot or a statue of a hoof. The next task was to get to Castelfranco Emilia by train. Frank and Margarita and Joe and Bill were given time penalties for taking a cab, which was against the rules. A Roadblock at the final stretch forced one team member to drive a Smart Car, while another was professionally driven in a sports car. Lenny and Karyn arrived last at the Pit Stop—Sant'Agata Bolognese—but were relieved to learn it was a non-elimination leg of the race.

In Episode 7, Frank and Margarita took the Fast Forward and skipped directly to the Pit Stop in Agra, Uttar Pradesh, India, while the other teams faced a "Glide" or "Ride" Detour to Ferrara, Italy. Rob and Brennan chose to hang glide there, while the others rode bicycles. The teams then returned to Rome to fly to New Delhi. Lenny and Karyn arrived last again, and this time they were eliminated. Karyn claimed that the experience had made her realize that she and Lenny weren't right for each other.

In Episode 8, the teams traveled from the Taj Mahal to the Palace of the Winds, in Jaipur, Rajasthan. The Detour required the teams to find a holy man traveling either by rowboat or elephant. From there, the teams traveled to the Karni Mata temple, in Deshnoke, then to Bikaner. A Roadblock in Bikaner made one member from each team walk through the Karni Mata temple of rats while wearing only socks on their feet. Nancy and Emily were the last to reach the Pit Stop—Laxmi Niwas Palace hotel—but discovered it was another non-elimination leg.

In Episode 9, the teams traveled to the Temple of Dawn in Bangkok, then faced a Detour requiring them to reach a monastery in Kanchanaburi, Thailand, by either bus or car. Nancy and Emily went after the Fast Forward, but lost out to Joe and Bill after failing to win a traditional competition of putting coins into 108 slots at the Temple of the Reclining Buddha. Finding themselves lagging behind, and completely exhausted, Nancy and Emily took a taxi to Kanchanaburi, earning a twenty-four-hour penalty for violating the rules of the Detour. A Roadblock made each team send one member through a pit of tigers, where they found a clue directing them to the Tiger Cave Temple, in Krabi. Joe and Bill were the last to arrive at the Pit Stop, but Nancy and Emily's penalty caused the mother-daughter team to be eliminated.

In Episode 10, the teams went to Thailand's Rai Leh Beach in search of "the king," which proved to be a rock formation. A Detour gave the teams the option to "Climb" or "Hike" the rocks, and each team opted for a rock climb. The Pit Stop was a boat rental company called Sea, Land and Trek, in Bor Tor, Au Luk. Joe and Bill arrived last, but were informed that it was a non-elimination leg.

In Episode 11, the teams journeyed from Thailand to Beijing. A Detour required the teams either to "Volley"—score five points against a Ping-Pong champion (chosen by Rob and Brennan, and Frank and Margarita), or to "Rally"—take a lengthy journey across Beijing by bus, motorcycle taxi, and rickshaw (chosen by Kevin and Drew, and Bill and Joe). The Roadblock was to eat traditional Chinese delicacies, such as chicken feet, beetle larvae, and squid. In a very close showdown, Kevin and Drew arrived last at the Tiantan Park Pit Stop and were eliminated.

In Episode 12, the teams began at Tiantan Park, where they retrieved a clue from a kite. They then traveled to the Great Wall of China, where they received a Detour. Each team opted to scale a short, steep staircase rather than a long, more level one at the Great Wall. They were next instructed to travel back to the United States, to Anchorage, via San Francisco and Seattle. Once in Alaska, they competed in a "Blanket Toss" Eskimo ritual and received a clue leading them to Matanuska Glacier, which a member of each team had to climb for the Roadblock task. No teams were eliminated in this episode.

In Episode 13, the three remaining teams completed the final challenge of the race—a Roadblock, in which one member of each team had to strip down to a bathing suit and submerge him or herself in the cold waters of Fish Lake, in Alaska. Then the teams traveled back to the final Pit Stop, Flushing Meadows Park, in New York City. Rob and Brennan finished first and won the race, earning $1 million. Frank and Margarita came in second, and Joe and Bill finished third.

RATINGS: In its first season, *The Amazing Race* drew in an average of 8.8 million viewers.

THE AMAZING RACE
(Season 2)

GENRE	Competition
FIRST TELECAST	3/11/2002
LAST TELECAST	5/15/2002
NETWORK	CBS
AIR TIME	Wednesdays, 9:00 p.m.
EPISODE STYLE	Story Arc

TALENT	Phil Keoghan (Host)
CAST	Chris Luca and Alex Boylan (Winners—lifelong friends); Tara Lynch and Wil Steger (2nd place—separated couple); Blake Mycoskie and Paige Mycoskie (3rd place—brother and sister); Oswald Mendez and Danny Jiminez (4th place—best friends); Gary Rosen and Dave Lepeska (5th place—former roommates); Mary Lenig and Peach Krebs (6th place—sisters); Cyndi Kalenberg and Russell Kalenberg (7th place—married pastors); Shola Richards and Doyin Richards (8th place—twin brothers); Peggy Kuhn and Claire Jinks (9th place—grandmothers); Hope Davis and Norm Davis (10th place—married parents); Deidre Washington and Hillary Washington (11th place—mother and daughter)
PRODUCTION COMPANIES	Bruckheimer Films and Earthview Inc., in association with Touchstone Television and Amazing Race Productions
CREATED BY	Jerry Bruckheimer; Bertram van Munster; Elise Doganieri
EXECUTIVE PRODUCERS	Jerry Bruckheimer; Bertram van Munster; Jonathan Littman; Hayma Screech Washington
CO-EXECUTIVE PRODUCERS	Amy Chacon; Evan Weinstein

Season 2's teams featured married parents Hope and Norm, sisters Mary and Peach, best friends Oswald and Danny, former roommates Gary and Dave, mother and daughter Deidre and Hillary, separated couple Tara and Wil, twin brothers Shola and Doyin, lifelong friends Chris and Alex, grandmothers Peggy and Claire, brother and sister Blake and Paige, and married pastors Cyndi and Russell.

In Episode 1, the race began in Pahrump, Nevada. The first clue sent the teams to Rio de Janeiro, Brazil, to find the statue of Christ the Redeemer. Most teams chose a

Detour, where they had to rappel down the face of Sugarloaf Mountain, while grandmas Peggy and Claire searched for the woman who inspired the song "The Girl from Ipanema." The Pit Stop was the *Tocorimé* yacht in Guanabara Bay, where Deidre and Hillary were the last team to arrive and the first team to be eliminated from the race.

In Episode 2, the teams were instructed to go to a Rio de Janeiro samba club. For the Detour, the teams hang glided from a mountain down to São Conrado Beach. Shola and Doyin played volleyball to earn the Fast Forward, which allowed them to advance directly to the Pit Stop at Iguaçu Falls, Brazil. The other teams took a speedboat ride into the falls for the Roadblock. Hope and Norm arrived last and were the second team eliminated from the race.

In Episode 3, the teams flew to South Africa to locate Nelson Mandela's former jail cell. The Detour had teams "Dance" with a local troupe for tips, or "Deliver" 250 pounds of fish. The Roadblock required one member from each team to buy a sheep's head and Epsom salts and to deliver the goods to a healer, who gave them a bitter brew to drink. After an airline travel snag, grandmas Peggy and Claire were the last to arrive at the Lanzerac Manor and Winery Pit Stop, and were the third team eliminated.

In Episode 4, the teams traveled to Namibia. On the Detour, they sandboarded down the Matterhorn Sand Dune in Swakopmund. The Roadblock required one of each team's members to haggle at a marketplace to acquire a collection of carved African animals. Oswald and Danny found the Fast Forward in the Swakopmund Hotel swimming pool, and the best friends went directly to the Pit Stop at Amani Lodge, near Windhoek, Namibia. After getting stuck in the sand, Shola and Doyin were last to check in and were the fourth team eliminated from the race.

In Episode 5, the teams headed from Namibia to Bangkok. The Roadblock forced one team member to crawl through a cave filled with bats and cockroaches. Cyndi and Russell's trouble finding the right water taxi during the Detour caused them to be the last to arrive at the Pit Stop in Ampawa, Thailand, making them the fifth team eliminated.

In Episode 6, the teams made their way to northern Thailand. At the Detour, each team opted for the "Boat" challenge (river rafting) rather than the "Beast" challenge (elephant riding). At the Roadblock, the teams had to wash chalk markings off an elephant's back. Chris and Alex arrived last at the Pit Stop—Karen Village, in Chiang Mai, Thailand, but were relieved to learn that it was a non-elimination leg of the race.

In Episode 7, the teams flew to Hong Kong. Gary and Dave beat Mary and Peach to the Fast Forward at Wong Tai Sin Temple, and the former roommates advanced directly to the Pit Stop onboard a junk in Victoria Harbour. At the Detour, Oswald and Danny opted to locate an herbal shop and drink foul-tasting tea, while the other teams chose to take taxis to a wishing tree. Tara outshined the competition in the Roadblock, which involved moving shipping containers with cranes. Mary and Peach were last to arrive at the Pit Stop and were the sixth team eliminated.

In Episode 8, the teams raced two legs, the first of which included a Hong Kong Detour with the option to row dragon boats or walk through the streets wearing ceremonial lion's heads. Afterward, the teams headed to Sydney, where the Roadblock involved deciphering Australian slang. Blake and Paige were the last ones to check in at the Pit Stop at Sydney's Museum of Contemporary Art, but were informed it was a non-elimination leg of the race. The second leg included a Detour to "Cool Down" and mine for opals in Coober Pedy, or to "Heat Up" by golfing under the blazing sun. Chris and Alex ate meat pies at Harry's Café de Wheels to earn the Fast Forward to the Pit Stop at an aboriginal camp outside Coober Pedy. The Roadblock was a boomerang-throwing exercise. Gary and Dave's Detour switch from "Cool Down" to "Heat Up" cost them the leg, as they were the last team to arrive at the Pit Stop, and were thus the seventh team eliminated.

In Episode 9, the teams flew to New Zealand, where they participated in the world's second-longest bungee jump, measuring 450 feet, at the Detour. Blake and Paige earned the Fast Forward in a speedboat race on the Shotover River, sending them directly to the Pit Stop—Inverary Sheep Station, at Canterbury Plains. The Roadblock required one member of each team to herd sheep by color. Oswald and Danny arrived last at the Pit Stop, but were spared, as it was another non-elimination leg.

In Episode 10, the teams remained in New Zealand, where they took a ferry to Picton, rappelled 350 feet into the Waitomo Caves on the Detour, and navigated ATVs on an off-road course near Auckland during the Roadblock. Tara and Will found the Fast Forward in the pit of a volcano at Mount Tarawera. Once again, Oswald and Danny arrived last, and this time they were eliminated from the race.

In Episode 11, the teams returned to the United States, flying to Maui, Hawaii, where they completed a pineapple-themed Detour and a snorkeling Roadblock, before arriving at the Pit Stop—Hui Aloha Church, in Maui. The three remaining teams then traveled through Alaska, en route to the final Pit Stop—Murray Circle, on East Fort Baker, overlooking San Francisco Bay, in California. Lifelong friends Chris and Alex won a tight footrace to the finish and won the $1 million prize, while Tara and Will finished second, and Blake and Paige came in a close third.

RATINGS: Season 2 of *The Amazing Race* brought in an average of 10.3 million viewers.

THE AMAZING RACE
(Season 3)

GENRE	Competition
FIRST TELECAST	10/2/2002
LAST TELECAST	12/18/2002
NETWORK	CBS
AIR TIME	Wednesdays, 9:00 p.m.
EPISODE STYLE	Story Arc
TALENT	Phil Keoghan (Host)
CAST	Flo Pesenti and Zach Behr (Winners—friends), Teri Pollack and Ian Pollack (2nd place—married parents); Ken Duphiney and Gerard Duphiney (3rd place—brothers); Derek Riker and Drew Riker (4th place—identical twins); John Vito Pietanza and Jill Aquilino (5th place—dating couple); Andre Plummer and Damon Wafer (6th place—friends); Aaron Goldschmidt and Arianne Udell (7th place—friends); Michael Ilacqua and Kathy Perez (8th place—long-distance couple); Heather Mahar and Eve Madison (9th place—roommates); Dennis Hyde and Andrew Hyde (10th place—father and son); Tramel Raggs and Talicia Raggs (11th place—brother and sister); Gina Diggins and Sylvia Pitt (12th place—moms)

PRODUCTION COMPANIES	Bruckheimer Films and Earthview Inc., in association with Touchstone Television and Amazing Race Productions
CREATED BY	Jerry Bruckheimer; Bertram van Munster; Elise Doganieri
EXECUTIVE PRODUCERS	Jerry Bruckheimer; Bertram van Munster; Jonathan Littman; Hayma Screech Washington
CO-EXECUTIVE PRODUCERS	Amy Chacon; Evan Weinstein

Season 3 featured twelve teams: friends Aaron and Arianne, friends Andre and Damon, father and son Dennis and Andrew, identical twins Derek and Drew, friends Flo and Zach, mothers Gina and Sylvia, roommates Heather and Eve, dating couple John Vito and Jill, brothers Ken and Gerard, long-distance couple Michael and Kathy, married parents Teri and Ian, and brother and sister Tramel and Talicia.

The race began in Florida Everglades National Park. Teams then flew from Miami to Mexico City to find the Angel of Independence Victory Column, where they were instructed to locate a man named Pablo based on a photo of him standing in front of a cathedral in Constitution Plaza Square. Ken and Gerard found the Fast Forward among a sea of typists, and advanced directly to the Pit Stop—Hacienda San Gabriel de las Palmas, in Morelos. The others had to choose between a "Wings" and a "Wheels" Detour, which sent them skydiving or riding a donkey cart. Gina and Sylvia were the last team to arrive at the Pit Stop, and were the first team eliminated from the race.

In Episode 2, the teams traveled within Mexico to Teotihuacan to climb the Pyramid of the Sun. From there, they took a bus to Cancún and a taxi to the San Marino Marina. Derek and Drew won the Fast Forward by flying on a rope by their feet with the Voladores, and advanced to the Pit Stop at the Diamante K bungalows, in Tulum. The Detour options were "Manpower" and "Horsepower," where teams kayaked or jet-skiied for the clue. After the Detour, the teams took a ferry to Chankanaab National Park, in Cozumel. For the Roadblock, teams dove into a dolphin lagoon to find the Pit Stop clue. Tramel and Talicia were the last to arrive at the Pit Stop, and were the second team eliminated.

In Episode 3, the teams flew to London. The Detour had them "Punt" a boat one mile down the River Cam, or "Bike" six miles through Cambridge. Teams took a bus to

Scotland and a taxi to the Highland Games, where the Roadblock required them to compete in a caber toss, hammer throw, and shot put. From there, the teams ran to the Pit Stop at Dunnottar Castle, near Stonehaven. Despite winning the Fast Forward by driving a tank through an obstacle course, Dennis and Andrew's extended delay in Mexico caused them to arrive last. They were the third team eliminated from the race.

In Episode 4, the teams found a message in a bottle at Stonehaven Harbour, which directed them to Porto, Portugal. An "Old School/New School" Detour had teams deliver wine by boat to one restaurant, or by truck to three restaurants. Then the teams traveled to a soccer stadium in Lisbon, where a Roadblock required them to block a penalty kick by a teenage soccer player. From there, teams traveled on foot to the Pit Stop, the Torre de Belém fortress. Aaron and Arianne arrived last, but Heather and Eve's time penalty for taking a cab instead of walking caused them to be the fourth team eliminated.

Episode 5 found the teams headed west of Lisbon to Cabo da Roca, in the Sintra-Cascais Natural Park, the westernmost point in continental Europe. The "Ropes" or "Slopes" Detour had teams descend a cliff by rappelling or by walking a long path. Next, the teams drove to Algeciras, Spain, where they boarded a ferry to Tangier, Morocco, then hopped a bus to Fez. The Roadblock required teams to find a clue among twenty-five offensive-smelling dye vats. From the ancient marketplace in Fez, the teams drove to the Pit Stop at the Borj-Nord fortress. Michael and Kathy's mistake of filling their diesel-fueled car with unleaded gasoline en route to Spain caused them to become the fifth team eliminated from the race.

In Episode 6, the teams drove to the Hassan II Mosque in Casablanca, took a train to Marrakech, then hailed a taxi to Palmeraie Oasis, in the desert. For the Detour, teams had to find an Arabic rubbing by riding horses or driving dune buggies. After translating the rubbing, they were directed to Café Glacier, where they sold five bowls of escargot to local customers for the Roadblock. Teri and Ian found the Fast Forward, which sent them directly to the Pit Stop in Riad Catalina. Aaron and Arianne lost the Fast Forward, and were the sixth team eliminated.

In Episode 7, teams flew to Munich, Germany, where they had to find a puppet next to the Friedensengel statue. Next, teams flew to Innsbruck, Austria, where the Detour had them ride with Olympic bobsledders or skate with a pair of Olympic ice skaters. Flo and Zach got the Fast Forward by finding a man surfing a standing wave.

The others rode a gondola to the Seegrube Station. A Roadblock required teams to descend more than two hundred feet to the ground on a rescue cable from the gondola. Andre and Damon were the last to arrive at the Pit Stop—the Neuschwanstein Castle in Füssen, Germany—and were the seventh team eliminated from the Race.

In Episode 8, teams took a trip to the Augustinerhof Farm, in Füssen. A clue in a bundle of hay sent the teams to Switzerland's Rheinfall, the largest waterfall in Europe. Then teams traveled by train to Zurich to find the Lindenhof town square. For the Detour, teams had to find the combination to a vault by counting Swiss currency in a jar or by retrieving the numbers from three downtown Zurich destinations. Next, the teams traveled by train to Grindelwald, where a Roadblock had them shoot an apple off a mannequin's head with a crossbow. John Vito and Jill were the last to arrive at the Pit Stop—Chalet Arnika, in Grindewald—but were relieved to find it was a non-elimination leg of the race.

In the first half of the two-hour Episode 9, teams traveled to a glacier gorge called the Gletscherschlucht. At the bottom of the gorge were keys to luxury cars, which they drove to the rural town of Kandersteg. There they loaded their cars onto an Alpine train bound for Red Bridge, at Adventure Park. For the Detour, teams bungee-jumped off the bridge or searched among seventy-five sheep to find keys hidden in the animals' bells. From there, they went to Château de Chillon, where the Roadblock had them assemble a Swiss army bicycle and pedal it to the first Pit Stop, at the steamship *Savoie*, in Montreux, Switzerland. Earlier, John Vito and Jill uncovered the Fast Forward by eating enough of a wheel of cheese to reveal a clue, allowing them to advance directly to the Pit Stop. Flo and Zach arrived last, but it was a non-elimination leg.

During the second hour of Episode 9, the teams took taxis to the Jet d'Eau fountain in Geneva. From there they flew to Kuala Lumpur, Malaysia, to find the Petronas Twin Towers, the largest towers in Asia. Then teams traveled by train to the Singapore National Orchid Garden to find a flower named after Margaret Thatcher. For the Detour, teams had to find a clue in the manatee pool at the Singapore Zoo or track down Singapore TV star Phua Chu Kang in a group of poorly labeled apartment buildings. Then teams drove to the Fountain of Wealth, in Suntec City, where a Roadblock had them run through the fountain to find a clue. John Vito and Jill, who won the first leg of Episode 9, arrived last at the Pit Stop at Mount Faber, and were the eighth team eliminated from the race.

In Episode 10, teams flew to Ho Chi Minh City, in Vietnam, to find the statue of Bac Ho, in Rex Square. From there, teams traveled to the rural Mekong Delta. The Detour gave teams the option of buying a water coconut at a floating marketplace or selling a basketful of fruit. Next, teams traveled to Ton Duc Thang, near the Saigon River, where a Roadblock required one member from each team to drive a bicycle taxi, pedaling the team partner to the Pit Stop at Café Thu Thiem. Derek and Drew arrived last, and were the ninth team eliminated from the race.

In the first half of the two-hour Episode 11 finale, teams took a four-hundred-mile train ride to the Imperial Palace in Hue, Vietnam. There they were instructed to go to a bridge in Da Nang. The Detour had teams cross the river either in "Basket Boats" or by riding across the bridge in "Basket Bikes" loaded with shrimp baskets. Then teams taxied to the boat quay in Hoi An and boated out to the middle of the river. For the Roadblock, teams used a traditional Vietnamese fishing platform to raise a fishing net containing the next clue. They then traveled to the Pit Stop at China Beach, in Hoi An. Flo and Zach arrived last, but were not eliminated from the race.

During the second hour of the finale, teams traveled to the Quang Minh Temple, where they learned they had to fly to Hawaii. In Kauai, teams strapped on parachutes at the top of Wailua Falls. For the Detour, they had to drop more than 150 feet to the pool below, or walk down a long path to the bottom of the falls. After that, they flew to Seattle, where they met at Kerry Park. From there, they went to the International Fountain at Seattle Center, near the Space Needle. For the Roadblock, teams arranged spinning animal faces that represented different tasks on a totem pole in the order in which they appeared this season. Flo and Zach crossed the finish line first and won the $1 million prize, with Teri and Ian in second and Ken and Gerard finishing third.

RATINGS: The third season of *The Amazing Race* gave CBS an average of 9.1 million viewers.

THE AMAZING RACE

(Season 4)

GENRE   Competition
FIRST TELECAST   5/29/2003

LAST TELECAST	8/21/2003
NETWORK	CBS
AIR TIME	Thursday, 8:00 p.m.
EPISODE STYLE	Story Arc
TALENT	Phil Keoghan (Host)
CAST	Reichen Lehmkuhl and Chip Arndt (Winners—gay and married); Kelly Parks and Jon Corso (2nd place—engaged couple); David Dean and Jeff Strand (3rd place—best friends); John Weiss and Al Rios (4th place—best friends and clowns); Chuck Shankles and Millie Smith (5th place—dating virgins); Tian Kitchen and Jaree Poteet (6th place—models and friends); Monica Ambrose and Sheree Buchanan (7th place—NFL wives); Steve Meitz and Dave Cottingham (8th place—air traffic controllers); Steve and Josh (9th place—father and son); Russell Brown and Cindy Duck (10th place—dating couple); Amanda Adams and Chris Garry (11th place—dating couple); Debra Carmody and Steve Carmody (12th place—married parents)
PRODUCTION COMPANIES	Bruckheimer Films and Earthview Inc., in association with Touchstone Television and Amazing Race Productions
CREATED BY	Jerry Bruckheimer; Bertram van Munster; Elise Doganieri
EXECUTIVE PRODUCERS	Jerry Bruckheimer; Bertram van Munster; Jonathan Littman; Hayma Screech Washington
CO-EXECUTIVE PRODUCERS	Amy Chacon; Evan Weinstein

Season 4 featured twelve teams: dating couple Amanda and Chris, best friends David and Jeff, married parents Debra and Steve, best friends and clowns John and Al, engaged couple Kelly and Jon, virginal dating couple Millie and Chuck, NFL wives Monica and Sheree, gay couple Reichen and Chip, dating couple Russell and Cindy, air traffic controllers Steve and Dave, father and son Steve and Josh, and model friends Tian and Jaree.

In Episode 1, the race began at Dodger Stadium, in Los Angeles, where the teams were instructed to fly to Milan, Italy. From there, they retrieved a clue at the top of the Dolomite Mountains. At the Detour, teams used a searchlight to find a key to start a snowmobile or crossed a steel cable bridge and used a zip line to fly across a 250-foot ravine. Afterward, they hiked to the Pit Stop, at the Hotel Lajadira in Cortina d'Ampezzo. Monica and Sheree took the Fast Forward and went directly to the hotel. Debra and Steve were the last to arrive, and were the first team eliminated from the race.

In Episode 2, teams snow-rafted down the ski jump at the Trampolino Olimpico, in Cortina d'Ampezzo. Then they traveled by train to the Ponte della Guglia bridge in Venice. For the "Waterway" or "Pathway" Detour, teams had to reach a plaza by gondola or on foot. Steve and Dave earned the Fast Forward by spotting it during a commedia dell'arte skit, and advanced to the Pit Stop—*Città di Padova* boat, in Venice. The other teams attended a masquerade at Palazzo da Mosto. For the Roadblock, teams had to photograph a doorman who was wearing a specific mask. Amanda and Chris arrived last at the Pit Stip, and were the second team eliminated from the race.

In Episode 3, teams traveled by train to Vienna, Austria, where a clue in the sewer instructed them to take a horse-drawn carriage to Schönbrunn Palace. For the Detour, teams had to choose between "Mozart" and "Beethoven," either dragging a double bass to the house where Mozart wrote *The Marriage of Figaro* or taking sheet music to the house where Beethoven wrote the "Heiligenstadt Testament." Steve and Josh won the Fast Forward by walking across a ballroom floor crowded with dancers while successfully balancing a tray of full Champagne glasses, and the duo advanced to the Pit Stop—Seeschloss Orth, in Gmunden, Austria. Meanwhile, the other teams went to the Donauturm spire, overlooking the Danube River. One member from each team bungeejumped off the spire during the Roadblock. Afterward, the teams traveled by train to Gmunden, to the Pit Stop. Russell and Cindy's inadvertent trip to Gmund rather than Gmunden caused them to arrive last, making them the third team eliminated.

In Episode 4, teams flew to Paris, where they boarded trains to the Le Mans racetrack. For the Roadblock, one member of each team performed a pitstop and rode a lap in a race car at the Bugatti Circuit. Teams then drove to Marseille, where they found a clue in the Phare de Sainte Marie lighthouse. From there they drove to the Gorges du Blavet, where the Detour offered the option "Ropes" or "Slopes"—rappelling versus hiking down a trail. Finally, the teams traveled to a two-hundred-year-old mansion at the Château des Alpilles, the Pit Stop, in Saint-Rémy-de-Provence. Tian and Jaree earned the Fast Forward by solving a puzzle at a museum near Marseille, and advanced directly to the Pit Stop. Steve and Josh arrived last, becoming the fourth team eliminated from the race.

In Episode 5, teams flew to Amsterdam to find the Magere Brug, a white bridge on the Amstel River. Then they boated to the Maritime/Scheepvaart Museum. For the Detour, teams carried cheese on stretchers or sifted through cow manure for the next clue. Chuck and Millie earned the Fast Forward by being strapped to the sails of the Molen Von Sloten windmill for ten revolutions. They proceeded directly to the Pit Stop, the Kasteel Muiderslot, in Muiden, the Netherlands. The other teams had to find a statue called *The Smoker* in the fishing village of Monnickendam. One member of each team had to catch twenty-five live eels for the Roadblock. Air traffic controllers Steve and Dave were the last to arrive at the Pit Stop, and were the fifth team eliminated from the race.

In Episode 6, teams traveled to Mumbai, India, where they went to Bollywood's Film City. During the "Suds" or "Duds" Detour, teams had to wash clothes by hand or locate a particular sari in a marketplace. From there, they went to Indo Universal Engineering, at Sassoon Docks, where the Roadblock instructed one member of each team to find twenty Palai fish in a fish market, and trade them for the next clue. Finally, the duos traveled to the Pit Stop, at the Gateway of India, in Mumbai, where Monica and Sheree's last-place finish made them the sixth team eliminated.

In Episode 7, the teams took a twenty-four-hour train ride to the Indian city of Ernakulam. Bulls dragged team members through mud and manure at the Roadblock at the sports field in Alleppey. The Detour offered team members the option of delivering yarn by elephant or chickens by bicycle. Teams concluded the leg at the Pitstop in rural Alleppey. Tian and Jaree were the last to arrive, and were the seventh team eliminated from the race.

In Episode 8, the teams traveled to Kota Kinabalu, Malaysia, where they were given a good-luck blessing from a priestess at Monsopiad Cultural Village. Teams then took a boat to a fishing trawler, where a Detour offered the options to "Net" fifteen fish in a pen or "Trap" lobsters. Next, at Manukan Island, one member from each team had to hit targets using a bow and arrow, blowpipe, and spear for the Roadblock. Kelly and Jon were the last to arrive at the Pit Stop, in Manukan Island, but were safe because it was a non-elimination leg.

In Episode 9, teams traveled within Malaysia to Kinabalu Park's Poring Hot Springs, where they walked on bridges more than one hundred feet above the ground before going to the Trushidup Palm Oil Plantation. Chip and Reichen beat Jon and Kelly to the Fast Forward by feeding four pieces of fruit to orangutans at the Sepilok Orangutan Rehabilitation Centre, in Sandakan. Meanwhile, the others stopped at the Detour, where they had to "Chop" down palm nut bunches or "Haul" the prickly bunches by wheelbarrow to a truck. At the Roadblock at Gomantong Caves, one member of each team climbed a fifty-foot ladder to get the final clue. Jon and Kelly overcame their Fast Forward mishap by reaching the Pit Stop at Sepilok Nature Resort before Millie and Chuck, who were the eighth team eliminated.

In Episode 10, the teams traveled to the Puu Jih Shih Temple, in Sandakan. They then flew from Kota Kinabalu to Seoul, South Korea, to locate Seoul Tower, in Namsan Park. Taxis took them to the Hanton River, in Sundam Valley, near the North Korean border. For the Roadblock, one member from each team swam through the partially frozen river. The teams then went to a subway station, where a Detour tested their "Strong Hands" or "Strong Stomachs." The duos had to break three stacks of boards with their hands at a Tae Kwon Do center or eat a large bowl of live octopus at a Korean restaurant. The Pit Stop was Seoul's Gyeongbokgung Palace. David and Jeff finished last, but stayed in contention because it was a non-elimination leg.

In Episode 11, the teams found their first clue hanging on a kite string at Hangang People's Park, at Yeouido Island, in Seoul. The clue sent them to a hotel penthouse in Brisbane, Australia. For the Detour, teams rappelled thirty feet down the side of the hotel or walked all the way down from the hotel and climbed up the stairs of another building to obtain the next clue. They then drove to the Underwater World aquarium, in Mooloolaba, where the Roadblock had them don scuba gear and retrieve a clue from a treasure chest. From there, it was a footrace to the Pit Stop at the Mooloolaba Yacht Club. Meanwhile, David and Jeff earned the Fast Forward by passing a lifeguard test to save a "victim," and advanced directly to the Pit Stop. Jon and Al were the last to reach the club, and were the ninth team eliminated from the race.

In Episode 12, the teams traveled to a woolshed in Ferny Hills. They then flew from Brisbane to Cairns, where they drove a car to Wild World Tropical Zoo, and where one member from each team photographed their partner feeding a crocodile. At Wangetti Beach, teams were given a Detour option to "Saddle Up" and ride horses or "Paddle" a kayak to a buoy. Then they drove outside Cairns to an adventure sports company, where they drove race buggies across a bumpy, muddy track for the Roadblock. The Pit Stop was fifty miles away, on Ellis Beach. Jon and Kelly finished last, but were safe because it was a non-elimination leg.

In Episode 13, the finale began with a trek to Tjapukai Aboriginal Cultural Park. From there, teams drove to Cairns International Airport and received a Detour instructing them to skydive ten thousand feet with an instructor or drive to a forest to locate a boat to travel to the skydive landing zone. Then they flew to the big island of Hawaii, where the Roadblock had them swim in Hilo's Kaulana Bay, retrieve a rock, break it, and read the clue hidden inside. The clue led teams to Hawaii Volcanoes National Park, from where they departed to find the anchor of the U.S.S. *Arizona,* in Phoenix. Afterward, teams went to Tempe's Sun Devil Stadium, where they solved a puzzle leading them to a particular seat containing the next clue. Finally, they arrived at Phoenix's Papago Park, where they rode mountain bikes to the finish line. Chip and Reichen arrived first, winning the $1 million prize, while Kelly and Jon came in second, and David and Jeff finished third.

RATINGS: Season 4 of *The Amazing Race* drew in an average of 8.4 million viewers.

THE AMAZING RACE
(Season 5)

GENRE	Competition
FIRST TELECAST	7/6/2004
LAST TELECAST	9/21/2004
NETWORK	CBS
AIR TIME	Tuesday, 10:00 p.m.
TALENT	Phil Keoghan (Host)

CAST Chip McAllister and Kim McAllister (Winner—married couple); Colin Guinn and Christie Woods (2nd place—dating couple); Brandon Davidson and Nicole O'Brian (3rd place—dating models); Linda Ruiz and Karen Heins (4th place—bowling moms); Kami French and Karli French (5th place—twins); Mirna Hindoyan and Charla Faddoul (6th place—cousins); Marshall Hudes and Lance Hudes (7th place—brothers); Bob Barron and Joyce Nicolo (8th place—senior Internet-dating couple); Jim McCoy and Marsha McCoy (9th place—father and daughter); Alison Irwin and Donny Patrick (10th place—dating couple); Dennis Frentsos and Erika Shay (11th place—previously engaged couple)

PRODUCTION COMPANIES Bruckheimer Films and Earthview Inc., in association with Touchstone Television and Amazing Race Productions

CREATED BY Jerry Bruckheimer; Bertram van Munster; Elise Doganieri

EXECUTIVE PRODUCERS Jerry Bruckheimer; Bertram van Munster; Jonathan Littman; Hayma Screech Washington

CO-EXECUTIVE PRODUCERS Amy Chacon; Evan Weinstein

Season 5 featured eleven teams: dating couple Alison (of *Big Brother 4*) and Donny, senior Internet-dating couple Bob and Joyce, dating couple Brandon and Nicole, cousins Mirna and Charla, married parents Chip and Kim, dating couple Colin and Christie, previously engaged Dennis and Erika, father and daughter Jim and Marsha, twins Kami and Karli, bowling best friends Linda and Karen, and brothers Marshall and Lance. This season introduced the "Yield" feature—whichever team used it could force one other team to stall for one hour. Each team could use the Yield advantage only once during the race.

In Episode 1, the teams began at the Santa Monica Pier, in California, where Jim injured his knee, requiring stitches. The teams flew to Uruguay, then took a bus to Punta del Este, to find a statue called *The Hand in the Sand.* From there, they took a ferry to Gorriti Island, leaving the next morning for a meat warehouse near the suburb of Maldonado, where each team had to carry a fifty-five-pound side of beef to a butcher shop. Alison and Donny were the first to reach the Yield, but chose not to use it. For the "Zips" or "Chips" Detour, teams had to pull themselves along a zip line from the top of a hotel or play twenty chips at a casino's roulette wheel. Then the teams took taxis to the Pit Stop—Casapueblo, in Punta Ballena. Chip and Kim had to return to retrieve a Route Marker they had missed, but they still finished ahead of Dennis and Erika, who arrived last and were the first team eliminated from the race.

In Episode 2, the teams traveled to Uruguay's capital, Montevideo, where they found clues hidden inside inflatable balls at the Shake Mega Disco. Next, the teams traveled to Buenos Aires, Argentina, where they found Evita Perón's tombstone, in Recoleta Cemetery. For the Detour, teams had to choose between walking eight dogs or finding a particular man among a group of tango dancers. They then went to Argentine ranch Estancia La Invernada, in San Antonio de Areco, where they retrieved a bandana from a calf's neck during the Roadblock. Finally, the teams took a carriage to the Pit Stop, an estate called La Porteña. Alison and Donny arrived last, and were the second team eliminated.

In Episode 3, the teams flew to San Carlos de Bariloche, a village at the base of the Andes Mountains. The mayor directed them to a chocolate factory, where they bit into thousands of chocolates in search of one with a white center. They then drove to Villa Catedral and took a gondola to the top of the mountain, where they encountered the Detour. In "Smooth Sailing" or "Rough Riding," teams had to paraglide or bike a rugged course down the mountain. Finally, they drove to the Pit Stop—Bahía López— where Jim and Marsha were the last to arrive, and the third team eliminated from the race.

In Episode 4, the teams took a one-thousand-mile bus ride back to Buenos Aires, followed by an eight-thousand-mile flight to St. Petersburg, Russia. At the battleship *Aurora,* teams had to find the gun that started the Russian Revolution. For the Detour, the teams blocked five shots from professional hockey players or drank a vodka shot while successfully balancing it on a sword. Then they traveled to the town of Pushkin to find the Old Tower Restaurant, where one member from each team ate a kilogram of caviar for the Roadblock. Upon completion, the teams took a sleigh to the Pit Stop at Catherine Palace. Bob and Joyce arrived last, and were the fourth team eliminated from the race.

In Episode 5, the teams took a train to St. Petersburg's Hermitage Museum, where they had to find Rembrandt's painting *The Return of the Prodigal Son*. A clue then directed them to fly to Cairo, Egypt, and to the Tower of Cairo. Colin and Christie earned the first Fast Forward by transporting a sarcophagus to a temple, and advanced to the Pit Stop—the Sphinx, in Giza. Meanwhile, the other teams went to the Giza Plateau, home to the three Great Pyramids. For the Roadblock, one member of each duo climbed into a watery tomb called the Osiris Shaft to retrieve a satchel. After solving a puzzle found within the satchel, teams headed to the Pit Stop. Linda and Karen arrived last, but were safe because it was a non-elimination round, but they were stripped of their money leading into the next leg.

In Episode 6, a clue in the Great Pyramids led the teams to Luxor, Egypt, then to the Karnak Temple, to find an ancient structure called the "mound of Creation." For the Detour, teams had to herd sheep onto a boat and sail them across the Nile or transport an urn of water by donkey. They then took taxis to Habu Temple, where they dug for a scarab for the Roadblock. Finally, they hurried to the Pit Stop at Crocodile Island. Marshall and Lance quit the race because of Marshall's severe knee pain; they were the sixth team eliminated.

In Episode 7, the teams flew to Nairobi, Kenya, and boarded a mystery flight to Kilimanjaro, Tanzania. From there they took a bus to the town of Mto Wa Mbu, where, for the Detour, they had the option of harvesting honey at a bee farm or delivering furniture. After traveling to the Kavishe Hotel in Kibaoni, one member from each team ate a large ostrich egg for the Roadblock. For their next challenge, teams zip-lined across a gorge to a Lake Manyara lookout, the Pit Stop. Charla and Mirna arrived last, and were the seventh team eliminated from the race.

In Episode 8, teams went to Dubai, United Arab Emirates. During the journey, Chip's refusal to pay a cabdriver the full fare resulted in Colin being sent to the police station. Colin finally paid the money, and he and Christie returned to the race. A clue on the heliport atop the Burj Al Arab hotel directed the teams to take a water taxi to the Port of Dubai. For the Detour, they skydived or drove four-by-four vehicles across the desert to the skydiving landing zone. Finally, teams went to the Pit Stop at a Bedouin oasis near Dubai, where last-place finishers Kami and Karli were relieved to learn it was a non-elimination leg.

In Episode 9, the teams traveled to Wild Wadi water park, where a clue instructed them to slide down Jumeirah Sceirah, a one-hundred-foot-high water slide. From there the teams flew to Kolkata, India, to find the Sahid Minar monument. Colin and Christie were the first to reach the second Yield, but chose not to use it. The teams also declined to use the Fast Forward, which would have required them to shave their heads. Then they traveled to the Globe Brick Factory, in Garia, where the Roadblock had them make twenty mud bricks. Next, teams took a train to Sealdah Station, where, for the Detour, they pushed an engineless taxi a half mile or found a specific stall in a large flower market where they would obtain a garland to release in the Ganges River. Finally, the teams headed to the Pit Stop at Victoria Memorial Hall. Brandon and Nicole finished last, but were surprised to learn it was the second consecutive non-elimination leg of the race.

In Episode 10, teams boarded a seven-thousand-mile flight to Auckland, New Zealand, where upon arrival, they drove two hundred more miles, to the Rotorua Museum. Colin and Christie once again declined to use the Yield, deeming it bad sportsmanship. For the "Clean" or "Dirty" Detour, teams white-water rafted a mile-long sledge course or scoured through a Hell's Gate mud pit for a clue. They then went to Rotorua's Matapara Farms, where the Roadblock required one member from each team to roll downhill in a giant inflatable ball called a zorb, then "walk" the zorb to the Pit Stop. Kami and Karli finished last, and were the eighth team eliminated from the race.

In Episode 11, teams drove 220 miles, to Auckland's Westhaven Marina, to find a particular yacht that had the Roadblock clue directing them to travel by boat to a bridge, climb a seventy-five-foot ladder, and retrieve a clue from the girders underneath the Auckland Harbour Bridge. The clue instructed teams to fly to Manila, Philippines, and from there travel to Malagueña Motors, in Cavite. Linda and Karen were the first to spot the Yield sign, but Chip and Kim opted to use it against Colin and Christie. Next, the teams decorated jeepnies (Filipino jitneys) and traveled to Victoria to find a giant duck statue. For the Detour, teams searched for a clue by plowing a field with oxen or herding one thousand ducks from one pen into another. Finally, teams raced to the Pit Stop—Coconut Palace, in Manila. After being Yielded, Colin and Christie finished last, but it was a non-elimination round, so they advanced to the finale.

In the two-part Episode 12 finale, teams went to Luneta Park to find a statue of Philippine hero José Rizal. They then boarded a charter flight to the island village of El Nido, where they took boats to find the island with a Philippine flag. Once they arrived, they donned snorkel gear and searched for the giant clam holding the next clue. For the Roadblock, one team member scaled the Lagen Wall by rope to retrieve a clue, then rappelled down. Linda and Karen were the last team to arrive at the Pit Stop at Lagen Island, and were the eighth team eliminated from the race.

To kick off the thirteenth and final leg, teams flew to snowy Calgary, Canada, and snowshoed one thousand feet to the top of the Continental Divide. From there, teams traveled to Olympic Park, in search of the Olympic cauldron. For the final Detour, teams had to "Slide" down the luge or "Ride" a bike down an Olympic ski slope. Upon completion, they flew to Dallas, Texas, then traveled to Fort Worth, in search of the stockyards. A clue at the center of a maze sent the teams to the finish line at Trammell Crow Park. Chip and Kim finished first and won the $1 million prize. Colin and Christie finished second, and Brandon and Nicole came in third.

RATINGS: The fifth season of *The Amazing Race* had an average of 10.3 million viewers.

THE AMAZING RACE
(Season 6)

GENRE	Competition
FIRST TELECAST	11/16/2004
LAST TELECAST	2/8/2005
NETWORK	CBS
AIR TIME	Tuesday, 9:00 p.m.
EPISODE STYLE	Story Arc
TALENT	Phil Keoghan (Host)
CAST	Freddy Holliday and Kendra Bentley (Winners—engaged models); Kris Perkins and Jon Buehler

(2nd place—long-distance dating couple); Adam Malis and Rebecca Cardon (3rd place—former couple); Hayden Kristianson and Aaron Crumbaugh, (4th place—dating models/actors); Lori Chestnut Harvey and Bolo Dar'tainain (5th place—married wrestlers); Jonathan Baker and Victoria Fuller (6th place—married couple); Gus McLeod and Hera McLeod (7th place—father and daughter); Don St. Claire and Mary Jean St. Claire (8th place—grandparents); Lena Jensen and Kristy Jensen (9th place—sisters); Meredith Tufaro and Maria Sampogna (10th place—best friends); Avi Schneier and Joe Rashbaum (11th place—friends)

PRODUCTION COMPANIES	Bruckheimer Films and Earthview Inc., in association with Touchstone Television and Amazing Race Productions
CREATED BY	Jerry Bruckheimer; Bertram van Munster; Elise Doganieri
EXECUTIVE PRODUCERS	Jerry Bruckheimer; Bertram van Munster; Jonathan Littman; Hayma Screech Washington
CO-EXECUTIVE PRODUCERS	Amy Chacon; Evan Weinstein

Season 6's eleven teams comprised former couple Adam and Rebecca, buddies Avi and Joe, grandparents Don and Mary Jean, engaged models Freddy and Kendra, father and daughter Gus and Hera, dating models/actors Hayden and Aaron, married couple Jonathan and Victoria, long-distance dating couple Kris and Jon, sisters Lena and Kristy, married wrestlers Lori and Bolo, and best friends Meredith and Maria.

In Episode 1, the teams flew from Chicago to the Keflavik International Airport, in Iceland, and then drove to the Seljalandsfoss waterfall to find a clue. From there, they continued their drive to Iceland's largest glacier, Vatnajökull, where a Detour gave them the option to scale a steep wall using ice picks or search an iceberg lagoon for a buoy with the next clue. Finally, they drove to the Blue Lagoon in Grindavik, the race's first Pit Stop. Adam and Rebecca were delayed after accidentally filling their car's diesel tank with unleaded gasoline, but they still beat Avi and Joe, who finished last and were the first team eliminated from the race.

In Episode 2, the teams flew to Oslo, Norway, where at the Roadblock, one member from each team zip-lined one thousand feet from the top of the Holmenkollen ski jump. (*Note:* The rules of the Roadblock had changed by this point, forbidding each team member from competing in more than six Roadblocks during the race.) The teams then traveled to the village of Brandbu, where they split into two groups for a Viking boat race. From there, they took a train to Voss, where they either rollerskiied on a course or participated in a stick- and axe-throwing competition for the Detour. Meredith and Maria were the last to reach the Pit Stop—Nesheimstunet Village, in Voss—and were therefore the second team eliminated from the race.

In Episode 3, the teams traveled to Stockholm, Sweden, in search of the Ice Bar, a nightclub made entirely of ice, where they slid shot glasses down a bar to hit a target. Next, at the world's largest IKEA store, the teams either counted the exact number of items in three bins or correctly assembled a desk for the Detour. Afterward, they took a train to Häggvik, then biked to a nearby farm. Hayden and Aaron, and Kris and Jon discovered the first Yield, but elected not to use it. For the Roadblock, one member of each team unrolled 270 hay bales to find the next clue. The teams returned to Stockholm to reach the Pit Stop—the ship the AF *Chapman*. After eight unsuccessful hours in the hay field, Lena was informed that she and Kristy were the third team eliminated from the race.

In Episode 4, the teams flew to Dakar, Senegal, to find Bel-Aire Cemetery, where a famous poet and former Senegalese president were buried. From there, the teams traveled to the fishing village of Kayar, where, for the Detour, they either caught fish from a boat or stacked fishing baskets on a table. In Lac Rose, one team member had to harvest enough salt to fill a twenty-five-gallon basket for the Roadblock. Finally, the teams took a ferry to the Pit Stop, at Île de Gorée, where last-place finishers Don and Mary Jean were happy to learn it was a non-elimination leg of the race.

In Episode 5, the teams went to the historic Slave House on Gorée Island, and then returned to Dakar, where they flew to Berlin, Germany. From there they took a train to the Berlin Wall, then went downtown to the Broken Chain sculpture. For the "Beers" or "Brats" Detour, teams searched a bar for coasters bearing their names and faces or traveled to a sausage factory to make a rope of five bratwurst links. For the Roadblock in Teufelsberg, one team member had to climb Devil's Mountain and race a soapbox derby car in less than thirty-seven seconds. After a footrace to the Pit Stop at Berlin's Brandenburg Gate, Don and Mary Jean finished last for the second leg in a row, and were thus the fifth team eliminated.

In Episode 6, the teams traveled to Checkpoint Charlie and Olympic Stadium in Berlin. For the Roadblock, one team member was strapped into a "hot rocket bungee" and sling-shot two hundred feet into the air. Next, the teams flew to Budapest, Hungary, and drove unreliable Trabants to the town of Eger. For the Detour, they either catapulted watermelons at a target or rolled cannonballs up a hill and stacked them in a pyramid. Then they returned to Budapest and to the Net Klub Internet Café, where the episode ended in a cliffhanger.

In Episode 7, the teams took taxis to the Heritage Rail Museum, where they had to race small motorized cars. Lori and Bolo won the Fast Forward by drinking pig's blood at a Transylvanian castle. The other teams headed to Margrit Island, where, for the Detour, they either attempted to score a goal against a Hungarian water polo player or rafted across the Danube River. From there, they went to Gundel, a one-hundred-year-old Budapest restaurant, where one member from each team had to eat twenty-four ounces of spicy soup. The leg ended with an uphill footrace to the Pit Stop at Fisherman's Bastion. Gus and Hera arrived last, and were the fifth team eliminated.

In Episode 8, the teams traveled to a winery in Budafok, where a clue directed them to fly to Corsica. Adam and Rebecca were the first to arrive at Napoleon's birthplace in Ajaccio, France, and they earned the Fast Forward by diving for a lobster trap on the ocean floor. They advanced to the Pit Stop at La Pietra in L'Île-Rousse. Meanwhile, the other teams encountered the Detour at Camp Raffalli, in Calvi, and either scaled a rock wall with an ascender rope or searched for a clue on a Zodiac boat among a sea of buoys. Next, the teams traveled to a winery in Zilia, where, for the Roadblock, one member of each team had to stomp enough grapes to fill five wine bottles. Hayden and Aaron were the last to arrive at the Pit Stop, but were safe because it was a non-elimination leg.

In Episode 9, the teams flew to Nice, France, where the first clue was hidden in the statue bust of King Albert I. From there, the teams traveled to Addis Ababa, Ethiopia, where, for the Detour, they either carried a thatched roof and installed it on a house or used mud to cover the wall of a house. Then they delivered two donkeys to St. George's Church in Lalibela, where Hayden and Aaron encountered the second Yield. Electing not to use it, they received the Roadblock, which instructed one team member to descend into the church to find a specific pendant on one of hundreds of worshippers. Then the teams went to the Pit Stop at nearby Lalibela Lookout. Jonathan and Victoria were the last to arrive, and were the sixth team eliminated from the race.

In Episode 10, the teams flew to Colombo, Sri Lanka, where, for the Detour, they climbed a tree and crossed a rope bridge to obtain liquor-making sap or scored a polo goal while riding an elephant. The teams then rode a bus to Dambulla, where the Roadblock had one team member climb more than one thousand steps to the top of Lion's Rock (using it as a vantage point from which to locate a flag), climb down to retrieve it, and along with their partner, bring it to the Pit Stop in Sigiriya. Lori and Bolo finished last, and were the seventh team eliminated from the race.

In Episode 11, the teams went to Shanghai, China, to find the Yu Yuan Gardens. From there, they took taxis to Huaneng Union Tower to find the next clue, as well as the Yield, which Freddy and Kendra used on Adam and Rebecca. For the Roadblock, one team member climbed a skyscraper and used a window washer's chair to clean a window, revealing the message "Tai Chi." From there the teams went to the Monument of the People's Heroes to find a master among a group of tai chi performers. At the Jiangpu Road Detour, teams carried bricks across a narrow plank or delivered more than four hundred pounds of ice to a fish market via tricycle. Thanks in part to the Yield, Adam and Rebecca were the last to arrive at the Pit Stop, Peace Hotel South Wing, but were spared when they learned it was a non-elimination leg of the race.

In the two-part Episode 12 finale, the teams took a train to Xi'an, then a taxi to Drum Tower, where, for the Detour, they either spray-painted a vehicle at a car factory or located two Chinese characters printed somewhere on ten bolts of fabric at a textile factory. Then they traveled to the Terracotta Warriors Museum, where a clue sent them to the north peak of Mount Hua, the site of the Roadblock. At the top, one team member had to find one of three thousand padlocks that could be opened by a key they had been given. Hayden and Aaron gave up and took a four-hour penalty, which caused them to be the eighth team eliminated from the race.

Next the teams flew to Honolulu, Hawaii, where at the Puu Ualakaa State Park

Detour, they searched more than one hundred thousand articles of clothing for a matching outfit or paddled an outrigger canoe on a two-mile course. After a skydiving Roadblock at Kamaka Air, the teams returned to Chicago. A clue at the top of the famous Water Tower directed them to Gino's East pizzeria, where they ate an entire deep-dish pizza for breakfast. Freddy and Kendra were first to cross the finish line at Ping Tom Memorial Park, and were awarded the $1 million prize. Kris and John finished second, and Adam and Rebecca came in third.

RATINGS: The sixth season of *The Amazing Race* brought in an average of 11.5 million viewers to CBS.

THE AMAZING RACE
(Season 7)

GENRE	Competition
FIRST TELECAST	3/1/2005
LAST TELECAST	5/10/2005
NETWORK	CBS
AIR TIME	Tuesday, 9:00 p.m.
EPISODE STYLE	Story Arc
TALENT	Phil Keoghan (Host)
CAST	Uchenna Agu and Joyce Agu (Winners—married couple); Rob Mariano and Amber Brkich (2nd place—engaged *Survivor* contestants); Ron Young and Kelly McCorkle (3rd place—dating POW and beauty queen); Meredith Smith and Gretchen Smith (4th place—retired couple); Lynn Warren and Alex Ali (5th place—boyfriends); Brian Smith and Greg Smith (6th place—brothers); Ray Housteau and Deana Shane (7th place—dating couple); Susan Vaughan and Patrick Vaughn (8th place—mother and son); Debbie Cloyed and Bianca Smith (9th place—

	friends); Megan Baker and Heidi Heidel (10th place—roommates); Ryan Phillips and Chuck Horton, (11th place—best friends)
PRODUCTION COMPANIES	Bruckheimer Films and Earthview Inc., in association with Touchstone Television and Amazing Race Productions
CREATED BY	Jerry Bruckheimer; Bertram van Munster; Elise Doganieri
EXECUTIVE PRODUCERS	Jerry Bruckheimer, Bertram van Munster; Jonathan Littman; Hayma Screech Washington
CO-EXECUTIVE PRODUCERS	Amy Chacon; Evan Weinstein

Season 7's eleven competitors were brothers Brian and Greg, friends Debbie and Bianca, boyfriends Lynn and Alex, roommates Megan and Heidi, retired couple Meredith and Gretchen, dating couple Ray and Deana, engaged *Survivor* contestants Rob and Amber, dating couple Ron and Kelly, best friends Ryan and Chuck, mother and son Susan and Patrick, and married couple Uchenna and Joyce.

In Episode 1, the teams began the race with a trip from Los Angeles to Cuzco, Peru, where a clue at a kiosk directed them to zip-line to the bottom of a gorge. For the Detour, teams either roped two llamas and led them to a pen or carried a basket with thirty-five pounds of alfalfa to a store. They then rode a delivery truck to the town of Pisac, and took a taxi back to Cuzco, to the Pit Stop, the 325-year-old church Convento de la Merced. Ryan and Chuck lost a footrace to the finish, and were the first team eliminated from the race.

In Episode 2, the teams began the leg with a shoe-shining task in Arequipa. They then traveled to Santiago, Chile, in search of a statue of the Virgin Mary at Cerro San Cristobal. For the "Shop" or "Schlep" Detour, they shopped for five ingredients for a chef or hauled a load of books to the Library of Congress. Megan and Heidi were the last team to reach the Pit Stop, at the Neptune fountain in Cerra Santa Lucia, and were the second team eliminated from the race.

In Episode 3, the teams drove through the Andes Mountains to Puente Viejo, in Argentina, where Rob and Amber encountered the first Yield but chose not to use it. For the Detour, teams rafted or biked a seven-mile course. Upon reaching Camp Suizo, a Roadblock required one member from each team to eat an Argentine meal consisting of four pounds of unusual cow parts. After Rob failed the Roadblock, he persuaded Ray and Deana and Meredith and Gretchen to fail it, too, with each accepting a four-hour penalty. Despite these setbacks, it was Debbie and Bianca who were last to arrive at the Pit Stop at Estância San Isidro horse ranch, and they were the third team eliminated from the race.

In Episode 4, the teams traveled to the town of Lunlunta to find Cabaña la Guatana gaucho ranch, where for the Roadblock, one team member had to ride a horse around barrels and spear a ring at the end of a course in forty seconds. Next, the teams traveled to Buenos Aires, where a man at the English Clock Tower sent them to the city of Tigre. For the Detour, at the docks, the teams located a specific shipwreck or navigated waterways to find a specific island. The Pit Stop was at the prestigious La Martina polo club, in Vicente Casares. Susan and Patrick arrived last, and were the fourth team eliminated from the race.

In the two-hour Episode 5, the teams flew to Johannesburg, South Africa, where, for the Detour, they rappelled into underground caves or delivered traditional items to five tribes. During the cave challenge, Gretchen fell and cut her face, requiring medical attention. Meanwhile, Ray and Deana opted to take the Fast Forward by crossing a dangerous walk suspension bridge, while the other teams drove to the Baragwanath Market in Soweto, where for the Roadblock, one member of each team purchased five items for a local orphanage. Meredith and Gretchen were last at the Pit Stop, on Kgakane Street in Soweto, but it was a non-elimination leg and they were only stripped of their money.

During the second hour of Episode 5, the teams traveled to Botswana, where one member from each team had to spear a moving target from twenty feet away for the Roadblock in Francistown. For the Detour, teams made flour by grinding corn or used straws to suck water from a pool and transferred it to a series of ostrich eggs. En route to the Detour, Brian and Greg's Jeep flipped, injuring their cameramen. While most teams stopped to check on them, Rob and Amber passed them by. This second leg culminated in a footrace to the Makgadikgadi Pans Pit Stop, where Brian and Greg finished first. Despite using the Fast Forward earlier, Ray and Deana were the last to arrive and were eliminated.

In Episode 6, teams traveled to a water tower in Sankuyo Village, where, for the

Detour, they carried items on their heads or milked goats. Next, the teams drove to the Khwai River and encountered the Roadblock, which required navigating the team's vehicle through a crocodile-infested river, and removing logs so the vehicle could drive through the bush. The Pit Stop was at the Khwai River Lodge, where Brian and Greg arrived last and were the fifth team eliminated from the race.

In Episode 7, the teams flew to Lucknow, India, to find the Bara Imambara Palace. Next, they headed to a steel emporium, where Rob and Amber talked Ron and Kelly out of using their Yield. For the Roadblock, one team member searched six hundred tin boxes for a clue, which directed them to take a rickshaw to a gas station in Aishbagh. For the "Solid" or "Liquid" Detour, teams transported coal on a flatbed bicycle to a store or delivered tea to five different employees in a crowded three-story office building. A surprise twist had the teams expecting a Pit Stop at the top of a Jodhpur building, but instead Phil gave them a clue to their next destination.

In Episode 8, the teams continued on the leg and went to the train station in Jodhpur, then to a clock tower in Sardar Marker. For the Detour, the teams transported a six-hundred-pound tiki elephant or dyed twenty sheets of fabric until the clue was revealed. Then they took an auto rickshaw to the Deora Krishi Farm, where, for the Roadblock, one member from each team maneuvered a camel-driven cart twice around a course. Meanwhile, Uchenna and Joyce earned a Fast Forward by shaving their heads, and advanced to the Pit Stop at Jaswant Thada, in Jodhpur. A visit to the wrong palace caused Lynn and Alex to finish last, and they were the seventh team eliminated from the race.

In Episode 9, the teams flew to Istanbul, Turkey, and took a ferry to the island of Kiz Kulesi, where they had to find one of four Travelocity roaming gnomes on the island. For the Detour, at Galata Kulesi tower, teams retrieved a box from a well and decoded a combination to unlock it or gathered enough locals to amass 2,500 kilograms. They then traveled to the Rumeli Hisari fortress, where the Roadblock required one member from each team to climb a rope ladder to retrieve a key unlocking the next clue. Ron and Kelly were last to reach the Pit Stop, at Rumeli Hisari lookout, but were relieved to learn it was a non-elimination leg.

In Episode 10, the teams flew to London, to find Abbey Road, and later traveled to the London Eye Ferris wheel, where they had to search for a clue flag located on a hotel roof. For the Detour, teams solved riddles in the subway, leading them to Sherlock Holmes's fictional residence at 221B Baker Street or hauled five 160-pound boats at a shipyard. At the Millennium Dome, Rob and Amber used the Yield on Ron and

Kelly. For the Roadblock, one member from each team drove a double-decker bus around a series of cones, then backed it into a parking space. The Pit Stop was at Potter's Field Park, where Meredith and Gretchen finished last and were the eighth team eliminated from the race.

In the two-hour Episode 11 finale, the teams flew to Kingston, Jamaica, and then to Frenchman's Cove, in Port Antonio, to find the next clue. For the Roadblock, one member from each team danced the limbo for the next morning's departure time. Then it was off to Grant's Level, in the hills, where, for the Detour, teams built a bamboo raft to cross the river or used an existing raft and pole to guide themselves on an eight-mile stretch of the Rio Grande. Uchenna and Joyce were the last to arrive at the first Pit Stop—at Round Hill, in Montego Bay—but were stripped of their money rather than eliminated.

During the second hour, the teams participated in an onion-chopping competition in Lucea. They then traveled to the Rose Hall Great House Resort and encountered the Detour, where they attempted a water obstacle course on horseback or golfed at a driving range. From there they flew to San Juan, Puerto Rico, and drove to the Castillo de San Felipe del Morro Fort, then to a sugar factory. For the Roadblock, one member from each team jumped off a thirty-foot bridge and swam to retrieve the next clue, which told the teams to fly to Miami, Florida. A brief stop at a cigar shop directed them to the finish line, at Bonnet House, in Fort Lauderdale. After an amazing fund-raising effort, Uchenna and Joyce finished first, winning the $1 million, with Rob and Amber in second, and Ron and Kelly in third.

RATINGS: The seventh season brought *The Amazing Race* its highest ratings, with an average of 13.0 million viewers.

THE AMAZING RACE: FAMILY EDITION
(Season 8)

GENRE	Competition
FIRST TELECAST	9/27/2005
LAST TELECAST	12/13/2005
NETWORK	CBS
AIR TIME	Tuesday, 9:00 p.m.

EPISODE STYLE	Story Arc
TALENT	Phil Keoghan (Host)
CAST	Linz Family (Winners—Nick, Alex, Megan, and Tommy; siblings); Bransen Family (2nd place—Walter, Elizabeth, Lauren, and Lindsay; father and daughters); Weaver Family (3rd place—Linda, Rebecca, Rachel, Rolly; widowed mother and children); Godlewski Family (4th place—Michelle, Sharon, Christine, Tricia; sisters); Paolo Family (5th place—Tony, Marion, DJ, Brian; parents and sons); Gaghan Family (6th place—Bill, Tammy, Billy, Carissa; parents and son and daughter); Schroeder Family (7th place—Mark, Char, Stassi, Hunter; father, stepmother, son, and daughter); Aiello Family (8th place—Tony, Kevin, Matt, David; father and sons-in-law); Rogers Family (9th place—Denny, Renee, Brittney, Brock; parents and son and daughter); Black Family (10th place—Reggie, Kim, Kenneth, Austin; parents and sons)
PRODUCTION COMPANIES	Bruckheimer Films and Earthview Inc., in association with Touchstone Television and Amazing Race Productions
CREATED BY	Jerry Bruckheimer; Bertram van Munster; Elise Doganieri
EXECUTIVE PRODUCERS	Jerry Bruckheimer; Bertram van Munster; Jonathan Littman; Hayma Screech Washington
CO-EXECUTIVE PRODUCERS	Amy Chacon; Evan Weinstein; Scott Einziger; Jon Kroll; Hayma Screech Washington; Carl Buehl

This season for the first time featured families—ten in teams of four. Because the age requirements were widened to include contestants as young as eight years old, the race traveled only largely within North America.

On the two-hour season premiere, the ten families began the race in New York City, where they were instructed to pick up camping supplies in SoHo. After finding the hot dog stand of Kevin O'Connor and Drew Feinberg from Season 1, the teams were directed to drive ninety-seven miles, to Washington Crossing, in Pennsylvania. There they re-created Washington's boat ride across the Delaware, rowing to the New Jersey riverbank to pick up a thirteen-star colonial flag. The next morning, teams faced the first Detour at Brubaker farm, in Mount Joy, where they either built a miniature watermill or transported an Amish buggy along a 1.5-mile course. Finally, the teams traveled to the Pit Stop—the Rohrer family farm in Lancaster. The Godlewski sisters were the first team to check in and claimed a $20,000 bonus. The Black family, including eight-year-old Austin, the youngest race participant, was the last team to check in, and the first eliminated from the race.

In Episode 2, the teams drove fifteen miles to the Haines Shoe House, in York, then received a clue directing them to Washington, D.C., to find another clue at the Reflecting Pool in front of the U.S. Capitol. The teams then drove to the Tidal Basin, near the Jefferson Memorial for the Roadblock, where one member from each team had to find a spy with a briefcase to get the next clue. Next, they drove to Welbourne Manor, in Middleburg, Virginia, for the Civil War–themed "Heat of the Battle" or "Heat of the Night" Detour, in which teams had to carry five injured soldiers or fill and light twenty kerosene lanterns. The Weaver family checked in first at the Pit Stop, winning a bonus trip to Bermuda. The Rogers family was the second team eliminated from the race.

In Episode 3, the teams flew from Washington, D.C., to Charleston, South Carolina, where they found their next clue in a gazebo in the Battery District. At the "Forrest Gump" or "Muddy Waters" Detour, teams either de-headed two hundred pounds of shrimp or drove an SUV through a muddy course. At the Charleston Visitors Center, the teams signed up for charter buses to an undisclosed destination eight hours away. At the Edward O. Buckbee Hangar at the U.S. Space and Rocket Center, in Huntsville, Alabama, two members from each team rode a centrifuge. The Bransen family arrived first at the Rocket Park Pit Stop, winning free gasoline for life. The Aiellos arrived last, and were the third team eliminated.

In Episode 4, the teams drove one hundred miles to Anniston, Alabama, and climbed the World's Largest Office Chair for the Roadblock. At the International Motorsports Hall of Fame, in Talladega, teams rode party bikes around the track. They then drove to Hattiesburg, Mississippi, to find the Southern Colonel trailer home dealership. For the Detour, at the Fairview Riverside State Park, in Madisonville, Louisiana, teams cut four slices off a twelve-inch log or played twenty-one against a riverboat dealer. For the second leg in a row, the Bransen family checked in first at the Pit Stop, Preservation Hall in New Orleans, winning a trip to Orlando. The Schroeders arrived last and were the fourth team eliminated from the race.

In Episode 5, the teams left the United States for Panama City, Panama, where they boarded a boat to the Smithsonian Tropical Research Institute, on Barro Colorado Island. Next, teams could complete the Detour or try for the season's only Fast Forward. The Gaghans and the Paolos went for the Fast Forward, tandem 140-foot bungee jumps. The Paolos completed the jumps first and advanced to the Miraflores Lockes Pit Stop, while the Gaghans returned to the research institute. At the Detour, teams delivered instruments to a local club or searched for wooden replicas of birds in the rain forest canopy. Then they traveled to the Estadio Juan Demóstenes Arosemena baseball stadium for the Roadblock, where one member from each team had to hit a pitch off a local Little Leaguer. The Godlewskis donned as much of their clothes as they could, figuring they'd have to give up everything but the clothes on their backs if it was a non-elimination leg—which it was, so they were safe.

In Episode 6, teams traveled six hundred miles by bus to San José, Costa Rica, where they picked up vans to drive thirty-five miles to find their next clue at the rim of an active volcano at Poas Volcano National Park. Next, teams drove to the Doka Estate coffee plantation, where they encountered the first of two Yields in the race. The Paolos arrived first and "Yielded" the Weavers. At the Roadblock, one member from each team had to find one red bean in eight hundred pounds of coffee beans. Then the teams drove to the beach town of Jaco, where, for the Detour, they either recovered Mayan relics or harvested fifteen bushels of bananas. For the second leg in a row, the Paolos arrived first at the Pit Stop—the malecón, in Quepos—where they won vehicles. The Gaghans finished last and were the fifth team to be eliminated.

In the two-hour Episode 7, the teams traveled to nearby Playa Maracas, where they swam out to a buoy to obtain their next clue, which directed them to take taxis to La Iglesia del Metal, in Grecia. For the Detour, teams painted cartwheels or transported sugarcane to a warehouse, where their next clue was hiding among many rum barrels. Next, the teams flew to Phoenix, Arizona, to the Bonderant SuperKart School, where one member from each team donned racing gear and drove fifty laps in a SuperKart for the Roadblock. The Godlewskis checked in first at the Pit Stop—the ranch at Fort McDowell Adventures, in Fountain Hill—winning a trip to Belize. The Bransens were the last to arrive, and lost everything but their passports and the clothes on their backs, since it was a non-elimination leg.

At the start of the next leg, the teams traveled to Mesa, Arizona, where one member from each performed a 360-degree loop in a fighter plane for the Roadblock. Next, the teams drove to Lipan Point, on the rim of the Grand Canyon, then to the Glen Canyon Dam, on the Colorado River, in Page, Arizona. For the Detour, teams used a compass to locate three islands or bailed water from a boat and carried it to shore. For the second leg in a row, the Godlewskis checked in first at the Pit Stop—a houseboat on Lake Powell—where they won a travel trailer. The Paolos arrived last and were the sixth team eliminated from the race.

In Episode 8, the teams traveled to Monument Valley, Utah, to John Ford's Point, where they boarded helicopters to Elephant Butte, in Arches National Park. In Moab, for the Detour, teams rappelled 270 feet into Bull Canyon or biked six miles. Next, the teams spent the night in Green River State Park, then traveled to Heber City, Utah, and Utah Olympic Park, in Park City, where the Weavers were "Yielded." For the Roadblock, one team member had to ski down a sixty-foot ramp. The Linz family arrived first at the Pit Stop—the rooftop of the Salt Lake City Public Library—winning a trip to Jackson Hole, Wyoming. The Weavers arrived last, but it was a non-elimination leg.

In Episode 9, teams inflated a hot air balloon at Park City High School, then rode across the valley. For the Detour, at the Heber Valley Railway, teams used antique tools to complete twenty feet of railway tracks or loaded four hundred pounds of coal by bucket into a steam locomotive. After stops at the eighty-seven-foot Bonneville Salt Flats sculpture called the *Tree of Utah* and at Bear Lake Rendezvous State Park, in Garden City, the teams encountered the Roadblock at Dunham Ranch, in Mt. Piney, Wyoming. Two members from each team rode horses to corral six cows. Next, the teams drove to Yellowstone National Park to watch Old Faithful erupt, then raced along Highway 287 to find the mat at the ranch at 15200, where Phil informed the teams that it wasn't a Pit Stop and that they had to keep racing.

In Episode 10, the teams traveled to the Turtle Ranch in DuBois, Wyoming, where they spent the night. At the "Pioneer Spirit" or "Native Tradition" Detour, teams either put wheels on a wagon, hooked it up to horses, and rode it a quarter mile or built a teepee using traditional tools. Next, the teams dressed up and took photos with Buffalo Bill in Cody, Wyoming. They then drove to Red Lodge Mountain golf course, in Montana. At the Roadblock, two members from each team rode a golf cart to hunt for four balls matching a particular color. Finally, the teams drove to Larry Arnold's Green Meadow Ranch, in Absarokee, where the Bransens checked in first at the Pit Stop, winning a Buick. The Godlewskis arrived last and were the seventh team eliminated from the race.

In the Episode 12 finale, the teams flew to Montreal, Canada, where they searched for a clue in the tunnels of the Underground City. At the "Slide It" or "Roll It" Detour, teams competed in curling or log rolling. At the American Pavilion, the teams were directed to an industrial park, where they had to find the door marked with the letter *J*. At the Roadblock, one member from each team had to complete a flying trapeze catch. At Parc Olympique, the teams searched fifty-six thousand seats for clue boxes designating the next morning's flight departure time to Toronto. After spotting a clue from the top of the CN Tower, the teams had to complete the final Detour, "Ship" or "Shoe," where they either sailed across Toronto Harbor and one team member climbed a one-hundred-foot mast to obtain a flag or they searched one hundred walkers for the pair of shoes matching the pair they had picked. Next, the teams drove to Queenston and boated to the Niagara River Whirlpool for their next clue, which directed them to their final destination, Lewiston, New York. For the final Roadblock, one member from each team had to piece together a giant seventy-one-piece jigsaw puzzle of North and Central America. Nick Linz beat Wally Bransen at the puzzle, and the Linz siblings checked in first at the Joseph Davis State Park Pit Stop, winning $1 million. The Bransens won the post-race "Final Amazing Challenge" (and a GMC Yukon), which aired only on CBS.com.

RATINGS: Episodes of *The Amazing Race: Family Edition* averaged 11.51 million viewers.

THE AMAZING RACE
(Season 9)

GENRE	Competition
FIRST TELECAST	2/28/2006
LAST TELECAST	5/17/2006
NETWORK	CBS
AIR TIMES	Tuesday, 10:00 p.m. (2/28–3/28); Wednesday, 8:00 p.m. (4/5–5/17)
EPISODE STYLE	Story Arc
TALENT	Phil Keoghan (Host)
CAST	BJ Averell and Tyler MacNiven (Winners—best friends); Eric Sanchez and Jeremy Ryan (2nd place—friends); Ray Whitty and Yolanda Brown-Moore (3rd place—dating); Joseph Meadows and Monica Cayce (4th place—dating); Fran Lazarus and Barry Lazarus (5th place—married forty years); Lake Garner and Michelle Garner (6th place—married parents); David Spiker and Lori Willems (7th place—dating); Danielle Turner and Dani Torchio (8th place—childhood friends), Wanda Lopez-Rochford and Desiree Cifre (9th place—mother and daughter); Lisa Hinds and Joni Glaze (10th place—sisters); John Lowe and Scott Braginton-Smith (11th place—lifelong friends)
PRODUCTION COMPANIES	Bruckheimer Films and Earthview Inc., in association with Touchstone Television and Amazing Race Productions
CREATED BY	Elise Doganieri; Bertram van Munster
EXECUTIVE PRODUCERS	Jerry Bruckheimer; Bert Van Munster; Elise Doganieri; Jonathan Littman

CO-EXECUTIVE PRODUCERS Amy Chacon; Evan Weinstein; Scott Einziger; Jon Kroll; Hayma Screech Washington; Carl Buehl,

Season 9 of *The Amazing Race* returned to the international format of the show, with eleven teams of two. The teams were buddies BJ and Tyler, lifelong friends John and Scott, couple Ray and Yolanda, parents Lake and Michelle, friends Danielle and Dani, sisters Lisa and Joni, dating twosome Joe and Monica, spouses Fran and Barry, mother and daughter Wanda and Desiree, friends Eric and Jeremy, and couple David and Lori.

In Episode 1, the teams began the race at Red Rocks Amphitheatre, outside of Denver, Colorado, then flew to São Paulo, Brazil. A clue on the rooftop of the Hotel Unique instructed teams to take a taxi to the Viaduto Santa Efigenia bridge. At the "Motor Head" or "Rotor Head" Detour, teams assembled a motorcycle or took a helicopter ride to a São Paulo building to find their next clue. They then attended a religious ceremony in a warehouse in the Santa Cecilia neighborhood. Eric and Jeremy were the first to check in at the Pit Stop—Estadio de Pacaembu—and won $10,000 each. John and Scott arrived last and were the first team eliminated from the race.

In Episode 2, the teams encountered their first Roadblock, at Edificio Copan, where they climbed the office building's fire escape and rappelled down four hundred feet. Next, the teams took three charter buses to Brotas, where they picked up Volkswagen Beetles. At the Detour, teams either pressed sugarcane and made ethanol from its distilled juice to use for fuel or used an ascender to climb a waterfall. The teams drove to the Pit Stop—Primavera da Serra, a nineteenth-century coffee plantation—where BJ and Tyler checked in first, winning a trip to Tahiti. "Glamazons" Lisa and Joni arrived last and were the second team eliminated.

In Episode 3, the teams zip-lined three hundred feet at a farm, then traveled to São Paulo, where they boarded planes to Moscow. At the Chaika Bassein water sports training facility, one member from each team jumped off the ten-meter platform, swam across the pool, and dove to the bottom to get the next clue. Next, the teams took taxis to the Novodevichy Monastery and found a clue in the Cathedral of the Virgin of Smolensk. For the Detour, the teams had to "Scour" fifteen hundred nesting dolls for ten clues or "Scrub" a public trolley bus. Eric and Jeremy arrived first at the mat at St. Basil's Cathedral, in Red Square, but Phil handed them another clue because the leg was not over.

In Episode 4, the teams flew to Frankfurt, Germany, where they boarded a train to Stuttgart to find Mercedes-Benz's flagship factory. They then had to ride on the "Wall of Death" at the factory's test track. Afterward, each team drove a Mercedes to Ellbach Field, near Bad Tölz, where one member from each searched under 150 Travelocity roaming gnomes for the Roadblock. At the Detour, at Bavaria Film Studios, in Grunewald, teams broke stunt bottles over one another's heads or performed a folk dance. Finally, Eric and Jeremy arrived first at the Pit Stop—the Siegestor peace monument, in Munich—where they traded their gnome for a trip to Africa. Wanda and Desiree finished last and were the third team eliminated from the race.

In Episode 5, the teams flew to Palermo, Italy, where they got a clue at the Teatro Massimo opera house. At the Castellammare del Golfo Detour, teams either carried a one-hundred-pound church bell up to the Chiesa di Santa Maria del Soccorso or searched clotheslines for one of sixteen marked pieces of laundry among twenty-four hundred articles of clothing. Next, the teams drove to Segesta, and hiked one mile to the ancient Greek amphitheater Teatro di Segesta, the site of this season's first Yield. The teams also learned that a Yield was ahead. For the Roadblock, one member from each team assembled a Greek statue containing two extra puzzle pieces. BJ and Tyler arrived first at the Pit Stop. Dani and Danielle, who were "Yielded" earlier, arrived last and were the fourth team eliminated.

In Episode 6, the teams drove to Catania, Sicily, to find Anfiteatro Romano, where they were given the Detour "Big Fish" or "Little Fish." Teams either carried a thirty-two pound swordfish through Catania's winding streets to the Storico la Pescheria market or sold four kilos of small Sicilian fish at the same market. Next, the teams drove to Siracusa, where one member from each team played "kayak polo" until scoring one goal for the Roadblock. Eric and Jeremy arrived first at the Fonte Aretusa Pit Stop, winning a cruise, while Dave and Lori arrived last and were the fifth team eliminated.

In Episode 7, the teams took a train to Rome, where a clue at the Trevi fountain instructed them to look for horse carriages near the Spanish Steps, where they were handed one half of a Leonardo Da Vinci Vitruvian Man. Next, the teams flew to Athens, Greece, and traveled to Agora, where Eric and Jeremy completed the Fast Forward and went directly to the Pit Stop—the Fortress of Rion. The others took a train to Isthmos Station, in Corinth, where one member from each team bungee-jumped 240 feet into the Corinth Canal for the Roadblock. At the Detour at the Ancient Stadium in Nemea, teams completed three ancient Olympic events or found nine pottery shards with Greek letters they translated into English to decipher a Greek city on a map. Lake and Michelle arrived last at the Pit Stop and were the sixth team eliminated from the race.

In Episode 8, the teams flew to Oman, where they climbed a giant incense burner in Riyann Park and then drove to a fishing village, Sur, for the "Camel" or "Watchtower" Detour. Teams either loaded a camel on a pickup truck and drove it to get the next clue or searched three towers for a scroll, which they drove to a silversmith who had the next clue. At the Roadblock in Al Hawiyah, one member from each team dug through 117 sand mounds in search of one of six *shuwas,* or underground ovens, cooking the lamb dishes they'd eat for dinner that evening. Finally, the teams drove to Jabreen Castle, in Nizwa, to the Pit Stop. Fran and Barry arrived first. BJ and Tyler were last, but were safe because it was a non-elimination leg of the race.

In Episode 9, the teams flew to Perth, Australia, to find the Kings Park War Memorial. Next, they took ferries from Fremantle to Rottnest Island for the Detour. Teams chose between dragging 40 large branches 126 yards across the beach to prevent erosion or searching 50 crayfish traps until catching a live crayfish. On the mainland, the teams traveled to the Fremantle Prison for the Roadblock, where one member from each team looked for batteries and a flashlight to help the team find a clue in underground tunnels. Eric and Jeremy were the first to arrive at the Pit Stop—the Fremantle Sailing Club, while Fran and Barry were last, and were thus the seventh team eliminated.

In Episode 10, the teams traveled to the Swan Bell Tower, in Perth, where they were directed to fly to Darwin and drive to the Crocodylus Park crocodile farm. After picking up a clue in a crocodile pool, teams drove to Batchelor, the site of the race's second Yield. BJ and Tyler "Yielded" Monica and Joseph, who were stalled while others did a tandem sky-dive jump for the Roadblock. Next, the teams drove to the Magnetic Termite Mounds, in Litchfield National Park, where for the Detour, they either hiked and swam one mile through a spider-infested river or off-roaded to the Lost City, where an aboriginal musician taught them how to play a didgeridoo. Finally, the teams drove to Lake Bennett Wilderness Resort, to the Pit Stop. Ray and Yolanda arrived first. BJ and Tyler were last, but were saved again by a non-elimination leg.

In Episode 11, the teams flew to Bangkok, Thailand, where they took a bus to the Three Spire Pagoda, the site of another Fast Forward. BJ and Tyler ate two large bowls of stir-fried grasshoppers and crickets, allowing them to go directly to the Pit Stop—Marble Temple, in Bangkok. At the Roadblock, one member from each team prepared a feast for the monkeys at the temple. At the Detour in Koh Kret Island's Buddha Garden, teams either transported seventy-two clay pots by balancing them on a wooden board or painted gold leaf on a Buddha statue for a shrine. Ray and Yolanda were the first to check in at the Pit Stop, and Monica and Joseph arrived last, and were thus the eighth team eliminated.

In Episode 12, the teams took taxis to the Royal Kraal elephant corral in Ayutthaya, then flew to Tokyo, where they drove to Shibuya, the busiest intersection in the world. At the Hachiko Statue Detour, the teams carried a traditionally dressed Japanese woman to a tea ceremony or assembled folding bicycles, which they rode to deliver two packages in Tokyo. After spending the night in sleep pods at the Capsule Land Hotel, the teams drove to Fujikyu Highland amusement park, where one member from each rode three rides while looking for a sign with a message that had to be relayed in order for the team to receive the next clue. Teams drove to Yamanakako, to the Pit Stop at Lake Yamanaka, where BJ and Tyler arrived first, while Ray and Yolanda arrived last, but were safe because it was a non-elimination leg.

In the Episode 13 finale, the teams flew to Anchorage, Alaska, and drove to Mirror Lake. There, for the Detour, they either drilled ten ice-fishing holes, which they then covered with an ice-fishing shack, or flew 150 miles on a bush plane to deliver medical supplies. At Kincaid Park, teams snow-shoed while looking for a clue directing them to fly to Denver, Colorado. At the Red Rocks Amphitheatre—the site where the race began—one member from each team had to find among 285 foreign flags the 9 representing the countries where they had traveled, then line them up in the order in which they visited those countries. BJ and Tyler arrived first at the final Pit Stop, winning $1 million. Eric and Jeremy finished second, while Ray and Yolanda were third.

RATINGS: *The Amazing Race 9* averaged 10.4 million overall viewers.

THE AMAZING RACE

(Season 10)

GENRE	Competition
FIRST TELECAST	9/17/2006
LAST TELECAST	12/10/2006
NETWORK	CBS
AIR TIME	Sundays 8:00 p.m.
EPISODE STYLE	Story Arc
TALENT	Phil Keoghan (Host)
CAST	Tyler Denk and James Breneman (Winners—models and recovering drug addicts); Rob Diaz and Kimberly Chabolla (2nd place—dating); Lyn Turk and Karlyn Harris (3rd place—single moms); Dustin-Leigh Konzelman and Kandice Pelletier (4th place—beauty queens); Erwin Cho and Godwin Cho (5th place—brothers); David Conley and Mary Conley (6th place—married); Peter Harsch and Sarah Reinertsen (7th place—recently dating); Tom Rick and Terry Consentino (8th place—boyfriends); Duke Marcoccio and Lauren Marcoccio (9th place—father and daughter); Kellie Patterson and Jamie Hill (10th place—cheerleaders); Vipul Patel and Arti Patel (11th place—married); Sa'eed Rudolph and Bilal Abdul-Mani (12th place—best friends)
PRODUCTION COMPANIES	Bruckheimer Films and Earthview Inc., in association with Touchstone Television and Amazing Race Productions
CREATED BY	Elise Doganieri; Bertram van Munster
EXECUTIVE PRODUCERS	Jerry Bruckheimer; Bert Van Munster, Elise Doganieri; Jonathan Littman

CO-EXECUTIVE PRODUCERS Amy Chacon; Evan Weinstein; Scott Einziger; Jon Kroll; Hayma Screech Washington; Carl Buehl

In Episode 1, the teams kicked off the race at Gas Works Park, in Seattle, Washington, where they learned they would be flying to Beijing, China. At the Gold House restaurant Roadblock, one member from each team ate all of the fish eyes out of a bowl of fish head soup. At the Meridian Gate of the Forbidden City, the teams were shocked to see Phil, who told Bilal and Sa'eed they were eliminated because they had arrived last. The next day, the teams traveled in World War II–era motorbike sidecars to a pedicab company, where, for the Detour, they either paved a forty-five-square-foot sidewalk or performed the Taiji Bailong relaxation technique. They then used rope to scale a wall to reach the Pit Stop at Juyongguan, a gateway to the Great Wall of China. James and Tyler arrived first, winning a bonus $10,000. Vipul and Arti arrived last and were thus the second team eliminated.

In Episode 2, the teams traveled by train to Ulan Bator, to the Choijin Lama Temple, for a clue leading them to Terelj. At the "Take It Down" or "Fill It Up" Detour at Gorkhi-Terelj National Park, teams had to take down a yurt dwelling's cover, roll it up, and put it on a camel or put four water containers on a hynik cart. At the Hotel Mongolia Roadblock, one member from each team shot a flaming arrow at a target 160 feet away. Peter and Sarah arrived first at the Pit Stop at the hotel and won a bonus trip for two. Jamie and Kellie didn't complete the Roadblock, never made it to the Pit Stop, and were thus the third team eliminated from the race.

In Episode 3, the teams flew more than 2,300 miles, to Hanoi, Vietnam, to find the Hoa Lo Prison, aka the "Hanoi Hilton." There they found former prisoner of war Sen. John McCain's flight suit and received a clue directing them to a flower shop in the Old Quarter. At the Roadblock, one team member sold enough flowers out of a bicycle to earn 80,000 Vietnamese dong, or about $5. Next, the teams took public buses to the tiny village of Vac and searched for the Dinh Vac Buddhist temple. At the Detour, teams formed wet coal into bricks for fuel or construced detailed birdcages. Erwin and Godwin arrive first at the Pit Stop—Canh Dong Dia, in Pho Vac. Tom and Terry arrived second and were surprised when Phil gave them a thirty-minute penalty for traveling by motorcycle (but they wound up finishing in eighth place), while Duke and Lauren arrived last and were the fourth team eliminated from the race.

In Episode 4, the teams received the leg's first clue via loudspeaker: "Attention racers! Taxi across the Red River to Ben Xe Gia Lam. Then, take a bus to Ben Xe Bai Chay. Then find the Hydrofoil Harbor." At the Roadblock in Ha Long, one member from each team used a mechanical ascender to climb ninety feet up the face of a rock, then rappel down. Next, the teams took motorboats to Sung Sot Cave for the "Over" or "Under" Detour: In Halong Bay, they rowed sampans to a provisions ship and delivered two loads of provision to a floating village or rowed sampans to an oyster farm to retrieve thirty underwater baskets. Rob and Kimberly were the first to arrive at the Soi Sim Island Pit Stop and won a pair of jet skis. Tom and Terry finished last and were the fifth team eliminated.

In Episode 5, the teams flew to Chennai, India, and traveled by bus to Vallavar Arts & Crafts, in Mamallapuram. At the "Wild Things" or "Wild Rice" Detour, teams helped move a marsh crocodile to a new pit or created a detailed floral design with colored rice powder. They then took a bus to Chennai, to Karthik Driving School. At the Roadblock, one member from each team took driver's education and completed an exam while driving on the left side of the busy streets. Peter and Sarah arrived first at the Chettinad House Pit Stop in Chennai, and won home gym systems. David and Mary arrived last, but were saved by a non-elimination leg. However, instead of losing their money and possessions, they were marked for elimination: if they didn't finish the next leg first, they'd incur a thirty-minute penalty while the other teams checked in.

In Episode 6, the teams flew to Kuwait City and drove to the Kuwait Towers, where they found the Roadblock and the first of two Fast Forwards. At the Roadblock, one member from each team climbed a ladder 610 feet up one of the towers, retrieved a satchel of puzzle pieces, and assembled a puzzle back on the ground. At the Fast Forward, wearing protective gear, David and Mary braved temperatures of more than one thousand degrees at a simulated oil well fire to receive a clue instructing them to travel directly to the Pit Stop at Al Sadiq Water Towers. Because they were marked for elimination but arrived first, they did not incur the thirty-minute penalty. Plus, they won a bonus trip to Jamaica. The other teams went to Souk Al-Gharabally for the Detour, where they filled and stacked ten, 110-pound bags of camel feed or raced a camel 140 yards by way of a voice-activated robotic jockey. Peter and Sarah arrived last at the Pit Stop, and were the sixth team eliminated.

In Episode 7, the teams flew to the small island nation of Mauritius, which is in the Indian Ocean, off the African coast. The teams drove two hundred miles to Grand Baie, and swam to the boat *Isla Mauritia* for the next clue. Next, they drove forty-nine miles to the Case Noyale Post Office, and Dustin and Kandice got in a fender-bender along the way. At the "Salt" or "Seat" Detour, teams searched three giant mounds of salt for a shaker or took a motorboat to an island where they looked for a flag to bring back. Dustin and Kandice arrived first at the Pitstop at Château Bel Ombre, winning motor scooters. David and Mary were again saved by a non-elimination leg, but were once again marked for elimination.

In Episode 8, the teams flew to the nearby island of Madagascar. In the capital, Antananarivo, they found the Black Angel statue at Lac Anosy, where they encountered a new game twist called the Intersection, in which each team had to pair up with another team and work together. Tyler and James paired with Rob and Kimberly, with the foursome vying for the Fast Forward, where they ate cow's lips at the Analakeley Market. Meanwhile, the other teams faced the "Long Sleep" or "Short Letter" Detour and delivered eight mattresses within Antananarivo or made twenty-eight pieces of paper. Once the Intersection was over, the teams traveled to Totohotohobato Ambondrona Analakeley for the Roadblock, where one team member searched for four specific rubber stamps from vendros. In this Roadblock, one member from each team had to search among dozens of rubber-stamp vendors. Finally, each team member who completed the Roadblock traveled to the Pit Stop—the Cathedral Andohalo—to meet his or her teammate. Dustin and Kandice arrived first, winning a bonus trip for two. David and Mary were marked for elimination, and because of their thirty-minute penalty, were the seventh team to be eliminated from the race.

In Episode 9, the teams flew to Helsinki, Finland, where they watched messages from home on computers at the Kappeli coffeehouse. Next, they traveled to Soppeenharjun koulu, in Ylöjärvi, for the "Swamp This" or "Swamp That" Detour, where they cross-country-skied or completed an obstacle course through a bog. They then took a train to Turku and drove to Lohja, to the Tytyri Limestone Mine. At the Roadblock, one member from each team rode a bike more than one mile into the mine and gathered a piece of limestone, which the team opened with tools. The teams returned to Helsinki, to Olympic Stadium, where they climbed the 236-foot Olympic Tower and rappelled face-first off the building. Once on the ground, the teams learned that the leg wasn't over and the episode was to be continued.

In Episode 10, the teams continued the leg and flew to Kiev, Ukraine, translated a Russian address, and drove to the military training Oster tank school, outside the city. For the Roadblock, one member from each team drove a Russian T-64 tank along a 1.2-mile course. Back in Kiev, for the "Make the Music" or "Find the Music" Detour, teams performed a rap at Dance and Groove Club or went to the Ukranian National Music Academy to look for sheet music by Tchaikovsky, and brought it to a pianist to play. Finally, the teams drove to the Pit Stop—the Great Patriotic War Museum. Tyler and James were first at the Pit Stop. Erwin and Godwin finished last and were the eighth team eliminated.

In Episode 11, the teams flew to Ouarzazate, Morocco, and drove four miles to the Antiquities du Sud antiques shop in the Kasbah district. They then drove to Atlas Studios, where Dustin and Kandice "Yielded" Lyn and Karlyn. At the Roadblock, one member from each team raced on a chariot while grabbing two flags matching the color on their horse. At the "Throw It" or "Grind It" Detour, at Café La Pirgola, in Idelssan, teams made two pots on a pottery wheel or ground olives and packed them in bags. Tyler and James arrived first at the Pit Stop—a nomadic Berber camp in the Atlas Mountains near Marrakech—where they won cell phones with free service. Dustin and Kandice arrived last and were saved by a non-elimination leg, but were nonetheless marked for elimination.

In Episode 12, the teams drove through the Atlas Mountains to Casablanca, to the Quartier des Habous. At the Roadblock, one team member prepared, cooked, and ate one pound of camel meat. Next, the teams flew to Barcelona, Spain, where they took taxis to Parc del Laberint. At the "Lug It" or "Lob It" Detour, teams walked more than one mile while wearing giant costumes or searched a huge pile of tomatoes for a clue. Rob and Kimberly were the first team to arrive at the Pit Stop—Palau Nacional de Montjuïc—and won a bonus trip. Dustin and Kandice, who were already marked for elimination, arrived last and were thus the ninth team eliminated.

In the Episode 13 finale, the teams flew to Paris, and went to the Eiffel Tower. They then took a train to Caen and traveled to the airport. At the final Roadblock, one team member performed a tandem thirteen-thousand-foot skydive with an instructor onto Omaha Beach, while his or her partner took a surprise aerial nosedive in a plane. The team members were reunited at a train station, where they boarded trains back to Paris to find Place de la Concorde. At the "Art" or "Fashion" Detour, teams either picked up paintings at an art studio and searched the square for an artist or made a jacket for a mannequin at the Anatomy fashion studio. Next, the teams flew to New York City to find the Daily News Building. They then walked to the East Village to find the *Alamo* sculpture. There they were directed to the final Pit Stop—St. Basil's Academy, in Garrison, New York. James and Tyler finished in first place, winning $1 million. Rob and Kimberly finished second, and Lyn and Karlyn finished third.

THE AMAZING RACE: ALL-STARS
(Season 11)

GENRE	Competition
FIRST TELECAST	2/18/2007
LAST TELECAST	5/06/2007
NETWORK	CBS
AIR TIME	Sundays 8:00 p.m.
EPISODE STYLE	Story Arc
TALENT	Phil Keoghan (Host)
CAST	Eric Sanchez and Danielle Turner (Winner—dating); Dustin-Leigh Konzelman and Kandice Pelletier (2nd place—beauty queens); Charla Turk and Mirna Harris (3rd place—cousins); Oswald Mendez and Danny Jimenez (4th place—best friends); Uchenna Agu and Joyce Agu (6th place—married); Joe Baldassare and Bill Bartek (7th place—life partners); Teri Pollack and Ian Pollack (8th place—married); Rob Mariano and Amber Mariano (9th place—married); David Conley and Mary Conley (10th place—married); Drew Feinberg and Kevin O'Connor (11th place—fraternity brothers); John Vito Pietanza and Jill Aquilino (12th place—dating)

PRODUCTION COMPANIES	Bruckheimer Films and Earthview Inc., in association with Touchstone Television and Amazing Race Productions
CREATED BY	Elise Doganieri; Bertram van Munster
EXECUTIVE PRODUCERS	Jerry Bruckheimer; Bert Van Munster; Elise Doganieri; Jonathan Littman
CO-EXECUTIVE PRODUCERS	Amy Chacon; Evan Weinstein; Scott Einziger; Jon Kroll; Hayma Screech Washington; Carl Buehl

In Episode 1, eleven teams from previous seasons of *The Amazing Race* flew from Miami, Florida, to Quito, Ecuador. They traveled by taxi to Plaza San Francisco, and then to Pim's Restaurant. At the Detour at Hacienda Yanahurco, in the Cotopaxi National Park, teams donned historical military uniforms and searched for missing uniform pieces or helped cowboys lasso and groom a wild horse. Rob and Amber arrived first at the Pit Stop—Mirador Cotopaxi, in the park. John Vito and Jill were the last team to arrive, and were thus the first All-Stars eliminated from the race.

In Episode 2, the teams flew to Santiago, Chile, where they took taxis to the headquarters of Codelco—the world's largest copper producer. At the Roadblock, the teams had to solve a word puzzle. Next, all the teams took the same flight to Calama, Chile, and traveled to Chuquicamata. At the "By Hand" or "By Machine" Detour, teams secured a two-ton tire to a dump truck or drove a front loader to transfer gravel. Next, they drove through the treacherous Valley of the Moon on their way to the Pit Stop—Valley of the Dead, in San Pedro de Atacama. Rob and Amber finished first again. Kevin and Drew were the last team to arrive, and were the second team eliminated from the race.

In Episode 3, the teams traveled to the San Pedro de Atacama church and received a clue directing them to fly to Puerto Montt, and then to drive to Metri. At the Roadblock, one member from each team jumped into a fish-breeding tank and transferred eighty flounder to another tank. Next, the teams traveled fifty miles to La Maquina, in Petrohue. At the Detour, teams rock-climbed forty feet or backtracked two miles to complete a two-and-a-half-mile white-water-rafting course. At the Playa Petrohue Pit Stop, Rob and Amber finished first for the third leg in a row. David and Mary arrived last and were the third team eliminated from the race.

In Episode 4, the teams flew to Punta Arenas, Chile, then traveled by taxi to Lord

Lansdale's shipwreck. At the Detour, teams went to the town center to retrieve a compass to help them locate the Nautilus building or built a signpost correctly writing out in chronological order the fourteen stops of Magellan's journey around the world. At the Roadblock, one member from each team had to sort mail to find a message from the past season's team at the Isla Redonda Post Office, in Ushuaia. Oswald and Danny were the first at the Pit Stop—Mastil de General Belgrano. Rob and Amber arrived last and were the fourth team eliminated from the race.

In Episode 5, the teams hiked the Marshall Mountain chain, retrieving a clue instructing them to fly to Maputo, Mozambique. At the Roadblock at Apopo training field, one member from each team used a rat to locate a deactivated mine. At the Praça dos Trabalhadores "Pamper" or "Porter" Detour, teams had to paint enough customers' fingernails at Maputo Central Market to earn thirty meticals (approximately one dollar) or fill ten, forty-five-pound bags with coal by hand, sew them closed, then carry a bag to a specific address. Charla and Mirna arrived first at the Pit Stop at Fortaleza de Maputo. Uchenna and Joyce arrived last, but were safe because it was a non-elimination leg; still, they were marked for elimination.

In Episode 6, the teams flew to Dar es Salaam, Tanzania, and traveled by dhow ferry to the island of Zanzibar. At the Zanzibar Town harbor Detour, teams pieced together a puzzle replicating a local-style Tinga Tinga artwork or loaded two fifty-pound logs onto a handcart and delivered them to a shipyard more than one mile away. At the Roadblock at the Maasai village in Kikungwi, one member from each team threw a wooden *rungu* weapon sixty-five feet at a clay target. For the second leg in a row, Charla and Mirna arrived first at the Pit Stop, at Ngome Kongwe, in Zanzibar Town. Uchenna and Joyce were penalized thirty minutes at the Pit Stop for arriving last on the previous leg, but were safe when Teri and Ian checked in after their penalty. Teri and Ian were the fifth team eliminated from the race.

In Episode 7, the teams flew to Warsaw, Poland, then traveled to Czapski Palace for the "Perfect Pitch" or "Perfect Angle" Detour. Teams went to Prymas Palace, tuned a grand piano and waited for a pianist to play a Chopin piece, or picked up a mannequin at Escada Boutique and brought it to the Panoramik Laboratory for an X ray revealing a clue. The teams then traveled to Lazienki Palace to the Pit Stop, where Dustin and Kandice arrived first. Joe and Bill arrived last, but were safe because it was a non-elimination leg; still, they were marked for elimination.

In Episode 8, the teams traveled by charter bus to Auschwitz-Birkenau, to the concentration camp, where they lit candles and paused for a moment of silence in honor of the victims of the Holocaust. Next, they encountered the Intersection, Fast Forward, and Detour at Jukiusz Slowacki Theatre, in Krakow, where each team paired with another. Oswald and Danny partnered with Uchenna and Joyce for the Fast Forward, where they counted stairs in two different towers, correctly added the numbers, then proceeded to arrive first at the Pieskowa Skala Pit Stop. Meanwhile, the other "Intersected" teams formed and ate Polish kielbasa or rolled out and made bagels to deliver to a restaurant. At the Roadblock, one member from each team dressed in authentic medieval armor and led a horse through a forest to a stable boy. Joe and Bill were marked for elimination, and their thirty-minute penalty cost them the leg. They were the sixth team eliminated from the race.

In Episode 9, the teams flew to Kuala Lumpur, Malaysia, then traveled to the Batu Caves, then to the Kampung Baru Mosque, where Dustin and Kandice "Yielded" Eric and Danielle. At the Detour, teams used the batik technique to dye a forty-five-square-foot cloth at Dewan Lama or searched six hundred boxes of cookies for one with a licorice center at Chow Kit Bomba. At the Roadblock in the Taman Sri Hartamas neighborhood, one member from each team biked around the neighborhood looking for enough recyclable newspapers to make a stack eight hands, or approximately six feet, high. Uchenna and Joyce missed a crucial flight connection and checked in at the Carcosa Seri Negara Pit Stop well after the other teams. They were the seventh team eliminated from the race.

In Episode 10, the teams flew to Hong Kong, then traveled to the Sun Wah Kiu Laundry, in Kowloon's Tsim Sha Tsui, site of the Fast Forward and the Detour. After Oswald and Danny completed a course with a stunt driver at a film set at the former Kai Tak Airport for the Fast Forward, they proceeded directly to the Pit Stop to check in first at Happy Valley Racecourse at the Hong Kong Jockey Club, on Hong Kong Island. At the "Kung Fu Fighting" or "Lost in Translation" Detour, teams climbed an eleven-story bamboo scaffold while being distracted by a Kung Fu battle or searched hundreds of Chinese signs to receive the next clue. At the Kennedy Town Roadblock, one member from each team had to kick down doors and pull Travelocity roaming gnomes across a pond. Eric and Danielle arrived last at the Pit Stop, but were safe because it was a non-elimination round; still, they were marked for elimination.

In Episode 11, the teams took turbojet ferries to Macau. At the Macau Tower, Oswald and Danny were short on cash, and made a deal with Dustin and Kandice to "Yield" Eric and Danielle for money. At the Roadblock, one member from each team performed the world's tallest sky jump off the Macau Tower. At the Lou Lim Ioc Gardens Detour, teams made two bundles of Chinese noodles or carried a dragon head and drum three quarters of a mile to a dragon boat on Nam Van Lake. Teams then drove mini-mokes to the Pit Stop—Trilho da Taipa Pequena 2000 Park, in Taipa—where Dustin and Kandice checked in first. Oswald and Danny checked in last, but it was a non-elimination leg.

In Episode 12, the teams flew to the island of Guam, then drove nine miles to Andersen Air Force Base, in Yigo. At the Detour, teams air-dropped five-hundred-pound care packages from transport planes or cleaned the wing of a B-52 bomber to a base sergeant's satisfaction. At the Roadblock at the U.S. Naval Base, on Orote Peninsula, one teammate performed a search-and-recue mission with a GPS. At the Fort Soledad Pit Stop in Umatac, Dustin and Kandice checked in first for the second leg in a row. Oswald and Danny finished last and were the eighth team eliminated.

In the Episode 13 finale, the teams flew to Honolulu, Hawaii. They took Jeeps to Kaumalapau Harbor, in Lanai, for the "Under" or "Over" Detour, where they swam to the floor of a cave to retrieve a clue or paddle-boarded to a buoy holding a clue. The teams then traveled to Shipwreck Beach, where they ran a mile and kayaked to get another clue. Then they flew to Oakland, California, to travel to their final destination, San Francisco. The final task at the city's mint tested each teammate's ability to think like his or her partner. Eric and Danielle arrived first at the final Pit Stop—the San Francisco Botanical Garden—winning $1 million. Dustin and Kandice finished second, while Charla and Mirna were third.

AMBUSH MAKEOVER

GENRE	Docudrama (Makeover)
FIRST TELECAST	9/23/2003
LAST TELECAST	9/12/2005
NETWORK	Syndicated

EPISODE STYLE	Self-contained
TALENT	William Whatley (Hairstylist); Nicole Williams (Makeup Artist); Mary Alice Haney (Style and Trends); Nancy Brensson (Fashion and Beauty); Anthony Perinelli (Stylist); Gigi Berry (Fashion and Style); Rob Talty (Hairstylist)
PRODUCTION COMPANY	Banyan Productions
EXECUTIVE PRODUCERS	Ray Murray; Susan Cohen-Dickler; Jan Dickler; Chris Rantamaki
PRODUCERS	Trisha Ward; Deb Whitcast
DIRECTOR	Daniel E. Hagan

Style agents, ranging from fashion experts to makeup artists to hairstylists, visited major U.S. cities finding people in need of an "ambush makeover." The targets were ordered to drop everything immediately for an exciting makeover adventure.

AMERICA'S CUTEST PUP

GENRE	Docusoap
FIRST TELECAST	4/7/2007
LAST TELECAST	6/9/2007
NETWORK	WE
EPISODE STYLE	Story Arc
CAST	Allen Haff (Host)
PRODUCTION COMPANY	Kaos Entertainment
EXECUTIVE PRODUCER	Megan Wilson

This canine beauty pageant featured thousands of adorable puppies from across the United States competing for the title of America's Cutest Puppy.

AMERICA'S FUNNIEST HOME VIDEOS

GENRE	Competition
FIRST TELECAST	1/14/1990
NETWORK	ABC
AIR TIMES	Sunday, 8:00 p.m. (1/1990–2/1993); Sunday, 7:00 p.m. (3/1993–5/1993); Sunday, 8:00 p.m. (5/1993–9/1993); Sunday, 7:00 p.m. (9/1993–6/1996); Sunday, 7:30 p.m. (6/1996–7/1996); Sunday, 7:00 p.m. (7/1996–12/1996); Sunday, 8:00 p.m. (1/1997); Sunday, 7:00 p.m. (2/1997); Sunday, 8:00 p.m. (3/1997); Sunday, 7:00 pm (4/1997–5/1997); Sunday, 8:00 p.m. (5/1997–9/1997); Monday, 8:00 p.m. (1/1998–8/1998); Saturday, 8:00 p.m. (7/1998–12/1998); Thursday, 8:00 p.m. (3/1999–4/1999); Saturday, 8:00 p.m. (5/1999–8/1999); Friday, 8:00 p.m. (7/2001–8/2001; 11/2001–9/2003); Sunday, 7:00 p.m. (9/2003–present)
EPISODE STYLE	Self-contained
TALENT	Bob Saget (Host, 1990–1997); John Fugelsang (Host, 1997–2001); Daisy Fuentes (Host, 1997–2001); Tom Bergeron (Host 2001–present); Ernie Anderson (Announcer, 1990–1996); Jess Harnell (Announcer, 1996–present)
PRODUCTION COMPANY	Vin Di Bona Productions
CREATED BY	Vin Di Bona
EXECUTIVE PRODUCERS	Vin Di Bona; Richard C. Brustein
CO-EXECUTIVE PRODUCERS	Todd Thicke; Terry Moore; Steve Paskay; Jerry Jaskulski
PRODUCERS	Michelle Narsaway; J. Elvis Weinstein; Barak Grass; Gary H. Grossman
SEGMENT PRODUCERS	Tim Stokes; Tara Cunn; Robin Felsen Von Halle

Based on a segment from the Japanese show *Fun TV with Kato-chan and Ken-chan*, *America's Funniest Home Videos* is ABC's longest-running comedy series. The show features candid, funny home movie clips sent in by viewers. The clips often include slapstick comedy, physical comedy, silly situations with pets and children, and practical jokes, and are peppered with funny narration by a host. At the end of each episode, the studio audience votes on their favorite video, with the winner earning $10,000. A $100,000 finale episode caps off each season, with each week's winner competing for the top prize.

AMERICA'S FUNNIEST PEOPLE

GENRE	Competition
FIRST TELECAST	9/1/1990
LAST TELECAST	8/1/1994
NETWORK	ABC
AIR TIME	Sunday, 8:30 p.m.
EPISODE	Self-contained
TALENT	Dave Coulier (Host); Arleen Sorkin (Host, 1990–1992); Tawny Kitaen (Host, 1992–1994)
PRODUCTION COMPANIES	Vin Di Bona Productions & ABC Productions
CREATED BY	Vin Di Bona
EXECUTIVE PRODUCER	Vin Di Bona
PRODUCER	Howard G. Malley
SEGMENT PRODUCERS	Cheryl Rhoads; Jill Baer
DIRECTORS	Steve Feld; Matthew Gaven; Steven Santos; Brady Connell; Lloyd Thaxton

A spinoff from *America's Funniest Home Videos*, *America's Funniest People* featured amateur videos of impressionists, comedians, dancers, pranksters, and the recurring "Jackalope" vignettes. Each week, the creator of the winning video won $10,000.

AMERICA'S GOT TALENT

GENRE	Competition (Talent)
FIRST TELECAST	6/21/2006
NETWORK	NBC
EPISODE STYLE	Story Arc
TALENT	Regis Philbin (Host—Season 1), Jerry Springer (Host—Season 2), David Hasselhoff (Judge), Piers Morgan (Judge), Brandy (Judge—Season 1), Sharon Osbourne (Judge 2—Season 2 to present)

CAST

Season 1 Finalists	Bianca Ryan (winner), The Millers, Taylor Ware, Realis, At Last, Rappin' Granny (Vivian Smallwood), The Passing Zone, Celtic Spring, All That, Quick Change
Season 2 Finalists	Terry Fator (winner), Cas Haley, Butterscotch, Julienne Irwin, Jason Pritchett, The Glamazons, Robert Hatcher, Sideswipe, The Calypso Tumblers, The Duttons
PRODUCTION COMPANIES	Syco Television, FremantleMedia
EXECUTIVE PRODUCER	Ken Warwick, Simon Cowell, Nigel Hall, Cecile Frot-Coutaz
PRODUCER	Megan Michaels, Adam Shapiro,
DIRECTOR	Russell Norman

America's Got Talent is a million-dollar search for America's next best amateur talent act. It features singers, dancers, magicians, comedians and other talents of all ages. For the audition round, each of the three judges has a button in front of them that they can press when they do not want the act to continue; the button rings an electronic bell and a large red "X" with the judge's name lights up over the stage. A louder, different sound indicates the third judge's button was pressed, and the contestant's performance is terminated.

Then, the judges are asked whether the contestant should continue to the next round, with the approval of two out of three judges required. From there, the contestant is either rejected or passed to the next round of performance. Ultimately, the finalists are determined by a home viewer vote. Twelve-year-old singer Bianca Ryan was the inaugural season's million-dollar winner.

Season two featured Jerry Springer as the show's new host and Sharon Osbourne taking Brandy's spot on the judging panel. The season got off to a heated start as Sharon stormed off the set after Piers' stinging criticism of the show's younger contestants. Ventriloquist Terry Fator won the second season's grand prize.

AMERICA'S MOST TALENTED KID
(aka The Search for the Most Talented Kid in America)

GENRE	Competition (Talent)
FIRST TELECAST	3/21/2003
LAST TELECAST	5/2/2003
NETWORK	NBC
AIR TIME	Friday, 8:00 p.m.
EPISODE STYLE	Story Arc
TALENT	Mario Lopez (Host); Lance Bass (Lead Judge); Maureen McCormick (Guest Judge); Sisqo (Guest Judge); Jermaine Jackson (Guest Judge); Daisy Fuentes (Guest Judge); Jamie Lynn Spears (Guest Judge); Tiffany (Guest Judge); Vivica A. Fox (Guest Judge); Lisa Ling (Guest Judge); Danny Bonaduce (Guest Judge)

CAST

Age 3–7 Group	Lil' Maxso; Kayla Weston; Cole Marcus; Evan Nagao; Brandy Panfilli; Lil' C

Age 8–12 Group	Brityn Martin; L. D. Miller; Lateefa Dooling; Cheyenne Kimball (Winner); Devin Downs; Chelsea Musick
Age 13–15 Group	Agape Chen; Laine Adley; Brandon Morgan; Kasey Butler; Diana Degarmo; Aaron Wedgeworth
PRODUCTION COMPANY	NBC Studios
EXECUTIVE PRODUCERS	Peter Johansen; Stuart Krasnow
DIRECTOR	Brad Kreisberg

Each episode of this song-and-dance competition featured twelve children grouped and competing in three age brackets: three to seven, eight to twelve, and thirteen to fifteen. Each week, the winners from the three age brackets returned for the finale to compete for $50,000 and the title of "America's Most Talented Kid." Competitors included future *American Idol* Season 3 runner-up Diana DeGarmo. The winner was singer/songwriter/guitarist Cheyenne Kimball, who was signed to Epic Records.

AMERICA'S MOST WANTED

GENRE	Docudrama
FIRST TELECAST	4/10/1988
NETWORK	Fox
AIR TIMES	Sunday, 8:00 p.m. (4/1988–8/1990); Friday, 8:00 p.m. (9/1990–7/1993); Tuesday, 9:00 p.m. (7/1993–1/1994); Saturday, 9:00 p.m. (1/1994–present)
EPISODE STYLE	Self-contained
TALENT	John Walsh (Host)
PRODUCTION COMPANY	STF Productions Inc.
PRODUCERS	Kenneth A. Carlson; Peter Gillespie; Lance Heflin; Cord Keller; Greg Klein; Peter Koper; Pam Lewis; Evan A. Marshall; Karen S. Shapiro; Paula C. Simpson; Sedgwick Tourison; Kurt Uebersax

DIRECTORS	Paul Abascal; Robert W. Brown; David H. Butler; Kenneth A. Carlson; Janice Cooke-Leonard; Philppe Denham; Mark Kohl; Stephan Menick; Peter Mullet; Alexander Pikas; Zachary Weintraub; Christopher Coppola; Hollywood Heard; Ralph Hemeecker; Martin Kunert; Gary Meyers; Jonathan Winfrey; Jeff Winn; Greg Yaitanes

America's Most Wanted highlights high-profile crimes in which the offenders have not yet been caught. Often the story of the crime is told through reenactments and interviews, and features crimes such as murder, rape, robbery, white-collar crimes, and terrorism. Following each presentation, host John Walsh gives viewers a phone number to call if they know the whereabouts of the criminal in question, to help law enforcment officials apprehend the fugitive. As of press time, the show has been responsible for the apprhension of 973 fugitives, and the recovery of 54 missing people, some of them children.

AMERICA'S NEXT PRODUCER

GENRE	Competition
FIRST TELECAST	8/18/2007
NETWORK	TV Guide Network
EPISODE STYLE	Story Arc
TALENT	Ananda Lewis (Host); David Hill (Judge); Matt Roush (Judge)
CAST	Gwen Uszuko (Winner); Bradley Gallo; Daniel Hosea, Jessica Iaccarino; Lindsay Liles; Adam Mutterperl; Sharon Nash; Steve "Schliz" Schleinitz; Evie Shapiro; Alphonso "Zo" Wesson
PRODUCTION COMPANY	Magic Elves Productions
PRODUCERS	Dan Cutforth; Jane Lipsitz

Ten aspiring video producers compete to see who possesses the best skills to create an original hit television series. Competitors take a concept through the development process while attempting to avoid elimination. Gwen Uszuko, twenty, won the competition, earning $100,000 and a development deal with TV Guide Network.

AMERICA'S NEXT TOP MODEL
(Cycle 1)

GENRE	Competition (Job)
FIRST TELECAST	5/20/2003
LAST TELECAST	7/15/2003
NETWORK	UPN
AIR TIME	Tuesday, 9:00 p.m.
EPISODE STYLE	Story Arc
TALENT	Tyra Banks (Host/Judge); Janice Dickinson (Judge); Kimora Lee Simmons (Judge); Beau Quillian (Judge); J. Alexander (Guest Judge); Steve Santagati (Guest Judge); Marilyn Gauthier (Guest Judge); Drew Linehan (Guest Judge); Douglas Bizarro (Guest Judge); Wyclef Jean (Guest Star); Loren Haynes (Guest Star); Alice Spivak (Guest Star); Brad Pinkert (Guest Star)
CAST	Adrianne Curry (Winner); Shannon Stewart (Runner-up); Elyse Sewell (8th eliminated); Robin Manning (7th eliminated); Kesse Wallace (6th eliminated); Giselle Samson (5th eliminated); Ebony Haith (4th eliminated); Nicole Panattoni (3rd eliminated); Katie Cleary (2nd eliminated); Tessa Carlson (1st eliminated)
PRODUCTION COMPANIES	10x10 Entertainment; Ty Ty Baby Productions
CREATED BY	Tyra Banks
EXECUTIVE PRODUCERS	Tyra Banks; Ken Mok

Ten aspiring supermodels lived together and competed in a series of demanding tests in hopes of winning the grand prize: a $100,000 contract with Revlon, a fashion spread in *Marie Claire* magazine, and a contract with Wilhelmina Models. Each episode culminated with host supermodel Tyra Banks and a panel of judges deliberating and then eliminating one of the women.

In Episode 1, viewers were introduced to the ten aspiring models, who moved into New York City's Flatotel. Extremely religious Robin didn't mesh well with the others. The girls were given Brazilian bikini waxes, then had to endure the cold January weather during a rooftop bikini photo shoot for JLo, by Jennifer Lopez. Shannon and Tessa were in the bottom two, but Tessa's lack of comfort in front of the camera caused her to be the first model eliminated.

In Episode 2, Giselle won the runway challenge and got to met special guest Wyclef Jean. The models then posed for *Stuff* magazine while wearing bikinis and standing behind glass with water pouring down it. Katie and Kesse were in the bottom two, and overly sexy Katie was the second model eliminated.

In Episode 3, the girls got makeovers, Elyse won a makeup application challenge, and everyone posed with a live snake in a photo shoot. After dinner, Adrianne got food poisoning and was rushed to the hospital, but toughed it out and went to judging so she wouldn't be eliminated. Ebony and Nicole were in the bottom two, but Nicole was the third model eliminated, after she skipped an important social event to talk to her boyfriend.

In Episode 4, the girls took acting classes, which paid off for Robin, who won a script-reading competition. Robin brought Shannon and Kesse to a spa as a reward. The girls then had to use their acting chops in a commercial for contact lenses. Giselle and Ebony were in the bottom two, and moisturizer-obsessed Ebony stumbled through her commercial take, and was the fourth model eliminated.

In Episode 5, the girls were concerned that Elyse might have an eating disorder. The model did the best in an interview with press member Steve Santagati, and picked Adrianne to share in her reward—they each had a loved one visit them in New York. Elyse saw her boyfriend, while Adrianne chose her mother. The girls then did a Reebok photo shoot, which emphasized jumping and midair poses. Elyse and Giselle were in the bottom two, and Giselle's lack of self-confidence led to her being the fifth model eliminated.

In Episode 6, the final five contestants were sent on a surprise trip to Paris, where they all had to move into one cramped apartment. Next was a Wonderbra lingerie photo shoot at the Eiffel Tower with model Brad Pinkert. The girls then went on a "go-see" challenge to the Wilhelmina offices, to audition for agents—a challenge Elyse won. Kesse and Adrianne were in the bottom two, and Keese was told she lacked "fire," and was thus the sixth model eliminated.

In Episode 7, the final four did a nude photo shoot, but religious Robin and shy Shannon refused to disrobe. Adrianne won a night on the town for being the most charming at a social event with Parisian bachelors, and chose Elyse to join her. Shannon and Robin were in the bottom two. Robin didn't put any effort into socializing, and her bad attitude helped her become the seventh model eliminated.

Episode 8 was a look back at how the final three contestants—Adrianne, Elyse, and Shannon—made it to the finale.

In the Episode 9 finale, the final three returned to New York to get catwalk tips from Tyra Banks. Elyse sleepwalked her way through a performance during a lecture on go-sees, and was the eighth model eliminated. Friends Shannon and Adrianne faced off at Kimora Lee Simmons's Baby Phat fashion show and faced the panel one final time. Adrianne's unpolished beauty beat Shannon's girl-next-door looks, and Adrianne Curry was crowned the winner.

RATINGS: The inaugural cycle of *America's Next Top Model* received an average of 3.8 million viewers for UPN.

AMERICA'S NEXT TOP MODEL
(Cycle 2)

GENRE	Competition (Job)
FIRST TELECAST	1/13/2004
LAST TELECAST	3/23/2004
NETWORK	UPN
AIR TIME	Tuesday, 9:00 p.m.
EPISODE STYLE	Story Arc

TALENT	Tyra Banks (Host/Judge); Janice Dickinson (Judge); Nigel Barker (Judge); Nole Marin (Judge)
CAST	Yoanna House (Winner); Mercedes Yvette (Runner-up); Shandi Sullivan (10th eliminated); April Wilkner (9th eliminated); Camille McDonald (8th eliminated); Sara Racey-Tabrizi (7th eliminated); Catie Anderson (6th eliminated); Xiomara Frans (5th eliminated); Jenascia Chakos (4th eliminated); Heather Blumberg (3rd eliminated); Bethany Harrison (2nd eliminated); Anna Bradfield (1st eliminated)
PRODUCTION COMPANIES	10x10 Entertainment; Bankable Productions
CREATED BY	Tyra Banks
EXECUTIVE PRODUCERS	Tyra Banks; Ken Mok

For Cycle 2, the number of models increased to twelve. The winner received a cosmetics campaign with Sephora, a fashion spread in *Jane* magazine, and a contract with IMG Models.

In Episode 1, the girls were whisked away to an aircraft carrier, where they had thirty minutes to apply makeup and dress for a photo shoot with members of the military. The next morning, Jenascia slept through her alarm and arrived late to a nude body-paint photo shoot. Jenascia and Anna were in the bottom two, and Anna, who refused to pose nude for the shoot, was cut.

In Episode 2, a personality clash between Camille and Yoanna continued, leading to a house meeting. J. Alexander gave the girls a crash course in runway walking, and Catie won a trip to Carmen Marc Valvo's cocktail party, and invited Camille and Mercedes to join her. The next day, the girls posed for a Steve Madden shoe advertisement, and later walked for the judges. Shandi and Bethany were in the bottom two. Despite Tyra Banks's comment that Shandi had the worst walk she'd ever seen, Bethany's lack of posing versatility made her the second model cut.

In Episode 3, the girls got hair makeovers, and an unhappy Catie cried after seeing her new pixie cut. Yoanna won the makeup application competition, and invited Sara, Xiomara, and April to a meal prepared by the rest of the girls. The next competition featured a photo shoot in a factory, where the girls were suspended by cables. Catie and Xiomara argued, and Catie passed out backstage. Xiomara and Heather were in the bottom two, and Heather's limited facial expression and difficulty looking older led her to become the third model eliminated.

In Episode 4, April won a fitness competition; then the girls' personal styles were evaluated. Catie cried again after being told her style was hooker-like. Betsey Johnson was a guest judge at a style competition where the girls had ten minutes to dress in one another's clothes. Shandi won, and invited Xiomara and Yoanna to have dinner with the Cycle 1 winner, Adrianne Curry. For the photo shoot competition, the girls portrayed celebrities. Catie and Jenascia were in the bottom two, and Jenascia was told she was too short, and was thus the fourth model eliminated.

In Episode 5, the girls were encouraged to reveal their innermost secrets during personality coaching. Judge Janice Dickinson decided that Mercedes's confession that she had lupus was the most honest, so Mercedes invited Sara on a shopping trip, where they received a surprise visit from their mothers. The girls then posed for an underwater photo shoot. Camille and Xiomara were in the bottom two. With two bad photo shoots in a row, Xiomara was the fifth model cut.

In Episode 6, the girls did a black-and-white photo shoot. Camille was upset because an allergic reaction caused her lips to swell. Later, April won an acting scene competition, and invited Catie to join her on a jewelry shopping spree. The final competition was a high-tech commercial for Rollitos chips. Camille and Catie were in the bottom two. Catie's unwillingness to demonstrate the necessary vulnerability during the shoots made her the sixth model eliminated.

In Episode 7, April won a choreographer's competition, and she invited Shandi and Sara to have dinner with members of the Wu-Tang Clan. Shandi's boyfriend accused her of being a hypocrite when she was picked up by a guy at a bar after telling her boyfriend not to date anyone while she was gone. The girls incorporated choreographed dance steps they had learned into a music video for Tyra's new single. Sara and Yoanna were in the bottom two, and Sara's lack of refined sexuality was the reason why she was the seventh model eliminated.

In Episode 8, the girls went to Milan, Italy, where they interviewed for modeling jobs. Later, judges watched videos from the models' interviews and made the girls defend their choices and actions. Then they did a photo shoot for Solstice sunglasses.

Mercedes and Camille were in the bottom two, and Camille's off-putting diva-like attitude led her to become the eighth model eliminated.

Episode 9 recapped the show to date, and included never-before-seen bonus footage.

In Episode 10, designer Stephen Fairchild outfitted the girls. Shandi won the high-fashion flea market challenge. She also confessed to her boyfriend that she had cheated on him with a male model. The competition involved a nude photo shoot, pairing Yoanna and Shandi as one team, and April and Mercedes as the other. Mercedes and April were in the bottom two. April's tendency to be overly analytical and not show enough emotion made her the ninth model eliminated.

In the Episode 11 finale, the girls dressed for a photo shoot in styles contrary to their normal look. Shandi was the tenth model eliminated, because of her lack of confidence. The judges and Dean and Dan Caten, from DSquared, made a surprise visit to evaluate the final two. The next day, Yoanna and Mercedes faced off in the DSquared final fashion show, and Yoanna House was declared the winner.

A special episode aired two months later, catching up with the models since they'd left the show.

RATINGS: Ratings spiked for the second cycle of *America's Top Model,* to an average viewership of 6.3 million.

AMERICA'S NEXT TOP MODEL
(Cycle 3)

GENRE	Competition (Job)
FIRST TELECAST	9/22/2004
LAST TELECAST	12/15/2004
NETWORK	UPN
AIR TIME	Wednesday, 8:00 p.m.
EPISODE STYLE	Story Arc
TALENT	Tyra Banks (Host/Judge); Janice Dickinson (Judge); Nigel Barker (Judge); Nole Marin (Judge);

	Jay Manuel (Photographer/Guest Judge);
	Jay Alexander (Runway Trainer/Guest Judge)
CAST	Eva Pigford (Winner); Camara "Yaya" Da Costa Johnson (Runner-up); Amanda Swafford (12th eliminated); Ann Markley (11th eliminated); Norelle Van Herk (10th eliminated); Nicole Borud (9th eliminated); Toccara Jones (8th eliminated); Cassie Grisham (7th eliminated) Kelle Jacob (6th eliminated); Jennipher Frost (5th eliminated); Laura "Kristi" Gromment (4th eliminated); Julie Titus (3rd eliminated); Leah Darrow (2nd eliminated); Magdalena Rivas (1st eliminated)
PRODUCTION COMPANIES	10x10 Entertainment; Bankable Productions
CREATED BY	Tyra Banks
EXECUTIVE PRODUCERS	Tyra Banks; Ken Mok

For Cycle 3, the number of models in the competition increased to fourteen. The winner received a $100,000 contract with CoverGirl, a fashion spread in *Elle* magazine, and a contract with Ford Models.

In Episode 1, a swimsuit modeling session kicked off the cycle. Toccara worried about her chances as a plus-size model, and Amanda admitted that she's legally blind. The next morning, Jay Manuel held a small photo shoot and announced the first set of cuts, which narrowed the field to the final fourteen competitors.

In Episode 2, the girls flew to New York and then to Jamaica, where they did a bikini photo shoot at a coral reef. Magdalena was the first model eliminated. The others returned to New York and paired up to room at the Waldorf-Astoria. The judges evaluated the photos from the Jamaica shoot, and Lean and Ann were in the bottom two. The judges said Ann looked "dead," and she was the second model eliminated.

In Episode 3, the girls received makeovers at the Peter Coppola salon. For their first test, they had ten minutes to get ready in the back of a limousine. Norelle won the competition, and invited Eva, Ann, and Kristi to an industry party. It was discovered that Cassie had bulimia, and she begged not to be eliminated. The next day, the girls didn't wear makeup for their photo shoot. They were then challenged to apply makeup in ten minutes, and were judged based on their complete post-makeover looks. Kelle and Julie were in the bottom two, and Julie was accused of lacking passion, therefore becoming the third model eliminated.

In Episode 4, J. Alexander gave the girls a runway lesson, and they participated in a Heatherette runway show. Eva won, and invited Ann and Kelle on an all-day yacht trip, where they met Cycle 2 winner, Yoanna House. Next, the girls posed wearing nothing but jeans in a Lee photo shoot, followed by a challenge to walk in shoes that were two sizes too small. Jennipher and Kristi were in the bottom two. Kristi's insecurities became apparent, and she was the fourth model eliminated.

In Episode 5, Janice Dickinson taught the girls the four basic swimsuit poses, then Tyra Banks had a one-on-one chat with each of them. The girls posed in the La Perla store window wearing lingerie. Kelle won the challenge and received $5,000 worth of lingerie, then selected Toccara and Amanda to receive $1,500 and $500 in lingerie, respectively. Next, the girls roller-skated during a Dooney and Bourke purse shoot. Jennipher and Kelle were in the bottom two. The judges said that Jennipher looked like she didn't want to be there, and she was the fifth model eliminated.

In Episode 6, Tyra discussed the importance of diet, and introduced plus-size model Kate Dillon. The first test sent the models to a boot camp, where they engaged in rigorous exercise. Yaya finished a staircase climb the quickest, and invited Toccara for a deluxe spa treatment. The next test had the models bouncing on trampolines while promoting an energy drink. Kelle and Ann were in the bottom two. Kelle was told her beauty didn't translate to photographs, and was the sixth model eliminated.

In Episode 7, the girls were sent on "go-sees" to five major New York designers, where they were judged on looks, walk, and personality. Yaya received the highest score, and invited Nicole to share a rack of clothes from the designers. The next test was to create two completely different personas, and perform at a fictional house of fashion. Toccara and Cassie were in the bottom two. Cassie was told she didn't look like she wanted to be there, and was the seventh model eliminated.

In Episode 8, the girls got fashion advice from stylist Rebecca Weinberg. Yaya won a red-carpet competition, and invited Norelle to a gourmet feast. The girls posed with a tarantula, then had to create a look around a hat. Ann and Toccara were in the bottom two. Toccara was blamed for mentally checking out, and was the eighth model eliminated.

In Episode 9, the girls performed a death scene opposite Taye Diggs. Yaya scored her fourth victory in a row, and chose Amanda to fly luxury-class with her to Tokyo, while the others flew coach. When they arrived, the models were given thirty minutes to learn their lines in Japanese for a Campbell's Soup commercial. Yaya and Nicole are in the bottom two, and unnoticeable Nicole was the ninth model eliminated.

Episode 10 recapped the highlights of the cycle.

In Episode 11, the girls were tested on their ability to learn a tea ceremony, and Yaya won again, inviting Amanda for a day at a hot springs. Later, Ann and Eva got into a fight. The next day, the girls wore kimonos for a T-Mobile photo shoot, then were tested on their ability to walk in the traditional Japanese dress. Ann and Norelle were in the bottom two, and Norelle was the tenth model eliminated.

In Episode 12, the girls put together a "Tokyo Street Style Outfit" using only a cell phone, atlas, and $200 worth of yen. Eva was declared the winner, and she and Ann received pearl necklaces. The girls then did an Anime-themed photo shoot. Finally, the judges gave them fifteen minutes to develop their own street style. Eva and Ann were in the bottom two. Ann was told she wasn't "bringing it," and was the eleventh model eliminated.

In Episode 13, the first test had the final three girls delicately lie on Zen rocks in a pool for a CoverGirl shoot. Afterward, Amanda was the twelfth model eliminated. For the first time, two African American models were in the final. Yaya and Eva competed in a Japanese-style runway show. In the final judging, Eva Pigford was applauded for shedding the chip from her shoulder, and was declared the winner.

A special episode aired the day before the Cycle 4 premiere, catching up on the latest news about the Cycle 3 models.

RATINGS: The third cycle of *America's Next Top Model* had an average of 5.0 million viewers.

AMERICA'S NEXT TOP MODEL
(Cycle 4)

GENRE Competition (Job)
FIRST TELECAST 3/2/2005

LAST TELECAST	5/18/2005
NETWORK	UPN
AIR TIME	Wednesday, 8:00 p.m.
EPISODE STYLE	Story Arc
TALENT	Tyra Banks (Host/Judge); Janice Dickinson (Judge), Nole Marin (Judge); Nigel Barker (Judge); Jay Alexander (Runway Trainer); Jay Manuel (Photographer)
CAST	Naima Mora (Winner); Kahlen Rondot (Runner-up); Keenyah Hill (12th eliminated); Brittany Brower (11th eliminated); Christina Murphy (10th eliminated); Michelle Deighton (9th eliminated); Tatiana Dante (8th eliminated); Tiffany Richardson (7th eliminated); Rebecca Epley (6th eliminated); Lluvy Gomez (5th eliminated); Noelle Staggers (4th eliminated); Brandy Rusher (3rd eliminated); Sarah Dankleman (2nd eliminated); Brita Petersons (1st eliminated)
PRODUCTION COMPANIES	10x10 Entertainment, Bankable Productions
CREATED BY	Tyra Banks
EXECUTIVE PRODUCERS	Tyra Banks; Ken Mok

For Cycle 4, the number of models in the competition remained at fourteen. The winner received a $100,000 contract with CoverGirl, a fashion spread in *Elle* magazine, and a contract with Ford Models.

In Episode 1, thirty-five girls arrived in Los Angeles for the first wave of auditions. The first cut narrowed the field to twenty, then, following a photo booth shoot, the final fourteen contestants were chosen.

In Episode 2, the girls learned that their home base would be in Los Angeles. Their first test was at the Paramount Studios lot, where they transformed themselves into movie aliens. They moved into a loft behind a showroom, then headed to a Privé salon for makeovers. Next, the girls showed off their makeovers while wearing only jeans. Brandy and Brita were in the bottom two. The judges claimed that Brita's beauty didn't translate to her photographs, and she was the first model eliminated.

In Episode 3, in the first test, the girls donned heels and ran the steps at the Los Angeles Coliseum. They then went to Kmart for a runway competition. Rebecca won, and invited Kahlen, Lluvy, Noelle, Naima, and Sarah to meet shoe designer Stuart Weitzman, where they each picked out a pair of shoes. In the morning, their test was to walk ten dogs for a flower shop ad. During the judging, Rebecca passed out and was taken to the hospital. Brittany and Sarah were in the bottom two. Sarah was the second model eliminated, because she lacked confidence in her looks and had a poor runway walk.

In Episode 4, the girls took a ballet class. At dinner that night, Tiffany lifted her alcohol ban, vomited, and passed out. The next day, former supermodel Beverly Johnson gave the girls inspirational advice. They were then tested to see how they handled a belligerent photographer at a tennis court photo shoot. Naima won the challenge and brought Kahlen and Tiffany with her to have dinner with tennis star Serena Williams. Next, the girls posed as the signs of the zodiac for a calendar shoot. Brandy and Lluvy were in the bottom two. Despite taking what the judges called the "worst picture in the history of this show," Lluvy wasn't eliminated. Brandy's failure to warm up during the shoots was the reason she was the third model eliminated.

In Episode 5, Michelle's face broke out in mysterious sores. At a makeup lecture, Jay Manuel fooled the girls by posing as an older man named Paul Thompson, while the man playing his "assistant" was actually Paul Thompson, makeup expert. Next the girls were told to make each other up in a natural way. Back at the loft, Noelle started a rumor that Michelle's sores were caused by flesh-eating bacteria, but it turned out to be a fairly routine condition called impetigo. The next day the models were challenged to assume different ethnicities for a "Got Milk?" ad while holding a three-year-old in their arms. Michelle was given a doll to hold instead of a baby, so that she wouldn't infect anyone with her condition. For the final judging, the girls were asked to apply makeup without the help of applicators, brushes, or mirrors. Lluvy and Noelle were in the bottom two. Noelle was told she wasn't "model-esque," and was the fourth model eliminated.

In Episode 6, Tyra Banks taught the girls about the business aspects of modeling and warned them against signing contracts without understanding them first. The girls were invited to a CoverGirl industry party, where they were secretly judged by the party's "guests." Keenyah won, and invited Brittany to accompany her for a night at a beachfront hotel. The next day the girls posed for photos while being pelted with artificial wind and rain. The final test involved creating, designing, and selling a perfume bottle. Rebecca and Lluvy were in the bottom two. Lluvy, who had been in the bottom two three consecutive times, was told she wasn't living up to her potential, and was the fifth model eliminated.

In Episode 7, the girls participated in a script-reading challenge. Naima was the best actress, and chose Tatiana and Michelle to share $10,000 worth of diamonds with her. The next day, the girls did a pillow fight photo shoot for Wonderbra with model Rib Hillis. At a shocking elimination, Tyra Banks dismissed both Rebecca and Tiffany, making them the sixth and seventh models eliminated. After Tiffany's nonchalant reaction to her elimination, Tyra launched into an angry tirade, calling her out for her reaction.

In Episode 8, the girls got a crash course in interviewing, and were tested when they had to interview rapper Eve. Christina won the challenge, and her interview was featured on *Entertainment Tonight*. The next day, the girls went to a cemetery for a photo shoot, in which they each had to embody one of the seven deadly sins. Kahlen was upset because she'd recently learned that one of her high-school friends had died, but she bravely completed the challenge. The final test was a mock press conference with the judges. Michelle and Tatiana were in the bottom two. Citing her lack of confidence and inarticulation, the judges made Tatiana the eighth model eliminated.

In Episode 9, the girls went to a wild animal park to learn how to behave like beasts. Brittany won the animal-posing competition, and invited Christina and Keenyah to stay with her at a luxury hotel during the girls' upcoming trip to South Africa. The other girls had to build their own tents and sleep out in the wilderness. The next test was to pose as a specific wild animal with a live crocodile. The final test was to demonstrate an array of emotions. Keenyah and Michelle were in the bottom two. The judges felt that Michelle wasn't strong enough to handle criticism in the fashion business, so she was the ninth model eliminated.

In Episode 10, the girls went on "go-sees" in South Africa. Keenyah won the challenge, and invited Brittany to join her for dinner at designer Craig Port's house. The next day, the girls were sent on a nature shoot, where they used natural items to create their outfits. At judgment, the girls were told to critique one another's photos, and revealed who they thought had the best and worst potential. Brittany and Christina were in the bottom two, and thanks to her icy persona, Christina was the tenth model eliminated.

In Episode 11, the girls learned traditional South African dance and performed it for an audience. Naima won the dance contest, earning thirty extra frames at her next photo shoot. She also gave Keenyah twenty extra frames, who gave Brittany ten extra frames. The next day, the girls took a trip to Nelson Mandela's prison cell. They then posed with male models at an ostrich farm photo shoot. There was a final dance and movement test at judgment the next day. Brittany and Naima were in the bottom two. Citing her dampening fire, the judges declared Brittany the eleventh model eliminated.

Episode 12 was a special recap episode featuring never-before-seen footage from the cycle.

In Episode 13, Tyra spoke one-on-one with the three remaining models, Kahlen, Keenyah, and Naima. The first test was an early-morning three-part shoot for Cover-Girl, including a commercial, a runway walk, and a still beauty shoot. Keenyah's lack of skills in posing and runway caused her to be the twelfth model eliminated. Naima and Kahlen faced off in the final runway show. Thanks to a stronger final performance, Naima Mora was crowned the winner.

RATINGS: Cycle 4 of *America's Next Top Model* had an average of 5.1 million viewers.

AMERICA'S NEXT TOP MODEL
(Cycle 5)

GENRE	Competition (Job)
FIRST TELECAST	9/21/2005
LAST TELECAST	12/14/2005
NETWORK	UPN
AIR TIME	Wednesday, 8:00 p.m.
EPISODE STYLE	Story Arc
TALENT	Tyra Banks (Host), Nigel Barker (Judge), Twiggy (Judge), J. Alexander (Judge/Runway Coach), Jay Manuel (Judge/Coach)
CAST	Nicole Linkletter (Winner); Nik Pace (Runner-up); Bre Scullark (11th eliminated); Jayla Rubinelli (10th eliminated); Kim Stolz (9th eliminated);

Lisa D'Amato (8th eliminated); Kyle Kavanagh (7th eliminated); Coryn Woitel (6th eliminated); Diane Hernandez (5th eliminated); Sarah Rhoades (4th eliminated); Cassandra Whitehead (3rd eliminated); Ebony Taylor (2nd eliminated); Ashley Black (1st eliminated)

PRODUCTION COMPANIES	10x10 Entertainment, Bankable Productions
CREATED BY	Tyra Banks
EXECUTIVE PRODUCERS	Tyra Banks, Ken Mok

For Cycle 5, the number of models in the competition was reduced by one, to thirteen. The winner received a $100,000 contract with CoverGirl, a fashion spread in *Elle* magazine, a cover photo shoot for *Elle Girl* magazine, and a contract with Ford Models.

Episode 1 was a special casting show, documenting how the final thirteen were chosen.

In Episode 2, thirty-six semifinalists arrived in Los Angeles to meet Tyra Banks. Thirteen finalists were chosen and moved into a boutique-themed L.A. mansion. The girls did their first runway show at a celebrity-filled *Life & Style* magazine party. For their first photo shoot, the girls dressed as superheroes and were suspended by wire. Ashley and Sarah were in the bottom two. The judges weren't impressed by Ashley's runway walk or her superhero photo, and she was the first model eliminated from the competition.

In Episode 3, the girls were given makeovers at the Louis Licari hair salon. The next day, they went to Beverly Hills, where they were given $500 to shop for their new styles. James St. James crowned Lisa the challenge winner, and she was allowed to keep her new outfit. For the photo shoot, each girl wore the same outfit as her partner, but posed separately. After the judges compared the photos, Diane and Ebony were in the bottom two, and Ebony was the second model eliminated.

In Episode 4, the girls' runway skills were tested in a rotating platform challenge in front of fashion designer Sue Wong. Bre won the challenge and got to borrow a gown once worn by Tyra Banks. Bre brought Kim, Coryn, Nik, and Jayla out to dinner with her. At the "fashion victim" photo shoot, each girl had to look fearful as she ran on a treadmill in front of a green screen. Jay Manuel wanted Cassandra to cut her hair shorter, but rather than completing her makeover, she opted to leave the competition. At the elimination ceremony, the girls' final test was to show the judges their signature runway walks. Kim and Sarah were in the bottom two, and Sarah's bad walk and lack of confidence made her the third model eliminated.

In Episode 5, the girls were given tips on hiding their flaws after they anonymously listed one another's imperfections. They then directed photographer Jay Goldbloom to shoot them in poses accentuating and concealing their flaws. Kyle won the challenge, and she invited Kim and Coryn to join her at a day spa. Later, former judge Janice Dickinson was a guest photographer for the extreme plastic surgery shoot. At elimination, the girls were grilled about their imperfections in a mock "go-see" with the judges. Bre and Diane were in the bottom two. Diane's hesitancy while addressing the judges led Tyra Banks to believe she wasn't being herself, and Diane was the fifth model eliminated.

In Episode 6, comedian Chris Spencer tested the girls' spokesmodel skills during a mock interview for the fake product Top Model Honey Banana Firming Mask. Kyle won the challenge, and she picked Nicole to join her in a VH1 *The Fabulous Life Of . . .* appearance. Next, the girls did a hectic commercial shoot, photo shoot, and press interview in thirty minutes with *Entertainment Tonight* correspondent Ryan Devlin. Nik and Coryn were in the bottom two. The judges said Coryn was beautiful and radiant, but her apparent sad demeanor made her the sixth girl eliminated.

In Episode 7, Tyra Banks surprised the girls with a raw "Vaseline-only," black-and-white photo shoot aimed at showing each model's inner beauty. Later, the girls ran an obstacle course in L.A.'s Griffith Park, then were immediately sent on a "go-see" with *Elle Girl* magazine editors. The next day, the girls posed as classic 1940s Vargas pinups to promote the Ford Fusion. At elimination, the girls had to pick out a sexy outfit and accessories on the fly. Bre and Kyle were in the bottom two. The judges weren't happy with her pinup shot or her sexy outfit, and she was the seventh girl eliminated.

Episode 8 was a recap episode of Cycle 5.

In Episode 9, the girls met Cycle 3 winner Eva Pigford at the Poodle Parlor photo studio, where she gave the girls modeling advice. The next day, the girls picked out an entourage of hair, makeup, and wardrobe people, who helped them prepare to convince talent agents they should win a guest role on UPN's *Veronica Mars*. Kim won the challenge. At a Hollywood Hills home, the girls posed for a photo shoot with MTV's *Wild Boyz*. At elimination, the girls posed with various objects, including a tube of toothpaste and a pair of sunglasses. Jayla and Nicole were in the bottom two, but for the first and only time, no one was eliminated. Instead, Tyra Banks revealed they'd all be going to London.

In Episode 9, the girls met *Entertainment Tonight* correspondent Kevin Frazier, who taught them about the paparazzi and keeping the model persona in public. In London, the girls took a double-decker bus tour of the city, then were tested on their paparazzi-handling skills when they were bombarded by photographers outside their hotel. For the photo shoot, the six girls posed crammed together in a phone booth. Jayla and Lisa were in the bottom two, and cocky Lisa was the eighth girl eliminated.

In Episode 10, the girls posed like statues in a park, and had to remain completely still for the entire photo shoot. Nik won the challenge and a $15,000 shopping spree at Harrods, a bonus she shared with Bre and Jayla. For the next photo shoot, the girls had to re-create classic works of art for Olay Quench body lotion. Bre and Nicole battled over cereal bars and Red Bull. Bre and Kim were in the bottom two, and the judges named Kim the ninth girl eliminated, thanks to her lack of consistency.

In Episode 11, the final four had to use their own clothes to create preppy, punk, mod, and Bollywood looks. Nik won the challenge, winning one hundred extra frames during her next photo shoot. She picked Nicole to win eighty extra frames, who picked Jayla to get sixty extra frames. Judge Twiggy taught the girls about British fashion, and sent them on "go-sees," where they were evaluated on photos and knowledge of the designers' styles. The next day, judge Nigel Barker photographed the models' Bollywood-inspired shoot. At elimination, the girls dressed up saris in more modern looks. Bre and Jayla were in the bottom two, and Jayla's mediocre photos and lackluster sari look made her the tenth girl eliminated.

In the Episode 12 finale, the final three—Nicole, Nik, and Bre—did a photo shoot and television commercial for CoverGirl. The next day, Bre was the eleventh girl eliminated. Then photographer Gilles Bensimon shot Nicole and Nik individually with Tyra Banks. For their final challenge, Nicole and Nik competed in a runway show wearing clothing by fashion designers Nargess Gharani and Vanya Strok. At the final elimination, Nicole was named winner.

AMERICA'S NEXT TOP MODEL
(Cycle 6)

GENRE	Competition (Job)
FIRST TELECAST	3/1/2006
LAST TELECAST	5/17/2006
NETWORK	UPN
AIR TIME	Wednesday, 8:00 p.m.
EPISODE STYLE	Story Arc
TALENT	Tyra Banks (Host); Nigel Barker (Judge); Twiggy (Judge); J. Alexander (Judge/Runway Coach), Jay Manuel (Judge/Coach)
CAST	Danielle Evans (Winner); Joanie Dodds (Runner-up); Jade Roda (11th eliminated); Sara Albert (10th eliminated); Furonda Brasfield (9th eliminated); Nnenna Agba (8th eliminated); Brooke Staricha (7th eliminated); Leslie Mencia (6th eliminated); Mollie Sue Steenis (5th eliminated); Gina Choe (4th eliminated); Kari Schmidt (3rd eliminated); Wendy Wiltz (2nd eliminated); Kathy Hoxit (1st eliminated)
PRODUCTION COMPANIES	10x10 Entertainment; Bankable Productions
CREATED BY	Tyra Banks
EXECUTIVE PRODUCERS	Tyra Banks; Ken Mok

For Cycle 6, the number of models in the competition remained at thirteen. The winner received a $100,000 contract with CoverGirl, a fashion spread in *Elle* magazine, and a contract with Ford Models.

In a special episode before the start of the cycle, viewers were caught up in the lives of previous *Top Model* winners Yohanna House (Cycle 2), Eva Pigford (Cycle 3), and Nicole Linkletter (Cycle 5).

In the Episode 2 casting special, a pool of thirty-two semifinalists was narrowed down to the final thirteen competitors.

In Episode 3, the girls participated in a mock press conference to challenge their public-speaking skills. Nnenna won the challenge, earning the first choice of the bedrooms in the contestants' Los Angeles mansion. In their first photo shoot, the girls were outfitted with skull caps to pose bald. Furonda and Kathy were in the bottom two, and Kathy was the first eliminated, because the judges thought she lacked potential.

In Episode 4, the girls got makeovers. With fashion and makeup tips from Cycle 4 winner Naima Mora, each girl chose a runway fashion befitting her individual style. Nnenna won the challenge, earning a $5,000 Nanette Lepore shopping spree, which she shared with roommates Gina and Jade. The girls posed among ice sculptures for their next photo shoot. Jade and Wendy were in the bottom two, and Wendy was the second girl eliminated, because the judges thought her photos didn't stand out.

In Episode 5, the girls had their first runway lesson, with J. Alexander. The next day, they wore giant, live, hissing Madagascar cockroaches while modeling Jared Gold fashions. Jade kissed a cockroach and won the challenge, earning a trip to the Sheri Bodell fashion show. She brought along Danielle, Mollie Sue, Nnenna, and Leslie. At the modern-day fairy-tale photo shoot, the girls had to stay composed while falling through midair. At elimination, they had to wear ten-inch high heels for a runway challenge; several girls tripped or fell. Gina and Kari were in the bottom two. It was Kari's failed effort on the runway that made her the third girl eiliminated.

In Episode 6, former *Top Model* judge Janice Dickinson and Cycle 5 contestant Lisa D'Amato gave the girls posing lessons. At the challenge, the girls used their skills in a Sears commercial shoot. Nnenna won the challenge, and got to keep all of the clothes from the shoot. The next day, the girls talked to Tyra Banks about their career goals beyond modeling, which was the theme of their next photo shoot. At elimination, the girls showed off three commercial poses using the clothes they had on, then wore fireman suits while producing edgy, editorial poses. Brooke and Gina were in the bottom two. The judges thought Brooke had more potential, so Gina was the fourth girl eliminated from the competition.

In Episode 8, the girls were given a lesson in improvisation techniques at the Groundlings Theatre. Their skills were put to the test when they performed improv sketches with actor Nick Cannon. Furonda won the challenge, earning a guest appearance on UPN's *Veronica Mars,* plus she and Nnenna filmed a public-service announcement for HIV prevention. Instead of a photo shoot, the girls again used their improv skills while taping a CoverGirl commercial. Mollie Sue and Jade were in the bottom two. Mollie Sue was the fifth girl eliminated because of her lack of personality.

In Episode 9, the girls learned about body movement on the runway, including a lesson on twirling from Richard and Ron Harris, the "Aswirl Twins." The models then tested their runway skills at a local church fashion show. Jade won the challenge, earning a $25,000 diamond ring. She chose to give another $10,000 ring to Furonda who in turn picked Nnenna to receive an $8,000 ring. At the Payless Shoes rooftop photo shoot, the models showed off their Krump dancing skills with Tommy the Clown and his Krumpers. At elimination, each girl had to strut her signature walk and perform a balance and posture test. Sara and Leslie were in the bottom two. Leslie's poor posture and presence made her the sixth girl eliminated.

In Episode 10, the girls were harshly critiqued by an actress playing an agent at the Strausberg Advertising agency. The girls were tested on how well they handled the cruel comments, and Jade won the challenge. She chose Nnenna to share her secret prize, which ended up being a visit from loved ones. There were two photo shoots during this episode. For one, the girls dressed as life-size dolls; for the other, Tyra instructed the girls on how to look beautiful while crying. Brooke and Jade were in the bottom two. Brooke was the seventh girl eliminated, because of her so-so performance overall.

In Episode 11, a public-relations expert trained the girls in handling the press. Nnenna won the next challenge, and chose Jade to join her in a day of pampering. The girls flew to Bangkok, Thailand, and for their first photo shoot abroad, they dressed as mermaids and posed hanging upside down over a floating market. At elimination, the girls had to showcase their personalities as models for the judges. Furonda and Nnenna were in the bottom two. The judges picked Nnenna to be the eighth girl eliminated because they thought her progress had halted and her overall performance had gone downhill.

Episode 12 was a recap show featuring never-before-seen clips from Cycle 6.

In Episode 13, the girls learned classical Thai dance moves, which they later performed for the judges and an audience. During the dance lesson, Danielle collapsed and was rushed to the hospital. The girls continued with the challenge, which Joanie won. She chose Sara to join her at a dinner with *Elle* Thailand publishing director Siri Udomritthruj. Against doctor's orders, a dehydrated Danielle checked herself out of the hospital to return to the competition. The girls traveled to the Thai jungle, where they posed on elephants for the Venus razor photo shoot. At elimination, the girls donned traditional Thai masks while attempting to convey emotions to the judges. Furonda and Jade were in the bottom two, and Furonda was the ninth girl eliminated, because of her inability to follow instructions.

In Episode 14, the girls went on "go-sees" and brought traditional, customary gifts to the Thai designers. Each girl got stuck in traffic during the challenge, arriving late for check-in, so no one won. The next day, the girls traveled to Phuket, where judge Nigel Barker photographed them in the surf. Danielle and Sara were in the bottom two, and Sara was the tenth girl eliminated, because of her stiff performance at the photo shoot.

In Episode 15 finale, the final three—Danielle, Joanie, and Jade—completed a CoverGirl photo shoot and television commercial. The next day, Jade, who had been in the bottom two five times, was the eleventh girl eliminated. For the final challenge, Danielle and Joanie competed in a Roj Singhakul runway show where the catwalk was a winding runway set over a pond. The judges chose Danielle as the winner.

AMERICA'S NEXT TOP MODEL
(Cycle 7)

GENRE	Competition (Job)
FIRST TELECAST	9/20/2006
LAST TELECAST	12/6/2006
NETWORK	The CW
AIR TIME	Wednesday, 8:00 p.m.
EPISODE STYLE	Story Arc
TALENT	Tyra Banks (Host); Nigel Barker (Judge); Twiggy (Judge); J. Alexander (Judge/Runway Coach); Jay Manuel (Judge/Coach)
CAST	CariDee English (Winner); Melrose Bickerstaff, (Runner-up); Eugena Washington (11th eliminated); Amanda Babin (10th eliminated); Michelle Babin (9th eliminated); Jaeda Young

(8th eliminated); Anchal Joseph (7th eliminated); Brooke Miller (6th eliminated); AJ Stewart (5th eliminated); Megg Morales (4th eliminated); Monique Calhoun (3rd eliminated); Megan Morris (2nd eliminated); Christian Evans (1st eliminated)

PRODUCTION COMPANIES	10x10 Entertainment; Bankable Productions
CREATED BY	Tyra Banks
EXECUTIVE PRODUCERS	Tyra Banks, Ken Mok

For Cycle 7, the first season to air on The CW, the number of models in the competition remained at thirteen. The winner received a $100,000 contract with CoverGirl, a fashion spread in and the cover of *Seventeen* magazine, and representation by Elite Model Management.

In the two-hour Episode 1, the thirty-three semifinalists were narrowed down to twenty-one. The girls participated in a nude photoshoot, and then thirteen finalists were chosen by the judges. At the first competition, the girls had to take the clothes off the backs of thirteen male models, and wear their new outfits on the runway. Melrose won, earning the chance to be "Diva for the Day" at the next photo shoot. At the contestants' house, there were only eleven beds for thirteen models. Monique sabotaged Eugena's bed, pouring water on it and pretending it was urine. At the photo shoot, each girl posed as a model stereotype. Melrose and Christian were in the bottom two. The judges thought Christian had less potential and her "model turned actress" stereotype photo was lackluster, so she was the first girl eliminated from the competition.

In Episode 2, the girls were made over, and several were unhappy with their new looks, including Jaeda, who thought her short hair made her look like a boy. For the challenge, the girls had to quickly put together an entire look, from makeup to wardrobe. Eugena won the competition, and posed for an exclusive photo shoot for CoverGirl's website, a prize she shared with CariDee and Jaeda. At the house, Monique spent hours on the phone, causing conflict with the other girls. At the photo shoot, the girls wore large wigs and hairpieces with moving parts. Megan and Jaeda were in the bottom two. Because of her flat photo, Megan was the second girl eliminated.

In Episode 3, Cycle 5's Bre Scullark was a special guest at the runway competition, where the girls wore vision-impairing masks and high heels while walking on broken slabs of concrete. AJ won the challenge, and chose CariDee and Megg to fly to Austin, Texas, with her to attend a star-studded Dennis Quaid Charity Weekend fashion show. A dehydrated Monique was taken to the hospital and missed the challenge where the girls rocked a catwalk suspended over water. The judges were unhappy that Monique couldn't tough out the challenge. She was in the bottom two with Eugena. Because the judges thought she wasn't driven, Monique was the third girl eliminated.

In Episode 4, a contortionist taught the girls about extreme posing, which they put to the test while showing off designer Bao Tranchi's fashions and jewelry. Eugena won the challenge, getting the $32,000 worth of jewelry that was being modeled. At the cirucs freak show photo shoot, the girls dressed up as Siamese twins, the bearded lady, and rubber girl, to name a few. Jaeda and Megg were in the bottom two, and Megg was the fourth girl eliminated, because she was unable to show her personality in a photo.

In Episode 5, former judge Janice Dickinson challenged the girls to interview her. Melrose won the competition, and joined the staff of *Entertainment Tonight,* interviewing stars on the red carpet. At the photo shoot, the girls were transformed into celebrity couples, including CariDee as Brad Pitt and Angelina Jolie, Michelle as Ellen DeGeneres and Portia de Rossi, and Brooke as Britney Spears and Kevin Federline. At judging, the girls' red-carpet interviewing skills were tested. AJ and Jaeda were in the bottom two, and former front-runner AJ was the fifth girl eliminated, as the judges thought she'd lost her competitive drive.

In Episode 6, Tyra Banks photographed the girls in a surprise photo shoot that highlighted their ability to look sexy and angry at the same time, as burlesque dancer and model, Dita Von Teese, offered tips. At a dinner party hosted by Elite Models' director, Cathy Gould, the models had to walk down a runway in the middle of the dinner table. For the third time, Melrose won, and invited Amanda, Michelle, and Brooke to join her at a *Seventeen* magazine photo shoot. Model Fabio posed with the girls at a mock romance novel cover shoot. Brooke and Eugena were in the bottom two. The judges weren't convinced Brooke had model potential, and on the night of her high-school graduation, she was the sixth girl eliminated.

Episode 7 was a Cycle 7 recap that featured never-before-seen footage of the girls.

In Episode 8, professional volleyball player and model Gabrielle Reece taught the girls about action and sports modeling. Then the girls posed with NASCAR driver Stanton Barrett while being photographed with a remote-controlled camera. Michelle won the task, and chose Amanda, CariDee, and Melrose to join in on her reward. The four girls had thirty seconds to put on as many articles of clothing as possible. Melrose won, getting $10,000 worth of clothes. At the photo shoot, the girls were made up as sexy space sirens modeling CoverGirl TrueBlend whipped foundation while flying at an indoor skydiving facility. At elimination, the girls had to pick random verbs and adverbs and act out the words, such as *swim frighteningly* or *dance aggressively*. Michelle and Anchal were in the bottom two. Thanks to her lack of self-confidence and commitment, Anchal was the seventh girl eliminated from the competition.

In Episode 9, acting coach Tasha Smith taught the girls how to break down their physical boundaries. CariDee won the silent film acting challenge, earning a guest spot on The CW's *One Tree Hill*. Tyra shocked the girls when she revealed they'd be going to Barcelona, Spain. Once in Europe, the girls met a group of male models, who joined them for dinner and the next challenge. The men and women paired up to film a commercial together, speaking only in Catalan. Jaeda's partner made a racist comment, which upset her. Overall, the girls had a difficult time memorizing their lines in Catalan; plus each had to kiss her partner in the commercial. CariDee and Jaeda were in the bottom two, and Jaeda's lack of improvement made her the eighth girl eliminated.

In Episode 10, Tyra warned the girls about the dark side of modeling. Then the models went on "go-sees" set up by Pancho Saula, the director of Elite Barcelona. Melrose won her fourth challenge, and picked CariDee to join her at a catered dinner at their apartment. Judge Nigel Barker was the photographer for the bullfighting photo shoot. At elimination, the girls had to reveal who among them they thought had the most and least model potential. Amanda was negatively singled out by the others, but her identical twin, Michelle, broke down in tears over her own insecurity and self-doubt about being a model. The twins were in the bottom two, but Amanda's drive won over the judges, and Michelle was the ninth girl eliminated.

In Episode 11, flamenco dancer Nacho Blanco taught the models the traditional Spanish dance. Eugena won the next day's dance competition and chose Amanda to share her prize—clothes worn at the Custo Barcelona Fall 2006 collection. At the photo shoot, the girls posed in pairs as nymphs floating underwater. A shivering CariDee prematurely abandoned the cold shoot, leaving her partner, Amanda, to finish the frames alone. Amanda and CariDee were in the bottom two. The judges worried that Amanda was too awkward and shy, so she was the tenth girl eliminated.

In the Episode 12 finale, the final three—CariDee, Eugena, and Melrose—met Cycle

6 winner Danielle Evans at the CoverGirl Double Lip Shine shoot. The judges questioned Eugena's passion, and she was the eleventh girl eliminated. At the final challenge, CariDee and Melrose faced off on the runway while dressed as ghostly brides in Victorio & Lucchino wedding gowns. CariDee mistakenly stepped on Melrose's dress, ripping a hole in the train, but Melrose recovered with confidence. The judges named CariDee the winner.

AMERICA'S NEXT TOP MODEL
(Cycle 8)

GENRE	Competition (Job)
FIRST TELECAST	2/28/2007
LAST TELECAST	5/16/2007
NETWORK	The CW
AIR TIME	Wednesday, 8:00 p.m.
EPISODE STYLE	Story Arc
TALENT	Tyra Banks (Host); Nigel Barker (Judge); Twiggy (Judge); J. Alexander (Judge/Runway Coach); Jay Manuel (Judge, Coach)
CAST	Jaslene Gonzalez (Winner); Natasha Galkina (Runner-up); Renee Alway (11th eliminated); Dionne Walters (10th eliminated); Brittany Hatch (9th eliminated); Jael Strauss (8th eliminated); Whitney Cunningham (7th eliminated); Sarah VonderHaar (6th eliminated); Diana Zalewski (5th eliminated); Felicia Provost (4th eliminated); Cassandra Watson (3rd eliminated); Samantha Francis (2nd eliminated); Kathleen DuJour (1st eliminated)
PRODUCTION COMPANIES	10x10 Entertainment; Bankable Productions
CREATED BY	Tyra Banks
EXECUTIVE PRODUCERS	Tyra Banks; Ken Mok

For Cycle 8, the number of models in the competition remained at thirteen. The winner received a $100,000 contract with CoverGirl, a fashion spread in and the cover of *Seventeen* magazine, and representation by Elite Model Management.

In the Episode 1 premiere, thirty-three semifinalists packed their bags for model boot camp in Los Angeles. After a photo shoot and a fashion quiz, the girls met Tyra Banks. The field was narrowed down to twenty contestants, then thirteen, who posed in a photo shoot depicting controversial political issues. Then the girls had three minutes to shop for outfits at Goodwill, which they later auctioned at a charity runway show. Jael won the challenge, as her ensemble got the highest bid. She signed her name on the ceremonial check given to charity. Jael and Kathleen were in the bottom two. While the judges criticized Jael for fearing success, they thought Kathleen had less potential, so she was the first girl eliminated.

In Episode 2, the girls joined J. Alexander and a high-school marching band, and were taught about the importance of timing and precision on the runway. Brittany won the prom fashion show runway challenge, earning a personalized trophy. At the photo shoot, the girls modeled as high-school clichés—e.g., the jock, the bookworm, the flirt. Natasha and Samantha were in the bottom two. Samantha's inexperience and lack of personality caused her to be the second girl eliminated from the competition.

In Episode 3, the girls were made over at a Beverly Hills salon. Brittany's new weave was painful, and Jael had most of her hair cut off. She also learned that a close friend at home had passed away. At the photo shoot, the girls were decorated as candy, such as gum balls, jelly beans, and candy canes. Diana and Cassandra were in the bottom two. The judges said Cassandra could not express her inner or outer beauty into a photo, and she was the third girl eliminated.

In Episode 4, posing instructor Benny Ninja taught the girls the art of "Voguing." At the next challenge, the girls had to quickly make their way through a tricky laser maze while being judged on their poses. Only Renee failed the challenge. Whitney's reward for winning was a $40,000 bracelet. At the photo shoot, the girls posed as gruesome crime scene victims. Felicia and Dionne were in the bottom two. Felicia was the fourth girl eliminated, after producing a weak photo and because of her overall declining performance.

In Episode 5, Elite Model Management director Cathy Gould taught the girls what they should and shouldn't wear. They were divided into groups to assemble and pose in their clothing lines. Whitney ignored Natasha's order that she stay within her group's platform, causing both to be disqualified. They would have won the challenge, but Sarah won instead, earning twice the amount of frames at the next photo shoot. The girls then posed as men alongside drag queens and Natasha finally impressed the judges. Diana and Whitney were in the bottom two. Diana's lack of enthusiasm made her the fifth girl eliminated.

In Episode 6, the girls gave themselves nicknames, which they then used at an industry party. Jael was thrown in the pool after annoying rapper 50 Cent, and Natasha jumped in after her. The drenched duo was mortified when they later met Tyra Banks's manager, Benny Medina. Dionne impressed Medina the most, and won a Keds spread in *Seventeen* magazine, to which she invited Jaslene and Whitney. The girls did their own hair and makeup for a photo shoot where they showed off four sides of their personalities. Tyra talked to the group, working out their issues with Renee. Whitney and Sarah were in the bottom two. The judges were disappointed with Sarah's overly posed photos, and made her the sixth girl eliminated.

In Episode 7, actress Tia Mowry gave the girls a quick acting class, and they were immediately given an acting challenge with Efren Ramirez ("Pedro" from *Napoleon Dynamite*). Renee won the challenge, and had Dionne share her prize, a T-shirt reading "I Voted for (contestant name)" and a family visit. Meanwhile, Natasha broke down over missing her daughter, but continued on in the competition. At the photo shoot, contestants from earlier cycles visited while the girls posed for shots representing some of the series' most memorable moments. The judges' favorites were Natasha and Brittany, while Jael and Whitney were in the bottom two. Whitney, who had been in the bottom two three weeks in a row, was the seventh girl eliminated, as the judges thought her beauty didn't transfer well to her photographs.

In Episode 8, Cycle 2 contestant April Wilkner and comedian Gary Riotto taught the girls interviewing skills. Next, the girls traveled to Sydney, Australia, where they interviewed locals while trying to speak in Australian slang. Natasha won the challenge, earning a chance to be a correspondent for *The Tyra Banks Show*. The girls spoke with an Australian accent while filming a CoverGirl commercial. Renee and Natasha were the standouts, while Brittany forgot her lines, and was in the bottom two, with Jael. Brittany's earlier, impressive photographs saved her, so Jael was the eighth girl eliminated.

Episode 9 was a recap episode that included never-before-seen footage of the girls.

In Episode 10, the final five went on "go-sees" to impress top Australian designers. Natasha and Brittany returned late and were disqualified, and Brittany blamed her taxi driver for her tardiness. Jaslene won the competition and picked Dionne to join her at a Nigel Barker photo shoot on top of the Sydney Harbour Bridge. Tyra Banks was the photographer for a swimsuit shoot in which the girls had to pose sensually for a women's magazine, and more seductively for a men's magazine. Dionne and Brittany were in the bottom two. Brittany's photos were better than Diane's, but her bad challenge feedback and poor personality and attitude made her the ninth girl eliminated.

In Episode 11, aboriginal teachers instructed the girls on self-expression and storytelling through dance. The final four used traditional body paint and costumes to help tell their life stories through dance. Dionne was bothered by the cold, while Renee won the challenge, sharing her pearl jewelry prize with Jaslene. Natasha's bout with the flu negatively affected her during the aboriginal dance photo shoot, while Renee and Jaslene impressed the judges with their shots.

At elimination, the girls revealed who among them they thought had the most and least potential. Natasha received the most criticism, but remained her optimistic self. She and Dionne were in the bottom two, and Dionne was the tenth girl eliminated, because she had the weaker portfolio.

In the Episode 12 finale, the final three shot a CoverGirl commercial and print ad. Renee's commercial was the best, but the judges thought she looked too mature in her photograph, so she was the eleventh girl eliminated. Jaslene and Natasha shot *Seventeen* magazine covers, and had individual chats with Tyra Banks before the final runway show. Jaslene improved throughout the runway challenge. Natasha's skirt fell off while walking, but she handled the mishap in a professional manner. At elimination, the judges were divided, but ultimately chose Jaslene as the winner.

AMERICA'S TOP COWBOY

GENRE Competition (Talent)
FIRST TELECAST 5/23/2007
NETWORK CMT

EPISODE STYLE	Story Arc
CAST	Trent Willmon (Host); Thomas Saunders (Judge); Kenny Call (Judge); Annie Bianco-Ellet (Judge)
TALENT	Mitch Coleman; Bradley Harter; Chad Klein; Jason Patrick; Jason Vohs; Scott Whinfrey

On this cowboy talent contest, contestants are judged on their cowboy skills in compulsory competitions and in freestyle events that showcase performance and execution. The eight cowboys compete for $50,000 and come from all walks of life.

AMERICAN CANDIDATE

GENRE	Docudrama
FIRST TELECAST	8/1/2004
LAST TELECAST	10/10/2004
NETWORK	Showtime
AIR TIME	Sunday, 9:00 p.m.
EPISODE STYLE	Story Arc
TALENT	Montel Williams (Host)
CAST	Park Gillispie (Winner); Keith Boykin; Bruce Friedrich; Chrissy Gephardt; Malia Lazu; Richard Mack; Joyce Riley; Kim Serafin; James Strock; Robert Vanech; Lisa Witter
PRODUCTION COMPANIES	Actual Reality Pictures; Showtime Networks
EXECUTIVE PRODUCERS	Tom Lassally; Jay Roach
PRODUCERS	Belisa Balaban; Adam Reed; William Ryan; Plowden Schumacher
DIRECTORS	Michael McNamara; Jonathan Chinn; Sebastian Doggart; Chip Goebert; Peter Krajewski

On documentary filmmaker R. J. Cutler's *American Candidate,* ten candidates from major political parties competed in challenges to determine who had the qualities and qualifications to be president of the United States. Real political experts advised the six male and four female candidates on their image, campaigns, and the challenges they faced while traveling by bus around the United States. Each week, the two candidates performing the worst debated against each other, with one voted out by the remaining contestants. Viewers voted for a winner at the end of the series. That winning candidate was Park Gillispie, who received a $200,000 cash prize and a chance to address the nation before the 2004 election.

AMERICAN CASINO

GENRE	Docudrama
FIRST TELECAST	6/1/2004
NETWORK	Travel Channel
EPISODE STYLE	Self-contained
CAST	Dawn LaGuardia (Director of Food and Beverage); Ninya Mae Perna (Hotel Manager); Matthew J. Sacca (Director of Player Development); Michael Tata (Vice President of Operations); David Demontmollin (Marketing Manager); Ralph Marano (Vice President and Assistant General Manager); Willie Bierlein (Executive Banquet Chef); Cheryl Rose (Director of Slot Operations); Wayne Shadd (Director of Marketing); Kelly Downey (Manager, Race and Sports Books); Joe Hasson (Vice President and General Manager); James Fricker (Pastry Chef); Joe Mulligan (Executive Chef); Bill Burt (Director of Casino Operations); Alex Peluffo (Banquet and Convention Operations Manager); Fred Tuerck (Assistant Security Manager)
PRODUCTION COMPANY	The Discovery Channel
EXECUTIVE PRODUCERS	C. Russell Muth; Craig Piligian; Andrea Richter; Ralph Wikke
PRODUCERS	Tim Calandrello; Alex Campbell; Jamie Campione; Michael Wunderle; Bob Schermerhorn

The Green Valley Ranch Resort and Spa in Henderson, Nevada, is the focus of this show highlighting the nonstop excitement and the behind-the-scenes action of the casino and resort business. Owned by brothers Lorenzo Fertitta and Frank Fertitta III, the ranch caters to celebrities and high rollers alike. One episode featured the memorial of Michael Tata, Green Valley Ranch Vice President, Operations, who was found dead at his home from an accidental drug overdose in July 2004.

AMERICAN CHOPPER

GENRE	Docudrama
FIRST TELECAST	3/31/2003
NETWORK	Discovery
EPISODE STYLE	Self-contained
CAST	Paul Teutul, Sr. (Owner of OCC); Paul Teutul, Jr. (Chief Designer and Fabricator); Vincent "Vinnie" Dimartino (Mechanic); Michael "Mikey" Teutel (Comic Relief); Keith Quill (Director of Operations); Richard Collard (Painter for NUB GRAFIX); Rick Petko (OCC Mechanic); Justin Barnes (Painter for J.B. Graphics); Christian Welter (OCC Mechanic); Cody Conell (OCC Mechanic)
PRODUCTION COMPANIES	Pilgrim Films & Television Inc.; Discovery Channel
EXECUTIVE PRODUCERS	Hank Capshaw; C. Russell Muth; Craig Piligian
PRODUCER	Alex Eastburg

This is a documentary series shot on location in Rock Tavern, New York, features Orange County Choppers, a custom motorcycle fabrication company. Camera crews capture the often contentious relationship between father, Paul Sr., son, Paul Jr., and their staff, as they create motorcycles that are one-of-a-kind works of art. Many of their pieces are auctioned at fund-raisers, including a bike built to benefit the families of U.S. troops seriously wounded or killed in Iraq and Afghanistan. Highlights include episodes with Jay Leno of *The Tonight Show,* who commissioned a modern version of his favorite classic bike, the 1939 Brough Superior; an *I Robot*–inspired bike for actor

Will Smith; and a bright yellow bike built for Lance Armstrong in honor of his record-setting victories in the Tour de France.

AMERICAN DREAM DERBY

GENRE	Competition
FIRST TELECAST	1/10/2005
LAST TELECAST	2/21/2005
NETWORK	GSN
EPISODE STYLE	Story Arc
TALENT	Steve Santagati (Host)
CAST	Deanna Manfredi (Winner); Chris Black; Susan Bosso; Eric Childers; Tara Clark; Aaron Coen; David Malatesta; Dean Pellegrin; Jewel Savage; Sara Slavin; Levar Thomas; Tara Walden
PRODUCTION COMPANY	Gonzo Productions
DIRECTOR	Tim Warren

In the first reality series to take a behind-the-scenes look at professional thoroughbred horse racing, contestants learned about buying, training, and working with racehorses at Santa Anita Park, in Arcadia, California. A final live, winner-take-all race was broadcast to determine who would be awarded all six horses, a contract with their trainer, and $250,000 in cash to fund a racing stable. The winner was Deanna Manfredi, a marketing consultant from Philadelphia. LeAnn Rimes sang the show's theme song, "You Take Me Home."

AMERICAN HIGH

GENRE	Docusoap
FIRST TELECAST	8/2/2000
NETWORKS	FOX (Episodes 1 and 2); PBS

AIR TIME	Wednesday, 9:00 p.m. (Fox run)
EPISODE STYLE	Story Arc
CAST	Kaytee Bodle; Shanna Davis; Scott Hinden; Allie Komessar; Brad Krefman; Mike "Kiwi" Langford; Suzy Lurie; Sarah Mages; Morgan Moss; Robby Nathan; Pablo Otavalo; Anna Santiago; Abby Schwartz; Tiffany Woods
PRODUCTION COMPANIES	Actual Reality Pictures; 20th Century Fox Television
EXECUTIVE PRODUCERS	R. J. Cutler; Cheryl Stanley; Erwin More; Brian Medavoy
PRODUCERS	Richard Bye; Jonathan Chinn; Nick Doob; Alison Ellwood; Jonathan Mednick; Molly O'Brien
CO-PRODUCER	Andrew Perry
DIRECTORS	R. J. Cutler; Alison Ellwood; Dan Partland

This documentary-style series filmed during the 1999–2000 school year at Highland Park High School, in Illinois. Fourteen students were given cameras to record video diaries about their feelings and experiences during their senior year. In 2001, the series won an Emmy for Outstanding Non-Fiction Program (Reality).

AMERICAN IDOL
(Season 1)

GENRE	Competition (Talent)
FIRST TELECAST	6/11/2002
LAST TELECAST	9/4/2002
NETWORK	FOX
AIR TIMES	Tuesday, 9:00 p.m.; Wednesday, 9:00 p.m.
EPISODE STYLE	Story Arc
TALENT	Ryan Seacrest (Host); Brian Dunkelman (Host); Paula Abdul (Judge); Simon Cowell (Judge), Randy Jackson (Judge)

CAST	Kelly Clarkson (Winner); Justin Guarini (Runner-up); Nikki McKibbin (8th eliminated); Tamyra Gray (7th eliminated); R. J. Helton (6th eliminated); Christina Christian (5th eliminated); Ryan Starr (4th eliminated); A. J. Gil (3rd eliminated); Jim Verraros (2nd eliminated); EJay Day (1st eliminated)
PRODUCTION COMPANIES	FremantleMedia North America; 19 TV Ltd.
CREATED BY	Simon Fuller and Simon Cowell
EXECUTIVE PRODUCERS	Simon Fuller; Nigel Lythgoe; Ken Warwick; Simon Jones; Cécile Frot-Coutaz
CO-EXECUTIVE PRODUCER	Brian Gadinsky
DIRECTOR	Bruce Gowers

Based on the UK hit *Pop Idol,* this songster talent contest follows judges Paula Abdul, Simon Cowell, and Randy Jackson as they search for the next pop music superstar in the United States. After weeks of audition rounds, the contestants selected by the judges perform for a live audience, and endure harsh criticism from the judges on Tuesday nights. One by one, television viewers vote off the contestants, who are eliminated on Wednesday nights. The last contestant remaining is crowned the winner, and receives a major recording and management contract.

On the series premiere, judges Paula Abdul, Simon Cowell, and Randy Jackson held auditions in seven U.S. cities, and eventually selected one hundred singers to advance to the next round.

In Episode 2, the singers performed in groups, learning various routines with little time to prepare. The 100 singers were narrowed down to fifty.

In Episode 3, the first group of ten singers performed, vying for the final ten audition spots. Tamyra Gray gave a sensational performance, while the judges thought Jim Verraros performed disappointingly.

In the Episode 4 results show, Tamyra won the first seat in the final group of ten, Ryan Starr took the second spot, and Jim shockingly earned the third seat.

In Episode 5, viewers were introduced to Justin Guarini and Kelly Clarkson, while Simon ripped female favorite A. J. Gil.

In Episode 6, Justin earned the fourth seat in the final ten. Kelly won a mild upset against Angela Peel to take the fifth seat, and A.J. pulled the second stunner of the season by earning the sixth seat.

In Episode 7, there were numerous poor performances, and Delano Cagnolatti was caught lying about his age. Randy threatened Simon after Simon accused the other judges of going too easy on the contestants.

In Episode 8, the judges continued to feud. Simon gushed over Christina Christian, who took the seventh seat in the finals. Nikki McKibbin wound up with the eighth seat, and EJay Day earned the ninth spot.

In Episode 9, five of the non-qualifiers—Kelli Glover, Christopher Aaron, Alexis, Angela Peel, and R. J. Helton—had one last chance to advance by attempting to earn a "wild card" from the judges. The unanimous recipient of the tenth and final spot was R.J.

Episode 10 featured a live studio audience. Hosts Ryan Seacrest and Bryan Dunkelman announced that each week's performances would have a theme. That week, all ten finalists performed Motown songs.

In Episode 11, Paula did a ventriloquism act with a cardboard cutout of Simon. EJay and Jim were the first two finalists cut.

Episode 12's theme was the 1960s. A.J., Justin, and Ryan delivered disappointing performances, and were reprimanded by Simon.

In Episode 13, A.J. was eliminated from the finals.

Episode 14's theme was the 1970s. Kelly's rendition of "Don't Play That Song" was the judges' favorite performance.

In Episode 15, Justin edged out Ryan, who gave a tearful good-bye.

Episode 16's theme was big band music. Kelly gave a standout performance with "Stuff Like That There," while Simon didn't think Nikki would survive the week.

In Episode 17, Christina was absent because she was hospitalized for stress. She was voted off, which made several of the contestants burst into tears.

Episode 18 featured Burt Bacharach night, with Bacharach himself there to collaborate with the contestants.

In Episode 19, R.J. and Nikki were in the bottom two, and R.J. was eliminated.

Episode 20's theme night was lifted—everyone sang two songs of their choice.

In Episode 21, favorite Tamyra was voted off.

In Episode 22, the final three—Justin, Kelly, and Nikki—each sang two songs, one they picked and one chosen by the judges. After Kelly's rendition of "Think Twice," Simon told her she was the best singer in the competition.

Episode 23 was a special hour-long results show. Nikki was eliminated, and received a standing ovation from the live studio audience.

Episode 24 took place at Hollywood's Kodak Theatre. Justin sang the original "Before Your Love," while Kelly sang her original "A Moment Like This." Justin reprised his earlier performance of "Get Here," while Kelly gave "Respect" another go. *Pop Idol* winner Will Young made a cameo. Finally, the original songs were flipped, as Justin performed "A Moment Like This," and Kelly sang "Before Your Love."

The Episode 25 finale featured several interviews, plus the five best and worst auditions. The ten finalists reunited to perform musical numbers. Finally, Kelly Clarkson was declared the winner, closing the show with another performance of her first single, "A Moment Like This."

RATINGS: The Tuesday edition of *American Idol* brought in an average of 21.5 million viewers, while the Wednesday edition had an average of 21.9 million viewers.

AMERICAN IDOL
(Season 2)

GENRE	Competition (Talent)
FIRST TELECAST	1/21/2003
LAST TELECAST	5/21/2003
NETWORK	FOX
AIR TIMES	Tuesday, 8:00 p.m.; Wednesday, 8:00 p.m.
EPISODE STYLE	Story Arc
TALENT	Ryan Seacrest (Host); Paula Abdul (Judge); Simon Cowell (Judge); Randy Jackson (Judge)
CAST	Ruben Studdard (Winner); Clay Aiken (Runner-up); Kimberley Locke (10th eliminated); Joshua Gracin (9th eliminated); Trenyce (8th eliminated); Carmen Rasmusen (7th eliminated);

Kimberly Caldwell (6th eliminated); Rickey Smith (5th eliminated); Corey Clark (4th eliminated); Julia DeMato (3rd eliminated); Charles Grigsby (2nd eliminated); Vanessa Olivarez (1st eliminated)

PRODUCTION COMPANIES FremantleMedia North America; 19 TV Ltd.

CREATED BY Simon Fuller and Simon Cowell

EXECUTIVE PRODUCERS Simon Fuller; Nigel Lythgoe; Ken Warwick; Simon Jones; Cécile Frot-Coutaz

CO-EXECUTIVE PRODUCER Brian Gadinsky

DIRECTOR Bruce Gowers

For Season 2 of *American Idol,* the number of finalists increased to twelve, and host Brian Dunkleman did not return, leaving Ryan Seacrest to perform hosting duties alone.

In Episode 1, Ryan and Season 1 contestant turned correspondent Kristin Holt recapped the Season 2 auditions held in New York, Miami, and Austin.

Episode 2 continued tracking auditions in Los Angeles and Detroit.

Episode 3 wrapped up national audition coverage in Atlanta and Nashville.

In Episode 4, those who'd passed the national tryouts flew to Los Angeles for the next round of auditions, at the Alex Theater. The field was narrowed to thirty-two contestants.

In Episode 5, Ryan gave a walk-through of the updated set, which included more cameras and a "family couch." The eight performers were Bettis Richardson, Charles Grigsby, J. D. Adams, Julia DeMato, Kimberly Caldwell, Lashundra Cobbins, Meosha Denton, and Patrick Forton.

Episode 6 was the first qualifying show. Unlike in the previous year, the three finalists were narrowed down to two, which meant Kimberly was left out as Charles and Julia made the cut.

Episode 7's eight performers were Clay Aiken, Candice Coleman, Rebecca Bond, Jacob John Smalley, Hadas, Ruben Studdard, Kimberley Locke, and Jennifer Fuentes. Meanwhile, Frenchie Davis, a promising early contender, was kicked off the show when producers discovered that she had posed topless for an adult website.

In Episode 8, Clay, Ruben, and Kimberley made the final three, and Ruben and Kimberley were chosen to move on.

Episode 9's eight performers were Equoia Coleman, George Trice, Jordan Segundo, Kimberly Kelsey, Louis Gazzara, Rickey Smith, Samantha Cohen, and Vanessa Olivarez.

In Episode 10, Vanessa, Rickey, and Equoia made the final three, and Vanessa and Rickey were chosen to advance.

Episode 11's final group of eight performers included Ashley Hartman, Chip Days, Corey Clark, Joshua Gracin, Juanita Barber, Nasheka Siddall, Patrick Lake, and Sylvia Chibiliti.

In Episode 12, Corey, Patrick, and Joshua were in the final three, and Corey and Joshua moved on. Ryan announced there would be a "wild card" selection show the next week, and Simon teased viewers about an exciting twist.

In Episode 13, the twist was revealed—there would be twelve finalists that season, instead of ten. The four "wild card" performers would be chosen by viewers and Simon, Randy, and Paula from these candidates: Aliceyn Coone, Carmen Rasmusen, Chip Days, Clay Aiken, Janine Falsone, Kimberly Caldwell, Nasheka Siddall, Olivia Mojica, and Trenyce.

In Episode 14, the "wild card" selections were revealed: America's "wild card" went to Clay, Randy's went to Kimberly Caldwell, Paula's went to Trenyce, and Simon's went to Carmen.

Episode 15 was a two-hour Motown label special featuring guest judge Lamont Dozier. Kimberley sang "Heat Wave"; Joshua sang "Baby I Need Your Lovin' "; Charles sang "How Sweet It Is"; Kimberly sang "Nowhere to Run"; Rickey sang "123"; Julia sang "Where Did Our Love Go?"; Clay sang "I Can't Help Myself"; Vanessa sang "You Keep Me Hanging On"; Corey sang "This Old Heart of Mine"; Carmen sang "You Can't Hurry Love"; Trenyce sang "Come See About Me"; and Ruben sang "Baby I Need Your Lovin' ".

In Episode 16, Vanessa was the first contestant voted off.

Episode 17 was a two-hour special featuring music from the movies, with guest judge Gladys Knight. Corey sang "Against All Odds"; Ruben sang "A Whole New World"; Trenyce sang "I Have Nothing"; Clay sang "Somewhere Out There"; Kimberly sang "Shoop Shoop Song"; Joshua sang "I Don't Want to Miss a Thing"; Carmen sang

"Hopelessly Devoted to You"; Charles sang "You Can Win"; Rickey sang "It Might Be You"; Julia sang "Flashdance! (What a Feeling)"; and Kimberley sang "Home."

In Episode 18, Charles was the second contestant voted off.

Episode 19's theme was country rock, featuring guest judge Olivia Newton-John. Joshua sang "Ain't Goin' Down Til' the Sun Comes Up"; Trenyce sang "I Need You"; Kimberley sang "I Can't Make You Love Me"; Corey sang "Drift Away"; Carmen sang "Wild Angels"; Rickey sang "I've Done Enough Dyin' Today"; Kimberly sang "Anymore"; Ruben sang "Sweet Home Alabama"; Julia sang "Breathe"; and Clay sang "Someone Else's Star."

In Episode 20, Julia was the third singer voted off.

Episode 21 featured a disco theme, with Verdine White as guest judge. Rickey sang "Let's Groove"; Carmen sang "Turn the Beat Around"; Kimberly sang "Knock On Wood"; Clay sang "Everlasting Love"; Trenyce sang "I'm Every Woman"; Ruben sang "Can't Get Enough of Your Love"; Kimberley sang "It's Raining Men"; and Joshua sang "Celebration." Meanwhile, Corey was kicked off the show after producers learned of his arrest for battery against his sister and for resisting arrest.

In Episode 22, the results show, it was revealed that none of the contestants would be voted off due to Corey's unexpected dismissal.

Episode 23's theme was Billboard No. 1 hits, and featured guest judge Lionel Richie. Clay sang "At This Moment"; Kimberley sang "My Heart Will Go On"; Rickey sang "Endless Love"; Kimberly sang "(Everything I Do) I Do It For You"; Joshua sang "Amazed"; Carmen sang "Call Me"; Trenyce sang "The Power Of Love"; and Ruben sang "Kiss and Say Goodbye."

In Episode 24, Rickey was the fifth person eliminated.

Episode 25's theme was Billy Joel songs, and was guest-judged by Smokey Robinson. Kimberly sang "It's Still Rock 'n' Roll to Me"; Ruben sang "Just The Way You Are"; Kimberley sang "New York State of Mind"; Carmen sang "And So It Goes"; Joshua sang "Piano Man"; Trenyce sang "Baby Grand"; and Clay sang "Tell Her About It."

In Episode 26, Kimberly Caldwell was the sixth contestant eliminated.

In a special Monday edition of Episode 27, Ryan interviewed the remaining finalists and recapped their performances to date.

Episode 28 featured songs written by Diane Warren. Kimberley sang "If You Asked Me To"; Clay sang "I Could Not Ask for More"; Trenyce sang "Have You Ever?"; Joshua sang "That's When I'll Stop Loving You"; Carmen sang "Love Will Lead You Back"; and Ruben sang "Music of My Heart."

In Episode 29, Carmen was the seventh singer voted out of the competition.

In Episode 30, each of the contestants sang two songs, one of which was written by guest judge Neil Sedaka. Ruben sang "Ain't Too Proud to Beg" and "Breaking Up Is Hard to Do"; Trenyce sang "Proud Mary" and "Love Will Keep Us Together"; Joshua sang "Then You Can Tell Me Goodbye" and "Bad Blood"; Kimberley sang "I Heard It Through the Grapevine" and "Where the Boys Are"; and Clay sang "Build Me Up Buttercup" and "Solitaire."

In Episode 31, Trenyce was the eighth contestant eliminated.

Episode 32 featured Bee Gees songs, and was guest-judged by Robin Gibb. Joshua sang "Jive Talkin'" and "To Love Somebody"; Clay sang "To Love Somebody" and "Grease"; Kimberley sang "I Just Want to Be Your Everything"; and "Emotion"; and Ruben sang "Nights on Broadway" and "How Can You Mend a Broken Heart."

Episode 33 was Joshua's last, as he was the ninth person voted off.

In Episode 34, each singer performed three songs. The first was drawn at random, the second was assigned by the judges, and the third was the contestant's choice. Kimberley sang "Band of Gold," "Inseparable," and "Anyone Who Had a Heart"; Ruben sang "Signed, Sealed, Delivered, I'm Yours," "Smile," and "If Ever You're in My Arms Again"; and Clay sang "Vincent," "Mack the Knife," and "Unchained Melody."

Episode 35 featured a guest performance by Season 1's Tamyra Gray, appearances by Justin Guarini and Kelly Clarkson, and a group medley by Kimberley, Ruben, and Clay. The show concluded with Kimberley being the tenth person cut from the show.

A special Monday edition on Episode 36 featured exposés on finalists Ruben and Clay.

In Episode 37, Paul Anka was the guest star. Ruben sang "A House Is Not a Home," "Imagine," and "Flying Without Wings"; and Clay sang "This Is the Night," "Here, There, and Everywhere," and "Bridge Over Troubled Water."

Episode 38 featured final performances by the two contenders. Ruben Studdard was crowned the winner.

RATINGS: Season 2 of *American Idol* had an average of 21.6 million viewers for its Tuesday edition, while the Wednesday edition had an average of 21.9 million viewers.

AMERICAN IDOL
(Season 3)

GENRE	Competition (Talent)
FIRST TELECAST	1/19/2004
LAST TELECAST	5/26/2004
NETWORK	FOX
AIR TIMES	Tuesday, 8:00 p.m.; Wednesday, 8:30 p.m.
EPISODE STYLE	Story Arc
TALENT	Ryan Seacrest (Host); Paula Abdul (Judge); Simon Cowell (Judge); Randy Jackson (Judge)
CAST	Fantasia Barrino (Winner); Diana DeGarmo (Runner-up); Jasmine Trias (10th eliminated); LaToya London (9th eliminated); George Huff (8th eliminated); John Stevens (7th eliminated); Jennifer Hudson (6th eliminated); Jon Peter Lewis (5th eliminated); Camile Velasco (4th eliminated); Amy Adams (3rd eliminated); Matthew Rogers (2nd eliminated); Leah LaBelle (1st eliminated)
PRODUCTION COMPANIES	FremantleMedia North America; 19 TV Ltd.
CREATED BY	Simon Fuller and Simon Cowell
EXECUTIVE PRODUCERS	Simon Fuller; Nigel Lythgoe; Ken Warwick; Simon Jones; Cécile Frot-Coutaz
CO-EXECUTIVE PRODUCER	Brian Gadinsky
DIRECTOR	Bruce Gowers

For Season 3, the number of finalists remained at twelve.

Episode 1 showcased the auditions in New York City.

Episode 2 continued audition coverage, as the scene shifted to Atlanta.

Episode 3 showed the selection process in Houston.

In Episode 4, the auditions came through Los Angeles and San Francisco, and

America was introduced to the infamous auditioner William Hung, who sang Ricky Martin's "She Bangs."

Episode 5 followed the audition process in Hawaii.

Episode 6 was a special show devoted to the auditions of contestants who never made it on the show—some for good reason.

In Episode 7, 117 finalists sang for the judges in Los Angeles. After a number of disappointing performances, thirty were cut.

In Episode 8, several of the eighty-seven finalists forgot lyrics, and the group was narrowed down to thirty-two.

In Episode 9, the first group of eight singers vying for two seats in the final twelve included Diana Degarmo, Marque Lynch, Ashley Thomas, Katie Webber, Erskine Walcott, Jennifer Hudson, Matthew Metzger, and Fantasia Barrino.

In Episode 10, Diana and Fantasia advanced to the final twelve.

Episode 11's eight performers were Jesus Roman, Lisa Leuschner, Kara Master, Briana Ramirez, Matthew Rogers, Noel Roman, Marisa Joy, and Camile Velasco.

In Episode 12, Camile and Matthew moved on to the final twelve.

Episode 13's eight contenders were Elizabeth Letendre, Eric Yoder, Amy Adams, Jon Peter Lewis, Charly Lowry, Jonah Moananu, Leah Labelle, and Latoya London.

In Episode 14, LaToya and Amy were picked for the final twelve.

Episode 15's final group of eight included Susie Vulaca, Heather Piccinini, John Preato, Tiara Purifoy, John Stevens, Jasmine Trias, George Huff, and Lisa Wilson.

In Episode 16, John Stevens and Jasmine locked down spots in the final twelve.

In Episode 17, the following singers earned a chance to qualify for the four "wild card" spots: Jennifer Hudson, Katie Webber, Marque Lynche, Matthew Metzger, Lisa Leuschner, Jon-Peter Lewis, Elizabeth Letendre, Leah Labelle, Eric Yoder, Susan Vulaca, George Huff, and Tiara Purifoy.

In Episode 18, the "wild card" votes went to Jon as America's choice, Jennifer as Randy's choice, Leah as Paula's choice, and George as Simon's choice.

Episode 19's theme was soul. Amy sang "You Make Me Feel Brand New"; Camile sang "Son of a Preacher Man"; Diana sang "Think"; Fantasia sang "Signed, Sealed, Delivered, I'm Yours"; George sang "(Sittin' on) the Dock of the Bay"; Jasmine sang "Inseparable"; Jennifer sang "Baby I Love You"; John sang "Lately"; Jon sang "Drift

Away"; LaToya sang "Ain't Nobody"; Leah sang "You Keep Me Hanging On"; and Matt sang "Hard to Handle."

In Episode 20, Leah was the first contestant voted out of Season 3.

For Episode 21's country theme, Diana sang "A Broken Wing"; George sang "I Can Love You Like That"; Fantasia sang "Always on my Mind"; John sang "King of the Road"; Jon sang "She Believes in Me"; Camile sang "Desperado"; Jennifer sang "No One Else on Earth"; Jasmine sang "Breathe"; Matthew sang "Amazed"; LaToya sang "Ain't Goin' Down Till the Sun Comes Up"; and Amy sang "Sin Wagon."

In Episode 22, Matthew was the second contestant eliminated.

In Episode 23, Nick Ashford and Valerie Simpson were guest judges for Motown night. Camile sang "For Once in My Life"; Jon sang "This Old Heart of Mine"; LaToya sang "Ooh Baby Baby"; Amy sang "Dancing in the Streets"; John sang "My Girl"; Jennifer sang "Heat Wave"; Jasmine sang "You're All I Need to Get By"; Diana sang "Do You Love Me?"; Fantasia sang "I Heard It Through the Grapevine"; and George sang "Ain't Too Proud to Beg."

In Episode 24, Amy was the third singer voted out.

Episode 25 featured the songs of Elton John, with the singer himself sitting in on rehearsals. For their performances, Fantasia sang "Something About the Way You Look Tonight"; Jon sang "Rocket Man"; Jasmine sang "Don't Let the Sun Go Down on Me"; John sang "Crocodile Rock"; Camile sang "Goodbye, Yellow Brick Road"; George sang "Take Me to the Pilot"; Diana sang "I'm Still Standing"; LaToya sang "Someone Saved My Life Tonight"; and Jennifer sang "Circle of Life."

In Episode 26, Season 1 contestant Tamyra Gray performed "Raindrops Will Fall." Camile was the fourth contestant eliminated from the competition.

In Episode 27, Quentin Tarantino was the guest judge for the movie theme week. George sang "Against All Odds"; Jon sang "Jailhouse Rock"; Jennifer sang "I Have Nothing"; Diana sang "My Heart Will Go On"; Fantasia sang "Summertime"; Jasmine sang "When I Fall in Love"; John sang "As Time Goes By"; and LaToya sang "Somewhere." Singer/songwriter Neil Sedaka was in the audience.

In Episode 28, Jon was the fifth eliminated, and Diana had her third showing in the bottom three.

Episode 29 featured Barry Manilow night, with Barry himself as guest judge. Diana sang "One Voice"; George sang "Trying to Get That Feeling Again"; Jennifer sang "Weekend in New England"; LaToya sang "All the Time"; Jasmine sang "I'll Never Love This Way Again"; John sang "Mandy"; and Fantasia sang "It's a Miracle."

Episode 30 again featured Barry Manilow. Jennifer was the sixth singer voted out, in what was considered a shocking elimination.

Episode 31 was Gloria Estefan night, with Gloria herself as guest judge. Fantasia sang "Get on your Feet"; George sang "Live for Loving You"; LaToya sang "Rhythm Is Gonna Get You"; Jasmine sang "Here We Are"; John sang "Music of My Heart"; and Diana sang "Turn the Beat Around."

In Episode 32, John was the seventh contestant voted out.

In Episode 33, the finalists each sang two songs on big band night. Diana sang "Someone to Watch Over Me" and "Come On, Get Happy"; George sang "Cheek to Cheek" and "What a Wonderful World"; LaToya sang "Too Close for Comfort" and "Don't Rain on My Parade"; Jasmine sang "The Way You Look Tonight" and "Almost Like Being In Love"; and Fantasia sang "Crazy Little Thing Called Love" and "The Rest of Your Life."

In Episode 34, George was the eighth contestant voted out.

Episode 35's theme was disco. Jasmine sang "Everlasting Love" and "It's Raining Men"; LaToya sang "Love You Inside and Out" and "Don't Leave Me This Way"; Fantasia sang "Knock on Wood" and "Holding Out for a Hero"; and Diana sang "This Is It" and "No More Tears (Enough is Enough)."

In Episode 36, LaToya was eliminated. The show also featured guest stars Donna Summer and Season 2 runner-up, Clay Aiken.

On a special Monday night episode, 37, Ryan heard the judges' take on Season 3, then the host interviewed the three finalists.

In Episode 38, the final three—Jasmine, Fantasia, and Diana—performed three songs, one personal choice, one chosen by the judges, and one picked by Clive Davis. Jasmine sang "Saving All My Love for You," "Mr. Melody," and "All By Myself"; Fantasia sang "Chain of Fools," "Fool in Love," and "Greatest Love of All"; and Diana sang "Ain't No Mountain High Enough," "Because You Loved Me," and "Don't Cry Out Loud."

In Episode 39, Jasmine was eliminated. The show also featured guest appearances by Season 1's Tamyra Gray and *Australian Idol* winner Guy Sebastian.

Episode 40 recapped the first three seasons of *American Idol*.

Episode 41 was a showdown between Diana and Fantasia. Diana sang "I Believe," "No More Tears," and "Don't Cry Out Loud," while Fantasia sang "All My Life," "Summertime" and her own version of "I Believe."

Episode 42 was the two-hour finale. After a parade of stars and much build-up, Fantasia Barrino won.

RATINGS: *American Idol* ratings increased again during Season 3, as the Tuesday edition averaged 25.7 million viewers, and the Wednesday edition brought in an average of 24.4 million viewers.

AMERICAN IDOL
(Season 4)

GENRE	Competition (Talent)
FIRST TELECAST	1/18/2005
LAST TELECAST	5/25/2005
NETWORK	FOX
AIR TIMES	Tuesday, 8:00 p.m.; Wednesday, 8:00 p.m.
EPISODE STYLE	Story Arc
TALENT	Ryan Seacrest (Host); Paula Abdul (Judge); Simon Cowell (Judge); Randy Jackson (Judge)
CAST	Carrie Underwood (Winner); Bo Bice (Runner-up); Vonzell Solomon (10th eliminated); Anthony Federov (9th eliminated); Scott Savol (8th eliminated); Constantine Maroulis (7th eliminated); Anwar Robinson (6th eliminated); Nadia Turner (5th eliminated); Nikko Smith (4th eliminated); Jessica Sierra (3rd eliminated); Mikalah Gordon (2nd eliminated); Lindsey Cardinale (1st eliminated)
PRODUCTION COMPANIES	FremantleMedia North America; 19 TV Ltd.
CREATED BY	Simon Fuller and Simon Cowell
EXECUTIVE PRODUCERS	Simon Fuller; Nigel Lythgoe; Ken Warwick; Simon Jones; Cécile Frot-Coutaz

CO-EXECUTIVE PRODUCERS Brian Gadinsky
DIRECTOR Bruce Gowers

For Season 4, the number of finalists remained at twelve.

Episode 1 kicked off with Sugar Ray's Mark McGrath guest-judging auditions in Washington, D.C.

Episode 2 documented the auditions held in St. Louis, Missouri.

Episode 3's guest judge was KISS frontman Gene Simmons, who oversaw auditions in New Orleans.

In Episode 4, Kenny Loggins was a guest judge at the Las Vegas auditions.

Episode 5 featured LL Cool J as the guest judge for auditions in Cleveland.

Episode 6 featured guest judge Brandy, who attended the California auditions in San Francisco and Los Angeles.

In Episode 7, nearly two hundred national qualifiers came to Hollywood for the first round of auditions.

In Episode 8, the number of contestants was cut to ninety-six at the Hollywood auditions.

In Episode 9, massive cuts were made, as the field narrowed from the seventies to the twenties.

Episode 10 concluded coverage of the Hollywood tryouts, and the contestant pool was trimmed down to twelve male and twelve female finalists.

Episode 11 featured performances by the top twelve male finalists: Anthony Fedorov, Anwar Robinson, Constantine Maroulis, David Brown, Harold "Bo" Bice, Jared Yates, Joe Murena, Jr., Judd Harris, Mario Vazquez, Nikko Smith, Scott Savol, and Travis Tucker.

Episode 12 featured performances by the top twelve female finalists: Amanda Avila, Aloha Mischeaux, Carrie Underwood, Celena Rae Batchelor, Janay Castine, Jessica Sierra, Lindsey Cardinale, Melinda Lira, Mikalah Gordon, Nadia Turner, Sarah Mather, and Vonzell Solomon.

In Episode 13, Jared, Judd, Melinda, and Sarah were eliminated from the competition.

Episode 14 featured performances by the remaining ten male finalists: Anthony

Fedorov, Anwar Robinson, Constantine Maroulis, David Brown, Harold "Bo" Bice, Joe Murena, Jr., Mario Vazquez, Nikko Smith, Scott Savol, and Travis Tucker.

Episode 15 featured performances by the remaining ten female finalists: Amanda Avila, Aloha Mischeaux, Carrie Underwood, Celena Rae Batchelor, Janay Castine, Jessica Sierra, Lindsey Cardinale, Mikalah Gordon, Nadia Turner, and Vonzell Solomon.

In Episode 16, four more contestants were cut: David, Joe, Celena, and Aloha.

In Episode 17, the eight male finalists performed: Anthony Fedorov, Anwar Robinson, Constantine Maroulis, Harold "Bo" Bice, Mario Vazquez, Nikko Smith, Scott Savol, and Travis Tucker.

In Episode 18, the eight female finalists performed: Amanda Avila, Carrie Underwood, Janay Castine, Jessica Sierra, Lindsey Cardinale, Mikalah Gordon, Nadia Turner, and Vonzell Solomon.

In Episode 19, another pair of males and a pair of females were voted out: Mario, Travis, Amanda, and Janay, leaving the top twelve Season 4 contestants.

Episode 20 was the first theme night, featuring songs of the 1960s. Jessica sang "Shop Around"; Anwar sang "A House Is Not a Home"; Mikalah sang "Son of a Preacher Man"; Constantine Maroulis sang "You've Made Me So Very Happy": Lindsey sang "Knock on Wood"; Anthony sang "Breaking Up Is Hard to Do"; Nadia sang "You Don't Have to Say You Love Me"; Bo sang "Spinning Wheel"; Vonzell sang "Anyone Who Had a Heart"; Scott sang "Ain't Too Proud to Beg"; Carrie sang "When Will I Be Loved"; and Nikko sang "I Want You Back."

Season 2 winner Ruben Studdard was in the audience for Episode 21, as Lindsey was the first of the top twelve to be eliminated.

Episode 22 featured appearances by Fred Bronson and Donny Osmond, and the theme was Billboard No. 1 hits. Anthony sang "I Knew You Were Waiting For Me"; Carrie sang "Alone"; Scott sang "Against All Odds"; Bo sang "Time in a Bottle"; Nikko sang "Incomplete"; Vonzell sang "Best of My Love"; Constantine sang "I Think I Love You"; Nadia sang "Time After Time"; Mikalah sang "Love Will Lead You Back"; Anwar sang "Ain't Nobody"; and Jessica sang "Total Eclipse of the Heart."

Episode 23 featured a rebroadcast of the previous episode's performances because the graphic at the end of that show had listed incorrect phone numbers for three of the singers.

In Episode 24, Mikalah was eliminated.

Episode 25's theme was 1990s music. Bo sang "Remedy", Jessica sang "On the

Side of Angels"; Anwar sang "I Believe I Can Fly"; Nadia sang "I'm the Only One"; Constantine sang "I Can't Make You Love Me"; Nikko sang "Can We Talk"; Anthony sang "Something About the Way You Look Tonight"; Carrie sang "Independence Day"; Scott sang "One Last Cry"; and Vonzell sang "I Have Nothing (If I Don't Have You)."

In Episode 26, Jessica was voted out.

Episode 27 featured songs from classic musicals. Scott sang "The Impossible Dream"; Constantine sang "My Funny Valentine"; Carrie sang "Hello, Young Lovers"; Vonzell sang "People"; Anthony sang "Climb Every Mountain"; Nikkok sang "One Hand, One Heart"; Anwar sang "If Ever I Would Leave You"; Bo Bice sang "Corner of the Sky"; and Nadia sang "As Long As He Needs Me."

Nikko was voted out in Episode 28. Season 3 winner Fantasia Barrino and Season 2 winner Ruben Studdard were in the audience.

In Episode 29, the contestants performed songs from the year they were born, and Daryl Hall and John Oates were guest judges. Nadia sang "When I Dream"; Bo sang "Free Bird"; Anwar sang "I'll Never Love This Way Again"; Anthony sang "Every Time You Go Away"; Vonzell sang "Let's Hear It for the Boy"; Scott sang "She's Gone"; Carrie sang "Love Is a Battlefield"; and Constantine sang "Bohemian Rhapsody."

Nadia was the fifth contestant eliminated in Episode 30.

Episode 31's theme was disco music. Constantine sang "Nights on Broadway"; Carrie sang "MacArthur Park"; Scott sang "Everlasting Love"; Anthony sang "Don't Take Away the Music"; Vonzell sang "I'm Every Woman"; Anwar sang "September"; and Bo sang "Vehicle."

In Episode 32, Anwar was sent home.

In Episode 33, the contestants performed songs from the past five years. Carrie sang "When God Fearin' Women Get the Blues"; Bo sang "I Don't Want To Be"; Vonzell sang "I Turn To You"; Anthony sang "I Surrender"; Constantine sang "How You Remind Me"; and Scott sang "Dance with My Father." Season 2 runner-up Clay Aiken and actress Heather Locklear were in attendance.

In Episode 34, Clay Aiken, Pamela Anderson, Elon Gold, Christopher Lloyd, Marissa Jaret Winokur, and Brian Scolaro watched as Constantine was eliminated from the competition.

In Episode 35, each of the remaining contestants performed one song by pop music producers Jerry Leiber and Mike Stoller, and one song from the Billboard Top 40 list. Anthony sang "Poison Ivy" and "Incomplete"; Scott sang "On Broadway" and

"Every Time You Go Away"; Vonzell sang "Treat Me Nice" and "When You Tell Me That You Love Me"; Bo sang "Stand By Me" and "Heaven"; and Carrie sang "Trouble" and "Bless the Broken Road."

Episode 36 was the end of the line for Scott, who was eliminated.

Episode 37's final four contestants performed one Nashville country song, and one song by Philadelphia soul pioneers Kenny Gamble and Leon Huff. Carrie sang "Sin Wagon" and "If You Don't Know Me By Now"; Bo sang "It's a Great Day to Be Alive" and "For the Love of Money"; Vonzell and "How Do I Live" and "Don't Leave Me This Way"; and Anthony sang "I'm Already There" and his version of "If You Don't Know Me By Now."

Episode 38 was Anthony's last, as he was eliminated.

In Episode 39, the remaining three contestants each sang three songs—one chosen by Clive Davis, one they chose themselves, and one chosen by the judges. Vonzell sang "I'll Never Love This Way Again," "Chain of Fools," and "On the Radio." Bo sang "Don't Let The Sun Go Down On Me," In a Dream," and "(I Can't Get No) Satisfaction." Carrie sang "Crying," "Making Love Out of Nothing At All," and "Man! I Feel Like a Woman!"

In Episode 40, Vonzell was eliminated, leaving Bo and Carrie to battle for the title.

Episode 41 was a special episode highlighting the world's worst auditions.

In Episode 42's showdown between Bo and Carrie, each sang the same two original songs, "Angels Brought Me Here" and "Inside Your Heaven."

Episode 43 began with Bo singing "Vehicle" and Carrie singing "Independence Day." Carrie Underwood was crowned the champion.

RATINGS: The fourth season brought *American Idol* its highest ratings to date, with an average of 27.3 million viewers for the Tuesday edition and 26.1 million viewers for the Wednesday edition. The finale brought in a staggering 30.3 million viewers.

AMERICAN IDOL

(Season 5)

GENRE   Competition (Talent)
FIRST TELECAST   1/17/2006

LAST TELECAST	5/24/2006
NETWORK	FOX
AIR TIMES	Tuesday, 8:00 p.m.; Wednesday, 9:00 p.m.
EPISODE STYLE	Story Arc
TALENT	Ryan Seacrest (host); Paula Abdul (judge); Simon Cowell (judge); Randy Jackson (Judge)
CAST	Taylor Hicks (Winner); Katherine McPhee (Runner-up); Elliott Yamin (10th eliminated); Chris Daughtry (9th eliminated); Paris Bennett (8th eliminated); Kellie Pickler (7th eliminated); Ace Young (6th eliminated); Bucky Covington (5th eliminated); Mandisa (4th eliminated); Lisa Tucker (3rd eliminated); Kevin Covais (2nd eliminated); Melissa McGhee (1st eliminated)
PRODUCTION COMPANIES	Fremantlemedia North America; 19 TV Ltd.
CREATED BY	Simon Fuller and Simon Cowell
EXECUTIVE PRODUCERS	Simon Fuller; Ken Warwick; Nigel Lythgoe; Simon Jones; Cécile Frot-Coutaz

The number of finalists remained at twelve for Season 5.

Episode 1 documented the national auditions in Chicago.

In Episode 2, viewers were treated to highlights from the Denver auditions.

Episode 3 featured auditions in Greensboro, North Carolina.

Episode 4 shared highlights from the San Francisco auditions.

Episode 5 showcased performances from the Las Vegas auditions.

Episode 6 featured the auditions from Austin.

The national auditions wrapped up in Episode 7 with a stop in Boston.

In Episode 8, the first round of finalists arrived in Hollywood to perform for the judges.

Episode 9 continued to chronicle the finalists' adventures in Hollywood as the top twenty-four were chosen.

In Episode 10, the judges named the final twelve males and twelve females who would compete on the show.

In Episode 11, the twelve female contestants performed live, and the American viewers began calling in their votes.

It was the guys' turn in Episode 12, as America decided which ten would be kept.

Episode 13 was the first results show, and Patrick, Stevie, Bobby, and Becky were sent home.

Episode 14 featured a new round of performances from the remaining females.

The remaining men performed in Episode 15 and awaited viewers' decisions.

In Episode 16, America's votes were revealed, and Brenna, Heather, Jose, and David were sent home.

With sixteen contestants left, Episode 17 featured the top eight females' performances, plus video clips highlighting the girls' lives.

In Episode 18, the top eight guys sang and shared details of their lives.

Episode 19 wrapped up the shows in the small studio, with a visit from Season 4 runner-up, Bo Bice. Will, Ayla, Kinnik, and Gideon were voted out.

The two-hour Episode 20 featured Stevie Wonder night. After spending a day with Stevie Wonder, the singers sang his songs. Ace sang "Do I Do"; Kellie sang "Blame It on the Sun"; Elliott sang "Knocks Me Off My Feet"; Mandisa sang "Don't You Worry 'Bout a Thing"; Bucky sang "Superstition"; Melissa sang "Lately"; Lisa sang "Signed, Sealed, Delivered"; Kevin sang "Part-Time Lover"; Katharine sang "Until You Come Back to Me"; Taylor sang "Living for the City"; Paris sang "All I Do"; and Chris sang "Higher Ground."

In Episode 21, Melissa McGhee was the first to go from the top twelve.

In Episode 22, the contestants sang songs from the 1950s, with a little help from Barry Manilow. Mandisa sang "I Don't Hurt Anymore"; Bucky sang "Oh Boy"; Paris sang "Fever"; Chris sang "I Walk the Line"; Katharine sang "Come Rain or Come Shine"; Taylor sang "Not Fade Away"; Lisa sang "Why Do Fools Fall in Love"; Kevin sang "When I Fall In Love"; Elliott sang "Teach Me Tonight"; Kellie sang "Walking After Midnight"; and Ace sang "In the Still of the Night."

Episode 23 featured a performance by Barry Manilow. Kevin Covais, affectionately known as "Chicken Little," was the second singer eliminated.

Episode 24's theme was songs from the twenty-first century. Lisa sang "Because of You"; Kellie sang "Suds in a Bucket"; Ace sang "Drops of Jupiter"; Taylor sang "Trouble"; Mandissa sang "Wanna Praise You"; Chris sang "What If"; Katharine sang

"The Voice Within"; Bucky sang "Real Good Man"; Paris sang "Work It Out"; and Elliott sang "I Don't Want to Be."

After a song from Wyclef Jean and Shakira on Episode 25, Lisa Tucker was voted out.

Kenny Rogers was the special guest on the country music–themed Episode 26. Ace sang "I Wanna Cry"; Kellie sang "Fancy"; Chris sang "Making Memories of Us"; Katharine sang "Bringing Out the Elvis"; Bucky sang "Best I Ever Had"; Paris sang "How Do I Live Without You"; Elliott sang "If Tomorrow Never Comes"; Mandisa sang "Any Man of Mine"; and Taylor sang "Take Me Home, Country Road."

In Episode 27, Kenny Rogers performed, and Mandisa was eliminated.

In Episode 28, members of the band Queen coached the remaining eight finalists on their choices from the Queen catalog. Bucky sang "Fat Bottomed Girls"; Ace sang "We Will Rock You"; Kellie sang "Bohemian Rhapsody"; Chris sang "Innuendo"; Katharine sang "Who Wants to Live Forever"; Elliott sang "Somebody to Love"; Taylor sang "Crazy Little Thing Called Love"; and Paris sang "The Show Must Go On."

In Episode 29, Bucky Covington was eliminated.

Rod Stewart invited the final seven to his home in Episode 30, offering assistance with numbers from the Great American Songbook. Chris sang "What a Wonderful World"; Paris sang "These Foolish Things"; Taylor sang "You Send Me"; Elliott sang "It Had to Be You"; Kellie sang "Bewitched, Bothered, and Bewildered"; Ace sang "That's All"; and Katharine sang "Someone to Watch Over Me."

In Episode 31, Rod Stewart performed, and Ace Young was voted out.

Episode 32 featured special guests Andrea Bocelli and David Foster, and the contestants chose love songs. Katharine sang "I Have Nothing"; Elliott sang "A Song for You"; Kellie sang "Unchained Melody"; Paris sang "The Way We Were"; Taylor sang "Just Once"; and Chris sang "Have You Ever Really Loved a Woman."

In Episode 33, Andrea Bocelli performed, while the seventh singer voted out was Kellie Pickler.

In Episode 34, the final five sang two songs, one from the year they were born and another off the Billboard charts. Elliott sang "On Broadway" and "Home"; Paris sang "Kiss" and "Be Without You"; Katharine sang "Against All Odds" and "Black Horse and Cherry Tree"; Chris sang "Renegade" and "I Dare You"; and Taylor sang "Play That Funky Music" and "Something."

After the group performance in Episode 35, Paris Bennett was eliminated.

Episode 36 followed the finalists on a trip to Graceland. Each sang two Elvis Presley tunes. Taylor sang "Jailhouse Rock" and "In the Ghetto"; Chris sang "Suspicious Minds" and "A Little Less Conversation"; Elliott sang "If I Can Dream" and "Trouble"; and Katharine sang "Hound Dog/All Shook Up" and "Can't Help Falling in Love."

In Episode 37, Chris Daughtry was eliminated, to gasps from the audience.

The final three sang three songs each in Episode 38: one chosen by the judges, one picked by Clive Davis, and one they chose themselves. Elliott sang "Open Arms," "What You Won't Do For Love," and "I Believe To My Soul." Katharine sang "I Believe I Can Fly," "Somewhere Over the Rainbow," and "I Ain't Got Nothing but the Blues." Taylor sang "Dancing in the Dark," "You Are So Beautiful," and "Try a Little Tenderness."

Episode 39 featured clips of the three finalists' homecomings. Elliott Yamin was the tenth contestant eliminated.

In Episode 40, Katherine and Taylor each performed two songs. Katherine sang "Somewhere Over the Rainbow" and "Black Horse and Cherry Tree," while Taylor sang "Levon" and "Living for the City." The show ended with Daniel Powter's performance of Season 5's farewell song, "Bad Day," and a montage of clips featuring all the finalists.

In Episode 41, the finale, the celebrity guest list included Live, Season 4 winner Carrie Underwood, Season 2 runner-up Clay Aiken, Toni Braxton, Prince, Meatloaf, and Burt Bacharach. In the end, Taylor Hicks was crowned the winner.

AMERICAN IDOL
(Season 6)

GENRE	Competition (Talent)
FIRST TELECAST	1/16/2007
LAST TELECAST	5/23/2007
NETWORK	FOX
AIR TIMES	Tuesday, 8:00 p.m.; Wednesday, 9:00 p.m.
EPISODE STYLE	Story Arc
TALENT	Ryan Seacrest (Host); Paula Abdul (Judge); Simon Cowell (Judge); Randy Jackson (Judge)

CAST	Jordin Sparks (Winner); Blake Lewis (Runner-up); Melinda Doolittle (10th eliminated); LaKisha Jones (9th eliminated); Chris Richardson (8th eliminated); Phil Stacey (7th eliminated); Sanjaya Malakar (6th eliminated); Haley Scarnato (5th eliminated); Gina Glocksen (4th eliminated); Chris Sligh (3rd eliminated); Stephanie Edwards (2nd eliminated); Brandon Rogers (1st eliminated)
PRODUCTION COMPANIES	FremantleMedia North America; 19 TV Ltd.
CREATED BY	Simon Fuller and Simon Cowell
EXECUTIVE PRODUCERS	Simon Fuller; Ken Warwick; Nigel Lythgoe; Simon Jones; Cécile Frot-Coutaz

The number of finalists remained at twelve for Season 6.

Episode 1 documented the national auditions in Minneapolis. Jewel was a guest judge.

In Episode 2, viewers were treated to what Simon Cowell called the worst auditions ever, in Seattle.

Episode 3 highlighted the Memphis auditions.

Episode 4 featured the New York auditions, with Carole Bayer Sager as guest judge.

Episode 5 showed promising auditions from Birmingham.

Olivia Newton-John was guest judge in the Los Angeles auditions.

The national auditions wrapped in Episode 7, with a stop in San Antonio.

Episode 8 featured auditions from around the country.

In Episode 9, the top twenty-four began the second round of auditions, in Hollywood.

In Episode 10, the judges revealed the top twelve males and top twelve females who would compete for America's votes.

In Episode 11, the twelve male contestants performed live, and viewers cast the first votes of the season.

It was the ladies' turn in Episode 12, as viewers voted on which ten would return the next week.

Episode 13 was the first results show, with Rudy, Paul, Nicole, and Amy sent home. The show also featured a performance by Season 3 winner Fantasia Barrino.

Episode 14 showcased a new round of performances from among the remaining males. Comedian Jeff Foxworthy was a special guest.

The remaining ladies performed in Episode 15.

In Episode 16, Nicholas, AJ, Leslie, and Alaina were sent home. Season 5's Kellie Pickler made an appearance to show off her new look and perform a song.

Episode 17 featured another round of performances by the male contestants.

Episode 18 showcased performances by the remaining eight females.

Season 5 winner Carrie Underwood performed in Episode 19. Antonella, Sabrina, Jared, and Sundance were the next contestants to go.

In Episode 20, the top twelve tackled a theme night with Diana Ross, who was on hand to coach the remaining hopefuls through their songs. Brandon sang "You Can't Hurry Love"; Melinda sang "Home"; Chris Sligh sang "Endless Love"; Gina sang "Love Child"; Sanjaya sang "Ain't No Mountain High Enough"; Haley sang "Missing You"; Phil sang "I'm Gonna Make You Love Me"; LaKisha sang "God Bless the Child"; Blake sang "You Keep Me Hangin' On"; Stephanie sang "Love Hangover"; Chris Richardson sang "The Boss"; and Jordin sang "If We Hold On Together."

Diana Ross performed in Episode 21. After joining Phil and Sanjaya in the bottom three, Brandon was the first of the top twelve to be sent home.

Episode 22 saw the contestants singing songs from the British Invasion, with Peter Noone coaching the boys and Lulu helping out the girls. Haley sang "Tell Him"; Chris Richardson sang "Don't Let the Sun Catch You Crying"; Stephanie sang "You Don't Have to Say You Love Me"; Blake sang "Time of the Season"; LaKisha sang "Diamonds Are Forever"; Phil sang "Tobacco Road"; Jordin sang "I Who Have Nothing"; Sanjaya sang "You Really Got Me"; Gina sang "Paint It Black"; Chris Sligh sang "She's Not There"; and Melinda sang "As Long as He Needs Me." This episode marked the appearance of Sanjaya superfan Ashley Ferl, often referred to as the "Crying Girl."

Lulu and Peter Noone performed in Episode 23, while Stephanie was the second of the top twelve to go.

In Episode 24, Gwen Stefani coached the contestants and chose their songs. LaKisha sang "Last Dance"; Chris Sligh sang "Every Little Thing She Does Is Magic"; Gina sang "I'll Stand by You"; Sanjaya sang "Bath Water"; Haley sang "True Colors"; Phil sang "Every Breath You Take"; Melinda sang "Heaven Knows"; Blake sang "Love Song"; Jordin sang "Hey Baby"; and Chris Richardson sang "Don't Speak."

In Episode 25, Gwen Stefani and Akon performed. Chris Sligh, Phil, and Haley were in the bottom three, and Chris was eliminated.

Tony Bennett coached the remaining finalists on classic American songs in Episode 26. Blake sang "Mack the Knife"; Phil sang "Night and Day"; Melinda sang "I Got Rhythm"; Chris sang "Don't Get Around Much Anymore"; Jordin sang "On a Clear Day"; Gina sang "Smile"; Sanjaya sang "Cheek to Cheek"; Haley sang "Ain't Misbehavin' "; and LaKisha sang "Stormy Weather."

In Episode 27, Phil, Haley, and Gina were in the bottom three, and Gina was eliminated. Michael Buble performed, filling in for an ill Tony Bennett.

In Episode 28, Jennifer Lopez coached the remaining eight finalists on their Latin music choices. Melinda sang "Sway"; LaKisha sang "Conga"; Chris sang "Smooth"; Haley sang "Turn the Beat Around"; Phil sang "Maria, Maria"; Jordin sang "Rhythm Is Gonna Get You"; Blake sang "I Need to Know"; and Sanjaya sang "Besame Mucho."

In Episode 29, Phil, Chris, and Haley were in the bottom three, and Haley was eliminated. The episode also featured a performance by Jennifer Lopez.

Martina McBride coached the remaining hopefuls for the country music–themed Episode 30. Phil sang "Where the Blacktop Ends"; Jordin sang "A Broken Wing"; Sanjaya sang, "Something to Talk About"; LaKisha sang "Jesus Take the Wheel"; Chris sang "Mayberry"; Melinda sang "Trouble Is a Woman"; and Blake sang "When the Stars Go Blue."

Episode 31 featured a performance by Martina McBride. Sanjaya was sent home after being in the bottom three with Blake and LaKisha.

Episode 32 was a lead-up to *Idol Gives Back,* with the final six singing inspirational songs. Chris sang "Change the World"; Melinda sang "There Will Come a Day"; Blake sang "Imagine"; LaKisha sang "I Believe"; Phil sang "The Change"; and Jordin sang "You'll Never Walk Alone."

In Episode 33, the *Idol Gives Back* special combined a traditional results show with an effort to help people around the world. Ellen DeGeneres co-hosted the show, which included performances by Josh Groban; Earth, Wind and Fire; Kelly Clarkson; Season 4 winner Carrie Underwood; Il Divo; Jack Black; and Rascal Flatts. Quincy

Jones led the top six in a song, and many celebrities appeared to help out the cause. In a surprising twist, Ryan announced that no one was being sent home, but two finalists would be voted out the following week.

In Episode 34, Jon Bon Jovi coached the final six in Bon Jovi songs. Phil sang "Blaze of Glory"; Jordin sang "Livin' on a Prayer"; LaKisha sang "This Ain't a Love Song"; Blake sang "You Give Love a Bad Name"; Chris sang "Dead or Alive"; and Melinda sang "Have a Nice Day."

After the group performance in Episode 35, Phil and Chris were eliminated. Jon Bon Jovi and Robin Thicke performed.

Episode 36 showcased a night of Bee Gees music, as Barry Gibb coached each of the final five through two numbers. Melinda sang "How Can You Mend a Broken Heart" and "Love You Inside and Out." Blake sang "This Is Where I Came In" and "You Should Be Dancing." LaKisha sang "Stayin' Alive" and "Run to Me." Jordin sang "To Love Somebody" and "Woman in Love."

Barry Gibb and Pink performed in Episode 37. LaKisha Jones was voted out.

In Episode 38, the final three sang three songs each: one chosen by the judges, one picked by the producers, and one they chose themselves. Jordin sang "Wishin' On a Star," "She Works Hard for the Money," and "I (Who Have Nothing)." Blake sang "Roxanne," "This Love," and "When I Get You Alone." Melinda sang "I Believe in You and Me," "Nutbush City Limits," and "I'm a Woman."

Episode 39 featured clips from the three finalists' homecoming trips, and performances by Elliott Yamin and Maroon 5. Melinda was eliminated.

In Episode 40, Jordin and Blake each performed a song they sang earlier in the season, as well as "This Is My Now," from the American Idol songwriting competition. Jordin sang "I (Who Have Nothing)," while Blake sang "You Give Love a Bad Name." Season 5's Chris Daughtry performed the Season 6 farewell song, "Home."

The Episode 41 finale featured celebrity appearances by Season 4 winner Carrie Underwood, Bette Midler, Joe Perry, Doug E. Fresh, Tony Bennett, Green Day, Gladys Knight, Smokey Robinson, Season 2 winner Ruben Studdard, Season 1 winner Kelly Clarkson, and Gwen Stefani. Finally, Jordin Sparks was crowned the winner.

AMERICAN INVENTOR

GENRE	Competition
FIRST TELECAST	3/16/2006
NETWORK	ABC
AIR TIMES	Thursday, 9:00 p.m. (3/2006–4/2006); Thursday, 8:00 p.m. (4/2006–5/2006); Wednesday, 9:00 p.m. (6/2007–8/2007)
EPISODE STYLE	Story Arc
TALENT	Matt Gallant (Host—Season 1), Nick Smith (Host—Season 2), Ed Evangelista (Judge—Season 1), Mary Lou Quinlan (Judge—Season 1), Doug Hall (Judge—Season 1), Peter Jones (Judge), Sara Blakely (Judge—Season 2), Pat Croce (Judge—Season 2); George Foreman (Judge—Season 2)

CAST

Season 1	Janusz Liberkowski (Winner—Spherical Safety Seat), Robert Amore (Toner Belt); Sharon Clemens (Restroom Door Clip); Darla Davenport-Powell (Here Comes Niya); Ed Hall (Word Ace); Mark Martinez (Sackmaster 2000); Sheryl McDonald (The Un-Brella); Francisco Patino (Double-Traction Bike); Jodi Pliszka (The Headliner); Joseph and Jennifer Safuto (Flushpure); Erik Thompson (Receiver's Training Pole); Jerry Wesley (EZ-X Portable Gym)
Season 2	Greg Chavez (Winner—Guardian Angel); Elaine Cato (The Six-in-One Backless Bra); Ricky DeReunnaux (HR Racers)
PRODUCTION COMPANIES	Syco Television; Peter Jones TV; Fremantlemedia

EXECUTIVE PRODUCERS	Peter Jones; Simon Cowell; Liz Bronstein; Siobhan Greene; Nigel Hall; Cécile Frot-Coutaz
PRODUCERS	Darren J. Paletz; Bob Gillan; James MacNab; John Petro; Kate Richter
DIRECTOR	Sharon Trojan Hollinger

Four judges—Ed Evangelista, Marylou Quinn, Peter Jones, and Doug Hall—picked twelve inventors and their products from a pool of hundreds to compete for the title of "American Inventor." Twelve contestants received $50,000 to work on their products, with the top four moving on to the finals. In the live finale, the four finalists presented thirty-second commercials for their inventions, and viewer votes declared the winner. Janusz Liberkowski, inventor of the Anecia Safety Capsule, a unique child's car seat based on the human womb, won the $1 million grand prize in cash and resources to help make his invention a reality.

There were cast and format changes in Season 2. Nick Smith took over as host, while returning judge Peter Jones was joined by Pat Croce, Sara Blakely, and George Foreman. The number of semifinalists was cut down to six, with each receiving $50,000 in development funding. Firefighter Greg Chavez and his invention of the Guardian Angel, a Christmas tree sprinkler system, received the grand prize.

AMERICAN JUNIORS

GENRE	Competition (Talent)
FIRST TELECAST	6/3/2003
LAST TELECAST	8/19/2003
NETWORK	FOX
AIR TIMES	Tuesday, 8:00 p.m.; Wednesday, 8:30 p.m.
EPISODE STYLE	Self-contained
TALENT	Ryan Seacrest (Host); Deborah Gibson (Judge); Gladys Knight (Judge); Justin Guarini (Guest Judge); Monica Arnold (Guest Judge); Nick Carter (Guest Judge); Ruben Studdard (Guest Judge)
CAST	Taylor Thompson (Final Group Member 1);

	Tori Thompson (Final Group Member 2); Chauncey Matthews (Final Group Member 3); Lucy Hale (Final Group Member 4); Danielle White (Final Group Member 5); Chantel Kohl (Finalist); Morgan Burke (Finalist); Jordan McCoy (Finalist); A. J. Melendez (Finalist); Katelyn Tarver (Finalist)
PRODUCTION COMPANIES	19 Entertainment; 19 Television; Fox Television; FremantleMedia Ltd.; FremantleMedia North America
CREATED BY	Simon Fuller
EXECUTIVE PRODUCERS	Cécile Frot-Coutaz; Simon Fuller; Nigel Lythgoe; Ken Warwick
PRODUCERS	Nikki Boella; Ron De Shay; Patrick Lynn
DIRECTOR	Bruce Gowers

The production team behind *American Idol* created this competition series for singers and dancers from ages six to thirteen. Twenty semifinalists traveled to Los Angeles to perform on television and before a panel of celebrity judges, then were split into two groups of ten for the semifinals. Viewers voted to determine which five from each group would advance to the top ten, then which five would win places in the musical act. Unlike *American Idol,* which features eliminations based on viewer votes, *American Juniors* took a different approach: the singers who received the most votes won spots in the group. The *American Juniors* debut single, "One Step Closer," peaked on the Billboard Singles sales chart at number six.

RATINGS: The Tuesday edition of *American Juniors* had an average of 7.8 million viewers, while on Wednesdays the show averaged 6.7 million.

AMERICAN PRINCESS

GENRE	Competition
FIRST TELECAST	8/7/2005
NETWORK	WE

EPISODE STYLE	Story Arc
TALENT	Mark Durden-Smith (Host); Jean Brooke-Smith (Judge); Richard Branson (Judge); Paul Burrell (Judge); Jodi Kidd (Judge); Catherine Oxenberg (Judge); Carol Sutherland
CAST	Michelle (Winner); Niqui (Runner-up); Angela C. (Top 10 Finalist); Atlanta (Top 10 Finalist); Carol S. (Top 10 Finalist); Crystal (Top 10 Finalist); Molly (Top 10 Finalist); Stephanie U. (Top 10 Finalist); Stephanie J. (Top 10 Finalist)
PRODUCTION COMPANY	Granada Television
EXECUTIVE PRODUCERS	Laura Fuest; Curt Northrup; Jeff Thacker
DIRECTOR	Leslie Garvin

Dubbed as a real-life *My Fair Lady,* this competition series featured a group of average American women competing to win the title of "American Princess" and a Harry Winston tiara valued at $1 million. Throughout the course of the series, the women received lessons in manners, dancing, and etiquette, in order to learn how to act like royalty. Each week, judges eliminated the women they deemed unfit, and in the end crowned Michelle the first "American Princess." This series was originally scheduled to be aired on NBC, but was pulled before it hit the air.

AMISH IN THE CITY

GENRE	Docusoap
FIRST TELECAST	7/28/2004
LAST TELECAST	9/21/2004
NETWORK	UPN
AIR TIME	Wednesday, 8:00 p.m.
EPISODE STYLE	Story Arc
CAST	Jonas Kurtz (Amish); Miriam Troyer (Amish); Mose Gingerich (Amish); Randy Stoll (Amish);

Ruth Yoder (Amish); Ariel (City Folk); Kevan
(City Folk); Meagan (City Folk); Nick (City Folk);
Reese (City Folk); Whitney (City Folk)

CREATED BY Jon Kroll

EXECUTIVE PRODUCERS Steven Cantor; Jon Kroll; Daniel Laikind

PRODUCERS Mary Belton; Mariam Jobrani; Lisa Lucas;
Brandy Menefee; Paul Frazier

Five Amish teenagers aged sixteen and older participated in their community's right-of-passage called *rumspringa,* which loosely translates as "running around." In this tradition, the young faithful are encouraged to explore a variety of taboo activities—ranging from drinking alcohol and smoking to far more serious escapades—before becoming officially baptised into the Amish religion. Living in the Hollywood Hills with six non-Amish urbanites, the Amish youths were encouraged to experience all that the shunned "English" (non-Amish) culture had to offer before they decided whether to return to the Amish community.

RATINGS: The UPN series brought in an average of four million viewers during its summer 2004 run.

ANCHORWOMAN

GENRE Docusoap

FIRST TELECAST 8/21/2007

LAST TELECAST 8/21/2007

NETWORK FOX

AIR TIME Tuesday, 8:00 p.m.

EPISODE STYLE Story Arc

CAST Dan Delgado; Phil Hurley; Annalisa Petraglia;
Lauren Jones

PRODUCTION COMPANIES Fox 21; G Group

EXECUTIVE PRODUCERS Brian Gadinsky; Chad Damiani; J.P. Lavin

CO-EXECUTIVE PRODUCER Josh Bingham

PRODUCERS	Amy Griggs; Amy Huggins
DIRECTOR	Mark S. Jacobs

Former *The Price Is Right* model, Miss New York, and WWE diva Lauren Jones traveled to Tyler, Texas, to become an anchorwoman at a local CBS affiliate. She learned to read a TelePrompTer and reported the nightly news on KYTX, Channel 19. The show was cancelled after only one episode. The remaining episodes are still available on Fox's website through Fox On Demand.

THE ANNA NICOLE SHOW

GENRE	Docudrama (Celebrity)
FIRST TELECAST	8/4/2002
LAST TELECAST	10/17/2004
NETWORK	E!
AIR TIME	Sunday, 10:00 p.m.
EPISODE STYLE	Self-contained
TALENT	Amanda Byram (Host/Narrator)
CAST	Anna Nicole Smith; Daniel Smith (Anna's son); Bobby Trendy (Anna's designer); Howard K. Stern (Anna's attorney); Kim Walther (Anna's assistant)
PRODUCTION COMPANY	E! Entertainment Television
EXECUTIVE PRODUCERS	Marcus J. Fox; Jeffrey Shore; Boyd Vico
PRODUCERS	Darren Ewing; Kevin Hayes; Mark McDermott

This show chronicled the life of the late Anna Nicole Smith. The series became a topic of watercooler conversations, as people speculated about the former Playboy "Playmate of the Year"'s odd behavior. Surrounded by her attorney, Howard K. Stern; her extremely loyal assistant, Kim; and her ever-present dog, Sugar Pie, Anna Nicole visited amusement parks, parties, and a tattoo parlor. Also captured was Anna at work, at the Kentucky Derby, and at award shows. The final show featured a slimmed-down Anna Nicole as she tried to reinvent herself once again.

ANYTHING FOR LOVE

GENRE	Docudrama (Romance)
FIRST TELECAST	6/16/2003
LAST TELECAST	9/11/2003
NETWORK	FOX
AIR TIMES	Monday, 9:00 p.m. (6/2003); Monday, 8:00 p.m. (6/2003–8/2003); Thursday, 8:30 p.m. (9/2003)
EPISODE STYLE	Self-contained
CAST	Mark L. Walberg (Host); Claudia DiFolco (Co-Host)
PRODUCTION COMPANY	Endemol Entertainment
EXECUTIVE PRODUCER	Paul Buccieri
DIRECTORS	R. Brian DiPirro; Jack Messitt

Sweethearts were reunited, and blossoming relationships tested, all in the name of love on this docudrama. Using different relationship tests, couples were given a chance to examine their potential sweetheart's fidelity and sincerity. Some tests involved hidden cameras, and some episodes featured marriage proposals.

THE APPRENTICE
(Season 1)

GENRE	Competition (Job)
FIRST TELECAST	1/8/2004
LAST TELECAST	4/15/2004
NETWORK	NBC
AIR TIME	Thursday, 9:00 p.m.
EPISODE STYLE	Story Arc
TALENT	Donald Trump; Carolyn Kepcher (Trump's Assistant); George Ross (Trump's Assistant); Robin Himmler (Trump's Secretary)

CAST	Bill Rancic (Winner); Kwame Jackson (Runner-up); Amy Henry (14th fired); Nick Warnock (13th fired); Troy McClain (12th fired); Heidi Bressler (11th fired); Katrina Campins (10th fired); Omarosa Manigault-Stallworth (9th fired); Ereka Vetrini (8th fired); Tammy Lee (7th fired); Jessie Conners (6th fired); Kristi Frank (5th fired); Bowie Hogg (4th fired); Sam Solovey (3rd fired); Jason Curis (2nd fired); David Gould (1st fired)
PRODUCTION COMPANIES	Mark Burnett Productions, in association with Trump Productions LLC
CREATED BY	Mark Burnett
EXECUTIVE PRODUCERS	Mark Burnett; Donald Trump
CO-EXECUTIVE PRODUCERS	Jay Bienstock

In *The Apprentice,* sixteen contestants compete against one another, completing tasks assigned to them by real estate mogul Donald Trump. Each week, Trump fires a candidate until he decides which person will win the grand prize—a job with the Trump Organization.

In Episode 1, the contestants were divided by gender into two teams of eight. The men named their team "Versacorp," while the women were "Protégé Corporation." For the first task, the teams sold lemonade on the streets of New York City. For outselling the men and winning the task, the women were invited to Donald Trump's penthouse suite. For losing the task, the men were sent to Trump's boardroom, where David was the first one eliminated after hearing Trump's trademark phrase, "You're fired!"

In Episode 2, the task was to design ads for the Marquis Jet Card. Protégé won the task, earning a dinner in Boston. Thanks to Jason's domineering leadership style and Sam's inability to focus, the men lost again, and Project Manager Jason was fired.

Episode 3's task was a shopping scavenger hunt, in which the teams had to negotiate for lower prices. The women of Protégé used their power of flirtation to win yet another task, earning dinner at the 21 Club. Versacorp's new project manager, Sam, was the next one fired.

The task in Episode 4 was to manage a Planet Hollywood restaurant for one night, and turn a larger profit than was made on the same night one year prior. The women were victorious again, winning a day of golf with Trump. The men lost their fourth straight task, and Bowie was fired.

Episode 5 began with a realignment, as project managers Nick and Kristi alternated in picking members for their new, now co-ed teams. The next task was to stage the most profitable flea market. The new Versacorp won and received a tour of Yankee Stadium, while Protégé's project manager, Kristi, got fired.

Love was in the air in Episode 6, as Nick and Amy became friendly. Versacorp won the task at hand by raising the most money for charity at a Sotheby's auction, and Protégé's Jessie was the next one fired.

Episode 7's task was to revamp apartments in New York City and find tenants to rent them for the highest possible percentage increase. Protégé finally got back in the winning column with a 27 percent rent increase, compared with Versacorp's 10 percent increase. Protégé went on a picnic at Trump's mansion in Bedford, New York, while Tammy was fired.

In Episode 8, the task was to market a new product called "Trump Ice" bottled water. Protégé won, and toured New York City in the Donald's private helicopter, while Versacorp's Ereka got fired.

Episode 9 challenged each team to select one bizarre or controversial artist whose work they believed would sell for the most money in an art gallery. Versacorp's artist outsold Protégé's by a whopping $13,600 to $869. Protégé's Omarosa suffered an emotional breakdown in the boardroom and was fired. For leading Versacorp to victory, Nick was awarded a private, ten-minute meeting with Trump.

Versacorp kept it going in Episode 10 by operating the most profitable rickshaw cab service, earning themselves a yacht ride around Manhattan. Protégé's boardroom meeting featured some criticism by Carolyn, and Heidi was fired.

Episode 11 was a recap show, in which Trump looked back on the first ten episodes, critiquing each of the fired contestants.

Episode 12's task was to attract the most gamblers to register at the Trump Taj Mahal casino. Protégé's victory earned them a stay in the hotel's best suite, plus $3,000 in gambling money. Meanwhile, in a close Versacorp boardroom decision, Katrina was fired.

In Episode 13, the task was to rent out the Trump World Tower penthouse for one night for the highest price—and for a *minimum* of $20,000. Versacorp won by securing a fee of $40,800, and earned a trip to the Donald's world-famous Mar-a-lago Club, in Florida. In a surprise, Amy's sister and Nick's father greeted them on the plane. Meanwhile, Protégé's Troy was the next fired.

Episode 14 subjected each of the final four candidates to individual interviews with Trump's closest advisers. Based on their opinions, Trump fired Nick and Amy, leaving Kwame and Bill to fight for the brass ring. Kwame's final task was to coordinate a Jessica Simpson concert, while Bill had to run a golf tournament. The episode ended in a cliffhanger, as Jessica was a no-show and Bill ran into storage problems on the course.

Episodes 15 and 16 aired back to back as the series finale. Kwame and Bill worked doggedly to make their respective projects a success. After much deliberation, Trump said "You're hired!" to Bill Rancic. Bill won a new car, a six-figure salary, and was assigned to oversee the building of a Chicago Trump Hotel instead of a California golf course.

RATINGS: The inaugural season of *The Apprentice* brought NBC an average of 20.7 million viewers.

THE APPRENTICE
(Season 2)

GENRE	Competition (Job)
FIRST TELECAST	9/9/2004
LAST TELECAST	12/16/2004
NETWORK	NBC
AIR TIME	Thursday, 9:00 p.m.
EPISODE STYLE	Story Arc
TALENT	Donald Trump; Carolyn Kepcher (Trump's Assistant); George Ross (Trump's Assistant); Robin Himmler (Trump's Secretary)
CAST	Kelly Perdew (Winner); Jennifer Massey (Runner-up); Kevin Allen (16th fired); Sandy Ferreira (15th fired); Ivana Ma (14th fired);

Andy Litinsky (13th fired); Maria Boren (12th fired); Wes Moss (11th fired); Chris Russo (10th fired); Raj Bhakta (9th fired); Elizabeth Jarosz (8th fired); Stacy Rotner (7th fired); John Willenborg (6th fired); Pamela Day (5th fired); Jennifer Crisafulli (4th fired); Stacie Jones Upchurch (3rd fired); Bradford Cohen (2nd fired); Rob Flanagan (1st fired)

PRODUCTION COMPANIES	Mark Burnett Productions in association with Trump Productions LLC
CREATED BY	Mark Burnett
EXECUTIVE PRODUCERS	Mark Burnett; Donald Trump; Jay Bienstock

In Season 2, the total number of contestants increased to eighteen. Also, the winning team's project manager earned exemption at the next challenge's boardroom, if their team lost the task.

In Episode 1, the women chose "Apex" as their team name, while the men called themselves "Mosaic." The first twist required each team to send one member to the other team to become that team's first project manager. The first task involved designing a new toy for Mattel. Apex's remote-control car with interchangeable parts was better received than Mosaic's line of action figures, earning the former a penthouse dinner with Trump and his then-fiancée, Melania Knauss. Mosaic's Rob was the first one fired, for not making himself useful enough during the task.

In Episode 2, Mosaic got revenge when a street-corner snafu helped their original ice-cream flavor, Donut, outsell Apex's Red Velvet. For their victory, Mosaic enjoyed Champagne and caviar, while Apex's Bradford was voted out for foolishly, to Trump's mind, waiving his exemption.

In Episode 3, Apex made a costly mistake by going $5,000 over budget in a task to promote a new flavor of Crest toothpaste. Mosaic was victorious and won a trip on the *Queen Mary II*. Stacie J.'s instability during critical moments led to her termination.

Episode 4's task was to open a new restaurant in twenty-four hours and receive the highest Zagat rating. Teams were given an open storefront, and had to choose a chef and decorate the space. Mosaic edged out Apex by a score of sixty-one to fifty-seven, and met former New York City mayor Rudy Giuliani as their prize. Apex project manager Jennifer C. made a controversial comment about two Jewish customers, and her poor leadership caused her to be the next fired.

Episode 5 challenged teams to pick a product, and outsell each other live on the QVC network. Mosaic's salesmanship with the DeLonghi Grill barely beat Apex's "It Works" home cleaner by a total of ten dollars. Mosaic attended a tennis match with John McEnroe and Anna Kournikova as their prize. Project manager Pamela was the next one fired.

Episode 6 featured a landslide victory by Apex in a task where teams designed and sold original clothing. Apex was rewarded with an invitation to a star-studded Hugo Boss party, while Mosaic's John was fired after he blamed Wes for a pricing error but failed to bring him along to the boardroom.

Episode 7 reshuffled the teams, as the incoming project managers picked three of their own team members to send to the other team. The task was to create a successful dog-based business. Both teams ran dog-washing businesses. The new Apex team won, and were rewarded with a meeting with New York City mayor Michael Bloomberg. Mosaic's Stacie R. was fired due to her constant complaining and unwillingness to accept responsibility.

Episode 8 challenged the teams to come up with a recruiting campaign for the New York City Police Department. Andy's emotional ad led Mosaic to victory, and his handiwork was publicly debuted in Times Square. Apex's project manager, Elizabeth, demonstrated poor leadership throughout, and was fired before she could even bring two teammates with her into the boardroom.

In Episode 9, the task was to renovate homes in Long Island and generate the largest appreciation in value. Previously fired candidates Rob and Jennifer C. assisted Mosaic, while Apex inherited the ousted Bradford and Stacie J. Mosaic won the task, earning a trip to Denise Rich's house in the Hamptons, while Raj's decision to turn a four-bedroom home into a three-bedroom led to his termination.

In Episode 10, Mosaic steamrolled Apex in a bridal shop sales competition, and was rewarded with an opportunity to purchase $50,000 in diamond jewelry. Apex's third straight trip to the boardroom resulted in project manager Chris's getting fired.

In Episode 11, Apex won the task of creating a new campaign for Levi's jeans.

Mosaic came unglued after Maria complained about not being picked as project manager, and existing project manager, Wes, did nothing to rectify it. Trump shocked everyone by firing both teammates.

In Episode 12, Apex won its second task in a row, designing a superior campaign and bottle for Pepsi Edge. They were rewarded with an opportunity to race Lamborghinis. Mosaic project manager, Andy, was fired for allowing himself to be trampled by his underlings.

Episode 13 featured a recap of the previous twelve episodes, with Trump critiquing each of the fired contestants.

In Episode 14, Mosaic nearly doubled Apex's revenue in a challenge, designing and selling M&M's M-AZING candy bars. Apex was rewarded with a trip to Chicago to meet the first winner of *The Apprentice,* Bill Rancic. Meanwhile, Ivana's mistake of flashing customers in an effort to sell the candy bars proved fatal, and Trump fired her.

Episode 15 began with a series of interviews with high-level executives from major companies, after which Kevin and Sandy were fired. For the final challenge, Jen managed a charity basketball game, while Kelly ran a polo match. Both were allowed to choose three previously fired contestants to assist them in their tasks.

Episodes 16, 17, and 18 aired as part of a three-hour finale. Trump sought the advice of the fired candidates and audience members in his hiring decision. Kelly Perdew was anointed the winner of *The Apprentice 2,* and chose to supervise the construction of a $4 billion project on Manhattan's West Side.

RATINGS: Season 2 of *The Apprentice* had an average of 16.1 million viewers each week.

THE APPRENTICE
(Season 3)

GENRE	Competition (Job)
FIRST TELECAST	1/20/2005
LAST TELECAST	5/19/2005
NETWORK	NBC
AIR TIME	Thursday, 9:00 p.m.

EPISODE STYLE	Story Arc
TALENT	Donald Trump; Carolyn Kepcher (Trump's Assistant); George Ross (Trump's Assistant); Robin Himmler (Trump's Secretary)
CAST	Kendra Todd (Winner); Tana Goertz (Runner-up); Craig Williams (15th fired); Alex Thomason (14th fired—Net Worth); Bren Olswanger (13th fired—Net Worth); Chris Shelton (12th fired—Net Worth); Angie McKnight (11th fired—Net Worth); Stephanie Myers (10th fired—Net Worth); Erin Elmore (9th fired—Net Worth); John Gafford (8th fired—Net Worth); Audrey Evans (7th fired—Net Worth); Tara Dowdell (6th fired—Net Worth); Michael Tarshi (5th fired—Magna); Kristen Kirchner (4th fired—Net Worth); Danny Kastner (3rd fired—Magna); Verna Felton (Quit); Brian McDowell (2nd fired—Net Worth); Todd Everett (1st fired—Magna)
PRODUCTION COMPANIES	Mark Burnett Productions, in association with Trump Productions LLC
CREATED BY	Mark Burnett
EXECUTIVE PRODUCERS	Mark Burnett; Donald Trump; Jay Bienstock
CO-EXECUTIVE PRODUCER	Kevin Harris

In Season 3, the contestants were divided into teams based on their educational background, "Street Smarts" vs. "Book Smarts."

In Episode 1, the team of college graduates picked the name "Magna" (as in "magna cum laude"), while those with only high-school diplomas dubbed themselves "Net Worth." Net Worth won the first task of marketing a new Burger King menu item while simultaneously running an actual Burger King franchise. For their efforts, they earned dinner at the 21 Club. Magna's project manager, Todd, was fired for poor leadership.

In Episode 2, Magna got their revenge by doing a better job of renovating a New Jersey motel and earning a higher customer rating. As a reward, they received a boating trip with Steve Forbes. Meanwhile, Project Manager Brian made it easy on Trump by admitting he had screwed up the most, and was the first fired.

In Episode 3, stressed-out Verna quit the show before the task even began. Net Worth ended up generating the most "buzz" for Nescafé's Tasters Choice coffee, earning a helicopter tour of Manhattan. Another project manager took the fall when Magna's Danny was fired.

In Episode 4, both teams failed to produce a satisfactory commercial for Dove body wash, as Magna's was too risqué, and Net Worth's was too safe. Both teams were sent to the boardroom, where Net Worth's project manager, Kristen, was fired.

Episode 5 challenged the teams to come up with the most successful mobile business using an Airstream trailer. Net Worth started a casting director service for actors, while Magna settled on a mobile massage parlor. Net Worth beat Magna, winning a $20,000 pearl shopping spree at Mikimoto. Meanwhile, Magna's Michael was fired for not working hard enough.

Magna won the task in Episode 6, creating a superior graffiti ad campaign for the new PlayStation 2 game, Grand Turismo 4. For winning, each of Magna's members had his portait taken by *Harper's Bazaar* photographer Patrick Demarchelier. A miscalculation by Net Worth's Tara led to her being the next one fired.

In Episode 7, Magna won its second task in a row by setting up the most profitable miniature golf course. The team's prize was a game of golf with Trump. Net Worth project manager Audrey was fired for failing to accept responsibility.

Net Worth lost its third straight task in Episode 8, as Magna outgained them nearly two to one in a hip-hop charity auction. Thanks to John's poor negotiating skills, he was the next one fired.

Episode 9 recapped previously unseen footage.

In Episode 10, Magna won again, as their box-designing clinic at Home Depot was more successful than Net Worth's cart-assembly presentation. As a reward, Magna experienced zero gravity during a Zero-G jet ride. Back at the boardroom, Erin's inappropriate comments to Trump's assistants got her fired.

The landslide continued in Episode 11, as Magna triumphed in a task designing a new pizza concept for Domino's Pizza. They sold the most pizzas, winning breakfast with Trump in his gold-plated apartment. Net Worth's project manager, Stephanie, was fired.

Magna won yet again in Episode 12, as they delivered a superior presentation to

American Eagle Outfitters for a new line of clothing. Magna's prize was a shopping spree at Bergdorf Goodman. For dropping the ball in Net Worth's presentation, Angie was fired.

In Episode 13, Magna designed the better brochure for Pontiac, and thus got to meet the New York Knicks. Going along with the advice of his assistants, Trump decided to fire Chris.

Magna's hot streak continued in Episode 14, as they designed a more sensible clutter-clearing device for Staples. For winning, Magna had breakfast at the Rainbow Room with Trump's assistants, Carolyn and George. Trump later accused Bren of lacking entrepreneurial spirit, and fired him.

Net Worth's collapse continued in Episode 15, as they made less than half the amount of money Magna made while selling commemorative T-shirts for Hanes's fiftieth anniversary. For their efforts, Magna flew combat planes and engaged in a virtual dogfight. For failing twice as project manager, Alex was fired by Trump.

In Episode 16, executives from four of the largest U.S. corporations interviewed the final three candidates, and singled out Craig as the next one who should be fired. For their final project, Kendra coordinated a video game tournament, while Tana organized the NYC 2012 Athlete Challenge, part of New York City's Olympics campaign. Each of the women was assigned three previously fired contestants to assist her.

In Episode 17, both women successfully pulled off their final projects, although Tana had more difficulty coordinating her team. The episode ended with Trump summoning both women to the boardroom, then asking to see all of the fired contestants.

In a special live Episode 18 finale, Trump said, "You're hired!" to Kendra Todd. She chose to renovate a Florida mansion, instead of coordinating the Miss Universe pageant.

RATINGS: The third season of *The Apprentice* had an average of 14.0 million viewers each week.

THE APPRENTICE

(Season 4)

GENRE Competition (Job)
FIRST TELECAST 9/22/2005

LAST TELECAST	12/15/2005
NETWORK	NBC
AIR TIME	Thursday, 9:00 p.m.
EPISODE STYLE	Story Arc
TALENT	Donald Trump; Carolyn Kepcher (Trump's Assistant); George Ross (Trump's Assistant); Bill Rancic (Fill-in for Ross); Robin Himmler (Trump's Secretary)
CAST	Randal Pinkett (Winner); Rebecca Jarvis (Runner-up); Felisha Mason (12th fired); Alla Wartenberg (11th fired); Adam Green (10th fired); Clay Lee (9th fired); Brian Madelbaum (8th fired); Marshawn Evans (8th fired); Markus Garrison (7th fired); Jennifer Murphy (6th fired); Josh Shaw (6th fired); James Dillon (6th fired); Mark Lamkin (6th fired); Kristi Caudell (5th fired); Toral Metha (4th fired); Jennifer Wallen (3rd fired); Chris Valetta (2nd fired); Melissa Holavach (1st fired)
PRODUCTION COMPANIES	Mark Burnett Productions, in association with Trump Productions LLC
CREATED BY	Mark Burnett
EXECUTIVE PRODUCERS	Mark Burnett; Jay Bienstock; Donald Trump; Conrad Riggs; Kevin Harris

Season 4 began with a group of eighteen contestants "hand-picked" by Donald Trump. The candidates included an inventor, an ex-NFL football player, and a Rhodes Scholar, as well as graduates from Wharton, Oxford, MIT, and even a few self-made millionaires.

In Episode 1, the candidates met one another at the Trump National Golf Club, in New Jersey, where the teams were divided by gender. The men called themselves "Excel," while the women named their team "Capital Edge." The first task was to create a new exercise class for Bally Total Fitness. The men's team barely won the task, although they elected not to give project manager Markus an exemption. Excel earned lunch with Trump at the Friar's Club. Capital Edge project manager, Kristi, brought one other team member to the boardroom, and Melissa was fired for being too negative.

In Episode 2, Capital Edge won the challenge of creating a new ad campaign for Lamborghini. For their reward, the women played hockey with the New York Islanders. Rebecca slipped on the ice and broke her ankle, leaving her future with the show in jeopardy. Excel project manager Chris decided to take only Markus with him to the boardroom. Unlike with Kristi, Chris's decision was seen as a mistake, and he was the second candidate fired.

In Episode 3, the teams produced and hosted a technology convention for senior citizens, featuring products from Best Buy. The men won, and passed toys out at a children's hospital for their reward. In an effort to prove that her broken ankle wasn't holding her back, Rebecca volunteered to be project manager. Broken televisions, misspelled lettering on cakes, and general incompetence were attributed to Capital Edge's devastating loss on the next task. While the team viewed Toral as the weakest member, her friendship with Rebecca saved her from a trip to the boardroom. Trump saw Rebecca's decision as a mistake, and she was fired.

Episode 4 challenged the teams to design a new promotional character for Dairy Queen. The women of Capital Edge designed a cartoon-like character named Zip, while the men of Excel came up with Ginny the Genie. While Mark was subjected to jeers for wearing a very feminine Genie costume, his team won, and got to play a game of baseball with the New York Mets. Toral's refusal to wear the Zip costume was the final straw, and she was fired for her ineffectiveness.

In Episode 5, the teams were commissioned to build a float for the Hollywood Holiday Parade promoting the film *Zathura*. Before they began, Trump gave the women an opportunity to take a member from the men's team, and they immediately chose Randal. Director John Favreau met with both teams, and was disappointed with Jennifer's inability to pronounce the name of the film. Excel was victorious, and won a recording session with Wyclef Jean. In the boardroom, Trump sent Kristi home because of her poor people skills.

Carolyn filled in for Trump in Episode 6, and Season 1 winner Bill Rancic took George's place. Carolyn's first task was to reshuffle the teams by letting the project managers pick three members of their team to send to the opposing side. The teams were then given the task of creating a display for Dick's Sporting Goods, focusing on a specific sport. Capital Edge chose golf, while Excel held a baseball clinic. Capital Edge won, earning a private jet ride to Montauk for a fishing trip and dinner on the beach. Excel failed to make enough sales, resulting in the biggest loss in the history of *The Apprentice*. For the first time, Trump fired four players at once: Jennifer M., Josh, James, and Mark.

In Episode 7, Excel choose to bring Randal to their group to even up the teams. With advice from Season 2 winner Kelly Perdew, the teams taught a new class for The Learning Annex. Randal led Excel in a "How to Stand Out" class, while Capital Edge's "Sex in the Workplace" tutorial immediately made people uncomfortable. Excel's victory earned them a shopping spree at Michael Kors. Clay's revelation that he was gay and a comment about Adam's being Jewish led to strife at Capital Edge. Ultimately, Markus's ineffectiveness came back to haunt him, and he was fired, prompting him to declare that his termination was "a railroad from the beginning."

In Episode 8, the teams designed a display for Best Buy to promote the latest *Star Wars* DVD release. Randal was the only Excel member who had seen a *Star Wars* film, which shifted the bulk of the work to him. Capital Edge won the task, but Clay's poor leadership led to his team deciding not to grant him an exemption. The team spent time with Season 1 winner Bill Rancic, and toured Trump Tower at City Place, in White Plains, New York. In the boardroom, Trump was flabbergasted that Brian, a New Yorker, hadn't accounted for traffic, which led to a missed meeting. Brian's mistake and Marshawn's shirking of her presentation responsibilities led to both of them being fired.

In Episode 9, Clay requested to switch to Excel, with Randal and Rebecca. Then, each three-person team worked to find a recording artist to write and perform an original song to be played on XM satellite radio. Capital Edge won the task, earning a private helicopter ride around Manhattan with Trump. Excel was sent to the boardroom, and after hearing about Clay's hindering exploits, Trump decided that and his past performance were enough to send him packing.

Episode 10 recapped the season so far.

Episode 11 challenged each team to get as many New Yorkers as possible to call an 800 number to receive a free sample of Shania Twain's new fragrance. Excel's Randal and Rebecca played hardball, buying the megaphones Capital Edge had reserved for themselves. Both teams hired people to wear promotional posters, and handed out the phone number. Randal and Rebecca won by only five phone calls, earning a horseback ride through Central Park and dinner with Shania Twain. For the first time in *Apprentice* history, Trump sent a project manager, Alla, back to the suite, and eventually fired Adam.

In Episode 12, the final four designed thirty-second commercials for a new Microsoft Office program. Capital Edge's ad was too wordy and hard to watch, so Rebecca and Randal of Excel were named the winners, earning a sailboat ride around New York City. In a very emotional boardroom, Felisha broke down, feeling betrayed by her teammate Alla. Both women were fired: Felisha for being too nice, and Alla for being too mean.

Episode 13 began with Randal and Rebecca picking their final teams over breakfast. Randal chose Mark, Marshawn, and Josh; Rebecca selected Chris, James, and her friend Toral. Randal organized an Outback Steakhouse–sponsored celebrity baseball game to benefit Autism Speaks, while Rebecca planned a Yahoo!-sponsored comedy night to benefit the Elisabeth Glaser Pediatric AIDS Foundation. At the end of the episode, Randal's event was plagued by bad weather, while Rebecca was forced to replace her emcee at the last minute.

Episode 14 gave viewers the thrilling conclusion. While Rebecca found another emcee, who did a great job, Randal was forced to move his event indoors and replace the game with a celebrity auction. Both events were successful, raising an impressive amount of money for the two charities, although both finalists were reprimanded for their individual mistakes. The show ended with the final two reflecting on their "journey" and preparing for the finale.

In the Episode 15 finale, Randal said that his perfect project manager record was more impressive than Rebecca's record of one win and two losses. Forced with a tough decision, Trump ultimately picked Randal as the winner. In an unprecedented move, he asked Randal if he should also hire Rebecca. To everyone's surprise, Randal told Trump that the show was not titled *The Apprenti,* and shot down the idea. Trump stuck with Randal's decision, and did not hire Rebecca.

THE APPRENTICE

(Season 5)

GENRE	Competition (Job)
FIRST TELECAST	2/27/2006
LAST TELECAST	6/5/2006
NETWORK	NBC
AIR TIME	Monday, 9:00 p.m.
EPISODE STYLE	Story Arc
TALENT	Donald Trump; Ivanka Trump (Trump's Assistant); Bill Rancic (Trump's Assistant); Donald Trump, Jr. (Trump's Assistant); Robin Himmler (Trump's Secretary)
CAST	Sean Yazbeck (Winner); Lee Bienstock (Runner-up); Allie Jablon (13th fired); Roxanne Wilson (13th fired); Tammy Trenta (12th fired); Michael Laungani (11th fired); Tarek Saab (10th fired); Charmaine Hunt (10th fired); Andrea Lake (9th fired); Leslie Bourgeois (8th fired); Lenny Veltman (7th fired); Bryce Gahagan (6th fired); Dan Brody (5th fired); Brent Buckman (4th fired); Theresa Boutross (3rd fired); Stacy Schneider (2nd fired); Jose "Pepe" Diaz (2nd fired); Summer Zervos (1st fired)
PRODUCTION COMPANIES	Mark Burnett Productions, in association with Trump Productions LLC
CREATED BY	Mark Burnett
EXECUTIVE PRODUCERS	Mark Burnett; Donald Trump
CO-EXECUTIVE PRODUCER	Jay Bienstock

Season 5 featured eighteen contestants once again "hand-picked" by Donald Trump, but this time included some non-American contestants. Teams were not divided by gender or education. This was the last season in New York, before the show moved to Los Angeles, and then back to New York for *The Celebrity Apprentice*. Project managers did not receive exemption from firing if their team won the task. Season 1 winner Bill Rancic and Trump's children Donald Jr. and Ivanka sat in as boardroom judges when Carolyn Kepcher and George H. Ross were unavailable.

In the Season 5 premiere episode, Trump chose Mensa member Tarek and Harvard Business School graduate Allie to be the project managers, and instructed them to choose their team members. Tarek picked Dan, Bryce, Charmaine, Lee, Leslie, Theresa, Lenny, and Summer—the team named "Gold Rush." Allie selected Tammy, Andrea, Michael, Sean, Pepi, Roxanne, Stacy, and Brent—called "Synergy." For the first task, the teams promoted Sam's Club warehouse stores through freebies and advertising with a Goodyear blimp. The team that sold or upgraded the most Sam's Club memberships won the task. Synergy sold forty-three, compared with Gold Rush's forty. Synergy's reward was lunch with Trump at the Wharton Club. In the boardroom, Gold Rush's Summer was the first fired, for not knowing when to keep quiet.

In Episode 2, the next task was to market the Gillette Fusion razor system through a text-messaging campaign. Gold Rush, headed by Lee, received 683 text messages, and Ivanka called the team "smart and impressive." Synergy, managed by Pepi, received 458 messages, and Bill Rancic blamed the team's late start and poor location. Gold Rush's reward was having the opportunity to work with Career Gear, a nonprofit company that supplies disadvantaged men with clothing to help get them back in the job market. In the boardroom, Trump told Synergy that "location is everything," and Stacy had picked the wrong location. She was fired, along with project manager Pepi, who lacked leadership skills and had lost the respect of his team.

In Episode 3, Gold Rush's Dan and Lee took two days off to observe the Jewish New Year. For the next task, each team organized a corporate retreat for General Motors executives to promote the 2007 Chevy Tahoe. Theresa was project manager for Gold Rush. The team lost the challenge because the GM executives thought they didn't have enough product knowledge. Synergy, led by Andrea, earned positive ratings from GM, and as their reward, got to swim with sharks at Atlantis Marine World, in Long Island. Trump blamed Gold Rush's failure on the lack of concept. Project manager Theresa was fired for being a bad leader.

In Episode 4, each team designed a billboard promoting Post Grape Nuts Trail Mix

Crunch Cereal. Post executives who judged the task found Synergy's ad too complex, but described Gold Rush's as brilliant. For their reward, project manager Charmaine and her team cooked with world-famous chef Jean-Georges. In the boardroom, Trump spared Synergy's project manager, Tammy, and fired Brent, who did not mesh well with the team.

In Episode 5, the teams gathered onboard a Norwegian Cruise Line ship to hear about the next task: to create a thirty-second commercial to promote Norwegian's Freestyle Cruising. Norwegian executives said both teams produced satisfactory ads in the three hours they were given, but found Synergy's voice-over ad clearer than Gold Rush's confusing text-based ad. Project manager Roxanne led Synergy to victory. The team earned a trip to a Brinks Security vault holding more than $100 million worth of diamonds, where they took home $30,000 worth. Gold Rush project manager Dan took Tarek and Lee to the boardroom, but Trump thought Lenny should have been there instead. Because of his bad decision, Dan was fired.

In Episode 6, Lee again skipped a task with Gold Rush, this time to observe Yom Kippur. For the next task, each team created a thirty-second jingle for Arby's Chicken Naturals. Arby's executives chose Synergy's song as the winner. Project manager Sean and his team sampled a six-course truffle-tasting menu at Alain Ducasse, at the Essex House. In the boardroom, Trump fired Gold Rush project manager Bryce, calling him a terrible leader.

In Episode 7, each team renovated and modernized a Boys and Girls Club recreational room. Project manager Michael led Synergy to the team's third consecutive victory, and as a reward they took an eight-year-old Make-A-Wish Foundation child on a shopping spree at Toys "R" Us. In the boardroom, Trump fired Gold Rush project manager Lenny for his poor leadership skills and bad decisions.

In Episode 8, Michael joined Gold Rush to even out the teams. For the task, each team helped launch 7-Eleven's new P'EatZZa Sandwich through a promotional giveaway based around 7-Eleven's Andretti Green Racing IndyCar. Gold Rush couldn't break its losing streak. They increased their 7-Eleven store's sales by 608 percent, while Synergy sold sandwiches at a lower price and increased their store's sales by 997 percent. Synergy project manager Andrea and her team flew on a private jet to Washington, D.C., to have breakfast at the historic Hay-Adams Hotel with New York senator Chuck Schumer. In the boardroom, Gold Rush project manager Leslie was fired, on her birthday, because she had set the sandwich price too high, leading to her team's loss.

A mid-season recap episode aired twice on CNBC. The show also offered sneak peeks at the upcoming Season 5.

In Episode 9, each team spent the day at Ellis Island to help create a souvenir tourist program sponsored by Ameriquest. Project manager Lee finally led Gold Rush to a win. The team raised $1,548.00, compared to Synergy's $843.40. For their win, Gold Rush played a round of golf with Trump and professional golfer Vijay Singh, plus they each won a set of golf clubs. Synergy project manager Allie was spared. Trump fired Andrea because she lacked business chemistry.

In Episode 10, each team threw a grand-opening event at a Hair Cuttery franchise. The team earning the biggest profit won. Project manager Tammy led Synergy to victory, making $1,005.47, compared to Gold Rush's $700.00. For their reward, Synergy helped Burt Bacharach write song lyrics. In the boardroom, Trump fired two candidates—project manager Charmaine, for bad leadership and laziness during the task, and Tarek, for insubordination and being hard to work with.

In Episode 11, the teams were restructured, leaving Gold Rush all-male and Synergy all-female. In the next task, teams sold Outback Steakhouse food at a tailgate party during a Rutgers University football game. Gold Rush used the Rutgers cheerleaders to promote their food, and earned $1,750. Synergy sold food in bulk and offered delivery, taking in $2,750. For their reward, project manager Roxanne and Synergy created signature wines at Raphael Winery in Long Island. In the boardroom, Gold Rush project manager Lee was spared, while Michael was fired because he had tried to share the Rutgers cheerleaders with the opposing team.

In Episode 12, each team created an interactive display for Microsoft's Xbox 360 in a Wal-Mart. The Microsoft and Wal-Mart executives said Synergy's display was inviting, but didn't promote a high-end purchase. Gold Rush's display was unfinished, but the executives liked that team's retail concept more. For their reward, Gold Rush project manager Sean and teammate Michael visited Dream Works Animation Studios, in Hollywood, where they did voice-overs for the animated film *Over the Hedge*. In the boardroom, Trump fired Synergy project manager Tammy for poor leadership and a bad design.

In Episode 13, each team designed four new uniforms for Embassy Suites hotels:

front desk, breakfast cook, suite keeper, and bellman. Gold Rush's fresh, comfortable designs won eighty-three votes from hotel employees, while Synergy's impractical, uncomfortable uniforms received only thirty-seven votes. Gold Rush project manager Lee and teammate Sean dined with Donald Jr. and Ivanka at Aquavit. In the boardroom, Trump fired Syngery project manager Roxanne and her teammate and friend Allie.

In Episode 14, Lee and Sean learned they were the final two. For the final task, they chose former candidates as their teammates. Lee picked Lenny, Pepi, and Roxanne to make up Gold Rush, while Sean took Andrea, Tammy, and Tarek for Synergy. Lee managed the Pontiac/Celebrity Hockey Game at Chelsea Piers, while Sean ran the Pontiac/Barenaked Ladies concert at the Trump Taj Mahal, in Atlantic City. At the end of the episode, Carolyn thought Lee was too laid back with Gold Rush. Meanwhile Synergy's Andrea mysteriously coughed up blood and was rushed to the doctor.

The Episode 15 finale was broadcast live from the Orpheum Theatre in Los Angeles. In their final tasks, Sean raised $40,000, while Lee managed only $30,000. Trump presented two possible jobs for the next apprentice: a hotel project in Hawaii or one in New York. Sean and Lee both said they would select the New York job if chosen as the apprentice. After Sean and Lee made their final pleas, Trump said he agreed with an NBC.com poll that had overwhelmingly sided with one candidate, Sean. "Lee, you're fired," Trump said, before saying his famous words to Sean, "You're hired!"

THE APPRENTICE: LOS ANGELES
(Season 6)

GENRE	Competition (Job)
FIRST TELECAST	1/17/2007
LAST TELECAST	4/22/2007
NETWORK	NBC
AIR TIMES	Sunday, 9:00 p.m. (1/2007–2/2007); Sunday, 10:00 p.m. (3/2007–4/2007)
EPISODE STYLE	Story Arc
TALENT	Donald Trump; Ivanka Trump (Trump's Assistant); Donald Trump, Jr. (Trump's Assistant)

CAST	Stefani Schaeffer (Winner); James Sun (Runner-up); Nicole D'Ambrosio (15th fired); Frank Lombardi (14th fired); Kristine Lefebvre (13th fired); Heidi Androl (12th fired); Tim Urban (11th fired); Angela Ruggiero (10th fired); Muna Heaven (9th fired); Surya Yalamanchili (8th fired); Jenn Hoffman (7th fired); Derek Arteta (6th fired); Aimee Trottier (5th fired); Aaron Altscher (4th fired); Marisa Demato (3rd fired); Michelle Sorro (quit); Carey Sherrell (2nd fired); Martin Clarke (1st fired)
PRODUCTION COMPANIES	Mark Burnett Productions, in association with Trump Productions LLC
CREATED BY	Mark Burnett
EXECUTIVE PRODUCERS	Mark Burnett; Donald Trump
CO-EXECUTIVE PRODUCER	Jay Bienstock

In season 6 the show moved to Los Angeles. The number of contestants remained at eighteen. Donald Trump's daughter Ivanka replaced a fired Carolyn Kepcher as a permanent boardroom judge and adviser, and his son Donald Jr. replaced George H. Ross. A new rule had the winning team's project manager keeping the role until the team lost a task. That project manager also sat in on the losing team's boardroom visit. After each task, the winning team (the "haves") slept inside a Beverly Hills mansion, while the losers (the "have nots") camped outdoors in "Tent City," which had no electricity or hot water. Trump's office/mansion was next door to the candidates' mansion.

In the season premiere, the candidates were forced to work together, to construct a large tent. The task determined the initial project managers, Heidi and Frank, who then performed a schoolyard-style pick to choose their teams. Heidi led "Kinetic," while Frank headed up "Arrow." Each team then ran a car wash to see which would make the most profit. Arrow lost by only $120. Kinetic earned dinner at Spago with Trump, Melania Knauss, Ivanka, and chef Wolfgang Puck. In the boardroom, Trump fired Martin, stating he'd be a better professor or lawyer than a businessman.

In Episode 2, the teams created a collection of swimsuits for designer Trina Turk, and the contestants modeled their pieces at a runway show. Heidi led Kinetic to another victory, earning $20,011, while Nicole led Arrow to make $19,616. For their reward, Kinetic was escorted by Trump to the Playboy Mansion for a pool party with with Hugh Hefner and the Playboy Playmates. The team was exempt from the next task. In the boardroom, Arrow's Carey was fired for his poor decision-making.

In Episode 3, Kinetic spent the evening at Loews Santa Monica Beach Hotel, while Arrow split into two teams to create Hollywood sightseeing bus tours. Aaron led James and Stefani, while Michelle managed Tim, Nicole, and Frank. Aaron's team won the task, receiving the highest approval rating from tour customers. There was no boardroom visit, because Michelle resigned from the competition, which Trump said was a bad decision.

In Episode 4, Surya, Aimee, and Marisa joined Arrow to even out the teams. For the next task, the teams created a new El Pollo Loco menu item, and ran a franchise for a day. Aaron led Arrow to victory, earning $488. The team won a private performance by Andrea Bocelli and a fireworks show. They also finally moved inside the mansion. Kinetic moved to Tent City. Project manager Heidi was spared, while Kinetic recommended that Trump fire Marisa. He did so.

In Episode 5, the teams harvested honey for Sue Bee Honey, to sell at Ralphs Supermarket. Kinetic sold $836.48 over Arrow's $775.48. Kinetic project manager Aimee and her team won basketball training with Kareem Abdul-Jabbar, James Worthy, and L.A. Lakers coach Phil Jackson and player Brian Cook. In the boardroom, Arrow targeted Surya as the scapegoat, but Trump fired project manager Aaron for his lack of leadership and poor strategy on the task.

In Episode 6, the teams had to get mall shoppers to sign up for Priceline.com. In two hours, more people signed up for Arrow's sweepstakes, despite Surya's poor leadership. The team won private surfing lessons and brunch, and teammates Tim and Nicole got romantic. Kinetic project manager Aimee was fired for not comprehending the mall's demographics.

In Episode 7, each team organized a promotional event for the Lexus LS 460 for VIP customers. Surya again led Arrow to victory, and the team won a chance to rap with Snoop Dogg. In the boardroom, Trump quickly fired Derek for calling himself "white trash." Project manager Jenn was also fired, for making poor decisions.

In Episode 8, each team produced a GNC-themed halftime show at a Los Angeles Galaxy soccer game. Kristine led Kinetic to victory, and the team won a round of golf with Trump at Trump National Golf Club, Los Angeles. Kinetic produces the better show for the win. For their reward, they enjoyed golf time with the Donald. In the boardroom, Trump said it was a hard decision to fire project manager Surya, who was an outcast among Arrow. However, he predicted that Surya would be successful in her future.

In Episode 9, each team produced a webisode soap opera promoting Soft Scrub Deep Clean Foaming Cleanser. James led Arrow to victory, earning the team a private meeting with California governor Arnold Schwarzenegger. In the boardroom, Kinetic project manager Kristine was spared when Trump fired Muna because she was too difficult to work with.

In Episode 10, James chose Nicole to join Kinetic. The teams competed to see which sold the most front-of-the-line passes and season tickets to Universal Studios Hollywood theme park. Arrow earned $32,000, outselling Kinetic by $7,000. Project manager James and the Arrow team won a helicopter ride above Los Angeles. Kinetic project manager Angela was fired for poor leadership skills and for not defending herself well.

In Episode 11, each team promoted Smartmouth mouthwash through an advertising insert in the *Los Angeles Times*. Heidi led Kinetic to victory, and the team received visits from loved ones as their reward. Project manager James led Arrow to the boardroom, where Trump fired Tim for his poor idea, his disloyalty to the team, and for allowing his romantic relationship with Nicole to interfere with his performance.

In Episode 12, the final six split into three teams of two, and Tent City was eliminated. The teams traveled to Las Vegas to create a promotional campaign for the city's Trump International Hotel and Tower. James and Stefani's "The Height of Luxury" presentation and brochure were hits. Frank and Heidi and Kristine and Nicole failed. Trump fired Heidi for her team's poor presentation, while Kristine was fired for putting the wrong phone number on her team's brochure.

In Episode 13, the final four met with four previous winners of *The Apprentice*. Then each team produced a sixty-second short film promoting Renuzit. James and Stefani were assisted by eliminated candidates Aaron and Angela; while Frank and Nicole chose Tim and Surya. In a special twist, Trump didn't fire anyone in the boardroom, and the final four were told they'd meet again in the live finale.

The Episode 14 finale was broadcast live from the Hollywood Bowl. Trump watched the teams' Renuzit spots again, polled the fired candidates, and listened to the final four plead their cases. He then fired Frank and Nicole. James and Stefani had a final verbal showdown. Trump told Stefani, "You're hired!" and the attorney was named the winner.

THE APPRENTICE: MARTHA STEWART

GENRE	Competition (Job)
FIRST TELECAST	9/21/2005
LAST TELECAST	12/21/2005
NETWORK	NBC
AIR TIME	Wednesdays 9:00 p.m.
EPISODE STYLE	Story Arc
TALENT	Martha Stewart; Charles Koppelman; Alexis Stewart
CAST	Dawna Stone (Winner—Matchstick); Bethenny Frankel (Runner-up—Primarius); Jim Bozzini (12th fired—Primarius); Marcela Valladolid (11th fired—Matchstick); Ryan Danz (11th fired—Matchstick); Leslie Sanchez (10th fired—Matchstick); Amanda Hill (9th fired—Matchstick); Howie Greenspan (8th fired—Primarius); Carrie Gugger (7th fired—Primarius); Sarah Brennan (7th fired—Primarius); David Karandish (6th fired—Matchstic); Jennifer Le (5th fired—Primarius); Dawn Silvia (4th fired—Matchstick); Shawn Killinger (3rd fired—Matchstick); Chuck Soldano (2nd fired—Matchstic); Jeff Rudell (1st fired—Matchstick)
PRODUCTION COMPANIES	Mark Burnett Productions; Martha Stewart Living Omnimedia; Trump Productions LLC
EXECUTIVE PRODUCERS	Donald Trump; Mark Burnett; Jay Bienstock; Martha Stewart

PRODUCERS   Luciana Brafman; Jeff Cole; Rob LaPlante;
Bill Pruitt; Thomas B. Ruff

A spinoff of Donald Trump's *The Apprentice*, Martha Stewart's show followed the same format as Trump's series, as candidates competed for a job with Martha Stewart Living Omnimedia, and were eliminated each week until a winner was chosen. The tasks reflected Stewart's areas of expertise: media, home renovation, entertaining, design, merchandising, technology, and style. Rather than saying, "You're fired," when a contestant was eliminated, Stewart said, "Goodbye." She also wrote a farewell letter to each fired contestant. Dawna Stone of St. Petersburg, Florida, was hired by Stewart to be development director of MSLO's *Body + Soul* magazine.

ARE YOU HOT?
THE SEARCH FOR AMERICA'S SEXIEST PEOPLE

GENRE	Competition
FIRST TELECAST	2/13/2003
LAST TELECAST	4/5/2003
NETWORK	ABC
AIR TIMES	Thursday, 9:00 p.m. (2/2003–3/2003); Saturday, 9:00 p.m. (4/2003)
EPISODE STYLE	Story Arc
TALENT	JD Roberto (Host); Rachel Hunter (Judge); Lorenzo Lamas (Judge): Randolph Duke (Judge)

CAST

Women   Chantille Boudousque (Winner); Aeriel; Amber; Brandy; Cari; Cherika; Crystal; Ivy; Jessica; Lisa; Nicki; Rachel; Renee; Sharee; Valerie; Wendy Lynn

Men	David Maxwell (Winner); Billy; Domenic; Dylan; Eric; Jameel; Jimmy; Jonathan; Ken; Kevin; Kevin; Luciano; Peake; Ryan; Shipley; Tony; Travis
PRODUCTION COMPANY	Next Entertainment Inc., in association with Telepictures Productions; ABC
EXECUTIVE PRODUCER	Mike Fleiss
CO-EXECUTIVE PRODUCERS	Scott Einzinger; Mike Nichols
PRODUCERS	Sean Olsen; Nelson Soler
DIRECTOR	Ken Fuchs

In this beauty contest, eight men and eight women were selected by a celebrity panel and an online viewer poll to determine who was the sexiest of the sexes. Judge Lorenzo Llamas used a laser pointer to indicate contestants' figure flaws. Chantille Boudousque and David Maxwell emerged as the winners.

Radio personality Howard Stern sued the parties involved for similarities between *Are You Hot?* and his own show, including the gimmick of using the laser pointer and the beauty pageant aspect of the contest. The executive producer of *Are You Hot?* had once been Stern's producer. The lawsuit was dismissed in August 2003.

ARMED AND FAMOUS

GENRE	Docusoap (Celebrity)
FIRST TELECAST	1/10/2007
LAST TELECAST	1/24/2007
NETWORK	CBS
AIR TIME	Wednesday, 8:00 p.m.
EPISODE STYLE	Story Arc
CAST	Jason "Wee-Man" Acuna; Erik Estrada; La Toya Jackson; Jack Osbourne; Trish Stratus
EXECUTIVE PRODUCER	Tom Forman
CO-EXECUTIVE PRODUCER	Jeff Krask

Five celebrities went to Muncie, Indiana, and were given a crash course in learning how to be a cop. After the three-week training session, they were given badges and became reserve officers. Viewers saw La Toya Jackson tasered as part of the training while Erik Estrada was called in to help resolve a domestic disturbance. CBS pulled the show after only three weeks on the air due to disappointing ratings for the series.

THE ASHLEE SIMPSON SHOW

GENRE	Docusoap (Celebrity)
FIRST TELECAST	6/16/2004
LAST TELECAST	3/30/2005
NETWORK	MTV
EPISODE STYLE	Story Arc
CAST	Ashlee Simpson; Joe Simpson (Ashlee's dad); Tina Simpson (Ashlee's mom); Jessica Simpson (Ashlee's sister—guest); Nick Lachey (Ashlee's brother-in-law—guest); Ryan Cabrera (Ashlee's boyfriend—guest)
EXECUTIVE PRODUCERS	Joe Simpson; Matt Anderson
PRODUCER	Charles Kramer
DIRECTORS	Matt Anderson; Casey Brumels; Shannon Fitzgerald; Kelly Welsh

This docusoap followed singer Jessica Simpson's younger sister Ashlee as she left home for the first time to embark on a pop music career. Ashlee broke up with her boyfriend and began dating singer Ryan Cabrera, who became the inspiration for her hit song "Pieces of Me." Battling insecurity and vocal problems, Ashlee emerged from her sister's shadow and became a legitimate recording artist, thanks in part to her family's support and guidance. Her first album, *Autobiography,* debuted with a No. 1 song on the Billboard charts in July 2004, and the disc later went platinum.

Season 2 included Ashlee's discredited lip-synching performance on *Saturday Night Live* and its aftermath, as Ashlee and her band launched their first nationwide tour. Other episodes featured Ashlee working with trainers and a vocal coach, performing at the Orange Bowl halftime show without a working earpiece (and being booed), and struggling to maintain her long-distance relationship with her boyfriend.

THE ASSISTANT

GENRE	Competition (Job)
FIRST TELECAST	7/12/2004
LAST TELECAST	8/30/2004
NETWORK	MTV
EPISODE STYLE	Story Arc
TALENT	Andy Dick
CAST	Melissa (Winner); Tanika Nicole Kennedy (Runner-up); Colin (eliminated in Episode 6); Mykell (eliminated in Episode 6); Stefani (eliminated in Episode 5); Anna (eliminated in Episode 5); Mark (eliminated in Episode 4); Ebony (eliminated in Episode 3); Sarah (eliminated in Episode 2); Jeff (eliminated in Episode 2); Nikeda (eliminated in Episode 1); Andrew (eliminated in Episodes 1 and 3)
PRODUCTION COMPANIES	MTV Productions; Superdelicious
EXECUTIVE PRODUCERS	Adam Cohen; Andy Dick; Cara Tapper; Joanna Vernetti
PRODUCER	Harve Levine
DIRECTORS	Kasey Barrett; Jeff Fisher

This competition featured comedian/actor Andy Dick and his irreverent brand of humor. Dick put twelve aspiring Hollywood wannabes through the difficult and sometimes absurd duties of a personal assistant, and one by one they were eliminated. Melissa won the coveted position, getting a new cell phone, a wardrobe, a car, and a job at MTV.

AVERAGE JOE

GENRE Competition (Dating)
FIRST TELECAST 11/3/2003
LAST TELECAST 7/27/2005
NETWORK NBC
AIR TIMES Monday, 10:00 p.m. (Seasons 1–3); Tuesday, 8:00 p.m. (Season 4, 6/2005–7/2005); Wednesday, 8:00 p.m. (Season 4, 7/2005)
EPISODE STYLE Story Arc
TALENT Kathy Griffin (Host—Season 1)

CAST

Season 1 Melana Scantlin (The Bachelorette); John Baumgaertner (Average Joe); Craig Campbell (Average Joe); Zach Cohen (Average Joe); Ken Danieli (Average Joe); Joe Fabiani (Average Joe); Jerry Ferrara (Average Joe); Jay Greenberg (Average Joe); Brad Holcman (Average Joe); Tareq Kabir (Average Joe); Michael Klein (Average Joe); David López (Average Joe); Dennis Luciani (Average Joe); Marc Marcuse (Average Joe); Adam Mesh (Average Joe); Michael Morelle (Hunk); Jason Peoples (Hunk/Winner); Alex Sabatini (Hunk); Walter Steffen (Average Joe)

Season 2 Larissa Meek (Bachelorette); Gil Hyatt (Hunk/Winner); Brian Worth (Average Joe/Runner-up); David Daskal (Average Joe); Theo Kousoulis (Hunk); Jim Frasseto (Hunk); Brian Glazer (Average Joe); Fredo LaPonza (Average Joe); Donato Ventresca (Average Joe); Michael Klein (Hunk); Michael Cardamone (Hunk); Michael Spitaletto (Average Joe); Pete Gaeth

(Hunk); Phuc Le (Average Joe); Robert Guichet;
C. J. Tippery (Average Joe); Justin Walsh
(Average Joe)

Season 3 Adam Mesh (Bachelor); Samantha Trenk (Winner);
Anna Merril; Elizabeth Griggs; Rachel Goetz;
Christine Morell; Sara Stone; Elizabeth Wood;
Summer Wesson; Rochelle Finkelstein;
Brittany Ducker; Jennifer Abrams; Amy Worth;
Jennifer Lifshitz; Tracilee Bennardello;
Jennifer Bolkin; Heather Caton; Stephanie Cahn;
Rebecca Butler; Courtney Butler

Season 4 Anna Chuboda (Bachelorette); Nathan Griffin
(Winner); Dante Alighire (Average Joe);
Jason Marcus (Average Joe); Harold Gold
(Average Joe); Josh Nachlas (Average Joe);
Bill Parks (Average Joe); Igor Zhivotovsky (Average
Joe); Joshua Smith (Average Joe); Nick Parlin
(Average Joe); Aaron Feldon (Average Joe);
Clay Ellis (Average Joe); Arthur Apicella (Average
Joe); Matt Hoffman (Average Joe); Chuck
Ardezzone (Average Joe); Daniel Boncel (Average
Joe); Aaron Clauset (Average Joe); Gino Cafarelli
(Average Joe); Damian Muziani (Average Joe);
Brad (Hunk); Carson (Hunk); Craig (Hunk); Greg
(Hunk); Josh (Hunk); Mike (Hunk); Rocky (Hunk)

PRODUCTION COMPANIES Krasnow Productions; NBC Studios
EXECUTIVE PRODUCER Stuart Krasnow
PRODUCERS Adam Vetri; Andrew Glassman; Grant Julian;
Nate McIntosh; Jason Raff
DIRECTORS Tony Croll; Jason Raff

In this competition a beautiful girl selected a potential suitor from a pool of "average-looking Joes," until good-looking guys were added to shake up the competition.

During Seasons 1 and 2, the female contestants selected the hunks instead of average-looking men. In Season 3, Season 1 runner-up Adam Mesh returned to select from a group of his biggest fans. The original format was restored in Season 4, but the show included makeovers for the average-looking men. Some former competitors—Fredo LaPonza, Brian Worth, and David Daskaloes—returned in the fourth season to train the new "Joes" before meeting with their potential dream date.

RATINGS: Season 1 of *Average Joe* brought in an average of 12.6 million viewers each week. The second season had an average of 11.1 million. Season 3 averaged 10.3 million people, while the fourth season had an average weekly viewership of 4.7 million.

X Y Z # A **B** C D E F G

FOX REALITY CHANNEL

A BABY STORY

GENRE	Docudrama
FIRST TELECAST	1998
NETWORK	TLC
EPISODE STYLE	Self-contained
PRODUCTION COMPANY	True Entertainment
EXECUTIVE PRODUCERS	Glenda Hersh (2002–2004); Terri Johnson (2002–2004); Steven Weinstock (2002–2004); Tara Sandler
SENIOR PRODUCERS	Lorri Leighton (2002–2004); Liz Naylor (2002–2004)
PRODUCERS	Audrey Bellezza (2003–2004); Lisa Mozo (2003–2004); Adrienne Hammel (2002–2003); Wayne Hackett; Christina Marra; Christina McElroy; Beth Simanaitis; Jackson Varady; Sadye White

Each episode of this long-running docudrama focuses on one expectant couple, following them up to and through their child's birth, exploring their hopes, dreams, and fears of impending parenthood.

THE BACHELOR

(Season 1)

GENRE	Competition (Dating)
FIRST TELECAST	3/25/2002
LAST TELECAST	4/25/2002
NETWORK	ABC
AIR TIME	Monday, 9:00 p.m.
EPISODE STYLE	Story Arc
TALENT	Chris Harrison (Host)
CAST	Alex Michel (The Bachelor); Amanda Marsh (Winner); Trista Rehn (Runner-up); LaNease Adams; Amy Anzel; Tina Chen; Daniela Ferdico; Lisa Gold; Jill Gosser; Cathy Grimes; Jaclyn Hucko; Kristina Jenkins; Alexa Jurgielewicz; Kimberly Karels; Denise Kellaher; Rachel Lanzilotto; Angela Lowery; Angelique Madrid; Paula Oliveira; Shannon Oliver; Wendi Plotnik; Melissa Reese; Rhonda Rittenhouse; Kathryn Sapienza; Christina Stencil; Amber West
PRODUCTION COMPANIES	Next Entertainment; Telepictures Productions
CREATED BY	Mike Fleiss
EXECUTIVE PRODUCER	Mike Fleiss
CO-EXECUTIVE PRODUCERS	Lisa Levenson; Kathy Wetherell; Jason A. Carbone; Scott Jeffress

This docudrama contest followed one man's quest for true love as he simultaneously dated twenty-five women from across the United States, narrowing his selection to the one he felt was right for him. At the conclusion of each episode, only those women who had received a single red rose from him continued to the next episode. At the conclusion of each season, it was up to the Bachelor to decide if he'd propose marriage to his chosen partner.

In Episode 1, viewers were introduced to bachelor Alex Michel. He hosted a cocktail party, where we met the twenty-five women competing to be his potential bride. After getting to know the bachelorettes, Alex presented roses to Kim, Cathy, Trista, Amy, Alexa, LaNease, Tina, Angelique, Rhonda, Christina, Katie, Amanda, Angela, Melissa, and Shannon. Those fifteen women moved into an oceanfront mansion, while the other ten returned home.

In Episode 2, the fifteen women, divided into groups of five, accompanied Alex on three dates. On Alex's first date, he traveled to Las Vegas with Angelique, Christina, Kathryn, LaNease, and Shannon. LaNease won the most money playing blackjack, earning a romantic gondola ride with Alex, where they kissed under a bridge. On his second date, he went to Palm Springs with Amanda, Amy, Angela, Melissa, and Trista. Alex and Amanda showered each other off after a mud bath, and Melissa sat on Alex's lap during the bus ride back to the mansion. On his third date, Alex cruised to Santa Barbara with Alexa, Cathy, Kim, Rhonda, and Tina, where he decided Rhonda seemed like marriage material. At the Rose Ceremony, Alex presented roses to Amanda, Cathy, Christina, Kim, LaNease, Rhonda, Shannon, and Trista.

In Episode 3, Alex's friends Stephanie and Sam created a compatibility test for the women. For scoring the highest, Amanda, Trista, and Shannon earned individual dates with Alex, while the lower scorers settled for a group date. During Alex's date with Amanda, they kissed several times and massaged each other. Alex enjoyed his date with Trista, but couldn't get a read on her feelings. On his date with Shannon, they ate a romantic dinner in the penthouse at the Four Seasons, and Alex gave her a matching necklace and earrings. On his group date, Alex and the ladies went horseback riding, where he connected emotionally only with Rhonda. At the Rose Ceremony, Alex presented a red rose to Amanda, Trista, Shannon, and Kim.

In Episode 4, each of the remaining four women took Alex home to meet her friends and family. Kim brought him speed-boating in Phoenix, where he generally got along with her family. Trista took him to St. Louis, where they kissed on her old high-school bleachers. Alex joined Amanda in Chanute, Kansas, where exhaustion was to blame for his not connecting with her parents. Finally, Alex went to Dallas to see Shannon, who seemed to ignore him in favor of showering her dog with attention. At the Rose Ceremony, Alex presented a rose to Shannon, Trista, and Amanda.

In Episode 5, Alex took each of the final three on an overnight date. He took

Amanda to New York City, where she professed her love for him, and they wound up covered in chocolate in a fantasy suite. Shannon and Alex went to Lake Tahoe, where she denied him a kiss and seemed hesitant to open up to him emotionally. Finally, he met Trista in Hawaii, where he confessed he wanted to date only her; but she was hesitant. At the Rose Ceremony, Alex gave roses to Amanda and Trista.

The Episode 6, "The Women Tell All" show reunited the twenty-three "dismissed" women, who gathered to talk about their experiences on *The Bachelor.*

In Episode 7, Alex brought both women home to Dallas to meet his family. During Trista's visit, she finally warmed up to him and agreed to spend the night. Amanda told Alex she was falling in love with him, and surprised him by putting on a French maid's outfit, and they retired to the bedroom. At the final Rose Ceremony, Alex presented his final rose to Amanda, who gleefully accepted.

In a special three and a half months later, Leanza Cornett interviewed Alex to learn how he had made his selection decisions.

A month and a half after that, a second special tied up the loose ends from the first season, revealing that Trista would star in her own spinoff, *The Bachelorette,* and introduced the five finalists to star in Season 2 of *The Bachelor.*

RATINGS: The first season of *The Bachelor* drew an average of 10.7 million viewers each week.

THE BACHELOR
(Season 2)

GENRE	Competition (Dating)
FIRST TELECAST	9/25/2002
LAST TELECAST	11/20/2002
NETWORK	ABC
AIR TIME	Wednesday, 9:00 p.m.
EPISODE STYLE	Story Arc
TALENT	Chris Harrison (Host)
CAST	Aaron Buerge (The Bachelor); Helene Eksterowicz (Winner); Angela; Cari; Christy; Heather Cranford; Hayley Crittenden; Kyla Dickerson;

Merrilee Donohue; Anindita Dutta; Erin; Fatima;
Frances; Gwen Gioia; Heather; Amber Johnson;
Camille Langfield; Liangy; Lori; Erin Lulevitch;
Dana Norris; Suzi Reid; Shannon; Brooke Smith;
Susie; Suzanne; Christi Weible

PRODUCTION COMPANIES	Next Entertainment; Telepictures Productions
CREATED BY	Mike Fleiss
EXECUTIVE PRODUCER	Mike Fleiss
CO-EXECUTIVE PRODUCERS	Lisa Levenson; Kathy Wetherell; Jason A. Carbone; Scott Jeffress

In Episode 1, the newest Bachelor, Aaron, a vice president of a bank chain, claimed to be the opposite of Season 1's bachelor, Alex. Aaron promised he didn't want to lead women on, and could envision popping the question by the end of the series. Aaron immediately took a liking to Christi, Gwen, and Brooke. At the Rose Ceremony, he presented a red rose to Angela, Anindita, Brooke, Christi, Dana, Erin, Frances, Gwen, Hayley, Heather E., Heather C., Helene, Kyla, Shannon, and Suzanne.

In Episode 2, the fifteen remaining women settled into a Malibu mansion. On Aaron's first group date, he went to the racetrack with Dana, Frances, Gwen, Heather E., and Helene. Gwen won a bet, and Aaron kissed her during a one-on-one balloon ride. On Aaron's second group date, he went to Napa Valley with Angela, Anindita, Christi, Erin, and Suzanne. During the trip, Suzanne mixed the best wine blend in a blind taste test, and she kissed Aaron in the wine cellar. On Aaron's third group date, he took Brooke, Hayley, Heather C., Kyla, and Shannon to Lake Powell, Arizona. Before the Rose Ceremony, Anindita and Frances announced that they didn't want roses, and eliminated themselves from the show. Aaron gave roses to Angela, Brooke, Christi, Gwen, Hayley, Heather C., Heather E., Helene, Kyla, and Shannon.

In Episode 3, Aaron's friends Ryan and Melissa gave the women a quiz, and Helene's and Brooke's answers earned them one-on-one dates. Aaron took Helene to the Hollywood Bowl, where they kissed under fireworks. Aaron and Brooke went to Big Bear Lake, where they kissed in a hot tub. On Aaron's next group date, he took Gwen, Hayley, and Kyla surfing, but failed to spark a romance. On the next group date, Aaron brought Angela, Christi, Heather C., Heather E., and Shannon to Disney's California Adventure, where Christi won a Skee-Ball game and took a private carousel ride with

Aaron. Back at the mansion, Helene admitted that Aaron had slipped her his phone number, in case she thought about leaving. At the Rose Ceremony, Aaron presented a red rose to Angela, Brooke, Gwen, Hayley, Heather C., and Helene. A bitter Christi confessed that she would have married Aaron, had he chosen her.

In Episode 4, host Chris Harrison told the girls that a personality test they took earlier had actually been a compatibility test, and Heather, Gwen, and Helene earned individual dates with Aaron. Heather and Aaron went to a spa in Santa Barbara, where they had a good time. Aaron took Gwen in a pumpkin-shaped carriage to dinner at a mansion, where they shared an intense conversation and a kiss. During Aaron's date with Helene, she advised him not to lead her on if he didn't think she'd win. On Aaron's group date, he took Angela, Brooke, and Hayley on a day cruise, and Aaron particularly enjoyed his conversation with Angela. At the Rose Ceremony, he gave roses to Angela, Brooke, Gwen, and Helene.

In Episode 5, each the remaining women took Aaron home to meet her family and friends. Gwen brought him to Buffalo, where he impressed her parents, and she decided he was worth getting emotionally involved with—at the risk of possible rejection and heartache. Aaron went to Philadelphia to see Helene, and romantic feelings blossomed. He joined Brooke in Alabama, where he impressed her stepfather enough to be invited into his University of Alabama shrine room. Angela brought Aaron to Kansas City, where her family seemed indifferent about meeting him. At the Rose Ceremony, Aaron presented a red rose to Gwen, Helene, and Brooke.

In Episode 6, Aaron went on romantic getaways to Kauai with Brooke, San Francisco with Gwen, and Aspen with Helene. On each date, they spent the night in the fantasy suite. At the Rose Ceremony, Aaron presented a red rose to Brooke and Helene.

In Episode 7, "The Women Tell All" special, those who didn't receive roses reunited and predicted whom Aaron would choose.

In Episode 8, Aaron made up his mind, presenting his final rose to Helene. He also proposed to her with a two-and-a-half-carat diamond ring, and she accepted.

Three months later, host Chris Harrison sat down with Aaron and Helene for a special interview, to discuss the events that had led to their breakup.

A month later, a special "Where are they now?" episode caught up with the stars from *The Bachelor* and *The Bachelorette*.

The following week, a special episode revealed Season 3's Bachelor, Andrew Firestone, and the twenty-five women who would be vying for his affections.

THE BACHELOR
(Season 3)

GENRE	Competition (Dating)
FIRST TELECAST	3/26/2003
LAST TELECAST	5/21/2003
NETWORK	ABC
AIR TIME	Wednesday, 9:00 p.m.
EPISODE STYLE	Story Arc
TALENT	Chris Harrison
CAST	Andrew Firestone (The Bachelor); Jen Schefft (Winner); Heather Barry; Kirsten Buschbacher; Jennifer Buttacavoli; Courtney Chan; Cristina Costa; Ginny Edwards; Elizabeth; Shannon Ford; Amy Greenspan; Kerri; Kristen; Tina Panas; Amy Plinska; Angela Polimeri; Rachel; Tiffany Sandels; Anne-Michelle Seiler; Tina Sevier; Audree Shelton; Stephanie; Amber Stoke; Christina Sztanko; Liz Terzo; Brooke Vermeulen
PRODUCTION COMPANIES	Next Entertainment; Telepictures Productions
CREATED BY	Mike Fleiss
EXECUTIVE PRODUCER	Mike Fleiss
CO-EXECUTIVE PRODUCERS	Lisa Levenson; Kathy Wetherell; Jason A. Carbone; Scott Jeffress

Episode 1 offered a peek at the audition process for the newest Bachelor. The winner was Andrew Firestone of the wealthy Firestone family. Once again, twenty-five women would compete for the Bachelor's affections.

In Episode 2, Andrew met his bachelorettes and mingled with them at a cocktail party. After some deliberation, he presented the first fifteen red roses to Amber, Amy P., Anne-Michelle, Audree, Christina, Cristina, Elizabeth, Heather, Jen, Kirsten, Liz, Rachel, Shannon, Tina P., and Tina S.

In Episode 3, the fifteen women move into the bachelorette pad. Andrew went on his first group date, with Amber, Christina, Kirsten, Liz, and Tina S., to a mud bath spa, where he invited Kirsten to get a massage with him. For his second group date, Andrew went to a basketball game with Amy, Audree, Elizabeth, Heather, and Rachel. He offered to kiss any woman who made a three-point shot, but none succeeded. On the last group date, he took Anne-Michelle, Cristina, Jennifer, Shannon, and Tina P. to Lake Tahoe. Cristina won the most while gambling, earning private time with Andrew. She asked him why she wasn't getting romantic vibes from him. At the Rose Ceremony, Andrew presented roses to Amber, Anne-Michelle, Audree, Cristina, Heather, Jen, Kirsten, Liz, Tina P., and Tina S.

In Episode 4, Andrew's friends Kevin and Shannon conducted a personality test on the women, and Amber and Kirsten won one-on-one dates with Andrew. Sparks didn't fly during Andrew's ice-skating date with Amber. During his yacht date with Kirsten, Andrew gave her a dress and jewelry, and they kissed. On Andrew's subsequent group date, with Anne-Michelle, Cristina, and Liz, he took them to a Moroccan restaurant with belly dancing. Later, he and Cristina kissed in a hot tub. Andrew took Audree, Heather, Jen, Tina P., and Tina S. to a ranch for their group date. "Wisconsin" Tina P. won private time with him after a mechanical bull-riding contest. At the Rose Ceremony, Andrew gave roses to Anne-Michelle, Cristina, Jen, Kirsten, Liz, and "Wisconsin" Tina.

In Episode 5, relationship experts selected three women to get one-on-one dates with Andrew, and three who would have to settle for a group date. Andrew's first one-on-one date was with Jen, in Palm Springs, where they kissed in the back of the limo. For his second date, with Kirsten, they went to a drive-in movie, and they also kissed. Andrew's last one-on-one date was with Anne-Michelle, for a fondue dinner, at which Anne-Michelle questioned him about his thought processes. At Andrew's tennis group date, with Christina, Liz, and Tina, the girls got a little competitive. At the Rose Ceremony, Andrew presented roses to Tina P., Kirsten, Jen, and Cristina.

In Episode 6, each of the remaining women took Andrew home to meet her family and friends. Tina brought Andrew to Wisconsin, where he had a brief meeting with her folks, and later he and Tina exchanged their first real kiss. Cristina further peppered Andrew with questions when he visited her in Newark, and he thought she was too nervous. Andrew saw Kirsten in Tampa, and romantic feelings blossomed, despite concerns she may not have been completely over her ex-boyfriend. Finally, Andrew went to Cleveland to see Jen, where they discussed mundane relationship issues, such as who would clean up after the dog. At the Rose Ceremony, Andrew presented a red rose to Kirsten, Tina P., and Jen.

Episode 7's "The Women Tell All" special featured a sit-down reunion with the women who did not receive roses.

In Episode 8, Andrew visited Utah with Kirsten, where they bobsledded, took a carriage ride, and ultimately spent the night together in the fantasy suite. Next, Andrew went to Scottsdale with Jen, where they went to a mud bath spa, kissed in the shower, and spent the night in the fantasy suite. Finally, Andrew and Tina P. went to Hawaii, and despite being afraid of getting hurt by him Tina spent the night in the fantasy suite as well. At the Rose Ceremony, Andrew presented a red rose to Jen and Kirsten.

In the Episode 9 finale, Andrew brought the final two women home to tour his family's California winery, where he told Kristen he had fallen in love with Jen, and presented Jen with the final red rose.

RATINGS: During the 2002–2003 season, *The Bachelor* drew in an average of 14.5 million viewers each week.

THE BACHELOR
(Season 4)

GENRE	Competition (Dating)
FIRST TELECAST	9/24/2003
LAST TELECAST	11/19/2003
NETWORK	ABC
AIR TIME	Wednesday, 9:00 p.m.
EPISODE STYLE	Story Arc
TALENT	Chris Harrison (Host)

CAST Bob Guiney (The Bachelor); Estella Gardinier (Winner); Kelly Jo Kuharski (Runner-up); Brooke Bradford; Lee-Ann Callebs; Christine; Shea Deeds; Mary Delgado; Jenny Hartgrove; Heather; Kristi Houston; Jennifer; Julie; Lanah; Lauren; Lindsay D.; Lindsay King; Antoinette Madonna; Misty; Meredith Phillips; Samantha; Shelly; Karin Smith; Stacey; Darla Whistler

PRODUCTION COMPANIES Next Entertainment; Telepictures Productions

CREATED BY Mike Fleiss

EXECUTIVE PRODUCER Mike Fleiss

CO-EXECUTIVE PRODUCERS Lisa Levenson; Kathy Wetherell; Jason A. Carbone; Scott Jeffress

Season 4 featured former *Bachelorette* runner-up Bob Guiney.

In Episode 1, Bob met the twenty-five women who would be competing for his attentions. During the first night's party, Bob shared his first kiss with Kelly Jo. Bob's mother, Nora, made a surprise appearance at the first Rose Ceremony, as Bob presented roses to Antoinette, Brooke, Estella, Jennifer, Jenny, Karin, Kelly Jo, Kristi, Lanah, Lindsay D., Lindsay K., Lee-Ann, Mary, Meredith, and Misty.

In Episode 2, Antoinette became very sick and was rushed to the hospital, where she worried she'd be at a disadvantage in the competition as a result. Bob went on his first group date with Brooke, Karin, Kelly Jo, and Meredith, enjoying time with them in San Francisco. On Bob's second group date, with Estella, Jennifer, Kristi, Lindsay D., and Misty, in Los Angeles, host Chris Harrison interrupted with the twist that it was an elimination date. Bob gave *white* roses to all of them except Lindsay D. For his third group date, Bob took Antoinette, Jenny, Lanah, Lee-Ann, Lindsay K., and Mary to Hollywood. At the Rose Ceremony, he presented a red rose to Antoinette, Brooke, Estella, Jenny, Karin, Kelly Jo, Lee-Ann, Mary, Meredith, and Misty.

In Episode 3, the remaining women voted for which woman they thought was most compatible with Bob, and the first one-on-one dates were chosen based on their responses. Meredith got the first one-on-one, and she and Bob rode horses on the beach. They kissed, but it was a bittersweet occasion for her, as her grandmother had just passed away. Mary, Kelly Jo, and Misty went on a group date to sing karaoke in their pajamas. Bob kissed Kelly Jo, but admitted to liking all three of them.

In Episode 4, Lee-Ann got the second one-on-one with Bob. They kissed on the *Queen Mary,* and Lee-Ann said she felt confident she'd get a rose. Estella, Karin, Jenny, Brooke, and Antoinette went on the second group date with Bob to an amusement water park, where Estella seemed to capture Bob's fancy. At the Rose Ceremony, Bob presented a red rose to Brooke, Estella, Kelly Jo, Lee-Ann, Mary, and Meredith.

In Episode 5, Bob's friends Greg, Katina, and Jamie moved into the house to decide whom would get the next three private dates with Bob. Mary was their first choice, and she and Bob went to a San Francisco Bay area amusement park. They kissed several times, and Mary admitted that she loved him. Estella and Bob traveled to Las Vegas for his second private date. She confessed she was falling for him, and he seemed excited to be with her. Kelly Jo got the third private date, to a bachelor pad, where they kissed in a hot tub. She also admitted she was falling for him. Brooke, Lee-Ann, and Meredith went on a group hot-air-balloon ride, where Bob said he liked all of them. At the Rose Ceremony, Bob presented roses to Estella, Kelly Jo, Mary, and Meredith.

In Episode 6, each of the remaining women took Bob home to meet her family and friends. Mary brought Bob to Tampa, and admitted she was in love with him, but he was less sure. In Wheaton, Illinois, Kelly Jo admitted it would break her heart if she didn't get a rose. Bob accompanied Meredith to her grandmother's grave in Portland, Oregon, and decided he loved her family. Finally, Estella brought Bob to Beverly Hills, where he impressed her mother by saying he wanted someone with a big heart. At the Rose Ceremony, he gave roses to Estella, Kelly Jo, and Mary.

In Episode 7, Bob went on dream dates with the final three. He escorted Kelly Jo to Anchorage, Alaska, where they rode a dogsled and spent the night in the fantasy suite. He and Mary went to Jackson Hole for a kayak adventure and massage. Their date also ended at the fantasy suite, but it was unclear if Mary spent the night. Then Estella and Bob traveled to Belize for a snorkeling adventure. Bob admitted he'd been thinking only of Estella all day, but as they went back to the fantasy suite, he had second thoughts about spending the night with her. At the Rose Ceremony, Bob presented roses to Estella and Kelly Jo.

Episode 8 was "The Women Tell All" episode, featuring the women who did not receive roses.

In Episode 9, Bob brought both women back to Long Lake, Michigan, to meet his family. Estella fell in love with his family, and told him to follow his heart. Kelly Jo impressed Bob, but his family wasn't sold on her. After a final date with each woman, Bob presented Estella with the final red rose. He gave her a ring, but it was not an engagement ring, since he didn't feel he was ready for the commitment.

During an hour-long "After the Rose" special, Estella and Bob made their first public appearance, and runner-up Kelly Jo confronted Bob in person with her feelings.

THE BACHELOR
(Season 5)

GENRE	Competition (Dating)
FIRST TELECAST	4/7/2004
LAST TELECAST	5/19/2004
NETWORK	ABC
AIR TIME	Wednesday, 9:00 p.m.
EPISODE STYLE	Story Arc
TALENT	Chris Harrison (Host)
CAST	Jesse Palmer (The Bachelor); Jessica Bowlin (Winner); Tara Huckeby (Runner-up); Amanda; Amber; Andrea; Anne-Catherine; Celeste; Debbie; DeShaun; Dolores; Francine; Jessica Holcomb; Holly; Jessica K; Jean Marie; Jenny M; Mandy Jeffreys; Julie; Katie; Kristin; Karen Lindsay; Kristin N; Mandy C; Rachel; Jenny Schiralli; Trish Schneider; Suzie Williams
PRODUCTION COMPANIES	Next Entertainment; Telepictures Productions
CREATED BY	Mike Fleiss
EXECUTIVE PRODUCER	Mike Fleiss
CO-EXECUTIVE PRODUCERS	Lisa Levenson; Kathy Wetherell; Jason A. Carbone; Scott Jeffress

Season 5 featured NFL New York Giants quarterback Jesse Palmer as the Bachelor.

In a special two-hour Episode 1, a new twist was revealed. One of Jesse's twenty-five bachelorettes was actually the wife of Jesse's best friend, who was acting as a spy and reporting back to Jesse. After meeting the women, Jesse had the opportunity to immediately give one rose to the woman who made the best first impression, and that was Trish. During the Rose Ceremony, Jesse accidentally presented a red rose to Katie when he really meant to give it to Karen. Chris allowed him to let Katie keep the rose and give a sixteenth rose to Karen. The other rose recipients were Amber, Anne-Catherine, Celeste, Jean Marie, Jess, Jessica B., Julie, Kristy, Mandy C., Mandy J, Jenny S., Suzie, and Tara.

In Episode 2, Jesse went sledding in Lake Tahoe on his first group date, with Celeste, Jessica B., Julie, Karen, Katie, Mandy J., and Tara. Of the seven, Jesse seemed most interested in Mandy J. Later, he went on a one-on-one dinner and opera date with first-impression rose recipient Trish. He was taken by her honesty, and the two shared a kiss. Jesse then went on his second group date, with Amber, Ann-Catherine, Jean Marie, Jenny S., Jesse, Kristi, Mandy C., and Suzie, where he foolishly revealed he used to "play the field." Viewers learned that Jenny S. was the spy. She warned Jesse that Trish was high maintenance, suggesting he go for Tara instead. Before the Rose Ceremony, Kristin told Jesse he wasn't right for her, which he appreciated because he had been planning to give her a rose. Instead, he presented roses to Jenny S., Jesse, Jessica B., Julie, Karen, Katie, Mandy J., Suzie, Tara, and Trish.

In Episode 3, the women took compatibility tests, and Suzie and Tara were selected for solo dates. After Jesse's dinner and movie date with Suzie, they kissed during the entire limo ride home. On Jesse's second solo date, with Tara, they went out for dinner and dancing, after which he kissed her and said he wanted to see her again. On Jesse's two-on-one pub and massage date with Mandy J. and Trish, he kissed both of them, but his affections for Mandy J. were stronger. On Jesse's group date with Jenny S., Jesse, Jessica B., Julie, Katie, and Karen, he and the women joined Habitat for Humanity to help build houses. Jenny S. informed Jesse that Trish had once slept with a married man. Jessica B. admitted that she was falling for Jesse, and the female Jesse came on too strong for the Bachelor's tastes. At the Rose Ceremony, Jesse decided to eliminate Jenny the spy, and he presented red roses to Jessica B., Karen, Mandy J., Suzie, Tara, and Trish.

In Episode 4, Jenny S. confessed to the girls that she had been a spy, and she selected Jessica B., Mandy J., and Tara to go on the next round of one-on-one dates. Jesse's picnic date with Jessica B. ended with their kissing at the Rose Bowl. His one-on-one cruise date with Mandy J. ended with their sharing a hot tub and kissing at sunset. On Tara's date, she became nervous and pulled away from a kiss. Jesse's elephant ride group date with Karen, Suzie, and Trish ended with Jesse kissing all three women. At the Rose Ceremony, Jesse presented a red rose to Jessica B., Mandy J., Tara, and Trish.

In Episode 5, each remaining woman took Jesse home to meet her family and friends. Jessica B. brought Bob to Huntington Beach, California, and she admitted she was falling for him, but her mother had reservations. Jesse went to Andrews, Texas, to see Mandy J., but to his disappointment, he didn't connect well with her family. Tara brought Jesse to Paul's Valley, Oklahoma, where he was nervous around her gun-toting father. Jesse also discovered that Tara had some emotional baggage. Bob went to Atlanta to see Trish, where he confronted her about her bad reputation. At the Rose Ceremony, he presented red roses to Jessica B., Mandy J., and Tara.

In Episode 6 "The Women Tell All" special, the women who didn't receive roses spilled their guts about Jesse and about what had gone on in the house.

In Episode 7, Jesse and the final three went on fantasy dates. While in Quebec City with Tara, they both admitted they were falling for each other, and wound up in the fantasy suite. On his trip with Jessica B. to the Bahamas, Jesse confessed to falling in love with her, as well as with someone else. Jessica overcame this enough to spend the night with him in the fantasy suite. In Washington, D.C., with Mandy J., the ousted Trish crashed the date and gave Jesse her room key. He declined the offer and spent the night with Mandy J., in the fantasy suite. At the Rose Ceremony, Jesse gave his final two roses to Jessica B. and Tara.

In Episode 8, two finalists visited Jesse's hometown of Indianapolis, Indiana. After shopping for engagement rings with both of them, Jesse made the decision to present his rose to Jessica, but he confessed he wasn't ready for marriage.

RATINGS: The 2003–2004 season of *The Bachelor* drew an average of 12.5 million viewers.

THE BACHELOR
(Season 6)

GENRE	Competition (Dating)
FIRST TELECAST	9/22/2004
LAST TELECAST	11/24/2004
NETWORK	ABC
AIR TIME	Wednesday, 9:00 p.m.
EPISODE STYLE	Story Arc
TALENT	Chris Harrison (Host)
CAST	Byron Velvick (The Bachelor); Jay Overbye (Runner-up); Mary Delgado (Winner); Tanya Michel (Runner-up) Abby; Alma; Amanda; Amy; Andrea; Ashley; Carolyn; Cheresse; Cynthia; Elizabeth; Heather; Jayne; Jennifer; Kelly; Kerry; Kristie; Kristin; Krysta; Leina; Lisa; Melinda; Natalie; Nicole; Susie; Wende
PRODUCTION COMPANIES	Next Entertainment; Telepictures Productions
CREATED BY	Mike Fleiss
EXECUTIVE PRODUCER	Mike Fleiss
CO-EXECUTIVE PRODUCERS	Lisa Levenson; Kathy Wetherell; Jason A. Carbone; Scott Jeffress

In Season 6, there was yet another twist. This time, there were *two* Bachelors, and the ladies got to choose which one they wanted to stay for the duration.

In Episode 1, host Chris Harrison introduced potential Bachelors Byron and Jay to the ladies' surprise. Everyone mingled, then there was a *women's* Rose Ceremony, during which the ladies decided to keep professional bass fisherman Byron, by a vote of eighteen to seven. Andrea had already fallen for Byron, and Krysta warned the other women not to mess with her. At Byron's first Rose Ceremony, he presented roses to Amanda, Andrea, Ashley, Cheresse, Cindy, Elizabeth, Jayne, Kelly, Kristie, Krysta, Leina, Natalie, Susie, Tanya, and Wende.

In Episode 2, Byron moved into a bungalow on the same grounds as the bachelorettes' house, and brought his dog, Sabrina, with him. Byron invited Cheresse on the first solo date, where they were treated to a private performance by R&B artist Brandy. Their evening ended with a kiss on the cheek. Byron returned to find notes and flowers at his door from Kristie and Krysta. He invited Jayne on the second solo date, where they went fishing and seemed to hit it off, but only hugged each other goodnight. Back at the house, Leina decided to leave the competition. Byron invited Natalie, Jayne, and Kristie for last-chance talks. At the Rose Ceremony, Byron presented roses to Amanda, Andrea, Cheresse, Cynthia, Elizabeth, Jayne, Kristie, Krysta, Susie, and Tanya.

In Episode 3, Byron invited Amanda on a one-on-one date, where they flew over the city in a vintage bomber plane, and ended the evening with a kiss. Prior to the date, a concerned Jayne approached Byron at his bungalow, asking him about his feelings. He assured her that he liked her. Byron went on a mystery date, which turned out to be with Heather from Season 2 of *The Bachelor* and Mary from Season 4. Back at the mansion, he chose Susie, Heather, and Cheresse for last-chance talks. At the Rose Ceremony, Byron presented a red rose to Andrea, Cheresse, Cynthia, Elizabeth, Jayne, Krysta, Mary, and Tanya.

In Episode 4, Cindy went to Byron's bungalow to get to know him better. Later, Byron invited Tanya for a one-on-one date at Newport Beach. They went to dinner and kissed. The next day, Byron invited Mary for a one-on-one date: a massage session. Byron was interested, but Mary seemed noncommittal. Later, he invited Elizabeth on a one-on-one date to the Long Beach Aquarium, but they didn't seem to have much chemistry. A group slumber party ensued with Byron, which included a game of "Truth or Dare." Mary worried Byron would disappoint her as Bob had in Season 4, so he took her outside to reassure her. Later, Jayne blocked Krysta's attempt to see Byron after hours. At the Rose Ceremony, Byron presented roses to Andrea, Cheresse, Cindy, Jayne, Mary, and Tanya.

In Episode 5, Byron had separate talks with Cheresse and Cindy, which led to kissing with both. Byron invited Mary for a one-on-one dinner date, which ended with a hot tub session and kissing. Next, Byron invited Jayne for a private sunset horseback ride, capped off with kissing. Jayne later told Byron she was having trouble living with the women, but he said it wasn't fair to let her stay over. Byron picked Tanya, Cindy, and Jayne for last-minute talks. At the Rose Ceremony, Byron gave roses to Cheresse, Cindy, Mary, and Tanya.

In Episode 6, Byron took the final four women on overnight fantasy dates. Mary and Byron went to Whistler Mountain in British Columbia, where she joined him in the fantasy suite. Byron took Tanya to Vancouver, and she confessed to voting for the Bachelor runner-up Jay. Tanya also joined Byron in the fantasy suite. Byron and Cheresse traveled to San Francisco, where she didn't join him in the fantasy suite. He promised not to hold it against her. Finally, he took Cindy to Sonoma, where she worried he wasn't over his ex-wife; nonetheless she joined him in the fantasy suite. At the Rose Ceremony, he presented a red rose to Cindy, Mary, and Tanya.

In Episode 7, each of the remaining women took Byron home to meet her family and friends. Tanya brought him to Plano, Texas, where he sidestepped personal questions from her friends. Also, Tanya and Byron kissed, but didn't really seem to connect. Byron went to Tampa to see Mary, where she said she was worried about getting hurt again. Cindy brought Byron to Hermosa Beach, California, where she said she had strong feelings for him; he was less committed. Finally, Byron had last-chance talks with all three women. At the Rose Ceremony, he presented a red rose to Mary and Tanya.

In Episode 8, Byron faced the women he rejected, where he discovered that Cindy was still upset over not getting picked. Bachelor runner-up Jay returned to find out which women had voted for him.

In Episode 9, Tanya's parents and Mary's mother came to the mansion, where Byron made a good impression on all of them. Next Tanya and Mary each visited Byron's home in Lake Mead, Nevada. Byron presented his final rose to Mary. He proposed marriage, and she accepted.

A special, live "After the Rose" episode aired immediately after the finale. Byron and Mary talked about their experience on *The Bachelor,* and Tanya confronted Byron.

THE BACHELOR
(Season 7)

GENRE	Competition (Dating)
FIRST TELECAST	3/28/2005
LAST TELECAST	5/16/2005
NETWORK	ABC
AIR TIME	Monday, 8:00 p.m.

EPISODE STYLE	Story Arc
TALENT	Chris Harrison (Host)
CAST	Charlie O'Connell (The Bachelor); Sarah B. (Winner); Krisily (Runner-up); Anitra; Brenda; Carrie; Danushka; Debby; Emlile; Geitan; Gina-Marie; Heather; Jenny; Kara; Katie; Kerry; Kimberley; Kindle; Krisily; Kristen; Kristina; Kristine; Kyshawn; Megan; Sarah W.; Siomara; Valerie
PRODUCTION COMPANIES	Next Entertainment; Telepictures Productions
CREATED BY	Mike Fleiss
EXECUTIVE PRODUCER	Mike Fleiss
CO-EXECUTIVE PRODUCERS	Lisa Levenson; Kathy Wetherell; Jason A. Carbone; Scott Jeffress

"Expect the unexpected" was the theme for Season 7. The Bachelor was actor Charlie O'Connell, the brother of actor Jerry O'Connell.

In Episode 1, the women were given five minutes to get ready before meeting Charlie for the first time. Anitra showed up wearing only a towel. Each woman had two minutes to talk to Charlie, and he gave two first-impression red roses to Sarah W. and Kerry. Then he had to cut five women. He told Kristina, Brenda, Debbie, Katie, and Heather to leave. Charlie's first group date with five women took place at a dive bar, where Kindle and Anitra earned roses. Charlie's second group date, with eight women, was at a nightclub, and uninvited Gina Marie crashed the party. Geitan opted to preserve her dignity and quit. Charlie gave his first rose to Krisily. He opted not to give out the second rose. His third group date involved volleyball and rock climbing, where Kara revealed she was a single mom, and Jenny and Kimberly earned roses. At the Rose Ceremony, Geitan returned, claiming that her previous decision to leave had been too hasty. Host Chris Harrison allowed the women to speak up, and they lashed out at one another. Charlie presented the remaining roses to Carrie, Gina Marie, Kara, Megan, and Sarah B., leaving twelve women in the house.

Episode 2 featured two solo dates and one ten-woman group date. In a special twist, one of the solo dates would result in the bestowing of a rose, while the other would end in instant elimination. Charlie picked Megan for the first one-on-one date to a restaurant, and she decided to dye her hair blonde beforehand. Charlie had a bad time on the date, and didn't give her a rose. He picked Sarah W. for the second one-on-one date, to a brewery, where he enjoyed himself and gave her a rose. Sarah boldly threw the rose away, saying it wasn't about the rose, it was about making a connection. Later, Charlie gave another rose to single mom Kara, by the pool, and another to Kimberley. At the Rose Ceremony, he presented the remaining roses to Anitra, Jenny, Kindle, Krisily, and Sarah B., leaving eight women in the house.

In Episode 3, Kimberley and Kara earned solo dates, while the rest settled on joining a group date. Charlie took Kimberley to an art gallery, and they ended up making out back at his place, where he gave her a rose. On the group date, Charlie took the women bowling. Later, he was too tired to take Kara out for the solo date that night, so they went ice-skating the next day, and Charlie cited his concerns about her being a single mom as his reason for not giving her a rose. At the Rose Ceremony, host Chris Harrison let the girls speak up again. Charlie presented his remaining roses to Anitra, Kindle, Krisily, Sarah B., and Sarah W.

In Episode 4, Charlie picked Sarah B. for a horseback-riding solo date, and after a post-ride conversation, he gave her a rose. On the group date, he took the women fencing, and Anitra earned a solo date for her fencing prowess. At dinner, they found that they had a lot of differences, and Charlie had too much to drink. He showed up at the women's house the next morning for a surprise Rose Ceremony, where he presented his remaining roses to Kimberley, Sarah W., and Krisily.

In Episode 5, each remaining woman took Charlie home to meet her family and friends. Sarah B. brought him to McKinney, Texas, where she privately told her sister she was strategically playing hard to get. Charlie went to Edmonton to see Kimberley, where they were ambushed by the ousted Jenny, and Kimberley's ex, each looking to reconcile. Sarah W. brought him to Corning, New York, where she had to explain why all the other women hated her. Finally, Charlie went to Providence to see Krisily, where he bonded with her family. At the Rose Ceremony, Charlie presented roses to Sarah B., Sarah W., and Krisily.

In Episode 6, Charlie went on a romantic getaway to Aruba with each of the three finalists. On his trip with Sarah W., she disrobed, and they kissed in the ocean. Charlie kissed Sarah B. for the first time, and they went back to the fantasy suite, but she didn't want to spend the night. His vacation with Krisily was the most romantic date of the three, and she eventually decided to stay at the fantasy suite. At the Rose Ceremony, Charlie presented roses to Krisily and Sarah B., after some confusion about *which* Sarah he'd selected.

In the Episode 7 "The Women Tell All" show, the contestants who were no longer in the running dished about the show.

In Episode 8's two-hour finale, Charlie met Krisily's and Sarah B.'s parents. Then host Chris Harrison announced a twist—after Charlie had one final date with each woman, he'd continue to date them in real life up until the live "After the Rose" special aired.

The live "After the Rose" special aired immediately after the finale. Charlie talked about all the dates and trips he had taken with Krisily and Sarah B. since the series ended. After a suspenseful buildup, he fought back tears as he gave his final rose to Sarah B.

RATINGS: In the 2004–2005 season, *The Bachelor* had an average viewership of 8.5 million.

THE BACHELOR: PARIS
(Season 8)

GENRE	Competition (Dating)
FIRST TELECAST	1/9/2006
LAST TELECAST	2/27/2006
NETWORK	ABC
AIR TIME	Mondays, 10:00 p.m.
EPISODE STYLE	Story Arc
TALENT	Chris Harrison (Host)
CAST	Travis Stork (Bachelor); Sarah S. (Winner); Moana (Runner-up); Ali D; Allie G; April; Cole; Cortney; Elizabeth; Jaime; Jehan; Jennifer; Kathy; Kristin; Kyle; Lisa; Liza; Princess; Sara H; Sarah B; Shiloh; Stephanie; Susan; Tara; Venus; Yvonne

PRODUCTION COMPANIES	Next Entertainment; Telepictures Productions
CREATED BY	Mike Fleiss
EXECUTIVE PRODUCERS	Mike Fleiss; Lisa Levenson; David Bohnert
CO-EXECUTIVE PRODUCERS	Ross Breitenbach; Tracey Finley; Donny Jackson; Sam Korkis; Tiffany McLinn Lore; Alycia Rossiter; Kerry Schmidt-Hardy; Nelson Soler; Monica Stock

Season 8 was set in one of the most romantic cities in the world—Paris. Once again, twenty-five women competed for the attention of this season's Bachelor, emergency room doctor Travis Stork.

In Episode 1, Travis was anxious to meet and mingle with the twenty-five women. He got a head start on the Rose Ceremony because during the party, he was able to give one rose to a woman he wanted to stay. The single rose made the other women nervous, as they competed for his attention. Travis was struck by excited Sarah B.'s cuteness, and she was the lucky recipient of the first rose. At the Rose Ceremony, Travis said he was the luckiest guy in the world, then gave roses to Cole, Moana, Jennifer, Elizabeth, Shiloh, Yvonne, Jehan, Susan, Tara Sarah S., and Kristen.

In Episode 2, host Chris Harrison informed the women there would be two group dates and one individual date, and on each date there would be a rose available. Kristen earned the first one-on-one date because she had received the final rose in the last Rose Ceremony. Harrison explained that if a woman didn't receive a rose during an individual date, she would be eliminated from the competition. During a double-decker bus tour around Paris with Jehan, Cole, Elizabeth, Yvonne, and Sarah S., Jehan was the lucky recipient of a rose. Back in the bachelorette pad, Jennifer found Kristen's date box, which informed her she'd join Travis on a Seine river cruise. Kristen was not given a rose on her date, though. Meanwhile, for the second group date, Jennifer, Moana, Susan, Tara, Shiloh, and Sarah B. went to Champagne country, and Tara received the rose. At the Rose Ceremony, Travis gave red roses to Moana, Sarah S., Jennifer, Sarah B., Shiloh, and Susan.

In Episode 3, Travis's fellow doctor friends Matt and Kevin flew to Paris to interview the final eight. The guys quizzed the women and asked them to showcase their talents. Susan won the solo date, getting an envelope to open with Travis. Matt and Kevin had written a note that read, "Nothing tests a relationship like finding your way through a foreign country." Travis and Susan had to find their way from the women's country manor to the Café de la Paix in Paris. There, Travis offered Susan a rose and a kiss. Back at the manor, Tara, Sarah S., Moana, Jehan, and Shiloh learned they'd fly to the French Riviera for an overnight group date on a yacht. Travis gave Moana the next rose. Then Sarah B. and Jennifer went camping with the Bachelor. Travis complimented Sarah B. on her beauty, and they kissed by the fire. She earned a rose, while Jennifer did not. At the Rose Ceremony, Susan, Sarah B., and Moana were already safe, and Jehan, Tara, and Sarah S. got the remaining roses.

In Episode 4, host Chris Harrison told the women there would be two one-on-one dates and one group date. Jehan got the first date box, which clued her in that she'd go on an Eiffel Tower picnic date with Travis. She informed Travis that she had been previously married, and didn't get a rose on her date, but returned to the house anyway. Next, Sarah B., Tara, Susan, and Moana were invited on a bike ride through the French countryside. There was no rose on the group date, but Moana won a bicycle race, earning a couples massage at a spa. Later that night, Sarah S. and Travis went on a date to the arts district, where she was given a rose. Sarah S. was the only woman safe at the Rose Ceremony, where Sarah B., Susan, and Moana earned the other flowers.

In Episode 5, Travis and the four women returned to North America to visit the women's hometowns. First, Travis saw Moana in San Clemente, California, where her family questioned his motives. Next, he flew to Winnepeg, Canada, to visit Sarah B., who introduced him to her welcoming family. Travis returned home to Nashville to see Sarah S. and her family, whom he invited to his home for dinner. Finally, he went to Durham, North Carolina, where Susan brought Travis home to meet her parents. Susan's mother was skeptical because her daughter had recently gotten out of an engagement. Travis returned to Paris, where he watched video messages from the final hour. At the Rose Cermony, Travis kept Susan, Moana, and Sarah S.

In Episode 6, Travis went on three exotic overnight dates. First, he met Moana in Venice, where they were attacked by playful pigeons in the famous Piazza San Marco. In Vienna, Travis gave Sarah the fantasy suite key, where they shared dinner and, finally, a kiss. Susan and Travis traveled to the French Alps, where they enjoyed a fondue dinner and a kissing session in a hot tub. Travis returned to Paris to watch three video messages. At the Rose Ceremony, Moana and Sarah S. got the final two roses.

In the Episode 7 finale, Travis enlisted the help of his family, who traveled to Paris to meet Moana and Sarah S. They were amazed to learn that Sarah S. and Travis lived less than one mile apart in Nashville. The family commented that they connected less with Moana. Then the girls' mothers arrived in Paris for a surprise shopping trip, where both picked out the same ring. Travis had his final date with Sarah, where they played tennis and shared a takeout dinner. Moana cooked a meal during her date with Travis. Before the final Rose Ceremony, Travis picked up the diamond rings chosen by the women. He met with Sarah first, and told her she was beautiful, smart, honest, and that she made him happy. After a fakeout, making her think she'd lost he kissed her and gave her the final rose, plus the diamond ring on a necklace.

THE BACHELOR: ROME
(Season 9)

GENRE	Competition (Dating)
FIRST TELECAST	10/3/2006
LAST TELECAST	11/27/2006
NETWORK	ABC
AIR TIME	Mondays, 10:00 p.m.
EPISODE STYLE	Story Arc
TALENT	Chris Harrison (Host)
CAST	Prince Lorenzo Borghese (Bachelor); Jennifer (Winner); Sadie (Runner-up); Agnese; April; Andrea; Carissa; Claudia; Cosetta; Ellen; Elyse; Erica; Gina; Heather; Jami; Jeanette; Jessica; Kim; Laura; Lisa; Meri; Renee; Rita; Rosella; Sarah; Tara
PRODUCTION COMPANIES	Next Entertainment; Telepictures Productions
CREATED BY	Mike Fleiss
EXECUTIVE PRODUCERS	Mike Fleiss; Lisa Levenson; David Bohnert
CO-EXECUTIVE PRODUCERS	Ross Breitenbach; Tracey Finley; Donny Jackson; Sam Korkis; Tiffany McLinn Lore; Alycia Rossiter; Kerry Schmidt-Hardy; Nelson Soler; Monica Stock

Season 9 was set in Rome, and starred Prince Lorenzo Borghese, a cosmetics entrepreneur. Once again, twenty-five women were competing for his love.

In Episode 1, the bachelorettes were surprised at home, where they were told they'd leave for Italy in less than twenty-four hours. At the opening party, Lorenzo had a tough time juggling twenty-five women at once. Host Chris Harrison then introduced two more bachelorettes—Agnese and Cosetta—local Italian women. Lorenzo gave his first-impression rose and a pair of earrings to Lisa. At a sunrise Rose Ceremony, Lorenzo sent fifteen women home, and gave out eleven roses, to Kim, Jeanette, Jami, Ellen, Sarah, Desiree, Jennifer, Gina, Erica, Sadie, and Agnese.

In Episode 2, the twelve remaining women split up to go on group dates with Lorenzo. At the Coliseum, Agnese taught Lorenzo how to say "kiss" in Italian. Then he and the others on the group date—Erica, Sadie, Ellen, and Jami—toured Rome on Vespas. Lorenzo gave the women beautiful party dresses, and later he got to know Sadie better, and presented her with a rose. The next day, Kim, Jeanette, Sarah, Desiree, Jennifer, and Gina traveled to a villa on the Mediterranean. Jennifer earned a rose, although Lorenzo told Gina she was one of his favorites. After a few cocktails, the group played bikini football on the beach. At the Rose Ceremony Lorenzo gave roses to Jeanette, Desiree, Jami, Gina, Agnese, and Erica.

Episode 3 featured a group date, a two-on-one date, and a solo date. The women performed an opera aria in Italian, and a singing instructor picked Jami to join Lorenzo for a glamorous opera date. She didn't get a rose because Lorenzo thought of her more as a friend. Next, Sadie, Desiree, Jeannette, Erica, Jennifer, Lisa, and Gina went on a group date to Tuscany, where Lorenzo gave a single rose to Jeannette. For his two-on-one date, Lorenzo had Erica and Agnese over for pizza. He told Erica he thought she wasn't being herself, so Agnese got the rose. At the Rose Ceremony, Sadie, Lisa, Jennifer, and Desiree earned roses.

Episode 4 featured one group date and two one-on-one dates, and those who received roses would also get hometown visits from Lorenzo to meet their families. Each woman was asked two questions: Who was the least deserving of becoming a princess? Who was the most insincere girl in the house? Previously eliminated bachelorette Erica was the surprise judge, and she chose Sadie for the first one-on-one date—a day of pampering. Sadie gave Lorenzo a San Diego Chargers jersey, a gift from her hometown, and he gave Sadie a rose. Desiree, Agnese, Jeanette, and Lisa dressed in togas for the group date, where Jeanette won a chariot race. Next, Lorenzo took Jennifer on the other private date, and she also received a rose. At the Rose Ceremony, Lisa and Agenese received the other two roses.

In Episode 5, Lorenzo visited Sadie in San Diego, where he met her close-knit family. Next, in Portland, Lorenzo and Lisa playfully painted an Italian fresco on her wall. In Miami, Lorenzo met Jennifer's family, and he was shocked when her father showed him his rifle. Finally, Lorenzo went to Venice to see Agnese's family. At the next Rose Ceremony, Sadie, Jennifer, and Lisa got flowers from Lorenzo.

Episode 6 featured three exotic overnight dates. In Gothenburg, Sweden, Lorenzo and Jennifer rode a roller-coaster at an amusement park, visited an ice bar, then spent the night in the fantasy suite. Then, Lisa and Lorenzo traveled to Budapest, where they went wine-tasting and listened to local music. Without even opening the envelope, Lisa agreed to spend the night in the fantasy suite with Lorenzo. In Sicily, Sadie and Lorenzo went scuba diving. Conservative Sadie told Lorenzo that spending the night in the fantasy suite would be a big deal, but she took the risk and stayed overnight with him. Back in Rome, at the Rose Ceremony, Lorenzo gave roses to Sadie and Jen.

In the Episode 7 finale, Lorenzo's parents, who had been married for forty years, met the final two bachelorettes. Jen was nervous to meet Princess Amanda and Prince Francesco, but she warmed up to them, telling them she pictured Lorenzo as her future husband. Sadie told his parents she loved Lorenzo's many facets. In an attempt to help Lorenzo make a decision, Amanda secretly arranged for both sets of parents to come to Rome, but this made for an awkward situation, for which he apologized to both women. Later, Lorenzo asked both girls' dads for their blessing. On their final date, Sadie and Lorenzo went sailing, and they saw a rainbow, prompting them to kiss. The next day, Jen and Lorenzo went horseback riding and had dinner at a private house. A thunderstorm struck, which Lorenzo felt was symbolic. Both women revealed they'd spend the rest of their lives with Lorenzo, but at the final Rose Ceremony, he gave Jennifer a rose and a ring, saying he could picture her as his wife. She said she'd fallen in love with him, and she was eager to move to New York City.

THE BACHELOR:
AN OFFICER AND A GENTLEMAN
(Season 10)

GENRE	Competition (Dating)
FIRST TELECAST	4/2/2007
LAST TELECAST	5/22/2007
NETWORK	ABC
AIR TIME	Mondays, 10:00 p.m.
EPISODE STYLE	Story Arc
TALENT	Chris Harrison (Host)
CAST	Andy Baldwin (Bachelor); Tessa (Winner); Bevin (Runner-up); Alexis; Amanda; Amber; Blakeny; Candace; Catherine; Danielle I.; Danielle V.; Erin; Jackie; Jeanette; Jessica; Kate; Linda; Lindsay; Nicole; Peyton; Stephanie T.; Stephanie W.; Susan; Tiffany F.; Tiffany W.; Tina
PRODUCTION COMPANIES	Next Entertainment; Telepictures Productions
CREATED BY	Mike Fleiss
EXECUTIVE PRODUCERS	Mike Fleiss; Lisa Levenson; David Bohnert
CO-EXECUTIVE PRODUCERS	Ross Breitenbach; Tracey Finley; Donny Jackson; Sam Korkis; Tiffany McLinn Lore; Alycia Rossiter; Kerry Schmidt-Hardy; Nelson Soler; Monica Stock

Season 10 featured twenty-five bachelorettes competing for the love of naval officer Andy Baldwin.

In Episode 1, Andy met the single women at a party on his thirtieth birthday. Andy said Stephanie T.'s smile and energy had earned her the first-impression rose. Blakeney and Lindsay showed their jealousy over Stephanie T.'s rose, while Peyton discovered that she and Andy shared the same birthday. At the Rose Ceremony, Andy sent home ten women, and gave out fourteen more roses. The recipients were Peyton,

Bevin, Kate, Alexis, Danielle I., Amber, Tiffany W., Tessa, Nicole, Susan, Amanda, Erin, Tina and Stephanie W. Eliminated Lindsay left the ceremony without saying goodbye, claiming that she was being sent home because she didn't have blonde hair and fake boobs. Then she bad-mouthed Andy, saying "he's short and his head is big and his teeth look fake," and called the show "fake and stupid." Meanwhile, inside, Andy and the bachelorettes toasted to the adventure ahead.

Episode 2 featured two group dates and one individual date. Since Stephanie got the first rose, she won the first individual date. After dinner on a yacht, Andy offered her a rose to stay in the competition, and she accepted it with a kiss. On the first group date, Nicole, Tiffany, Alexis, Stephanie from Kansas, Bevin, Amanda, and Tessa rode the mechanical bull at the Saddle Ranch Chop House. Then each woman chose an evening gown to wear to dinner with Andy, which was followed by a hot tub session. Andy picked Tiffany to spend more time with him after the group date. Then Kate, Susan, Erin, Tina, Amber, Danielle, and Peyton went to a hotel on the beach in Santa Monica for a mini triathlon, which Amber won, earning time alone with Andy. At the Rose Ceremony, Tessa, Danielle, Bevin, Amber, Stephanie, Kate, Nicole, Tina, Peyton, Amanda, and Erin each received a rose, while Alexis, Susan, and Tiffany were sent home.

In Episode 3, the women were woken up by a drill sergeant and attended bachelorette boot camp. Bevin was a model soldier, until she injured her ankle during the tire obstacle course. Andy diagnosed a displaced fracture, and surprised her with a rose. She later returned to the house on crutches. Both Stephanies, Nicole, Amber, and Tina went on the first group date, to Glen Ivy Hot Springs Spa. For the second group date, Kate, Danielle, Erin, and Amanda drove race cars. Tessa and Peyton received a two-on-one date in San Diego, at the USS *Midway* naval aircraft carrier, where they had a candlelit dinner. Tessa received a rose from Andy, and Peyton was sent home. At the Rose Ceremony, Andy gave roses to Amber, Danielle, Stephanie from Kansas, Tina, Kate, Nicole, and Stephanie from South Carolina, while Amanda and Erin were sent home.

Episode 4 featured two group dates and an individual date, and everyone flew on a private jet to Lake Tahoe. Nicole, Danielle, Stephanie from Kansas, and Bevin went on a casino group date, and Andy chose Bevin to spend more time with him. At the hotel suite, Tessa, Kate, Tina, and Stephanie from South Carolina found out they'd be playing in the snow with Andy during their date. While on the slopes, Kate joined

Andy on a gondola. Later, he picked Tina to spend more time with him after skiing. During his solo date with Amber, they kissed in the hot tub, and he gave her a rose. At the Rose Ceremony, Andy gave flowers to Tessa, Danielle, Bevin, Tina, and Stephanie from Kansas, while Kate, Stephanie from South Carolina, and Nicole were sent home.

In Episode 5, there was one group date and two individual dates where no roses would be given out. During lunch on his yacht, Andy divided his time among brunettes Tina, Amber, and Tessa, and blondes Bevin, Danielle, and Stephanie. On the first individual date, Andy and Stephanie learned about wines. Then Andy, Amber, Bevin, Tina, and Danielle built a playground for charity. Before their solo date, Andy gave Tessa a Chopard diamond necklace and earrings, and took her shopping for a dress. At the Rose Ceremony, Andy gave flowers to Bevin, Amber, Tessa, and Danielle, while Stephanie and Tina were sent home.

In Episode 6, Andy visited the final four girls' hometowns. In Seattle, Bevin admitted that she was once married, and he thanked her for her honesty, but secretly admitted that it bothered him. Later he met her family and kissed her goodbye. In Bethel, Connecticut, he met Danielle's family, and she told him she thought it was fate that they meet. She also kissed him goodbye, and admitted after her college boyfriend passed away, she'd thought she'd never fall in love again—until she met Andy. In Washington, D.C., Tessa introduced Andy to her family and best friend, who grilled him with so many questions, he stepped away from the dinner table to do the dishes. In Sugar Land, Texas, Andy met Amber at the grade school where she teaches. She admitted that her relationship with her parents was rocky, so her aunt made a surprise visit to meet Andy. At the Rose Ceremony, Andy gave roses to Tessa, Bevin, and Danielle, and Amber was sent home.

In Episode 7, the final three women visited Andy in Hawaii, where he took each one to the Pearl Harbor Memorial. Andy met Tessa in Kauai, for a zip-line ride and some relaxing moments in a hammock. They spent the night in the romantic fantasy suite. Then, Andy and Danielle went on a catamaran ride, which was followed by a psychic reading. They also spent the night in the fantasy suite. During an adventurous date with Bevin, they kayaked, hiked, jumped off a waterfall, and enjoyed a private luau. In the fantasy suite, she fed him strawberries with whipped cream, and they slow-danced. Andy's best friend, Gatsby, flew to Kauai to help Andy choose his final two, which turned out to be Bevin and Tessa.

In the Episode 8 finale, Andy returned to his hometown, Lancaster, Pennsylvania, where his family met the final two bachelorettes. His mother was mesmerized by the beauty of Tessa, who felt at home with her and the rest of the family. Andy told his parents that Bevin had overcome many obstacles, and his mother said that Andy seemed more connected to her. Back in Hawaii, Andy took Bevin on a helicopter ride. Later, she cooked him dinner and gave him a card that said she wanted to spend her life with him. For his last date with Tessa, they rode horses on the beach and swam at sunset. They ate dinner, and he read a note she'd written that said she believed they were meant to be together. Bevin arrived first at the final Rose Ceremony, where Andy told her she wasn't the one. She cried, and told him she'd never forget him. Tessa arrived, and Andy got down on one knee and asked her to marry him. She accepted his proposal, and he offered her the final red rose.

The next night, *The Bachelor: After the Final Rose* special aired, and Andy and Tessa were interviewed, as were Danielle, Amber, and Stephanie T.

THE BACHELORETTE
(Season 1)

GENRE	Competition (Dating)
FIRST TELECAST	1/8/2003
LAST TELECAST	2/19/2003
NETWORK	ABC
AIR TIME	Wednesday, 9:00 p.m.
EPISODE STYLE	Story Arc
TALENT	Chris Harrison (Host)
CAST	Trista Rehn (Bachelorette); Ryan Sutter (Winner); Charlie Maher (Runner-up); Jamie Blyth; Brian Ching; Peter Dizdar; Duane; Eric; Rob Fayard; Jack French; Bob Guiney; Greg H.; Brian Hrouda; Brian K.; Matt; Michael; Paul; Brook Pemberton; Jeff Popovich; Josh; Brian Sander; Greg Todtman; Chris Tunnessen; Wayne; Russell Woods
PRODUCTION COMPANIES	Next Entertainment; Telepictures Productions

CREATED BY	Mike Fleiss
EXECUTIVE PRODUCER	Mike Fleiss
CO-EXECUTIVE PRODUCERS	Jason A. Carbone; Daniel Goldberg; Scott Jeffress; Lisa Levenson; Clay Newbill; Sally Ann Salsano

This spinoff of *The Bachelor* featured the runner-up contestant from season one, Trista Rehn, looking for true love among twenty-five male suitors.

In Episode 1, viewers were reintroduced to Trista. She hosted a cocktail party for her twenty-five would-be mates, and presented roses to the fifteen men who would be advancing.

In Episode 2, the men separated into groups of five, and each group joined Trista on a shared date. The first group visited Las Vegas, where Russell hit it off best with Trista. The second group went to a day spa, where Trista and Ryan talked about marriage. The third group attended a San Diego Chargers game, where Greg and Charlie both got in some quality time. At the Rose Ceremony, Trista presented roses to Charlie, Bob, Greg T., Ryan, Michael, Rob, Jamie, and Russell.

In Episode 3, Trista's friends Missy, Sara, and Shannon devised a compatibility quiz for the guys. Trista went on three individual dates. She took a blimp ride with Russell, went to a water park and a salon with Charlie, and visited Sea World with Ryan. She took the rest of the guys to the racetrack and the beach. Ryan's poem was a big hit, and Trista rewarded him with a kiss. At the Rose Ceremony, Trista gave roses to Charlie, Russell, Ryan, and Greg T.

In Episode 4, each of the remaining guys took Trista home to meet his family and friends. Ryan brought her to Vail, where she slid down the pole at the fire station and they kissed at sunset. Greg took Trista to New York for a motorcycle ride through Central Park, dinner, and finally a visit to his apartment, where he sang to her. Trista went to San Francisco, to see Russell, where he introduced her to his family. In Flagstaff, Trista met Charlie's mother. The Rose Ceremony fell on Trista's thirtieth birthday. Ryan gave her another poem and an original painting. Greg performed a rap song and gave her the lyrics to all of the songs he'd sung to her. Russell gave her a photo he took of a sunset. Finally, Charlie gave her a silver frog, hoping she'd find her Prince Charming. Trista presented rosees to Ryan, Charlie, and Russell.

In Episode 5, Trista traveled to Seattle with Ryan, where they spent the night in the fantasy suite. Next she traveled to Sedona with Russell, where he accused her of putting up emotional walls between them. Finally, she traveled to Cabo San Lucas with Charlie, where they also spent the night in the fantasy suite. Trista presented a rose to Ryan and Charlie.

In the Episode 6 reunion, all the guys who didn't receive a rose predicted whom Trista would choose.

In Episode 7, Trista took the two finalists home to St. Louis to meet her family and friends. Charlie fared well in a question-and-answer session with her family. Ryan overcame his nerves and professed his love for Trista to her father, asking his permission to marry her. Back in Los Angeles, both guys shopped for an engagement ring for Trista. At the Rose Ceremony, Ryan proposed to Trista and she accepted, giving him her final rose.

RATINGS: The first season of *The Bachelorette* brought in an average of 16.7 million viewers each week.

THE BACHELORETTE
(Season 2)

GENRE	Competition (Dating)
FIRST TELECAST	1/14/2004
LAST TELECAST	2/25/2004
NETWORK	ABC
AIR TIME	Wednesday, 9:00 p.m.
EPISODE	Story Arc
TALENT	Chris Harrison (Host)
CAST	Meredith Phillips (Bachelorette); Ian McKee (Winner); Matthew Hickl (Runner-up); Aaron; Brad Andrzejewski; Damon Bowers; Andy Chang; Anselm Clinard; Sean Denham; Eliot; Rick Enrico; Todd Hedrick; Harold Hersh; Cory Higgins; Brian Holden; Keith Kormanik; Lanny Lawrence; Marcus; Ryan Morelli; Jeff O'Quinn; Ryan Reeve;

Chris Ritter; Robert; Chad Schlee; Justin Sherrod; Trevor

PRODUCTION COMPANIES	Next Entertainment; Telepictures Productions
CREATED BY	Mike Fleiss
EXECUTIVE PRODUCER	Mike Fleiss
CO-EXECUTIVE PRODUCERS	Jason A. Carbone; Daniel Goldberg; Scott Jeffress; Lisa Levenson; Clay Newbill; Sally Ann Salsano

Season 2 featured Meredith, who wasn't selected by Bob during Season 4 of *The Bachelor,* looking for love among twenty-five bachelors.

In Episode 1, Meredith met her twenty-five suitors, several of whom gave her gifts. Host Chris Harrison explained that one of her fifteen roses was a white one, which would allow the recipient to go on a solo date with her. She presented the white rose to Rick, and the red roses to Brad, Chad, Damon, Eliot, Harold, Ian, Lanny, Marcus, Matthew, Robert, Ryan M., Ryan R., Sean, and Todd.

In Episode 2, on the first group date, Meredith went ATV riding with Brad, Chad, Harold, Marcus, Matthew, Ryan M., and Sean. Everyone wanted private time with her. Meredith and Rick went bowling on their solo date. They agreed to a bet: if Rick won the game, she'd give him a rose; if he lost, she would eliminate him. Rick lost the match, but she kissed him on the limo ride back anyway. Meredith went horseback riding on the second group date with Damon, Eliot, Ian, Lanny, Robert, Ryan R., and Todd. Todd won a cow-rustling challenge, earning private time with Meredith. At the Rose Ceremony, Meredith presented roses to Brad, Chad, Ian, Lanny, Matthew, Rick, Ryan M., Ryan R., Sean, and Todd.

Episode 3 featured a solo date, a two-on-one group date, and a seven-on-one group date. Based on compatibility tests the men took earlier, Ian earned the solo date. He and Meredith went to Chinatown, where they kissed. On the two-on-one date, Meredith took Ryan M. and Todd to the Santa Barbara Zoo, after which she confessed she'd probably give only one of them a rose. On the seven-on-one date, Meredith took the remaining guys to a hockey game. There was a new bet: whoever got the most hockey pucks past the Mighty Ducks team goalie would get private time with her. Matthew won, and she kissed him during their private moment together. At the Rose Ceremony, Meredith was conflicted, so host Chris Harrison allowed her to retain seven (not six) suitors. She gave roses to Brad, Chad, Ian, Lanny, Matthew, Ryan M., and Sean.

In Episode 4, contestant Kelly Jo from season four of *The Bachelor* and Meredith's friend TJ arrived to help Meredith evaluate the men's love letters, and selected which three suitors would go on solo dates. Chad got the first solo dates, a romantic gondola ride during which they kissed under a bridge. Matthew earned the second solo date, a small plane ride over the wine country, followed by a fireside dinner, where they kissed. Lanny earned the third solo date, in which he prepared dinner at Meredith's house, after which they kissed on the couch. On the next group date, Meredith went golfing with Brad, Ian, Ryan M., and Sean. Ian and Meredith kissed in a hammock, and she admitted that he "melted" her. At the Rose Ceremony, she gave roses to Chad, Ian, Lanny, and Matthew.

In Episode 5, each of the four finalists took Meredith home to meet his family and friends. Matthew brought her to Houston, where she won over his family. In Buffalo, Meredith was surprised that Chad lived with his mom, but she said that he was everything she'd been looking for in a romantic partner. Ian brought her to New York City to meet his brother and best friend, but curbed her expectations when he said he had no plans to propose to her if she picked him. Lanny brought her to Dallas, where, to her chagrin, she learned that he comes from a strict religious family. At the Rose Ceremony, she presented a rose to Chad, Ian, and Matthew.

In Episode 6, Meredith headed to Puerto Rico for overnight dates with each of the three finalists. She met Ian in San Juan, where they talked about his wariness of marriage, yet wound up spending the night at the fantasy suite. Next, Meredith met Chad on a boat in the marina, where his hesitation cost him a passionate kiss, but they, too, ended up in the fantasy suite. Finally, Meredith greeted Matthew on the beach, where they got along so well they cancelled their scheduled plans and went directly to the fantasy suite. At the Rose Ceremony, Meredith gave roses to Ian and Matthew.

The Episode 7 tell-all reunited the twenty-three eliminated men to discuss the show, and make their predictions on the outcome.

In Episode 8, Meredith brought each of the two finalists to Portland, Oregon, to meet her family and friends. While in town, both men bought engagement rings. Meredith presented her final rose to Ian. He dropped to one knee and proposed, and Meredith accepted.

A special live "After the Final Rose" episode featured the first public appearance by Meredith and Ian, as well as an appearance by runner-up Matthew.

RATINGS: Season 2 of *The Bachelorette* had an average of 11.5 million viewers each week.

THE BACHELORETTE
(Season 3)

GENRE	Competition (Dating)
FIRST TELECAST	1/10/2005
LAST TELECAST	2/28/2005
NETWORK	ABC
AIR TIME	Monday, 8:00 p.m.
EPISODE STYLE	Story Arc
TALENT	Chris Harrison (Host)
CAST	Jen Schefft (Bachelorette); Jerry (Winner); John Paul (Runner-up); Andrew; Andy; A.W.; Ben; Chris C.; Chris M.; Collin; David; Eric H.; Eric T.; Fabrice; Jason; Josh; Keith; Kevin; Mark; Matt L.; Matt M.; Michael; Ryan Sh.; Ryan Sm.; Stu
PRODUCTION COMPANIES	Telepictures; Warner Brothers; Next Entertainment
CREATED BY	Mike Fleiss
EXECUTIVE PRODUCER	Mike Fleiss
CO-EXECUTIVE PRODUCERS	Jason A. Carbone; Daniel Goldberg; Scott Jeffress; Lisa Levenson; Clay Newbill; Sally Ann Salsano

In Season 3, hopeless romantic Jen Schefft looked to find a new beau, after her relationship with former Bachelor Andrew Firestone didn't pan out in Season three of *The Bachelor*. For Season 3 of *The Bachelorette,* the show moved to New York City, and Jen helped select her twenty-five suitors.

In Episode 1, Jen's friends Michelle and Abby posed as waitresses to spy on the suitors at the opening party. Her friends selected Keith to receive Jen's first-impression rose, resulting in a solo date with Jen. At the Rose Ceremony, Jen gave roses to A.W.,

Ben, Fabrice, Jason, Jerry, John Paul, Josh, Mark, Matt, Michael, Ryan Sh., Ryan Sm., Stu, and Wendell.

In Episode 2, Jen went sightseeing on her first group date, with A.W., Ben, Fabrice, Jason, Jerry, Michael, and Ryan Sm., but no romantic sparks flew. On her one-on-one date with Keith, they took a horse-drawn carriage to a restaurant, and Jen admitted she was having trouble being herself. Following her second group date, to a Knicks game with John Paul, Josh, Mark, Matt, Ryan Sm., Stu, and Wendell, she said she thought her future husband was among the group. Back at the house, the guys became rowdy, and the cops showed up after Jerry shouted into a megaphone. Before the Rose Ceremony, Jason admitted he was a virgin. Jen presented roses to Ben, Fabrice, Jerry, John Paul, Josh, Keith, Ryan Sh., and Wendell.

Episode 3 featured a "shirts versus skins" basketball game in the park, after which host Chris Harrison announced that the highest (John Paul) and lowest scorer (Fabrice) from the winning team had each earned a solo date with Jen. On Jen's solo date with Fabrice, they were treated to a private performance by Vanessa Williams at the Cotton Club. Fabrice shed a tear while talking about his ex. He then shocked Jen by trying to kiss her, and she pushed him away. On Jen's solo date with John Paul, they flew to the Mohegan Sun Casino in Connecticut and got massages. They didn't kiss, but Jen said it was the best first date she'd ever had. She and the remaining guys went on a group date to Central Park, where they played football, and Jerry kissed her during a private moment on a rowboat. At the Rose Ceremony, Jen gave roses to Ben, Fabrice, Jerry, John Paul, Ryan Sh., and Wendell. Fabrice was upset that he was the last one presented with a rose.

In Episode 4, the guys competed for two one-on-one dates by writing anonymous letters to Jen. Ryan earned the first solo date, and he and Jen went for a ride on a NYFD fire truck. Later, they kissed in her hot tub. Jerry earned the second solo date. At a romantic jazz club, Jerry and Jen danced and shared a long kiss. On Jen's next group date, she sent the remaining guys on a race to get a bouquet at the top of the Empire State Building, which Wendell won. Later, Fabrice quit the show, claiming that there was no passion between him and Jen. At the Rose Ceremony, Jen presented roses to Jerry, John Paul, Ryan, and Wendell.

In Episode 5, each of the remaining suitors took Jen home to meet his family and friends. John brought Jen to Oklahoma City, where he bought her cowboy boots and they kissed for the first time. In Medford, Oregon, Ryan and Jen went ice skating, and she got along well with his family. In Chicago, Wendell's mother opined that her son seemed to like Jen more than she liked him. Finally, Jen met Jerry in Rochester, New York, where there was a power outage, and Jen learned how to introduce herself in sign language to Jerry's deaf mother. At the Rose Ceremony, Jen presented roses to Jerry, John Paul, and Ryan.

In Episode 6, Jen went on romantic overnight dates with the finalists. In Bermuda, John Paul agreed to spend the night in the fantasy suite, as fireworks exploded over the beach. Jen went with Jerry to Hilton Head, where they spent time in the fantasy suite, even though they both felt something wasn't quite right. In Cape Cod, Ryan admitted he was ready for marriage, and they spent the night in the fantasy suite. At the Rose Ceremony, Jen presented roses to Jerry and John Paul.

The Episode 7 tell-all reunited the twenty-three eliminated suitors to discuss the show.

In Episode 8, Jen brought the two finalists to Cleveland to meet her family and friends. John Paul impressed her folks by bringing her mom a gift, and describing his investment successes. Jerry didn't impress them as much, but Jen's attraction to him was stronger. Jen's friends Abby and Michelle concluded that John Paul's feelings for her were stronger and more apparent than Jerry's. Jen went on one final date with each guy. At the Rose Ceremony, John Paul proposed to her, but Jen declined and presented the final rose to Jerry.

A special live "After the Final Rose" episode featured previous footage of Jerry proposing to Jen. Shockingly, Jen rejected his proposal, deciding to just remain friends. They fielded questions from the audience, and speculation ran rampant that she had met someone else since the show.

RATINGS: The third season of *The Bachelorette* had an average weekly viewership of 8.7 million.

BACK TO THE GRIND

GENRE Docusoap
FIRST TELECAST 7/18/2007
NETWORK TV Land

EPISODE STYLE Self-contained
PRODUCTION COMPANY Michael Levitt Productions
EXECUTIVE PRODUCERS Michael Levitt; Eugene Pack
PRODUCER Beth Einhorn

On each half-hour episode of this docusoap, iconic TV performers such as Betty White, Erik Estrada, and Sherman Hemsley performed the real-life versions of their classic television characters' jobs.

BALDWIN HILLS

GENRE Docusoap
FIRST TELECAST 7/10/2007
NETWORK BET
EPISODE STYLE Self-contained
CAST Ashley; Daymeon; Garnette; Gaven; Gerren; Jordan; Makenzy; Moriah; Roqui; Sal; Staci; Willie
PRODUCTION COMPANY McCommera Filmworks, Inc.
EXECUTIVE PRODUCERS Michael McNamara; Sheri Maroufkhani; Bill Rademakers; Mark Brown
PRODUCERS Mark Bobadilla; Hashim Williams
DIRECTOR Michael McNamara

This docusoap follows the lives of eleven upper-middle-class African American teenagers growing up in a posh Los Angeles neighborhood known as the black Beverly Hills. The half-hour series documented the kids going to school, partying, and shopping.

BAM'S UNHOLY UNION

GENRE Docusoap
FIRST TELECAST 1/30/2007

LAST TELECAST	4/30/2007
NETWORK	MTV
EPISODE STYLE	Self-contained
CAST	Bam Margera; Melissa (Missy) Rothstein; Phil Margera; April Margera; Brandon (Dico) DiCamillo; Rake Yohn; Jessica Rothstein; Marian Rothstein; Amanda Rothstein
PRODUCTION COMPANY	MTV Productions
EXECUTIVE PRODUCERS	Michael Bloom; Joe DeVito; Terry Hardy
PRODUCER	Joseph Frantz

This program chronicled the wedding planning and nuptials of professional skateboarder and *Jackass* star Bam Margera and his childhood sweetheart, Melissa Rothstein.

BANDS ON THE RUN

GENRE	Competition (Talent)
FIRST TELECAST	4/1/2001
LAST TELECAST	7/8/2001
NETWORK	VH1
EPISODE STYLE	Story Arc
CAST	Josh Dodes Band; Soulcracker; Flickerstick; Harlow
EXECUTIVE PRODUCERS	Dan Cutforth; Jane Lipsitz; Lauren Zalaznick
CO-EXECUTIVE PRODUCER	Annie Imhoff
DIRECTORS	Craig Borders; Brendon Carter; Mark Perez

This competition featured four unsigned bands traveling around the United States on a limited budget. The band earning the least amount of money from live performances was eliminated. Texas rock band Flickerstick won $50,000 cash, $100,000 in music gear, a showcase performance for music representatives, and production of a music video, which was played on VH1.

BANDS REUNITED

GENRE	Docudrama (Celebrity)
FIRST TELECAST	1/19/2004
LAST TELECAST	11/11/2004
NETWORK	VH1
EPISODE STYLE	Self-contained
TALENT	Aamer Haleem (Host)
CAST	Berlin; Romeo Void; A Flock of Seagulls; Klymaxx; Frankie Goes to Hollywood; Kajagoogoo; Extreme; Dramarama; The Alarm; Squeeze; Haircut 100; New Kids on the Block; ABC; The English Beat; The Motels; Scandal; Vixen; Information Society
PRODUCTION COMPANY	Evolution Film and Tape
EXECUTIVE PRODUCERS	Kathleen French; Ken Fuchs; Lisa Knapp; Julio Kollerbohm; Eddie October; Douglas Ross; Kim Rozenfeld
CO-EXECUTIVE PRODUCER	David Rupel
PRODUCERS	Richard Blade; Jeff Bowler; Steve Jones
DIRECTORS	Steve Jones; David Charles Sullivan

On this docudrama, host Aamer Haleem and his crew ambushed retired rock 'n' roll band members in the hopes of reuniting the groups for another performance. Some musicians were excited at the prospect, while others were angry, embarrassed, and unable to get past the reasons their band broke up. The bands that successfully reunited were Berlin, Flock of Seagulls, Kajagoogoo, The Alarm, Haircut 100, The English Beat (who performed as The Beat), The Motels, Scandal, and Vixen.

BATTLE FOR OZZFEST

GENRE	Competition (Talent)
FIRST TELECAST	10/25/2004

LAST TELECAST	1/10/2005
NETWORK	MTV
AIR TIME	Monday, 10:30 p.m.
EPISODE STYLE	Story Arc
TALENT	Ozzy Osbourne (Judge); Sharon Osbourne (Judge)
CAST	A Dozen Furies; Cynder; Manntis; Final Drive; Beyond All Reason; Guilt By Association; Sicks Deep; Trauma Concept
EXECUTIVE PRODUCER	Greg Johnston
CO-EXECUTIVE PRODUCER	Frank Rehwaldt
PRODUCERS	Frank Rehwaldt; Rick Telles; Dan Murphy; Nate McIntosh; Marcus Fox; Tom Becker
DIRECTORS	Gary Pennington; Lisa Caruso; Rick Telles; Kelly Welsh

Eight bands competed for one spot on the Ozzfest 2005 tour. Sharon and Ozzy Osbourne judged bands to find the one most prepared, both mentally and physically, as well as hardcore enough to handle the demands of the tour. Online voters chose A Dozen Furies as the winner. The band won a record deal, gear, and money to cover their tour expenses.

BATTLE OF THE NETWORK REALITY STARS

GENRE	Competition (Celebrity)
FIRST TELECAST	8/17/2005
LAST TELECAST	9/21/2005
NETWORK	Bravo
AIR TIME	Wednesday, 9:00 p.m.
EPISODE STYLE	Story Arc
TALENT	Mike Adamle (Host); Trishelle Cantella (Reporter);

Omarosa Manginault-Stallworth (Reporter); Bob Guiney (Reporter)

CAST

Team Underdog Bradford Cohen (Winner—originally Team Miz); Nikki McKibbin (Winner—originally Team Chip); Brian Worth (Winner—originally Team Chip); Rachel Love Fraser (Winner—originally Team Coral); Adam Mesh (originally Team Coral); Mirna Hindoyan (Winner—originally Team Miz)

Team Miz Michael Mizanin (Runner-up—Captain); Valerie Penso (Runner-up); Burton Roberts (Runner-up); Heidi Bressler (Runner-up—originally Team Coral); Richard Hatch (Runner-up); Ryan Starr (Runner-up)

Team Chip Chip McAllister (eliminated in Episode 6—Captain); Kim McAllister (eliminated in Episode 6); Matt Gould (eliminated in Episode 6); Sue Hawk (eliminated in Episode 6); Theo Vonkurnatowski (eliminated in Episode 6); Will Kirby (eliminated in Episode 6)

Team Coral Coral Smith (eliminated in Episode 4—Captain); Melissa Howard (eliminated in Episode 4); Will Wikle (eliminated in Episode 4); Evan Marriott (eliminated in Episode 4); Tina Panas (eliminated in Episode 4—originally Team Gervase); Gervase Peterson (eliminated in Episode 4—original captain for Team Gervase)

Team Gervase/Jonathan *Jonathan Baker (eliminated in Episode 3—became captain in Episode 2); Mike Malin (eliminated in Episode 3); Victoria Fuller (eliminated in Episode 3); Wendy Pepper (eliminated in Episode 3); Brittany Brower (eliminated in Episode 3); Chris Russo (eliminated*

*in Episode 3); David Daskal (eliminated in
Episode 3/joined in Episode 2); Jerri Manthey
(eliminated in Episode 3/joined in Episode 2);
Duncan Nutter (eliminated in Episode 2);
Charla Faddoul (eliminated in Episode 2—
originally Team Miz)*

PRODUCTION COMPANY TWI
EXECUTIVE PRODUCERS Robert Horowitz; Steve Mayer

The classic '70s celebrity competition returned to television in 2005 with a few reality
twists. In *Battle of the Network Reality Stars,* four teams comprised of thirty-two reality
stars from sixteen shows—unlike the original series, which featured three teams. Classic
challenges included an "obstacle course," a "dunk tank," and "Simon Says." Unlike the
Battle from the seventies and eighties which featured self-contained specials, the new
Bravo version spanned the course of six episodes, each with many surprises.

In Episode 1, the bottom three teams voted off one team member, who was then
surprisingly switched to another team. In Episode 2, the lowest-scoring team eliminated two of its members. After a bit of team shifting, reality stars Jerri Matheney and
David Daskal were brought in to fill in the open spots. In Episodes 3 and 4, the lowest-
scoring teams were eliminated, and Team Underdog, which consisted of previously
eliminated contestants, was introduced. In the end, Team Underdog won, earning
$10,000 for each team member.

BEAUTY AND THE GEEK

GENRE Competition
FIRST TELECAST 6/1/2005
NETWORKS The WB (Seasons 1 & 2); The CW (Season 3)
AIR TIMES Wednesday, 8:00 p.m. (Season 1); Wednesday,
9:00 p.m. (Season 2), Wednesday, 8:00 p.m.
(Season 3)
EPISODE STYLE Story Arc

TALENT   Brian McFayden (Host—Season 1); Mike Richards (Host—Seasons 2 and 3)

CAST

Season 1   Chuck Munon (Winner—Geek) and Caitlin Stoller (Winner—Beauty); Richard Rubin (Runner-up—Geek) and Mindi Emanuel (Runner-up—Beauty); Shawn Bakken (5th eliminated—Geek) and Scarlet Garcia (5th eliminated—Beauty); Bill Lambing (4th eliminated—Geek) and Lauren Bergfeld (4th eliminated—Beauty); Brad Hooker (3rd eliminated—Geek) and Krystal Tini (3rd eliminated—Beauty); Joe Hanson (2nd eliminated—Geek) and Erika Rumsey (2nd eliminated—Beauty); Eric Chase (1st eliminated—Geek) and Cheryl Elliott (1st eliminated—Beauty)

Season 2   Cher Tenbush (Winner—Beauty); Josh Herman (Winner—Geek); Brittany Knott (7th eliminated—Beauty); Joe Block (7th eliminated—Geek); Jennipher Johnson (6th eliminated—Beauty); Ankur Mehta (6th eliminated—Geek); Sarah Coleman (5th eliminated—Beauty); Wes Wilson (5th Eliminated—Geek); Danielle Gonzalez (4th eliminated—Beauty); Karl Hench (4th eliminated—Geek); Tristin Clow-Thomsen (3rd eliminated—Beauty); Chris Saroki, (3rd eliminated—Geek); Thais Soares (2nd eliminated—Beauty); Tyson Mao (2nd eliminated—Geek); Amanda Horan (1st eliminated—Beauty); Brandon Blankenship (1st eliminated—Geek)

Season 3   Megan Hauserman (Winner—Beauty);

Alan "Scooter" Zackheim (Winner—Geek);
Cecille Gahr (7th eliminated—Beauty); Nate Dern
(7th eliminated—Geek); Jenny Lee Berns
(6th eliminated—Beauty); Niels Hoven
(6th eliminated—Geek); Nadia Underwood
(5th eliminated—Beauty); Mario Muscar
(5th eliminated—Geek); Erin Gipson
(4th eliminated—Beauty) Andrew "Drew"
Sawa (4th eliminated—Geek); Andrea Ciliberti
(3rd eliminated—Beauty); Matt Herman
(3rd eliminated—Geek); Sheree Swanson
(2nd eliminated—Beauty); Piao Sam (2nd
eliminated—Geek); Tori Elmore (1st eliminated—
Beauty); Sanjay Shah (1st eliminated—Geek)

PRODUCTION COMPANIES Katalyst; 3 Ball Productions
CREATED BY Nick Santora
EXECUTIVE PRODUCERS Nick Santora; Ashton Kutcher; Jason Goldberg;
John Foy; Todd A. Nelson; J. D. Roth
DIRECTOR Brian Smith

Billed as a "social experiment" rather than a reality dating show, this program paired seven female beauties, who hadn't focused on academics, with seven smart guys, who lack the confidence and social savvy to date pretty girls. Each episode featured a task testing the beauties' knowledge, such as a spelling bee and geography quiz. There was also a task testing the geeks' social skills, such as a dance competition or a contest to see who could get more girls' phone numbers. The winner of each task nominated a couple to go to the elimination round, where the beauties and geeks faced off, one-on-one, on topics based on the episode's tasks. At the end of the series, the team left standing split a $250,000 cash prize.

Chuck and Caitlin were the winners of Season 1, which was set in Los Angeles.

Season 2's challenges included public speaking, party planning, photography, shopping, and strip poker in Las Vegas. Cher and Josh won Season 2, earning $250,000.

New challenges awaited the third season's competitors, as the beauties were tested on rocket science and car repair; while the geeks secured girls' phone numbers and participated in a dance competition. Finalist Nate, who didn't like his partner, Cecille, encourage the rest of the contestants to vote for their competitors, Megan and Scooter. Winning by a vote of eight to two, Megan and Scooter shared a prize of $250,000. In a season three shocker, the eliminated contestants voted as to which team of beauty and geek would win the grand prize.

BEG, BORROW AND DEAL

GENRE	Competition
FIRST TELECAST	9/17/2002
LAST TELECAST	8/19/2003
NETWORK	ESPN
EPISODE STYLE	Story Arc
TALENT	Rich Eisen (Host—Season 1); Summer Sanders (Host—Season 2)

CAST

Season 1	Kelli Zink (Winner—Team Cobi); Josh Gates (Winner—Team Cobi); Juliet Rogulewski (Winner—Team Cobi); John "Bubba" Britton (Winner—Team Cobi); Julian Bryce (Team Contact); Katie Carzola (Team Contact); Tony Farina (Team Contact); Aubrey Aquino (Team Contact)
Season 2	Doug Landis (Winner—Team Exodus); Stacey Harman (Winner—Team Exodus); Greg Matzek (Winner—Team Exodus); Eric Raine (Winner—Team Exodus); Charles Porter (Team Cake); Annmarie Sairrino (Team Cake); Kristen Mott (Team Cake); Kerri Kasem (Team Cake)
PRODUCTION COMPANIES	Broken Twig Productions, Inc.; Mandt Bros.
EXECUTIVE PRODUCERS	Michael Mandt; Neil Mandt

PRODUCERS	Andi Ward; Israel DeHerrera; Gary Jarjoura; Paul Pawlowski; Tony Scheinman; Holy Buchan; Liz Fine; Karla K. LeCroix; Andi Ward
DIRECTOR	Neil Mandt

In this competition, which was shot across the United States in fourteen days, two teams of four players were dropped off in New York City's Times Square with only the clothes on their backs and their driver's licenses. Their goal was to complete ten sports-related tasks from a list of forty challenges. Teams were not allowed to have money or cell phones, and had to try to negotiate and navigate their way to the final destination in the shortest amount of time. The Season 1 final destination was Alcatraz Island; Season 2's was Mount Rushmore. The winning team received two all-expenses-paid trips to four championship sporting events in the next year. Team Cobi won Season 1, while the Season 2 winners were Team Exodus.

BEING BOBBY BROWN

GENRE	Docucomedy (Celebrity)
FIRST TELECAST	6/30/2005
LAST TELECAST	8/25/2005
NETWORK	Bravo
EPISODE STYLE	Self-contained
CAST	Bobby Brown; Whitney Houston; Bobbi Kristina Brown
PRODUCTION COMPANIES	B2 Entertainment; Brownhouze Entertainment; World of Wonder
EXECUTIVE PRODUCERS	Tracey Baker; Frances Berwick; Rachel Smith; Christopher Tricarico; Darin Chavez
CO-EXECUTIVE PRODUCERS	Bobby Brown; Tommy Brown
PRODUCER	Wanda Shelley
DIRECTOR	Stephanie Black

This docucomedy followed the life of singer Bobby Brown and his wife, Whitney Houston. The show featured Bobby's release from jail, their family trips to London and the Bahamas, and Bobby treating Whitney to a special Mother's Day. Whitney often dominated the show, and popularized her catchphrase, "Hell to the no!"

THE BENEFACTOR

GENRE	Competition
FIRST TELECAST	9/13/2004
LAST TELECAST	10/25/2004
NETWORK	ABC
AIR TIME	Monday, 8:00 p.m.
EPISODE STYLE	Story Arc
TALENT	Mark Cuban (Host/The Benefactor)
CAST	Femia (Winner); Dominic (Runner-Up); Linda Caruso; Tiffany Weisser; Mario Mendez; William; Kevin; Rich; Laurel; Latane; Shawn; Chris; Christine; Spencer; Grayson
PRODUCTION COMPANIES	Dog Fight Industries Inc.; 12 Yard; 2929 Productions
EXECUTIVE PRODUCERS	Todd Wagner; David Young; Clay Newbill
DIRECTORS	Jim Morton; Molly O'Rourke; Karen Segal; Robert Sizemore

Dallas Mavericks owner, billionaire Mark Cuban put sixteen competitors to the test for a chance to win $1 million. The tests were based on Cuban's own struggles, and were designed to illustrate the contestants' creativity, competitiveness, values, and entrepreneurial spirit. When a competitor was asked to leave the show, Cuban said his catchphrase, "Sorry, your million-dollar dream just ended." Femia won the $1 million prize.

RATINGS: *The Benefactor* had an average of 4.4 million viewers during its fall 2004 run.

BEST FRIEND'S DATE

GENRE	Docudrama (Dating)
FIRST TELECAST	12/3/2004
LAST TELECAST	2/11/2005
NETWORK	Noggin/The N
AIR TIME	Friday, 8:30 p.m.
EPISODE STYLE	Self-contained
TALENT	Nick Slatkin (Host); Tika Sumpter (Host)
PRODUCTION COMPANY	De Oliveira Entertainment Group
CREATED BY	Adam Tobin
EXECUTIVE PRODUCER	Rick de Oliveira
CO-PRODUCER	Adam Tobin
SEGMENT PRODUCER	J. P. LaClette
DIRECTOR	Brian Crance

In this docudrama, the best friend of a single teenage contestant selected a blind date from four potential suitors for his or her pal. Once the contestant met the suitor, the two went on an unconventional date, and were put in silly, somewhat embarrassing situations. At the end of the date, the single teen had to decide if he or she would date the best friend's pick again.

BIG BROTHER
(Season 1)

GENRE	Competition
FIRST TELECAST	7/5/2000
LAST TELECAST	9/29/2000
NETWORK	CBS
AIR TIMES	Monday, 8:00 p.m.; Tuesday, 8:00 p.m.; Wednesday, 8:00 p.m.; Friday, 8:00 p.m.; Saturday, 8:00 p.m.

EPISODE STYLE	Story Arc
TALENT	Julie Chen (Host); Regina Lewis (AOL Correspondent); Drew Pinsky (Health and Human Relations Expert)
CAST	Eddie McGee (Winner); Josh Souza (1st Runner-up); Curtis Kin (2nd Runner-up); Jamie Kern (7th evicted); George Boswell (6th evicted); Cassandra Waldon (5th evicted); Brittany Petros (4th evicted); Karen Fowler (3rd evicted); Jean Jordan (2nd evicted); William "Mega" Collins (1st evicted)
PRODUCTION COMPANY	Endemol
EXECUTIVE PRODUCERS	John De Mol; Douglas Ross; Paul Romer
CO-EXECUTIVE PRODUCERS	Greg Stewart; Rupert Thompson; Kathleen French
DIRECTOR	Terry Donohue

Based on the hit Dutch series, Season 1 of *Big Brother* featured ten strangers living together in a house filled with cameras and microphones, twenty-four hours a day, seven days a week, for eighty-seven days, competing for a $500,000 grand prize. The House Guests were isolated from the outside world during their stay, living off only the bare essentials, in terms of food and supplies. During the series, they participated in a variety of physical and mental challenges, which determined what food the guests would eat and who would be Head of Household. The Head of Household had his or her own room, and more luxuries than the rest of the house. Each week, House Guests nominated two of their own for banishment, and home viewers evicted House Guests each week through call-in votes. Eddie McGee was voted the winner by viewers, earning a cash prize of $500,000.

RATINGS: The first season of *Big Brother* brought CBS an average of 9.6 million viewers each Monday night. The Tuesday edition had an average of 8 million viewers each week. Wednesday's show had an average of 16.1 million viewers. Friday's edition had an average of 7.3 million viewers. The Saturday edition had an average of 5.3 million viewers.

BIG BROTHER 2

GENRE	Competition
FIRST TELECAST	7/5/2001
LAST TELECAST	9/20/2001
NETWORK	CBS
AIR TIMES	Tuesday, 8:00 p.m.; Thursday, 8:00 p.m.; Saturday, 8:00 p.m. (later, 9:00 p.m.)
EPISODE STYLE	Story Arc
TALENT	Julie Chen (Host)
CAST	Will Kirby (Winner); Nicole Schaffrich (Runner-up); Monica Bailey (9th eliminated); Hardy Ames-Hill (8th eliminated); Bill "Bunky" Miller (7th eliminated); Krista Stegall (6th eliminated); Kent Blackwelder (5th eliminated); Mike "Boogie" Malin (4th eliminated); Shannon Dragoo (3rd eliminated); Autumn Daly (2nd eliminated); Justin Sebik (Removed from the house by producers); Sheryl Braxton (1st eliminated)
PRODUCTION COMPANY	Endemol
CREATED BY	John de Mol
EXECUTIVE PRODUCERS	Paul Römer, Douglas Ross; Arnold Shapiro
CO-EXECUTIVE PRODUCERS	Kathleen French; Greg Stewart; J. Rupert Thompson; Don Wollman
DIRECTOR	Terry Donohue

For Season 2, *Big Brother* raised the starting number of House Guests to twelve. Unlike the first season, in which viewers voted for eviction, a rotating Head of Household nominated two candidates, and the House Guests' vote decided who was evicted.

In Episode 1, Nicole established herself as the dominant House Guest, Hardy was the house heartthrob, and Bunky secretly confessed that he was gay. The first Food Challenge directed all twelve House Guests to squeeze themselves and a load of groceries into an SUV. They succeeded, winning the groceries. Kent won the SUV for being the last one to exit, despite Autumn's plea that she and her son really needed a vehicle. Kent later tried to form a male alliance against the women. Mike was chosen as the first Head of Household after winning a "wheel of adjectives" game.

In Episode 2's Luxury Challenge, the House Guests searched a mud-filled pool for twelve keys with their names on them. They found all twelve keys in six minutes, winning access to a hot tub. Mike nominated Sheryl and Nicole for eviction, intentionally picking the nicest person to go against Nicole in an effort to evict her.

In Episode 3, Will initiated a twenty-four-hour group fast to test everyone's will-power. Autumn dropped out after only three hours, while Will, Shannon, and Justin lasted the longest. Will developed an interest in Shannon, which wasn't initially recip-rocated. Bunky admitted to homophobic Kent that he was a homosexual, which Kent eventually accepted. The Food Challenge had eleven of the House Guests spell names of food using their bodies. Everyone won steaks after Head of Household Mike success-fully read the word *filet* from an elevated chair. Sheryl and Nicole worried about whom would be voted off.

In Episode 4, Justin was expelled from the house for physically threatening the other House Guests. Mike, Will, and Shannon formed an alliance called "Chill Town," so Kent allied the remaining five in a group called "Real People." During the vote, Chill Town selected Nicole, but Real People retaliated by unanimously voting for Sheryl, making her the first evicted House Guest.

Episode 5 began with a relieved Nicole unpacking her bags, while Mike worried that his ploy to evict her might come back to haunt him. Autumn accused Mike of ulterior motives, so that she would vote for Nicole. Mike denied this, and accused Au-tumn of coming on to every guy in the house. Autumn and Shannon fought over workout advice, prompting Shannon to leave a bag of potato chips on Autumn's bed, though they later reconciled. The Head of Household competition tested everyone's knowledge of their housemates, a challenge Krista won. The Food Challenge had the men and women guess their estimated weights, then step on a scale and test their ac-curacy. The men won by a pound, earning groceries for the week, while the women had to eat nothing but peanut butter and jelly. The episode ended with Krista nominating Autumn and Kent for eviction.

In Episode 6, the women earned a barbecue dinner for winning a battle of the sexes bull-riding Luxury Challenge. Krista beat Mike in an America's Choice viewer vote on who should get a gourmet birthday dinner and a greeting from home, but she invited Mike to celebrate with her. Autumn and Kent each made pleas to be allowed to stay in the house.

In Episode 7, Nicole attempted to join the Chill Town alliance, while Shannon started warming up to Will, drawing concern from her boyfriend at home. Autumn was unanimously eliminated seven to zero, and left without saying goodbye. Hardy won a numerical housemate knowledge challenge, becoming the new Head of Household.

Episode 8 featured a Food Challenge in which each House Guest wrote three wanted food items on yellow balls. These balls, along with others labeled with food items, were lobbed over the fence. Each time someone caught a ball, that House Guest won the food labeled on it. Kent and Bunky formed a surprising alliance called "The Untouchables," while Hardy, Monica, and Krista appeared to be working together. Hardy nominated Chill Town's Will and Shannon for eviction, strategically splitting apart the two lovebirds.

In Episode 9, Will and Shannon vowed that whoever remained in the house would target Hardy. For the Luxury Challenge, the House Guests were divided into Red and Blue teams to see which team could remove its clothes, send them across a clothesline, and put them back on first. Bunky, Nicole, Kent, and Shannon prevailed and got their real clothes professionally cleaned. Shannon got revenge on Hardy by cleaning a toilet with his toothbrush. The producers scolded her for causing a health hazard, so she threw the top of the toothbrush away and told Hardy she'd accidentally broken it. Hardy learned the truth from Krista, and he and Shannon had a heated confrontation.

In Episode 10, Shannon persuaded everyone to vote for her, so Will could stay. Knowing they were about to be split up, Shannon and Will dressed up for a "date" at a private table. Meanwhile, Krista turned away Mike's attempts to share a bed with her, but ended up kissing him. Shannon's wish was fulfilled when she was evicted. Just before she left, she told Will, "I'll see you soon." Kent became the next Head of Household by winning the game Higher/Lower, in which the House Guests guessed whether the numerical answers to questions were higher or lower than the ones host Julie Chen gave them.

In Episode 11's Food Challenge, each of the eight House Guests was assigned one of seven food groups, and had to correctly answer two out of three questions to win items from that food group. The House Guests won five of the seven food groups, with

Monica losing the dairy products and Krista failing on fruit. Mike overheard Krista saying her dream date was Dracula, so he dressed like a vampire and waited in her bed. Amused by his ploy, Krista eventually got into bed with him. Kent nominated Krista and Mike for eviction, and Mike accused Kent of betraying him after Mike protected him.

In Episode 12, Monica won a CD-tossing Luxury Challenge, earning a personal stereo system and a Michael Jackson CD. Hardy won an America's Choice viewer vote, and got to make a three-minute phone call to his grandmother. Some House Guests believed the house was haunted, so they used a spirit board with vague results. Nicole complained that she was doing all the housework, which didn't sit well with the others.

In Episode 13, Mike was evicted, and shared a goodbye kiss with Krista. Hardy became Head of Household again after winning a trivia game about the seven remaining housemates.

In Episode 14, Krista and Will took Mike's departure hard. The Food Competition awarded each House Guest his or her favorite meal for dinner if he or she could drink the entire meal after it was liquefied in a blender. Kent struggled to quit smoking, while Will told Nicole that he thought she was falling in love with him. Nicole tested Will's resolve by pretending to get undressed and join him in the shower, but walked away at the last minute. Hardy emotionally announced Will and Kent as his nominees for eviction.

Episode 15's Luxury Challenge was a battle of the sexes, as the blindfolded men and women rescued dummies from the house. The women won, rescuing three dummies first, earning a choice of a prize valued at up to one hundred dollars. Krista sent flowers to Mike, while Will sent flowers to Shannon. An America's Choice vote sent a pot-bellied pig named Ophelia to the house. At the house meeting, nominee Kent urged everyone to nominate Hardy as soon as they became Head of Household.

In Episode 16, Julie Chen asked Bunky why he had never been nominated for eviction, and Bunky guessed it was because he was not as big a threat as the others. Kent lost a unanimous eviction vote, which he rationalized by claiming he was tired of his housemates' indecency and was ready to leave anyway. Nicole became the new Head of Household after winning a key sliding game.

Paranoia reigned supreme in Episode 17, as everyone wondered whom he could really trust. Nicole nominated Krista and Monica for eviction. Up to this point in the competition, Monica had been inconspicuous, as she hadn't been nominated and had never won Head of Household.

In Episode 18, the House Guests received a trampoline from an America's Choice viewer vote, and said goodbye to Ophelia the pig. Monica and Krista wondered who would be the next to go.

In Episode 19, the HouseGuests discussed how they planned to spend the $500,000 prize. Krista's plans were for naught, as she was evicted by a vote of three to zero, which upset Monica and Bunky. There was no Head of Household competition, as the remaining House Guests were left to mull over the latest eviction.

In Episode 20, Will cried because he'd let down Mike, Shannon, and Krista. In the Luxury Challenge, the House Guests competed to see who would be first to retrieve movie tickets frozen in a block of ice. Bunky won, and picked Monica to join him for a screening of *American Pie 2*. In the Food Challenge, each House Guest found a jar of peanut butter. Julie Chen secretly tried to bribe each House Guest with money, in exchange for making the rest of the house eat only peanut butter and jelly all week. Bunky and Hardy accepted the bribes, but only Bunky got the money because the lid of his peanut butter jar had a lower number than Hardy's. Julie Chen informed the contestants that someone had accepted a $5,000 bribe, but Bunky was too terrified to admit he was the one.

In Episode 21, Bunky finally admitted that he had accepted the bribe. Hardy also admitted to accepting the bribe, only to lose it to Bunky. The Head of Household competition involved a geography quiz about the evicted housemates. The first player to drive a radio-controlled car to the correct state on a giant U.S. map, knocking over a flag, won a point. Bunky and Hardy advanced to round two, where Hardy became the new Head of Household by beating Bunky in an obstacle course based on their former housemates' order of eviction. Bunky won the America's Choice question and received a letter from his husband, Greg. Each House Guest recorded a sixty-second message to send to a loved one.

Episode 22 began with the House Guests ending their four-day peanut butter and jelly diet with a fast-food meal. After a Food Challenge using building blocks to construct towers. Bunky feared he'd get nominated for eviction for playing hardball with Hardy in a cigarette trade. Hardy made a deal with Will not to nominate him, if Will agreed never to nominate Hardy and Nicole together. But Hardy nominated Will anyway, along with Bunky.

Episode 23's Luxury Challenge required the House Guests to design a doll in their own likeness, then float it over the Big Brother fence in a basket using balloons. Nominees Will and Bunky finished first and second, earning a helicopter trip over Los Angeles. The America's Choice vote gave all the House Guests, a sportswear shopping spree, allowing them to keep whatever they were able to put on in ninety seconds. Nicole and Will talked and seemed to patch things up just before the eviction vote.

Episode 24 featured a live eviction, in which Hardy voted out Bunky in a tie breaker. The Head of Household competition tested the House Guests, ability to keep a hand on a key for the longest time while lying together on an outdoor bed without falling asleep. They all refused Julie's bribe of a Santa Barbara spa weekend, and the episode ended in a cliffhanger.

Episode 25 kicked off with an airplane banner message from Nicole's husband, Jeff, who was upset over Internet rumors that she and Will were romantically involved. The show allowed Nicole to webcast a live message to Jeff, reassuring him that nothing had happened. Meanwhile, the three Head of Household competitors rejected a bribe of a limo ride to a fast-food restaurant. Nicole was eliminated while trying to pull back the covers that Will had stolen from her. Will agreed to take his hand off the key in exchange for "either his wildest fantasy or worst nightmare," making Monica the new Head of Household. Will's "prize" turned out to be an empty, three-foot-tall peanut butter jar prop from a previous challenge. A Food Challenge allowed the House Guests to keep whatever items they could carry through a tricky obstacle course. Monica nominated Nicole and Hardy for eviction.

Nicole's marital concerns were alleviated in Episode 26 when her husband, Jeff, sent a second airplane banner message saying he loved her. An America's Choice vote turned the backyard into a "winter wonderland," and a snowball fight ensued. In a surprise Luxury Challenge, the House Guests competed against four former *Survivor* contestants. Each team had to spell their respective show's name using building blocks while being tied to their teammates. Then they had to retrieve four keys from an ice cube–filled pool, and extinguish four torches. The Survivors won the challenge and split $15,000. A second Luxury Challenge paired each House Guest with a Survivor in a code-cracking competition. Hardy and Sue finished first, and Hardy was allowed to go online and see fan websites that had been created in his honor. The Survivors finally departed, leaving Will to think about whom to evict.

In Episode 27, Will was the only eligible voter, since Monica was Head of Household and Nicole and Hardy were nominees. Will evicted Hardy. Since only three House Guests remained, the next Head of Household got to choose whom to evict. The Head of Household competition required contestants to match adjectives supplied by evicted House Guests with current House Guests. Will won round one, with round two coming up next.

In Episode 28, the producers decided to inform the House Guests of the September 11 terrorist attacks. The House Guests were reassured that their family members had been contacted and all were safe, except Monica's cousin, Tabitha, who worked in the World Trade Center and couldn't be reached. Julie caught up with the evicted House Guests and found out what they had been up to. Back at the house, Monica was eliminated from the Head of Household competition in round two. Will lost a round-three trivia challenge pertaining to events that had transpired in the house, making Nicole the final Head of Household. Nicole evicted Monica, and Will was left in the final two.

Episode 29's finale began with Nicole explaining her strategy of being true to herself, while Will admitted that his plan was to lie to everyone, and lose all challenges. The evicted House Guests discussed their experiences, during which they aired their beefs with their fellow housemates, and Krista accepted Mike's surprise wedding proposal. Evictees asked Will and Nicole one final question, before casting their votes for the final winner. Before the results were announced, Will and Nicole were each allowed to nullify the vote of one evictee who they believed had voted against them. Will astutely nullified Bunky's vote for Nicole, and Nicole nullified Shannon's vote for Will. The remaining votes were revealed, and Will was declared the $500,000 winner.

RATINGS: The Tuesday edition brought in an average of 9.0 million viewers. Thursday's show had an average of 9.1 million viewers, while the Saturday edition had an average of 5.7 million viewers.

BIG BROTHER 3

GENRE	Competition
FIRST TELECAST	7/10/2002
LAST TELECAST	9/25/2002
NETWORK	CBS

AIR TIMES	Wednesday, 9:00 p.m.; Thursdays, 8:00 p.m.; Saturday, 8:00 p.m.
EPISODE STYLE	Story Arc
TALENT	Julie Chen (Host)
CAST	Lisa Donahue (Winner); Danielle Reyes (Runner-up); Jason Guy (11th eliminated); Amy Crews (10th eliminated after returning to the house in week 6; 3rd eliminated); Marcellas Reynolds (9th eliminated); Roddy Mancuso (8th eliminated); Gerald "Gerry" Lancaster (7th eliminated); Chiara Berti (6th eliminated); Josh Feinberg (5th eliminated); Eric Ouellette (4th eliminated); Tonya Paoni (2nd eliminated); Lori Olsen (1st eliminated)
PRODUCTION COMPANIES	Arnold Shapiro and Alison Grodner Productions, in association with Endemol Entertainment
CREATED BY	John de Mol
EXECUTIVE PRODUCERS	Paul Römer; Arnold Shapiro; Allison Grodner
CO-EXECUTIVE PRODUCER	Don Wollman
DIRECTOR	Terry Donohue

In Episode 1, the twelve contenders moved into the house, where Josh, the waiter, instantly assumed the role of leader, causing friction with fashion stylist Marcellas. Jason and Amy hit it off, thanks to their Southern roots, and media buyer Danielle was wary of Lisa, who seemed more innocent than she was. In the first Food Challenge, the male House Guests paired up with females, and each duo carried as much food as they could up a tree and into their oversize bird's nest, keeping whatever they brought. Host Julie Chen revealed that the pair that sat in their nest the longest would win $3,000 for every week they remained in the house. Jason and Lori won the cash challenge. Meanwhile, Josh formed an alliance with the first three pairs eliminated. Danielle and Gerry became the house "mom and dad." Lisa won a House Guest trivia challenge to become the first Head of Household.

In Episode 2, Eric hit on Lisa, and Marcellas was afraid to reveal his homosexuality. The first Luxury Competition involved entering a pool of slime, switching bathing suits with someone of the opposite sex, and racing to the finish line. Everyone crossed the line within six minutes, winning hot tub access. Josh's and Marcellas's strong personalities made them immediate targets, while Jason won over the ladies by confessing he was a virgin. Lisa's two nominees for the first eviction were Marcellas and Lori.

Episode 3's Food Competition involved writing names of desired foods on eggs and tossing them over a wall to someone of the opposite sex. Each egg safely caught in a basket earned that person whatever food was written on it. Later, Roddy and Chiara began flirting, while the other guys talked strategy. Lisa explained a new twist called the Veto Challenge, whose winner could remove one nominee from the chopping block and remain immune from the Head of Household's replacement nomination. The first Veto Challenge involved shooting air guns at mannequins that looked like the House Guests. Gerry won Veto power after Head of Household Lori awarded him the tie breaker over Marcellas.

In Episode 4, the House Guests competed in a Luxury Challenge for a Hawaiian luau. The two nominees Marcellas and Lori picked teammates to identify six items that had been removed from the house. Marcellas's team finished first and won the luau. Ironically, Josh used most of the house food to cook a feast for the losing team. Amy turned down Tonya and Chiara's request that she join them in the shower, while Gerry used his Veto on Marcellas, who he believed was a victim of racism and homophobia. Lisa nominated Amy as his replacement. Several housemates objected to Gerry's implication that they were racist homophobes, making Gerry a marked man for the next week.

In Episode 5, Lori was evicted in a five-to-four vote, forfeiting Jason's chance at the $3,000-per-week prize. *Big Brother 2* contestants Nicole, Hardy, Autumn, and Kent made cameo appearances in prerecorded clips. Marcellas won a house trivia competition to become the new Head of Household.

Episode 6 began with Marcellas forbidding anyone from talking to him about his nomination strategy. The girls participated in a bikini contest, using peanut butter to keep their suits in place. Then the guys strutted their stuff, and Chiara and Roddy were voted Mr. and Mrs. Big Brother. They had their first kiss later that night. Danielle's team lost to Roddy's in a brownie-eating weight-gain Food Challenge, forcing them to eat nothing but peanut butter and jelly that week. Marcellas nominated Josh and Tonya, explaining that Tonya was a pawn to help ensure Josh's eviction.

Episode 7 featured a challenge in which each of the eleven House Guests received one box; only one of the boxes held the Veto medallion. The House Guests bartered goods and services to acquire as many boxes as possible. Danielle ended up with six boxes and the Veto medallion, which she decided not to use. The first America's Choice question awarded exercise equipment to the winner of a human bowling challenge. Danielle won, choosing an elliptical trainer for the house.

In Episode 8, alliance paranoia started to build. In a pretaped segment, *Big Brother 2* contestants Monica, Sheryl, Bunky, and Will visited, and Monica revealed that her cousin had never been found after the World Trade Center attack. Tonya was evicted, presumably because she didn't lobby as hard as Josh to remain in the house. Roddy became the new Head of Household by winning a true-false House Guest trivia game.

In Episode 9, the romance between Eric and Lisa heated up, while Chiara became affectionate with Jason, despite already being involved with Roddy. The Food Competition was a life-size Batik puzzle game, where every piece represented a food House Guests could win by fitting it into a container. Roddy nominated Marcellas and Amy for eviction, with Amy seemingly the biggest target.

Episode 10 featured a secret new alliance between Danielle and Jason, who between them had access to every one of the other housemates. An America's Choice question asked which House Guest should be awarded a gourmet dinner date with the housemate of his or her choice. Surprisingly, Marcellas was declared the winner, despite two other romances in the house. Marcellas chose Amy to join him for a lobster and scallop feast. Danielle, Marcellas, Jason, Gerry, and Josh formed an alliance to target the couples. Eric earned Veto Power by winning an oversize game of pool, but elected not to use it.

Amy was unanimously evicted, seven to zero in Episode 11. Outsider Gerry became the next Head of Household by winning a House Guest trivia game.

In Episode 12, the House Guests were uneasy because they couldn't figure out Gerry's strategy. Marcellas gave facials to Eric, Roddy, and Jason; then Eric and Lisa shared an intimate kiss. In the "Name That Tune"–like Food Competition, team members faced off one-on-one to challenge one another to eat as many food items as possible in two minutes. Danielle, Josh, Roddy, and Chiara lost the game and had to eat peanut butter and jelly for a week. Gerry nominated Eric and Lisa for eviction, threatening to split the lovebirds.

Episode 13 was lucky for Chiara, who earned Veto Power by winning a game called "TurnOver," in which players moved one space at a time over a chessboard-like grid, turning over the square they'd just left, until they had no space left to step. Once again, the Veto Power went unused. Jason cried as he read a letter from his mom, his award for winning an America's Choice question.

Episode 14 was Eric's last, as Gerry selected him with the tie breaker vote. Chiara became the next Head of Household by winning a game called "Gutterball," which involved rolling a bowling ball as close to the gutter as possible without it going in.

Episode 15 featured a life-size game of "Ballast" as the Food Competition, where House Guests tried to remove cylinders from a stack without causing the stack to fall, earning the food labeled on the cylinder. A big twist was revealed, as the House Guests learned that one of the four evictees would return to the house. Chiara sent Roddy and Josh to the chopping block, with Josh appearing to be everyone's target.

Episode 16 began with Roddy talking Josh out of leaving the house voluntarily, although Josh figured he was a goner. Lisa won Veto power by chronologically ordering a series of house events shown on the plasma screen, but again the Veto was not used.

Josh was unanimously evicted, in a vote of five to zero, in Episode 17. Host Julie Chen held a challenge to determine which of the four evictees would return to the house. Step one asked the evicted House Guests how much of the $500,000 they would be willing to forfeit; Lori lost for offering only $50,000. Step two asked the evicted House Guests how many days they would be willing to eat only peanut butter and jelly; Tonya lost for offering only twenty-one days. Julie then revealed that neither evictee would have to forfeit money, or eat peanut butter and jelly, after all, and the House Guests voted to have Amy return instead of Eric. The Head of Household Challenge tested who could sit the longest in an oversize bathtub, even after Chiara poured sixty squid into it.

In Episode 18, Amy became Head of Household by outlasting everyone in the bathtub, enduring the addition of seaweed, pond scum, and electric eels.

During Episode 19's Food Challenge, the House Guests donned skimpy bathing suits and entered a wind chamber, where they caught food vouchers and stuffed them into their clothes. Two House Guests failed to catch ten vouchers, so everyone earned only two days of peanut butter and jelly. The Luxury Challenge had the House Guests hunt down eighteen CD covers, which revealed that Sheryl Crow was about to perform in their backyard. Amy later nominated Chiara and Roddy for eviction. Gerry regained Veto power by winning a Slip 'n Slide distance contest, but once again the Veto went unused.

In Episode 20, Roddy and Chiara braced for their separation. They decided to end their romance, but agreed to pursue a friendship once they left the house. A tearful Chiara was evicted four to one. The Head of Household Challenge was a quote-recalling game. Jason won and became Head of Household for the first time.

In Episode 21, the House Guests mourned the loss of Chiara. Marcellas was convinced that Gerry was in love with him. The Food Challenge involved transporting eighteen doughnuts through a series of seven obstacle-course work stations. Jason conferred with other House Guests about his nomination strategy, eventually choosing Gerry and Amy.

In Episode 22, each House Guest adopted and decorated a garden gnome. For the Veto Challenge, each gnome was suspended above the ground by three strings. When a contestant answered a question correctly about another House Guest, that contestant's suspension string was cut. If his or her gnome crashed to the ground, that House Guest was eliminated from the challenge. Jason's gnome was the last one hanging, so he won Veto Power, which he did not use. Danielle won the America's Choice question vote and was able to view video from her family.

Episode 23 featured a fake-out by Julie Chen during the eviction vote, when she announced that Amy would stay (which meant that Gerry was evicted). Marcellas became the first two-time Head of Household, after winning a true-false trivia game.

In Episode 24, the Food Challenge involved a search through hundreds of pies to find seven medallions, which represented the days everyone would eat peanut butter and jelly. The House Guests barely found all seven medallions within the ninety-second time limit, then Roddy started a pie fight. Danielle and Lisa discovered they both knew sign language, and began silently strategizing. Marcellas nominated Roddy and Amy for eviction.

During the Episode 25 Veto competition, the House Guests navigated an obstacle course while balancing a block on their heads. Amy won and stunned Roddy by not using her Veto, breaking her earlier promise to save him.

In Episode 26, Amy began to unravel, thanks in part to a booze binge. Despite everyone's disgust with her, Roddy was unanimously evicted, three to zero. An America's Choice question gave everyone a shopping spree, letting the House Guests keep whatever they could put on in ninety seconds. Jason became Head of Household after winning a video quiz.

Episode 27 was a special live two-hour show. Marcellas and Lisa both thought they were safe with Jason in charge. A new twist called the Golden Power of Veto was introduced, which allowed a player to remove him or herself from the nomination block. The Food Challenge involved a dinner party in which the House Guests had to eat disgusting foods. After being unable to eat many of the food items, they were forced to eat peanut butter and jelly for several days that week. Jason nominated Marcellas and Amy for eviction. In the Golden Veto Challenge, the contestants crossed a field of laser beams and touched photos of the evicted House Guests in the order of their eviction. They were given time penalties for breaking a laser beam or getting the order wrong. Marcellas finished fastest, and won the Golden Veto, but elected not to use it, leaving the decision to the group. This proved to be a fatal strategy, as Marcellas was evicted by a two-to-one vote. Danielle earned her first Head of Household title by winning a trivia test about the housemates.

Episode 28 began with a Luxury Competition, in which the House Guests had to find four cell phones hidden in the house, earning them each a three-minute phone call home and a $1,000 gift for a loved one. Amy accepted a $10,000 bribe from Julie Chen, depriving everyone else of their gift and phone call. For the Food Challenge, the House Guests donned sponge suits to absorb water from large kiddie pools and transfer it to seven smaller pools. Each pool filled to a certain level earned them a theme meal. The House Guests won five of the seven available meals. Danielle put Lisa and Amy on the eviction block, which gave Jason the one and only vote.

In Episode 29, the House Guests rode hydraulic surfboards during the Luxury Challenge. Jason and Amy stayed on for the longest combined time, earning them a Cruise on the Pacific Ocean. Lisa won the America's Choice question, earning an Internet chat with her fans. Eric logged on to chat with Lisa, confirming they'd go to San Francisco together once she was out of the house.

In Episode 30, the origin of Jason and Danielle's ten-week alliance was revealed. The two consulted, and Jason ultimately evicted Amy.

In Episode 31, Lisa won round one of the Head of Household Challenge by holding her key the longest during a storm. Jason won round two, in which the competitors had to arrange photos of the House Guests in the order of their eviction, fill a water bucket by wringing out a wet towel, eat a peanut butter and jelly sandwich, and arrange House Guests' photos in the order they'd received Veto power. Lisa defeated Jason for the ultimate Head of Household title in round three by correctly matching more House Guests' quotes to the people they were talking about. An emotional Lisa decided to evict Jason from the house, keeping Danielle in the final two.

In the Episode 32 finale, the ten evicted House Guests returned and openly talked about their experiences and relationships on the show. They voted Lisa the $500,000 winner of *Big Brother 3*, in a nine-to-one tally over Danielle.

RATINGS: The Wednesday edition of Season 3 had an average of 9.8 million viewers each week. Thursday's show had an average of 8.7 million viewers. Saturday's show had an average of 6.0 million viewers.

BIG BROTHER 4

GENRE	Competition
FIRST TELECAST	7/8/2003
LAST TELECAST	9/24/2003
NETWORK	CBS
AIR TIMES	Tuesday, 8:00 p.m.; Wednesday, 9:00 p.m.; Friday, 8:00 p.m.
EPISODE STYLE	Story Arc
TALENT	Julie Chen (Host)
CAST	Jun Song (Winner); Alison Irwin (Runner-up); Robert Roman (10th eliminated); Erika Landin (9th eliminated); Jee Choe (8th eliminated); Jack Owens, Jr. (7th eliminated); Justin Giovinco (6th eliminated); Nathan Marlow (5th eliminated); Dana Varela (4th eliminated); David Lane (3rd eliminated); Michelle Maradie (2nd eliminated); Amanda Craig (1st eliminated)

PRODUCTION COMPANIES	Arnold Shapiro and Alison Grodner Productions, in association with Endemol Entertainment
CREATED BY	John de Mol
EXECUTIVE PRODUCERS	Paul Römer; Arnold Shapiro; Allison Grodner
CO-EXECUTIVE PRODUCER	Don Wollman
DIRECTOR	Terry Donohue

Episode 1 began with only eight House Guests, who moved into the *Big Brother 4* house and chose bedrooms. Jun, Alison, and Dana were immediately drawn to good-looking Nathan. The first Food Challenge split everyone into two teams, with members standing on their own beam. Each time a House Guest answered a true-false question incorrectly, his team's beam was raised one foot in the air. No one fell off the beams, so everyone won groceries. Then host Julie Chen dropped a bombshell—five of the House Guests' exes would be moving into the house. The eight initial House Guests made a pact to vote off all the exes. The exes arrived and were shocked to find the others in the house. The exes were Amanda (Scott's ex-fiancée), Justin (Alison's ex-boyfriend), Jee (Jun's first love), Michelle (David's virgin high-school girlfriend), and Robert (who had cheated on Erika).

In Episode 2, the five exes were given Bed Passes, which allowed them to take any bed and force the former occupant to sleep on a couch or cot. Robert took Alison's bed in the room where his ex, Erika, was sleeping, and Jee took Dana's bed, angering both women. In the "Love Room," Jun and Amanda shared a bed, as did Nathan and Michelle. The Luxury Competition required the House Guests to drench themselves in green slime and transfer it to a bucket. By filling the bucket, they would win access to the hot tub. Mini-alliances began to form, including Alison's phony pact with her ex, Justin. The Head of Household Competition paired the House Guests into "sitters" and "kneelers." If a kneeler took his or her knee off a button, then the sitting partner was doused in fish guts and the team was eliminated. Runners-up Robert and Justin bowed out when Alison vowed not to nominate them, giving her and Nathan the win. Odd man out Scott selected winning teammate Nathan to be the Head of Household.

In Episode 3, the girls started to eye David, Robert, Scott, Justin, and Jee, while the guys were interested in nineteen-year-old Michelle. The Food Challenge paired up the House Guests and made one member estimate the other's weight in potatoes. Only three teams came within twenty-five pounds, earning three food groups for the house. Later, some House Guests played a racy game of Truth or Dare. Scott told his ex, Amanda, that he still had feelings for her, and was upset when Nathan nominated her and Jee for eviction.

In Episode 4, Dana won a knot-untying challenge, earning Power of Veto. Nathan and Alison seemed to be growing close, although she claimed it was merely strategic. Racked by his feelings for Amanda, Scott snapped and went into a furniture-tossing rant, which got him expelled from the house. David and Amanda slept together the night before her eviction, a first in U.S. *Big Brother* history.

In Episode 5, Erika's fight with her ex, Robert, caused her to break down in tears. Amanda and David got romantic in the Head of Household Room. Alison's current boyfriend, Donny, got upset when he saw footage of his girlfriend kissing Nathan. The duplicitous Dana decided not to use her Veto, and Scott's ex, Amanda, was unanimously evicted. Jee became Head of Household by winning a challenge involving figuring out the majority opinion on various House Guests.

In Episode 6, Dana was pissed off about everything, which angered her housemates. For the Food Challenge, the House Guests had to identify mystery meats and vegetables in five casseroles. The team of Alison, Justin, Erika, Jack, and Jun won the challenge and earned quality food, while the others were stuck with peanut butter and jelly. Jee nominated Erika and Michelle for eviction, although Michelle was perceived as a pawn to ensure that Erika got ousted.

In Episode 7, Jun celebrated her birthday with a cake, but only the Food Challenge winners were allowed to eat it. Several girls staged a swimsuit fashion show, using salad ingredients for bikinis. David earned Power of Veto for winning at "Duckball," a game of throwing rubber duckies into or near a bucket. David elected not to use the Veto.

Episode 8 revealed a secret alliance between exes Jee and Jun, who strategized in Korean. An emotional Michelle was shockingly evicted by a six-to-two vote. Dana won a buzz-in trivia contest and became the new Head of Household.

Episode 9 featured flirting between Dana and Justin. The house excelled in the Food Challenge, catching several parachuting capsules from the sky and earning much-needed food. Dana ignored her alliances by nominating a vengeful Alison and retired FBI agent Jack, who called *Big Brother* "tougher than being in the middle of the cold war."

In Episode 10, Dana's former allies turned against her for breaching their pact.

Alison was thrilled when Nathan earned Power of Veto by winning the "Niagara Balls" challenge. The Luxury Competition required contestants to spin in a chair for thirty seconds, then dizzily walk with a full Champagne glass on a tray without dropping it. Figure skater Alison won, and invited Nathan to a private gourmet dinner. He later used his Veto to take Alison off the chopping block, and Dana replaced her with David.

Nathan became a target in Episode 11, after having vetoed Dana's nomination of Alison. Replacement nominee David vowed to nominate Nathan and Alison if he won Head of Household to split them up. David never got the chance, as he was evicted by a five-to-two vote. Alison won the next Head of Household Challenge by dropping Ping-Pong balls into a cylinder.

In Episode 12, the House Guests expressed concern over Nathan and Alison's winning streak in the Luxury, Veto, and Head of Household competitions. Nathan's momentum continued, as he teamed with Jun, Justin, and Jack to win a pipe-laying Food Challenge, condemning the losers to a week of peanut butter and jelly. Alison separately offered to spare Jun and Justin from nomination, in exchange for their returning the favor if they became Head of Household. They both agreed, except Jun made it clear that Nathan would not receive the same immunity. Nevertheless, Alison nominated Jun as a pawn against fellow nominee Dana.

In Episode 13, Jack, Nathan, Erika, and Alison conspired to eliminate Justin. Meanwhile, Alison was playing the field, having kissed Justin, Dave, and Nathan. Exes Jun and Jee warmed up to each other, but hid it so their alliance would remain secret. Nathan's "metrosexual" behavior led others to wonder if he was gay. Jee performed a ceremony to honor the anniversary of his father's death. Robert earned Veto Power by winning a modified life-size version of Battleship, but opted not to use it.

In Episode 14, the inseparable Justin, Jee, and Robert earned the nickname the "Three Stooges," for their comedic antics. During the live eviction, difficult Dana was eliminated by an unsurprising, unanimous six-to-zero vote. Justin became the new Head of Household after winning a competition that involved identifying which House Guests had said certain quotes before entering the house.

In Episode 15, Justin's Head of Household status made the Three Stooges a formidable alliance. The Food Challenge had House Guests dressing up as the foods they were trying to win. Jun and Jee began "fighting" as a cover for their alliance. Justin nominated Jack and Nathan for eviction, citing them as "big threats."

In Episode 16, Nathan accused Alison of betraying him, which she secretly confessed she was willing to do. The stench of Justin's favorite (but unwashed) pair of shorts offended his housemates. The Luxury Challenge required House Guests to remove their swimsuits to reveal sewn-in letters, and hang them on a clothesline to spell out a secret word. As they undressed, a pipe dumped foam all over them, which only partially hid their nudity. They spelled out the word *laundry,* and won laundry service for the next week. The Veto Competition was a life-size game of "Quoridor," in which players tried to cross the life-size game board by forming pathways and blocking their opponents. For the second week in a row, Robert won Veto Power and declined to use it.

Double-dealing and paranoia plagued Episode 17, as no one appeared to be trustworthy. Nathan was the next victim, as he was unanimously evicted, five to zero. The Head of Household Competition challenged the House Guests to squeeze into a series of steel cages, the first of which could hold six people, the second only four, and the last only two. Whichever of the two remaining competition finalists stayed locked in the cage the longest would become the new Head of Household.

Episode 18 began with Erika winning the Head of Household Challenge, after convincing runner-up Jee to sell out his alliance and leave the cage in exchange for immunity. The Food Challenge was an exotic seafood eating competition. Five of the seven House Guests ate their "delicacy" to earn five days of food, while Alison and Justin failed, and thus condemned the house to two days of peanut butter and jelly. Eager to break up the Three Stooges, Erika nominated Justin and Robert for eviction.

In Episode 19, the House Guests learned Alison and Jun had been playing both sides in their alliances, so Alison and Jun formed a secret alliance to combat the others. The Veto Competition required each player to videotape portraits of the thirteen House Guests in the order in which they won the "Golden Veto." Jun was the fastest to tape the correct order, and won Veto Power, but declined to use it. America's Choice selected Robert to receive a letter from his daughter.

Episode 20 was Justin's last, as he was evicted by a vote of three to one. Jee won a bocce ball competition to become Head of Household for the second time.

In Episode 21, an upset Alison was convinced she'd be the next evicted. Robert told Jack he was safe, but suspiciously asked him not to tell his alliance mate, Erika. Meanwhile, sexual frustration drove everyone crazy. Jee won Veto Power by being the only one to accept host Julie Chen's terms that the rest of the housemates eat peanut butter and jelly for one week. The annoyed House Guests deduced that Jee was the one who had screwed them over, and made him a target.

In Episode 22, Jee nominated Jack and Erika for eviction to break up their alliance. There was a special competition in which hundreds of garden gnomes were smashed, with the goal of discovering three golden tickets before a disqualifying black ticket appeared. Jee won—his third win in a week—and earned a daily meal from McDonald's for the entire week. He shared his first meal with Jack. Meanwhile, the three women formed a secret alliance. The Luxury Competition for a high-speed shopping spree had the House Guests dressing in primal outfits and "sacrificing" articles of their housemates' clothing to the fire. Later, after hearing Erika's and Jack's pleas, Jee decided not to use his Veto.

Episode 23 featured a live eviction, which Jack lost by a two-to-one vote. Jun became the new Head of Household by winning a quiz about items that had "disappeared" from the house. Her reward was a trip to the MTV Video Music Awards, her first time out of the house in fifty-four days.

At the start of Episode 24, a guilty-feeling Jee vowed to join the others on their all–peanut butter and jelly diet, but Alison caught him sneaking food from the storage room. During the Food Challenge, the House Guests placed in a tube in alphabetical order colored balls with the names of food written on them. Their award was those foods. Finally, there was a Veto Challenge to guess where Jun was. After three clues, Alison correctly guessed the MTV Video Music Awards, and won Veto Power.

Jun returned from the VMAs in Episode 25, and Alison tried to convince her to join an all-female alliance. Instead, Jun nominated Alison for eviction alongside Jee.

In Episode 26, Alison used her Veto to nix her nomination, and Robert was picked to replace her. Robert got lucky, as Jee was unanimously evicted, two to zero. Robert's luck further improved when he won the Head of Household Challenge by correctly completing the most statements from the evicted jurors.

In Episode 27, Robert was pleased to be Head of Household, since he was the only male left in the house. In an attempt to gain Robert's favor, Jun gave him a massage. For the Food Challenge, the housemates decorated piñatas stuffed with pesos. The pesos were redeemed for four-star dinners for the balance of the week. Robert nominated Alison and Jun for eviction.

Paranoia reared its head again in Episode 28, as Alison woke up at 1:00 a.m. to find Erika and Jun strategizing. Alison stayed up with them for more than a half hour to thwart their conspiracy against her. The Veto Challenge involved a four-sided pyramid, with steps representing each week in the house. Each time a player correctly placed placards of that week's original two nominees on a step, it lit up and let the player move to the next step. Alison was elated to win the challenge, flaunting her Veto Power. Later, she and Jun earned a flight in the Goodyear Blimp for being the fastest two to finish the Luxury Competition obstacle course. Robert won the America's Choice Question and received a phone call from his daughter.

Episode 29 began with round one of the final Head of Household Competition. Each housemate was forced to hold his or her key while performing a balancing act during an artificial snowstorm. Jun bowed out after an hour, and Robert agreed to quit when Alison told him she was "99 percent sure" she'd take him with her to the final two. Later, the House Guests opened a mysterious gift box to reveal a mime, who shadowed and tormented them all day. The Luxury Challenge was to hurl Velcro balls at the mime, and be the first to get three to stick; Robert won. For his reward, he invited Alison to a private house screening of the unreleased movie *Runaway Jury*. He also earned a trip to the film's red-carpet premiere that October.

In Episode 30, Robert won yet another America's Choice question, and was awarded with a live Internet chat with *Big Brother 4* fans. Jun won round two of the Head of Household Competition, a complex recall game about the other House Guests.

In Episode 31, Jun decided to throw the tie breaker round three of the Head of Household Competition, in which the housemates were asked to guess how their respective exes had answered a series of questions. Alison won the Head of Household. In a live vote, she evicted Robert, breaking her promise to take him to the final two because she feared the jurors would favor him in the final vote.

Episode 32 was a recap show of *Big Brother 4* to date.

In Episode 33, the evicted House Guests reviewed every moment from the show, learning for the first time of all the secret alliances, romances, and betrayals. After some emotional exchanges, the jurors returned to the house and gave Jun and Alison a surprisingly cold reception. In a "lesser of two evils" compromise, Jun was voted the $500,000 *Big Brother 4* champion by a six-to-one vote, with Alison's lone vote coming from Nathan.

RATINGS: The Tuesday edition had an average of 8.8 million viewers. Wednesday's edition of Season 4 had an average of 9.5 million viewers. Friday's show had an average of 7.1 million viewers.

BIG BROTHER 5

GENRE	Competition
FIRST TELECAST	7/6/2004
LAST TELECAST	9/21/2004
NETWORK	CBS
AIR TIMES	Tuesday, 9:00 p.m.; Thursday, 8:00 p.m.; Saturday, 9:00 p.m.
EPISODE STYLE	Story Arc
TALENT	Julie Chen (Host)
CAST	Drew Daniel (Winner); Michael "Cowboy" Ellis (Runner-up); Diane Henry (12th eliminated); Jennifer "Nakomis" Dedmon (11th eliminated); Karen Ganci (10th eliminated); Marvin Latimer (9th eliminated); Adria Klein (8th eliminated); Natalie Carroll (7th eliminated); Will Wikle (6th eliminated); Jase Wirey (5th eliminated); Scott Long (4th eliminated); Holly King (3rd eliminated); Lori Valenti (2nd eliminated); Mike Lubinski (1st eliminated)
PRODUCTION COMPANIES	Arnold Shapiro and Alison Grodner Productions, in association with Endemol Entertainment
CREATED BY	John de Mol
EXECUTIVE PRODUCERS	Paul Römer; Arnold Shapiro; Allison Grodner
CO-EXECUTIVE PRODUCERS	Don Wollman; Rich Meehan
DIRECTOR	Terry Donohue

Season 5 was nicknamed "Project DNA: 'Do Not Assume.'"

In Episode 1, the thirteen House Guests arrived to discover they'd be sleeping on concrete slabs. Marvin assumed the role of emcee, while the "out there" Jennifer (aka Nakomis) appeared to be the first target. The Food Challenge involved scaling a double-helix structure and plucking off balls labeled with food items. Lori's ball contained a key, which opened a chest containing $10,000. She accepted the money, on the condition that her housemates lose all the food they had just earned. Jase, Drew, Scott, and Michael (aka "Cowboy," and not to be confused with Mike) formed the "Four Horsemen" alliance. Will told Lori he's gay, and was worried about "the Alpha Male contingent." In a shocker, Michael and Nakomis learned they had the same father. The Head of Household Challenge divided the house into pairs. One member of each pair walked on a treadmill, while the other answered questions. Each incorrect answer raised his or her partner's treadmill speed. If the treadmill partner couldn't keep up, he or she fell backward into mud. Jase and Scott were the last team standing, and odd man out Will picked Jase for Head of Household.

In Episode 2, Michael and Nakomis told everyone they were brother and sister, which some housemates dismissed as fiction. Jase found a plasma screen in his Head of Household room that allowed him to see everything going on in the house, but without volume. The Luxury Challenge required making a life-size margarita, using Michael as the lime. The House Guests' win earned them the key to the hot tub and a Mexican meal. Jase nominated Mike and Nakomis for eviction.

In Episode 3, Mike persuaded Holly to throw the Veto Challenge, a flamingo-ringing competition. Scott defeated Jase and Mike to win the Power of Veto, but opted not to use it. Meanwhile, Adria, Diane, Nakomis, and Lori formed an all-female alliance against the men.

Mike was unanimously evicted at the start of Episode 4. Marvin won the Head of Household Challenge by best guessing how the majority of the House Guests had answered questions. Guy Dedmon was introduced as Mike and Nakomis's father, and stated that he was thrilled to learn he had a son. Another twist was revealed: Adria admitted she'd been secretly switching places in and out of the house with her identical twin, Natalie. If the twins avoided eviction for five weeks, they'd both be allowed to enter the game as separate competitors.

In Episode 5, Marvin nominated Holly and Lori for eviction because they were both strong players. During the Food Challenge, the House Guests used slingshots to shoot rubber chickens into baskets representing food groups, while avoiding the "Bad Egg" baskets. Will hit a Bad Egg basket, causing everyone to lose all the food they'd earned. The group managed to get a few more food items before time ran out, but Will became a target. The Four Horsemen worried about Jase's loyalty after he took a romantic bath with Holly, but Holly later accused Jase of trying to manipulate her. Meanwhile, Scott and Michael developed a strange "metrosexual" bond.

In Episode 6, Nakomis rejected Michael's attempt to have her join the Four Horsemen, revealing that she couldn't stand him. Will and Karen schemed to vote out Holly. Jase won the Veto Challenge by untangling a one hundred-foot rope, threading it through a series of walls and placing his Veto ring on a post at the end. Jase used his Veto to remove Holly from the chopping block, and Marvin chose Karen to replace her. Diane and Will both developed a crush on Drew, while Scott became the new house target.

In Episode 7, Marvin revealed that his nominations would break up the Lori-Karen-Will alliance. Lori was evicted, but not before she was told of Adria and Natalie's stunning switcheroo. Drew won Head of Household in a number-based trivia game called "High-Low."

In Episode 8, Drew and Diane begin to have romantic feelings, but still didn't completely trust each other. Drew nominated Holly and Nakomis for eviction. Jase and Scott were upset that Drew had chosen Holly. Everyone ate well after a successful Food Challenge, forming food names out of letters from alphabet soup. Scott flirted with Holly in the hot tub, and Drew became suspicious of Jase's double dealing.

In Episode 9, Nakomis earned the Veto after winning a bluffing-based betting game, and took herself off the chopping block. Drew surprisingly nominated Adria in her place, when everyone thought he'd choose Marvin. During an argument with Holly, Diane revealed the Four Horsemen alliance, drawing Jase's wrath. When Drew didn't defend her, Diane cut all ties with him. Cowboy Jase and Scott also voiced their dissatisfaction with Drew.

In Episode 10, Holly was evicted in a surprising seven-to-one vote, which upset Jase. Holly learned of the Adria/Natalie secret. During the Head of Household Challenge, each House Guest stood in front of a cardboard cutout of his or her likeness, and had to hold down a button on the cutout's mouth for as long as possible.

After a record-breaking nine and a half hours of button-pressing, Diane won Head of Household in Episode 11. She nominated Scott and Jase for eviction.

In Episode 12, Adria, Nakomis, Diane, and Will discovered the spy plasma screen in the Head of Household Room. They wondered why Drew had never told Diane about it. Jase won Veto Power in a piggy bank–filling game, while Scott and Jase conspired against Diane. Jase took himself off the chopping block, and Diane replaced him with Marvin.

Scott was evicted in a four-to-three vote in Episode 13. Adding to the intrigue, it was revealed that Drew and Diane also had identical twins, but they had not been in the house. Then host Julie Chen revealed that one of the House Guests had been secretly switching places with his or her twin. After much speculation, Natalie walked in and revealed that she was Adria's twin. Nakomis won Head of Household in a true-false game about objects in the house.

In Episode 14, everyone reacted to the twins' revelation, while Cowboy worried he'd be the next one voted out. Jase's new strategy was to be so annoying that people would want to bring him to the final two to guarantee their own victory. The Food Competition involved diving face-first into a table of pies to find hidden cards redeemable for food. Nakomis nominated Diane and Marvin for eviction.

In Episode 15, Drew was hesitant about continuing his romance with Diane. She suggested they start up a "single birth versus twins" alliance. Jase was clueless that others were scheming against him, until Cowboy broke the news. Drew won a balloon-popping Veto Challenge and took Diane off the block, and Nakomis nominated Jase as a replacement.

Episode 16 was Jase's last, as everyone except Cowboy voted to evict him. It was a bitter experience for the former Four Horsemen leader, until he reunited with Holly and had to decide if they should continue their relationship. Adria became the new Head of Household after winning a variation of a shuffleboard game.

In Episode 17, the Food Competition was a hamburger-making contest, and was won by Michael, Will, Nakomis, and Karen, forcing Drew to stay on his week-long peanut butter and jelly "fast." Adria nominated Marvin and Will for eviction.

In Episode 18, Adria won Veto Power in a Christmas gift–opening challenge. Drew, Diane, and Will won the Luxury Competition by creating a red carpet out of scraps, then searching a bowl of M&M's to find the golden one. Their award was a trip to a screening of the movie *Without a Paddle*. Not surprisingly, Adria didn't use her Veto, since she had made the nominations earlier.

In Episode 19, Will lost a tie breaker and was evicted from the house. Nakomis became the new Head of Household after winning a competition identifying which House Guests had uttered a series of quotes.

Nakomis was angry at Adria in Episode 20 for breaking her promise by nominating Will and casting his tie-breaking eviction vote. During the Food Challenge, the House Guests tried to consume their favorite meal in less than three minutes, after it had been "homogenized" in a blender. Six of the seven House Guests succeeded, earning food for the house for six days. The house won steaks and fitness equipment in the Luxury Competition. Nakomis nominated Adria and Natalie for eviction, holding them responsible for double-crossing Will.

In Episode 21, Adria won Veto Power by figuring out which House Guests' faces made up the jumbled images on a JumboTron. Adria took herself off the block, so Nakomis nominated her half-brother, Cowboy, figuring he'd be a pawn against hated twin Natalie.

In Episode 22, Drew tried to persuade Diane to form a twin alliance with Adria and Natalie, but Diane wasn't interested. America's Choice picked a thrilled Marvin for a walk-on role on *The Young and the Restless,* one of his favorite shows. Nakomis's eviction strategy worked to perfection, as Natalie was voted out four to one, sparing Cowboy. Marvin was the new Head of Household after winning a putting game.

Adria and Cowboy were nominated again in Episode 23. Cowboy won another America's Choice vote, and was awarded an opportunity to speak with his fiancée. Karen won the Golden Veto Power in an ice-chipping competition, but didn't use it.

In Episode 24, Marvin successfully drove a wedge between Drew and Diane by getting her to kiss his chest, which Drew found out about. Then Adria was unanimously evicted from the house. On her way out, she launched into a tirade against the other House Guests, vowing to form an alliance with her sister on the final jury. Drew won the Head of Household Competition, a true-false trivia game using chemical reactions to determine if someone was right or wrong.

In Episode 25, trust issues prompted Drew to nominate Diane for eviction, alongside the dangerous Marvin. Diane won Veto Power in a modified Skee-Ball game and took herself off the block. Drew nominated Nakomis in her place, as a pawn to get Marvin eliminated. Drew's plan was successful, as Marvin was the second House Guest voted out within forty-eight hours. Nakomis became Head of Household after answering questions about items missing from the house.

In Episode 26, Nakomis nominated Drew and Cowboy for elimination. Diane won Veto Power by freeing herself from a cage, and took Drew off the block. Nakomis chose Karen to replace Drew.

In Episode 27, Karen made her departure. Later, Drew won a Head of Household Competition in which the House Guests had to determine the chronology of certain events.

Episode 28 featured a Luxury Challenge of burning housemates' unfashionable clothing items, in exchange for a shopping spree for new clothes. Drew put Diane and Nakomis up for eviction.

In Episode 29, Cowboy won Veto Power by plugging in lights in the order in which everyone else had earned Veto Power. Cowboy shocked his half-sister by removing Diane from the block instead. Part one of three of the final Head of Household challenge was won by Drew, which required the House Guests to stand on a platform and hold on to their keys during a simulated earthquake.

In Episode 30, Cowboy won part two of the final Head of Household Competition by best matching two House Guests with previous quotes. In part three, Drew won Head of Household after best completing a sentence the way the jury did. He stunned Diane by evicting her, viewing her as a threat.

The jury convened in Episode 31 and revisited the first eleven weeks of the show. In a close vote decided by tie breaker Will, Drew was declared the $500,000 winner of *Big Brother 5*.

RATINGS: Season 5's Tuesday edition had an average of 9.0 million viewers. The Thursday show had an average of 8.9 million viewers. The Saturday edition had an average of 6.0 million viewers.

BIG BROTHER 6

GENRE	Competition
FIRST TELECAST	7/7/2005
LAST TELECAST	9/16/2005
NETWORK	CBS
AIR TIMES	Tuesday, 9:00 p.m.; Thursday, 8:00 p.m.; Saturday, 8:00 p.m.
EPISODE STYLE	Story Arc
TALENT	Julie Chen (host)

CAST	Maggie Ausburn (Winner); Ivette Corredero (Runner-up); Janelle Pierzina (13th Eliminated); April Lewis (12th eliminated); Howie Gordon (11th eliminated); Beau Beasley (10th eliminated); James Rhine (9th eliminated); Rachel Plencer (8th eliminated); Jennifer Vasquez (7th eliminated); Kaysar Ridha (6th eliminated after returning to the house in week 6; 4th eliminated); Sarah Hrejsa (5th eliminated); Eric "Cappy" Littmann (3rd eliminated); Michael Donnellan (2nd eliminated); Ashlea Evans (1st eliminated)
PRODUCTION COMPANIES	Arnold Shapiro and Alison Grodner Productions, in association with Endemol Entertainment
CREATED BY	John de Mol
EXECUTIVE PRODUCERS	Paul Römer; Arnold Shapiro; Allison Grodner
CO-EXECUTIVE PRODUCERS	Don Wollman; Rich Meehan
DIRECTOR	Terry Donohue

Season 6 was labeled the "Summer of Secrets." Each of the fourteen House Guests started the game in a secret pair, not realizing that everyone else was also paired up. If the secret pair was kept intact until the end of the game, the record grand prize would be $1 million, with the runner-up getting $250,000. If the pair was broken up, the usual $500,000 grand prize would be given out, with a $50,000 runner-up prize.

In Episode 1, the Orange Team won groceries for a week after beating the Blue Team by throwing the most coconuts into a Big Kahuna mouth from a surfboard. Rachel, from the Orange Team, won Head of Household by staying the longest on the surfboard. She nominated the Blue Team's Ashlea and Kaysar for eviction.

In Episode 2, Howie's vanity was exposed, while gay Beau thought Howie might be bi-curious. Head of Household Rachel discovered a remote control in her room that revealed a TV feed of a mysterious Gold Bedroom. She also discovered a secret panel leading to a doorway and the key to the hot tub. While everyone got in the hot tub to soak, Rachel revealed her findings, and the House Guests spun a bottle for the right to sleep in the Gold Bedroom. Only three pairs of two could compete for Veto Power, so Head of Household Rachel chose Maggie as her partner, while nominees Ashlea and Kaysar chose Howie and Eric (aka Cappy), respectively. Rachel won the Veto Challenge by untangling ropes in a jungle gym to get the Veto Medallion. Rachel almost changed her nominee to Jennifer, whom she thought was sneaking around her Head of Household room, but decided to keep things as they were.

The home viewers learned in Episode 3 that the "secret pairs" had preexisting friendships, and in James and Sarah's case, they were a real-life couple. Sarah was unhappy when James strategically flirted with some of the other women. Ashlea was evicted by a nine-to-two margin, and was told about the secret pairs. Cappy became the next Head of Household by winning a speed-based true-false competition.

Cappy's frequent crying spells raised some suspicions in Episode 4, while some were unhappy with Michael's flirtatious ways. Ivette fashioned a Slip 'n Slide out of trash bags. Beau playfully climbed on Kaysar while he was asleep, annoying him. The Food Challenge tested the House Guests' ability to eat disgusting concoctions in exchange for real food. Cappy nominated Michael and Janelle for eviction.

In Episode 5, the guys staged a muscle-flexing show for the ladies. Michael teased Cappy about his short stature, and the housemates restrained Eric from attacking Michael. James earned Veto Power by winning a zip-line race, but declined to use it.

Michael cleared the air with Eric in Episode 6, but not before most of the house had turned against him—except Janelle, who started a secret romance with him. But the romance was short-lived, as Michael was evicted by a nine-to-one vote. Kaysar won Head of Household in a competition based on predicting the majority's answer to questions.

In Episode 7, Ivette admitted to April that she was having a relationship with a woman named Maggie, without specifying whether it was the same Maggie who was in the house. Howie claimed that he practiced the Jedi arts. The house lost a spelling bee Food Challenge and was stuck with peanut butter and jelly for the week. Kaysar nominated James and Maggie for eviction.

New table coasters in Episode 8 contained a clue to unlocking the Gold Room's safe, leading the housemates to unsuccessfully count the number of seas on a world map. James and Sarah were welcomed into Kaysar's alliance after confessing to their real-life relationship. The Veto Challenge involved a life-size chess game where players moved like the pieces, and were eliminated when they had nowhere to move. James won Veto Power when Kaysar strategically threw the game, and used it to remove himself from the block. Kaysar replaced James with Eric.

Episode 9 revealed Kaysar's position as puppetmaster, as Eric was strategically eliminated. Maggie became Head of Household after winning a contest to roll a ball close to, but not into, a hole.

In Episode 10, Maggie struck a deal to spare Rachel and Howie from nomination, provided they agreed not to nominate her the following week. Everyone won the Food Competition, which featured a *Match Game*-like challenge. The House Guests also received the combination to one Gold Room safe, which revealed peanut butter and jelly sandwiches, but Janelle's sandwich gave her immunity from peanut butter and jelly for the rest of her stay. Howie later went on a "date" with Beau, demonstrating that he'd do anything to win the game. Maggie nominated Kaysar and James for eviction.

In Episode 11, Sarah won Veto Power by throwing balls at a television to turn the power on and change the channel. Every House Guest selected a gum ball from a machine, six of which were "admission tickets" to the Luxury Challenge. Rachel, Jennifer, and Sarah enjoyed a movie premiere and snacks after screwing lightbulbs into a marquee to reveal the words *sold out*. Sarah used her Veto to remove James from the block, and Maggie nominated Janelle in her place.

Kaysar was evicted in Episode 12. The new target seemed to have shifted to James. Howie became the new Head of Household after winning a rapid-fire trivia game, where a correct answer allowed him to eliminate an opponent. Host Julie Chen announced that America's Choice would vote one of the evictees back into the house.

In Episode 13, Rachel was upset that she threw the Head of Household Challenge so Howie could win, only to have him cozy up with Maggie's "Powder Puff" alliance. During the Food Challenge, two teams ate as much candy off a conveyor belt as possible. Janelle, Ivette, Maggie, April, and Beau were condemned to peanut butter and jelly for a week, after they let the most candy go by uneaten. Rachel, Howie, April, and Maggie agreed on a two-week mutual immunity deal, in exchange for nominating James. Howie nominated James and Sarah for eviction, threatening to split the couple.

In Episode 14, James won the Veto Challenge, where the goal was to fill a piñata with the most candy without going over twenty pieces. James took himself off the block, and Howie replaced him with Ivette, as a "pawn" to evict Sarah.

In Episode 15 Sarah was evicted. Host Julie Chen revealed that Kaysar had been picked by America's Choice to reenter the house. The Head of Household Challenge involved each House Guest leaning on a pressure cooker button for as long as possible.

In Episode 16, Jennifer won Head of Household for holding down her button for fourteen hours. This occurred after she made a deal with Kaysar for him to give her the Head of Household. As the contestants released their buttons, they each opened a box. The contents ranged from lavish gifts to spoiled food. Jennifer nominated Rachel and Janelle for eviction.

In Episode 17, the question of whether James would be back-doored loomed, and Kaysar and Maggie celebrated their birthdays. The Power of Veto involved a coaster toss, which Rachel won. Maggie declared that she really wanted to eliminate Kaysar because she didn't like the fact that he returned to the house, and he was nominated for eviction.

Kaysar was evicted for a second time in Episode 18. Tempers flared when April called Janelle a gold digger. A determined Janelle won Head of Household. Host Julie informed Janelle it was a double-eviction week, and without hesitation, Jennifer and Maggie were nominated.

In Episode 19, Janelle won the Power of Veto, taking Maggie off the block and replacing her with Ivette. By a five-to-one vote, Jennifer left the house. Beau won a Head of Household memory game, and his alliance celebrated.

In Episode 20, Beau and his alliance worried that the longer James stayed, the harder it would be to evict him. Rachel and Howie were nominated, but James became the spoiler when he won the aquatic-themed Veto Challenge.

Rachel was unanimously voted out in Episode 21. April, whom Howie had nicknamed "Busto," won a tie-breaker Head of Household against Janelle, and the Friendster alliance stayed in power as the Sovereign Survivors were left to lick their wounds and strategize. April made a strategic play and put Howie and Janelle up for eviction.

As Episode 22 unfolded, April asked that Janelle and Howie not select James for the Veto competition, at which Janelle earning a special Silver Veto prize—a trip to the Bahamas. April won the Veto, and replaced Janelle with her real target, James. Janelle also won "America's Choice" and received a telephone call from her boyfriend.

Episode 23 featured Jen and Rachel in the sequestered jury house. James made a last-ditch effort to secure votes, but he met his fate in a unanimous vote and was evicted. Howie won the bowling-themed Head of Household Challenge. He spent only one night in the Head of Household Room, as it was another double-eviction week, and Ivette and Beau were nominated.

Howie was excited to receive two Jedi light sabers in his Head of Household Room in Episode 24. Holly King from *Big Brother 5* surprised the House Guests at the casino-themed Power of Veto Competition. Maggie won, but didn't use the Veto. Beau was evicted by another unanimous vote. Ivette won the next Head of Household competition, a question-and-answer contest called Magnetic Attraction.

Episode 25 began with Ivette cheerfully declaring to anyone who could hear that she wanted Janelle and Howie out of the house. She nominated them, despite Janelle's plea that she nominate April. Janelle won the Morph-O-Matic Power of Veto, dashing Ivette's dream of evicting her next. Janelle took herself off the block and April was nominated, but felt safe, as her alliance was only after Howie.

In Episode 26, Julie Chen congratulated April for not smoking on what was then Day 38 in the house. James joined the other evicted House Guests in the jury house, followed by Beau. Howie was evicted by a vote of two to one, and the unstoppable Janelle won the "Before or After" Head of Household competition.

In Episode 27, April told everyone she couldn't wait to have sex with her husband. Janelle and Ivette bonded over talk of babies. Janelle tried to make friends with the remaining "Nerd Herd" of friends, hoping for future votes. Janelle won the America's Choice reward, earning a visit to the set of CBS's *Two and a Half Men*. Janelle and April compared plastic surgery procedures, as part of Janelle's strategy to put doubts in the minds of Ivette and Maggie about April's loyalty. Janelle put Maggie and Ivette up for nomination.

Howie arrived at the jury house, a house already divided as to who should win *Big Brother 8*. Episode 28 took an unexpected turn when Ivette won the "Missing Link" Power of Veto. April became upset when Ivette celebrated her victory too enthusiastically, as Janelle was forced to put April up for eviction. April was evicted, and the final three—Ivette, Maggie, and Janelle—began the final Head of Household competition, "The Key to Being Safe."

In Episode 29, Janelle dropped the key first round of the Head of Household competition, and Maggie was distracted. Ivette won round one, and two scooters as a bonus. Janelle won the second round, a padlock question-and-answer challenge.

Janelle told Ivette she would take her to the final two if she won, and said she shouldn't take Maggie to the finals because then she'd lose. The last round involved guessing how the jurors had answered a question posed to them earlier. Maggie could only listen as Janelle and Ivette competed. After a nail-biting tie breaker, Ivette won and selected Maggie to go to the final two. Janelle told Julie that Ivette had just made a $500,000 mistake.

In the Episode 30 finale, Ivette and Maggie recalled the good and bad times, and the strategies and sorrows, during "The Summer of Secrets." The jury was still divided as to who would win. For the last time, the jury addressed Ivette and Maggie, peppering them with comments, some quite unfavorable. Beau, James, and Janelle voted for Ivette, while Rachel, Howie, April, and Jennifer cast the winning votes for Maggie, who received $500,000 in a four-to-three *Big Brother 6* victory.

RATINGS: Season 6's Tuesday edition had an average of 8.3 million viewers. The Thursday edition had an average of 7.8 million viewers. The Saturday showing had an average of 5.2 million viewers.

BIG BROTHER: ALL-STARS
(Season 7)

GENRE	Competition
FIRST TELECAST	6/21/2006
LAST TELECAST	9/12/2006
NETWORK	CBS
AIR TIMES	Sunday, 8:00 p.m.; Tuesday, 8:00 p.m.; Thursday, 8 p.m.
EPISODE STYLE	Story Arc
TALENT	Julie Chen (Host)
CAST	Mike "Boogie" Malin (Winner); Erika Landin (Runner-up); Janelle Pierzina (11th evicted); Will Kirby (10th evicted); "Chicken" George Bosworth (9th evicted); Danielle Reyes (8th evicted); James Rhine (7th evicted);

Marcellas Reynolds (6th evicted); Kaysar Ridha (5th evicted); Diane Henry (4th evicted); Jase Wirey (3rd evicted); Jennifer "Nakomis" Dedmon (2nd evicted); Alison Irwin (1st evicted)

PRODUCTION COMPANIES	Arnold Shapiro and Alison Grodner Productions, in association with Endemol Entertainment
CREATED BY	John De Mol
EXECUTIVE PRODUCERS	Paul Romer; Arnold Shapiro; Alison Grodner
CO-EXECUTIVE PRODUCER	Don Wollman
DIRECTOR	Terry Donohue

The first episode reintroduced viewers to twenty former House Guests: George, Bunky, Will, Mike, Monica, Marcellas, Lisa, Danielle, Erika, Dana, Alison, Jase, Jennifer, Diane, Howie, Janelle, Kaysar, James, Michael, and Ivette were all nominated. At the end of the episode, host Julie Chen told viewers that the top three men and top three women to receive the most viewer call-in votes would be guaranteed a spot in the house.

In Episode 2, Julie revealed that producers had decided to increase the occupant count from twelve to fourteen. Starting with the women, Janelle's was the first key handed out, followed by Erika's. Nakomis was next up, trailed by the feisty Diane. Next, Julie announced the top four men: Howie, followed by Kaysar. James and Jase were also lucky ones. After some excitement, Julie revealed the final keys. Will was the first called, followed by Danielle, Marcellas, Alison, Mike "Boogie," and "Chicken" George. Before the first Head of Household competition, Julie announced that for the first time, and for that week only, there would be two Heads of Household, who would have to share not only a room and privileges, but also nomination duties. If the two did not agree on the nominees, both Heads of Household would be placed on the block. For the competition, the House Guests were split into two groups, with one launching objects at the opposing group, who were placed atop slippery pedestals on a spinning platform. When the dust settled, Jase and Janelle were crowned dual Heads of Household, and wasted no time nominating Alison and Danielle.

In Episode 3, the Power of Veto Competition was announced. With Jase and Janelle already in the competition, Alison spun the wheel for another competitor, winning King Kaysar. Danielle spun and got George. The House Guests dove for Power of

Veto symbols in a Dumpster full of rotting garbage. The first player to find six Veto symbols and place them in their tray won the Veto. But first the HouseGuests were covered with peanut butter and jelly sandwiches, hair remnants from the drains of the old *Big Brother* houses, and a stew of rancid food and water. When the drama subsided, Janelle emerged as the first Veto winner. At the Veto ceremony that evening, she announced she wouldn't use her power.

In Episode 4, Alison was the first All-Star evicted in an eight-to-two vote. The "Alison Rules" Head of Household Competition required knowledge of the newly evicted House Guest. Everyone had to guess how Alison had answered a series of questions—a challenge won by Kaysar.

During the Episode 5 Food Competition, the House Guests were given bibs and split up into three teams of two. The competition required the teams to search for rats hidden in slop and transfer them to a cage using their teeth. After a messy race, the Red Team emerged as the winner, meaning Mike, Will, George, Jase, Diane, and Erika would eat well that week. Meanwhile, the Blue Team feasted on the remains of the competition slop for the entire week. At the nomination ceremony, Nakomis and Diane were on the block.

During the Episode 6 Power of Veto competition, the players teed off with oversize golf clubs to both win and give away "Veto Balls." The last remaining golfer, or the player with the lowest number of Veto Balls won. Erika was victorious, but opted not to use the Veto.

Nakomis was eliminated in Episode 7. During the "Pay Attention" Head of Household Competition, the House Guests watched images of the first four Head of Household Competitions, then went outside for a quiz. James and Danielle faced off in a tense tie breaker. James won, and was crowned the new Head of Household.

During the Episode 8 "Holey Moley" Food Competition, pairs maneuvered a bowling ball up a wide ramp to win food for the house, plus a catered meal of their choice. If the ball fell into a hole, the House Guests had to eat whatever food section that represented: including slop, veggies and beer, bread and kumquats, and meat and ice cream. James and Erika, Diane and Boogie, Kaysar and Howie, and Jase and George won feasts for the house. Danielle and Will won bread and kumquats, and veggies and beer. "Beauty Queens" Marcellas and Janey scored only veggies and beer. The episode ended with James nominating George and Will.

In the Episode 9 Veto Competition, players were randomly chosen: James picked Kaysar, Will chose Boogie, and George drew Jase. During the "How Bad Do You Want It" Competition, a thermometer listed six tasks. As each task was revealed, the six competing House Guests held up either a red ball, to refuse the task, or a green ball, to agree to it. The last remaining House Guest won the Power of Veto. When George agreed to eat slop for the rest of his stay, he was awarded the Power of Veto over Kaysar. At the Veto ceremony, George unsurprisingly saved himself, and James nominated Jase as a replacement.

Jase was evicted by a vote of nine to zero in Episode 10. During the "Define and Dismiss" Head of Household Competition, the first House Guest to buzz in and correctly answer a question was able to eliminate another House Guest, but an incorrect answer resulted in elimination. The questions revolved around words written on a wall inside the house: *Love, Hate, Betrayal, Honesty, Loyalty,* and *Deceit.* Janelle answered the final question correctly and was Head of Household for a second time.

In Episode 12, the "Food Fight" Food Competition, the House Guests entered a padded ring where balls rained down. Whoever caught the lone "star ball" won food privileges, and could tag someone to eat slop for the following week. Boogie won the first ball, choosing Marcellas to eat slop for the week. Howie caught the next star ball, and put Will on slop. With the next star ball, Kaysar relegated George to the slop diet, and James put Diane on slop with his star ball. Danielle captured the final ball, putting Erika on slop. In an entertaining nomination ceremony, Janelle picked Erika and Mike Boogie.

In Episode 13, Janelle woke up everyone the night before the Veto Competition to pick players. After pulling House Guest's Choice, Janey picked Howie as her partner. Erika randomly drew Diane, and Mike pulled House Guest's Choice, picking Will. After being awakened by phone calls from viewers every fifteen minutes, the House Guests got a final wake-up call at 5:00 a.m., this time announcing the Power of Veto Competition. The House Guests hustled into the backyard, where each took a seat on an electric chair for the "Torture Test." Words or phrases pertaining to the game were spelled out backward on plasma screens. The first player to get three correctly identified words won the Veto, but an incorrect answer resulted in elimination. For every correct answer, the House Guest could choose a torture device from the torture table and use it on a competitor to foil their concentration. Once plied with a torture device, a player had to endure it for the rest of the game. Mike Boogie was victorious, leaving little doubt whom he'd use the Veto on. Before the Veto ceremony, the Luxury Competition was announced, and the prize was a private screening of *Talladega Nights: The Ballad of Ricky Bobby*. The House Guests were told that even those on food restrictions would be allowed to have refreshments during the movie if they were on the winning team. Team Shake and Team Bake assembled, and the backyard was set up like a pit crew area with a full-size NASCAR vehicle on a spinning podium in the center. The team members began inside the car while it spun around. As it slowed, they had to jump out of the car and perform crew duties. Team Shake had the fastest time, winning the reward. Finally, when Mike used the Veto on himself, Janelle nominated Diane.

Diane was voted out in a seven-to-one vote in Episode 14. The surviving House Guests assembled in the backyard for the Head of Household Competition. The aim of the game was to hang onto a large web of ropes positioned in the middle of the yard. Julie revealed that the evening would kick off a week's worth of competitions. Throughout the week, the House Guests would be further tempted with five golden eggs. Three of the eggs contained a slop-free food pass; the power to cancel an eviction vote, good for one week; or $10,000. The other two eggs were rotten. Only House Guests who intentionally dropped out of the competition were eligible to choose from among the eggs. The last House Guest remaining in the web would be crowned the new Head of Household. The episode ended in a cliffhanger.

In a true test of endurance, in Episode 15, Danielle won Head of Household, but the big winner was George, who received the slop pass as a gift from Marcellas. After a day of scheming, Danielle nominated Janelle and James in an attempt to "shake things up."

Before the Episode 16 Veto Competition, Danielle drew first, pairing up with Will. Janelle chose Marcellas, and James pulled Boogie's name. The Veto Competition was a "grave" affair, with the players exiting the house to find themselves in a faux graveyard. They were told to lie down in their open "graves," and to refrain from speaking or moving. Each player started with forty points, and would be tempted with prizes and punishments that would either add or subtract points from their total. The player with the most points at the end of the game won the Power of Veto. Janelle displayed no shame in gaining points by putting the entire household on cold water and army cots for a week. Danielle sacrificed her comfort for twenty-four hours in solitary confinement to win nine points. James gave up points to win the margarita party and a phone call from home. Kaysar, Howie, and George were relegated to slop for the entire week, as Janelle was announced the Veto winner. It was no surprise when she used the Veto on herself, prompting Danielle to nominate Kaysar.

In a live elimination ceremony, Kaysar was sent home by a five-to-one vote in Episode 17. For the Head of Household Competition, "The Ghosts of Seasons Past," Julie explained that through a series of true-false questions, the House Guests would be tested on their knowledge of past House Guests. A House Guest who answered incorrectly or was slowest to answer was eliminated, and the last person standing was the new Head of Household. Erika was faster than the rest, and won. Julie then announced the Coup d'Etat: Whoever won this power would have the ability to overthrow the Head of Household and replace their nominations on the spot at any of the next three evictions. However, only the winning House Guest would know what they had won, and the power would remain secret until it was used.

Episode 18 was fraught with controversy over the Head of Household Competition and its results, as the House Guests complained loudly about faulty buzzers. Suddenly, over the PA system, Executive Producer Alison Grodner informed the House Guests that there had indeed been technical difficulties during the prior Head of Household Competition, and as a result the competition would need to be replayed. By answering a series of questions regarding the séance the night before, the housemates would again compete for the power, a competition that left Janelle as the new Head of Household. When the House Guests returned inside after the competition, they discovered a sheep in their living room. Danielle wanted to name it Dolly after the sheep cloned in Scotland. Danielle figured that the clue must be DNA, meaning "Do Not Assume." She ran into the Diary Room to give her "official answer" to the Coup d'Etat competition. The Food Competition was announced, and Janelle introduced the Big Brother Bakery. The House Guests were ordered to create seven different slop dishes in less than one hour. A panel of special guests would judge the dishes on taste, creativity, and originality. At the end of the hour, they had seven dishes, one for each day of the week. The judges were introduced: former House Guests Jun, Marvin, and Nicole. The housemates ended up with food for every day except Wednesday. At the nomination ceremony, Janelle put Danielle and Erika on the block.

In Episode 19, the House Guests had a tough time figuring out what the Coup d'Etat clues added up to. Exiting the house for the second clue, the House Guests saw a giant needle and thread. Later, Janelle called everyone to the Veto Competition. She drew Will, Erika chose Marcellas, and Danielle picked James. At the "Anything You Can Do I Can Do" Veto Competition, Nicole from *Big Brother 2* was the surprise host. With a little help from James, Danielle won the Power of Veto. During the ceremony, Danielle surprised no one by saving herself, forcing Janelle to nominate Marcellas in her place.

Episode 20 featured a blast from the past when everyone dressed up for the "prom." Julie recapped the Coup d'Etat Competition, and Mike was asked to go to the Diary Room, where he was informed that he had won the Coup d'Etat with his answer "You reap what you sow." Julie explained that he could use the Veto Power anytime in the next three evictions. At the vote, Julie revealed to the House Guests that someone had won the Coup d'Etat. She asked if the winner wanted to use the power, but no one stood up, so the nominees stated their cases. Marcellas was unanimously voted out, and headed to the sequester house. Julie announced that it was a double eviction week, with the next House Guest going home that Sunday. The Head of Household Competition looked like a high-school prom night based on what "senior superlative" titles America voted for each of the House Guests to receive, such as "Most Likely to Succeed." If a player answered correctly, they advanced a step from their starting square. If they answered incorrectly, they stayed put. The first House Guest to reach his or her final square would be the new Head of Household. In a tie breaker, Chicken George got closer to the answer than Danielle, and won Head of Household. George had to stand immediately and reveal his two new nominees. Stunned, he hoisted James and Erika onto the block.

In Episode 21, George called everyone to the living room to pick players for the Veto Competition. He drew Howie's name, Erika picked Danielle, and James pulled out Will's name. During the "Gnome Is Where the Veto Is" Competition, the House Guests carried their Veto symbol from one stump across to a winning spike on a distant stump, while locked into ankle restraints tethering them to where they stood. To unlock the restraint, they had to grab a key hanging out of reach by using tape and the left-over items from past Veto competitions. James reached his bag, freeing himself first to win the Power of Veto. After James saved himself, George surprisingly filled the void with Howie, who was voted out of the house. "The Return of the Gnomes" Head of

Household Competition was in a question-and-answer format. The House Guests answered questions by placing their heads in a hole marked True or False. An incorrect answer meant a pie in the face and elimination. Mike, once again, won a crucial Head of Household.

As the House Guests gathered around the tiny kitchen table in Episode 22, Boogie brought out the keys for the nominations. As expected, Janelle and James were on the block, but they didn't have much time to mope before they had to pick players for the Power of Veto Competition. Boogie drew House Guest's Choice and partnered up with Will, Janey picked Danielle's name, and James chose Erika. The setup "is kind of like musical chairs," Janey explained, with the House Guests racing to scavenge through the jungle for "voodoo dolls," each labeled with a letter. Questions were asked about past *Big Brother* All-Stars. To show their answer, the players had to find the doll with the letter matching the House Guest's name, race with it to a large stone slab, and offer it as a sacrifice. There was an added twist, though, as each question meant one less stone slab was available where sacrifices could be made, meaning one House Guest was eliminated with every question. After the final question (and a broken fingernail), Janey was the first to return with the correct doll, and won the Veto. That evening, she saved herself, and Mike had no choice but to put George in the vacant seat.

In Episode 23, viewers were offered a peek at life for Marcellas in the sequester house, and how it changed when Howie showed up. Back at the main house, James was voted out by a three-to-one margin. For the "But First" Head of Household Competition, the House Guests judged whether the statements Julie read were true or false. To indicate a true response, they stepped up on a podium; if they thought the answer false, they stepped down. The competition was a short one, with Erika winning Head of Household.

For the Episode 24 Food Competition, the House Guests went into the storage room to discover outfits for bees, birds, and flowers. Will and Boogie grabbed the bee costumes, Danielle and Janelle donned the bird costumes, and Erika and George took on the flower outfits. The birds and the bees had to dive into a nectar pool, absorb as much nectar as possible, then return to the flowers to squeeze out as much as possible. Their flower helpers assisted with the squeezing. The luxuries and food up for grabs included a trampoline, a slop pass for a week, beer and wine, and Christmas in August. When the final bell rang, the House Guests assembled to find out that while they'd missed out on bread, cereal, desserts, and dairy, they were awarded with the trampoline, Christmas in August, a five-star dinner, and beer and wine. Later, at the nomination ceremony, George and Janelle were put on the block.

In Episode 25, Christmas in August was delivered by a special guest, actor Neil Patrick Harris of CBS's *How I Met Your Mother*. The next day, Erika asked the House Guests to assemble in the living room, where everyone pulled a number to determine the order of the Power of Veto Competition. In this competition, partial images of two evicted House Guests flashed on a large video screen. The first player to correctly identify the two House Guests would win the Veto. Janelle was victorious, winning her fourth Veto. She saved herself from elimination, and Erika sent her former ally, Danielle, to the chopping block.

In Episode 26, Danielle was eliminated by a unanimous vote. Then, the House Guests had to play an entire week in one hour. Very quickly, Janelle won "The Battle of the Sexes" Head of Household Competition, a series of questions about events that had taken place in the *Big Brother* house that summer. Janelle nominated George and Erika. For the "I'm Knots about Veto" Power of Veto Competition, each House Guest was attached to a rope with two large knots in the middle. At the end of the rope was a Veto symbol. The first player to untie the knots, remove the Veto symbol, then hit a buzzer was the winner. Erika won, and immediately removed herself from the block. Janelle nominated Mike Boogie, and George was quickly voted out of the house.

In Episode 27, the final four commented on how impressed they were with themselves for making it so far. Janey announced the Head of Household Competition, "The Big Brother Bowl," which consisted of a series of questions based on what day specific events had taken place in the house. The House Guests wrote their answers on their yard marker, and based on the amount they were over or under the correct number, they were penalized points. Players with a correct answer did not have to move away from the end zone. Mike won the competition, boosting his confidence even more. Left with little choice, he nominated Janelle and Erika.

With a hurricane headed for the jury house in Episode 28, the jury was moved to safer quarters, but George wasn't safe from Hurricane Howie when he moved in. Back at the house, for the "When the Stars Align" Power of Veto Competition, the backyard was set up with four sectioned-off private areas, one for each House Guest. Each player had to put the ten faces of the evicted House Guests around their ten-point stars to solve the puzzles written on each point. Once all the stars were correctly aligned, the House Guests pressed a buzzer to signal that they were finished. Janelle won the Veto, saving herself and securing her spot in the final three. Mike then made the tough decision to nominate Will, which led to Will's eviction. Julie then announced part one of the three-part "Mount HoH" Head of Household Competition. Even though Boogie was the outgoing Head of Household, he was still eligible to play. Each House Guest had to climb onto one side of a volcano, turn around, and face forward with his back to the volcano. Once there, he had to grab a large key above him. The aim of the game was to remain on the volcano, holding on to the key with both hands, without letting his feet or keys touch the mat below. The last person left on the volcano automatically advanced to the final round of the three-part competition. Moments after the start, Boogie jumped off the volcano, confident that the winner would take him to the final two. Soon after, Janelle took her hand off the key, making Erika the winner of round one.

During episode 28, the second part of the final Head of Household Competition, "Fly by Night," was unveiled after dark. The House Guests entered the backyard to find laser beams, smoke, and a GM Pontiac Solstice convertible hanging high above the ground. Pictures of the past six winners of *Big Brother* were placed around the upper rim of the circular scaffolding. The players were hooked into harnesses and hoisted high over the ground to the scaffolding rim. They had to swing from each point where a House Guest's face was pictured along the circle's rim to the next, directing the laser beams off the mirrors at each location to point to each *Big Brother* winner, in the proper order. Mike's big effort paid off, leaving him to face Erika in the third part of the competition. The final round of the three-part final Head of Household Competition took place inside the house. Julie announced she'd be reading six statements made by members of the jury while they were in the house. For each statement, she read two possible endings, and the players guessed which was correct. In the end, Mike Boogie was declared the final Head of Household, and he sent Janelle to the last jury seat.

In the Episode 29 finale, Julie Chen led the jury members and the other evicted House Guests down memory lane before announcing that Mike "Boogie" Malin was the $500,000 winner of *Big Brother All-Stars*. Janelle was awarded $25,000 by an America's Choice vote.

BIG BROTHER 8

GENRE	Competition
FIRST TELECAST	7/5/2007
LAST TELECAST	9/18/2007
NETWORK	CBS
AIR TIMES	Sunday, 8:00 p.m.; Tuesday, 9:00 p.m.; Thursday, 8:00 p.m.
EPISODE STYLE	Story Arc
TALENT	Julie Chen (Host)
CAST	"Evil" Dick Donato (Winner); Daniele Donato (Runner-up); Zach Swerdzewski (11th Evicted); Jameka Cameron (10th evicted); Eric Stein (America's Player—9th evicted); Jessica Lynne Hughbanks (9th evicted); Amber Siyavus (8th evicted); Jen Johnson (7th evicted); Dustin Erikstrup (6th evicted); Kail Harbick (5th Evicted); Nick Starcevic (4th evicted); Mike Dutz, (3rd evicted); Joe Barber (2nd evicted); Carol Journey (1st evicted)
PRODUCTION COMPANIES	Alison Grodner Productions, in association with Endemol Entertainment
CREATED BY	John De Mol
EXECUTIVE PRODUCERS	Conrad Green; Shirley Jones; Ruth Wrigley
PRODUCERS	Heather Darroch; Alex Dundas; Gigi Eligoloff; Lee Hupfield; Tim Quicke; Frank Rehwaldt; Simon Welton
DIRECTORS	Simon Hepworth; Helen Downing; Martin Lord

Season 8 featured an *Alice in Wonderland*-inspired theme. The house had oversize and undersize bedrooms. The backyard featured animal-shaped topiaries and a spinning teacup, along with a pool and hot tub. Running eighty-one days, the season featured two twists. One, the "Biggest Nemesis," introduced the drama of three sets of enemies living together: ex-boyfriends Joe and Dustin, estranged daughter and father Danelie and Dick, and ex–best friends Carol and Jessica. There was also a second twist, "America's Player." This twist had House Guest Eric attempting to carry out the wishes of the viewers. He received his directive when he visited the Diary Room. Season 8 also featured *Big Brother: After Dark,* to be broadcast on the premium cable network, Showtime Too, from midnight to 3:00 a.m. Eastern Time. On *After Dark,* viewers could watch live footage directly from the *Big Brother* house. The show was delayed to other areas of the country, and was censored only for slanderous remarks or music copyright infringement issues. Viewers of *After Dark* got an earful as Dick's "Evil Dick" persona was evident in all his profanity-laced, spitting, yelling, and strategizing moments. He even revealed that he had conspired with his son, Vincent, to receive a coded letter from home while sequestered, giving him clues about whom he shouldn't trust in the house. The producers decreed that Dick's coded letter didn't violate any rules, as this method of communication had not been contemplated by the production company.

During week one, the first eleven House Guests arrived, and as they were getting to know one another, host Julie Chen informed them that three other House Guests would be added to the mix. During the first Head of Household Competition, everyone but Nick played a true-or-false question game involving a spinning mechanical mushroom. Kail and Eric won, and behind a one-way mirror, the three House Guests selected Kail as the Head of Household. The three "enemies" entered the living room. All were upset, but Daniele, visably shaken upon seeing her father, Dick, later formed a secret alliance with him. Kail, leader of the Mrs. Robinson Alliance—Mike, Zach, and Nick—nominated Amber and Carol for eviction. Eric was told to make up a traumatic story about his past to tell Kail, which he did. Daniele and Nick grew closer, and Jen became jealous. Daniele won the first Power of Veto, but didn't use it.

During week two, in a ten-to-one vote, Carol was evicted from the house. Eric helped secure her eviction with his vote. Self-obsessed and unpopular Jen won the Head of Household Competition, and put Daniele and Dick up for nomination. The women lost the "Name That Pie" Food Competition, and had to eat slop for the week. Eric was told to target Jessica for eviction, and discussed it with Jen. Daniele once again won the Power of Veto, and used it to save herself. Joe was put on the block. Eric was then instructed to sleepwalk into Joe's bed, which he attempted to do, but failed.

During week three, Joe was evicted in a nine-to-one vote, helped by Eric. Dick warned Kail that she had plastered a big target on her back with her alliance. Dick won the "Getting Schooled" Head of Household true-or-false game, and Eric tried to influence Jen's nomination, and succeeded. Jen playfully wrestled with Eric and won, and all were rewarded in a new Food Challenge. Zach livened up the boredom in the house by streaking. Eric vandalized Jen's bed by squirting mustard on her pillow and shirt, without being discovered. Jen and Dick were the last two standing in an *Alice in Wonderland*–inspired Power of Veto Competition, where Dick tried to psych out Jen. It didn't work, and she won the Power of Veto and used it, allowing Mike to be put up for elimination. Dick warned Daniele that he didn't trust Nick, and didn't like her relationship with him.

During week four, Eric's campaign to oust Kail failed, and Mike was voted out seven to two. The home audience met Daniele's boyfriend, Kris, who said he trusted Daniele, despite evidence of a budding "showmance" between her and Nick. "The Eliminator" Head of Household Competition was won by Dustin, who nominated Kail and Jen for eviction. Eric won another challenge, asking for Jen's nomination. Dick continued to upset the household, yelling and playing practical jokes on people. Some House Guests went back on slop, and Jameka won the Power of Veto, keeping her vow to save Jen. Nick was put up for eviction in her place. Eric was given the task of introducing a new catchphrase into the household, "I'd do that for a dollar!" He completed the task.

In week five, Eric's campaign to get rid of Kail failed again, as Nick was voted out six to two. Daniele was upset, but Dustin hoped it played out that way, as he wanted to backdoor Nick. Daniele won Head of Household as a banner flew overhead, causing the House Guests to question the game. Amber burst into tears, again. Jen tried to bargain, but America wanted her to be nominated, and she was, alongside Kail. Daniele realized that Eric was "the weasel," responsible for odd votes and unusual behavior, and shared her theory with Dick and Jessica. Jen won the Power of Veto, and Eric was put up for nomination. Eric was told to promise Jessica he'd be in the final two with her. Dick made temporary peace with Jen, promising not to put her up if she didn't nominate Daniele the next week.

Kail was evicted by a four-to-three vote in week six. Swearing on her child's life, Amber wanted Eric evicted, but Jessica won Head of Household, and nominated Dick and Daniele. Eric failed at a task to flatter Dick incessantly. In a move to protect Daniele, Dick continued to annoy the House Guests, hoping to get them to like Daniele and hate him. Dick vowed that if he won Power of Veto, he would take Daniele off the block, which he did. Eric was told to try to target Dustin, who chose prizes over trying to win the Veto. Eric failed at his task of giving Jessica the silent treatment.

During the seventh week, evicted House Guest and Dustin's former boyfriend, Joe, remarked that Dustin's personality was his downfall. The Eric/Jessica/Dick/Daniele alliance was formed under the watchful eye of Zach. In a surprise vote, Dustin was eliminated four to two, and Dick declared, "I just pulled off the biggest coup. Ha ha! See ya!" But did he? Eric was told to get Amber nominated. Daniele won Head of Household, and she nominated Amber and Jameka, the self-proclaimed good people. Eric was also told to give his childhood stuffed animal to Jessica, which she lovingly accepted. Daniele won the Power of Veto, and took Amber off the block, backdooring her real target, Jen. Daniele and Amber won a trip out of the house to participate as contestants on the CBS game show *Power of 10*, where Amber won $1,000. Eric was instructed to perform his easiest task: get Jen evicted.

In week eight, Jen, wanting to go out in a blaze of glory, stole and destroyed Dick's cigarette stash. A heated argument took place in the backyard, where Jen claimed that Dick burned her with a remaining cigarette. The House Guests watched some of Amber and Daniele's appearance on *Power of 10*, then Jen was unanimously evicted by a vote of six to zero. Jessica escaped the fate of the dunk tank to win Head of Household. Amber revealed to Jessica that Jen had told her Eric had a girlfriend back home. Eric went to the Head of Household room and smoothed things out with Jessica. The House Guests got naked in a pile of bubbles to solve a puzzle, in order to earn a clothing shopping spree—which the girls won. Eric campaigned to have Amber nominated. His mission was accomplished, with Zach also going up for eviction. Amber and Jameka prayed for Amber to stay. Eric won the Power of Veto, and declined to use it. He completed the America's Player task of kissing Jessica, and she whispered to him, "It's about time!"

In the ninth week, America's Player Eric was told to get Amber evicted, and his mission was accomplished with a three-to-one vote. Dick and Zach started talking mutual strategy. America wanted Eric to get Jameka nominated. Zach won Head of Household and put Jessica and Jameka up for nomination. Eric was conflicted, but didn't reveal he was America's Player to Jessica, who asked him many questions. Daniele won Power of Veto, hosted by All-Star Janelle. Together with Dick, Danielle formed a new alliance, excluding Eric and Jessica, and including Zach. America's Player asked Eric to mimic Dick, with hysterical results. America wanted Eric to vote for Jameka to be evicted, and he desperately campaigned to keep Jessica in the house. Daniele did not use her Power of Veto.

The tenth week brought a surprise to the HouseGuests: a "Fast Forward" episode where two House Guests would be eliminated. Jessica was the first to go, in a two-to-one vote. Dick won an accelerated Head of Household competition, and Eric jokingly asked if he would put Daniele up, a task he was given as America's Player. He failed to get Daniele nominated, and was nominated with Jameka. Zach won Power of Veto, and let the nominations stand. Eric was evicted in a two-to-zero vote. Zach won the next Head of Household, and Dick and Daniele were betrayed, with both put up for nomination. Viewers were treated to a look at some of the jurors at their secret location, sequestered from the events that had transpired. Daniele won another Power of Veto, equaling the record set by All-Star Janelle. Daniele took Dick off the block, as thanks for his having done the same for her earlier in the game. Jameka was evicted by Daniele's solo vote. The first of the three-part final Head of Household Competition began with Zach, Dick, and Daniele perched on a makeshift carrot. The three remaining House Guests had to jump over a mechanical rabbit while holding on to a key hanging over their heads. Within a few minutes, the House Guests were sprayed with cold water as each attempted to be the last competitor standing.

In the eleventh week, Daniele was the first to slip off the carrot. For what turned out to be a little more than seven hours, Zach and Dick shivered as more water rained down on them. In the end, Daniele told her father, Dick, that she loved him, and that it was okay if he let go of the key. Reluctantly, he stepped down, and Zach won the first of three competitions to determine the Head of Household. An exhausted Dick competed against Daniele in a round-two puzzle competition. Daniele really wanted to go to round three, and Dick assured her that if he won, he could defeat Zach in the third round. Meanwhile, back at the juror house, Eric and Jessica continued their romance. The final Head of Household contest was a question-and-answer challenge, and Dick defeated Zach, who became the final House Guest to check in to the juror house. Dick and Daniele celebrated their position in the finals, and prepared themselves for the questions the evicted House Guests would ask. Daniele was afraid they'd see her as weak, riding on Dick's coattails. Dick assured her that she was an excellent game player, winning vital Head of Household and Veto competitions. The jurors' questions delved into Daniele's personal life, which upset her. Eric was told to vote for Dick. The identity of America's Player Eric and all his mischievous deeds were revealed, much to everyone's surprise. On Day 81, the jury cast a five-to-two vote, awarding Dick $500,000 as the winner of *Big Brother 8*. He received votes from Eric, Dustin, Amber, Zach, and Jessica.

BIG MAN ON CAMPUS

GENRE	Competition (Dating)
FIRST TELECAST	12/15/2004
LAST TELECAST	1/19/2005
NETWORK	The WB
AIR TIME	Wednesday, 9:00 p.m.
EPISODE STYLE	Story Arc
TALENT	Whitney Drolen

CAST

The Men	Matt (Big Man on Campus); Billy; Michael; Nick; Marcus; Jeff
The Women	Michaela (Campus Queen/Winner); Jessica; Aimee; Morgan; Diamond; Jessica L.; Kelly N.; Kelly D.; Kat; Alexandra; Kristina; Natalie; Melissa; Jaime; Jen
PRODUCTION COMPANY	Next Entertainment, in association with Telepictures Productions
EXECUTIVE PRODUCER	Mike Fleiss
CO-EXECUTIVE PRODUCERS	Leslie Radakovich; Tracy Mazuer
DIRECTORS	Ken Fuchs; Jason Harper

Billed as "the ultimate collegiate wish-fulfillment dating series," *Big Man on Campus* asked fifteen beautiful college girls from the University of Central Florida, in Orlando, to find "the hottest man on campus." Once Matt was chosen as "Big Man on Campus," there was a twist. He took out, rated, and got to know the fifteen young women at various outings and romantic dates before selecting his "Campus Queen," Michaela.

RATINGS: *Big Man on Campus* brought in an average of 1.7 million viewers each week during its winter run.

THE BIGGEST LOSER

GENRE	Competition (Endurance/Makeover)
FIRST TELECAST	10/19/2004
NETWORK	NBC
AIR TIME	Tuesday, 8:00 p.m.
EPISODE STYLE	Story Arc
TALENT	Caroline Rhea (Host); Bob Harper (Trainer); Jillian Michaels (Trainer—Seasons 1 and 2); Kim Lyons (Trainer—Season 3)

CAST

Season 1   Ryan Benson (The Biggest Loser—lost 122 lbs.); Kelly Minner (Runner-up—lost 79 lbs.); Gary Deckman (lost 71 lbs.); Dave Fioravanti (lost 71 lbs.); Andrea Baptiste (lost 59 lbs.); Kelly McFarland (lost 72 lbs.); Aaron Semmell (lost 61 lbs.); Lisa Anderone (lost 57 lbs.); Matt Kamont (lost 64 lbs.); Maurice Walker (lost 64 lbs.); Lizzeth Davalos (lost 22 lbs.); Dana Disilvio (lost 22 lbs.)

Season 2   Matt Hoover (The Biggest Loser—lost 157 lbs.); Seth Word (Runner-up—lost 123 lbs., won $50,000); Suzy Preston (Third Place—lost 95 lbs., won $25,000), Ryan Kelley (lost 78 lbs.); Jen Kersey (lost 91 lbs.); Suzanne Mendonca (lost 87 lbs.); Shannon Mullen (lost 108 lbs.);

	Kathryn Murphy (lost 161 lbs.); Andrea Overstreet (lost 75 lbs.); Nick Gaza (did not attend final weigh-in); Ruben Hernandez (lost 81 lbs.); Jeff Levin (lost 153 lbs.); Pete Thomas (lost 185 lbs., won $100,000, lost highest percentage of weight); and Mark Yesitis (lost 165 lbs.)
Season 3	Erik (The Biggest Loser—lost 214 lbs.); Brian (Runner-up—lost 156 lbs., won $100,000); Amy (lost—106 lbs.); Bobby (lost 96 lbs.); Marty (lost 146 lbs.); Melinda (lost 64 lbs.); Tiffany (lost 51 lbs.); Heather (pregnant, weight wasn't measured); Jennifer (lost 100 lbs.); Kai (lost 118 lbs.); Ken (lost 161 lbs.); Nelson (lost 69 lbs.); Pam (lost 68 lbs.); Wylie (lost 129 lbs.) Jaron (lost 160 lbs.), and Adrian (lost 58 lbs.); Poppi (not picked for the regular season; won $50,000)
PRODUCTION COMPANIES	Reveille LLC; 25/7 Productions; 3 Ball Productions; NBC Universal Television Studio
EXECUTIVE PRODUCERS	Ben Silverman; Dave Broome; J. D. Roth; John Foy; Todd A. Nelson
CO-EXECUTIVE PRODUCERS	Mark Koops; Howard Owens; Troy Searer
DIRECTOR	Brian Smith

Twelve overweight competitors—six men and six women—formed two teams, and with the assistance of a team trainer, attempted to lose weight through diet and exercise. One team trained in a boot-camp setting, while the other took a calmer approach. A competitor was eliminated after the weigh-in, as the team that lost the lowest percentage of weight had to vote someone out. The Biggest Loser was the person who lost the highest percentage weight, winning a grand prize of $250,000.

The Biggest Loser: Special Edition began on January 4, 2006. Instead of the usual twelve to fourteen strangers competing, the special edition featured contestants who already knew one another. Instead of spending months at the ranch, and then continuing to lose weight at home, the *Special Edition* contestants spent only eleven days at the ranch, then returned home for several months. At the end, the contestants returned to be weighed, and one team was declared the winners.

RATINGS: Season 1 of *The Biggest Loser* had an average of 10.3 million viewers each week.

BLIND DATE

GENRE	Docudrama (Dating)
FIRST TELECAST	9/1999
NETWORK	Syndicated
EPISODE STYLE	Self-contained
TALENT	Roger Lodge (Host)
PRODUCTION COMPANIES	Bobwell Productions; Gold Coast Entertainment; Renegade 83
EXECUTIVE PRODUCERS	David Garfinkle; Thomas Klein; Matthew Papish; Jay Renfroe
CO-EXECUTIVE PRODUCERS	Rob Dames; Harley Tat
PRODUCER	Brandy Menefee
CO-PRODUCERS	Glen Freyer; Gary Lucy; David Pullano
SEGMENT PRODUCERS	Stephen Berger; Mason Brown; Bryan Bultz; Nancy Cohen; Gregor Collins; Jay Erickson; Stan Evans; Luciana Fields; Archie Gips; Kim Hoffman; Alverta Jentimane; Kevin Katakoa; Karen Korn; Matt Odgers; Jon Peper; Eric Peterkofsky
DIRECTORS	Chad Baron; Ryan Cummings; Joel Ratz; Vincent Cariati

Camera crews follow couples as they go on blind dates. The dates are played back while pop-up-style graphics add commentary to the romantic and not-so-romantic proceedings. The show has spawned three DVD sets and a Pay-per-View special of the show's racier moments called, *Blind Date Uncensored.*

BLOW OUT

GENRE	Docusoap (Job)
FIRST TELECAST	6/8/2004
NETWORK	Bravo
AIR TIME	Tuesday, 9:00 p.m.
EPISODE STYLE	Story Arc
CAST	Jonathan Antin (Owner, Jonathan Salon); Tish Rourke (Manicurist); Alyn Topper (Hairstylist and Colorist); Daniel Owens (Stylist); Michael Solis (Stylist/Colorist); Kiara Bailey (Stylist); Annie Covell (Receptionist); Jason Low (Stylist); Brandon Martinez (Stylist—Season 1); Alicia Grandstedt (Stylist/Colorist—Season 1); Jenn MacDonald (Stylist, Colorist and Extensions Expert—Season 1)
PRODUCTION COMPANIES	Reveille LLC; Magna Global Entertainment; Arnold Shapiro and Alison Grodner Productions
EXECUTIVE PRODUCERS	Allison Grodner; Frances Croke Page; Arnold Shapiro; Ben Silverman, Mechelle Collins, Kevin Dill
SEGMENT PRODUCER	Steven Bortko
PRODUCERS	Jeff Anderson Munkres; Elaine Frontain Bryant; Lisa Caruso; Kevin Dill; Mark Koops; Rob Lee; H. T. Owens; Derrick Speight
DIRECTOR	Kevin Dill

On this docusoap, celebrity hairstylist Jonathan Antin allowed cameras to document the struggles and staffing conflicts he faced as he opened his new Beverly Hills salon. In addition to Antin, the show followed his team of stylists, including Brandon, a cocky bad boy whose brash ways ended up getting him fired. In Season 2, the show featured Antin launching his own line of hair care products. In Season 3, Antin struggled to maintain his businesses, as well as cope with being a father to his newborn son, Asher.

BOARDING HOUSE: NORTH SHORE

GENRE	Docudrama
FIRST TELECAST	6/18/2003
LAST TELECAST	7/23/2003
NETWORK	The WB
AIR TIME	Wednesday, 8:00 p.m.
EPISODE STYLE	Self-contained
TALENT	Josh Faure-Brac (Narrator)
CAST	Sunny Garcia; Myles Padaca; Damien Hobgood; Danny Fuller; Veronica Kay; Holly Beck; Chelsea Georgeson
PRODUCTION COMPANIES	Mark Burnett Productions; Basic Elements
EXECUTIVE PRODUCERS	Lisa Berger; Mark Burnett; Lisa Hennessy
PRODUCERS	David C. Brown; Leslie Garvin; Cherie Marquez; Bruce Toms

Shot on location on the island of Oahu, Hawaii, this docudrama featured personalities from the pro surfing world, who allowed cameras to chronicle their culture and competitions as the surfers lived under the same roof.

BOOT CAMP

GENRE	Competition (Endurance)
FIRST TELECAST	3/28/2001
LAST TELECAST	5/23/2001
NETWORK	FOX
AIR TIME	Wednesday, 9:00 p.m.
EPISODE STYLE	Story Arc
TALENT	Leo McSweeney (Drill Instructor); Tony Rosenbum (Drill Instructor); Dave Francisco (Drill Instructor);

	Annette Taylor (Drill Instructor); Don LaFontaine (Narrator)
CAST	Jen Whitlow (Winner); Ryan Wolf (Runner-up); Alfonso Moretti, Jr. (eliminated in Episode 7); Jennifer Moretty (eliminated in Episode 7); Leigh Dana Jackson (eliminated in Episode 6); Kasi Brown (eliminated in Episode 6); Katie Coddington (eliminated in Episode 5); Shawn Yaney (eliminated in Episode 5); Jack Lauder (eliminated in Episode 4); Jodi Hutak (eliminated in Episode 4); Mark Meyer (eliminated in Episode 3); David Thomson (medically discharged in Episode 3); Rebecca Ann Haar (eliminated in Episode 2); Sue Yen Pupo (eliminated in Episode 2); John Park (eliminated in Episode 1); Jane Katherine (quit in Episode 1)
PRODUCTION COMPANIES	Granada Entertainment USA; LMNO Productions
EXECUTIVE PRODUCERS	Bill Paolantonio; Marcus Plantin; Eric Schotz; Scott Messick
PRODUCERS	Paige Morrow; Alex Rader; Royce Toni; Tim Warren
DIRECTORS	Scott Messick; Chris Pechin

Using an elimination/competition format, this program followed real-world drill instructors as they put sixteen "recruits" through the rigors of authentic military training. The challenges included obstacle courses and confidence-building missions. Judged by their peers, the weakest civilian in the squad was given his marching orders. In a twist, the person voted out picked another recruit to eliminate. The remaining two recruits, Ryan Wolf and Jen Whitlow, competed in The Gauntlet—a grueling event that tested their physical and mental skills. The results of The Gauntlet, combined with a final vote, determined the winner. Jen Whitlow won the grand prize of $500,000, while Ryan Wolf took home the second place prize of $100,000.

RATINGS: *Boot Camp* drew an average audience of 11 million viewers during its spring 2001 run.

BORN TO DIVA

GENRE	Competition (Talent)
FIRST TELECAST	4/28/2003
LAST TELECAST	5/22/2003
NETWORK	VH1
EPISODE STYLE	Story Arc
TALENT	Ron Grant (Judge); Ken Komisar (Judge); Cory Rooney (Judge); Tommy Mottola (Judge); Patti LaBelle (Judge); Kelly Rowland (Judge); Lisa Stansfield (Judge); Gloria Estefan (Judge); T-Boz and Chilli (Judge); Jacob Neal (Diva Team—Hairstylist); Misa Hylton-Brim (Diva Team—Fashion Stylist); Kenn Hicks (Diva Team—Vocal Coach)
CAST	Tarralyn Ramsey (Atlanta Diva—winner); Towanda Charmaine Cofield, (Philadelphia Diva); Tomey Sellars (Miami Diva); Sasha Allen (New York Diva); Eno Uffort (London Diva)
PRODUCTION COMPANY	Bunim-Murray Productions
EXECUTIVE PRODUCERS	Mary-Ellis Bunim; Julio Kollerbohm; George Moll; Tommy Mottola; Jonathan Murray; Kim Rozenfeld
CO-EXECUTIVE PRODUCER	Julie Pizzi
PRODUCER	Kristin Mean
DIRECTOR	Rico Martinez

This talent competition was a quest to find an unknown female singer with megastar potential. A winner from each city was selected by a panel of music stars and industry professionals. The five finalists attended a week-long "Diva Boot Camp" and met with stylists to prepare them for their final performance in Las Vegas, on *VH1 Divas Duets*. Online voting by viewers determined the winner. Tarralyn Ramsey won the competition and a recording/management deal with Tommy Mottola's label.

BOY MEETS BOY

GENRE	Competition (Dating)
FIRST TELECAST	7/29/2003
LAST TELECAST	9/2/2003
NETWORK	Bravo
EPISODE STYLE	Story Arc
TALENT	Dani Behr (Host)
CAST	James Getzlaff (Bachelor); Andra Stasko (James's best friend); Wes Culwell (Winner—gay); Franklin (straight); Brian Hay (gay); Sean (eliminated in Episode 4—straight); Darren O'Hare (eliminated in Episode 4—gay); Robb MacArthur (eliminated in Episode 4—gay); Dan Wells (eliminated in Episode 3—straight); Michael Godinez (eliminated in Episode 3—straight); Matthew (elminated in Episode 3—gay); Jim (eliminated in Episode 2—straight); Paul (eliminated in Episode 2—straight); Marc (eliminated in Episode 2—gay); Chris Wilson (eliminated in Episode 1—gay); Brian Austin (eliminated in Episode 1—straight); Jason Tiner (eliminated in Episode 1—gay)
PRODUCTION COMPANY	Evolution Film & Tape Inc.
CREATORS	Dean Minerd; Douglas Ross; Tom Campbell
EXECUTIVE PRODUCERS	Frances Berwick; Kathleen French; Amy Introcaso; Dean Miners; Douglas Ross; Greg Stewart
CO-EXECUTIVE PRODUCERS	Tom Campbell; Kirk Marcolina
PRODUCER	Mario Yates
DIRECTORS	Becky Smith; Catherine McCarthy; S. Leo Chiang

Following the format established by *The Bachelor,* this first gay dating series had a twist: not all the suitors were gay. A single gay male contestant and fifteen suitors resided in separate accommodations under one roof. It was up to the contestant to eliminate all but one suitor. If he selected a legitimately gay man to date, the two won an adventure-packed vacation to New Zealand and $25,000. If he selected a masquerading straight man, the straight man won the $25,000. In the end, James chose Wes, one of the gay suitors, thereby winning the cash and the romantic trip.

BRAT CAMP

GENRE	Docusoap
FIRST TELECAST	7/13/2005
LAST TELECAST	8/24/2005
NETWORK	ABC
AIR TIME	Wednesday, 9:00 p.m.
EPISODE STYLE	Story Arc
CAST	Tony Randazzo (Sage Walk Leader—Glacier Mountain Wolf/Narrator); Scott Fitzwater (Therapist—Fire Bear); J. Huffine (Clinical Director—Flying Eagle); Cindy Fogel (Therapist—Mother Raven); Frank (Reluctant Bison Charging, 15); Isaiah Alrcon (Obsidian Snow Leopard, 17); Lexie (Insightful Fawn Growing, 17); Lauren (Flying Fire Fox, 17); Heather (Painted Butterfly, 16); Nick (Insightful Young Hawk, 14); Shawn (River Carving Canyon, 17); Jada Chabot (Spring Robin Searching, 15); Derek (Emerging Frog, 14)
PRODUCTION COMPANY	Arnold Shapiro; Alison Grodner Productions
EXECUTIVE PRODUCERS	Arnold Shapiro & Allison Grodner; Peter Casely-Hayford; Jamie Isaacs; Claudia Milne; Mark Rowland
SENIOR PRODUCER	Robin Groth
DIRECTOR	Ross Brettenbach

Based on the *Brat Camp* series from the United Kingdom, nine teenagers with disciplinary issues were sent by their parents to Sage Walk Wilderness School, in Oregon, for fifty days. Once the teens completed their stay, their parents hoped their behavior and mental attitudes would have changed so they could return to their families without anger and resentment. In the finale, it was revealed that most of the teens had changed for the better as a result of their time at the camp, with the exception of Jada, who had been caught smoking marijuana

BREAKING BONADUCE

GENRE	Docusoap (Celebrity)
FIRST TELECAST	9/11/2005
NETWORK	VH1
EPISODE STYLE	Story Arc
CAST	Danny Bonaduce; Gretchen Bonaduce; Isabella Bonaduce; Dante Bonaduce; Garry Corgiat
PRODUCTION COMPANIES	VH1 Productions; 3 Ball Productions
EXECUTIVE PRODUCERS	J. D. Roth; John Foy; Todd A. Nelson; Jeff Olde; Claire McCabe; Kim Rozenfeld; Danny Bonaduce; Gretchen Bonaduce; Brandon Riegg; Troy Searer; Jeff Krask
DIRECTOR	Mark Jacobs

The Partridge Family's Danny Bonaduce and his wife, Gretchen, got married seven hours into their first date. Throughout their fifteen years of marriage, the couple has weathered addiction, infidelity, life-changing moments, and everyday frustrations. Originally conceived as a glimpse into their unusual marriage, *Breaking Bonaduce* followed the family's trials and tribulations as Danny descended into drug, alcohol, and sex addiction, and a trip back to rehab. In addition, the couple attended therapy sessions to deal with their problems. The series reached an especially riveting point when Danny attempted suicide. In the show's second season, Gretchen asked Danny to move out of their house, but invited him back by the finale.

BRIDEZILLAS

GENRE	Docudrama
FIRST TELECAST	1/27/2003
NETWORKS	FOX (one-hour special); WE (series)
EPISODE STYLE	Self-contained
TALENT	Mindy Burbano (Host/Narrator)
EXECUTIVE PRODUCERS	Sam Brick; David Green; Mary Pelloni
PRODUCERS	Paul Kolsby; Jenny McGonigal; Carrie Certa; Pamela Covais; Ron Davis; Maria Galatin; Elisa M. Rothstein; Deborah J. Whitcas; Mario Yates
DIRECTOR	Paul Kolsby

Camera crews followed future brides on their "emotional-roller coaster" experience preparing for their "perfect" wedding day. *Bridezillas* followed the brides as they went from sweet to certifiable.

BRITNEY AND KEVIN: CHAOTIC

GENRE	Docudrama (Celebrity)
FIRST TELECAST	5/17/2005
LAST TELECAST	6/14/2005
NETWORK	UPN
AIR TIME	Tuesday, 9:00 p.m.
EPISODE STYLE	Self-contained
CAST	Britney Spears; Kevin Federline
EXECUTIVE PRODUCERS	Britney Spears; Kevin Federline; Susan Zirinsky

Pop star Britney Spears's home videos were turned into this personal account of her courtship with dancer Kevin Federline, a relationship that blossomed into marriage. The series ended with the world premiere of Britney's video for "Someday (I Will Understand)."

BSTV

GENRE	Docudrama (Hoax)
FIRST TELECAST	5/15/2005
NETWORK	VH1
EPISODE STYLE	Self-contained
TALENT	Paul Garner; Jim Cashman; Nichole Lennstrom; Paul Greenberg; Stephanie Escajeda; Steve Mallory; Brandon Johnson; Marc Wootton
PRODUCTION COMPANY	VH1, in conjunction with Ealing Studios
CREATED BY	Paul Garner
EXECUTIVE PRODUCERS	Paul Garner; Jim Biederman; Jill Leiderman; Michael Hirschorn; Jim Ackerman
PRODUCERS	C. K. Gillen; Elizabeth Belew; Paul Allen
DIRECTOR	C. K. Gillen

Civilians and television personalities unknowingly auditioned for a fake reality series in this hoax show. Improvisational comedy actors portrayed the show's producers, and tried to elicit reactions from those auditioning. Some of the reality stars who were duped in this series included Evan Marriott, Nick Warnock, Jenna Lewis, and Kimberly Caldwell.

BUT CAN THEY SING?

GENRE	Competition (Talent)
FIRST TELECAST	10/30/2005
LAST TELECAST	12/4/2005
NETWORK	VH1
EPISODE STYLE	Story Arc
CAST	Ahmet Zappa (Host); Tony Michaels (Dance Instructor); Jackie Simley-Stevens (Vocal Coach); Rachel Riggs (Vocal Coach)

TALENT	Michael Copon (Winner); Carmine Gotti Agnello (Runner-up); Morgan Fairchild (2nd Runner-up); Bai Ling (eliminated in 5th episode); Antonio Sabato, Jr. (eliminated in 4th episode); Larry Holmes (eliminated in 3rd episode); Joe Pantoliano (eliminated in 2nd episode); Myrka Dellanos (eliminated 2nd episode); Kim Alexis (eliminated 2nd episode)
PRODUCTION COMPANY	Granada Television USA
EXECUTIVE PRODUCERS	Jay Karas; Antonia Mattia; Curt Northrup; Jeff Olde
PRODUCER	Kate Richter
DIRECTORS	Alan Carter; Steve Paley

In an *American Idol*–like competition, nine celebrities tested out their singing skills. Coached by vocal and dance instructors, they then performed live in front of a studio audience. Home viewers voted online for their favorite performer, and the winner's favorite charity received $50,000. Actor Michael Copon won the grand prize for the Shaken Baby Alliance.

BUZZKILL

GENRE	Docucomedy (Hoax)
FIRST TELECAST	6/18/1996
NETWORK	MTV
EPISODE STYLE	Self-contained
TALENT	Dave Sheridan; Travis Draft; Frank Hudetz
PRODUCERS	Paul Cockerill; Greg Johnston
DIRECTOR	Jason Sands

The *Candid Camera* genre was done guerrilla-style in this hidden-camera show for MTV, in which a team of three comedians traveled America to carry out pranks. Their tricks included having people model silly clothes, offering ridiculous safety tips to people on Miami Beach, and watching reactions as people become the "victims" of bad voodoo spells in New Orleans.

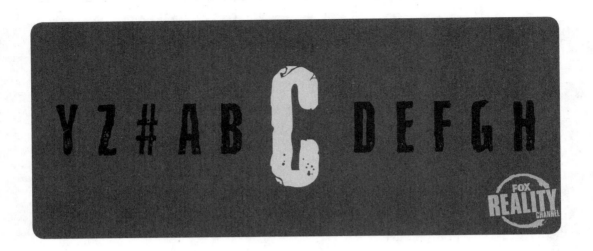

CAESARS 24/7

GENRE	Docudrama
FIRST TELECAST	1/10/2005
LAST TELECAST	7/16/2005
NETWORK	A&E
EPISODE STYLE	Self-contained
PRODUCTION COMPANIES	Cypress Point Productions; 44Blue Productions Inc.
EXECUTIVE PRODUCERS	Stuart Zwagil; Gerald W. Abrams; Rasha Drachkovitch; Michael R. Goldstein
DIRECTORS	Autumn Doerr; Joke Fincioen; Julie Jorgensen; James Lockart; Biagio Messina; C. Webb Young

Shot on location in Las Vegas, *Caesars 24/7* focused on the employees of Caesars Palace as they interacted with tourists and the "regulars." Episodes featured the employees supervising weddings and bachelor parties, entertaining high rollers, and hosting a boxing event.

CAMP REALITY

GENRE	Competition
FIRST TELECAST	1/30/2007
NETWORK	Fox Reality Channel
EPISODE STYLE	Story Arc
TALENT	Burton Roberts (Host)
CAST	Scott Long; Michelle Deighton; Jonny Fairplay; Brennan Swain; Ryan "Ryno" Opray; Rebecca Cardon; John "JP" Palyok; Coral Smith; Nikki McKibben; Adam Larson; Tamie Sheffield; Toni Ferrari
CREATED BY	Burton Roberts
EXECUTIVE PRODUCERS	Burton Roberts; Bob Boden

Though hosted by *Survivor* alum Burton Roberts, this docudrama features no eliminations and no manipulations. Roberts brings together twelve fellow reality stars from shows such as *The Amazing Race* and *American Idol* to Big Bear, California, to compete in various challenges, ranging from archery to paintball to milk chugging.

CANDID CAMERA

GENRE	Docucomedy (Hoax)
FIRST TELECAST	9/1991 (Syndicated)
LAST TELECAST	4/24/2005
NETWORK	Syndicated (1991–1992); CBS (2/1998–9/2000); PAX (1/2001–4/2005)
EPISODE STYLE	Self-contained
TALENT	Dom Deluise (Host—syndicated); Eva LaRue Callahan (Co-host—syndicated); Peter Funt (Host—CBS & PAX); Suzanne Somers (Co-host—CBS); Dina Eastwood (Co-host—PAX)

PRODUCTION COMPANY	King World Productions (syndicated)
EXECUTIVE PRODUCER	Peter Funt
PRODUCER	Phil Gurin
DIRECTORS	George Elanjian, Jr. (syndicated); Sean McNamara (syndicated); Lenn Goodside (CBS and PAX); Ron de Moraes (CBS and PAX)

This grandfather of reality shows was revived in the early 1990s, as *Candid Camera* once again set up hidden cameras to capture the reactions of ordinary people in outrageous pranks. Just like the original show, the revived series' pranks involved simple circumstances, such as malfunctioning equipment or odd characters, such as an airport security agent who asked a man to go through an X-ray machine as part of the screening process. New segments in this updated version included "Then and Now," in which classic pranks were re-created with modern victims.

CANNONBALL RUN 2001: RACE ACROSS AMERICA

GENRE	Competition
FIRST TELECAST	8/5/2001
LAST TELECAST	8/9/2001
NETWORK	USA
EPISODE STYLE	Story Arc
TALENT	Bill Weir (Host); Krista Herman (Co-host); Lee Reherman (Co-host)
CAST	Carlton Denning (Winner—Hip Hop with Pop); HemDee Kiwanuka (Winner—Hip Hop with Pop); David Vargas (Winner—Hip Hop with Pop); Matt Deane (2nd place—Third Wheel); Jane Norris (2nd place—Third Wheel); Dana Walker (2nd

place—Third Wheel); Princess Davis (3rd place—Alpha Gamma Grandma); Steve Ponce (3rd place—Alpha Gamma Grandma); Mike Grofsky (3rd place—Alpha Gamma Grandma); Susan Hawk (eliminated in Episode 4—The Castaways); Jeff Varner (eliminated in Episode 4—The Castaways); Kaya Wittenburg (eliminated in Episode 4—The Castaways); Steve England (eliminated in Episode 3—Hog Wild); Tom Kreon (eliminated in Episode 3—Hog Wild); Jacquelyn Simone (eliminated in Episode 3—Hog Wild); Marc Harrison (disqualified in Episode 2—Forbidden Fruit); Jodi Ann Patterson (disqualified in Episode 2—Forbidden Fruit); Natalia Sokolova (disqualified in Episode 2—Forbidden Fruit)

PRODUCTION COMPANIES Brass Ring Entertainment; Checkered Flag Productions; GRB Entertainment Inc., USA Cable Network; USA Network Inc.

EXECUTIVE PRODUCERS Cris Abrego; Thomas Augsberg; Gary R. Benz; Beau Flynn; Dawn Parouse; Rick Telles; Brock Yates

PRODUCER Ben Samek

DIRECTOR Rick Telles

Loosely based on the hit movie of the same name, this competition featured six teams of three who hit the road from New York to Los Angeles, encountering challenges during a race to the finish line. Cast members included reality stars Kaya Wittenburg, from *Temptation Island*, and Susan Hawk and Jeff Varner, of *Survivor*. The $75,000 winners of the race were Hip Hop with Pop's HemDee Kiwanuka, David Vargas, and Carlton Denning.

CARPOCALYPSE

GENRE	Competition (Makeover)
FIRST TELECAST	2/26/2005
NETWORK	Spike TV
EPISODE STYLE	Self-contained
PRODUCTION COMPANIES	Film Garden; Mess Media
CREATED BY	Brigham Cottan; Edwin Saenz
CO-EXECUTIVE PRODUCER	Ross Kaiman
PRODUCERS	Brigham Cottan; Jamie Iracleanos; Joe Marotta
DIRECTOR	Edwin Saenz

Competitors armed with just a few days and a few hundred dollars turned junkyard parts into demolition derby machines on this competition series. The match-ups involved an array of vehicles, including RVs, school buses, and taxis. The winner of the derby took home a cash prize.

THE CASINO

GENRE	Docudrama (Job)
FIRST TELECAST	6/15/2005
LAST TELECAST	8/29/2004
NETWORK	FOX
AIR TIME	Monday, 9:00 p.m.
EPISODE STYLE	Story Arc
CAST	Tom Breitling (Owner, Golden Nugget); Timothy Poster (Owner, Golden Nugget); Zach Conine (Assistant); Dee Conton (Director of Casino Marketing); Joe Leone (Entertainment Director); John Sunstrum (Casino Host); Tommy Sunstrum (Dealer/Host); Matt Dusk (Singer)

PRODUCTION COMPANY	Mark Burnett Productions
CREATED BY	Mark Brunett; James Bruce; Conrad Riggs
EXECUTIVE PRODUCERS	Mark Brunett; James Bruce; Conrad Riggs; Robert Lieberman; Trent Othick
PRODUCERS	Ariana Squar; Zachary Weintraub; Chris Nee; Mark Mori; Roy Bank; Mark Burg; Freddy Deane; Oren Koules

This job-related docudrama followed entrepreneurs Timothy Poster and Thomas Breitling, who at age thirty-two sold their company, Travelscape.com, to Expedia for $105 million and bought the Golden Nugget Las Vegas Hotel and Casino. The friends' goal was to bring the "Rat Pack" glamor of yesteryear to their new business gamble. Cameras followed everything from what it took to make a casino, to getting a gaming license, to booking talent, to handling staffing woes, and ultimately, to keeping the customers satisfied throughout around-the-clock drama.

RATINGS: This Mark Burnett venture brought in an average of 4.4 million viewers a week for FOX.

CELEBRITY COOKING SHOWDOWN

GENRE	Competition
FIRST TELECAST	4/17/2006
LAST TELECAST	4/22/2006
NETWORK	NBC
EPISODE STYLE	Story Arc
TALENT	Alan Thicke (Host); Gael Greene (Judge); Colin Cowie (Judge); Govind Armstrong (Coach); Cat Cora (Coach); Wolfgang Puck (Coach)
CAST	Cindy Margolis (Winner); Patti LaBelle; Gabrielle Reece; Chelsea Cooley; Big Kenny; Alison Sweeney; Tony Gonzalez; Tom Arnold; Ashley Parker Angel

PRODUCTION COMPANIES	Bad Boy Worldwide Entertainment Group; Reveille Productions
EXECUTIVE PRODUCERS	Sean "P. Diddy" Combs; David A. Hurwitz; Ben Silverman
PRODUCERS	Sean Atkins; Angela Heller; Russ Ward; Brad Wollack

Celebrities teamed up to cook with professional chefs, then had their creations judged by an event planner and a food critic. At the end of each show, viewers voted on who they thought prepared the best meal. The first three episodes ran on consecutive nights, with the winner from each night advancing to the finals. Due to low ratings, the show was nearly canceled before completion, but NBC aired the final two episodes.

CELEBRITY DUETS

GENRE	Competition (Talent)
FIRST TELECAST	8/29/2006
LAST TELECAST	9/29/2006
NETWORK	FOX
AIR TIME	Friday, 9:00 p.m.
EPISODE STYLE	Story Arc
TALENT	Wayne Brady (Host); David Foster (Judge); Marie Osmond (Judge); Little Richard (Judge)
CAST	Alfonso Ribeiro (Winner), Lucy Lawless, Cheech Marin, Carly Patterson, Lea Thompson, Chris Jericho, Hal Sparks, Jai Rodriguez
PRODUCTION COMPANY	Syco Television
EXECUTIVE PRODUCERS	Simon Cowell; Arthur Smith
PRODUCERS	Sean Atkins; Angela Heller; Russ Ward; Brad Wollack
DIRECTOR	Bruce Gowers

Established singers, such as Aaron Neville, Michael Bolton, and Toby Keith paired with celebrities unaffiliated with the music industry. The professionals instructed their celebrity partners, and the two performed duets for judges, a live audience, and home viewers, who voted on their favorites each week. Actor Alfonso Ribeiro of *The Fresh Prince of Bel-Air* was voted the $100,000 winner, a prize he donated to Fresh Start, an organization that provides plastic surgery for children with birth defects.

CELEBRITY FIT CLUB

GENRE	Competition (Makeover)
FIRST TELECAST	1/9/2005
NETWORK	VH1
EPISODE STYLE	Story Arc
TALENT	Ant (Host); Dr. David Katz (Health Expert—Season 1); Marisa Peer (Hypnotherapist); Harvey Walden IV (Fitness Trainer); Dr. Ian Smith (Health Expert—Season 2)

CAST

Season 1	Daniel Baldwin; Kim Coles; Joe Gannascoli; Judge Mablean Ephriam; Biz Markie; Ralphie May; Mia Tyler; Wendy Kauffman
Season 2	Wendy Kaufman; Willie Aames; Jani Lane; Phil Margera; Victoria Jackson; Toccara Jones; Gary Busey
Season 3	Kelley LeBrock; Countess Vaughn; Bizarre; Gunnar Nelson; Jeff Conaway; Chastity Bono; Tempestt Bledsoe; Young MC; Bruce Vilanch
Season 4	Bonecrusher; Carnie Wilson; Nicholas Turturro; Erika Eleniak; Tina Yothers; Vincent Pastore; Angie Stone; Ted Lange
Season 5	Ross Mathews; Maureen McCormick; Dustin Diamond; Tiffany; Warren G; Da Brat; Cledus T. Judd; Kimberley Locke

PRODUCTION COMPANY	Granada Entertainment
EXECUTIVE PRODUCERS	Dagmar Charlton; Curt Northrup
DIRECTOR	R. Brian DiPirro

Shot over fourteen weeks, this competition followed eight overweight celebrities as they were divided into two teams and challenged to get into shape. Each episode featured a weigh-in, and rivalries heated up among the stars.

CELEBRITY MOLE

GENRE	Competition (Celebrity)
FIRST TELECAST	1/8/2003
LAST TELECAST	12/18/2004
NETWORK	ABC
AIR TIME	Wednesday, 10:00 p.m.
EPISODE STYLE	Story Arc
TALENT	Ahmad Rashad (Host)

CAST

Season 1 (Hawaii)	Kathy Griffin (Winner); Frederique Van Der Wal (The Mole); Erik Von Detten; Stephen Baldwin; Corbin Bernsen; Michael Boatman; Kim Coles
Season 2 (Yucatan)	Dennis Rodman (Winner); Angie Everhart (The Mole); Mark Curry; Tracy Gold; Keshia Knight Pulliam; Stephen Baldwin; Corbin Bernsen; Ananda Lewis
PRODUCTION COMPANY	Stone-Stanley Productions
EXECUTIVE PRODUCERS	Luis Barreto; Grant Johnson; Scott A. Stone; David G. Stanley; Clay Newbill (Season 2)
PRODUCER	Tim Bock
DIRECTOR	Sean Travis

In this spin-off of *The Mole* series, six celebrities played mental and physical games for two weeks to determine who among them had been hired by the producers to be the secret saboteur—the "Celebrity Mole." Games added money to a cumulative cash pot. Following each round, players took a quiz with questions designed to uncover the mole's identity. The star with the least number of correct answers was "executed" and had to leave the game. In the end, the celebrity who guessed correctly won the money in the cash pot when the true identity of the celebrity mole was revealed. Season 1's winner was comedian Kathy Griffin, while former NBA player Dennis Rodman won Season 2.

CELEBRITY PARANORMAL PROJECT

GENRE	Docudrama
FIRST TELECAST	10/22/2006
LAST TELECAST	12/17/2006
NETWORK	VH1
EPISODE STYLE	Self-contained
PRODUCTION COMPANY	51 Minds Entertainment
EXECUTIVE PRODUCERS	Cris Abrego; Mark Cronin; Ben Samek
PRODUCERS	Fred Birckhead; Zach Kozek; Devon Platte
DIRECTOR	Zach Kozek

In this docudrama, stars visited haunted sites to investigate paranormal activities. In each episode, a team of five celebrities had to track down the ghosts haunting a spooky location. With the help of modern technology, the celebrities documented their terrifying journey.

CHAINS OF LOVE

GENRE	Competition (Dating)
FIRST TELECAST	4/17/2001
LAST TELECAST	5/22/2001

NETWORK	UPN
AIR TIME	Tuesday, 8:00 p.m.
EPISODE STYLE	Self-contained
TALENT	Madison Michele (Host)
PRODUCTION COMPANY	Endemol
PRODUCERS	Bryan Bultz; Archie Gips; Matt Odgers; Bradford Schultze; Jude Weng

Based on a Dutch dating show involving five strangers, this competition physically chained four women to one good-looking man for four days. Each day, one woman was unchained and eliminated from the competition. The winning female received $10,000. The series was originally scheduled to air on NBC but was dropped by the network before it aired.

CHASING FARRAH

GENRE	Docudrama (Celebrity)
FIRST TELECAST	3/23/2005
LAST TELECAST	4/27/2005
NETWORK	TV Land
EPISODE STYLE	Story Arc
TALENT	Farrah Fawcett
PRODUCTION COMPANY	Windmill Productions
EXECUTIVE PRODUCERS	Marta M. Mobley; Craig J. Nevius; Sal Maniaci
PRODUCER	Nancy Valen
DIRECTOR	Craig J. Nevius

A behind-the-scenes look at the 1970s television icon and sex symbol Farrah Fawcett recorded the chaos that ensued as she traveled with an entourage from Hollywood to her birthplace in Texas, with stops along the way in Miami and New York. The series featured an episode with Farrah's former partner, Ryan O'Neal, in an unflinching look into their private lives.

CHEATERS

GENRE	Docudrama
FIRST TELECAST	09/2000
NETWORK	Syndicated
EPISODE STYLE	Self-contained
TALENT	Tommy Habeeb (Host); Tommy Grand (Host, 2000–2003); Joey Greco (Host, 2004-Present)
PRODUCTION COMPANIES	Direkt Produktions; Goldstein/Habeeb Entertainment
EXECUTIVE PRODUCER	Bobby Goldstein
PRODUCERS	Billy Tears; John McCalmont; Tommy Habeeb
DIRECTOR	John McCalmont

This docudrama focused on cheating spouses. Armed with incriminating video evidence, the show's host, along with his camera crew, bodyguards, and the victim confronted the cheaters on-camera, often catching them off-guard, leading to heated results.

CHEERLEADER NATION

GENRE	Docusoap
FIRST TELECAST	3/2006
NETWORK	Lifetime
EPISODE STYLE	Story Arc
CAST	Donna (Coach); Eric (Parent); Saleem (Choreographer); Terri (Parent); Teresa (Parent); Alexa; Amanda; Ashley; Ayrica; Chelsea; Kaitlin; Katie; Megan; Nicole; Ryan
PRODUCTION COMPANIES	Fox Television; Lifetime Television
EXECUTIVE PRODUCER	Laurie Girion

This docusoap followed Lexington, Kentucky's, Paul Laurence Dunbar High School cheerleading squad's long road to a national championship. The show featured the squad's families, too, and delved into the world of parenting these ambitious teenagers.

CHEYENNE

GENRE	Docusoap
FIRST TELECAST	5/31/2006
LAST TELECAST	6/19/2006
NETWORK	MTV
EPISODE STYLE	Self-contained
CAST	Cheyenne Kimball
PRODUCTION COMPANY	MTV Productions
EXECUTIVE PRODUCERS	Rod Aissa; Lois Clark Curren; Jesse Ignjatovic

Cheyenne chronicle the daily drama that unfolded as Cheyenne Kimball made the transition from small-town girl to big-time rock star after winning the *America's Most Talented Kid* competition.

CHUCK WOOLERY: NATURALLY STONED

GENRE	Docusoap (Celebrity)
FIRST TELECAST	6/15/2003
LAST TELECAST	7/27/2003
NETWORK	GSN
EPISODE STYLE	Story Arc
TALENT	Scott Parkin (Narrator)
CAST	Chuck Woolery

PRODUCTION COMPANY Laurelwood Productions; Red Skies Entertainment
EXECUTIVE PRODUCER Phil Gurin

On this docusoap the game show host took viewers behind the scenes of his professional life at the taping of "Lingo" and at the rap-video remake of his Top 40 radio hit "Naturally Stoned" (recorded with the group Avant Garde). The series also included a peek into a TV shopping channel where Woolery experienced an overwhelming response to his "Motolure" product.

CLEAN SWEEP

GENRE Docudrama (Makeover)
FIRST TELECAST 9/13/2003
NETWORK TLC
EPISODE STYLE Self-contained
TALENT Stacey Dutton (Host—Season 1); Tava Smiley (Host—Season 2); Angelo Surmelis (Designer); Shelli Alexander (Organizer); Valerie Bickford (Designer); Molly Luetkemeyer (Designer); Peter Walsh (Organizer—Season 2); Kelli Ellis (Designer—Season 2); James Saavedra (Designer—Season 2)
PRODUCTION COMPANY Evolution Film & Tape Inc.
EXECUTIVE PRODUCERS Kathleen French; Dean Minerd; Douglas Ross; Susan Seide; Greg Stewart
PRODUCER Deborah Markoe-Klein
DIRECTORS Laurent Malaquais; Hans van Riet; Deborah Markoe-Klein

A team of design experts persuaded couples to clean the clutter out of their homes or workplaces in this makeover show. On a budget, two rooms were transformed into functional, stylish spaces. Along the way, viewers were given tips to enable them to complete the projects shown on the series.

THE CLUB

GENRE	Docudrama
FIRST TELECAST	11/10/2004
NETWORK	Spike TV
EPISODE STYLE	Self-contained
CAST	Ed Williams (Owner); Allison Melnick (Party Promoter); Chuckie (Director of Food and Beverage); Joe (General Manager); Jessie (The Hostess); Michael (The Efficiency Expert); Michelle (Server); Stacey (Server); Andrea (Server); Jackie (Server); Marc (Marketing); Sean (VIP); Walter (Bartender); Lenny (Bar Back); Brian (VIP host)
PRODUCTION COMPANY	Reveille Productions
EXECUTIVE PRODUCERS	Kevin Dill; Tracy Dorsey; Mark Koops; H. T. Owens; Robert Riesenberg; Greg Shapiro; Ben Silverman
PRODUCERS	Josh Bingham; Duncan McLean

On *The Club,* Ed Williams renovated his Las Vegas nightclub, Ice, attempting to make it the hottest spot in the city. Tension brewed as he brought Los Angeles promoter Allison Melnick into the fold. Melnick and her abrasive manner caused much conflict among the staff during the show.

COLD TURKEY

GENRE	Competition
FIRST TELECAST	10/3/2004
LAST TELECAST	5/17/2005
NETWORK	PAX
AIR TIMES	Sunday, 10:00 p.m. (Season 1); Tuesday, 9:00 p.m. (Season 2)

EPISODE STYLE	Story Arc
TALENT	A. J. Benza (Host)

CAST

Season 1   Calvin Smith; Francesca Sloan; D. J. Henderson; Carol Patterson; Cory Cataldo; Keith Jones; Amy Hall; Chechulae McDonald; Karen McCauley

Season 2   Leslie Reeder (Team Maverick); Greg Rizzo (Team Maverick); A. J. Ramirez (Team Maverick); Brad Robinson (Team Maverick); Jessie Gibson (Team Iron Fist); Pete Chen (Team Iron Fist); Christian Driggs (Team Iron Fist); Michelle Angevine (Team Iron Fist); Brenda (Team Iron Fist); Linda Reinecke (dropped out); Chelsea Merrick (dropped out)

PRODUCTION COMPANIES	NBC Productions; Visual Frontier Inc.
CREATED BY	Jeremy Wallace
EXECUTIVE PRODUCERS	Stuart Krasnow; Murray Valeriano; Jeremy Wallace; Kevin Williams
DIRECTOR	Darren Ewing

Chain smokers live under the same roof for twenty-four days while trying to quit smoking. Dr. Will Kirby, the winner of *Big Brother 2*, made guest appearances on the series. Those who stuck it out split a cash prize. In Season 1, all the smokers survived the competition, splitting a cash prize of $99,510. In Season 2, the participants were split into two teams: Team Maverick and Team Iron Fist. Team Maverick split $32,000, while Team Iron Fist split $63,500.

COLLEGE HILL

GENRE	Docudrama
FIRST TELECAST	1/28/2004

LAST TELECAST	5/12/2005
NETWORK	BET
EPISODE STYLE	Story Arc
TALENT	Scott Parkin (Narrator)

CAST

Season 1 (Southern University)	Delano, Jabari, Nina Shalondrea, Stacey
Season 2 (Langston University)	Stacey Stephens; Arthur "Israel" Doyle; Brittani Lewis; Coti Farley; Alva "Peaches" Jasper; Nafiys Blakewood; Tanisha Taylor; John Walker
Season 3 (Virginia State University)	Deirdra Tyrone-Davis; Audrina Clyde; Rodney Henry; Arlando Whitaker; Ray Cunningham; Bianca Olivo; Anya Holland; Will Grishaw
Season 4 (University of the Virgin Islands)	Idesha Browne; Vanessa Hamilton; Devon "Chicky" Luis; Andres St. Kitts; Fallon Favors; Krystal Lee; Jaron "J.T" Bets; Willie McMiller
College Hill Interns (Chicago)	Letia Walker; Jenna Nia Bailey; Kathy Harris; Tationna Boiser; Ivy Box; Spencer Humphrey; Marc Reece; Maurice Andrews; Lonnie Abernathy; Kasheef Wyzard
PRODUCTION COMPANY	Edmonds Entertainment
EXECUTIVE PRODUCERS	Christopher Scott Cherot; Tracey E. Edmonds; Michael McQuarn
PRODUCERS	Ron De Shay; Tracey E. Edmonds
CO-PRODUCERS	Michael McQuarn; Julian M. Lloyd; Emerlynn Lampitoc
DIRECTORS	Christopher Scott Cherot; Tamika Lamison; David Seligman; Melvin James; Dana Klein; Brian Krinsky; Matthew Ruecker

This first African American reality drama, season 1 featured eight college co-eds living together while attending Southern University in Louisiana. The series followed a *Real World*–type format, but centered on students at a historically African American university. The second season was taped at Langston University in Oklahoma. The third season took place at Virginia State University, in Ettrick, Virginia. Season 4 was filmed at the University of the Virgin Islands, in St. Thomas. *College Hill Interns,* a 2007 spin-off series, followed students during a summer internship in Chicago.

COLONIAL HOUSE

GENRE	Docudrama
FIRST TELECAST	5/7/2004
NETWORK	PBS
EPISODE STYLE	Story Arc
CAST	Jeff Lin (Company Servant); Dave Verdecia (Head of Verdicia House); Debbie Verdecia (Dave's wife); Maddison Verdecia (Dave's daughter—oldest child); Tony Verdecia (Dave's son—middle child); Emily Verdecia (Dave's daughter—youngest child); David Wyers (Governor's son—youngest child); Jeff Wyers (Governor—episodes 1–5); Tammy Wyers (Governor's wife); Bethany Wyers (Governor's daughter—oldest child); Amy Wyers (Governor's daughter—middle child); John Voorhees (Hunter and Negotiator); Giacomo Voorhees (John's son); Michelle Rossi-Voorhees (John's wife); Craig Tuminaro: (Company Servant); Danny Tisdale (Oldest Freeman—head of the Freemen's household); Dominic Muir (Freeman/Quartermaster); Jack Lecza: (Cape Merchant and Treasurer—Episodes 6–8); Paul Hunt (Servant to the Governor/Company Servant); Amy-Kristina Herbert (Widow); Don Heinz (Lay Preacher/Assistant Governor—Episodes 1–5); Governor—Episodes

	6–8); Clare Samuels (Indentured Servant [Cook] to the Governor); Don Wood (Freeman/Assistant Governor); Jonathon Allen (Indentured Servant to the Lay Preacher's family); Julia Friese (Indentured Servant to the Governor's family/Company Servant); Carolyn Heinz (Lay Preacher's wife)
PRODUCTION COMPANIES	Thirteen/WNET Communications Group; Wall to Wall Television Ltd.
EXECUTIVE PRODUCERS	Beth Hoppe; Leanne Klein
PRODUCER	Nicholas Brown
DIRECTORS	Sally Aitken; Nick Brown; Kristi Jacobson; Philippa Ross

The production team behind *The 1900 House* and *Frontier House* turned their attention to life in seventeenth-century America in this docudrama. Participants live for five months on the East Coast, eating, dressing, and working like the first American settlers. Oprah Winfrey devoted one of her shows to her *Colonial House* visit, but it was not a part of the PBS series.

COMBAT MISSIONS

GENRE	Competition
FIRST TELECAST	1/16/2002
NETWORK	USA
EPISODE STYLE	Story Arc
TALENT	Rudy Boesch (Base Commander); James D. Dever (Sergeant Major); Heather Cunningham (Camp Medic)
CAST	Dexter Fletcher (Winner—Bravo Squad); Rod Teeple (Delta Squad, Team leader); Baz (Delta Squad, Team Leader 2); George Ciganik (Delta Squad replacement); Garth Estadt (Delta Squad);

Scott Helvenston (Delta Squad); William Nissen (Delta Squad replacement); Rod Nutter (Delta Squad); John Winn (Delta Squad); Jeff Byers (Bravo Squad); Steve Claggett (Bravo Squad); Mark Corwin (Bravo Squad); Bob Kain (Bravo Squad); Sean Sirker (Bravo Squad replacement); Jody Taylor (Bravo Squad); Ed Bugarin (Charlie Squad, Team Leader); Cade Courtley (Charlie Squad replacement, Team Leader 2); Ossie Crenshaw (Charlie Squad); Jeff Everage (Charlie Squad); Ken Greaves (Charlie Squad); John Potter (Charlie Squad); Jonathan Weber (Charlie Squad replacement); Wilson Wong (Charlie Squad replacement); Justin Young (Charlie Squad); Dan O'Shea (Alpha Squad, Team Leader); Mark Jackson (Alpha Squad); Eric Johnson (Alpha Squad replacement); Frank Monestere (Alpha Squad); Scott Oates (Alpha Squad); Harald Zundel (Alpha Squad replacement); Chris Pate (Alpha Squad); Mell Spicer (Alpha Squad); Darrell Pfingsten (Shadow Squad); Santos Hernandez (Shadow Squad); Christopher Gilbertson (Shadow Squad)

PRODUCTION COMPANY	Mark Burnett Productions
EXECUTIVE PRODUCER	Mark Burnett
CO-EXECUTIVE PRODUCER	Cord Keller
PRODUCERS	Larry Barron; Brian Crance

Producer Mark Burnett's (*Survivor, The Apprentice*) competition series tested the skills of twenty-four contestants drawn from the ranks of the Delta Force, Green Beret, Marine Recon, Navy SEALs, Police SWAT, and CIA Special Operations. The show's host was decorated ex–Navy SEAL and former *Survivor: Borneo* contestant Rudy Boesch. As each team lost, one member was eliminated. Dexter Fletcher won the $250,000 grand prize. Contestant Scott Helvenston, later working as a contract guard, was killed outside Fallujah, Iraq, when his convoy was hit by rockets.

THE COMPLEX: MALIBU

GENRE	Competition (Makeover)
FIRST TELECAST	8/30/2004
LAST TELECAST	10/8/2004
NETWORK	FOX
AIR TIME	Monday, 8:00 p.m.; Friday, 8:00 p.m.
EPISODE STYLE	Story Arc
TALENT	Tyler Harcott (Host); Lourdes Marie Barros (Designer—Judge); David Kessler (Real Estate Broker—Judge); Jason Marshall (Architect—Judge)
CAST	Steve Shepley and Nicole Forslund (Winners); Barney and Rose (Runners-up); Dave and Ana (Runners-up); Scott and Sam (2nd Runners-up); Brad Plumley and Lew Gallow (eliminated in Episode 4); Carl Abrasmon and Kim Sarubbi (eliminated in Episode 3); Erik and Jayna (eliminated in Episode 2); Sanyika and Monique (eliminated in Episode 1)
PRODUCTION COMPANIES	FremantleMedia North America; Chaos Theory
EXECUTIVE PRODUCERS	Ted Haimes; Robin Feinberg
PRODUCERS	John Ennis; Rebecca Hertz; Eden Gaha
DIRECTOR	Craig Borders

Inspired by the hit Australian show *The Block*, this competition pitted eight couples against one another for a cash prize that was awarded to whoever did the best job of restoring and redecorating a four-unit apartment. Each week the couple had to renovate a specific room in their apartment unit. At the end of each episode, a panel of judges, including an architect, an interior designer, and a real estate agent, evaluated the remodeling work and how much value it added to the unit. A contestant vote determined which two couples were put up for eviction each week. Of those two couples, the one whose remodeling added the least value to their unit was eliminated. The series culminated in a building's sale at an auction. The winners were Steve and Nicole, whose prize was $317,250, the net profit from the sale of all four apartment units at the final auction. The show's theme song was the Talking Heads hit "Burning Down the House."

CON

GENRE	Docucomedy (Hoax)
FIRST TELECAST	4/2005
NETWORK	Comedy Central
EPISODE STYLE	Self-contained
TALENT	Skyler Stone; Zach Johnson; Dave Keyes
PRODUCTION COMPANY	Comedy Central Films
CREATED BY	Skyler Stone
EXECUTIVE PRODUCERS	Skyler Stone; Rick de Oliveira
CO-EXECUTIVE PRODUCERS	Chris Cox; Matt Sloan
PRODUCER	J. C. Spink
DIRECTOR	Peter Delasho

Self-proclaimed con artist Skyler Stone divulges the secrets of his profession in this docucomedy. Each episode features a specific prank, which ranges from trying to enter a ski resort for free, to persuading models to clean his apartment by posing as a photographer doing a shoot about housecleaning. Stone often convinces store owners to give him products for free by promising them they'll be featured in a film or television show, which only means they end up on *Con*.

THE CONTENDER

GENRE	Competition
FIRST TELECAST	3/7/2005
NETWORK	NBC, ESPN
AIR TIMES	Monday, 9:30 p.m. (3/2005); Thursday, 10:00 p.m. (3/2005) Sunday, 8:00 p.m. (3/2005–5/2005); Tuesday, 8:00 p.m. (5/2005)
EPISODE STYLE	Story Arc
TALENT	Sylvester Stallone (Host/Mentor—Season 1); Sugar Ray Leonard (Host/Mentor)

CAST

Season 1 Sergio Mora (Winner); Peter Manfredo (Runner-up); Anthony Bonsante; Jesse Brinkley; Brent Cooper; Juan De La Rosa; Miguel Espino; Jeff Fraza; Joey Gilbert; Alfonso Gomez; Ahmed Kaddour; Jimmy Lang; Jonathan Reid; Tarick Salmaci; Ishe Smith; Najai Turpi

Season 2 Grady Brewer (Winner); Steve Forbes (Runner-up); Nick Acevedo; Norberto Bravo; Cornelius Bundrage; Gary Balletto; Micheal Stewart; Freddy Curiel; Andre Eason; Aaron Torres; Vinroy Barrett; Rudy Cisneros; Michael Clark; Ebo Elder; Jeff Fraza; Walter Wright

PRODUCTION COMPANIES Dream Works SKG; Mark Burnett Productions; Rogue Marble, ESPN

EXECUTIVE PRODUCERS Sylvester Stallone; Mark Burnett; Jeffrey Katzenberg; Bruce Beresford-Redman; Lisa Hennessy; Ron Wechsler

PRODUCERS Eric Van Wagenen; Matt Van Wagenen; Fred Peabody; Al Berman; Peter Woronov

DIRECTOR Michael Simon

Producer Mark Burnett (*Survivor, The Apprentice*), along with hosts actor Sylvester Stallone and boxing legend Sugar Ray Leonard, gave sixteen boxing hopefuls a chance to have a boxing career and to win $1 million. Cameras followed the competitors as they trained, fought, and struggled with their real-life fears, boxing their way through the competition, hoping to earn a spot in the finale. Prior to the series' debut, aspiring prizefighter/competitor Najai Turpin committed suicide in Philadelphia. A tribute episode was dedicated to Turpin during the run of the show. In the final match, between Sergio Mora and Peter Manfredo, Mora emerged as the champion, earning the $1 million prize.

The Contender 2 aired on ESPN, and the season culminated in a final match at Los Angeles' Staples Center, broadcast live on September 26, 2006. Grady Brewer beat Steve Forbes for the $500,000 prize.

COOKING UNDER FIRE

GENRE	Competition
FIRST TELECAST	4/27/2005
LAST TELECAST	7/20/2005
NETWORK	PBS
AIR TIME	Wednesday, 8:00 p.m.
EPISODE STYLE	Story Arc
TALENT	Ming Tsai (Judge); Todd English (Judge); Michael Ruhlman (Judge); Michael Castner (Announcer)
CAST	Katie Hagan-Whelchel (Winner); John Paul Abernathy; William "Billy" Barlow; Michael Duronslet; Blair King; Sara Lawson; Matthew Leeper; Autumn Maddox; Yannick Marchand; Jennifer McDermott; Russell Moore; Katsuji Tanabe
PRODUCTION COMPANIES	Lance Reynolds Productions; A Better Machine; WGBH Lifestyle Productions
EXECUTIVE PRODUCERS	W. Lance Reynolds; John Rieber; Laurie Donnelly
PRODUCERS	Luke Crafton; Jen Sneider
DIRECTOR	John Rieber

This cooking competition series featured twelve contestants who traveled across the country learning culinary skills and dealing with the pressures of the restaurant business. Katie Hagan-Whelchel won the contest and a chef position at a prestigious New York City restaurant.

COPS

GENRE	Docudrama
FIRST TELECAST	3/11/1989
NETWORK	FOX
AIR TIMES	Saturday, 9:00 p.m. (3/1989–6/1989); Saturday, 8:00 p.m. (6/1989–7/1990); Saturday, 9:00 p.m. (8/1990–7/1991); Saturday, 8:00 p.m. (7/1991–present)
EPISODE STYLE	Self-contained
TALENT	Harry Newman (Announcer)
PRODUCTION COMPANIES	20th Century Fox Television; Barbour/Langley Productions
CREATED BY	John Langley
EXECUTIVE PRODUCERS	Malcolm Barbour; John Langley
PRODUCERS	Jimmy Langley; Hank Barr; Paul Stojanovich; Andrew Thomas

This granddaddy of current reality shows premiered on the FOX network in 1989, accompanied by its catchy, signature reggae tune by Inner Circle, "Bad Boys." This non-hosted, non-narrated show was "filmed on location with the men and women of law enforcement." All action was filmed from the point of view of the participating law enforcement authorities. The series visited more than 140 U.S. cities, and filmed in Hong Kong, London, and the former Soviet Union.

CORKSCREWED: THE WRATH OF GRAPES

GENRE Docusoap
FIRST TELECAST 11/22/2006
NETWORK Fox Reality Channel
EPISODE STYLE Story Arc
TALENT Nigel Lythgoe, Ken Warwick; Cain Devore (Narrator)
PRODUCTION COMPANIES Talent TV; Magic Pictures Inc.
EXECUTIVE PRODUCERS John Kaye Cooper, Elaine Gallagher; Bob Boden
CO-EXECUTIVE PRODUCER Kris Lythgoe

Renowned reality producers and childhood friends Nigel Lythgoe and Ken Warwick followed their dreams of owning their own vineyard in this original Fox Reality Channel series.

Nigel and Ken began as dancers on a British television show before breaking into the world of television production. They shot to fame producing *American Idol* and had separate success with *So You Think You Can Dance* (Nigel) and *America's Got Talent* (Ken).

Their success in producing hit shows didn't quite translate to producing grapes and wine at their new multimillion-dollar investment in Paso Robles, California. The purchase was originally going to be a joint venture with *American Idol* creator Simon Fuller and *Idol* personalities Simon Cowell, Randy Jackson, and Ryan Seacrest, but the four withdrew, leaving Nigel and Ken as the remaining owners of the 168-acre vineyard.

They found troubles at every turn as wild boars, fires, and gophers threatened to devour their valuable crops, and ate away at their profits. As if that wasn't enough, they also had to deal with fitting in and gaining the trust of the Paso Robles community. The two were perceived as designer brand–wearing, big-shot outsiders from Hollywood by the laid-back jeans-clad residents of the central California small town. Eventually, the two were welcomed as fellow citizens, and their fortunes turned around as they were able to produce a successful crop by the end of the series.

In addition to seeing Nigel and Ken's adventure in the world of the wine business, viewers got a taste of show business as cameras took them behind the scenes of *So You Think Can Dance* and *America's Got Talent*. Each episode featured cameos by popular personalities, such as Regis Philbin, David Hasselhoff, and Cat Deeley.

COWBOY U

GENRE	Competition
FIRST TELECAST	1/16/2004
NETWORK	CMT
EPISODES	Story Arc
TALENT	Rocco Wachman (Professional Cowboy); Judd Leffew (Bull Rider); Shawn Stephens (Champion Team Roper)

CAST

Season 1	Dani Armstrong; David Bauman; Megumi Hosogai; Brandie Lyons; Frank Prather; Amir Raziq; Chris Shurley; Elli Wooten
Cowboy U "Molokai"	Sal Williams (Winner); Brian; Candy; Corey; Fawn; George; Rachel; Tera
Cowboy U "Colorado"	Sal Williams (Winner); Brian; Candy; Corey; Fawn; George; Rachel; Tera
PRODUCTION COMPANY	Traige Entertainment, Inc.
EXECUTIVE PRODUCERS	Steve Kroopnick; Stu Schreiberg; David Wechter; Jennifer Orme
PRODUCERS	Jon Hotchkiss; Sarah Kane; Tim Gaydos; Chris W. King
DIRECTOR	David Wechter

This competition series featured a cowboy boot camp for city slickers. Four men and four women became working ranch cowboys, learning how to rope a steer, barrel-race, and ride a twelve-hundred-pound bull in the hopes of earning the $25,000 prize, champion belt buckle, and custom-made *Cowboy U* saddle. Six seasons of the show have aired, set in Arizona; California; Colorado; Moloka'i, Hawaii, Oklahoma; and Texas.

CRASH TEST

GENRE	Competition (Hoax)
FIRST TELECAST	2/24/2004
LAST TELECAST	12/20/2004
NETWORK	Spike
AIR TIME	Tuesday, 9:30 p.m.
EPISODE STYLE	Self-contained
EXECUTIVE PRODUCER	Sergio Myers
PRODUCER	Katherine Dore
DIRECTORS	Miles Kahn; Jennifer Langheld

On *Crash Test,* to earn points, two uninvited guests attended a series of events and had to perform a variety of stunts without getting caught or forced to leave. The competitor who won the most points advanced to the next level of competition The reward for these surreptitious activities was the title of "Ultimate Crasher."

CRISS ANGEL: MINDFREAK

GENRE	Docudrama
FIRST TELECAST	7/20/2005
NETWORK	A&E
EPISODE STYLE	Self-contained
CAST	Criss Angel
PRODUCTION COMPANIES	Angel Productions Incorporated; TVX
EXECUTIVE PRODUCERS	Bradley Anderson; Mack Anderson; Dave Baram; Michael Blum; Nancy Dubuc; Steven Lenchner; Rob Sharenow

PRODUCERS	Nicholas Amendolare; Will Raee
DIRECTOR	Michael Yanovich

On his docudrama, Criss Angel demonstrates his visionary approach to the art of magic. Dubbed "the new Houdini," Angel specializes in mentalism, hypnosis, illusion, and escape. Illusions included Criss being set ablaze for forty-six seconds with very little protection, and his levitating people on the street.

CUPID

GENRE	Competition (Dating)
FIRST TELECAST	7/9/2003
LAST TELECAST	9/16/2003
NETWORK	CBS
AIR TIME	Wednesday, 10:00 p.m.
EPISODE STYLE	Story Arc
TALENT	Brian McFayden (Host); Simon Cowell
CAST	Lisa Shannon (Bachelorette), Kimberly Tarter (Lisa's best friend); Laura Restum (Lisa's best friend), Hanke Stepleton (Winner); Robert Amstler (Runner-up); Evan Hook (8th eliminated); Dominic Mancini (7th eliminated); Brian Renda (6th eliminated); Joe Nardulli (5th eliminated); Ken Jones (4th eliminated); Paul Stancato (3rd eliminated); Scott Schwartz (2nd eliminated); Rob Wiles (1st eliminated)
PRODUCTION COMPANIES	FremantleMedia; Cupid Productions, Inc.
CREATED BY	Simon Cowell
EXECUTIVE PRODUCERS	Simon Cowell; Craig Piligian
CO-EXECUTIVE PRODUCER	Teri Kennedy
PRODUCERS	Eden Gaha; Nicole Gaha; Yolanda Parks
DIRECTORS	Craig Borders; Bruce Gowers

This series created by *American Idol* judge Simon Cowell followed Lisa Shannon and her two best friends, Kimberly and Laura, as Lisa tried to find the perfect mate. The series began with a cross-country search, with hundreds of men trying to impress Lisa and her friends. The three women narrowed the field to ten bachelors, who later moved into a home in the Hollywood Hills. Then Lisa went on a series of dates with the men, as her friends watched and critiqued. Home viewers determined who should stay and who was to be eliminated, and eventually chose Hank as Lisa's mate. In the live finale, Hank was given the opportunity to propose to Lisa and marry her to claim a $1 million dowry. Hank decided that while he wanted to continue seeing Lisa, proposing was not right at the time.

THE CUT

GENRE	Competition
FIRST TELECAST	6/9/2005
LAST TELECAST	9/7/2005
NETWORK	CBS
AIR TIME	Thursday, 9:00 p.m.
EPISODE STYLE	Story Arc
TALENT	Tommy Hilfiger (Host)
CAST	Chris Cortez, (Winner); Princess Warren (Runner-up); Elizabeth Saab (Runner-up); Felix Arguelles (13th eliminated); Wes Davis (12th eliminated); Deanna Bonin (11th eliminated); Shauna Storey (10th eliminated); Rob Walker (9th eliminated); Jessica Dereschuk (8th eliminated); Jeff Berin (7th eliminated); James Wolfe (6th eliminated); Julie O'Connor (5th eliminated); Tommy Walton (4th eliminated); Chris Sherrill (3rd eliminated); Vlada Drukh (2nd eliminated); Amy Salinger (1st eliminated)
PRODUCTION COMPANIES	Lions Gate Television; Pilgrim Films and Television
CREATED BY	Craig Piligian; Darren Maddern

EXECUTIVE PRODUCERS	Craig Piligian; Peter Connolly
CO-EXECUTIVE PRODUCERS	Darren Maddern; Eli Frankel
PRODUCERS	Joe Coleman; Sean M. Kelly; Alison Sandler
DIRECTOR	Rick Ringbakk

Sixteen designers competed for an opportunity to have their fashion lines produced under the Tommy Hilfiger label on *The Cut*. The contestants lived together in a Manhattan loft and faced a series of challenges presented to them by Hilfiger himself. The challenges tested not only their design skills but also their business and marketing savvy. Each week, Hilfiger eliminated one candidate based on his or her performance in a challenge. In the final episode, the remaining three designers showcased their designs in window displays at Macy's Herald Square. Hilfiger ultimately selected Chris Cortez as the winner of the grand prize.

DAISY DOES AMERICA

GENRE	Docudrama
FIRST TELECAST	12/6/2005
LAST TELECAST	1/17/2006
NETWORK	TBS
EPISODE STYLE	Self-contained
CAST	Daisy Donovan
PRODUCTION COMPANY	Coquette Productions
EXECUTIVE PRODUCERS	Courteney Cox Arquette; David Arquette; Brad Kuhlman; Jim Biederman; Daisy Donovan
PRODUCERS	Stephen Castagnola; Thea Mann; Spencer Millman
DIRECTORS	Amanda Blue; C. K. Gillen; Ivan Voctor

Comic actress and British socialite Daisy Donovan learned about life in the United States as she searched for her piece of the American dream in this docudrama.

DALLAS: SWAT

GENRE Docudrama

FIRST TELECAST 1/5/2006

NETWORK A&E

EPISODE STYLE Self-contained

CAST Johnny Baker (Dallas); J. D. Byas (Dallas); Steve Claggett (Dallas); Robert Cockerill (Dallas); J. T. Curtis (Dallas); Christian D'Alesandro (Dallas); Richard Emberlin (Dallas); Eddie Fuller (Dallas); Larry Gordon (Dallas); Joe A. Guzman (Dallas); Paul Junger (Dallas); Randy Lancaster (Dallas); Keith Reig (Dallas); Terigi Rossi (Dallas); Todd Stratman (Dallas); Andre Taylor (Dallas); Misty VanCuren (Dallas); Todd Welhouse (Dallas); Jonathan (Ricochet) Bibbs (Detroit); Jason (Diesel) Brasgalla (Detroit); Larry (Smooth); Kevin "Condor" Shepherd (Detroit); Larry Davis (Detroit); Sean "Woody" Howitt (Detroit); Joe "Brain" Weekley (Detroit); Jim Carmody (Kansas City); Aaron Hendershot (Kansas City); Charles "Chip" Huth (Kansas City); Joe McHale (Kansas City); Brian Tomanio (Kansas City); Bryan Truman (Kansas City)

PRODUCTION COMPANY A&E Television Network

EXECUTIVE PRODUCER Laura Fleury

PRODUCERS C. Webb Young; Neil A. Cohen; Xackery Irving

Dallas SWAT followed the busy, stressful lives of the Dallas SWAT team law enforcement officers. From intense missions to downtime at home, the show chronicled how job pressure affected the team members' lives. In the Season 2, the series began profiling the Detroit and Kansas City SWAT teams.

DAMAGE CONTROL

GENRE	Competition (Hoax)
FIRST TELECAST	3/6/2005
NETWORK	MTV
EPISODE STYLE	Self-contained
TALENT	Pierre Bouvier (Host); Devin Ratray; Jennifer Johnson; Rizwan Manji; Ben Morrison; Paul Sutera; Brian Huskey; Rue DeBona; Jamie Benge; Lisa Dodd
PRODUCTION COMPANY	Tiger Aspect
EXECUTIVE PRODUCERS	Drew Pearce; Rico Martinez
PRODUCERS	Justin Booth; Vince D'Orazi; Bechara Gholam; Frank Sutera
DIRECTOR	Claudia Frank

Based on a British television series, *Damage Control* follows parents who conspire with the show's producers to leave their teenage child home alone for a weekend. Hidden cameras capture each teens' reaction to various compromising situations. The parents secretly watch the action from the house next door, and win $1,000 every time they correctly guess how their child will behave. When the parents return home, they question the child about what occurred. If the teen confesses, the family is awarded more money.

DANCE FEVER

GENRE	Competition (Talent)
FIRST TELECAST	7/13/2003
LAST TELECAST	8/24/2003
NETWORK	ABC Family
AIR TIME	Sunday, 7:00 p.m.

EPISODE STYLE	Story Arc
TALENT	Eric Nies (Host); Hammer (Judge); Carmen Electra (Judge); Jamie King (Judge); Lisette Bustamante (Preliminary Judge/Coach); Carrie Anne Inaba (Preliminary Judge/Coach)
CAST	Live in Color (Winner); All That (Finalist); B-Boy Crumbs (Finalist); Souther Belles (Finalist); Funk & Fusion (Finalist); Ryan and Diana (Finalist)
PRODUCTION COMPANIES	Merv Griffin Entertainment; Nash Entertainment; Bob Bain Productions
CREATED BY	Merv Griffin
EXECUTIVE PRODUCERS	Merv Griffin; Bob Bain; Bruce Nash
PRODUCERS	Paul Flattery; Amy Baker

Based on the wildly successful disco competition show from the 1970s, the twenty-first-century version of *Dance Fever* featured dance teams and individuals as they vied for a $100,000 grand prize at a dance-off in Las Vegas. Live in Color emerged as the grand champions of this show.

DANCING WITH THE STARS
(Season 1)

GENRE	Competition (Talent)
FIRST TELECAST	6/1/2005
LAST TELECAST	7/6/2005
NETWORK	ABC
AIR TIME	Wednesday, 8:00 p.m.
EPISODE STYLE	Story Arc
TALENT	Tom Bergeron (Host); Lisa Canning (Hostess); Len Goodman (Judge); Carrie Ann Inaba (Judge); Bruno Tonioli (Judge)

CAST	Kelly Monaco and Alec Mazo (Winners); John O'Hurley and Charlotte Jorgensen (Runners-up); Joseph McIntyre and Ashly DelGrosso (4th eliminated); Rachel Hunter and Jonathan Roberts (3rd eliminated); Evander Holyfield and Edyta Sliwinska (2nd eliminated); Trista Sutter and Louis Van Amstel (1st eliminated)
PRODUCTION COMPANY	BBC Worldwide America
CREATED BY	Eric Morley (created the original British version *Strictly Come Dancing*)
EXECUTIVE PRODUCERS	Conrad Green; Richard Hopkins
DIRECTOR	Alex Rudzinski

In this competition based on the format of the British series *Strictly Come Dancing,* celebrities are paired with professional ballroom dancers, who teach them routines which the two then perform each week before a panel of judges. The judges scores are combined with the home viewers' votes, and each week the couple who scores the lowest is eliminated. The final two couples compete in the finale for the *Dancing With the Stars* disco ball trophy.

In Episode 1, the couples danced either the cha-cha or the waltz. Edyta Sliwinska and boxer Evander Holyfield; Charlotte Jorgensen and actor John O'Hurley; and Ashly DelGross and singer Joey McIntyre performed the cha-cha, while Louis Van Amstel and "Bachelorette" Trista Rehn Sutter; Jonathan Roberts and model Rachel Hunter; and Alec Mazo and actress Kelly Monaco danced the waltz. Rachel and Joey tied for the lead, with twenty points, Evander and Trista earned eighteen, John scored seventeen, and Kelly rounded out the bottom with a thirteen.

In Episode 2, the pairs performed the rumba and the quickstep, and it was the final time the six teams competed together. John placed first, with twenty-six points; Rachel scored twenty-four; Joey got twenty-one; Trista earned nineteen; and Kelly got seventeen. Evander and Edyta's fourteen points put them in last place. At the end of the show, viewers were encouraged to vote for their favorites.

Trista and Louis were the first couple to be eliminated, in Episode 3. John and

Rachel performed the tango, while Evander, Joey, and Kelly danced the jive. Rachel led the pack with twenty-six points; John scored twenty-four; Joey had twenty-two; Kelly earned twenty-one; and Evander came in last, with thirteen.

Evander and Edyta were voted out in Episode 4. All of the dancers performed the samba. Kelly surprised everyone, earning twenty-six points. Rachel wasn't far behind, with twenty-five. John scored twenty-one, and Joey got twenty.

After combining the judges' scores with viewer votes, Rachel and Jonathan were eliminated in Episode 5. John, Joey, and Kelly performed the paso doble and the fox-trot. John finished first, with a combined score of fifty-four. Kelly earned forty-seven, while Joey scored forty-five.

In Episode 6, Joey and Ashly were eliminated. John and Kelly faced off in the finale, performing two dances each. John and Charlotte scored fifty-four points, while Kelly and Alec took the edge, with fifty-five points. For the finale, the judge's votes weighed more heavily than those of the audience, which led to much anger among fans when Kelly and Alex were declared the winners.

Because of the outcry over the unfairness of the finale, Kelly Monaco and John O'Hurley returned for a "dance-off." Based on audience votes alone, John was declared the winner.

DANCING WITH THE STARS
(Season 2)

GENRE	Competition (Talent)
FIRST TELECAST	1/5/2006
LAST TELECAST	2/26/2006
NETWORK	ABC
AIR TIMES	Thursday, 8:00 p.m.; Friday, 8:00 p.m.
EPISODE STYLE	Story Arc
TALENT	Tom Bergeron (Host); Samantha Harris (Hostess); Len Goodman (Judge); Carrie Ann Inaba (Judge); Bruno Tonioli (Judge)
CAST	Drew Lachey and Cheryl Burke (Winners);

Jerry Rice and Anna Trebunskaya (Runners-up);
Stacy Keibler and Tony Dovolani (8th eliminated);
Lisa Rinna and Louis Van Amstel (7th eliminated);
George Hamilton and Edyta Sliwinska
(6th eliminated); Tia Carrere and
Maksim Chmerkovskiy (5th eliminated);
Master P and Ashly DelGrosso (4th eliminated);
Giselle Fernández and Jonathan Roberts
(3rd eliminated); Tatum O'Neal and Nick Kosovich
(2nd eliminated); Kenny Mayne and Andrea Hale
(1st eliminated)

PRODUCTION COMPANY BBC Worldwide America

CREATED BY Eric Morley (created the original British version
Strictly Come Dancing)

EXECUTIVE PRODUCERS Conrad Green; Richard Hopkins

DIRECTOR Alex Rudzinski

Season 2 added a results show, which aired on the nights following the performances. These shows included additional performances by professional dancers and guest musicians.

In Episode 1, female celebrities and their professional partners performed the waltz, while the men danced the cha-cha. Singer Drew Lachey scored twenty-four points, while TV journalist Giselle Fernandez and Academy Award winner Tatum O'Neal tied, with twenty-three. Actress and former WWE diva Stacy Keibler earned twenty-two points; former NFL player Jerry Rice got twenty-one; actress Lisa Rinna scored nineteen; actor George Hamilton took eighteen; ESPN anchorman Kenny Mayne had thirteen; and rapper Master P was at the bottom, with twelve. Master P was a last-minute replacement for his son, Lil' Romeo, who couldn't perform because of an injury.

In Episode 2, Burt Bacharach performed, while Drew and Cheryl danced again. Kenny and Andrea were the first pair eliminated.

In Episode 3, after a quickstep rumba, Stacy finished first, with twenty-nine; Drew earned twenty-seven points; Giselle got twenty-four; Jerry received twenty-three;

George and Tia tied, with twenty-seven; Lisa took twenty; Tatum got seventeen; and Master P remained in last place, with sixteen points.

Jesse McCartney performed in Episode 4, while Tatum and Nick were eliminated.

In Episode 5, the eight pairs danced the jive or the tango. Drew and Stacy tied for first, with twenty-seven points. Lisa moved up, earning twenty-five points, while George and Giselle tied with twenty-two. Jerry scored nineteen, and again Master P finished in last place, with fourteen points.

The Style Elements Club professional dance troupe performed in Episode 6. Giselle and Jonathan were the third couple eliminated.

In Episode 7, the couples chose either the foxtrot or the paso doble. Drew took top honors, with twenty-eight points; Stacy and Lisa tied with twenty-six; Tia scored twenty-five; Jerry got twenty-four; George earned twenty-one; and Master P scored a record low, with only eight points.

The Pussycat Dolls sang their hit singles "Don't Cha" and "Sway" in Episode 8. Finally, Master P and Ashley were eliminated.

In Episode 9, the pairs performed the samba, then danced a group salsa. Stacy earned the season's first perfect score of thirty. Drew came in second, with 27. Lisa scored twenty-five points; George earned twenty-four; Jerry received twenty-three; and Tia finished last, with twenty-two points.

Barry Manilow performed in Episode 10, then Tia and Maksim were the fifth couple eliminated.

In Episode 11, the couples performed two numbers chosen from among jive, tango, paso doble, quickstep, or rumba. Drew and Stacy both scored perfect thirties. Lisa came in second, with twenty-seven points; while Jerry and George tied with twenty-three points.

In Episode 12, Bill Medley and his daughter, McKenna, sang a duet, and a group of Maksim's students performed a routine. George and Edyta were the sixth couple eliminated.

In Episode 13, the stars were given their choice of one ballroom routine and one Latin. Drew and Stacy tied for first again, with combined scores of fifty-five. Lisa finished in second, with fifty-three, and Jerry cames in last, with forty-one.

In Episode 14, Michael Buble performed, and Lisa and Louis were the seventh couple eliminated.

In Episode 15, the final three couples chose a favorite dance for one performance;

the other was a freestyle routine. Drew scored perfect thirties on both performances. Stacy scored thirty and twenty-six; while Jerry received twenty-six and twenty-seven.

In the Season 2 finale, the three remaining couples performed another routine. While Stacy scored a perfect thirty, Drew earned just twenty-seven. Stacy was eliminated, giving Jerry Rice and Anna Trebunskaya who earned twenty-seven on their last routine, second place. Finally, Drew Lachey and Cheryl Burke were crowned the winners.

DANCING WITH THE STARS
(Season 3)

GENRE	Competition (Talent)
FIRST TELECAST	9/12/2006
LAST TELECAST	11/15/2006
NETWORK	ABC
AIR TIMES	Tuesday, 8:00 p.m.; Wednesday, 8:00 p.m.
EPISODE STYLE	Story Arc
TALENT	Tom Bergeron (Host), Samantha Harris (Hostess), Len Goodman (Judge), Carrie Ann Inaba (Judge), Bruno Tonioli (Judge)
CAST	Emmitt Smith and Cheryl Burke (Winners); Mario Lopez and Karina Smirnoff (Runners-up); Joey Lawrence and Edyta Sliwinska (8th eliminated); Monique Coleman and Louis Van Amstel (7th eliminated); Jerry Springer and Kym Johnson (6th eliminated); Sara Evans and Tony Dovolani (withdrew during sixth week); Willa Ford and Maksim Chmerkovskiy (5th eliminated); Vivica A. Fox and Nick Kosovich (4th eliminated); Harry Hamlin and Ashly DelGrosso (3rd eliminated); Shanna Moakler and Jesse DeSoto (2nd eliminated); Tucker Carlson and Elena Grinenko (1st eliminated)

PRODUCTION COMPANY	BBC Worldwide America
CREATED BY	Eric Morley (created the original British version *Strictly Come Dancing*)
EXECUTIVE PRODUCERS	Conrad Green; Richard Hopkins
DIRECTOR	Alex Rudzinski

The scoring system changed in Season 3 of *Dancing with the Stars*. The viewer votes still factored in 50 percent of the scores, but the judges' scores were added, and the pairs earned points based on the percentage of total points given to all performers.

In Episode 1, the ten celebrity/professional pairs were introduced. The men danced the cha-cha, while the women performed the foxtrot. Actor Mario Lopez gained an early lead with twenty-six points. Former NFL player Emmitt Smith earned twenty-four points. Singer Willa Ford and actress Vivica A. Fox tied with twenty-two points. Actor Joey Lawrence received twenty-one; actress Monique Coleman scored nineteen; former Miss USA Shanna Moakler took eighteen; actor Harry Hamlin got seventeen; talk show host Jerry Springer earned sixteen; singer Sara Evans received fifteen; and MSNBC news anchor Tucker Carlson finished last, with twelve points.

Tom Jones performed in Episode 2, and Tucker and Elena were the first pair eliminated.

In Episode 3, the men danced the quickstep, and the women performed the mambo. Joey took first, with twenty-nine points. Monique came in second, with twenty-six points. Emmitt and Vivica tied with twenty-four. Willa earned twenty-three, Shanna received twenty-two, and Mario, Sara, and Harry tied with twenty-one. Jerry finished last, with nineteen.

Julio Iglesias performed and professionals danced in Episode 4. Shanna and Jesse were the second pair to go.

In Episode 5, the eight remaining couples danced a jive or a tango. Monique and Vivica tied for first with twenty-seven points. Sara finished second with twenty-five points, while Mario, Joey, Willa, and Harry tied with twenty-two. Jerry received twenty-one points, and Emmitt finished last, with nineteen points.

The Scissor Sisters performed in Episode 6. Harry and Ashly were the third couple eliminated.

In Episode 7, dancers danced either the paso doble or the waltz. Mario scored the highest yet, with twenty-nine points. Willa finished second, with twenty-eight. Joey received twenty-seven, while Emmitt, Monique, and Vivica tied with twenty-four. Jerry got twenty-two, and Sara finished last, with twenty points.

Nick Lachey and Los Lonely Boys both performed in Episode 8. Vivica and Nick were the fourth pair to leave.

In Episode 9, the pairs danced the samba and the rumba in tribute to Carnivale. Mario, Emmitt, Monique, and Willa tied for first, with twenty-seven points. Joey finished with twenty-five. Jerry and Sara tied for last, with twenty-two points.

Rod Stewart gave a performance, and professionals danced in Episode 10. Willa and Maksim were the fifth team eliminated.

For Episode 11, the remaining couples danced a ballroom style they hadn't yet performed, plus they did a group freestyle dance. Sara Evans withdrew from the show, which she exclusively discussed with host Tom Bergeron. Mario finished first, with twenty-eight points. Emmitt was right behind, with twenty-five points, while Joey earned twenty-four, Monique got twenty-three, and Jerry finished last, with eighteen.

In Episode 12, Lionel Richie sang a few hits. Since Sara had withdrawn from the competition, no couples are eliminated.

Episode 13 featured two rounds: ballroom and Latin. The scores from these rounds were added to the judges' scores from the previous week, for a total possible score of ninety points. Mario hung on to the lead, with a combined score of eighty-four. Emmitt was close behind, with eighty-two. Joey got eighty-one, Monique earned seventy-seven, and Jerry again finished last, with sixty-four.

Martina McBride performed in Episode 14. Jerry and Kym were eliminated

The final four couples performed one ballroom-style dance and one Latin dance in Episode 15, styles they repeated in the following week. Mario's hot streak continued, as he scored fifty-seven points. Emmitt and Joey tied for second, with fifty-four, while Monique received fifty-three.

In Episode 16, Il Divo performed, and contestant Willa Ford returned to sing. Monique and Lewis were the next couple eliminated.

In Episode 17, the final three pairs performed their favorite ballroom and Latin dances. Mario, Emmitt, and Joey all received a near-perfect score of fifty-nine.

In Episode 18, Pet Shop Boys performed a retro number. Then Joey and Edyta were sent packing.

Emmitt and Mario performed three dances each in Episode 19. They repeated their favorite routines from the season, and Mario danced the paso doble, while Emmitt picked the mambo. Both Mario and Emmitt performed the samba to the same song in a "Dancing" first. Finally, each did a freestyle dance. The judges again gave both pairs the same score, a near-perfect eighty-nine.

In the Episode 20 finale, all of the couples returned to perform again. Then Emmitt Smith and Cheryl Burke won the disco ball trophy.

DANCING WITH THE STARS
(Season 4)

GENRE	Competition (Talent)
FIRST TELECAST	3/19/2007
LAST TELECAST	5/22/2007
NETWORK	ABC
AIR TIMES	Monday, 8:00 p.m.; Tuesday, 8:00 p.m.
EPISODE STYLE	Story Arc
TALENT	Tom Bergeron (Host); Samantha Harris (Hostess); Len Goodman (Judge); Carrie Ann Inaba (Judge); Bruno Tonioli (Judge)
CAST	Apolo Anton Ohno and Julianne Hough (Winners); Joey Fatone and Kym Johnson (Runners-up); Laila Ali and Maksim Chmerkovskiy (9th eliminated); Ian Ziering and Cheryl Burke (8th eliminated); Billy Ray Cyrus and Karina Smirnoff (7th eliminated); John Ratzenberger and Edyta Sliwinska (6th eliminated); Heather Mills and Jonathan Roberts (5th eliminated); Clyde Drexler and Elena Grinenko (4th eliminated); Leeza Gibbons and Tony Dovolani (3rd eliminated) Shandi Finnessey and Brian Fortuna (2nd eliminated); Paulina Porizkova and Alec Mazo (1st eliminated)
PRODUCTION COMPANY	BBC Worldwide America

CREATED BY   Eric Morley (created the original British version
Strictly Come Dancing)
EXECUTIVE PRODUCERS   Conrad Green, Richard Hopkins.
DIRECTOR   Alex Rudzinski

In Episode 1 of Season 4, the ten pairs of dancers were introduced. The men performed the cha-cha, while the women danced the foxtrot. 'N Sync member Joey Fatone took an early lead with twenty-four points. Boxer Laila Ali scored twenty-three points. Olympic short track speed skater Apolo Anton Ohno and actor Ian Ziering tied, with twenty-one points. Former Miss USA Shandi Finnessey and former supermodel Paulina Porizkova tied with nineteen. Charity campaigner Heather Mills, who has a prosthetic leg, scored eighteen points. Actor John Ratzenberger got seventeen, NBA legend Clyde Drexler earned sixteen, talk show host Leeza Gibbons received fifteen, and actor/singer Billy Ray Cyrus finished last, with thirteen points.

In Episode 2, the men danced the quickstep, and the women performed the mambo. Laila took over the lead, with twenty-seven points. Apolo scored twenty-six points; Joey and Heather tied with twenty-four; Ian got twenty-two; while John, Paulina, Billy Ray, and Leeza tied, with twenty-one. Shandi received twenty, and Clyde came in last place, with eighteen points.

Episode 3 featured a recap of Season 4's first two performances.

Dionne Warwick performed while the professionals danced in Episode 4. Paulina and Alec were the first pair eliminated from Season 4.

In Episode 5, the eight remaining pairs did a jive or a tango. Joey, Leeza, Heather, and Ian tied for first, with twenty-four points each. Apolo finished in second, with twenty-three. Shandi, Laila, and Billy Ray tied, with twenty-one. John earned twenty points, while Clyde finished last, with sixteen.

In Episode 6, Josh Groban, Ciara, and Survivor performed. Shandi and Brian were the second team eliminated.

In Episode 7, the pairs danced the paso doble or the waltz. Joey took first, with twenty-eight points. Apolo scored twenty-six; Ian earned twenty-four points; Heather got twenty-three; while Billy Ray and Laila tied, with twenty-one. John and Leeza also tied, with sixteen, while Clyde came in last with fifteen.

In Episode 8, Season 2 winner Drew Lachey returned to dance with Cheryl Burke to the music of Big and Rich. Leeza and Tony were the third team to go.

The remaining dancers learned a rumba or a samba in Episode 9. Apolo earned a perfect score of thirty; Laila got a twenty-eight; Joey received a twenty-five; Ian earned a twenty-four; Heather picked up twenty-one; John got eighteen; Billy Ray scored seventeen; and Clyde again finished last, with thirteen.

In Episode 10, Macy Gray sang and Lisa Rinna returned to dance a tribute to Broadway. Clyde and Elena were the fourth couple eliminated.

Episode 11 featured a group swing dance followed by an individual Latin number. The dancers were judged only on their Latin dance. Apolo and Laila tied for first place, with a score of twenty-eight. Joey came in a close second, with twenty-seven. Ian got twenty-four; Heather picked up twenty-three; and John finished last, with nineteen. Season 3 contestant Jerry Springer also made an appearance.

Joss Stone and the cast of the film *Dreamgirls* performed, while Jimmy Kimmel offered his witty opinions in Episode 12. Heather and Jonathan were the fifth team eliminated.

The final four couples danced one ballroom-style dance and one Latin dance in Episode 13. Apolo continued his hot streak, with fifty-eight points. Joey finished second, with fifty-five, while Laila received a fifty-three. Ian earned forty-seven points, and Billy Ray finished last, with a thirty-eight.

In Episode 14, Meatloaf performed. John and Edyta were the sixth team to go.

The remaining three couples danced their favorite ballroom style, plus a Latin dance in Episode 15. Apolo took first again, with fifty-eight. Joey scored fifty-five points. Laila got fifty-three, Ian received forty-seven, and Billy Ray finished last again, with a thirty-eight.

In Episode 16, Nelly Furtado performed, and Billy Ray and Karina were the seventh team eliminated.

The semifinals began in Episode 17, as the couples chose a favorite ballroom and a favorite Latin dance. Joey and Laila tied, with a perfect score of sixty. Apolo finished a close second, with fifty-nine points, with Ian trailing with fifty-eight.

In Episode 18, Enrique Iglesias performed while Joaquin Cortes did an accompanying dance. Ian and Cheryl were the eighth team sent home.

In Episode 19, the final three couples danced one freestyle number and another of the judges' choice. Apolo earned fifty-eight points. Joey scored a fifty-six, and Laila got a fifty-five.

In the Season 4 finale, the couples returned to dance once more, and the final three pairs performed one final number. Apolo, Joey, and Laila all scored perfect thirties, which was combined with the previous night's scores. Apolo and Julianne were crowned the winners.

DATE MY MOM

GENRE	Competition (Dating)
FIRST TELECAST	11/15/2004
NETWORK	MTV
EPISODE STYLE	Self-contained
EXECUTIVE PRODUCERS	Mark Koops; Kallissa Miller; H. T. Owens
PRODUCERS	Dianne Martinez; Jennifer Stander
DIRECTOR	Adam Goldberg

On this dating competition one bachelor platonically went out with three mothers. His goal was to get to know the moms in the hopes of figuring out which of their daughters he'd most want to date.

DATE PATROL

GENRE	Docudrama (Dating)
FIRST TELECAST	9/20/2003
NETWORK	TLC
EPISODE STYLE	Self-contained
TALENT	Peggy Bunker (Host); Stephanie Raye (Communications); Mark Edgar Stephens (Body Language); Terrence Charles (Style); Tracy Cox (Relationship Expert—Season 2)
PRODUCTION COMPANY	FremantleMedia
EXECUTIVE PRODUCERS	Jane Rimer; Char Serwa; Ronnie Weinstock
PRODUCERS	Molly M. Fowler; Teri Klein; Karen Kunkel; Gabriel Roth; Madeleine Solano

Based on the British show *Date Squad,* this series followed a team of experts as they coached single people in personal style, body language, and communication skills in hopes of helping them attract a date. Each episode began with a subject going on a "demo date" monitored by the Date Patrol. Following the date, the experts pointed out any missteps the subject made. Then each Date Patrol coach tutored the subject during a four-week period. After the training and a makeover, the subject had to go out on a real date while being monitored again by the Date Patrol. If the date was going well, the subject could secretly hit a button to cut off the surveillance cameras and let the date proceed without the Date Patrol, but if the subject still needed help, the Date Patrol intervened.

THE DATING EXPERIMENT

GENRE	Docudrama (Dating)
FIRST TELECAST	6/25/2003
LAST TELECAST	7/16/2003
NETWORK	ABC
AIR TIME	Wednesday, 10:00 p.m.
EPISODE STYLE	Self-contained
TALENT	Hector Elizondo (Narrator)
PRODUCTION COMPANIES	ABC-Greengrass Productions; D S Entertainment, in association with Vin Di Bona Productions
EXECUTIVE PRODUCERS	Vin Di Bona; Daniel Schwartz
CO-EXECUTIVE PRODUCERS	Terry Moore; Steve Paskay; Kathy Wetherell
DIRECTOR	Gretchen Warthen

Based on the Japanese show *The Future Diary,* this dating docudrama featured men and women agreeing to have a red diary guide them on a journey to find true love. The participants were not allowed money or contact with family or friends during the process. The question loomed: Would participants continue to date once the diary no longer controlled their actions?

DEADLIEST CATCH

GENRE Docudrama

FIRST TELECAST 4/12/2005

NETWORK Discovery

EPISODE STYLE Self-contained

TALENT Mike Rowe (Narrator)

CAST Jerry "Corky" Tilley (Captain—*Aleutian Ballad*);
Scott Templin (*Aleutian Ballad*); Clayton Custer
(*Aleutian Ballad*); Nicole Tilley (*Aleutian Ballad*);
Carl Powers (*Aleutian Ballad*); Gary Edwards
(Captain—*Big Valley*); Jeff Weeks (Captain—
Billikin); Phil Harris (Captain—*Cornelia Marie*);
Jake Harris (Bait Boy—*Cornelia Marie*);
(Roger Jensen (First Mate—*Cornelia Marie*);
(Dave Millman (Deckhand—*Cornelia Marie*);
Dan Gilbert (Deckhand—*Cornelia Marie*); Walt
Dauderis (Deckhand—*Cornelia Marie*); Tony
LaRussa (Captain—*Fierce Allegiance*); Pete Liske
(Captain—*Lady Alaska*); Vince Shavender
(Captain—*Lucky Lady*); Rick Quashnick
(Captain—*Maverick*); Donna Quashnick (Cook—
Maverick); Blake Painter (Engineer—*Maverick*);
Mike Johnson (Deckhand—*Maverick*);
Justin Gifford (Deckhand—*Maverick*);
Hiram Johnson (Deckhand—*Maverick*); Sig
Hansen (Captain—*Northwestern*); Edgar Hansen
(Deckboss—*Northwestern*); Noirman Hansen
(Deckhand—*Northwestern*); Nick Mavar, Jr.
(Deckhand—*Northwestern*); Rick McLeod
(Engineer—*Northwestern*); Jim Stone (Captain—
Retriever); Stein Eric Nyhammer (Captain—

Rollo); Corey Arnold (Deckhand—*Rollo*):
Matt Sullivan (Deckhand—*Rollo*); Bryan Greer
(Engineer—*Rollo*); Christian Kirk (First Mate—
Rollo); Roger Strong (Captain—*Saga*); Larry
Hendricks (Captain—*Sea Star*); John Hillstrand
(Captain—*Time Bandit*); Andy Hillstrand
(Captain—*Time Bandit*); Neil Hillstrand (*Time
Bandit*); Mike Fourtner (Deckhand—*Time Bandit*);
Tom Miller (Deckhand—*Time Bandit*); Coleman
Anderson (Captain—*Western Viking*)

PRODUCTION COMPANIES	Discovery Network; Original Productions
EXECUTIVE PRODUCER	Thom Beers
PRODUCERS	Brian Knappmiller; Patrick Costello; Cameron Glendenning; Larry Law; Chris Nee; Johnny Petillo; Chris Smith

The Deadliest Catch follows fishing ships and their crews during dangerous crab fishing seasons. The show emphasizes the danger to the crews of these ships. Each episode focuses on a story or situation that occurred on one or more ships, and provides the backstory and particular activities of one or two crew members, particularly the greenhorns (inexperienced crew members) on several ships.

DESTINATION STARDOM

GENRE	Competition (Talent)
FIRST TELECAST	8/23/1999
LAST TELECAST	7/23/2000
NETWORK	PAX
EPISODE STYLE	Self-contained
TALENT	Lisa Canning (Host); Kala'i Miller (Host)
PRODUCTION COMPANY	Entertainment Studios
EXECUTIVE PRODUCERS	Byron Allen; Al Masini

PRODUCERS	April Masini, Marco Orsini; Sam Riddle, Paul Van Wormer
DIRECTOR	Tony Charmoli

Shot on location in Hawaii, this competition followed talented hopefuls from around the world as they competed in six performance categories for a grand prize of $500,000. The voting was determined by the live in-studio audience. Grammy Award winners Los Lonely Boys competed as a family act on the series.

DIARY OF AN AFFAIR

GENRE	Docudrama (Romance)
FIRST TELECAST	10/9/2004
NETWORK	Style
EPISODE STYLE	Self-contained
PRODUCTION COMPANY	Linda Ellman Productions
EXECUTIVE PRODUCERS	Mark Efman; Linda Ellman; Mark Farrell; Christopher Meindl
PRODUCERS	Mike Pack; Kelly Shacklett

Cameras chronicled the confessions of men and women who were having extramarital affairs on *Diary of an Affair.* As the stories were recounted, viewers witnessed drama, passion and remorse surrounding the affairs and learned about any repercussions of the various indiscretions.

DICE: UNDISPUTED

GENRE	Docusoap
FIRST TELECAST	3/4/2007
LAST TELECAST	1/1/2008
NETWORK	VH1

EPISODE STYLE	Story Arc
CAST	Andrew Dice Clay; Eleanor Kerrigan
PRODUCTION COMPANY	Fox Television Studios
EXECUTIVE PRODUCERS	Andrew Dice Clay; Danny Salles
PRODUCERS	Danny Hayes; Scott Mlodzinski

This docusoap followed comedian Andrew Dice Clay as he struggled to recapture his past popularity while dealing with his fiancée and two sons.

DINNER: IMPOSSIBLE

GENRE	Docudrama
FIRST TELECAST	1/24/2007
NETWORK	Food Network
EPISODE STYLE	Self-contained
CAST	Chef Robert Irvine; George Krall; George Gelati
PRODUCTION COMPANY	Dolce Vita Productions
EXECUTIVE PRODUCERS	Marc Summers; Brian O'Rielly,
CO-EXECUTIVE PRODUCER	Alan Blassbert
PRODUCERS	Amy Van Vessem; Arnie Baker; Matt Berkowitz; Mary Beth Anderson; Jeanine Pavuk
DIRECTORS	Scott Preston; Dana Calderwood; Ryan Craig

Classically trained chef Robert Irvine and his two sous-chefs are given a specific culinary task each week to complete within a certain period of time, while overcoming obstacles along the way. Tasks have included making dinner for 150 passengers aboard a luxury locomotive, creating an eighteenth-century meal in Colonial Williamsburg, Virginia, and preparing a meal on a deserted island in the Bahamas.

DOG: THE BOUNTY HUNTER

GENRE	Docudrama (Job)
FIRST TELECAST	8/6/2003
NETWORK	A&E
EPISODE STYLE	Self-contained
CAST	Duane "Dog" Chapman; Beth Smith (Bondsman); Leland Chapman (Dog's son); Tim Chapman (Bondsman); Duane Lee Chapman (Dog's son)
PRODUCTION COMPANIES	A&E Television Network, Inc.; Hybrid Films
EXECUTIVE PRODUCERS	Daniel Elias; David Houts; Boris Lee Krutonog; Neil A. Cohen; Nancy Dubuc; Rob Sharenow
PRODUCERS	Po Kutchins; Allan Title
DIRECTORS	David Houts; Andrew Dunn; Jayson Haedrich

This spin-off from the A&E series *Take This Job,* follows real-life bounty hunter Duane "Dog" Chapman and his colorful family and associates as they apprehend fugitives, principally on the islands of Hawaii.

Duane, Leland, and Tim Chapman were arrested in mid-September 2006 on kidnapping charges dating back to 2003, when the bounty hunters went to Mexico to capture Andrew Luster, who was evading multiple counts of rape. Mexican authorities wanted Luster handed over to them, denied Chapman and his gang permission to leave the country, declared them fugitives from justice, and tried to get them extradited to Mexico for sentencing. A&E aired a special on the matter called *Dog: The Family Speaks,* which was one of the highest-rated specials for the network.

DR. 90210

GENRE	Docudrama (Makeover)
FIRST TELECAST	7/11/2004
NETWORK	E!

EPISODE STYLE	Self-contained
CAST	Dr. Richard Ellenbogen; Dr. Robert M. Rey; Dr. Linda Li; Dr. Jason Diamond; Dr. Gary Alter; Dr. Robert Kotler; Dr. Steven Svehlak; Dr. Daniel Yamini; Dr. Tony Youn
PRODUCTION COMPANY	E!
EXECUTIVE PRODUCERS	Donald Bull; Rick Leed
PRODUCERS	Carmen Mitcho; Jennifer Morton; Brenda Coston

This makeover docudrama features the professional and personal lives of noted Beverly Hills plastic surgeons, along with the stories of their patients and cosmetic surgical procedures.

DR. G: MEDICAL EXAMINER

GENRE	Docudrama (Job)
FIRST TELECAST	7/23/2004
NETWORK	Discovery Health Channel
AIR TIME	Friday, 9:00 p.m.
EPISODE STYLE	Self-contained
TALENT	Jeff Colt (Narrator)
CAST	Jan Garavaglia (Dr. G)
PRODUCTION COMPANY	Atlas Media Corporation
EXECUTIVE PRODUCER	Bruce David Klein
PRODUCERS	Christopher Carlson; Craig Coffman; Brenna C. McCarthy; Jerry Tully; Jennifer Usdan

On *Dr. G: Medical Examiner,* stories from the files of Florida deputy chief medical examiner Dr. Jan Garavaglia are dramatized as she gathers information to solve real-life cases.

DREAM JOB

GENRE	Competition (Job)
FIRST TELECAST	2/24/2004
LAST TELECAST	3/20/2005
NETWORK	ESPN
EPISODE STYLE	Story Arc
TALENT	Stuart Scott (Host); LaVar Arrington (Judge); Kit Hoover (Judge); Al Jaffee (Judge); Tony Kornheiser (Judge); Stephen A. Smith (Judge—Season 2); Woody Paige (Judge—Seasons 2 and 3)

CAST

Season 1 Mike Hall (Winner/Student—Glen Ellyn, Ill.); Chet Anekwe (Computer Programmer—Queens, N.Y.); Maggie Haskins (Student—Chicago, Ill.); Aaron Levine (Student—Calabasas, Calif.); Kelly Milligan (Attorney—Kearney, Nev.); Michael Quigley (Auto Supplies—Yeadon, Penn.); Lori Rubinson (Marketing Executive—Suffern, N.Y.); Zach Selwyn (Actor—Tuscon, Ariz.); Casey Stern (Executive Recruiter—Massapequa, N.Y.); Nick Stevens (Writer/Comedian—Braintree, Mass.); Alvin Williams (Retail Manager—Tuscaloosa, Al.); Chris Williams (Attorney—Roxbury, Mass.)

Season 2 David Holmes (Winner/Student—Uniontown, Ohio); Valerie Hawrylko (Management Consultant—Oakton, Va.); Brian Startare (Health Care Manager—Glassboro, N.J.); Anish Shroff (Radio Host—Bloomfield, N.J.); Grant Thompson

(Actor—Los Angeles, Calif.); Joe Voyticky (Attorney—Brooklyn, N.Y.); K. C. James (Accountant—Los Angeles, Calif.); Jason Ashworth (Assistant Tour Manager—New Freedom, Penn.); Winston Bell (Banker—Cleveland, Ohio); Jason Horowitz (Student—West Bloomfield, Mich.); Stephanie Rich (Travel Coordinator—Arlington, Texas); Whitney Scott (Sports Information Assistant—Lockwood, Mo.)

Season 3   Dee Brown (Winner/Boston Celtics—Jacksonville, Fla.); Gerald Wilkins (Orlando Magic); Dennis Scott (Orlando Magic); J. R. Reid (Charlotte Hornets); Matt Bullard (Houston Rockets); Darryl Dawkins (Philadelphia 76ers)

PRODUCTION COMPANY   Jumbolaya Productions
EXECUTIVE PRODUCERS   Tiffany Trigg; Mary-Jane April; Mark Shapiro
CO-PRODUCERS   Carol Silver; Bob Chesterman

This competition featured a group of contestants competing for a spot on ESPN's *Sportscenter* team. Each show tested the candidates' skills in sportscasting-related challenges, such as calling play-by-plays on a game or using a Telestrator. Judges were ESPN personalities and sports journalists who offered critiques, while home viewers voted on who would advance and who would be cut. Season 1's winner was Mike Hall, a journalism student from the University of Missouri. Season 2's winner was David Holmes, a journalism student from Kent State University. Season 3 added a twist: all of the contestants were all former NBA pros. That season's winner was former Boston Celtic Dee Brown.

DRIVING FORCE

GENRE   Docusoap
FIRST TELECAST   7/17/2006
NETWORK   A&E

EPISODE STYLE	Self-contained
CAST	John Force; Ashley Force; Brittany Force; Courtney Force; Laurie Force
PRODUCTION COMPANY	Schmaguuli LLC
EXECUTIVE PRODUCERS	Stephen Hopkins; Dan Partland; David Schermerhorn; Brent Travers
PRODUCERS	Sarah Skibitzke; Brigid Kelly

This docusoap focused on John Force, one of the most dominant National Hot Rod Association (NHRA) drag racers and funny car champions, as he reconnected with his daughters, who are in their twenties. The girls have decided to follow in their father's footsteps, competing as drivers for John Force Racing.

THE DUDESONS

GENRE	Docudrama
FIRST TELECAST	6/6/2006
LAST TELECAST	9/24/2006
NETWORK	Spike TV
EPISODE STYLE	Self-contained
CAST	Hannu-Pekka Parviainen; Jukka Hilden; Jarno Laasala; Jarno Leppala
PRODUCTION COMPANY	Oy Rabbit Films Ltd.
EXECUTIVE PRODUCER	Jarno Laasala
DIRECTOR	Jarno Laasala

This Finnish series portrayed the lives of four best friends living on The Dudesons Ranch, located close to the Arctic Circle. This *Jackass*-style show featured crazy stunts, comedy, broken bones, lost thumbs, numerous near-death experiences, and one pet pig.

ED MCMAHON'S NEXT BIG STAR

GENRE	Competition (Talent)
FIRST TELECAST	9/9/2001
LAST TELECAST	8/25/2002
NETWORK	PAX
AIR TIME	Sunday, 6:00 p.m.
EPISODE STYLE	Story Arc
TALENT	Ed McMahon (Host)
EXECUTIVE PRODUCERS	Ed McMahon; George Schlatter
PRODUCER	Jeff McMahon

Taped at the MGM Grand Hotel in Las Vegas, this competition featured contestants from various fields of talent, including singing, modeling, dancing, and comedy. Future star Ryan Pinkston, from *Punk'd* was the winner of the "Best of Dance" category.

ELIMIDATE

GENRE	Competition (Dating)
FIRST TELECAST	9/2001
NETWORK	Syndication
EPISODE STYLE	Self-contained
PRODUCTION COMPANY	Dawn Syndicated Productions, in association with Telepictures Productions
EXECUTIVE PRODUCER	Alex Duda
PRODUCERS	Alicia Good; Carrie Brown; Timothy J. Hamilton; Julie Heimler; Jeff Hudson; Marci Klein; Sheila Rosenbaum; Jubba Sayid; Andrew Scott; Jeff Zimmer

Four suitors vie to win the heart of the person they are dating on *elimiDATE*. Cameras record the comments each suitor makes about the others as they rate one another's chances of being the suitor selected to win the date.

Before Constantine Maroulis became a finalist on Season 4 *American Idol*, he was a winning competitor on *elimiDATE*.

ENDURANCE

GENRE	Competition
FIRST TELECAST	10/5/2002
NETWORK	NBC
EPISODE STYLE	Story Arc
TALENT	J. D. Roth (Host)
PRODUCTION COMPANY	3 Ball Productions
CREATED BY	J. D. Roth; Todd A. Nelson
EXECUTIVE PRODUCERS	J. D. Roth; Grady Candler
CO-EXECUTIVE PRODUCERS	John Foy; Erin Wanner

PRODUCERS   Bill Hochhauser; Elayne Cilic; Johanna Rowe
DIRECTOR   Tim Warren

On *Endurance,* twenty kids ages twelve to fifteen divided into ten teams of two are taken to an exotic location to compete against one another in mental and physical challenges. In each episode, the participants face two missions: an Endurance Mission and a Temple Mission. Winners of the Endurance Mission win pieces of the Pyramid of Endurance, while teams winning the Temple Mission earn the right to nominate two teams to go head-to-head at the Temple of Fate. At the Temple of Fate, the two nominated teams face a final challenge, with the losing team is eliminated from the competition. The sole surviving team wins a trip.

THE ENTERTAINER

GENRE   Competition
FIRST TELECAST   1/23/2005
NETWORK   E!
EPISODE STYLE   Story Arc
TALENT   Wayne Newton (Host)
CAST   Delisco (Winner); Jennifer Joseph; Theresa Bruneau; Jacquie Aquines; Nathan Burton; Marla Schultz; Paul Sperrazza; Joe Trammel; Dave Russ; Sarah Darling
PRODUCTION COMPANIES   E! Entertainment Television; Kandor Entertainment; LivePlanet
EXECUTIVE PRODUCERS   Howard Barish; Lee Brownstein; Wayne Newton; Larry Struber; Larry Tanz
DIRECTOR   Lee Brownstein

Mentored by Wayne Newton, ten newcomers were challenged mentally, physically, and creatively throughout a ten-week period to see if they had what it took to become Las Vegas entertainers. New York–based singer Delisco won the $1 million contract and a spot in Wayne Newton's Las Vegas extravaganza.

EXTREME DATING

GENRE	Competition (Dating)
FIRST TELECAST	7/29/2002
LAST TELECAST	9/10/2004
NETWORK	Syndication; FX
EPISODE STYLE	Self-contained
TALENT	Jillian Barberie (Host)
PRODUCTION COMPANY	Wheeler/Sussman
EXECUTIVE PRODUCERS	Sharon Sussman; Burt Wheeler
PRODUCERS	Matt Iseman; Dan Riley; Mykelle Sabin; Daniel Adam Smith; Erich Recker
DIRECTORS	Dan Riley; Daniel Adam Smith

This competition revealed what happens when a man or woman's former mates are allowed to interfere with their love life. Each episode depicted two dates during which two of the man's ex-girlfriends or the woman's ex-boyfriends eavesdropped. The object of the show was to have the ex-partner persuade the date not to go out a second time with the ex. A free second date was awarded if the mate didn't listen to the ex-partners. If the ex-partners won, they were awarded a prize. Humorous graphics and captions added commentary to the action.

EXTREME MAKEOVER

GENRE	Docudrama (Makeover)
FIRST TELECAST	4/23/2003
LAST TELECAST	7/16/2007
NETWORK	ABC
AIRTIMES	Thursday, 9:00 p.m. (4/2003–4/2004); Wednesday, 10:00 p.m. (4/2004–5/2004); Thursday, 8:00 p.m. (6/2004–12/2004); Thursday, 9:00 p.m.

	(1/2005–4/2005); Thursday, 8:00 p.m. (7/2005–8/2005); Monday, 9:00 p.m. (7/2007)
EPISODE STYLE	Self-contained
TALENT	Sam Saboura (Host/Stylist); Sissy Biggers (Host—Season 1)
PRODUCTION COMPANIES	Lighthearted Entertainment; New Screen Entertainment
EXECUTIVE PRODUCERS	Charles A. Bangert; Louis H. Gorfain; Julie Laughlin; Jacqui Pitman; Howard Schultz
PRODUCERS	Peter Steen; Janis Biewend; Mary Clayton; Hank O'Karma; David Schewel
DIRECTORS	Charles A. Bangert; Shanda Sawyer

On this makeover docudrama, people underwent extensive makeovers, consisting of procedures such as plastic surgery, Lasik surgery, and cosmetic dentistry. Professionals coached them on hair, makeup, and fitness. The show also helped some participants realize their dreams once their makeovers were complete.

EXTREME MAKEOVER: HOME EDITION

GENRE	Docudrama (Makeover)
FIRST TELECAST	2/15/2004
NETWORK	ABC
AIR TIMES	Sunday, 8:00 p.m. (2/2004–7/2004); Sunday 9:00 p.m. (7/2004–9/2004); Sunday, 8:00 p.m. (9/2004–present)
EPISODE STYLE	Self-contained
TALENT	Ty Pennington (Leader/Carpenter); Paul DiMeo (Designer); Preston Sharp (Crew); Dawson Connor (Crew); Paige Hemmis (Carpentry/Nuts and Bolts); Alle Ghadban (Crew); Eduardo Xol (Landscape); Michael Moloney (Interiors/Glamour);

Constance Ramos (Building/Planning); Tracy Hutson (Shopping/Style); Ed Sanders (Construction)

PRODUCTION COMPANIES	Endelmol; Lock and Key Productions
EXECUTIVE PRODUCERS	Craig Armstrong; Tom Forman
CO-EXECUTIVE PRODUCERS	Luis Barreto; Denise Cramsey; Janelle Fiorito; Star Price
PRODUCERS	Emily Sinclair; Diane Korman; Mark Rains; Andrew Lipson
DIRECTORS	David Dryden; Patrick Higgins

Not your typical makeover show, this one features families facing hardship. Some of the family members have medical problems, others just need assistance because of circumstances they could not overcome on their own.

The "Home Makeover" crew surprises a lucky family with an early morning bullhorn announcement that their home is about to be made over. The family leaves their property for a complimentary vacation while the crew, volunteers, and a few specialists, in just seven days, renovate and revitalize—and in some cases raze and completely rebuild—the family's home, landscape, and lifestyle. Some of the makeovers have included installing an elevator in a home, designing a special-needs environment for a deaf mom and dad with an autistic/blind son, and creating an ultraviolet-free living space, both indoors and outdoors, for a little girl allergic to the sun.

Neighbors and the workers all cheer as the family arrives home from their vacation to see their incredible new home. Once the excitement starts to wind down, Ty and his crew often have one more surprise gift for the family, in the form of scholarships, mortgage payoffs, or celebrity visits.

A spinoff series of specials called *How'd They Do That?* followed some of the *Extreme Makeover: Home Edition* episodes, detailing how the renovations were completed.

THE EX-WIVES CLUB

GENRE	Docudrama
FIRST TELECAST	5/28/2007
LAST TELECAST	6/25/2007
NETWORK	ABC
AIR TIME	9:00 p.m.
EPISODE STYLE	Self-contained
TALENT	Shar Jackson; Marla Maples; Angie Everhart
PRODUCTION COMPANY	Glassman Media
EXECUTIVE PRODUCERS	Lewis Fenton; Andrew Glassman
DIRECTOR	Tony Croll

Each episode of *The Ex-Wives Club* focused on a man and a woman who had endured a devastating divorce, watching them as they let go of the past, rebuilt their self-esteem, and ventured out into the world again.

FAKE-A-DATE

GENRE	Competition (Hoax/Dating)
FIRST TELECAST	3/17/2004
NETWORK	GSN
EPISODE STYLE	Self-contained
TALENT	Evan Marriott (Host)
PRODUCTION COMPANY	Montana Productions
EXECUTIVE PRODUCERS	Paul Buccieri; Jenny Daly; Tim Puntillo
DIRECTOR	Patrick Higgins

Joe Millionaire's Evan Marriott played the role of host on *Fake-a-Date,* a show featuring one contestant who went on a date with two people of the opposite sex. The twist was that only one was really looking for love. The other already had a significant other and was playing to win a trip. If the contestant chose the person looking for love, the two went on a trip together. However, if the contestant picked the faker, the faker won the trip with his or her real significant other.

FAKING THE VIDEO

GENRE	Competition (Hoax)
FIRST TELECAST	5/24/2004
LAST TELECAST	6/28/2004
NETWORK	MTV
EPISODE STYLE	Story Arc
TALENT	Lance Barber (Billy the Fake Director); Smith Cho (Wardrobe Mistress); Stephanie Courtney (Fake Producer); Mikey Day (Fake PA)
CAST	Diana (Winner); Doug (Runner-up); Rikki (eliminated in Episode 5); Thurston (left in Episode 3); Sean; Casey
CREATED BY	Danny Salles
EXECUTIVE PRODUCERS	Danny Salles; Lois Curren; Rod Aissa
CO-EXECUTIVE PRODUCER	Chris Curry
DIRECTOR	Arthur Borman

In this hoax show six young hopefuls looking to work in Hollywood got their big break landing a job on a music video shoot, working with Bubba Sparxxx, J. C. Chasez, Michelle Branch, Monica, Nick Lachey, Omarion, and Sleepy Brown. But there was a twist: There was no real music video. It was all a hoax to see which candidate had what it took to get his foot in the door. The six contenders were eliminated, one by one, while unwittingly competing for a cash prize and the opportunity to work with music director Wayne Isham.

FAME

GENRE	Competition (Talent)
FIRST TELECAST	5/28/2003
LAST TELECAST	7/23/2003

NETWORK	NBC
AIR TIME	Wednesday, 8:00 p.m.
EPISODE STYLE	Story Arc
TALENT	Debbie Allen (Host); Joey Fatone (Host); Carnie Wilson (Judge); Johnny Wright (Judge); JoJo Wright (Judge)
CAST	Harlemm Lee (Winner); Shannon Bex; Brandon O'Neal; Serena Henry; Allyson Arena (eliminated in Episode 9); Moy (eliminated in Episode 9); "Tyce" Diorio (introduced in Episode 7; eliminated in Episode 9); Justin Jacoby (eliminated in Episode 8); Alex Boyd (eliminated in Episode 8); Jamisen Tiangco (eliminated in Episode 7); Raymond Lee (eliminated in Episode 7); Lauren Hildebrandt (eliminated in Episode 6); Gary Adams (eliminated in Episode 6); Carolyn Zeppa (eliminated in Episode 4); Johannes Williams (eliminated in Episode 4); Sean Dolan (eliminated in Episode 4); Christine Evangelista (eliminated in Episode 3); Alexis Adler (eliminated in Episode 3); Dion Watson (eliminated in Episode 3); Todd Evans (eliminated in Episode 2); Ryan Chotto (eliminated in Episode 2); Michelle Livigne (eliminated in Episode 2); McKenzie Thomas (eliminated in Episode 1); Judy Ho (eliminated in Episode 1); Danny Alvarez (eliminated in Episode 1)
PRODUCTION COMPANIES	MGM Television; Stone Stanley Entertainment
EXECUTIVE PRODUCERS	Jeff Margolis; David G. Stanley; Scott A. Stone
PRODUCER	Debbie Allen
DIRECTOR	Jeff Margolis

Fame actress Debbie Allen selected twenty-four male and female dancer/singers to compete in this elimination talent competition. The winner, Harlemm Lee, won a prize package that included a recording contract with W.I.R.E. Records, a first-class suite at the W Hotel in New York for one year, and a year's training at Debbie Allen's dance academy.

THE FAMILY

GENRE	Competition
FIRST TELECAST	3/4/2003
LAST TELECAST	9/10/2003
NETWORK	ABC
AIR TIMES	Tuesday, 10:00 p.m. (3/2003); Wednesday, 10:00 p.m. (7/2003–9/2003)
EPISODE STYLE	Story Arc
TALENT	George Hamilton (Host); Andrew Lowrey (The Butler); Ringo Allen (The Social Secretary); Linda Levis (The Head Housekeeper); Franck Porcher (The Chef); Jill Swid (The Stylist)
CAST	Anthony (Winner—cousin); Mike (cousin); Maria (cousin); Melinda (cousin); Mike (cousin); Robert (cousin); Jill (cousin); Ed (cousin); Dawn Marie; Michael (uncle); Donna (aunt)
PRODUCTION COMPANIES	Arnold Shapiro and Allison Grodner Productions; Buena Vista Productions
EXECUTIVE PRODUCERS	Arnold Shapiro; Allison Grodner; Mindy Moore
DIRECTORS	Bryan O'Donnell; Danny Salles

An extended family shared a luxurious Palm Beach estate as they competed for a $1 million grand prize on *The Family*. In a twist, the household staff secretly judged the actions of the family as a different contestant was eliminated each week. Cousin Anthony won the prize, and promised to split the winnings with all the family members who participated on the series.

FAMILY BONDS

GENRE	Docudrama
FIRST TELECAST	3/17/2004
NETWORK	HBO
EPISODE STYLE	Self-contained
CAST	Tom Evangelista (The Boss); Flo Evangelista (wife); Chris Evangelista (nephew); Dana Giassakis (daughter); Sal Evangelista (teenager); Frankie Evangelista (kid); Dawn Carfora (sister-in-law); Jimmy Carfora (brother-in-law); Kim Persinger (sister-in-law); Dan Boswith
PRODUCTION COMPANIES	Cactus Three; HBO; Stick Figure Productions
EXECUTIVE PRODUCERS	Nancy Abraham; Steven Cantor; Daniel Laikind; Sheila Nevins
CO-EXECUTIVE PRODUCERS	Julie Goldman; Krysanne Katsoolis; Caroline Stevens
CO-PRODUCER	Pax Wassermann
DIRECTOR	Steven Cantor

This docudrama followed the lives of the Evangelistas and their business, All-City Bail Bonds. The show focused on their bounty-hunting adventures, and their home and family life.

FAMILY BUSINESS

GENRE	Docudrama (Makeover)
FIRST TELECAST	2/21/2003
NETWORK	Showtime
EPISODE STYLE	Story Arc
CAST	Adam Glasser (aka Seymore Butts); Lila Glasser (Adam's mother); Stevie Glasser (Adam's cousin)

PRODUCTION COMPANIES	Maxwell Productions; Arnold Shapiro and Allison Grodner Productions; Showtime Networks Inc.
EXECUTIVE PRODUCERS	Jay Blumenfield; Allison Grodner; Anthony Marsh
PRODUCERS	Ross Breitenbach; Jason Cooper; Steven Bortko
DIRECTORS	Jay Blumenfield; Anthony Marsh

Single father Adam Glasser produces, distributes, and sometimes stars in his own very controversial adult films. Known to his legion of fans as "Seymore Butts," Glasser goes behind-the-scenes of the pornography industry. His mother and bookkeeper, Lila, insisted that she wants nothing more for him than to meet a nice girl and settle down. Comic relief is supplied by Glasser's cousin Stevie.

FAMILY PLOTS

GENRE	Docudrama
FIRST TELECAST	4/19/2004
NETWORK	A&E
EPISODE STYLE	Story Arc
CAST	John Greeney (Funeral director/Apprentice Embalmer); David Moravee (Funeral Director); Matt Nickoley (Assistant Funeral Director); Rick Sadler (Mortuary Manager); Emily Vigney (Office Manager/Funeral Director in Training/youngest sister); Chuck Wissmiller (Funeral Assistant/Remover/father); Melissa Wissmiller (Assistant Funeral Director/eldest sister)
PRODUCTION COMPANY	A&E Television Networks Inc.
EXECUTIVE PRODUCER	David Houts

This real-life version of *Six Feet Under* centered on a family who ran a mortuary in Poway, California. Some family members prepared the dead for burial or cremation, while others counseled the grieving family members on making funeral arrangements for their loved ones.

THE FASHIONISTA DIARIES

GENRE	Competition
FIRST TELECAST	8/1/2007
NETWORK	Soapnet
EPISODE STYLE	Story Arc
CAST	Andrew Kanakis; Bridget; Janjay; Nicole; Rachel Jacoby; Tina; Charlotte (Mentor); Brandon (Mentor); Kathleen (Mentor); and Mandie (Mentor)
PRODUCTION COMPANIES	Go Go Luckey; Buena Vista Productions
EXECUTIVE PRODUCERS	Mike Maloy; Suzanne Myers; Jody Raida; Gary Auerbach; Hulie Auerbach; Jenny Daly

Set in New York City, this competition followed five girls and a guy, all in their twenties, as they tried to prove themselves working at entry-level tasks in the competitive world of the fashion, beauty, and publishing industries. Along the way, they endured high stress and harsh criticism from their demanding new bosses, with the ultimate goal of winning the prize of an assistant position at one of the mentors' companies.

FAT MARCH

GENRE	Competition
FIRST TELECAST	8/6/2007
LAST TELECAST	9/10/2007
NETWORK	ABC
AIR TIME	Monday, 9:00 p.m.
EPISODE STYLE	Story Arc
TALENT	Lorrie Henry (Trainer); Steve Pfiester (Trainer)
CAST	Chantal; Jami Lyn; Kimberly; Loralie; Shea; Wendy; Anthony; Matt; Michael; Sam; Shane
PRODUCTION COMPANY	Ricochet

EXECUTIVE PRODUCER Nick Emmerson
CO-EXECUTIVE PRODUCERS Kirsty Robson; Julie Laughlin

Twelve overweight people set off on a "Fat March," beginning at the Boston Marathon starting line and ending in Washington, D.C. The participants and their two fitness trainers walked more than 570 miles, passing through nine states, with the goal of shedding unwanted pounds and getting fit along the way. In addition, they competed for a prize pool of $1.2 million. Stressing teamwork, the competition awarded more money as the number of people who finished increased.

FEAR

GENRE Competition
FIRST TELECAST 2/18/2001
LAST TELECAST 5/27/2002
NETWORK MTV
EPISODE STYLE Self-contained
TALENT Dan Gifford (Web Voice)
PRODUCTION COMPANY MTV Networks
CREATED BY Martin Kunert; Eric Manes
EXECUTIVE PRODUCERS Dawn Parouse; Beau Flynn; Eric Manes; Martin Kunert
CO-EXECUTIVE PRODUCER George Verschoor
PRODUCERS Cris Abrego; Robert Cardenas
DIRECTORS Luis Barreo; David Parks; George Verschoor; Rick Telles

Shot in a style reminiscent of *The Blair Witch Project,* this competition featured six young investigators exploring abandoned spooky locations around the world as they attempted to explain the unexplainable.

FEAR FACTOR

GENRE	Competition (Endurance)
FIRST TELECAST	6/11/2001
LAST TELECAST	9/12/2006
NETWORK	NBC
AIR TIMES	Monday, 8:00 p.m. (6/2001–8-2001; 1/2002–9/2005); Tuesday, 8:00 p.m. (12/2005–2/2006; 6/2006–9/2006)
EPISODE STYLE	Self-contained
TALENT	Joe Rogan (Host)
PRODUCTION COMPANIES	Endemol Entertainment USA; Evolution Film & Tape Inc.; Lock and Key Productions; Pulse Creative
EXECUTIVE PRODUCERS	John de Mol; Matt Kunitz; David A. Hurwitz;
CO-EXECUTIVE PRODUCERS	Kathleen French; Douglas Ross; J. Rupert Thompson; Greg Stewart
PRODUCERS	Rich Brown; Michael J. Glazer; Tom Herschko; Scott Larson
DIRECTOR	J. Rupert Thompson; Randall Einhorn

In this endurance competition competitors were given three unusual and extreme physical stunts to complete. The second stunt often involved eating or drinking something vile, or interacting with creepy creatures. In the final round, the competitor who completed the task in the shortest amount of time won $50,000. Some competitors featured couples, such as a husband and wife or pairs of friends. Over the years, many episodes were devoted to a theme, such as Las Vegas, twins, Miss USA, or the film *Psycho*.

FIGHT FOR FAME

GENRE	Competition (Talent)
FIRST TELECAST	6/5/2005
LAST TELECAST	8/7/2005
NETWORK	E!
AIR TIME	Sunday, 10:00 p.m.
EPISODE STYLE	Self-contained
TALENT	Greg Meyer (Agent—Judge); Adam Lieblein (Agent—Judge); Marki Costello (Casting Director—Judge)
CAST	Brianna Konefall; David Petruzzi; Jillian Pollock; Joseph Ferrante; Monique Pardo; Emeka Nnadi; Kate Woodruff; Jamie Everett; Dominic Prietto; Heather Goins; Candace Pittman; Jonathan Kowalsky; Sean Lyons; Sophia Shalmoni; Kelsey Barney; Nina Kaczorowski; Myla Martin; Ashley Smith; Kaki West; Nikki Zeno; Nina Kaczorowski; Steve Coombs; Omar Regan; Sahra Silanee; Michael Antonacci; Jon Garman; Cameron Goodman; David Kobzantsev; Amy Rosoff; Angel Monroe; Dylan Vox; Raquel Rischard; Pam Levin; J. Lee; Justin Andersch; Lindsay Gareth; Lisa Fleming; Michelle Pirraglia; Sean Klitzner; Drew Broadrick; Chad Chaney; Rachelle Franklin; Jackie Maddison

A group of wannabe actors vied for roles on TV shows and in movies and commercials. The competitors performed monologues and scenes, and discussed their dreams of stardom. In each episode one talented person was selected to be represented by a Hollywood talent agency.

FIGHT GIRLS

GENRE	Competition
FIRST TELECAST	8/7/2006
NETWORK	Oxygen
EPISODE STYLE	Story Arc
TALENT	Master Toddy (Head Trainer)
CAST	Felice Herrig; Kerry Vera; Jeanine Jackson; Jennifer Tate; Michelle Waterson; Miriam Nakamoto; Ardra Hernandez; Dawn Boyd; Lisa King; Gina Carano
PRODUCTION COMPANY	Mess Media
EXECUTIVE PRODUCERS	Scott Messick; Thomas Weber
PRODUCERS	Jennifer Ferrara; Anneli Gericke; Marla Roberts

On *Fight Girls,* seven American female fighters lived and trained in Las Vegas for the chance to fight in a Muay Thai championship match in Thailand.

FILM FAKERS

GENRE	Docudrama (Hoax)
FIRST TELECAST	11/10/2004
NETWORK	AMC
AIR TIME	Wednesday, 10:00 p.m.
EPISODE STYLE	Self-contained
CREATED BY	Dave Noll
EXECUTIVE PRODUCER	Mark Perez
PRODUCERS	Suzanne Molinaro; Marla Puccetti
DIRECTOR	Mark Perez

Novice actors were given an opportunity to perform in a low-budget film, but there was a twist—it was all a hoax, and there was no movie. The production crew, who were in on the secret, set out deliberately to undermine the film, causing chaos on the set and unnerving the inexperienced actors.

FILM SCHOOL

GENRE	Docusoap (Job)
FIRST TELECAST	9/10/2004
LAST TELECAST	11/12/2004
NETWORK	IFC
AIR TIME	Friday, 10:30 p.m.
EPISODE STYLE	Story Arc
CAST	Alrick Brown; Barbara Klauke; Leah Meyerhoff; Vincenzo Tripodo
PRODUCTION COMPANY	Film 101 Inc.
CREATED BY	Nanette Burstein
EXECUTIVE PRODUCERS	Nanette Burnstein; Debbie DeMontreux; Ed Carroll
PRODUCERS	Jordan Roberts; Sharon Barnes
DIRECTORS	Nanette Burstein; Tamas Bojtor; Rebecca Cammisa; Sybil Dessau; Greg Orselli

Four film students from New York University's Tisch School of the Arts allowed cameras to capture the grueling process of making their ten-minute thesis films on this docusoap. The series was not a filmmaking competition; rather, it allowed viewers to observe the casting, budgeting, logistic considerations, and personal drama that go into moviemaking.

FILTHY RICH: CATTLE DRIVE

GENRE	Docucomedy (Celebrity)
FIRST TELECAST	6/14/2005
NETWORK	E!
EPISODE STYLE	Story Arc

CAST

The Kids	Courtenay Semel; Haley Giraldo; Alex Quinn; Brittny Gastineau; Fabian Basabe; Shanna Ferrigno; Noah Blake; Alexander Clifford; George Foreman III; Kourtney Kardashian
The Ranchers	Wayne Iacovetto (Ranch Owner); Jerad Iacovetto (Ranch Hand); Maria Schnell (Ranch Hand); Joshua Smith (Trail Boss)
PRODUCTION COMPANY	Base Camp Films
CREATED BY	Joe Simpson; Jason Felts; Justin Berfield
EXECUTIVE PRODUCERS	Joe Simpson; Brady Connell; Justin Berfield; Jason Felts; James A. Jusko
CO-EXECUTIVE PRODUCERS	Douglas C. Forbes
PRODUCER	Heath Luman
DIRECTOR	Randall Einhorn

The children of the rich and famous left behind their privileged lifestyles and headed to the open range as they assisted on a one-hundred-mile cattle drive at a ranch in Steamboat Springs, Colorado. *Filthy Rich: Cattle Drive* cast members included the children of George Foreman, Lou Ferrigno, Pat Benatar, Robert Blake, and the CEO of Yahoo!. The kids performed not-so-glamorous tasks such as helping a cow give birth.

FIRE ME, PLEASE!

GENRE	Competition (Hoax)
FIRST TELECAST	6/7/2005
LAST TELECAST	7/5/2005
NETWORK	CBS
AIR TIME	Tuesday, 9:00 p.m.
EPISODE STYLE	Self-contained
TALENT	Dave Holmes (Host)
PRODUCTION COMPANY	LMNO Productions
EXECUTIVE PRODUCERS	Bill Paolantonio; Eric Schotz

CO-EXECUTIVE PRODUCERS	Dan Funk
PRODUCER	Steve Durgin

Two contestants began new jobs on the same day, with the same goal: to be fired from the job as close to 3:00 p.m. as possible, without being fired later than that. The employer didn't know its premises had been set up with hidden cameras to capture the action. The contestant who accomplished the task won $25,000.

FLAVOR OF LOVE

GENRE	Competition (Dating)
FIRST TELECAST	8/6/2006
NETWORK	VH1
EPISODE STYLE	Story Arc
TALENT	Flavor Flav (Bachelor)

CAST

Season 1   Nicole Alexander (Winner—aka Hoopz); Tiffany Pollard (Runner-up—aka New York); Courtney Jackson II (aka Goldie); Brooke Thompson (aka Pumkin); Jefandi Cato (aka Georgia); Kim Manning (aka Peaches), Tikka Rain (aka Sweetie); Xotchitl Rodriguez (aka Miss Latin); Amber Kemp (aka Shellz); Leilene Ondrade (aka Smiley); Schatar Sapphira Taylor (aka Hottie); Crystal Athena Stevenson (aka Serious); Abigail Kintanar (aka Red Oyster); Thela Brown (aka Rain)

Season 2   London Charles (Winner—aka Deelishis); Tiffany Pollard (Runner-up—aka New York); Becky Johnston (aka Buckwild); Neveah Crawford (aka Krazy); Kelly Jay Jenkins (aka Beatuful);

Larissa Hodge (aka Bootz); Tarasha Lee (aka Bamma); Tykeisha Thomas (aka Somethin); Yanay Yancy (aka Hood); Shay Johnson (aka Buckeey); Britney Morano (aka Tiger); Jasmine Dare (aka Payshintz); Renee Austin (aka H-Town); Bettie Brown (aka Nibblz); Saaphyri Windsor (no nickname); Ronnise Clark (aka Choclate); Darra Boyd (aka Like Dat); Jennifer Toof (aka Toastee); Jesselynn Desmond (aka Wire), Maria Dunbar (aka Spunkeey)

PRODUCTION COMPANY 51 Minds Entertainment

EXECUTIVE PRODUCERS Mark Cronin; Cris Abrego; Ben Samek; Matt Odgers

PRODUCERS Michelle Brando; Lauren A. Stevens

DIRECTORS Zach Kozek; Robert Sizemore

After his failed romance with actress Brigitte Nielsen on VH1's *Strange Love,* rapper Flavor Flav now looks for a new romance on *Flavor of Love.* Twenty single women move into a Los Angeles mansion to compete for the bachelor's attention. Flav gives each woman a nickname to more easily remember her, such as New York, Pumkin, Red Oyster, and Hoopz. He dates the women, trying to find out which ones are there for him, and not his money. Hoopz won Flav's heart in Season 1, and he gave her a set of gold teeth.

Flav and Hoopz eventually broke up, and he returned to VH1 for Season 2 of the show, which billed itself as focusing on the truth. Flav's challenges again were set up to identify the gold diggers and the fakes. Season 1 contestant New York returned as a contestant, and ended up in the final two, with Deelishis. Flav chose Deelishis as the Season 2 winner, but they, too, broke up, and Season 3 was under way.

FLAVOR OF LOVE GIRLS: CHARM SCHOOL

GENRE	Competition (Talent)
FIRST TELECAST	4/15/2007
LAST TELECAST	7/1/2007
NETWORK	VH1
EPISODE STYLE	Story Arc
TALENT	Mo'Nique (Host); Keith Lewis (Judge); Mikki Taylor (Judge)
CAST	Saaphyri Windsor (Winner); Shay Johnson/Buckeey (Finalist); Leilene Ondrade/Smiley (Finalist); Becky Johnston/Buckwild (Finalist); Brooke Thompson/Pumkin (9th eliminated); Larissa Aurora/Bootz (8th eliminated); Darra Boyd/Like Dat (7th eliminated); Schatar Sapphira Taylor/Hottie (6th eliminated); Courtney Jackson II/Goldie (5th eliminated); Cristal Athena Stevenson/Serious (4th eliminated); Jennifer Toof/Toastee (3rd eliminated); Heather Crawford/Krazy (2nd eliminated); Thela Brown/Rain (1st eliminated)
PRODUCTION COMPANY	51 Minds Entertainment
EXECUTIVE PRODUCERS	Mark Cronin; Chris Abrego; Ben Sarnek
DIRECTOR	Robert Sizemore

Thirteen contestants from the first two seasons of *Flavor of Love* were taught proper etiquette. Actress and model Mo'Nique was host. The winner of the competition, Saaphyri, won $50,000 and the title of "Charm School Queen."

FLIPPED

GENRE	Docudrama
FIRST TELECAST	8/6/2001
NETWORK	MTV
EPISODE STYLE	Self-contained
PRODUCTION COMPANY	Arnold Shapiro and Allison Grodner Productions
CREATED BY	Arnold Shapiro
EXECUTIVE PRODUCER	Arnold Shapiro
PRODUCERS	Allison Grodner; Karen Duzy; Nicole Solomon
DIRECTOR	Kevin Dill

Teens spent twenty-four hours in somebody else's shoes in an attempt to give them a reality check. In one episode, a sixteen-year-old changed places with her mother and had to tend to her mother's household chores as well as go to her mom's job. Other episodes dealt with serious issues such as drugs and discrimination.

FLIPPING OUT

GENRE	Docusoap
FIRST TELECAST	7/31/2007
NETWORK	Bravo
EPISODE STYLE	Self-contained
CAST	Jeff Lewis; Zoila Chavez; Jenni Pulos; Chris Elwood; Stephen Bowman; Ryan Brown
PRODUCTION COMPANY	Authentic Entertainment
EXECUTIVE PRODUCERS	Lauren Lexton; Tom Rogan
CO-EXECUTIVE PRODUCER	Billy Taylor
PRODUCERS	Jairus Cobb; Ben Faulks; Gregg Paine
DIRECTOR	Jairus Cobb

This docusoap followed the life and antics of one of Los Angeles' most colorful real estate speculators, obsessive-compulsive businessman Jeff Lewis. The show also featured the exploits of employees and friends.

FOOD FIGHT

GENRE	Competition
FIRST TELECAST	5/22/2003
NETWORK	Food Network
EPISODE STYLE	Self-contained
TALENT	JD Roberto (Host)
PRODUCTION COMPANY	Tentmakers Entertainment
EXECUTIVE PRODUCERS	Scott Galloway
SEGMENT PRODUCER	Lisa Weiss

Two teams battle in a timed cooking competition shot on location in regions with a distinctive food style. The teams are assigned a main course and twenty dollars to shop for specific ingredients to make their dishes stand out. A panel of local food experts judge the competition.

FOR BETTER OR FOR WORSE

GENRE	Docudrama
FIRST TELECAST	5/24/2003
NETWORK	TLC
EPISODE STYLE	Self-contained
CAST	Kathleen McClellan (Host—Seasons 1 and 2); Alicia Davis (Host—Season 3); Sally Steele (Wedding Planner); Alana Barone (Wedding Planner); Jonathan Dane (Wedding Planner Assistant); Jake Hanover (Wedding Planner

Assistant); Heidi Popp (Wedding Planner
Assistant); Yifat Oren (Wedding Planner);
Matt O'Dorisio (Wedding Planner); Erika Shay
(Wedding Planner); Angie Bloom Hewitt
(Wedding Planner); Jackson Lowell (Wedding
Planner); Alan Dunn (Wedding Planner)

PRODUCTION COMPANY	Nash Entertainment
EXECUTIVE PRODUCERS	Debra Weeks; Bruce Nash; Robin Nash
PRODUCERS	Babette Pepaj; Dan Perry; Shirley Jackson
DIRECTOR	Chris Wilson

Guided by a wedding planner, family members were given $5,000 and one week to create the perfect setting for a wedding. The couple getting married had no input regarding the planning of the ceremony.

FOR LOVE OR MONEY

GENRE	Competition (Dating)
FIRST TELECAST	6/2/2003
LAST TELECAST	8/9/2004
NETWORK	NBC
AIR TIME	Monday, 9:00 p.m.
EPISODE STYLE	Story Arc
TALENT	Jordan Murphy (Host)

CAST

Season 1 Rob Campos (The Bachelor); Erin Brodie (Winner); Catherine; Cristy C.; Christina; Kelly Ford; Laura Hamil; Cristy H.; Paige Jones; Kirstin; Staci Lai; Lauren; Alima Ravenscroft; Tracy; Melissa Wehrman

Season 2 Erin Brodie (The Bachelorette); Chad Viggiano (Winner); Dustin; Chad F.; Deric; Munch; Richard; Victor; Dan; Chris; Paul, Thomas; Eric; Sean; Greg

Season 3 Preston Mercer (The Bachelor); P. J. Spillman (Winner); Rachel Veltri (Runner-up); Johanna; Melayne; Melody; Tiniesha; Andrea Langi; Ali; Heather; Beth; Monica; Leslie; Jamie; Rebekah

Season 4 Rachel Veltri (Bachelorette); Andrea Langi (Bachelorette—eliminated in Episode 1); Caleb Janus (Winner); Alex; Dave K.; Dave S.; Jai; Wes; Rudy; Morgan; Chad; Ben; Brian; Josh; Steve; Mike

PRODUCTION COMPANIES Nash Entertainment; 3 Ball Productions
EXECUTIVE PRODUCERS Bruce Nash; J. D. Roth; John Foy; Todd Nelson
CO-EXECUTIVE PRODUCER Adam Greener
PRODUCERS Bonner Bellew; Ellayne Cilic; Tim Eagan; Shye Sutherland
DIRECTOR Brian Smith

Fifteen women (Seasons 1 and 3) or men (Seasons 2 and 4) were forced to choose between their possible soul mates or $1 million. Each season offered new twists.

In Season 1, the chosen bachelorette, Erin Brodie, was given the choice between the bachelor who picked her, Rob Campos, or a check for $1 million. She chose the check.

Season 2 began immediately after Season 1, as Brodie was given the chance to double her $1 million if she could persuade a new bachelor she'd picked to choose her instead of $1 million. She picked Chad Viggiano, and he chose her instead of the money. Erin decided to split with him the additional $1 million she won.

Season 3 featured a new twist: Each woman was assigned a check ranging from $1 to $1 million. The women did not know the value of the checks, but the bachelor, Preston Mercer, did. If the woman Preston chose kept her check instead of him, she got to keep the value of the check. If the woman Preston chose took him instead of the money, he had to decide whether he wanted to keep the woman or take her check. In the end, Preston chose P.J., and stuck with her, rather than taking her check, which was worth $1.

In Season 4, two bachelorettes from the previous season competed for a spot as the chooser. At the end of the season opener, the man voted to keep Rachel Veltri as their chooser. In the end, she chose Caleb Janus, and both decided to give up a check for $1 million in exchange for love.

FOREVER EDEN

GENRE	Competition (Romance)
FIRST TELECAST	3/1/2004
LAST TELECAST	4/9/2004
NETWORK	FOX
AIR TIMES	Monday, 9:00 p.m. (3/2004; Friday, 9:00 p.m. (4/2004)
EPISODE STYLE	Story Arc
TALENT	Ruth England (Host)
CAST	Wallace Luyten; Chris; Claudia; Kassie Miller; David Lovejoy; Brooke; Liz; Neveen (banished in Episode 10); Jason Wehner (banished in Episode 10); Michelle (left in Episode 8); Michael (banished in Episode 6); Shawna Frazier (banished in Episode 5); Jordan (banished in Episode 4); Khalilah (left in Episode 3); Mary Chamberlin (banished in Episode 2); Craig Rice (banished in Episode 2); Matt
PRODUCTION COMPANIES	Mentorn; A. Smith and Co.
CREATED BY	Howard Davidson; Phil Roberts
EXECUTIVE PRODUCERS	Tom Gutteridge; Arthur Smith; Charles Thompson; Bruce Toms; Kent Weed
CO-EXECUTIVE PRODUCER	Andrew Scheer
PRODUCER	Ben Samek

In this competition set in the tropical resort of Portland, Jamaica, single men and women left their day-to-day lives and families behind to live in the lap of luxury. There were twists designed to reveal secrets that might get the ten competitors banished. For each week a competitor stayed, he or she earned money. After being banished, a contestant gave half of his or her coins to one of the remaining players. Whenever a contestant "threw in the towel," and decided to exit Eden, he or she lost all of the money accumulated.

FORTY DEUCE

GENRE	Docusoap
FIRST TELECAST	4/7/2005
LAST TELECAST	4/28/2005
NETWORK	Bravo
EPISODE STYLE	Story Arc
CAST	Ivan Kane ("Forty Deuce" owner); Suzy Champagne (Ivan's wife/Business Partner); Vai Au-Harehoe (Dancer); Carolina Cerisola (Dancer); Melissa Chiz (Dancer); Kiva Dawson (Dancer); Dakota Ferreiro (Dancer); Erin Giraud (Dancer); Carolyn Pace (Dancer); Tracy Phillips (Dancer); Jade Ruggiero (Dancer); Victoria Taylor (Dancer)
PRODUCTION COMPANY	The Zalman King Company
PRODUCERS	Martha Adams; Patrick Davenport
CO-PRODUCER	Champagne Suzy

Successful nightclub owner Ivan Kane and his wife/business partner, Champagne Suzy, allowed cameras to capture the glitz and glamour involved in the opening of their latest venture, Forty Deuce, at Mandalay Bay, in Las Vegas. Non-nude burlesque dancers performed in an atmosphere with the look and feel of an upscale 1920s speakeasy. Zalman King (*Nine ½ Weeks, Red Shoe Diaries*) directed.

FRATERNITY LIFE

GENRE	Docusoap
FIRST TELECAST	2/26/2003
NETWORK	MTV
EPISODE STYLE	Story Arc

CAST

Season 1	Alex; Dan; Earl; Jarreau; Paul; Stephen (voted out); Tim
Season 2	Robbie; Slater; Jon; Bryant; Chris; Drew; Kenny B.
EXECUTIVE PRODUCERS	Russell Heldt; J. J. Jamieson
PRODUCERS	Joey Castillo; Lauralee Jarvis; Jeff Keirns; Joshua Klinman; Shannon Owen
DIRECTORS	Brian Krinsky; Michelle Brando; Sean Rankine; Robert Sizemore; Rollen Torres; Jeff Fisher; Kathy Wetherell

This college docusoap follows the drama that young men encounter as they rush, pledge, and eventually become members of a fraternity. Season 1 featured the Sigma Chi Omega fraternity house at the University of Buffalo, New York. Season 2 followed the same process at the Delta Omega Chi House at the University of California, in Santa Cruz.

FRESHMAN DIARIES

GENRE	Docusoap
FIRST TELECAST	8/31/2003
LAST TELECAST	11/2/2003
NETWORK	Showtime
EPISODE STYLE	Story Arc

CAST Rashan; Jochen; Casey; Kyle; Luis; Neil McGurk; Josh McGinnis; Arlette; Kelly; Laura; Shannon; Michael; Natasha; Memo; Nicole; Courtney; Claire
PRODUCTION COMPANY Actual Reality Pictures
EXECUTIVE PRODUCER R. J. Cutler

The documentary-style program followed a distinctly different group of students armed with video cameras, as they experienced their first year of studies at the University of Texas at Austin. The show ended prematurely, reportedly due to financial reasons.

FRONTIER HOUSE

GENRE Docusoap
FIRST TELECAST 4/29/2002
LAST TELECAST 5/1/2002
NETWORK PBS
EPISODE STYLE Story Arc
TALENT Kathryn Walker (Narrator)
CAST Tracy Clune; Conor Clune; Justin Clune; Aine Clune; Gordon Clune; Erin Patton; Mark Glenn; Karen Glenn; Kristen McLeod; Nate Brooks; Mark Patton
EXECUTIVE PRODUCERS Alex Graham; Beth Hoppe; Mark Saben
PRODUCERS Nicholas Brown; Maro Chermayeff; Simon Shaw
DIRECTORS Nicholas Brown; Maro Chermayeff

Inspired by the British series *1900 House,* this docusoap featured three modern-day American families from California, Boston, and Tennessee, who arrived by covered wagon to live for five months in the rustic Montana wilderness as settlers did in 1883. They had to churn their own butter, make their clothes, live off the land, and learn to coexist.

GASTINEAU GIRLS

GENRE	Docudrama (Celebrity)
FIRST TELECAST	2/1/2005
LAST TELECAST	2/7/2006
NETWORK	E!
AIR TIME	Tuesday, 8:00 p.m.
EPISODE STYLE	Self-contained
TALENT	Lisa Gastineau (Mother); Brittny Gastineau (Daughter); Lou Martini, Jr. (Doorman)
PRODUCTION COMPANIES	E! Entertainment Television; True Entertainment
EXECUTIVE PRODUCERS	Glenda Hersch; Steven Weinstock; Ann Lewis; Sara Nichols
CO-EXECUTIVE PRODUCER	Chad Greulach
PRODUCERS	Jerry Kolber; Julie Bob Lombardi
DIRECTORS	Lisa Caruso; Mark Perez; Miles Kahn

Former model and ex-wife of NFL star Mark Gastineau, Lisa and her daughter, Brittny, were the New York socialites, best friends, and occasional rivals featured in this docudrama. Their doorman, Lou, was the series commentator as mother and daughter searched for love, fame, and good shopping.

GENE SIMMONS FAMILY JEWELS

GENRE	Docucomedy
FIRST TELECAST	8/7/2006
NETWORK	A&E
EPISODE STYLE	Story Arc
CAST	Gene Simmons; Shannon Tweed; Nick Simmons; Sophie Simmons
PRODUCTION COMPANIES	A Day With; A&E Television Network; Big Machine Design; Gene Simmons Company; The Greif Company
EXECUTIVE PRODUCERS	Adam Reed; Nancy Dubuc; Leslie Greif; Deidre O'Hearn; Gene Simmons
CO-EXECUTIVE PRODUCERS	Chad Greulach; Adam Freeman
PRODUCERS	David Price; Ben Hatta
DIRECTORS	Adam Reed; Adam Freeman

KISS frontman, rock legend Gene Simmons, opened the home he shared with girlfriend and former Playmate of the Year Shannon Tweed and their two children as cameras captured their domestic life on this docucomedy. Viewers followed Gene on his numerous business meetings, including music and Indycar ventures. Season 2 chronicled his and Shannon's plastic surgeries.

GENE SIMMONS' ROCK SCHOOL

GENRE	Docucomedy (Celebrity)
FIRST TELECAST	8/19/2005
NETWORK	VH1

EPISODE STYLE	Story Arc
TALENT	Dee Snider (Narrator); Gene Simmons
PRODUCTION COMPANY	RDF Media
EXECUTIVE PRODUCER	Grant Mansfield
PRODUCERS	Jo Crawley; Theodore Kim
DIRECTORS	Ros Ponder; Abigail Priddle

On *Gene Simmons' Rock School,* the KISS frontman traveled to the United Kingdom for six weeks to transform a group of classically trained preteen students from Christ's Hospital boarding school into a rough-around-the-edges rock band.

GET PACKING

GENRE	Competition (Dating)
FIRST TELECAST	10/3/2003
LAST TELECAST	12/23/2004
NETWORK	Travel Channel
AIR TIME	Friday, 10:00 p.m.
EPISODE STYLE	Self-contained
TALENT	Michelle Beadle (Host); Fabrizio Brienza (Coach); Janet Jorgulesco (Coach); Veronica Milchorena (Coach); Sixto Nolasco (Coach); Patty Rothstein (Coach); John Solomon (Coach); Freddy Stebbins (Coach); Tracie Wright
PRODUCTION COMPANY	NorthSouth Productions
PRODUCER	Marvin Cigel
DIRECTOR	Marvin Cigel

In this dating competition, two single men or women vied to win a romantic trip with a mystery date. With the help of coaches, singles snooped around their potential date's home for ten minutes. Based on information they gathered, they were given $1,000 and three hours to shop for items they thought their potential date would need, and packed the contents into a suitcase. The mystery date then examined the suitcase to determine who would win the free getaway.

GET THIS PARTY STARTED

GENRE	Docudrama (Makeover)
FIRST TELECAST	2/7/2006
LAST TELECAST	2/14/2006
NETWORK	UPN
AIR TIME	Tuesday, 9:00 p.m.
EPISODE STYLE	Self-contained
TALENT	Kristin Cavalleri (Host); Ethan Erickson (Host); Lara Shriftman (Special Events Coordinator)
PRODUCTION COMPANY	Allison Grodner Productions
EXECUTIVE PRODUCER	Allison Grodner

Get This Party Started captured the drama and excitement as friends and family worked with party planners to throw a surprise event in honor of their loved one. Nothing was spared to make the lucky person's dreams come true. The series was canceled after only two episodes.

THE GIRLS NEXT DOOR

GENRE	Docudrama
FIRST TELECAST	8/7/2005
NETWORK	E!
EPISODE STYLE	Self-contained
CAST	Hugh Hefner; Holly Madison; Bridget Marquardt; Kendra Wilkinson
PRODUCTION COMPANY	Prometheus Entertainment

CREATED BY	Kevin Burns
EXECUTIVE PRODUCER	Kevin Burns
CO-EXECUTIVE PRODUCER	Bryan O'Donnell
SENIOR PRODUCERS	Jennifer Colbert; Scott Hartford

Set in the Playboy Mansion, *The Girls Next Door* follows the lives of Hugh Hefner and his three girlfriends, Holly, Bridget, and Kendra. Episode highlights have included a look at Midsummer Night's Dream, the infamous summer party held each year at the mansion; a *Playboy* pictorial shoot of Hef's girlfriends; and a Playmate birthday party at Hef's Palms suite in Las Vegas.

GOD OR THE GIRL

GENRE	Docusoap
FIRST TELECAST	4/16/2006
NETWORK	A&E
AIR TIMES	Sundays 9:00 p.m.
EPISODE STYLE	Story Arc
TALENT	Dan DeMatte; Mike Lechniak; Steve Horvath; Joe Adair
PRODUCTION COMPANY	The Idea Factory
EXECUTIVE PRODUCERS	Neil A. Cohen; Stephen David; David Eilenberg; Darryl M. Silver; Mark Wolper
PRODUCER	Maren S. Patterson

This five-part miniseries followed four twentysomething men as they decided between becoming a Catholic priest or settling down with a woman to start a family. At the end of the series, only one man, Steve, entered the seminary. Two of the others incorporated religion into their lives, as Dan became a youth minister and Joe became a lay minister, while Mike became a teacher.

GREASE:
YOU'RE THE ONE THAT I WANT

GENRE Competition (Talent)

FIRST TELECAST 1/7/2007

LAST TELECAST 3/25/2007

NETWORK NBC

EPISODE STYLE Story Arc

TALENT Billy Bush (Host); Denise Van Outen (Co-Host); David Ian (Judge); Jim Jacobs (Judge); Kathleen Marshall (Judge)

CAST

Dannys Max Crumm (Winner); Austin Miller (Runner-up); Derek Keeling (5th eliminated); Chad Doreck (4th eliminated); Kevin Greene (3rd eliminated); Jason Celaya (2nd eliminated); Matt Nolan (1st eliminated)

Sandys Laura Osnes (Winner); Ashley Spencer (Runner-up); Allie Schulz (5th eliminated); Kathleen Monteleone (4th eliminated); Kate Rockwell (3rd eliminated); Juliana Hansen (2nd eliminated); Ashley Andrson (1st eliminated)

PRODUCTION COMPANIES BBC Worldwide; Nederlander Television & Film Productions; Phoenix Productions

EXECUTIVE PRODUCERS All Edgington; David Ian; Louis A. Stroller; Paul Teledgyy

DIRECTOR Nick Murray

This competition series set out to find a new Danny Zuko and Sandy Dumbrowski for a Broadway revival of "Grease" set to premiere later that year. The series began with a number of cross-country auditions judged by Broadway director and choreographer Kathleen Marshall, "Grease" co-writer Jim Jacobs, and producer David Ian.

After a series of semi-finals, the judges narrowed down the field of fifty to the six young men and six young women that would make up the competition's finalists.

Each week, the finalists would perform before a live studio audience and the panel of judges. Home viewers would vote on their favorite Sandy and Danny each week and the two from each group that received the lowest votes would battle it out in a sing-off the following week. The judges would then determine which Danny and which Sandy from each sing-off would be eliminated.

The final winners were determined solely by the home audience's vote and America decided that Minnesota native Laura Osnes would play the new Sandy and California's Max Crumm would play the new Danny.

The new production of "Grease" starring Laura and Max premiered August 19, 2007, at the Brooks Atkinson Theatre.

THE GREAT AMERICAN DREAM VOTE

GENRE	Competition
FIRST TELECAST	3/27/07
TELECAST	3/28/07
NETWORK	ABC
EPISODE STYLE	Self-contained
TALENT	Donny Osmond (Host)
PRODUCTION COMPANY	Warner Horizon Television
EXECUTIVE PRODUCER	Mike Fleiss
PRODUCER	Derek Che
DIRECTOR	Lisa Levenson

The show featured contestants who wanted their dream to come true. The studio audience would pick the two finalists; those at home would select the winner via Internet voting. Despite the premiere's *Dancing with the Stars* lead-in, it drew very disappointing ratings. ABC cancelled the show after only two episodes.

GREAT PRETENDERS

GENRE	Competition (Talent)
FIRST TELECAST	10/1/1998
NETWORK	ABC Family
EPISODE STYLE	Self-contained
TALENT	Stacy Ferguson; Pamela Covais; Scott Sternberg
PRODUCER	Doug Turner
DIRECTOR	Barry Glazer

Girl group Wild Orchid hosted this teen lip-sync show in which a studio audience judged the best performance, and the pseudo singer with the most votes was inducted as the top Great Pretender of the episode. Wild Orchid member Stacy Ferguson went on to become better known as Fergie.

GROWING UP GOTTI

GENRE	Docucomedy
FIRST TELECAST	8/2/2004
NETWORK	A&E
EPISODE STYLE	Story Arc
CAST	Victoria Gotti; Frank Agnello (Victoria's son); John Agnello (Victoria's son); Carmine Agnello, Jr. (Victoria's son); Luigi (Victoria's handyman); Robert (Victoria's assistant)
EXECUTIVE PRODUCERS	Victoria Gotti; Gary R. Benz; Michael Branton; Judith Regan; William Stanton
CO-EXECUTIVE PRODUCERS	Banks Tarver; Craig Spirko
PRODUCER	Mitchell Rosenbaum

Growing Up Gotti followed the lives of Victoria Gotti, daughter of the late mob boss, John Gotti, and her three teenage sons, Carmine Jr., John, and Frank. Victoria gave viewers an unprecedented look into her life—one filled with the same challenges and conflicts most divorced mothers face while raising teenagers. Scenes included Victoria moving forward in her life while dating, trying Botox, and keeping her sons out of trouble.

HEAD 2 TOE

GENRE	Docudrama (Makeover)
FIRST TELECAST	2/14/2004
LAST TELECAST	4/16/2005
NETWORK	Lifetime
EPISODE STYLE	Self-contained
TALENT	Tanika Ray (Host)
PRODUCTION COMPANY	Pie Town Productions
EXECUTIVE PRODUCERS	Tara Sandler; Scott Templeton
CO-EXECUTIVE PRODUCER	Julie Stern
PRODUCERS	Matthew Beirne; Taha Howze; Ron Mackovich; Robbie White

Two women who knew each other gave each other makeovers while blindfolded. At the reveal, the blindfolds were removed and each woman reacted to the other's styling suggestions.

HELL DATE

GENRE	Docusoap
FIRST TELECAST	7/9/2007
NETWORK	BET
EPISODE STYLE	Self-contained
CAST	Farelle Walker; Kiya Roberts; Donnivin Jordan
PRODUCTION COMPANIES	Peter M. Cohen Productions
EXECUTIVE PRODUCERS	Peter M. Cohen; James DuBose
CO-EXECUTIVE PRODUCER	Lesley Wolff

On *Hell Date,* an unsuspecting single man or woman is sent on a date with an actor whose job it is to make the single's blind date hilarious.

HELL'S KITCHEN

GENRE	Competition (Job)
FIRST TELECAST	5/30/2005
NETWORK	FOX
AIR TIME	Monday, 9:00 p.m.
EPISODE STYLE	Story Arc
TALENT	Gordon Ramsay (Chef/Judge); Scott Liebfried (Sous-Chef); Mary Ann Salcedo (Sous-Chef)

CAST

Season 1	Michael (Winner); Ralph (Runner-up); Andrew; James; Elsie; Christopher; Jessica; Mary Ellen; Carol Ann; Dewberry; Jeff; Wendy
Season 2	Heather (Winner); Viginia (Runner-up); Polly; Rachel; Sara; Maribel; Tom; Giacomo; Garrett; Gabe; Larry; Keith

Season 3	Rock Harper (Winner); Bonnie Muirhead (Runner-up); Aaron Song; Brad Miller; Eddie Langley; Josh Wahler; Vinnie Fama; Jen Yemola; Joanna Dunn; Julia Williams; Tiffany Nagel; Melissa Firpo
PRODUCTION COMPANIES	Granada Entertainment USA; A. Smith & Co. Productions; Upper Ground Enterprises
EXECUTIVE PRODUCERS	Paul Jackson; Arthur Smith; Kent Weed; Daniel Soiseth; Natalka Znak
PRODUCERS	Pete Tartaglia; Jordan Beck; Ben Hatta
DIRECTOR	Tony Croll

Based on the British series of the same name, *Hell's Kitchen* features world renowned, often volatile, chef Gordon Ramsay as he trains twelve aspiring chefs to learn the restaurant business. The participants are divided into two teams, and face a series of challenges as they open a new restaurant in Hollywood. They are judged based on performance, Chef Ramsay's observations during the dinner service challenges, and by the customer report cards filled out at the restaurant. At the end of each episode, Chef Ramsay eliminates a contestant on the losing team. Michael was the winner of Season 1, and his prize was his own restaurant. In the second season, Heather was named senior chef of Terra Rosa, at the Red Rock Resort Spa and Casino, in Las Vegas. Season 3 winner, Rock, became a head chef at Green Valley Ranch Resort and Spa, in Las Vegas.

HE'S A LADY

GENRE	Competition (Hoax)
FIRST TELECAST	10/19/2004
LAST TELECAST	11/23/2004
NETWORK	TBS
AIR TIME	Tuesday, 10:00 p.m.
EPISODE STYLE	Story Arc
TALENT	Tony Frassand (Host); John Salley (Judge); Morgan Fairchild (Judge); Debbie Matenopolous (Judge)

CAST	David (Winner—"Wynona"); Albert (1st runner-up—"Alberta"), Donnell (2nd Runner-up—"Raven Nightshade"); Cree (eliminated in Episode 5—"Carmen"), Michael (eliminated in Episode 4—"Scarlett"); Dan (eliminated in Episode 3—"Gisele"), Ryan (eliminated in Episode 2—"Sunshine"); Nathan (eliminated in Episode 1—"Amber"), Patrick (eliminated in Episode 1—"Lilly"), Rick (eliminated in Episode 1—"Chiquita"), Sam (eliminated in Episode 1—"Samantha")
PRODUCTION COMPANY	Evolution Film and Tape, Inc.
PRODUCERS	Joycelyn Di Palma; Babette Pepaj
DIRECTORS	Katherine Brooks; Glen Taylor

Eleven male contestants thought they were recruited to compete on a reality show called *All-American Man*. The twist: it was all a hoax; the show was fake. The men competed to see who could best walk, talk, and dress like a lady, for a $250,000 "prize." Challenges included being a bridesmaid in a wedding and competing in a modeling contest judged by Frederique. Celebrity judges voted David, aka "Wynona," the winner.

HEY PAULA

GENRE	Docusoap
FIRST TELECAST	6/28/2007
NETWORK	Bravo
EPISODE STYLE	Story Arc
TALENT	Paula Abdul
PRODUCTION COMPANIES	Scott Sternberg Productions; Bravo Cable
EXECUTIVE PRODUCER	Lenid Rolov
PRODUCERS	Ken Abraham; Paula Abdul; Scott Sternberg
DIRECTOR	Jason Sands

This docusoap chronicle of the private, often wacky life of singer, dancer, and *American Idol* judge Paula Abdul, followed Abdul as she prepared for another season of the FOX series, while developing the movie *Bratz* and her perfume and cosmetics line.

HGTV DESIGN STAR

GENRE	Competition (Job)
FIRST TELECAST	7/23/2006
NETWORK	HGTV
EPISODE STYLE	Story Arc
TALENT	Clive Pearse (Host), Cynthia Rowley (Judge); Martha McCully (Judge); Vern Yip (Judge)
CAST	David Bromstad (Winner); Alice Fakier (Runner-up); Tym De Santo (eliminated in Episode 7); Temple McDowell (eliminated in Episode 6); Teran Evans (eliminated in Episode 5); Donna Moss (eliminated in Episode 5); Teman Evans (eliminated in Episode 4); Vanessa De Leon (eliminated in Episode 3); Joseph Kennard (eliminated in Episode 2); Ramona Jan (eliminated in Episode 1)
PRODUCTION COMPANIES	HGTV
EXECUTIVE PRODUCERS	James Bolosh; Amy Quimby; Sally Ann Salsano
PRODUCERS	Pam LaLima; Kyle Simpson
DIRECTOR	Scott Jeffress

Ten aspiring designers tried to impress an expert panel of judges and home viewers with their personalities and designs on *HGTV Design Star*. David Bromstad of Miami was voted the winner, and was the recipient of his own HGTV show.

HIDDEN HOWIE

GENRE	Docucomedy (Celebrity)
FIRST TELECAST	8/18/2005
NETWORK	Bravo
EPISODE STYLE	Self-contained
CAST	Howie Mandel; Julie Warner (Howie's wife)
PRODUCTION COMPANIES	3 Arts Entertainment Production Company; Jar Productions Production Company
EXECUTIVE PRODUCERS	Howie Mandel; Neal Israel; Alan R Cohen; Alan Freedland; Peter Tilden; Michael Rotenberg
CO-EXECUTIVE PRODUCER	Robert J. Visciglia
PRODUCERS	Michael Platt; Barry Safchik
CO-PRODUCER	Rich Thurber
DIRECTOR	Neal Israel

Comedian, husband, and father Howie Mandel balanced his home and work life while providing funny man-on-the-street encounters to a talk show on *Hidden Howie*. Part fiction, part reality, this series featured real hidden-camera footage of Howie and the public.

HIGH SCHOOL REUNION

GENRE	Docusoap
FIRST TELECAST	1/5/2003
NETWORK	The WB
AIR TIMES	Sunday, 9:00 p.m. (Seasons 1 and 2); Tuesday, 9:00 p.m. (Season 3)
EPISODE STYLE	Story Arc
TALENT	Mike Richards (Host)

CAST

Season 1   Dan B. (The Player); Patricia B. (The Gossip); Amy C. (The Chubby Cheerleader); Sarah C.

	(The Bitchy Girl); Natasha D. (The Popular Girl); Chris E. (The Misfit); Dave G. (The Bully); Jason G. (The Pipsqueak); Maurice G. (The Loner); Tim G. (The Artist); Holly H. (The Shy Girl); Jeff K. (The Class Clown); Dan P. (The Jock); Maya P. (The Homecoming Queen); Ben R. (The Nerd); Nicole R. (The Tall Girl); Summer Z. (The Flirt)
Season 2	LouAnn (The Homecoming Queen); Johnny (The Quarterback); Denise (The Ex); Gabe (The Jock); Lenny (The Geek); Laura (The Drama Queen); T.J. (The Redneck); Heather C. (The Ugly Duckling); Jessica (The Teen Mom); Chris (The Class Clown); Jeralyn (The Wallflower); Daniel (The Gay Guy); Tre (The Player); Trevor (The Pipsqueak); Amanda (The Sophomore Flirt); Heather F. (The Sophomore Vixen); Stacy (The Sophomore Sweetheart)
Season 3	Nikol (The Good Girl); John (The Loud Mouth); Loretta (The Dream Girl); Jim (The Jock); Jen (The Predator); Torie (The Hot Sister); Tara (The Baby Sister); Kristian (The Nerd); Matt (The Dork); Carin (The Fat Girl); Brien M. (The Rebel); Gianni (The Basketball Star); Jaime (The Obsessed Ex); Nikki (The Head Cheerleader); Ezequiel (The Shy Guy)
PRODUCTION COMPANY	Next Entertainment Inc., in association with Telepictures Productions
CREATED BY	Mike Fleiss
EXECUTIVE PRODUCERS	Mike Fleiss; Mike Nichols
PRODUCER	Kelly Welsh
DIRECTORS	Martin Hilton; Robert Sizemore

Former high-school classmates were surprised to be reunited for two weeks in Oahu, Hawaii, on *High School Reunion*. They received "hall passes" to go on adventures to explore their relationships. Season 1 featured students from Oak Park River Forest High School in Illinois, Class of 1992. Season 2 spotlighted a ten-year reunion of classmates from Round Rock High School in Austin, Texas. The show's third and final season documented a ten-year reunion of students from Cardinal Gibbons High School in Fort Lauderdale, Florida.

HI-JINKS

GENRE	Docucomedy (Hoax)
FIRST TELECAST	8/12/2005
NETWORK	Nickelodeon
AIR TIME	Tuesday, 9:30 p.m.
TALENT	Leila Sbitani (Host)
PRODUCTION COMPANY	Banyan Productions
CREATED BY	Joe Boyd
EXECUTIVE PRODUCERS	Joe Boyd; Susan Cohen-Dicker; Korea Stein-Solomon; Jan Dickler; Ray Murray; Kim Rosenblum

Teachers and parents got the last laugh on kids with pranks of their own on *Hi-Jinks*. Some segments featured celebrities, such as Meredith Viera and Susan Sarandon, getting in on the joke.

THE HILLS

GENRE	Docusoap
FIRST TELECAST	5/31/2006
NETWORK	MTV
EPISODE STYLE	Story Arc
CAST	Lauren "LC" Conrad; Heidi Montag; Audrina Patridge; Whitney Port; Jordan Eubanks; Brian Drolet; Jason Wahler; Brody Jenner; Spencer Pratt
PRODUCTION COMPANIES	MTV Productions

EXECUTIVE PRODUCERS	Adam Divello; Tony DiSanto; Liz Gateley
PRODUCER	William Langworthy
DIRECTORS	Jason Sands; Matthew Testa

This spin-off of *Laguna Beach: The Real Orange County,* follows Lauren Conrad and friends and their dramatic lives in Los Angeles, California. Lauren also interns at *Teen Vogue* magazine.

HIT ME BABY ONE MORE TIME

GENRE	Competition (Celebrity/Talent)
FIRST TELECAST	6/2/2005
LAST TELECAST	6/30/2005
NETWORK	NBC
AIR TIME	Thursday, 9:00 p.m.
EPISODE STYLE	Self-contained
TALENT	Vernon Kay (Host)

CAST

Episode 1	Arrested Development (Winner—Episode 1); A Flock of Seagulls (Episode 1); CeCe Peniston (Episode 1); Loverboy (Episode 1); Tiffany (Episode 1)
Episode 2	Vanilla Ice (Winner—Episode 2); Haddaway (Episode 2); The Knack (Episode 2); The Motels (Episode 2); Tommy Tutone (Episode 2)
Episode 3	Irene Cara (Winner—Episode 3); Cameo (Episode 3); Howard Jones (Episode 3); Sophie B. Hawkins (Episode 3); Wang Chung (Episode 3)
Episode 4	Thelma Houston (Winner—Episode 4); Billy Vera (Episode 4); Club Nouveau (Episode 4); Glass Tiger (Episode 4); Greg Khin (Episode 4);

Episode 5	PM Dawn (Winner—Episode 5); Animotion (Episode 5); Juice Newton (Episode 5); Missing Persons (Episode 5); Shannon (Episode 5)
PRODUCTION COMPANY	Granada America
EXECUTIVE PRODUCERS	Paul Jackson; Curt Northrup; Michael Agbabian; Dwight D. Smith; Daniel Soiseth; Stewart Morris
PRODUCERS	Alle Brown; Erik Himmelsbach; Jason Lenzi
DIRECTOR	Jonathan Bullen

Based on the British show of the same name, *Hit Me Baby One More Time* featured musical acts who had been out of the spotlight singing two songs, one a classic of their own and the other a contemporary tune. A studio audience vote each night determined the winner, and prize money was given to the winning singer's favorite charity.

THE HITCHHIKER'S CHRONICLES

GENRE	Docudrama
FIRST TELECAST	6/27/2003
NETWORK	FX
EPISODE STYLE	Self-contained
CAST	Elysia Skye (Driver)
PRODUCTION COMPANIES	Brass Ring Entertainment; Greystone TV
CREATED BY	Tod Dahlke
EXECUTIVE PRODUCERS	Tod Dahlke; Ben Samek; Rick Telles; Cris Abrego

Inspired by HBO's *Taxicab Confessions*, *The Hitchhiker's Chronicles* documented the backseat experiences of young adults hitching rides on spring break and on the July 4th weekend around South Padre Island, Texas, and in Canada and France.

HOGAN KNOWS BEST

GENRE	Docudrama (Celebrity)
FIRST TELECAST	7/10/2005
NETWORK	VH1
EPISODE STYLE	Self-contained
CAST	Terry "Hulk" Hogan; Linda Hogan (Terry's wife); Brooke Hogan (Terry's daughter); Nick Hogan (Terry's son)
PRODUCTION COMPANY	Pink Sneakers Productions
EXECUTIVE PRODUCER	Kimberly Belcher Cowin
PRODUCER	John Ehrhart
DIRECTOR	Scott Bennett

Following in the footsteps of *The Osbournes, Hogan Knows Best* followed the life of wrestling superstar and father Terry "Hulk" Hogan, and his family in their twenty thousand-square-foot estate in Florida. Vignettes included Hulk enforcing curfew on his teenage kids, keeping a watchful eye on potential suitors for his daughter, Brooke, and moving the family to Miami to help Brooke jump-start a singing and recording career.

HOME DELIVERY

GENRE	Docudrama (Makeover)
FIRST TELECAST	9/13/2004
NETWORK	Syndicated
EPISODE STYLE	Self-contained
TALENT	Egypt; Sukanya Krishnan; Stephanie Lydecker; John Sencio
PRODUCTION COMPANY	6th Avenue Productions
PRODUCERS	Amy Rosenblum; Marc Victor
CO-EXECUTIVE PRODUCER	Paul Faulhaber

Everyday people with compelling stories were surprised by the "Home Delivery" team who performed transforming life makeovers, enabling the contestants to have the resources they needed to help themselves or others.

HOOKING UP

GENRE	Docusoap
FIRST TELECAST	7/14/2005
LAST TELECAST	8/11/2005
NETWORK	ABC
AIR TIME	Thursday, 9:00 p.m.
EPISODE STYLE	Story Arc
CAST	Amy; Kelly; Christen; Cynthia; Claire; Lisa; Kristin; Reisha; Maryam; Shelly; Sonja
EXECUTIVE PRODUCER	Terence Wrong
CO-PRODUCERS	Rad Hebert; Bryan Taylor

Shot for one year in New York City, *Hooking Up* followed the lives of eleven women from ages twenty-five to thirty-eight, and their online dating trials and tribulations. The women came from all walks of life, and included Reisha, a technology consultant; and Lisa, a gynecologist. The show followed the singles from their first online hello to meeting their dates' parents.

HOUSE RULES

GENRE	Competition (Makeover)
FIRST TELECAST	10/10/2003
NETWORK	TBS
EPISODE STYLE	Story Arc
TALENT	Mark L. Walberg (Host); Shad Bogany (Realtor—Judge); Kelly West (Designer—Judge); Stephen K. Hann (Builder—Judge)

CAST	Bill Fernandez and Cindy Fernandez (Winners— Blue Team); Adam Wells and Katie Wells (Red Team); Joey Smith and Rebecca Stephens (Silver Team)
PRODUCTION COMPANY	Evolution Film & Tape Inc.
EXECUTIVE PRODUCERS	Tracy Dorsey; Kathleen French; Toni Gallagher; Dean Minerd; Robert Riesenberg; Douglas Ross; Greg Stewart
PRODUCER	Howard C. Bauer
DIRECTOR	Jason Carey

This twelve-week competition series focused on three couples. Each couple renovated a house that they could ultimately win as a prize. The participants earned their weekly allowance by participating in themed games judged by a panel of expert builders and designers. Home viewers voted Bill and Cindy the winning couple.

HOUSTON MEDICAL

GENRE	Docudrama
FIRST TELECAST	6/18/2002
LAST TELECAST	7/23/2002
NETWORK	ABC
AIR TIME	Tuesday, 10:00 p.m.
EPISODE STYLE	Self-contained
TALENT	Jeff Colt (Narrator)
CAST	Crystal Cassidy, M.D.; James "Red" Duke, M.D.; Billy Gill, M.D.; Bill Gormley, M.D.; Patrick Green; Mark Henry, M.D.; Michael Kent, M.D.; Noel Kowis; Terri Major-Kincade, M.D.; Alicia Mangram, M.D.; Jonathon McCracken; Donna Purselley; Marnie Rose, M.D. Mary Sharkey; Kirk Spencer; Tricia Thompson; Drue Ware, M.D.; James Wheless, M.D.

PRODUCTION COMPANY	Greengrass Productions
PRODUCERS	Janis Biewend; Robin Groth; Mitchell Horn; Tracey Washington Bagley
DIRECTORS	Joel Schwartzberg Stanley Taylor; Charles A. Bangert

Dubbed a nonfiction version of the scripted TV series *ER,* this documentary-style drama portrayed the real-life stories of doctors, hospital staff, patients, and their families and friends in the critical-care and level-one trauma centers in Houston's Memorial Hermann Hospital.

HOW CLEAN IS YOUR HOUSE?

GENRE	Docucomedy (Makeover)
FIRST TELECAST	9/6/2004
NETWORK	Lifetime
EPISODE STYLE	Self-contained
TALENT	Kim Woodburn (Host); Aggie McKenzie (Host)
PRODUCTION COMPANY	FremantleMedia
EXECUTIVE PRODUCER	Tracy Verna
CO-EXECUTIVE PRODUCER	Jeff Collins
SENIOR PRODUCER	Bob Kirsh
PRODUCERS	Casey Brumels; Norm Green; Cindy Kain; Melanie Rowland
DIRECTOR	Evan Stone

This U.S. version of the hit British show *How Clean Is Your House?* reveals the dirtiest homes in America. Cleaning experts Kim Woodburn and Aggie McKenzie inspect homes and scold residents for their disgusting living conditions. Then Kim and Aggie spend the episode teaching the homeowners how to clean up their mess. A cleaning team helps to complete the makeover process. Kim and Aggie return to the homes two weeks after the major cleanup to see if the residents are keeping up with their cleaning duties.

HOW DO I LOOK?

GENRE	Docudrama (Makeover)
FIRST TELECAST	1/16/2004
NETWORK	The Style Network
EPISODE STYLE	Self-contained
TALENT	Finola Hughes (Host)
PRODUCTION COMPANY	The Style Network
EXECUTIVE PRODUCER	Deana Delshad
CO-EXECUTIVE PRODUCER	Tracey Finley
SUPERVISING PRODUCER	Tracey Benger
DIRECTOR	Chris Wilson

On *How Do I Look?* a female contestant plays dress-up with three of her closest friends and relatives while on a shopping spree. As part of the experience, the friends and relatives dress the contestant the way they've always wanted her to look.

HOW TO GET THE GUY

GENRE	Docusoap
FIRST TELECAST	6/12/2006
LAST TELECAST	7/3/2006
NETWORK	ABC
AIR TIME	Monday, 10:00 p.m.
EPISODE STYLE	Self-contained
TALENT	JD Roberto (Love Coach), Teresa Strasser (Love Coach)
CAST	Anne (The Girl Next Door); Alissa (The Dreamer); Michelle (The Career Girl); Kris (The Party Girl)
PRODUCTION COMPANIES	Deacon Productions; Scout Productions
EXECUTIVE PRODUCER	David Collins; David Metzler

PRODUCER Kevin Finn; Ryan Crow
DIRECTOR Rich Kim

Four young, beautiful, single women tackled the trials and tribulations of love while following the advice of love coaches. The women declared they were open and ready to do whatever it took to find true love in San Francisco.

I HATE MY JOB

GENRE	Docudrama
FIRST TELECAST	11/9/2004
LAST TELECAST	1/12/2005
NETWORK	Spike
EPISODE STYLE	Self-contained
TALENT	Reverend Al Sharpton (Host); Stephanie Raye (Co-Host)
PRODUCTION COMPANY	RDF Media
EXECUTIVE PRODUCER	Joe Houlihan
DIRECTORS	Scott Jason Farr; Andres L. Porras

Mentored by former presidential candidate and civil-rights activist Al Sharpton and psychologist Stephanie Raye, eight men from various walks of life were given the opportunity to leave behind their nine-to-five jobs for three months to pursue their dream careers. Some of the job switches included a casino dealer who wanted to be a cartoonist, a handyman who wanted to be a hockey coach, and a manure shoveler who wanted to be a male model.

I LOVE NEW YORK

GENRE	Competition (Dating)
FIRST TELECAST	1/8/2007
LAST TELECAST	4/15/2007
NETWORK	VH1
EPISODE STYLE	Story Arc
TALENT	Tiffany Pollard (New York/Bachelorette); Mauricio Sanchez (Chamo); Michelle Patterson (Sister)
CAST	Patrick Hunter (Winner—aka Tango); Kamal Givens (aka Chance); Ricky Perillo (aka Romance); David Amerman (aka 12 Pack); Jason Rosell (aka Heat); Lee Marks (aka Boston); Kevin John (aka Bonez); Sandro Padrone (aka Rico); Hashim Smith (aka Trendz); William Lash (aka Onix); Randy Richwood (aka Wood); Josh Gallander (aka White Boy); Kevin Watson (aka T-Weed); LaMonty Council (aka Pootie); Darin Darnell (aka Ace); Bryant Covert (aka Jersey); Ahmad Givens (aka Real); Tyrone (aka Tbone); Thomas (aka TMoney); Chase Irwin (aka Token)
PRODUCTION COMPANY	51 Minds Entertainment
EXECUTIVE PRODUCERS	Mark Cronin; Cris Abrego; Ben Samek
PRODUCERS	Michelle Brando; Lauren A. Stevens; Chris Carlson
DIRECTOR	Robert Sizemore

On this dating competition, New York, the arch nemesis among the bachelorettes on Seasons 1 and 2 of *Flavor of Love,* returned to VH1 to find love. With the help of her mother, Sister Patterson, and her assistant, Chamo, New York dated twenty bachelors until she found her man, Tango. But the Season 1 winner broke up with New York on the reunion show. She again returned to find a new love on *I Love New York 2,* where she met her man, Tailor Made.

I MARRIED A PRINCESS

GENRE	Docusoap (Celebrity)
FIRST TELECAST	4/1/2005
NETWORK	Lifetime
EPISODE STYLE	Story Arc
CAST	Catherine Oxenberg; Casper Van Dien; India Oxenberg; Cappy Van Dien; Grace Van Dien; Maya Van Dien; Celeste Van Dien
PRODUCTION COMPANY	New Wave Entertainment
EXECUTIVE PRODUCERS	Christen Harty Schaefer; Barry Katz
DIRECTORS	Christen Harty Schaefer

The glamorous and hectic lives of *Dynasty* actress and real-life royal Catherine Oxenberg and her husband, actor Casper Van Dien (*Starship Troopers*), were featured on this docusoap. The couple were shown parenting their blended family of five children at their Malibu home.

I WANNA BE A SOAP STAR

GENRE	Competition (Talent)
FIRST TELECAST	10/16/2004
NETWORK	SoapNet
EPISODE STYLE	Story Arc
TALENT	Cameron Mathison (Host); Debbi Morgan (Actress—Judge); Mark Teschner (Casting Director/Judge—Season 1); Michael Bruno (Talent Manager/Judge); Judy Blye Wilson

(Casting Director/Judge—Season 2); Julie Madison (Judge—Season 3); Hogan Sheffer (Writer/Judge—Season 4); Mary Beth Evans (Actress/Judge—Season 4)

CAST

Season 1	Mykel Shannon Jenkins (Winner); Alisia Geanopulos; Maya D. Gilbert; Robyn Hyden; Brianna Konefall; Nick Steele; Mark Teschner; Kent Winfrey
Season 2	Alec Musser (Winner); Maiesha; Christina; Joe; Isaak; Prudence; Alia; Farley; Nicole; Toussaint; Sean; Cathy
Season 3	Mike Jerome (Winner); Shamika Cotton; BethAnn Bonner; Lauren Ryland; Lindsey Spruill; Michael Albanese; Lukas Hassel; Dean Cochran; Ayinde Jones; Kelly McGarry
Season 4	Patricia; Bo; Yves; Ashley; Corey; Jimena; Justin; Joyce; Monica; Travis
PRODUCTION COMPANIES	LMNO Productions, Soapnet
EXECUTIVE PRODUCERS	Lisa Bourgoujian; Bill Paolantonio; Eric Schotz
PRODUCER	Gary Lucy
DIRECTOR	Neil DeGroot

A group of aspiring actors live together on a soap opera set and compete in various acting assignments for a role on the daytime drama *General Hospital* (Season 1), *All My Children* (Season 2), and *One Life to Live* (Season 3). Season 3's BethAnn Bonner was later given a contract for a role on *One Life to Live*. Season 4 offered the winner a contract on the daytime drama *Days of our Lives*. A panel of experts from the acting and television fields judges the aspiring actors.

I WANT A FAMOUS FACE

GENRE	Docudrama (Makeover)
FIRST TELECAST	2/1/2004
NETWORK	MTV
EPISODE STYLE	Self-contained
TALENT	Jessica Chesler (Narrator)
PRODUCTION COMPANY	Pink Sneaker Productions
EXECUTIVE PRODUCERS	Lauren Lazin; Dave Sirulnick

MTV camera crews documented twelve young men and women who made the decision to have elective cosmetic surgery to look like a famous celebrity on *I Want a Famous Face*. Some surgeries were successful, while others produced disastrous results. The psychological aspects of plastic surgery were also explored. In one episode, actress Drew Barrymore counseled a twenty-three-year-old woman against undergoing surgery to look like her. A follow-up show, *MTV News Now: They Wanted a Famous Face*, revisited the patients to find out if their lives had changed for the better following surgery.

I WANT TO BE A HILTON

GENRE	Competition
FIRST TELECAST	6/21/2005
LAST TELECAST	8/9/2005
NETWORK	NBC
AIR TIME	Tuesday, 9:00 p.m.
EPISODE STYLE	Story Arc
TALENT	Kathy Hilton (Host)
CAST	Jaret Elwood (Winner); Yvette Brown; Julianne "Jules" Levita; Latricia Lindsey; John "J.W." Whitehead; John Colonna; Anna Poonkasem;

	Jabe Robinson; Vanessa Kemling;
	Jaclyn "Jackaay" Watt; Alain "Alan" Constantine;
	Niki Pais; Rashad El Amin; Brenden Martin
PRODUCTION COMPANY	Endemol USA
EXECUTIVE PRODUCERS	Paul Buccieri; Jason Hervey; Danny Salles;
	Rick Hilton
DIRECTOR	Chris Donovan

In a series inspired by the format of *The Apprentice,* Kathy Hilton, mother of Paris Hilton, invited fourteen young adults to compete for the opportunity to live like a member of her family, on *I Want to Be a Hilton.* Divided into the Park and Madison teams, competitors acquainted themselves with high-society culture, fashion, and charity events to win the grand prize of a $200,000 trust fund, a new apartment, a stylish wardrobe, and the opportunity to live the good life. Jaret Elwood was the winner.

I WITNESS VIDEO

GENRE	Docudrama
FIRST TELECAST	8/16/1992
LAST TELECAST	7/10/1994
NETWORK	NBC
AIR TIMES	Sunday, 8:00 p.m. (8/1992–9/1993); Sunday, 7:00 p.m. (9/1993–7/1994)
EPISODES STYLE	Self-contained
TALENT	Patrick Van Horn (Host—Season 1); John Forsythe (Host—Season 2)
EXECUTIVE PRODUCER	Terry Landau

I Witness Video spotlighted viewer-submitted videos of dramatic situations, such as natural disasters, crime scenes, and animal attacks. Critics commented that this show was the antithesis of the much lighter-fare *America's Funniest Home Videos.*

I'D DO ANYTHING

GENRE	Competition
FIRST TELECAST	9/28/2004
NETWORK	ESPN
EPISODE STYLE	Self-contained
TALENT	George Gray (Host)
PRODUCTION COMPANIES	ESPN Original Entertainment; Trans World International, Inc., Mess Media
EXECUTIVE PRODUCERS	Scott Messick; Steve Mayer; Bob Horowitz

Contestants competed, elimination style, in outrageous and sometimes dangerous physical challenges in order to help land a sports fantasy gift for a friend or relative on *I'd Do Anything*. Three stunts were split into the categories of pain, shame, and insane.

I'M A CELEBRITY, GET ME OUT OF HERE!

GENRE	Competition (Celebrity)
FIRST TELECAST	2/19/2003
LAST TELECAST	3/5/2003
NETWORK	ABC
EPISODE STYLE	Story Arc
TALENT	John Lehr (Host)
CAST	Cris Judd (King of the Jungle); Melissa Rivers (9th eliminated); "Stuttering" John Melendez (8th eliminated); Bruce Jenner (7th eliminated); "Downtown" Julie Brown (6th eliminated); Tyson Beckford (5th eliminated); Nikki Schieler-

Ziering (4th eliminated); Maria Conchita Alonso (3rd eliminated); Alana Stewart (2nd eliminated); Robin Leach (1st eliminated)

EXECUTIVE PRODUCERS Natalka Znak; Alexander Gardiner; John Saade
PRODUCER Richard Cowles
DIRECTOR: Steve Beim

Based on the British import of the same name, *I'm a Celebrity, Get Me Out of Here!* chronicled the adventures of ten celebrities who left behind their glamorous lifestyles to rough it in the Australian rain forest in order to win prize money for the charities of their choice.

Each installment featured "The Bush Tucker Trial," in which one celebrity had the opportunity to win extra food for the rest of the group. Viewers voted to determine the outcome. The ultimate "King of the Jungle" was choreographer Cris Judd, the former husband of actress/singer Jennifer Lopez.

According to the television tabloid show *Celebrity Justice* contestant "Downtown" Julie Brown filed a lawsuit against ABC and the show's production company for $500,000 in damages as a result of injuries and scarring she sustained from numerous bites from leeches while competing in "The Bush Tucker" challenges. (As of press time, the outcome of the lawsuit was still pending.)

I'M STILL ALIVE!

GENRE Docucomedy (Hoax)
FIRST TELECAST 4/14/2004
LAST TELECAST 5/19/2004
NETWORK UPN
EPISODE STYLE Self-contained
TALENT Jim Forbes (Narrator)
PRODUCTION COMPANY A. Smith and Co.
EXECUTIVE PRODUCERS Arthur Smith; Kent Weed
CO-EXECUTIVE PRODUCER Michael Miller

I'm Still Alive! featured stories of people who escaped life-threatening situations. These recollections were illustrated with both CGI reenactments and real footage from the events. The harrowing events highlighted in the show included failed stunt attempts, train derailments, and plane crashes.

ICE ROAD TRUCKERS

GENRE	Docusoap
FIRST TELECAST	6/17/2007
NETWORK	History Channel
EPISODE STYLE	Self-contained
CAST	T. J. Tilcox; Hugh Rowland; Rick Yemm; Alex Debogorski; Jay Westgard; Drew Sherwood
PRODUCTION COMPANY	Original Productions
EXECUTIVE PRODUCERS	Thom Beers; Dolores Gavin

Ice Road Truckers follows six men for two months while they perform what is considered to be one of the world's most dangerous jobs. In Season 1 viewers watched them haul supplies to diamond mines over frozen lakes doubling as roads, roadways that had killed many truckers.

IN A FIX

GENRE	Docudrama (Makeover)
FIRST TELECAST	2/2/2004
NETWORK	TLC
EPISODE STYLE	Self-contained
TALENT	Marc Goldberg
CAST	Deborah DiMare (Designer); Franzella Guido (Designer); Nani Vinken (Designer); Justin Brown (Crew Member); Marc Bartolomeo (Crew Member);

Jennie Lyn Bernston (Crew Member); Gregory Carey (Crew Member); James Lunday (Crew Member); Danny Paul (Crew Member) Evette Rios (Designer); Don Wood (Crew Member)

PRODUCTION COMPANY	NorthSouth Productions
EXECUTIVE PRODUCERS	Charlie DeBevoise; Mark Hickman
PRODUCERS	Roseann Pascale; Marvin Blunte; Gary Carr; Thom Hinkle; Robert Latorre; Nick O'Gorman

Viewers unable to complete their home improvement projects due to a lack of skill, time, or money were invited to contact *In a Fix* for assistance. Four-to-six person crews gave home makeovers to viewers selected by the show's producers. Crews completed repairs and renovations, and provided some surprises.

IN SEARCH OF THE PARTRIDGE FAMILY

GENRE	Competition (Talent)
FIRST TELECAST	9/5/2004
LAST TELECAST	10/17/2004
NETWORK	VH1
EPISODE STYLE	Story Arc
TALENT	Todd Newton (Host); David Cassidy; Danny Bonaduce; Shirley Jones; Carrie Ann Inaba (Choreographer)
CAST	Leland Grant (Keith finalist—Winner); David Petruzzi (Keith finalist); Teddy Geiger (Keith finalist); Lucais Reilly (Keith finalist); Paul Carpenter (Keith finalist); Jonathan Redford (Keith finalist); James Snyder (Keith finalist); Sutter Zachman (Keith finalist); Spencer Tuskowski

(Danny finalist—Winner); Keaton Savage (Danny finalist); Chris Farach (Danny finalist); Clayton Griffin (Danny finalist); Blayze Dawson (Danny finalist); Peabo Powell (Danny finalist); Alex Oyen (Danny finalist); Matt Vrchota (Danny finalist); Emily Stone (Laurie finalist—Winner); Alexis Mero (Laurie finalist); Alana Allen (Laurie finalist); Allison Considine (Laurie finalist); Rachel Kimsey (Laurie finalist); Christina P. Grace (Laurie finalist); Allison Miller (Laurie finalist); Essie Shure (Laurie finalist); Suzanne Sole (Shirley finalist—Winner); Krissy Todd (Shirley finalist); Julie Wittner (Shirley finalist); Mary Kay Twargowski (Shirley finalist); Dee Nelson (Shirley finalist); Gabrielle Wagner (Shirley finalist); Judy Guinosso (Shirley finalist); Lisa Arnold (Shirley finalist)

PRODUCTION COMPANIES Jeff Margolis Productions; Sony Pictures Television

EXECUTIVE PRODUCERS David Cassidy; Jeff Margolis

PRODUCERS Dave Boone; Jon Macks; Michael McCullough; Mick McCullough; Gloria Fujita O'Brien

DIRECTOR Alan Carter

In Search of the Partridge Family producers traveled the country searching for actor/singers who resembled those who played the original Keith (David Cassidy), Laurie (Susan Dey), Danny (Danny Bonaduce), and Shirley (Shirley Jones) on *The Partridge Family*. Once in the finals, the contestants received makeovers and went through boot camp–style training to win a chance to be in the pilot for a new *Partridge Family* series. The winners were Leland Grant as Keith Partridge, Emily Stone as Laurie Partridge, Spencer Tuskowski as Danny Partridge, and Suzanne Sole as Shirley Partridge.

INKED

GENRE	Docudrama
FIRST TELECAST	7/20/2005
NETWORK	A&E
AIR TIME	Friday, 8:00 p.m.
EPISODE	Self-contained
CAST	Carey Hart (Co-Founder); Thomas Pendelton (Co-Owner); Monica (Shop Manager); Clark North (Tattoo Artist); Quinn (Greeter); Dizzle (Apprentice); Eric "Big E" Pele (Tattoo Artist)
PRODUCTION COMPANIES	Foglight Entertainment; Fox Studio; Insomnia Media Group
EXECUTIVE PRODUCERS	Gregg Backer; Jeff Bowler; Matthew Ginsburg
CO-EXECUTIVE PRODUCERS	Lewis Fenton; Jennifer Lange; Bret Saxton; Heather Urgan
SENIOR PRODUCERS	Joseph Gomes; Pam LaLima
DIRECTORS	Gregg Backer; Jeff Bowler; Lewis Fenton

Extreme motocross champion Carey Hart's tattoo shop is the focus of *Inked*. Cameras follow the diverse group of clientele and staffers at Hart & Huntington Tattoo Company in the Palms Casino Resort in Las Vegas. The stories behind the tattoos requested by the customers are featured in the series, as well as the show's cast of characters, including Dizzle, the young apprentice who aspires to be a tattoo artist; and Clark, the senior artist who lost one of his eyes in an accident. Some of the celebrities who have visited Hart's shop include 'N Sync member Lance Bass, professional skateboarder Tony Hawk, and former NBA player Dennis Rodman.

INTERSCOPE PRESENTS "THE NEXT EPISODE"

GENRE	Competition (Talent)
FIRST TELECAST	11/14/2003
NETWORK	Showtime
EPISODE STYLE	Story Arc
TALENT	Cee-Lo (Host); 50 Cent (Host); Wyclef Jean (Host); X Zibit (Host);
CAST	Spitfya (Winner—Los Angeles finalist); Trek Life (Los Angeles finalist); Quest M.C.O.D.Y. (Detroit finalist); J. Hill (Detroit finalist); Ness Lee (Atlanta finalist); Tonsmoccon (Atlanta finalist); Chocolate Thai (New York finalist); Diabolic (New York finalist): Young Blake (Philadelphia finalist); L.P. (Philadelphia finalist)
EXECUTIVE PRODUCERS	Paul Rosenberg; Jimmy Iovine; Gillian Fleer; Gene Kirkwood; Randy Sosin
CO-EXECUTIVE PRODUCER	Moses Edinborough
DIRECTOR	Moses Edinborough

Inspired by the rap contests in the film *8 Mile,* this talent competition traveled to five cities as two rappers participated in a five-round battle to perform various styles of rapping (a cappella, beat box, with a live drummer, DJ Drops Beat, and an overall final round). Judges were rappers and rap personalities. The series culminated with a winner-takes-all freestyle rap battle.

INTERVENTION

GENRE	Docudrama
FIRST TELECAST	3/6/2005
NETWORK	A&E
EPISODE STYLE	Self-contained
PRODUCTION COMPANIES	Daring Productions; GRB Entertainment
EXECUTIVE PRODUCERS	Gary R. Benz; Michael Branton; Bryn Freedman
PRODUCERS	Peter Steen; Janis Biewend; Mary Clayton; Hank O'Karma; David Schewel

Intervention examines the lives of addicts and the effect their addiction has on their family and friends. Each episode ends with a professional interventionist working with family and friends to urge the addict to seek treatment.

INVASION IOWA

GENRE	Docusoap (Hoax)
FIRST TELECAST	3/29/2005
LAST TELECAST	4/1/2005
NETWORK	Spike
EPISODE STYLE	Story Arc
PRODUCTION COMPANY	GRB Entertainment Inc.
CREATED BY	Rhett Reese
EXECUTIVE PRODUCERS	Gary R. Benz; Mary Jester; J. Holland Moore; Everett Reese; Rhett Reese; William Shatner; Paul Wernick
PRODUCERS	Mary Jester Astor; Andrew Green; Brendon Carter; J. Holland Moore
DIRECTOR	Brendon Carter

Inspired by the success of their duplicitous series *Joe Schmo,* the same production team set its sights on Riverside, Iowa, population 928, in *Invasion Iowa.* Riverside's citizens were fooled into believing their town was about to be the location for a new sci-fi/action-adventure film starring William Shatner. A group of actors and Shatner arrived from Hollywood and parodied the attitudes and bad manners some people expect from moviemakers. Local people were hired to work on the crew and act in the nonexistent film. Once the town's citizens were let in on the joke, the city of Riverside was given $100,000.

INVASION OF THE HIDDEN CAMERAS

GENRE	Docucomedy (Hoax)
FIRST TELECAST	7/12/2002
LAST TELECAST	8/9/2002
NETWORK	FOX
AIR TIME	Friday, 8:00 p.m.
EPISODE	Self-contained
TALENT	Doug Stanhope (Host)
PRODUCTION COMPANY	Rocket Science Laboratories
EXECUTIVE PRODUCER	Chris Cowan
DIRECTOR	Jeffrey A. Fisher

Invasion of the Hidden Cameras was another spin on the hidden-camera prank genre, with the gags often bordering on the extreme and outrageous. Host Doug Stanhope participated in many of the jokes, which included playing a prank on a clown by sending him to a funeral staged by the show, and having a man test his new liver at a bar.

IRON CHEF AMERICA

GENRE	Competition
FIRST TELECAST	1/16/2005
NETWORK	Food Network

EPISODE	Self-contained
TALENT	Alton Brown (Commentator); Mark Dacascos (The Chairman); Bobby Flay (Iron Chef); Mario Batali (Iron Chef); Masaharu Morimoto (Iron Chef); Kevin Brauch (Floor reporter)
PRODUCERS	John Bravakis; Steve Kroopnick

Based on the hit Japanese show *Iron Chef,* this cooking competition features chefs battling with stateside Iron Chefs—such as Bobby Flay, Mario Batali, and Masaharu Morimoto—in Food Network's Kitchen Stadium. The chefs must cook with a "secret ingredient," and similar to the Japanese show, they have only one hour to prepare as many dishes as possible. Their menus are presented to a panel of judges, who declare a winner, who is either the Iron Chef or the challenger.

THE IT FACTOR

GENRE	Docusoap
FIRST TELECAST	1/6/2002
NETWORK	Bravo
EPISODE STYLE	Story Arc

CAST

Season 1 (New York)	Miranda Black; Kevin Bulla; Katheryn Winnick; Michaela Conlin; Godfrey; Daisy Eagan; Queen Esther; Chelsea Lagos; P. J. Mehaffey; Latarsha Rose; Jimmy Smagula; Nathan Wetherington
Season 2 (Los Angeles)	Krystal; LisaRaye; Jennifer Ann Massey; Jeremy Renner; Daniel Louis Rivas; Sara Rivas; Josh Waters; De'Angelo Wilson; Maria Costa
PRODUCTION COMPANY	Zanzibar Productions
EXECUTIVE PRODUCERS	David Clair; Lauren Friedland; Nicole Torre
PRODUCER	Megan Sanchez-Warner

The It Factor followed the lives of young actors trying to make it big in the entertainment field. Season 1 featured twelve competitors as they experienced the nerve-wracking process of attending casting calls and auditions in the New York City entertainment industry. Cast members Godfrey and Miranda have had major acting roles since starring on the series.

Season 2 followed actors looking for their big break in Los Angeles. The cast included former pop star Krystal, and brother and sister Sara and Danny. Other aspiring actors in the Los Angeles season included De'Angelo, who was discovered by Denzel Washington, and LisaRaye who appeared in Ice Cube's movie *The Players Club*. The second season focused on the actors as they made their way through the pilot season.

JACKASS

GENRE	Docudrama
FIRST TELECAST	10/1/2000
NETWORK	MTV
EPISODE STYLE	Self-contained
CAST	Johnny Knoxville; Bam Margera; Steve-O; Chris Pontius; Ryan Dunn; Brandon Dicamillo; Ehren McGhehey; Preston Lacy; Jason Acuña; Dave England; Jess Margera; Dimitry Elyashkevich; Chris Raab; Jeff Tremaine; Rick Kosick; Trip Taylor; Stephanie Hodge; Manny Puig
PRODUCTION COMPANY	Dickhouse Productions
EXECUTIVE PRODUCERS	Carol Eng; Spike Jonze; Johnny Knoxville; John Miller; Jessica Swirnoff
PRODUCER	Trip Taylor

A hit for MTV, *Jackass* featured a group of guys, some of whom were stuntmen and extreme sports enthusiasts, who performed outrageous acts for laughs, often deliberately inflicting pain on each other and themselves for kicks. Stunts were often executed with a hidden, handheld camera capturing passersby's reactions. This series was the inspiration for *Viva La Bam* and *Wildboyz,* and spawned two films.

THE JAMIE KENNEDY EXPERIMENT

GENRE	Docucomedy (Hoax)
FIRST TELECAST	1/13/2002
LAST TELECAST	7/15/2004
NETWORK	The WB
AIR TIMES	Sunday, 8:30 p.m. (1/2002–3/2002); Sunday, 9:30 p.m. (4/2002–5/2002); Thursday, 8:00 p.m. (5/2002–6/2002); Thursday, 8:30 p.m. (7/2002–9/2002); Thursday, 9:00 p.m. (9/2002–1/2003); Thursday, 9:30 p.m. (1/2003–2/2003); Thursday, 9:00 p.m. (2/2003–7/2003); Wednesday, 9:00 p.m. (6/2003–7/2003); Thursday, 8:00 p.m. (8/2003–9/2003); Thursday, 8:30 p.m. (9/2003–11/2003); Thursday, 9:00 p.m. (11/2003–7/2004)
EPISODE STYLE	Self-contained
TALENT	Jamie Kennedy (Host)
PRODUCTION COMPANIES	Big Ticket Television; Warner Bros. Television; Bahr-Small Productions; Karz Entertainment
EXECUTIVE PRODUCERS	Fax Bahr; Garry Campbell; Brian Hartt; Mike Karz; Jamie Kennedy; Adam Small
PRODUCERS	Walter Barnett; Jim Biederman; Tim Gibbons; Richard King; Josh H. Etting
CO-PRODUCERS	David Franzke; Karen Thornton
DIRECTORS	Michael Dimich; Tim Gibbons; Andrew Kozar

In *The Jamie Kennedy Experiment* the young comedian and actor played hidden pranks on members of the unsuspecting public. Kennedy often wore a disguise and played one of the characters involved in the pranks, such as a rapper similar to the one he portrayed in the movie *Malibu's Most Wanted,* and Virginia Hamm, an advice talk show host.

THE JANICE DICKINSON MODELING AGENCY

GENRE	Docusoap
FIRST TELECAST	6/6/2006
NETWORK	Oxygen
EPISODE STYLE	Story Arc
TALENT	Janice Dickinson; Nathan Fields; Peter Hamm
PRODUCTION COMPANIES	FremantleMedia North America; Krasnow Productions
EXECUTIVE PRODUCERS	Janice Dickinson; Stuart Krasnow; Kevin Williams
DIRECTOR	Darren Ewing

On *The Janice Dickinson Modeling Agency,* supermodel Dickinson, an *America's Next Top Model* and *Surreal Life* alum, juggles motherhood and business as she searches among hundreds of aspiring models, finds financial backing, and establishes a reputation for her new modeling agency.

JOE MILLIONAIRE
(Season 1)

GENRE	Competition (Dating/Hoax)
FIRST TELECAST	1/6/2003
LAST TELECAST	2/24/2003
NETWORK	FOX
AIR TIME	Monday, 9:00 p.m.

EPISODE STYLE	Story Arc
TALENT	Alex McLeod (Host); Paul Hogan (The Butler/Narrator); Mark L. Walberg (Reunion Host)
CAST	Evan Marriott (Joe Millionaire); Zora Andrich (Winner); Sarah Kozer (Runner-up); Melissa Mowery (eliminated in Episode 5); Melissa Jo "Mojo" Hunter (eliminated in Episode 4); Alison Senior (eliminated in Episode 3); Dana Cassasa (eliminated in Episode 2); Heidi Crowe (eliminated in Episode 2); Dayana (eliminated in Episode 2); Brandy (eliminated in Episode 2); Katie (eliminated in Episode 2); Amanda Hale (eliminated in Episode 2); Amy (eliminated in Episode 1); Andrea Croton (eliminated in Episode 1); Melissa W. (eliminated in Episode 1); Katy (eliminated in Episode 1); Gretchen (eliminated in Episode 1); Erica (eliminated in Episode 1); Jennifer (eliminated in Episode 1); Mary (eliminated in Episode 1)
PRODUCTION COMPANY	Rocket Science Laboratories
EXECUTIVE PRODUCERS	Chris Cowan; Jean-Michel Michenaud
CO-EXECUTIVE PRODUCER	Liz Bronstein
PRODUCERS	Steve Sobel; Alan Wieder; Ray Giuliani

Joe Millionaire took the reality dating format to a new level with a major twist. Twenty women flew to France thinking they were on a romance show to gain the hand of a multimillionaire named Evan Warner. The catch was that "multimillionaire" Evan was actually Evan Marriott, a construction worker earning only $19,000 a year. On hand to guide Evan through his journey was butler Paul Hogan, who also served as the show's narrator.

In Episode 1, the twenty women moved in to a French château and met Evan, who arrived on horseback to greet them. The episode concluded with a ball, where Evan danced with each woman to get to know her better. After the ball, he gave pearl necklaces to the twelve women he wanted to see again, while he sent home Andrea, Amy, Melissa W., Katy, Gretchen, Erica, Mary, and Jennifer.

Episode 2 featured three group dates. Melissa M., Sarah, Brandy, and Dana picked grapes with Evan at a French vineyard. Mandy, Mojo, Katie, and Amanda accompanied him on a train date, where they had to shovel coal to fuel the train. Heidi, Dayana, Zora, and Alison went horseback riding with him but had to clean out the stables. At the end of the dates, Evan gave sapphire necklaces to his top five picks: Melissa M., Mojo, Sarah, Zora, and Alison. These five went on a trip to Paris with him.

In Episode 3, Evan's final five went on individual dates with him in Paris. Evan and Mojo went to the Moulin Rouge. Sarah learned tango dancing with him. Melissa M. and Evan visited the Eiffel Tower. Then Zora and Evan went out for dinner, which included awkward conversation. Then they went on a walk, with music provided by a live string quarter. Evan slipped, mentioning he had been on a construction tractor just weeks before. Fortunately for him, the comment didn't spark anything from Zora. Alison and Evan went on a boat trip down the Seine, and she basically admitted she was not really interested in him. This eased the tension between them, and they left for Notre Dame. At the elimination ceremony, Evan gave an emerald necklace to each of the women except Alison.

Evan and the final four women returned to the château in Episode 4, and they all went on individual dates. Sarah and Evan went on a bike ride that concluded with an infamous walk in the forest at night. While nothing was explicitly said, something that sounded like slurping was heard offscreen. Melissa M. and Evan remained at the château for their date and cooked dinner together. Zora and Evan went on a horseback riding date in the woods. The date continued with them hopping in a hot tub, only to be joined later by Melissa M., Sarah, and Mojo. Then Evan and Mojo learned how to fence. Later, at the château, Mojo presented Evan with a puzzle of herself and a poem. Evan gave a ruby necklace to each of the women, except for Mojo.

In Episode 5, Evan and the final three took off for more individual dates. He and Melissa M. went to Cannes, where they talked on the beach, and Evan revealed tips on how to heal cuts with super glue. He and Zora flew to Corsica, where they had dinner and relaxed in the hotel pool. He and Sarah headed to Nice, where after dinner she dropped by his hotel room to spend time with him to "look at the moon." During this episode, Evan had a panic attack about having to lie to the women, and had to be calmed down by producer Ray Guiliani. He then gave a diamond pendant to Zora and Sarah, sending home Melissa M.

Episode 6 featured a recap interspersed with footage of Evan going on final walks with Sarah and Zora before making his final decision. The episode ended with butler Paul summoning the women for Evan's announcement.

Episode 7 was a two-hour finale. During the first hour, the women were profiled, and Evan revealed what they had been doing since the show finished taping. The second hour featured Evan's final decision and his confession that he wasn't a millionaire. He chose Zora, revealing that he was really a construction worker. He asked her to meet him in the ballroom later that evening to let him know if she'd still continue seeing him. She showed up and told him she wanted to keep seeing him. Then Paul carried a covered tray into the ballroom and said there was one final twist. He opened the tray to reveal a check for $1 million dollars to be split between them, giving the show a bit of a fairy-tale happy ending.

One week later, FOX aired a reunion special hosted by Mark L. Walberg. The nineteen eliminated women met for the first time since the end of the show's taping.

JOE MILLIONAIRE
(Season 2)

GENRE	Competition (Dating/Hoax)
FIRST TELECAST	10/20/2003
LAST TELECAST	11/24/2004
NETWORK	FOX
AIR TIME	Monday, 9:00 p.m.
EPISODE STYLE	Story Arc
TALENT	Samantha Harris (Host); Paul Hogan (The Butler/Narrator)
CAST	David Smith (Joe Millionaire); Linda Kazdova (Winner—quit in Episode 4/returned in Episode 6); Cat (Runner-up); Petra (eliminated in Episode 8); Anique (eliminated in Episode 6); Olinda

(eliminated in Episode 5); Giada (eliminated in Episode 5); Kristyna (eliminated in Episode 5); Alessia (eliminated in Episode 4); Lina (eliminated in Episode 4); Linda (quit in Episode 4); Karolina (eliminated in Episode 3); Tereza (eliminated in Episode 3); Jerusha (eliminated in Episode 2); Johanna (eliminated in Episode 2); Yassamin (eliminated in Episode 2)

PRODUCTION COMPANY Rocket Science Laboratories

EXECUTIVE PRODUCERS Chris Cowan; Jean-Michel Michenaud

This sequel to the original *Joe Millionaire* starred David Smith, a twenty-four-year-old rodeo cowboy from Texas who made only $11,000 a year. Fourteen European women competed for David in Italy, where they were told his family was in the oil business, and that his net worth was more than $80 million.

In Episode 1, the women and David traveled to the Italian countryside, where the women partied for several days. The episode concluded as David was introduced to them.

Episode 2 focused on a ball, where David met each woman one at a time. He eliminated three women: Johanna, Jerusha, and Yassimin, despite his misgivings about Lina.

Episode 3 featured group dates. David took Kristina, Giada, and Olina for a pottery lesson and dinner. Anique, Tereza, Cat, and Lina went on a bike riding date with him in Lucca. The date included a picnic lunch, where they became more acquainted. Alessia, Karolina Petra, and Linda accompanied David for a day at the leaning tower of Pisa. David gave sapphire necklaces to all but two women, Karolina and Tereza.

In Episode 4, the women got a taste of David's life in Texas when he gave them each cowboy-related gifts and brought them to a ranch in Tuscany, where they had to clean horse stables. The other women became envious of Linda when she grew closer to David. This prompted her to leave the competition, which left David feeling dejected. He presented emerald necklaces to all of the women except Lina and Alessia.

During the two-hour Episode 5, David went on individual dates with the remaining women. He and Petra went to Florence, where they took a walk to the Ponte Vecchio and ate dinner. Cat and David went to a sauna and finished their spa date with dinner. David and Giada went on a date to an old perfurmery. On Kristyna and David's date, they rode down the river and later had dinner. He and Olinda had lunch in Florence, while he and Anique enjoyed a romantic dinner. Ruby necklaces were handed out in the next elimination ceremony, and Giada and Kristyna were eliminated.

The second hour of Episode 5 featured more one-on-one dates with the final four, this time in Rome. Petra and David took a romantic walk around the city. He and Anique made wishes at the Trevi Fountain and ate lunch at a café. His and Cat's dinner date concluded with Champagne on the balcony of his hotel suite. He and Olinda dressed up in gladiator costumes for a chariot ride, dueled in Roman ruins, then returned to his hotel room. Diamond pendants were handed out at the elimination ceremony, where Olinda was eliminated.

During the two-hour Episode 6, Anique and David rode a helicopter to Portofino, where he bought her a handbag and they ate dinner. They ended the evening in his room, where David asked the cameraman to leave to give them privacy. The cameraman left, but the audio recording continued. David and Petra began their date at the beach and had dinner in Sardinia. He and Cat dined outside during sunset in Capri. After dinner, they headed to David's hotel room, where they shared a bubble bath.

As a surprise, when David returned to the villa, he was given some time to spend at the ranch, but not alone with his horse, Hurricane. Linda, who had voluntarily left the show in episode four, was at the ranch, too. Then Paul informed David that all three women could stay, or he could go forward with the elimination ceremony. If he went ahead with the elimination, Linda would be brought back. David chose to bring back Linda, and aquamarine and diamond necklaces were handed out at the next elimination ceremony. Cat and Petra received them, while Anique was sent home, and Linda was brought back into the mix.

In the second hour, the women met in Venice. Petra and David went on a dinner date, and he gave her bracelets. They were then serenaded by an opera singer, and took a boat ride back to the hotel. David and Linda began their date with breakfast, then walked along a pier. He and Cat went on a gondola ride and finished the evening in his hotel room. Linda saw them and became jealous. Cat and Linda received diamond bracelets, while Petra went home.

The two-hour Episode 7 finale began with a recap of the season. Linda and David had lunch during their final date, while Cat's final date was over a candlelight dinner. David chose Linda, then revealed he was not a millionaire. He asked Linda to meet him that night if she still wanted to be with him. He waited for her that evening, but she never arrived. He returned to Texas and saw a letter from her explaining her decision. Then she emerged from his house to greet him, telling him she wanted to be with him. Paul emerged and handed Linda a check for $250,000, and gave the deed to the ranch to David.

THE JOE SCHMO SHOW

GENRE	Docucomedy (Hoax)
FIRST TELECAST	9/2/2003
LAST TELECAST	8/10/2004
NETWORK	Spike TV
EPISODE STYLE	Story Arc
TALENT	Ralph Garman (Host—Season 2, as Derek Newcastle)

CAST

Season 1 Matt Kennedy Gould (Joe Schmo); Melissa Yvonna Lewis (Asleigh Rivera, "The Rich Bitch"); David Hornsby (Steve "The Hutch" Hutchinson, "The Asshole"); Angela Dodson (Molly Crabtree, "The Virgin"); Franklin Dennis Jones (Earl Bradford, "The Veteran"); Nikki Davis (Gina Price, "The Schemer"); Lance Krall (Carols "Kip" Calderas, "The Gay Guy"); Brian Keith Etheridge (Brian, "The Buddy"); Kristen Wiig (Patricia "Dr. Pat" Lane, "The Quack")

Season 2 Tim Walsh (Joe Schmo); Ingrid Wiese (Jane Schmo, "The Schmo Turned Actress"); Tim Herzog (Austin, "The Bachelor"); Valerie Azlynn (Piper, "The Bachelorette"); Jonathan Torrens (Gerald, "The

Gotta-be-Gay Guy"); Natsha Leggero (Rita, "The Drunk"); Kevin Kirkpatrick (Bryce, "The Stalker"); Jessica Makinson (Eleanor, "The Weeper"); Steve Mallory (Ernie, "The Heir"); Grtechen Palmer (Ambrosia, "The Bitch"); Jon Huertas (T.J., "The Playah"); Jana Speaker (Cammy, "The Moron")

PRODUCTION COMPANY	Stone Stanley Entertainment
CREATED BY	Rhett Reese
EXECUTIVE PRODUCERS	Rhett Reese; Anthony Ross; David G. Stanley; Scott A. Stone; Paul Wernick
PRODUCER	Andrew Green
DIRECTORS	Danny Salles (Season 1); Sean Travis (Season 2)

In this hoax show, Matthew Kennedy Gould signed on for a reality show called *Lap of Luxury,* in the hope of winning $100,000 by living in a mansion in Southern California. The twist was that *Lap of Luxury* wasn't a real show, and his fellow contestants were really actors representing classic reality-show stereotypes, such as "the buddy" or "the virgin." Matthew had to endure bizarre challenges such as sumo wrestling and "Hands on a High-Priced Hooker," a spoof of reality-show endurance challenges, where Matthew had to hold his hand on a prostitute longer than any of the other contestants. In the Season 1 finale, Matthew thought he'd lost in the final vote to Hutch, but host Ralph Garman received word that someone in the room wasn't whom he appeared to be. Hutch and the rest of the cast revealed to Matthew that they were actors. Ralph explained to Matthew the premise of the show and informed him that he'd get to keep all the prizes.

The second season featured Tim and Ingrid, two "real" people who had agreed to appear on the reality show *Last Chance for Love,* which was actually a fake relationship show, with actors portraying other competitors. In Episode 4, Ingrid suspected that the show was something other than what she signed up for, and was paid $100,000 to join the rest of the cast and not reveal the truth to Tim. A new Jane Schmo, Amanda, was added to the cast. Tim and Amanda didn't know the show was a parody reality-comedy show until the final episode. Like the first season, after the joke was revealed to them, they were told that whatever prizes and cash they had earned was theirs to keep.

RATINGS: The first season finale was seen by more than 3 million viewers, bringing Spike its highest ratings up to that point.

JUNKYARD WARS

GENRE	Competition
FIRST TELECAST	9/13/1998
LAST TELECAST	8/8/2004
NETWORK	TLC
EPISODE STYLE	Self-contained
TALENT	Lisa Rogers (Host—2002); Tyler Harcott (Host—2001); George Gray (Host—2001); Cathy Rogers (Host—1999–2002); Robert Llewellyn (1998–2002); Rossi Morreale (Host); Greg Bryant (Judge)
EXECUTIVE PRODUCERS	Alexandra Middendorf; Martin Davidson; David Frank; Jason Gibb; Cathy Rogers
PRODUCERS	Alison Turner; Al Edgington; Nathaniel Grouille; Bill Hobbins; Ross Kaiman; Rupert Parker
DIRECTORS	Andrew Greenberger; Ross Kaiman; Marc Marriott; Cathy Rogers; Alison Turner

Based on the British show *Scrapheap Challenge, Junkyard Wars* featured two teams who were given one day to create magnificent machines using discarded items found in a junkyard. Remade items included rockets, gliders, cannons, and diving suits.

JUST FOR LAUGHS

GENRE	Docucomedy
FIRST TELECAST	7/17/2007

NETWORK	ABC
AIR TIMES	Tuesday, 8:00 p.m. and 8:30 p.m.
EPISODE STYLE	Self-contained
EXECUTIVE PRODUCERS	Pierre Girard; Troy Miller
CO-EXECUTIVE PRODUCERS	Tracy Baird; Michael Weinberg
PRODUCER	Jacques Chevalier
DIRECTOR	T. T. Miller

Unsuspecting victims were the targets of funny, hidden-camera tricks and practical jokes on this docucomedy.

JUVIES

GENRE	Docusoap
FIRST TELECAST	2/1/2007
NETWORK	MTV
EPISODE STYLE	Self-contained
CAST	Mary Beth Bonaventura
PRODUCTION COMPANIES	Calamari Productions; Intuitive Entertainment; MTV/Remote Productions
EXECUTIVE PRODUCERS	Kevin Dill; Karen Grau; Lily Neumeyer
PRODUCER	John Salcido
DIRECTOR	Melissa Kennedy

The gritty *Juvies* took place at Indiana's Lake Country Juvenile Center, where first-time offenders waited to discover their fates. With unprecedented access, the series followed the offenders' day-to-day lives in the center and in court, while they waited for a judge to decide their futures.

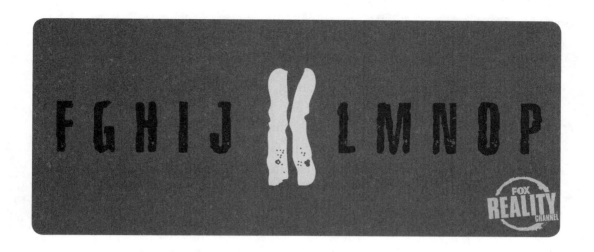

KATHY GRIFFIN:
MY LIFE ON THE D-LIST

GENRE	Docucomedy (Celebrity)
FIRST TELECAST	8/3/2005
EPISODE STYLE	Self-contained
CAST	Kathy Griffin, John Griffin (Kathy's dad), Maggie Griffin (Kathy's mom); Jessica Zajicek (Kathy's assistant); Tony Tripoli (one of Kathy's best gays—Season 1); Dennis Hensley (one of Kathy's best gays—Season 1); Matt Moline (Kathy's ex-husband)
PRODUCTION COMPANY	Picture This Television
EXECUTIVE PRODUCERS	Marcia Mule; Bryan Scott; Lisa M. Tucker; Kathy Griffin; Frances Berwick; Amy Introcaso-Davis; Rachel Smith Series; Cori Abraham
PRODUCERS	Beth Wichterich; Matthew Lahey
DIRECTORS	Matthew Lahey; Toby Oppenheimer

This peek into the life of comedian, actress, and pop culture junkie Kathy Griffin. In Season 1, cameras followed Griffin's stand-up live shows and her red-carpet coverage of the Oscars for the E! network. They also captured "D-List" moments, such as when hardly any fans showed up for a DVD signing, or Griffin's recollection of Star Jones's distaste for her after her appearance on *The View*. The show also featured Griffin's home life with her then-husband, Matt, and frequent visits by her mother and father, and her "favorite gays," Dennis and Tony. In Season 2, Griffin traveled to Iraq to perform for the U.S. troops. Other episodes featured her leap back into the dating world, mourning the death of her father, and inviting her mother to live with her. A highlight from Season 3 was her trip to England, where she deliberately fell out of a car to get her photo in the tabloids. *My Life on the D-List* was nominated for the 2006 and 2007 Emmys for Outstanding Reality Program, and won the award in 2007.

KATIE & PETER

GENRE	Docusoap
FIRST TELECAST	4/21/2007
NETWORK	E!
EPISODE STYLE	Self-contained
CAST	Katie Price, Peter Andre
EXECUTIVE PRODUCERS	Nick Bulien; Neville Hendricks
PRODUCER	Simon Harries
DIRECTORS	Simon Harries; Rachel Rosen; Stephen Lennhoff

Britain's hottest celebrity couple, model Katie Price and musician Peter Andre, juggle work, family, and time for romance on *Katie & Peter*.

KEPT

GENRE	Competition
FIRST TELECAST	5/29/2005
LAST TELECAST	8/4/2005

NETWORK	VH1
EPISODE STYLE	Story Arc
TALENT	Jerry Hall
CAST	Seth Frye (Winner); Maurizio Farhad; Jason Fromer; Ricardo Medina, Jr.; Frank Trigg; Slavco Tuskaloski; Devonric; Brian Bergdoll; Jon Benarroch; Anwar Jenkins; Austen Earl; Michael Biloto
EXECUTIVE PRODUCERS	Michael Canter; Sam Korkis; Kim Rozenfeld; Brandon Riegg; Julio Kollerbohm; Mark Ganshirt; Debbie Adler Myers
PRODUCER	Jason Kooper
DIRECTOR	G. T. Taylor

Jerry Hall, the fortysomething former model and ex-wife of Rolling Stone's frontman Mick Jagger, turned the tables on traditional reality shows when she chose a younger man to be her escort. Twelve men in their mid-twenties and early thirties competed for the opportunity to be a "kept" man, and to win a six-figure allowance for one year. Seth won the competition.

KICKED OUT

GENRE	Docudrama
FIRST TELECAST	9/6/2005
NETWORK	ABC Family
EPISODE STYLE	Self-contained
PRODUCTION COMPANY	Rocket Pictures
EXECUTIVE PRODUCER	Jim Berger
CO-EXECUTIVE PRODUCER	James Flint
PRODUCERS	Nicole Solomon; Danny Shaner
DIRECTOR	James Flint

Parents got revenge on their slacker kids when they literally *Kicked Out* their free-loading children. For ten days, the slackers were sent off to their own place, where they had to find a job to pay the bills and get their chores done without the aid of their parents.

KILL REALITY

GENRE	Docusoap
FIRST TELECAST	7/25/2005
LAST TELECAST	9/12/2005
NETWORK	E!
EPISODE STYLE	Story Arc
CAST	Rob Cesterino; Josh Souza; Jenna Lewis; Jon Dalton (aka Jonny Fairplay); Ethan Zohn; Trishelle Cannatella; Jenna Morasca; Stacie Jones Upchurch; Bob Guiney; Stephen Hill; Reichen Lehmkuhl; Tonya Cooley; Trish Schneider; Lewis; Toni Ferrari
PRODUCTION COMPANY	Creative Light Entertainment
EXECUTIVE PRODUCERS	Russell Heldt; Rich Tackenberg; Scott Zakarin

On *Kill Reality,* fourteen former reality-show stars convened to produce and act in the independent horror film *The Scorned.* Madness and drama ensued as the players lived and worked together under one roof.

KING OF CARS

GENRE	Docusoap
FIRST TELECAST	4/4/2006
NETWORK	A&E
EPISODE STYLE	Self-contained
CAST	Josh Towbin (Chop); Will Tooros (Chilly Willy); Prem Singh (Blue Genie); Mark Deeter (Bob the Builder)

PRODUCTION COMPANY	A&E Television Networks
EXECUTIVE PRODUCERS	Josh Towbin; Daniel Elias; David Houts
PRODUCERS	Dan Flaherty; Julie Lei; Adriana Pacheco; Robert Palumbo
DIRECTORS	Andrew Dunn; Daniel Elias; Po Kutchins

King of Cars follows thirty-year-old Josh "Chop" Towbin, aka "The King of Cars," as he runs his Las Vegas car dealership. Chop's wacky infomercial, *The Chopper Show,* has garnered him a cult following in Sin City. The A&E series features a behind-the-scenes look at the busy Dodge dealership to see how the deals are made. When he's not at the dealership, Chop is often balancing his roles as father, rap impresario, and Vegas player.

KING OF THE JUNGLE

GENRE	Competition
FIRST TELECAST	10/13/2003
NETWORK	Animal Planet
AIR TIME	Tuesday, 8:00 p.m.
EPISODE STYLE	Story Arc
TALENT	Jeff Corwin (Host/Judge—Season 1); Madison Michele (Host)

CAST

Season 1	Kelly Diedring (Winner); Adam; Aletris; Christina; Ed; Ernie; Jamie; Jarrod; Jennifer; Jeremy; John; Mike
Season 2	Tony Stallings (Winner); Bee; Cherry; Cynthia; Henry; Jacob; Jennifer; Lang; Lindsay; Patrick; Roberto; Shannon
PRODUCTION COMPANY	Jupiter Entertainment
EXECUTIVE PRODUCERS	Stephen Land (Season 1); Geoffrey Proud (Season 1); Kathleen French (Season 2); Douglas Ross (Season 2); Greg Stewart (Season 2)
DIRECTORS	Steven J. Santos (Season 1); Jack Farrell (Season 2)

Shot on location in Fort Pierce, Florida, *King of the Jungle* featured twelve animal experts competing for the opportunity to host their own wildlife program on Animal Planet. Season 1's winner was Kelly Diedring, and Tony Stallings won Season 2.

KNIEVEL'S WILD RIDE

GENRE	Docudrama (Celebrity)
FIRST TELECAST	4/5/2005
NETWORK	A&E
EPISODE STYLE	Self-contained
CAST	Robbie Knievel; Bill Rundle (Robbie's best friend); Krysten Knievel (Robbie's daughter); "Master" Brian Gates (Bodyguard); Todd (Ramp Builder); Pete (Utility Guy); Dan "Zuck" Zucker (Manager); Roman (Mechanic); Dan Haggerty; Spanky Spangler (Stunt Coordinator); Jon Simanton (Opening Act)
PRODUCTION COMPANIES	Screaming Flea Productions; A&E Television Network
EXECUTIVE PRODUCERS	Matt Chan; Lisa Knapp; Nancy Dubuc; Robert Sharenow
DIRECTOR	Stephen Hens

Robbie Knievel, son of the legendary motorcycle daredevil Evel Knievel, hit the road with his ragtag biker crew and real-life family to execute life-or-death motorcycle jumps on *Knievel's Wild Ride*. Emotions ran high during the series, which included conflicts with Robbie's dad and quieter times with his daughter, Krysten.

KNOCK FIRST

GENRE	Docudrama (Makeover)
FIRST TELECAST	10/6/2003
NETWORK	ABC Family

EPISODE STYLE	Self-contained
TALENT	Shane Booth (Designer); Taniya Nayak (Designer); Carrie Roy (Carpenter); Patty Benson (Carpenter); Jano Badovinac (Designer); Andy Hampton (Carpenter)
PRODUCTION COMPANY	Scout Productions
EXECUTIVE PRODUCERS	David Collins; Michael Williams
CO-EXECUTIVE PRODUCER	C. Fitz
DIRECTOR	Brian Robel

Teenage children and their friends, guided by a professional team of designers and carpenters, had forty-eight parent-free hours to lend outdated rooms a party atmosphere on *Knock First*.

LA INK

GENRE	Docusoap
FIRST TELECAST	8/7/2007
NETWORK	TLC
EPISODE STYLE	Self-contained
CAST	Kat Von D (Katherine von Drachenberg)
PRODUCTION COMPANY	Original Media
EXECUTIVE PRODUCERS	Pamela Deutsch; Charlie Corwin
PRODUCERS	Ben Salter; Kerry Carlock; Timothy J. Hamilton; Cat Rodriguez
DIRECTOR	Luis Barreto

In this spin-off of TLC's *Miami Ink,* tattoo artist Kat Von D sets up shop in her hometown of Los Angeles.

LAGUNA BEACH: THE REAL O.C.

GENRE	Docusoap
FIRST TELECAST	9/28/2004
NETWORK	MTV
EPISODE STYLE	Story Arc
TALENT	Jeff Colt (Narrator)
CAST	Stephen Coletti (Seasons 1 and 2); Kristin Cavalleri (Seasons 1 and 2); Lauren Conrad ("L.C.") (Seasons 1 and 2); Talan Torriero (Seasons 1 and 2); Jessica Smith (Season 2); Alex Murrel (Season 2); Jason Wahler (Season 2); Taylor Cole (Season 2); Lo Bosworth (Season 1); Morgan Olsen (Season 1); Christina Schuller (Season 1); Trey Phillips (Season 1); Tessa Keller (Season 3); Raquel "Rocky" Donatelli (Season 3); Kyndra Mayo (Season 3); Cami Edwards (Season 3); Cameron Brinkman (Season 3); Chase Johnson (Season 3); Breanna Conrad (Season 3); Kelan Hurley (Season 3); Lexie Contursi (Season 3),
EXECUTIVE PRODUCERS	Dave Sirulnick; Gary Auerbach; Tony DiSanto; Liz Gateley; Wendy Riche
PRODUCERS	Tina Gazzerro; Todd Darling; Morgan J. Freeman; Jason Sands
DIRECTORS	Hisham Abed; Mark Petersen; George Plamondon; Jason Sands

Shot on location in a wealthy seaside town, *Laguna Beach: The Real O.C.* follows the lives of eight privileged teens nearing the end of their senior year of high school. The drama runs high as the teens party, fall in and out of relationships, and contemplate their futures. While *Laguna Beach* is indeed a reality show, it is shot and edited like a scripted drama, giving it the feel of a prime-time soap opera, such as *The O.C.* By the third season, most of the original cast members had grown up and moved on, such as Lauren Conrad, star of MTV's *The Hills,* as a new group of teens were featured on the show.

LAS VEGAS GARDEN OF LOVE

GENRE	Docudrama
FIRST TELECAST	3/21/2005
LAST TELECAST	5/9/2005
NETWORK	ABC Family
EPISODE STYLE	Self-contained
CAST	Johnny Manvilla; Cheryl Luell (Johnny's cousin); Barb Ludwig (Johnny's aunt); Chuck Ludwig (Johnny's uncle); Rob Manvilla (Johnny's dad); Craig Luell (Cheryl's husband); Jojo Manvilla (Johnny's brother)
PRODUCTION COMPANIES	Schmaguuli; Cedar Ridge Entertainment; iCandy Productions, as iCandy TV Inc.; ABC Family Channel
CREATED BY	Stephen Hopkins; David Schermerhorn; Brent Travers
EXECUTIVE PRODUCERS	Stephen Hopkins; Brent Travers; David Schermerhorn
CO-EXECUTIVE PRODUCERS	Sandy Cohen; Mark Angotti
PRODUCERS	Charles Kramer; Sarah Skibitzke; Mark Cole; Gregory Ross

Las Vegas Garden of Love followed the often wacky day-to-day occurrences at Garden of Love, a family-owned wedding chapel in Las Vegas through the eyes of its fifteen-year-old videographer, Johnny.

LAST COMIC STANDING

GENRE Competition (Talent)

FIRST TELECAST 6/10/2003

NETWORKS NBC; Comedy Central

AIR TIMES Tuesday, 9:00 p.m. (Seasons 1–4); Wednesday, 9:00 p.m. (Season 5)

EPISODE STYLE Story Arc

TALENT Jay Mohr (Host—Seasons 1 and 2) Anthony Clark (Host—Seasons 3 and 4); Bill Bellamy (Season 5); Colin Quinn (Judge—Seasons 1 and 2); Ross Mark (Judge—Seasons 1 and 2); Bob Read (Judge—Seasons 1 and 2); Caroline Rhea (Judge—Season 1); Joy Behar (Judge—Season 1); Buddy Hackett (Judge—Season 1); Joe Rogan (Judge—Season 1); Mo'Nique (Judge—Season 1); Victoria Jackson (Judge—Season 1); Phyllis Diller (Judge—Season 1); Aisha Tyler (Judge—Season 1); Kim Coles (Judge—Season 2); Drew Carey (Judge—Season 2); Brett Butler (Judge—Season 2); Tess Drake (Judge—Season 2); Anthony Clark (Judge—Season 2); Rich Vos (Judge—Season 2); Alonzo Bodden (Judge—Season 5); Ant (Judge—Season 5); Kathleen Madigan (Judge—Season 5)

CAST

Season 1 Dat Phan (Winner); Ralphie May (Runner-up); Rich Vos (8th eliminated); Cory Kahaney (7th eliminated); Tess Drake (6th eliminated); Geoff Brown (5th eliminated); Dave Mordal (4th eliminated); Rob Cantrell (3rd eliminated); Tere Joyce (2nd eliminated); Sean Kent (1st eliminated):

Season 2 John Heffron (Winner); Alonzo Bodden (Runner-up); Gary Gulman (2nd Runner-up); Kathleen Madigan (7th eliminated); Tammy Pescatelli (6th eliminated) Corey Holcomb (5th eliminated); Jay London (4th and 8th eliminated; returned as a wildcard); Ant (3rd eliminated); Todd Glass (2nd eliminated); Bonnie McFarlane (1st eliminated)

Season 3 Alonzo Bodden (Winner); Rich Vos; Dave Mordal; John Heffron; Gary Gulman (eliminated in Episode 7); Todd Glass (eliminated in Episode 7); Tess Drake (eliminated in Episode 7); Geoff Brown (eliminated in Episode 7); Kathleen Madigan (eliminated in Episode 6); Jay London (eliminated in Episode 6); Dat Phan (eliminated in Episode 6); Ralphie May (eliminated in Episode 6); Ant (eliminated in Episode 5); Sean Kent (eliminated in Episode 5); Tammy Pescatelli (eliminated in Episode 4); Rob Cantrell (eliminated in Episode 4); Corey Holcomb (eliminated in Episode 3); Tere Joyce (eliminated in Episode 3); Jessica Kirson (eliminated in Episode 2); Cory Kahaney (eliminated in Episode 2)

Season 4 Josh Blue (Winner); Ty Barnett (Runner-up); Chris Porter (2nd Runner-up); Michelle Balan (5th eliminated); Roz (4th eliminated); Kristin Key (3rd eliminated); Rebecca Corry (3rd eliminated); Bil Dwyer (2nd eliminated); Joey Gay (2nd eliminated); Stella Stolper (1st eliminated), April Macie, (1st eliminated), Gabriel Iglesias (disqualified)

Season 5 Jon Reep (Winner); Lavell Crawford (Runner-up); Amy Schumer; Gerry Dee; Ralph Harris (6th eliminated); Doug Benson (5th eliminated); Matt Kirshen (4th eliminated); Debra DiGiovani

	(3rd eliminated): Dante and Gina Yashere (1st and 2nd eliminated)
EXECUTIVE PRODUCERS	Peter Engel; Rob Fox; Barry Katz; Jay Mohr; Dan Cutforth; Jane Lipsitz
CO-EXECUTIVE PRODUCERS	Al Edgington; Laurie Girion; Javier Winnik
PRODUCERS	Cori Fry; Javier Winnik; Brittany Lovett; Phil Silver; Molly O'Rourke; Brian Szot; K. P. Anderson
DIRECTORS	Rob Fox; Chuck Vinson; Tony Sacco; Craig Spirko; Kenny Hull

Last Comic Standing sets out to find the funniest person in America. The ten finalists live together and compete in head-to-head stand-up routines in front of a live studio audience, who determines which comics will advance to the finals. Season 1 culminated in a final stand-up showdown in which home viewers voted for the winner. Dat Phan was awarded his own stand-up special on Comedy Central, a development deal with NBC, and an appearance on *The Tonight Show*.

Season 2 was marred by controversy when the celebrity talent scouts discovered that their votes in the preliminary round of competition had not been considered, in favor of the producer's final vote. Season 2 winner was John Heffron.

Season 3's "Battle of the Best" tournament featured the finalists from the first two seasons. Each week, competitors were eliminated based on who had earned the least number of viewer votes, and the comic who received the most votes was awarded $50,000. Winner Alonzo Bodden was awarded a grand prize of $250,000. Due to lackluster ratings, NBC canceled the show before the last episode of the third season aired. The final episode was later aired on Comedy Central rather than NBC.

Season 4 comics lived on the *Queen Mary* ocean liner in Long Beach, California. For the first time in the series, a comic was disqualified. Gabriel Iglesias broke the rules by sending an e-mail from the ship. Anthony Clark replaced Jay Mohr as host of the show. Comedian Josh Blue, whose jokes often center on his cerebral palsy, was the Season 4 winner. The season also included the "Last Comic Downloaded" online competition, which was won by Theo Von of MTV's *Road Rules*.

Season 5 featured an international group of comics, with finalists from Australia and England. Bill Bellamy was the new host. Winner Jon Reep received an NBC Universal contract, a Bravo television special, and $250,000.

As of press time, Season 6 auditions were under way.

THE LAST RESORT

GENRE	Docusoap (Relationship)
FIRST TELECAST	8/11/2002
NETWORK	ABC Family
EPISODE STYLE	Story Arc
TALENT	Kalai Miller (Host); Tess Hightower (Therapist); Dr. Roger A. Rhoades (Therapist); Dr. Lynn Ianni (Relationship Coach)
PRODUCTION COMPANY	Fisher Entertainment
PRODUCERS	Kevin F. Anderson; Suzanne Pate; Amy Wruble

On *The Last Resort,* four couples traveled to Hawaii to try to rekindle their affection for each other and save their relationships. Couples participated in counseling sessions, took sunset cruises and carriage rides, and enjoyed romantic candlelit dinners.

THE LAW FIRM

GENRE	Competition
FIRST TELECAST	7/28/2005
LAST TELECAST	10/8/2005
NETWORK	NBC; Bravo
AIR TIME	Thursday, 9:00 p.m. (NBC run)
EPISODE STYLE	Story Arc
TALENT	Roy Black (Host)
CAST	Mike Cavalluzzi (Winner); Olivier Tallieu (Runner-up); Aileen Page (eliminated in Episode 7); Deep Goswami (eliminated in Episode

6); Christopher Smith (eliminated in Episode 5); Keith Bruno (eliminated in Episode 4); Barrett Elizabeth Rubens (eliminated in Episode 3); Regina Silva (eliminated in Episode 3); Elizabeth Bradley (eliminated in Episode 2); Anika Harvey (eliminated in Episode 2); Jason Adams (eliminated in Episode 1); Kelly Chang (eliminated in Episode 1);

PRODUCTION COMPANIES	Renegade 83, Inc., in association with David E. Kelley Productions and 20th Century Fox Television
CREATED BY	David E. Kelley
CO-EXECUTIVE PRODUCERS	Jay Renfroe; Jonathan Pontel; David E. Kelley; David Garfinkle; Adam Greener
PRODUCERS	Julia Silverton; Missy Hughes; Rachel Kirshenbaum
DIRECTOR	Cord Keller

Prolific prime-time television creator David E. Kelley (*The Practice*, *Ally McBeal*) turned his attention to the real-life drama of the courtroom in this competition series. Twelve lawyers divided into two teams competed against each other, trying actual cases in a court that was legally binding. Top legal analyst and attorney Roy Black selected who would be eliminated on each episode, and in a twist, the ousted lawyer could be from either the losing or the winning team. Winner Mike Cavalluzzi received a grand prize of $250,000. After two episodes, NBC pulled the plug on the show, and the remaining episodes aired on Bravo.

RATINGS: In its two airings on NBC, *The Law Firm* had an average of 4.5 million viewers.

LIE DETECTOR

GENRE	Docudrama
FIRST TELECAST	3/8/2005
LAST TELECAST	6/28/2005

NETWORK	PAX
AIR TIMES	Tuesday, 9:00 p.m. (3/2005–4/2005); Tuesday, 8:00 p.m. (4/2005–6/2005); Sunday, 6:00 p.m. (4/2006–6/2006)
EPISODE STYLE	Self-contained
TALENT	Rolonda Watts (Host); Ed Gelb (Polygraph Administrator)
PRODUCTION COMPANY	Mark Phillips Philms & Telephision
EXECUTIVE PRODUCER	Mark Phillips
PRODUCER	Rick Davis

People who hoped to clear their names voluntarily submitted to polygraph examinations on *Lie Detector*. The premiere episode featured a lie detector test conducted on Paula Jones, the former Arkansas state employee who sued President Bill Clinton for sexual harassment. Jones passed her test. The veracity of this series was called into question by critics.

LISA WILLIAMS: LIFE AMONG THE DEAD

GENRE	Docudrama
FIRST TELECAST	10/12/2006
NETWORK	Lifetime
CAST	Lisa Williams (Self); D. C. Douglas (Narrator)
PRODUCTION COMPANIES	Merv Griffin Entertainment; Kimo Jagger Productions; LAD Productions
EXECUTIVE PRODUCERS	Raymond J. Brune; Yann Debonne; Merv Griffin; Andrew Yani
CO-EXECUTIVE PRODUCERS	Michael Shevloff
PRODUCERS	Bob Schermerhorn; Shannon Vandermark
DIRECTORS	Bob Schermerhorn; Brett P Jenkins; Yann DeBonne

On *Lisa Williams: Life Among the Dead,* the British medium and clairvoyant Williams traveled to the United States to use her supernatural gifts to talk to the dead and give information to their surviving loved ones.

LITTLE PEOPLE, BIG WORLD

GENRE	Docudrama
FIRST TELECAST	3/4/2006
NETWORK	TLC
EPISODE STYLE	Self-contained
TALENT	Matt Roloff; Amy Roloff; Jeremy Roloff; Zach Roloff; Molly Roloff; Jacob Roloff
PRODUCTION COMPANY	Gay Rosenthal Productions
EXECUTIVE PRODUCERS	Paul Barrosse; Joseph Freed; Gay Rosenthal
PRODUCERS	Billy Cooper; Matthew Lahey; Cynthia Matzger; Ann Suckow

Little People, Big World follows the daily lives of the Roloff family: parents Matt and Amy, and their four children, Zach, Jeremy, Molly, and Jacob. Matt, Amy, and Zach have dwarfism, while Jeremy, Molly, and Jacob are average height. Zach and Jeremy are twins, despite the fact that they are not both little people. In the third season, many of the episodes followed the story of Jacob's pumpkin-launching trebuchet accident and his recovery.

LIVE LIKE A STAR

GENRE	Docudrama (Makeover)
FIRST TELECAST	6/22/2004
NETWORK	Syndication
EPISODE STYLE	Self-contained
TALENT	Colin Cowie (Party Planner); Gerry Garvin

(Celebrity Chef); Gregory Joujon-Roche (Celebrity Trainer); Jennifer Rade (Celebrity Stylist); Lash Fary (Celebrity Shopper); Laurie Bailey (Celebrity Party Planner); Leslie Sachs (Celebrity Interior Designer); Roshumba (Supermodel); Stuart Gilchrist (Celebrity Interior Designer)

PRODUCTION COMPANIES	Wheeler-Sussman Productions; Small Cages Productions
EXECUTIVE PRODUCERS	Burt Wheeler; Glen Freyer
PRODUCER	Tracey Finley
DIRECTOR	Jeff Rifkin

Two people got a little "Hollywood touch" added to their lives on this makeover series. Highlights ranged from people fulfilling their dreams of becoming head chef for a day at a Hollywood hot spot, to having their wedding arranged by a celebrity event planner.

LIVING LAHAINA

GENRE	Docusoap
FIRST TELECAST	4/17/2007
LAST TELECAST	5/2/2007
NETWORK	MTV
EPISODE STYLE	Self-contained
CAST	Kimo Kinimaka; Sean Souza; Alex "Gator" Altamirano; Casey Cameron; Dave Ball; Matt Allen
EXECUTIVE PRODUCER	Jesse Ignjatovic
PRODUCERS	Patrick Murphy; Cat Rodriguez
DIRECTOR	Michael Lange

Filmed on location in Hawaii during a three-month period, *Living Lahaina* focused on a group of twentysomething surf instructors and their father figure–boss at the Royal Hawaiian Surf Academy.

LONG WAY ROUND

GENRE	Docusoap
FIRST TELECAST	10/28/2004
NETWORK	Bravo
EPISODE STYLE	Story Arc
TALENT	Ewan McGregor; Charley Boorman
PRODUCTION COMPANIES	Bravo Networks; Elixir Films; Image Wizard Television
EXECUTIVE PRODUCERS	Ewan McGregor; Charley Boorman; David Alexanian; Russ Malkin; Frances Berwick; Jamila Hunter
PRODUCER	Alexis Alexanian
DIRECTORS	David Alexanian; Russ Malkin

Actor Ewan McGregor and his best friend, Charley Boorman, documented their twenty-thousand-mile motorcycle tour around the globe on *Long Way Round*. The duo had only minimal assistance from mass transit to get them across oceans. They filmed their adventure with their own handheld video cameras, with camera crews meeting them at certain stops.

LOOKING FOR LOVE: BACHELORETTES IN ALASKA

GENRE	Competition (Dating)
FIRST TELECAST	6/2/2002
LAST TELECAST	7/7/2002
NETWORK	FOX
AIR TIME	Sunday, 9:00 p.m.

EPISODE STYLE	Story Arc
TALENT	Steve Santagati (Host)
CAST	
The Bachelorettes	Andrea; Cecile; Karen; Rebekah; Sissie
The Bachelors	Bob; Brad; Brent; Doug; Jack; Jason; Jeff; Jim; Keith; Kristian; Kurt; Matt; Michael; Mike; Patrick; Terence; Thaddeus; Tim; Troy; Will
PRODUCTION COMPANIES	Fox Television Network; LMNO Productions
EXECUTIVE PRODUCERS	Bill Paolantonio; Scott Messick; Eric Schotz

Shot on location in Alaska, this competition had five single women take their pick of fifty eligible local men. Each woman selected one man to "keep on ice" as a suitor. Then the remaining men competed for the chance to romance the other women in the wilderness. None of the short-term relationships resulted in marriage.

LOST

GENRE	Competition
FIRST TELECAST	9/5/2001
LAST TELECAST	12/30/2001
NETWORK	NBC
AIR TIME	Wednesday, 8:00 p.m.
EPISODE STYLE	Story Arc
CAST	Lando Hawkins and Carla Antonino (Winners—Race 1); Joe Gulla and Courtland Bascon (Race 1); Tami Becker and Celeste Weaver (Race 1); Dan Wells and Laurie Zink (Winners—Race 2); Bob Hayden and Fred Agee (Race 2); Donna and Veronica (Race 2)
PRODUCTION COMPANIES	Conaco; Jumbolaya Productions; NBC Studios; Windfall Films
EXECUTIVE PRODUCERS	David Dugan; Nancy Stern
CO-EXECUTIVE PRODUCERS	Mary-Jane April; A. J. Morewitz; Jeff Ross

Three teams of two unrelated contestants were blindfolded and dropped in a secret location in this competition. During their training before the drop, the contestants' cell phones, money, and any other tools that could be used to help them were confiscated. By the time of the drop, they were equipped with only ten dollars, minimal food and water, and a few helpful supplies. The contestants had to use deduction, common sense, and bargaining to make their way back to the Statue of Liberty in New York City. The first team to reach the Statue of Liberty split a grand prize of $200,000. Each member of the winning team also won a new car. The series consisted of two three-episode races. The first race had contestants dropped in Mongolia. Lando Hawkins and Carla Antonino won the race. The second race dropped contestants in Bolivia. Dan Wells and Laurie Zink were the second race's champions. While intended to be a three-episode arc, the second race was condensed into a two-episode arc during its initial airing on NBC.

LOVE IS IN THE HEIR

GENRE	Docudrama
FIRST TELECAST	11/28/2004
LAST TELECAST	1/31/2005
NETWORK	E!
EPISODE STYLE	Story Arc
CAST	Ann Claire Van Shaick; Michael T. Scheinberg (Ann Claire's assistant); Mandana Pahlbod (Ann Claire's sister); Shahboz Pahlbod (Ann Claire's father); Beatrice Anne Pahlbod (Ann Claire's mother)
EXECUTIVE PRODUCER	Steven Michaels
PRODUCER	Nikki Boella
DIRECTOR	Katherine Brooks

Princess Ann Claire, a descendant of the last shah of Iran, dreamed of becoming a country music singing star. To avoid being financially cut off by her wealthy family, she agreed to stop her rebellious ways, get a job as a country singer, and find a man worthy of her father's approval on this docudrama. The final installment revealed that the princess was unable to realize her dream of getting a record deal or a man.

LOVE U

GENRE	Docudrama (Romance)
FIRST TELECAST	4/11/2003
LAST TELECAST	5/16/2003
NETWORK	TLC
EPISODE STYLE	Story Arc
TALENT	Marki Costello (Host)
PRODUCTION COMPANY	Termite Art Productions
EXECUTIVE PRODUCER	Erik Nelson
PRODUCERS	Rachael Pihlaja; Jennifer Stocks
DIRECTOR	James Taylor

On *Love U,* couples on the threshold of marriage enrolled themselves in a prenuptial boot camp, going on field trips and doing homework assignments designed to test their relationship and compatibility. On the final "Judgment Day," marriage counselors and clinical experts observed the couples on videotape, interviewed them in person, and offered their opinions on the probability of a successful marriage.

MAD MAD HOUSE

GENRE	Competition
FIRST TELECAST	3/1/2004
LAST TELECAST	4/29/2004
NETWORK	Sci Fi
EPISODE STYLE	Story Arc
TALENT	Fiona Horne (Witch); Iya Ta'Shia Asanti (Voodoo Priestess); Don Henrie (Vampire); Art Aguirre (Modern Primitive); David "Avocado" Wolfe (Naturist)
CAST	Jamie Etheridge (Winner); Nicole Ferrera (Runner-up); Eric Lindquist (8th eliminated); Loana Huynh (7th eliminated); Noel Shankel (6th eliminated); Tim McGhee (5th eliminated); Bonnie Dobkin (7th eliminated); Brent Ellis (3rd eliminated); Kelly Keefe (2nd eliminated); Hamin Phillips (1st eliminated)

PRODUCTION COMPANY	A. Smith and Co.
EXECUTIVE PRODUCERS	Arthur Smith; Kent Weed
CO-EXECUTIVE PRODUCER	Tony Yates
PRODUCER	Cyndi Hubach
DIRECTOR	Brian Smith

Five people who lived alternative lifestyles tested ten ordinary people to live in their booby-trapped, spooky house in *Mad Mad House*. The ordinary people were tested to see who was the most open and tolerant of the others' unconventional lives, and the "alts" voted them out one by one. Jamie won the $100,000 grand prize.

MADE

GENRE	Docudrama
FIRST TELECAST	8/3/2002
NETWORK	MTV
EPISODE STYLE	Self-contained
PRODUCTION COMPANY	MTV
EXECUTIVE PRODUCER	Bob Kusbit
CO-EXECUTIVE PRODUCERS	Rob Dames; Harley Tat
PRODUCERS	Matthew Blaine; Josh Haygood; Allison Howard; Elizabeth Mcdonald
DIRECTORS	Matthew Blaine; Josh Haygood; Elizabeth Mcdonald

Made gives teens the opportunity to live their dreams while discovering a little something about themselves along the way. With the help of a "Made Coach" the teens achieve some of their goals, while other goals become character-building adventures.

MADE IN THE USA

GENRE	Competition
FIRST TELECAST	9/14/2005
LAST TELECAST	10/14/2005
NETWORK	USA
EPISODES	Story Arc
TALENT	Todd Newton (Host); Nolan Bushnell (Judge); Karim Rashid (Judge); Joy Mangano (Judge)
CAST	Chris Spencer and Sammy Davis (Winners); Justin Marty and Joshua Pace; Joe and Lisa Byles; Landon Worthington and Marvin Dinovitz; Scott and Doug Krentz; Quintana Kemp and Jessica Prasse;
PRODUCTION COMPANIES	10 by 10 Entertainment; Home Shopping Network, Inc.
EXECUTIVE PRODUCERS	Ken Mok; James Lima
PRODUCERS	J. Paul Buscemi; Javier Winnik; Heather Cocks; Richard Glatzer; Johanna Rowe

On *Made in the USA*, inventors from across the nation competed for the opportunity to sell their products on the Home Shopping Network. After an open casting call, the field of inventors was narrowed to six teams of two. The teams participated in a number of challenges that involved developing their sales and marketing skills and perfecting their inventions. Three judges determined who would be eliminated each week based on team performance. The series culminated with the final three teams presenting their products as home viewers determined the champion. Chris Spencer and Sammy Davis, with their "Hydromax System," a device designed to hydrate football players while playing a game, were the winners, earning a one-year contract with HSN.

MADE PRESENTS: CAMP JIM

GENRE	Docusoap
FIRST TELECAST	10/2003
NETWORK	MTV
EPISODE STYLE	Story Arc
CAST	Jim McMullan (Coach); Meredith; Jennifer; Danielle; Candace; Emlee; Elizabeth; Tara; Kyle; Kristen; Jeff
PRODUCTION COMPANY	MTV Productions
EXECUTIVE PRODUCERS	Raoul Rosenberg; Andrew Hogel; Jonathan M. Singer
PRODUCER	Gina Glickman
DIRECTORS	Kasey Barrett; Cynthia Matzger; Donald Bull

On *Made Presents: Camp Jim,* fifteen wannabe professional cheerleaders were instructed by all-star cheerleading coach Jim McMullan for two weeks. The show was a spin-off of the "I Want to Be A Cheerleader" episode of *Made,* which focused on teenage girls who tried out for their schools' cheerleading squads.

A MAKEOVER STORY

GENRE	Docudrama (Makeover)
FIRST TELECAST	10/11/2000
NETWORK	TLC
EPISODE STYLE	Self-contained
TALENT	Dan Brickley (Coach); Alison Freer (Coach); Moses Jones (Coach); Gretchen Monahan (Coach)
PRODUCTION COMPANY	Banyan Productions
EXECUTIVE PRODUCER	Richard Monahan
PRODUCER	Amy Van Vessem

Another in the line of *Story* series on TLC, this docudrama featured subjects undergoing full makeovers by a team of coaches. The recipients were given new wardrobes, hair, and makeup.

MAKING IT BIG

GENRE	Docudrama
FIRST TELECAST	4/24/2005
LAST TELECAST	6/5/2005
NETWORK	Oxygen
EPISODE STYLE	Self-contained
TALENT	Linda Kaplan Thaler (Host); Howard Dell (Host)
PRODUCTION COMPANY	Wildly Sophisticated Television Inc.
PRODUCER	Sue Ridout
DIRECTORS	Tara Hungerford; Jennifer Little

On *Making it Big,* Madison Avenue branding guru Linda Kaplan Thaler advised six aspiring professionals on their specific career paths: chef, choreographer, hairstylist, fashion designer, wedding planner, and entertainment reporter. The contestants were given challenges to overcome in order to win an apprenticeship with a business icon from their chosen field.

MAKING NEWS: TEXAS STYLE

GENRE	Docusoap
FIRST TELECAST	6/11/2007
NETWORK	TV Guide Network
EPISODE STYLE	Self-contained
CAST	Kara Lee; Allyson; Melissa; Tatum; Jay
PRODUCTION COMPANY	Nick Davis Productions
EXECUTIVE PRODUCER	Nick Davis
DIRECTOR	Steve Bronstein

Making News: Texas Style took a behind-the-scenes look at the people who report and produce the news from a small, local CBS affiliate, KOSA-TV, in Odessa, Texas.

MAKING THE BAND

GENRE	Docusoap (Job)
FIRST TELECAST	3/24/2000
LAST TELECAST	3/30/2002
NETWORKS	ABC (Seasons 1 and 2); MTV
AIR TIMES	Friday, 9:30 p.m. (3/2000–5/2000); Friday, 9:00 p.m. (5/2000–9/2000); Friday, 8:00 p.m. (Season 2) (ABC run)
EPISODE STYLE	Story Arc
TALENT	Louis J. Pearlman (Music Producer)
CAST	Eric Michael Estrada; Dan Miller (replaced Ikaika); Trevor Penick; Jacob Underwood; Ashley Parker Angel; Ikaika Kahoano (Season 1—quit the band)
PRODUCTION COMPANIES	Bunim-Murray Productions; MTV Productions; Trans Continental Pictures
EXECUTIVE PRODUCERS	Mary-Ellis Bunim; Jon Murray
PRODUCERS	Cris Abrego; Jennifer Lange; Ken Mok; Jonathan M. Singer
DIRECTORS	Luis Barreto; Paul Morzella; C. B. Harding; Teri Kennedy

Making the Band starred music mogul Louis J. Pearlman (Backstreet Boys, 'NSync) as he cast his new, pop boy band, O-Town. Cameras captured the tension involved in turning strangers into a hit-making musical group. O-Town's debut single, "Liquid Dreams," made music history when it entered the Billboard singles sales charts at number one.

MAKING THE BAND 2

GENRE	Docusoap (Job)
FIRST TELECAST	10/19/2002
LAST TELECAST	5/13/2004
NETWORK	MTV
EPISODE STYLE	Story Arc
TALENT	Sean "P. Diddy" Combs (Music Producer)
CAST	Sara Stokes; Lynese "Babs" Wiley; Lloyd "Ness" Mathis; Frederick Watson; Rodney "Chopper" Hill
PRODUCTION COMPANIES	Bad Boy Worldwide Entertainment Group; Bunim-Murray Productions (2002–2003); MTV Networks; MTV Productions; Trans Continental Pictures
EXECUTIVE PRODUCERS	Mary-Ellis Bunim (2002–2003); Jon Murray (2002–2003); Sean "P. Diddy" Combs; Rick de Oliveira
PRODUCERS	Jac Benson II; Kenny Hull; Phil Robinson
DIRECTORS	Diane Houslin; Kenny Hull; Zo Wesson; Leola Westbrook

On *Making the Band 2,* music entrepreneur and rapper Sean "P. Diddy" Combs put aspiring singers through boot camp–style training in New York City, culminating in a recording contract as he created a new hip-hop group. The competitors' personal dramas and conflicts behind the music were also featured. The Season 1 winners were Sara, Babs, Lloyd, Frederick, Chopper, and Dylan—named "Da Band." In Season 2, the band learned to get along, hired a manager, and began recording. Season 3 kicked off as the band members met music journalists impressing them with their personalities and music. P. Diddy warned them that once their song was released, things could get tough because of the demands of being on the road touring. By the final episode, Da Band had disbanded.

MAKING THE BAND 3

GENRE Docusoap (Job)

FIRST TELECAST 3/3/2005

LAST TELECAST 8/10/2006

NETWORK MTV

EPISODE STYLE Story Arc

TALENT Sean "P. Diddy" Combs (Music Producer); Johnny Wright (Judge); Laurie Ann Gibson (Judge); Doc Holiday (Judge); Phil Robinson (Judge)

CAST Shannon Bex (Season 2—Winner); Wanita "D. Woods" Woodgette (Season 2—Winner); Aubrey O'Day (Seasons 1 and 2—Winner); Aundrea Fimbres (Seasons 1 and 2—Winner); Dawn Angelique Richard (Season 2—Winner); Michelle Livigne (Season 1); Malika (Season 2); Martii (Season 1); Francesca (Season 1); Lavante (Season 1); Tyra (Season 1); Kristen (Season 1); Patty (Season 1); Yahaira (Season 1); Bethany (Season 1); Mylah (Season 1); Shantae (Season 1); Roxy (Season 1); Nicole (Season 2); Paschun (Season 1); Celeste (Season 1); Erika (Season 1); Leche (Season 1); Aileen (Season 1); Sammy (Season 2); Tokiko (Season 2); Amber (Season 2); Jennifer (Season 2); Tiffany (Season 2); Chelsea (Season 2); Cindy (Season 2); Kaui (Season 2); Jasmine (Season 2); Melissa (Season 2); Kelli (Season 2); Dominique (Season 2); Denosh (Season 2); Bennett (Season 2); Taquita (Season 2); Thorn (Season 2)

PRODUCTION COMPANIES Bad Boy Worldwide Entertainment Group; MTV Networks; MTV Productions

EXECUTIVE PRODUCERS Sean "P. Diddy" Combs; Ted Iredell

CO-EXECUTIVE PRODUCER	Perry Dance
PRODUCER	Kenny Hull
DIRECTORS	Dana Klein; Matthew Ruecker; Leola Westbrook; Kenny Hull; Zachary Isenberg; Sean Rankine

In the third edition of *Making the Band*, Sean "P. Diddy" Combs set out to create the next great girl group. As in Season 2, the finalists were sent to New York City to live in an apartment while they endured grueling training and auditions to determine who would get a spot in the group. At the end of the first season, it was determined that none of the girls had what it took to make it into the group. However, three of the finalists—Aubrey, Malika, and Aundrea—were allowed to return in the second season, where the audition process continued.

In Season 2, a new group of finalists was split into two bands: SHE (She Has Everything) and Chain 6. Aubrey, Shannon, Wanita, Aundrea, and Dawn were chosen as the final five in the finale.

In Season 3, the band chose the name Danity Kane, and after much rehearsing, on August 22, 2006, they released their first, self-titled album, which peaked at No. 1 on the Billboard charts within three weeks of its release.

MAN VS. WILD

GENRE	Docudrama
FIRST TELECAST	11/10/2006
NETWORK	Discovery Channel
EPISODE STYLE	Self-contained
CAST	Bear Grylls (Host)
PRODUCTION COMPANY	Diverse Productions
EXECUTIVE PRODUCERS	Mary Donahue; Rob MacIver
DIRECTORS	Scott Tankard; Mike Warner

On *Man vs. Wild*, adventurer Bear Grylls strands himself in popular wilderness destinations, locations where tourists often become lost or in danger. While navigating his way back to civilization, he demonstrates local survival techniques, such as getting out of quicksand in the Moab Desert, negotiating perilous jungle rivers in Costa Rica, crossing ravines in the Alps, and avoiding sharks off Hawaii.

MANHUNT

GENRE	Competition
FIRST TELECAST	8/3/2001
LAST TELECAST	9/7/2001
NETWORK	UPN
AIR TIME	Friday, 8:00 p.m.
EPISODE STYLE	Story Arc
TALENT	John Cena (Hunter—"Big" Tim Kingman); Raye Hollitt (Hunter—Rain); Kala'i Miller (Hunter—Koa)
CAST	Wesley Ace; Ed Anthony Budzius; Karen Cha; Lucas Ford; Elizabeth Forsyth; Lyzz Forsyth; Nicole Gordillo; Romey Jakobson; Mandy Kaplan; Jacqueline A. Kelly; Jim Lee; James McCaughley; Joe McMullen
EXECUTIVE PRODUCERS	Edward Barbini; Chris Crowe; Bob Jaffe

Shot on location in Kauai, Hawaii, and Griffith Park in Los Angeles, *Manhunt* featured twelve contestants navigating the wilds of Hawaii to get from one end of the island to the other without getting shot three times by paintball guns. Once eliminated, the women had their ponytails clipped off, while the men had to shave their heads. Once the series was shot, producers were told to reshoot and replay certain games. The competitors were told they had to do this to receive money for their efforts in Hawaii. So, the contestants put bandanas on their heads to cover their hair growth since the series ended. While Nicole Gordillo was awarded $250,000, the show became the subject of FCC complaints for alleged manipulation in the show's production.

MANHUNT:
THE SEARCH FOR AMERICA'S MOST
GORGEOUS MALE MODEL

GENRE	Competition
FIRST TELECAST	10/13/2004
LAST TELECAST	11/30/2004
NETWORK	Bravo
EPISODE STYLE	Story Arc
TALENT	Carmen Electra (Host); Marisa Miller (Judge); Bruce Hulse (Judge)
CAST	Jon Jonsson (Winner); Rob Williams (Runner-up); Kevin Peake (Embedded Model); Tate Arnett; Brian Bernie; Ron Brown; Hunter Daniel; Matt Lanter; Kevin Osborn; Blake Peyrot; Paulo Rodriguez; John Stallings; Maurice Townsell; Seth Whalen
PRODUCTION COMPANY	Visual Frontier, Inc.
EXECUTIVE PRODUCERS	Stuart Krasnow; Denise Cramsey; Robert Horowitz
PRODUCER	Karen Gorman
DIRECTOR	Darin Ewing

Ordinary American men were recruited to compete for a chance to win a $100,000 contract with a top international modeling agency on *Manhunt: The Search for America's Most Gorgeous Male Model*. Each week, a wannabe model was eliminated, as the men competed in the boardroom, in nightclubs, on runways, and at a nude photo shoot. The twist was that real-life model Kevin Peake (who had also been a contestant on ABC's *Are You Hot?*) infiltrated the group and secretly reported back to the producers on who he thought should stay or go. Jon Jonsson won the grand-prize contract.

THE MANSION

GENRE	Competition (Makeover)
FIRST TELECAST	10/2/2004
LAST TELECAST	11/18/2004
NETWORK	TBS
EPISODE STYLE	Story Arc
TALENT	Mark L. Walberg (Host); Cassandra Dunson (Judge); Tom Stempfley (Judge); Tim Carter (Judge);
CAST	Dan (Winner); Amanda; Andy; Elvis; Jeff; Kim; Michele; Sando
PRODUCTION COMPANY	Evolution Film & Tape, Inc.
EXECUTIVE PRODUCERS	Kathleen French; Jill Garelick; Dean Minerd; Douglas Ross; Greg Stewart; Larry Struber
DIRECTORS	Pete Tartaglia; Kevin Bray; Adam N. Duke; Marty Graff

A historic Cincinnati, Ohio, mansion in need of major remodeling was the focus on this makeover competition. Each week, the competitors were given a budget and a rebuilding assignment to complete. Judges awarded cash prizes to them for their efforts. Viewers gave the winning vote to Dan, who earned keys to the mansion and a $50,000 bonus.

MARRIED BY AMERICA

GENRE	Docusoap (Celebrity)
FIRST TELECAST	3/3/2003
LAST TELECAST	4/14/2003
NETWORK	FOX
AIR TIMES	Monday, 9:00 p.m., Thursday, 9:00 p.m.

EPISODE STYLE	Story Arc
TALENT	Sean Valentine (Host); Jenn Berman (Expert— Marriage and Family Therapist); Ms. P (Expert); Don Elium (Expert—Marriage and Family Counselor)
CAST	Billie Jeanne and Tony (didn't get married); Jill and Kevin; Stephen and Denise (3rd eliminated); Jennifer and Xavier (2nd eliminated); Matt and Cortez (1st eliminated)
PRODUCTION COMPANIES	20th Century Fox; Rocket Science Laboratories
EXECUTIVE PRODUCERS	Chris Cowan; Jean-Michel Michenaud; Ted Haimes
CO-EXECUTIVE PRODUCER	Kathy Wetherell
DIRECTOR	Bob Levy

Five single men and women who had never met became engaged to be married by viewers playing matchmaker. The engaged couples moved into a house together and began planning their weddings. Viewers watched the couples do everything from selecting wedding attire and rehearsing the ceremony to holding their scandalous bachelor and bachelorette parties. Marriage experts evaluated the relationships as they viewed tapes from the house and eliminated couples each week if they were deemed incompatible. In the end, two couples remained: Billie Jeanne and Tony, and Jill and Kevin. A wedding was set up for each of them in the finale. Viewers voted for the couple they felt would be most likely to get married—and the couple who did had an opportunity to win a new house and $500,000. Jill and Kevin were the top vote-getters, but since they didn't get married, they didn't receive the prize. Tony also opted out of marrying Billie Jeanne, leaving her at the altar.

This was the first reality show to be fined by the FCC for indecency over an episode featuring pixilated strippers and a woman licking whipped cream off a man's nipple. FCC commissioners voted unanimously to fine each of the 169 FOX stations that aired the program $7,000, a fine totaling $1,183,000. FOX Broadcasting Company spokesperson Joe Earley said, "We disagree with the FCC's decision and believe the content was not indecent." Later, a blogger at buzzmachine.com reported that the

FCC had received 90 complaints, rather than the 159 they claimed. The complaints came from only 23 people, and all but two letters were virtually identical.

MASTER OF CHAMPIONS

GENRE	Competition
FIRST TELECAST	6/22/2006
LAST TELECAST	7/20/2006
NETWORK	ABC
AIR TIME	Thursday, 8:00 p.m.
EPISODE STYLE	Self-contained
TALENT	Chris Leary (Host); Lisa Dergan-Podsednik (Co-Host); Oksana Baiul (Judge); Steve Garvey (Judge); Jonny Moseley (Judge)
PRODUCTION COMPANIES	Nippon Television; Y27 Entertainment
EXECUTIVE PRODUCERS	Tim Crescenti; Yoshiro Yasuoka; Isao Zaitsu; Jonas Larsen; Anthony Ross
PRODUCERS	Anthony Fiorino; Sean M. Kelly
DIRECTOR	Michael Dimich

On each week of *Master of Champions,* six competitors with unique talents faced off to determine who was the best. Contestants participated in challenges such as the International Human Fireworks, Interpretive Pizza Tossing, Blindfolded Foot Archery, the Extreme Unicycle Obstacle Course, and Amazing Drift Driving. A panel of three judges, all professional sports champions, determined the winner. The series was based on the show *World Records,* by NTV in Japan.

MEET MISTER MOM

GENRE	Docucomedy
FIRST TELECAST	8/2/2005

LAST TELECAST	9/7/2005
NETWORK	NBC
AIR TIMES	Tuesday, 8:00 p.m.; Wednesday, 8:00 p.m.
EPISODE STYLE	Self-contained
PRODUCTION COMPANIES	Reveille LLC; Full Circle Entertainment; James Bruce Productions
CREATED BY	Kim Campoli
EXECUTIVE PRODUCERS	Ben Silverman; Robert Riesenberg; James Bruce
PRODUCER	Kenneth A. Carlson

On *Meet Mister Mom,* everyday dads were put to the test, when two families' mothers were sent away on a surprise vacation. The dads had to pick up the slack and play mom for the week, while also completing specific tasks, such as cooking a themed meal for surprise guests or organizing a backyard pool party. The moms watched the chaos via video, and in the end, one of the two families was declared the winner and received a cash prize for their victory.

MEET MY FOLKS

GENRE	Competition
FIRST TELECAST	7/22/2002
LAST TELECAST	8/25/2003
NETWORK	NBC
AIR TIMES	Monday, 10:00 p.m. (7/2002–8/2002); Wednesday, 8:00 p.m. (7/2002); Saturday, 8:00 p.m. (8/2002); Saturday, 10:00 p.m. (9/2002) (1/2003–2/2003); Monday, 9:30 p.m. (3/2003); Monday, 10:00 p.m. (6/2003–8/2003)
EPISODE STYLE	Self-contained
PRODUCTION COMPANIES	Nash Entertainment; Satin Productions; NBC Studios
EXECUTIVE PRODUCERS	Bruce Nash; Scott Satin

CO-EXECUTIVE PRODUCER	Andrew Jebb
PRODUCERS	Tim Scott; Aliyah Silverstein
CO-PRODUCER	Eric Waddell
DIRECTORS	Lauren Alvarez; Chris Donovan; C. B. Harding

Inspired by the 2000 film *Meet the Parents,* this competition followed three suitors dating the single grown child of two loving parents. Following a series of interviews, meetings with former sweethearts, and a lie detector examination, the parents chose which suitor won a date with their child.

MEET THE BARKERS

GENRE	Docudrama (Celebrity)
FIRST TELECAST	4/6/2005
LAST TELECAST	2/27/2006
NETWORK	MTV
EPISODE STYLE	Self-contained
CAST	Travis Barker; Shanna Moakler (Travis's wife); Landon Barker (Travis and Shanna's son); Atian De La Hoya (Shanna's daughter); Alabama Barker (Travis and Shanna's daughter)
PRODUCTION COMPANY	MTV Productions
EXECUTIVE PRODUCERS	Lois Curren; Rod Aissa; Jesse Ignja
DIRECTORS	Kelly Welsh; Katherine Brooks; Cameron Glendenning; Dana Klein

Opposites attracted and married on *Meet the Barkers,* the MTV series that starred newlyweds Travis Barker, the mohawk-wearing, tattooed drummer from Blink 182, and his bride, former Miss USA, actress Shanna Moakler. In the series, the couple learned to balance partying, parenthood, and careers.

In the second season, Travis and Shannon spent most of their time preparing for the arrival of their new baby daughter, Alabama, who was born in the finale. In August of 2006, Travis filed for divorce and the couple split.

MEET THE MARKS

GENRE	Docucomedy
FIRST TELECAST	7/17/2002
LAST TELECAST	7/31/2002
NETWORK	FOX
AIR TIME	Wednesday, 8:30 p.m.
EPISODE STYLE	Self-contained
TALENT	Joe O'Connor (Joe Marks): Cathy Shambley (Cathy Marks); Patrick Cavanaugh (Patrick Marks); Kaitlin Olson (Kaitlin Marks); Tara Nulty (Tara)
PRODUCTION COMPANY	Vin Di Bona Productions
EXECUTIVE PRODUCER	Vin Di Bona
CO-EXECUTIVE PRODUCER	Jeff Eastin
CO-PRODUCERS	Erik Fleming; Gerry Cohen
DIRECTOR	Gerry Cohen

Meet the Marks was a hybrid sitcom and reality show. The sitcom element featured the Marks family, portrayed by actors living in a house. The reality element involved real people who visited the house not knowing that the family members were actually actors. Some of the unsuspecting victims included a tutor who was asked to do a commercial with Ed McMahon and a clown who was asked to do a striptease for the Markses' daughter.

MERGE

GENRE	Docudrama
FIRST TELECAST	10/3/2003

NETWORK	Lifetime
EPISODE STYLE	Self-contained
TALENT	Lisa Rinna (Host); Bobby Trendy (Decorator); Jennifer Farrell (Decorator); John Mack (Decorator); Ronnie Kerr (Carpenter); Jonathan Redford (Carpenter)
PRODUCTION COMPANY	Dalaklis-McKeown Entertainment
EXECUTIVE PRODUCERS	Chuck Dalaklis; Theresa McKeown
CO-EXECUTIVE PRODUCER	Robert Asher
PRODUCERS	Andrew Greenberger; Kathy Landsberg; Alison Martino; Fred Villari
DIRECTORS	Lee Abbott; Christopher Bavelles; Jeff Fisher; Andrew Greenberger; Fred Villari

Merge featured a newly married couple as they moved into their new home. Host Lisa Rinna and a team of decorators helped them figure out which of their individual belongings they would keep and which they would trash. The "merge" took place while the newlyweds went on their honeymoon.

THE MESSENGERS

GENRE	Competition
FIRST TELECAST	7/23/2006
LAST TELECAST	8/27/2006
NETWORK	TLC
EPISODE STYLE	Story Arc
TALENT	Tim Bader (Host); Richard Greene (Judge); Robert V. Schuller (Judge)
CAST	Daneea Badio (Winner); Angelica Osborne (Runner-up); Cornelious Flowers (Runner-up); Darryl Van Leer (8th eliminated); Iman Mafi (7th eliminated); Robert Rutherford

(5th eliminated); Karen Michel (4th eliminated);
Zahava Zaidoff (3rd eliminated); Kent Healy
(2nd eliminated); Floyd Nolan (1st eliminated)

PRODUCTION COMPANY	Original Productions
EXECUTIVE PRODUCERS	Thom Beers; Elizabeth Browde
PRODUCER	Deboriah Dupree

This competition series set out to find America's next great inspirational speaker. At the conclusion of each episode, one person was eliminated by the studio audience's vote. The winner, Daneea Badio, received a publishing deal and was given the chance to host her own TLC television special.

MILLION DOLLAR LISTING

GENRE	Docusoap
FIRST TELECAST	8/29/2006
LAST TELECAST	10/4/2006
NETWORK	Bravo
EPISODE STYLE	Self-contained
CAST	Chris Cortazzo; Michael Wegmann; Shannon McLeod; Scotty Brown; Carol Bird; Lydia Simon; Madison Hildebrand; Ray Schuldenfrei; Dia Schuldenfrei; Chase Campen
PRODUCTION COMPANY	World of Wonder
EXECUTIVE PRODUCERS	Fenton Bailey; Randy Barbato
PRODUCER	Michaline Babich

Million Dollar Listing followed the trials and tribulations of two real estate companies. Each episode showcased a real estate listing from Hollywood and one from Malibu, from the beginning of the selling process and moving toward the coveted close. The show featured the ups and downs of real estate involving a dozen of California's biggest and best homes as they were put on the housing market.

MINDING THE STORE

GENRE	Docucomedy (Celebrity)
FIRST TELECAST	7/10/2005
LAST TELECAST	9/9/2005
NETWORK	TBS
EPISODE STYLE	Story Arc
CAST	Pauly Shore; Mitzi Shore (Pauly's mother); Sammy Shore (Pauly's father); Dean Gelber (Pauly's best friend/Manager of The Comedy Store); Tommy Morris (Talent Booker); Marlon Hernandez (Handyman/Sidekick); Sara Wasserman (Pauly's Personal Assistant); Marc Hatchell (Pauly's friend)
PRODUCTION COMPANIES	Arnold Shapiro & Allison Grodner Productions; Bayonne Entertainment
EXECUTIVE PRODUCERS	Allison Grodner; Rob Lee; Arnold Shapiro

The world-famous Comedy Store on Sunset Strip was the setting for *Minding the Store,* which followed former MTV star Pauly Shore as he revamped both his own image and that of the comedy club founded by his parents.

MIRACLE WORKERS

GENRE	Docusoap
FIRST TELECAST	3/6/2006
LAST TELECAST	4/3/2006
NETWORK	ABC
AIR TIME	Monday, 8:00 p.m.
EPISODE STYLE	Self-contained
TALENT	Redmond Burke (Chief of Pediatric Cardiovascular

Surgery); Billy Cohn (Director of Minimally
Invasive Surgical Technology); Janna Bullock
(Registered Nurse); Tamara Houston (Registered
Nurse)

PRODUCTION COMPANIES	Dream Works Television; Renegade 83 Entertainment
EXECUTIVE PRODUCERS	Justin Falvey; Darryl Frank; David Garfinkle; Jay Renfroe
PRODUCERS	Jonathan Cornick; Dennis Principe, Jr.
DIRECTORS	Jim Hunziker; Gary Shaffer

Each episode of *Miracle Workers* followed two stories of ordinary people who didn't have access to the medical procedures that could forever change their lives. A prominent team of doctors and specialists tackled these seemingly overwhelming medical problems. Patients' lives changed as the professionals used modern medical technology to heal those most in need. The medical team restored not only the patients' health, but also their hope in living a full life.

MISS SEVENTEEN

GENRE	Competition (Job)
FIRST TELECAST	10/17/2005
LAST TELECAST	12/19/2005
NETWORK	MTV
EPISODE STYLE	Story Arc
CAST	Atoosa Rubinstein (Host)
TALENT	Jennifer Steele (Winner); Jessica (Runner-up); Sasha; Jill; Julie; Connie; Savannah; Briann; Leah; Amber; Ashley; Brittney; Caroline; Kristen; Maria; Nicole; Skylar
PRODUCTION COMPANY	MTV Productions
EXECUTIVE PRODUCER	Greg Johnston

PRODUCER Jordan Doran

DIRECTORS Kasey Barrett; Lisa Caruso; Alan Finn; Shannon Fitzgerald

Seventeen ambitious American girls moved to New York City to compete in weekly character-testing and building challenges under the watchful eye of *Seventeen* magazine editor-in-chief, Atoosa Rubenstein. Grand-prize winner Jennifer Steele received a college scholarship and a paid internship at *Seventeen*.

MISSION: MAN BAND

GENRE Docusoap

FIRST TELECAST 8/6/2007

LAST TELECAST 9/10/2007

NETWORK VH1

EPISODE STYLE Story Arc

CAST Bryan Abrams; David Bermejo; Bryan Michael Cox; Rich Cronin; Matt Downham; Chris Kirkpatrick; Kristina Knowles; Katies McNeil; Jeff Timmons

PRODUCTION COMPANIES Kandokids Films; Tijuana Entertainment

EXECUTIVE PRODUCERS John Foy; Tony Harding; Kennedy; Troy Searer

PRODUCERS Peter Herschko; Andrea Murphy; Scott Zabielski

DIRECTOR Tony Croll

On *Mission: Man Band,* a supergroup of former boy band members from 'N Sync, 98 Degrees, LFO, and Color Me Badd was formed. For one month, the new group, Sureshot, tried to recapture the fame they enjoyed in their heyday. They performed at an Orlando Magic halftime show in January 2007 and were booed by the crowd.

MODEL CITIZENS

GENRE	Docudrama (Makeover)
FIRST TELECAST	10/4/2004
LAST TELECAST	12/27/2004
NETWORK	PAX
AIR TIME	Monday, 8:00 p.m.
EPISODE STYLE	Self-contained
TALENT	Larissa Meek (Host)
PRODUCTION COMPANY	First Television
EXECUTIVE PRODUCERS	Bradley Anderson; Mack Anderson
PRODUCER	Jerry Decker
DIRECTORS	Liz Cook; Camie Holmes

Shot on location in Chicago, Los Angeles, San Diego, and New Hampshire, this make-over series followed successful male and female models as they performed manual labor to beautify local communities in need.

A MODEL LIFE
WITH PETRA NEMCOVA

GENRE	Docusoap
FIRST TELECAST	7/13/2007
NETWORK	TLC
EPISODE STYLE	Story Arc
CAST	Petra Nemcova; Abigail; Angelika; Beatrice; Lucia; Michelle; Valeria
PRODUCTION COMPANIES	25/7 Productions; The Mattola Company
EXECUTIVE PRODUCERS	Jeb Brein; Dave Broome; Sara Kozak; Tommy Mattola
PRODUCER	Matt Westmore

On *A Model Life with Petra Nemcova,* Czech supermodel Nemcova was host and mentor to six girls from different countries, helping them understand what it took to be a model. Nemcova gave them lessons in everything from nutrition to dealing with difficult photographers. The girls were evaluated by NEXT Modeling, which determined who would receive contracts with the agency.

THE MOLE

GENRE	Competition
FIRST TELECAST	1/9/2001
NETWORK	ABC
AIR TIMES	Tuesday, 8:00 p.m. (1/2001–2/2001); Wednesday, 8:00 p.m. (2/2001); Friday, 8:00 p.m. (9/2001–10/2001); Tuesday, 9:00 p.m. (5/2002–8/2002)
EPISODE STYLE	Story Arc
TALENT	Anderson Cooper (Host)

CAST

Season 1	Steven Cowles (Winner); Kathryn Price (The Mole); Manuel Herrera; Afi Ekulona; Wendi Wendt; Henry Wentz; Jennifer Biondi; Kate Pahls; Charlie McGown; Jim Morrison
Season 2	Dorothy Hui (Winner); Bill McDaniel (The Mole); Ali Gorman; Heather Campbell; Katie Mills; Patrick Guilfoyle; Lisa Noller; Darwin Conner; Michael "Bribs" Brbiesca; Rob Nelson; Myra Brown; Bob Paulhus; Elavia Bello; Al Spielmen
PRODUCTION COMPANY	Stone-Stanley Productions
CREATED BY	Bart De Pauw; Michiel Evlieger; Tom Lenaerts; Michel Vanhove
EXECUTIVE PRODUCERS	Rick Tubbax; Clay Newbill; David G. Stanley; Scott Stone

PRODUCERS Doug DeLuca; Sue Langham
DIRECTORS Craig Borders; Paul Morzella

Based on a Belgian show, *The Mole* involved a group of players, one of whom was secretly working with the show's producers as a spy. Players endured mental and physical challenges to get clues as to who was "the mole" and to add money to the grand prize. In each episode, the player scoring the lowest on a computerized exam about The Mole's identity was "executed" and had to leave the game. The contestant scoring the highest on the final exam won the grand prize.

MONSTER GARAGE

GENRE	Docudrama (Makeover)
FIRST TELECAST	6/23/2002
NETWORK	TLC
EPISODE STYLE	Self-contained
TALENT	Jesse James (Host); Tom Prewitt (Painter)
EXECUTIVE PRODUCERS	Thom Beers; Tracy Green
PRODUCERS	Joseph Mulcrone; Evan Aaronson; Jeff Conroyl; Fred Golding; Andrew Greenberger; Jesse James; Hildie Katibah; Hugh King; Larry Law; Brian Lovett
DIRECTOR	Dylan O'Brien

Hosted by outlaw biker Jesse James, whose West Coast Choppers was first spotlighted on the Discovery Channel series *Motorcycle Mania*, *Monster Garage* captured the imagination of both gearheads and non–car enthusiasts alike as vehicle building, modifying, and fabrication were taken to a new level. When a car was successfully transformed into a showcase vehicle, the team won a tool chest with $3,400 worth of Mac tools. A few of the customized vehicles included garbage trucks, street sweepers, and cars that made beer, popped wheelies, shook trees, and even flew.

MONSTER HOUSE

GENRE	Competition (Makeover)
FIRST TELECAST	6/2/2003
LAST TELECAST	8/19/2005
NETWORK	Discovery
AIR TIME	Friday, 8:00 p.m.
EPISODE STYLE	Self-contained
TALENT	Steve Watson (Host); Tara Stephenson (Decorator)
EXECUTIVE PRODUCERS	Thom Beers; Scott Hallock; Kevin Healey
PRODUCERS	Tom Bellos; David Burris; Jeanne Dresp; Jennifer Herschberg; Brian Knappmiller; Jeff Kuntz; Dean Ollins; Chris Peeler; Aron T. Plucinski
DIRECTORS	Tom Bellos; Wendy Calhoun; Paul Harrison; Clarie Scanlon; Rob Worsoff

A five-member team of builders had five days to transform a simple home into a themed residence on *Monster House*. If the crew got the job done, they won a toolbox filled with expensive power tools. Themes the builders created included race car, Las Vegas, old English, hacienda, medieval castle, the seventies, "Under the Sea," Paris, and a dog mansion.

MOTORMOUTH

GENRE	Competition (Talent)
FIRST TELECAST	10/26/2004
NETWORK	VH1
EPISODE STYLE	Self-contained
TALENT	Zane Lamprey (Host—pilot episode)
EXECUTIVE PRODUCERS	Toni Gallagher; Paul Hardy; Russell Heldt
PRODUCER	Damla Dogan
DIRECTORS	Paul Hardy; James Flint

Played for laughs and shot in more than forty cities around the United States, this hidden camera series had friends set up friends, capturing unsuspecting participants as they sang along to a car radio.

MR. PERSONALITY

GENRE	Competition (Dating)
FIRST TELECAST	4/1/2003
LAST TELECAST	5/19/2003
NETWORK	FOX
AIR TIME	Monday, 9:00 p.m.
EPISODE STYLE	Story Arc
TALENT	Monica Lewinsky (Host)
CAST	Hayley Arp (The Bachelorette); Will Dyck (Winner); Chris Berg (Runner-up); Brian Caroliss; Joseph Vincent; Trevor Olsen; Ted Burker; Pete Chen; Michael Checkoleigh; Noe Garza; Michael Limeau; Tim Plant; Bill Mason; Jim; Stan; Robert Poden; Jonny Marquez; Aaron Brady; Robert Fedariqui; Richard Collins
PRODUCTION COMPANIES	Nash Entertainment; The G Group
CREATED BY	Bruce Nash; Robert Kosberg
PRODUCER	Brian Gadinsky
DIRECTOR	Adam Briles

This dating/elimination reality series from Bruce Nash (*Meet My Folks, Who Wants to Marry My Dad?*) asked the age-old question: Do looks really matter? Bachelorette Hayley Arp was introduced to twenty male suitors who wore masks to hide their appearance. Hayley didn't see her prospective date's face until after she'd made her final selection. In the end, Hayley chose Will Dyck. The show was hosted by Monica Lewinsky.

MR. ROMANCE

GENRE	Competition (Talent)
FIRST TELECAST	3/14/2005
LAST TELECAST	4/18/2005
NETWORK	Oxygen
EPISODE STYLE	Story Arc
TALENT	Fabio (Host)
CAST	Randy Ritchwood (Winner); Bruce Blauer; Justin Dryer; Hakan Emden; Mark Mast; Tony Catanzaro; Charles Gladish; Adam Hatley; Scott Alexander; Tom Jay Jones; Chris Gonzalez; Andrew Larsen
CREATED BY	Gene Simmons
EXECUTIVE PRODUCERS	Leslie Greif; Jude Weng
CO-EXECUTIVE PRODUCER	Fernando Mills
PRODUCERS	Julie Frankell; Mimi Freedman; Cindy Guyer
DIRECTOR	Jude Weng

This pageant-style series featured twelve handsome men competing for $50,000 and the opportunity to appear on the cover of a Harlequin romance novel. The final judging by a panel of romance specialists and celebrity judges was done in front of an all-female live audience. The winner was Randy Ritchwood.

MTV'S BURNED

GENRE	Docudrama (Hoax)
FIRST TELECAST	3/29/2003
NETWORK	MTV
EPISODE STYLE	Self-contained
TALENT	Rachel Sterling (Host)
PRODUCTION COMPANIES	MTV Networks; Remote Productions

CREATED BY Jack Merrick; Grant Mitchell; Colman Dekay
EXECUTIVE PRODUCERS Damon Harman; John J. Hermansen;
Sam Sokolow
DIRECTOR Damon Harman

Using hidden cameras, girls on spring break caught unsuspecting flirtatious guys on *MTV's Burned*. The guys were later invited back to the MTV house, where everyone watched the footage.

MTV'S FANATIC

GENRE Docudrama (Celebrity)
FIRST TELECAST 7/6/1998
NETWORK MTV
EPISODE STYLE Self-contained
PRODUCER Jacqueline Beaudette
DIRECTORS Jacqueline Beaudette; Jason A. Carbone;
Chad Greulach; Mike Nichols; Joel K. Rodgers;
Ben Samek

Viewers got a chance to meet their idols on *MTV's FANatic*. The unsuspecting fan was ambushed by the *FANatic* crew and taken away to meet their idol. Celebrities who met their diehard fans included Tara Lipinski, Van Halen, and Stevie Nicks.

MTV'S LITTLE TALENT SHOW

GENRE Competition (Talent)
FIRST TELECAST 9/18/2006
LAST TELECAST 10/5/2006
NETWORK MTV
EPISODE STYLE Self-contained

CAST	Laurie Ann Gibson (Judge); Kimberley Locke (Judge); Bryan Dattilo (Judge); Matt Cedeno (Judge); Sean Kanan (Judge)
PRODUCTION COMPANY	MTV Productions
EXECUTIVE PRODUCER	Michael Canter
PRODUCER	Todd "Spider" Chambers

On each episode of *MTV's Little Talent Show,* seven performers sang, danced, and acted in three rounds of competition. A rotating panel of celebrity judges included Constantine Maroulis and Kimberly Locke of *American Idol.* The judges evaluated the performances and picked two contestants to compete in the final "Triple Threat Round." Performers had to combine their singing, dancing, and acting skills, and the winner earned $500 and the title of that day's most talented performer.

MTV'S THE 70S HOUSE

GENRE	Competition (Talent)
FIRST TELECAST	7/5/2005
LAST TELECAST	9/6/2005
NETWORK	MTV
EPISODE STYLE	Story Arc
TALENT	Bill Dwyer (Burt Van Styles); Natasha Leggero (Dawn); Aaron Lee (Voice of Oscar)
CAST	Andrew (winner); Joey Mendicino (Runner-up); Peter Asencio; Geo; Ashley; Hailey; Howard; Lee; Linda Khristine; Sarah Bray; Corey Hartwyk; Ruben
PRODUCTION COMPANY	Superdelicious
CREATED BY	Aaron Lee
EXECUTIVE PRODUCERS	Joanna Vernetti; Cara Tapper; Adam Cohen
CO-EXECUTIVE PRODUCER	Aaron Lee
CO-PRODUCERS	Rich Kim; Robert Sizemore
DIRECTOR	Robert Sizemore

This social experiment series put twelve modern-day young adults into a house straight out of the 1970s. The residents were forced to wear the clothes and listen to the music of the seventies, watch black-and-white television, and learn to dial a rotary phone, all while facing challenges, such as learning how to disco. At the end of each episode, the two residents deemed "not seventies enough" faced off in a seventies-themed elimination round in which they played Operation or competed in a game such as *The $10,000 Pyramid.* Guiding them along their groovy journey were polyester-clad game show host Burt Van Styles; swinging seventies housewife Dawn; and Oscar, the mysterious disembodied voice that doled out the residents' challenges each week. Andrew was victorious, winning a prize package including a 2005 Volkswagen Beetle and an Apple iPod Photo.

MURDER

GENRE	Competition
FIRST TELECAST	7/31/2007
NETWORK	Spike
EPISODE STYLE	Self-contained
CAST	Tommy Le Noir (Host); Dr. Howard Oliver
PRODUCTION COMPANY	Bunim-Murray Productions
EXECUTIVE PRODUCERS	Jonathan Murray; Kevin Lee
PRODUCERS	Ben Salter; Nara Walker; Kevin Mendonca

On *Murder,* two teams of three investigators faced off to correctly solve cases of cold-blooded homicides in the United States.

MURDER IN SMALL TOWN X

GENRE	Competition
FIRST TELECAST	7/24/2001
LAST TELECAST	9/4/2001
NETWORK	FOX

AIR TIME	Tuesday, 9:00 p.m.
EPISODE STYLE	Story Arc
TALENT	Gary Fredo (Host/Lead Investigator); Pat Battistini (Ferry Owner G. D. Thibodeaux); Heather Campbell (Diner Owner Samantha Larabee); Don Chastain (General Hayden De Beck); Joy Claussen (Postmistress Leita Rose-Blodgett); Jennifer Dibert (Merchant Mary Elizabeth); Caitlin Keats (Prudence Connor); Shishir Kurup (X-Ray the Cabdriver); Jennifer Tung (Attorney Deanna Harris); George Hall (C. R. Flint); Jack McCabe (Nate Flint); Christopher Liam Moore (Reporter Frank Kovick); Sarah Morris (Abigail "Abby" Flint); Moira Walley (Carmen Flint); Cory Pendergast (Jimmy Tinker); Damara Reilly (Lillian "Lil" Tinker); Terence Paul Winter (Police Chief Dudley Duncan); Cathy Shambley (Dr. Neva Bowden); Kent George (Reverend Rusty Crandall); Tom Stechschulte (Businessman William Lambert); Tim Walkoe (Mayor Emerson Bowden); Barney Martin (Gonzo); Ronnie Warner (Sunset Club Owner Drew Chambers); Sam Witwer (First Mate Moe Zaleski); William L. Nelson (Lodge Owner Bill Thompson); Sarah Slean (Sunset Club Performer); Andrea Clark (Tate Kovich); Randy Clark (Bouncer 1); Steve Mellor (Bradford Ferris); William Nelson (Hotel Manager); Roger Segien (Bouncer 2)
CAST	Angel Juarbe, Jr. (Winner); Kristen Kirchner; Katie Kloecker; Lindsey Labrum; Andrew Landan; Brian Porvin; Alan Frye; Stacey Carmona; Shirley King; Jeff Monroe
EXECUTIVE PRODUCERS	George Verschoor; Gordon Cassidy; Robert Fisher, Jr.
PRODUCER	Page Feldman

DIRECTORS Gary Auerbach; Todd Darling; Mark Miks; David Parks; Gary Pennington; Craig Spirko; George Verschoor

On *Murder in Small Town X,* improvisational actors played suspects and witnesses as contestants tried to solve a fictional murder for a grand prize of $250,000 and a 2002 Jeep Liberty Sport. The winner, Angel Juarbe, Jr., a New York City firefighter, perished in the World Trade Center collapse just one week after the final episode aired.

MUSIC BEHIND BARS

GENRE	Docudrama
FIRST TELECAST	10/18/2002
NETWORK	VH1
EPISODE STYLE	Self-contained
TALENT	Dylan McDermott (Host)
PRODUCTION COMPANY	Arnold Shapiro & Allison Grodner Productions
EXECUTIVE PRODUCERS	Arnold Shapiro; Allison Grodner
CO-EXECUTIVE PRODUCERS	Jay Blumenfield; Anthony Marsh
PRODUCERS	Nicole Solomon; Seth Cohen

The gritty *Music Behind Bars* features bands that form within prison walls at penitentiaries around the country. Each episode focuses on a specific band and a key event affecting them, such as a band member leaving because of parole, or the group organizing a concert. In addition to following the band, the show delves into the members' lives, from how they wound up in prison, to how music has changed their lives.

MY BARE LADY

GENRE	Docusoap
FIRST TELECAST	12/7/2006
NETWORK	Fox Reality Channel
EPISODE STYLE	Story Arc
TALENT	Sasha Knox; Nautica Thorne; Chanel St. James; Kirsten Price; Christopher Biggins (Coach); Jeff Harding (Narrator)
PRODUCTION COMPANY	Zig Zag Productions
EXECUTIVE PRODUCERS	Danny Fenton; Jes Wilkins; Bob Boden
PRODUCERS	David P. Beitchman; Dave Winnan
DIRECTOR	Dave Winnan

This outrageous Fox Reality Channel original asked the question: Can adult film stars make it in the world of legitimate theater?

My Bare Lady began with one of the most unique auditions in reality television history. Auditioning in front of casting directors, porn star after porn star was asked not only to read lines from *Romeo and Juliet* but also to fake an orgasm for the panel. The results were often hilarious, sometimes embarrassing, but always riveting.

Eventually, four of the adult film stars were selected by a British casting director and sent to the United Kingdom, where they attended a professional acting school in London. The four also lived together in a local flat. The show revealed all as the four went through rigorous training and rehearsals while preparing for a showcase at the Garrick Theatre, in London's famed West End district. *My Bare Lady* captured the drama on and offstage, even while romance bloomed as Sasha grew close with one of the Romeos in her class.

In the series' exciting climax, things came to a head with the showcase. The four performed a musical number and acting scenes, but it was Kirsten who landed the coveted role of Juliet in the *Romeo and Juliet* scene that served as the centerpiece of the presentation.

The series proved to be a wild success, especially on the Internet, as millions downloaded one clip of Sasha's unique lap dance take on *Romeo and Juliet*.

MY BIG FAT OBNOXIOUS BOSS

GENRE	Competition (Hoax)
FIRST TELECAST	11/7/2004
LAST TELECAST	12/12/2004
NETWORK	FOX
AIR TIME	Sunday, 9:00 p.m.
EPISODE STYLE	Story Arc
TALENT	William August (Mr. N. Paul Todd); Jamie Denbo (Jamie Samuels, Executive Vice President); Shannon Hall (Executive Assistant); David Jahn (David Hickman, COO); Kent Sublette (Kent Todd, the boss's son); Tamara Clatterbuck (Lynn Todd); Danielle Schneider (Danielle Todd); Ken August (Kent Todd)
CAST	Annette Dziamba (Winner); Michael Gregorio (Runner-up); Damian Dolyniuk (eliminated in Episode 9); Kerry McCloskey (eliminated in Episode 8); David Harper (eliminated in Episode 8); Douglas Dennard (eliminated in Episode 7); Whitney (eliminated in Episode 6); Robert Hospidor (eliminated in Episode 5); Tonia (eliminated in Episode 4); Elli Frank (eliminated in Episode 3); Christy (eliminated in Episode 2); Daniel (eliminated in Episode 1)
PRODUCTION COMPANIES	Rocket Science Laboratories; 20th Century Fox Television
EXECUTIVE PRODUCERS	Chris Cowan; Jean-Michel Michenaud
PRODUCERS	Alan Weider; Steve Sobel

In this parody of *The Apprentice*, twelve competitors humiliated and embarrassed themselves hoping to land a dream job. The twist was that it was all a hoax: no job existed. Fictional boss Mr. N. Paul Todd (an anagram for "Donald Trump") divided the competitors into two teams and gave them impossible-to-understand tasks. Making the actual decision of who stayed in the game was a monkey spinning a wheel. After being let in on the joke, winner Annette Dziamba was awarded $350,000.

MY BIG FAT OBNOXIOUS FIANCE

GENRE	Docucomedy (Hoax)
FIRST TELECAST	1/19/2004
LAST TELECAST	2/23/2004
NETWORK	FOX
AIR TIME	Monday, 9:00 p.m.
EPISODE STYLE	Story Arc
TALENT	Claudio Fiolco (Host); Steven Bailey (Steve Williams—the Groom); Richard Kuhlman (Richard Williams); Laura Henry (Laura Williams); Kristina Hayes (Kristina Williams); James Grace (Jimmy Haize)
CAST	Randi Coy (The Bride); Bruce Coy (Randi's father); Catherine Coy (Randi's mom); Melanie Coy (Randi's sister); Patrick Coy (Randi's brother); Bobby Coy (Randi's brother)
PRODUCTION COMPANY	Rocket Science Laboratories
EXECUTIVE PRODUCERS	Chris Cowan; Jean-Michel Michenaud
CO-EXECUTIVE PRODUCER	Ray Giuliani
PRODUCER	Joel K. Rodgers
CO-PRODUCERS	Alan Wieder; Steve Sobel
DIRECTOR	Bryan O'Donnell

From the makers of *Joe Millionaire*, *My Big Fat Obnoxious Fiance* fooled Arizona schoolteacher Randi Coy into thinking she was on a reality show in which she and another "contestant," Steve Williams, had to fool their families into thinking they had become engaged. The bigger twist was that Steve Williams was actually Steven Bailey, an actor hired by the producers to push Randi and her family's buttons.

In Episode 1, Randi was told that she would have to convince her family that she was in love with Steve and would be getting married to him in twelve days. What she didn't know was that Steve was actually an actor paid to be as annoying as possible.

In Episode 2, Steve and Randi visited a wedding planner, and tried on wedding clothes. The next day Randi gave Steve a list of things he needed to change, and they visited a sex therapist.

In Episode 3, Randi's best friend, Anna, met Steve. Randi tried to do yoga with Steve. Then he got a makeover. Steve introduced Randi to his family, played by actors, and announced that they were engaged.

In Episode 4, Randi announced to her family that she and Steve were engaged to be married in three days.

In Episode 5, Randi attempted to persuade her family to come to the wedding. While Randi and her mother visited the wedding planner, Steve was fitted for his tux.

In the series finale, it rained on the wedding day. As the Coy family prepared for the ceremony, Randi's sister, Melanie, was very upset with Randi. People began arriving for the wedding. Patrick and Bobby wore kilts because of the Coys' Irish heritage. All of Randi's family attended, and no one objected. When the time came for Steve to say, "I do," he said he couldn't, and told everyone that it was not a real wedding. He explained to them what the show was about, then revealed that he and his family were actually actors. He gave a speech about the Coys' love for one another and gave them checks: $500,000 for Randi, and $500,000 for the rest of her family. Randi's family forgave her, and they watched a clip from when Randi first met Steve.

MY FAIR BRADY

GENRE	Docucomedy (Celebrity)
FIRST TELECAST	09/11/2005
NETWORK	VH1
EPISODE STYLE	Story Arc
CAST	Christopher Knight (Himself); Adrianne Curry (Herself); Florence Henderson (Herself)
PRODUCTION COMPANIES	Mindless Entertainment; 51 Pictures; VH1 Productions
CREATED BY	Mark Cronin; Cris Abrego

EXECUTIVE PRODUCERS	Mark Cronin; Cris Abrego; Jeff Olde; Jill Modabber
CO-EXECUTIVE PRODUCERS	Ben Samek; Jacquie Dincauze
PRODUCERS	Chris Brewster; Christopher Knight
DIRECTORS	Zach Kozek; Robert Sizemore

This spin-off from *The Surreal Life,* featured the blossoming relationship between *Brady Bunch* actor Christopher Knight and *America's Next Top Model* winner Adrianne Curry, twenty-five years Knight's junior. The couple moved in together, and at the end of Season 1, Chris asked Adrianne to marry him.

The second season, subtitled *We're Getting Married,* focused on the couple's preparations for their wedding day, which occurred in the final episode.

MY LIFE AS A SITCOM

GENRE	Competition (Talent)
FIRST TELECAST	1/20/2003
NETWORK	ABC Family
EPISODE STYLE	Story Arc
TALENT	Dave Coulier (Judge); David Faustino (Judge); Maureen McCormick (Judge)
CAST	Zaccagnino Family (Winner); Mozian Family; Almeida-Miller Family; Lucas Family; Sampson Family; Fontaine Family; Mac-Gregor Gordon Family; Bollmann Family
PRODUCTION COMPANY	Nash Entertainment
CREATED BY	Bruce Nash; Jonathan Prince
EXECUTIVE PRODUCERS	Bruce Nash; Michael Canter; Harlan Freedman; Jeff Krask; David Perler
PRODUCERS	Rachel Powell; Pamela Lane; Frank Murgia
DIRECTORS	Darren Ewing; James Flint

My Life as a Sitcom searched America to find everyday people living as the quintessential sitcom family. The contestants were narrowed to eight finalists, with the Zaccagnino family winning the series and the opportunity to tape a sitcom pilot based on their lives.

MY OWN

GENRE	Competition (Dating)
FIRST TELECAST	9/1/2005
NETWORK	MTV
EPISODE STYLE	Self-contained
PRODUCTION COMPANY	Toy Plane Industries
EXECUTIVE PRODUCER	Billy Rainey
PRODUCERS	Sharon Lord; Michele Barnwell; Katherine Brooks; Jen Friesen
DIRECTOR	Gary Shaffer

On *My Own,* a celebrity-obsessed single person met a group of six contestants resembling that celebrity. The contestants competed to win a date with the fan. After several rounds of competition, including a live singing performance, the contestant most like the celebrity won the date with the fan.

MY SUPER SWEET 16

GENRE	Competition (Talent)
FIRST TELECAST	1/1/2005
NETWORK	MTV
EPISODE STYLE	Self-contained
PRODUCERS	Ira Fields; Tara Higgins; Azon Juan
DIRECTOR	Azon Juan

My Super Sweet 16 features fifteen-year-old girls from affluent families as they plan their sweet-sixteen birthday parties. Drama and excitement surround each girl's party, as guests are eager to see if the birthday girl's dream party will come off successfully.

NANNY 911

GENRE	Docudrama
FIRST TELECAST	11/3/2004
LAST TELECAST	2/23/2007
NETWORK	FOX
AIR TIMES	Wednesday, 9:00 p.m. (11/2004–1/2005); Monday, 8:00 p.m. (3/2005–7/2005); Wednesday, 9:00 p.m. (9/2005–10/2005); Monday, 9:00 p.m. (12/2005); Wednesday, 9:00 p.m. (1/2006); Friday, 8:00 p.m. (3/2006); Friday, 8:00 p.m. (9/2006–2/2007)
EPISODE STYLE	Self-contained
TALENT	Fraser Brown (The Butler); Deborah Carroll (Nanny Deb); Stella Reid (Nanny Stella); Yvonne Shove (Nanny Yvonne); Lillian Sperling (Nanny Lillian)
PRODUCTION COMPANY	Granada Entertainment USA
EXECUTIVE PRODUCER	Paul Jackson
PRODUCER	Jack Walworth

DIRECTORS Stacey Travis; Suzanne Ali; Michaline Babich; Karyn Benkendorfer; Richard Hall; Tim Eagan; Michael E. Gretza; Sue Kolinsky; Tarin Laughlin; Thomas Loureiro; Gerry McKean; Michael Rotman; Meg Ruggiero; Jamie Schutz; Michael Shevloff; Bruce Toms

Each episode of *Nanny 911* featured a family with child-rearing problems. A live-in nanny came to the family's rescue, teaching the parents and the children effective ways to avoid temper tantrums and adopt proper table manners. The show ended with hugs all around, and the nanny left the family having corrected the problems.

NASHVILLE STAR

GENRE Competition (Talent)
FIRST TELECAST 3/8/2003
NETWORK USA
EPISODE STYLE Story Arc
TALENT Wynonna (Host—Season 4), Cowboy Troy (Co-Host—Season 4); LeAnn Rimes (Host—Season 3); Nancy O'Dell (Host—Seasons 1 and 2); Bret Michaels (Judge—Season 3); Phil Vassar (Judge—Season 3): Anastasia Brown (Judge—Season 3); Billy Greenwood (Judge—Season 2); Brett Warren (Judge—Season 2); Brad Warren (Judge—Season 2); Robert Oermann (Judge—Season 1); Tracy Gershon (Judge—Seasons 1 and 2); Charlie Robinson (Judge—Season 1)

CAST

Season 1 Buddy Jewell (Winner); John Arthur Martinez (Runner-up); Miranda Lambert (2nd Runner-up);

Brandi Gibson (9th eliminated); Brandon Silveira (8th eliminated); Amy Chappell (7th eliminated); Jamey Garner (6th eliminated); Prentiss Varnon (5th eliminated); Travis Howard (4th eliminated); Tasha Valentine (3rd eliminated); Kristen Kissling (2nd eliminated); Anne Louise Blythe (1st eliminated)

Season 2 Brad Cotter (Winner): George Canyon (Runner-up); Matt Lindahl (9th eliminated); Lance Miller (8th eliminated); Jennifer Hicks (7th eliminated); Brent Keith (6th eliminated); Marty Slayton (5th eliminated); Sheila Marshall (4th eliminated); Mal Rogers (3rd eliminated); Stacy Michelle (2nd eliminated); Gregory DeLang (1st eliminated)

Season 3 Erika Jo (Winner); Jason Meadows (Runner-up); Jody Evans (2nd Runner-up); Jayron Weaver (7th eliminated); Justin David (6th eliminated); Jenny Farrell (5th eliminated); Tamika Tyler (4th eliminated); Casey Simpson (3rd eliminated); Christy McDonald (2nd eliminated); Josh Owen (1st eliminated)

Season 4 Chris Young (Winner); Casey Rivers (Runner-up); Nicole Jamrose (2nd Runner-up); Matt Mason (7th eliminated); Jared Ashley (6th eliminated); Kristen McNamara (5th eliminated); Melanie Torres (4th eliminated); Monique LeCompte (3rd eliminated); Shy Blakeman (2nd eliminated); Jewels Hanson (1st eliminated)

PRODUCTION COMPANIES Hoosick Falls Productions; Picture Vision; Reveille Productions

EXECUTIVE PRODUCERS Mark Koops; H. T. Owens; Ben Silverman; George Verschoor; Jeff Boggs

PRODUCERS Gordon Cassidy; David Parks; Jason Sands; Jon Small; Teri Weinberg; Damon Zwicker

DIRECTOR Michael Simon

Nashville Star features a cross-country search to find America's next big country star. Each season begins with nationwide auditions that narrow the thousands of hopefuls down to the finalists. After the audition shows, contestants compete week after week while living together in a Nashville house called Chez Twang. While judges critique the contestants, it is up to the viewers to decide who is eliminated each week, and who wins a Sony Music Nashville recording contract. Season 1's winner was Buddy Jewell; Season 2's was Brad Cotter; Season 3's champion was Erika Jo; and the winner of Season 4 was Chris Young. In Season 4, Bret Michaels was replaced with a series of guest judges, such as Naomi Judd, Patti LaBelle, and Larry the Cable Guy.

NEWLYWEDS: NICK & JESSICA

GENRE	Docudrama (Celebrity)
FIRST TELECAST	8/19/2003
LAST TELECAST	3/30/2005
NETWORK	MTV
EPISODE STYLE	Self-contained
CAST	Jessica Simpson; Nick Lachey; Drew Lachey (Nick's brother); Ashlee Simpson (Jessica's sister); Joe Simpson (Jessica's dad); Tina Simpson (Jessica's mom)
PRODUCTION COMPANY	MTV Productions
EXECUTIVE PRODUCERS	R. Greg Johnston; Rod Aissa
PRODUCERS	Sue Kolinsky; Shari Brooks; Larry Rudolph; Joe Simpson; Todd C. Stevens
DIRECTORS	Matt Anderson; Katherine Brooks; Donald Bull; Ron Flaherty; Marcus Fox; Marla Hopkin; Sarah K. Pillsbury; Todd C. Stevens

Newlyweds: Nick & Jessica chronicled the first year of the celebrity marriage of former 98 Degrees singer Nick Lachey and pop star Jessica Simpson. Jessica struggled with the challenges of married life—and life in general. Famous humorous Jessica moments included her misunderstanding that "Chicken of the Sea" was a brand of canned tuna, not chicken, and her refusal to eat Buffalo wings because she "doesn't eat buffalo."

The second season began as Nick and Jessica celebrated their first wedding anniversary in Atlantic City and New York. Viewers learned how messy Jessica was and what a neat freak Nick could be. The couple's busy work schedule included the launch of Jessica's "Dessert" line of edible beauty products, and her follow-up hit song "Take My Breath Away."

The third and final season highlighted Jessica and Nick's second wedding anniversary, dog training, Jessica's preparation for her role in the movie *The Dukes of Hazzard,* several family holiday gatherings, and their decision whether to move from their first home.

NEWPORT HARBOR: THE REAL ORANGE COUNTY

GENRE	Docusoap
FIRST TELECAST	8/13/2007
NETWORK	MTV
EPISODE STYLE	Story Arc
CAST	Chrissy; Clay; Allie; Grant; Chase; Taylor; and Sasha
PRODUCTION COMPANY	Go Go Luckey Productions
EXECUTIVE PRODUCERS	Gary Auerbach; Tony DiSanto; Liz Gateley; Dave Sirulnick

This high-school reality drama features a new location with all the conflict of its predecessor, *Laguna Beach.* The series follows a group of wealthy high-school seniors living in an affluent area of Southern California as they deal with love and heartbreak.

NEXT

GENRE	Competition (Dating)
FIRST TELECAST	4/4/2005
NETWORK	MTV
EPISODE STYLE	Self-contained
EXECUTIVE PRODUCERS	Kallissa Miller; Jacqui Pitman; Howard Schultz
PRODUCERS	Kristi Fraijo; Liz Givens; Dianne Martinez; Victoria Mercado
DIRECTOR	Adam Goldberg

Each episode of *Next* features five timed speed dates. If a date fizzles in the first few seconds, the person meeting the potential suitor yells, "Next!" to end the date. If the date goes past the one-minute mark, the suitor wins a cash prize. If the date lasts the full five minutes, the suitor decides between having a second date or taking a cash prize. When contestants aren't on their speed date, they hang out in the *Next* bus, which is wired for video and sound to capture all of their dishy comments.

NEXT ACTION STAR

GENRE	Competition (Talent)
FIRST TELECAST	6/14/2004
LAST TELECAST	7/28/2004
NETWORK	NBC
AIR TIMES	Monday, 10:00 p.m. (6/2004); Tuesday, 8:00 p.m. (6/2004–7/2004); Wednesday, 8:00 p.m. (7/2004)
EPISODE STYLE	Story Arc
TALENT	Tina Malve (Host); Victoria Burrows (Judge); Louis Morneau (Judge); Alan Schechter (Judge);

Scot Boland (Judge); John Einsohn (Judge); Marki Costello (Judge); Howard Fine (Acting Coach)

CAST Corrine Van Ryck de Groot (Winner); Sean Carrigan (Winner); Jared Elliot (Runner-up); Jeanne Bauer (Runner-up); Melisande Amos (eliminated in Episode 9); John Keyser (eliminated in Episode 9); Mae Moreno (eliminated in Episode 8); Mark Nilsson (eliminated in Episode 8); Linda Borini (eliminated in Episode 6); Harold "House" Moore (eliminated in Episode 6); Greg Cirulnick (eliminated in Episode 5); Somere Sanders (eliminated in Episode 5); Santino Sloan (eliminated in Episode 4); Viviana Londono (quit in Episode 4); Todd Farr (eliminated in Episode 3); Young Chu (eliminated in Episode 3); Krista Coyle (eliminated in Episode 3); Michelle Lee (eliminated in Episode 3); Laura Douglas (eliminated in Episode 3); Matt Miller (eliminated in Episode 3); Austene Clark (eliminated in Episode 2); Brittany Istre (eliminated in Episode 2); Dan Wells (eliminated in Episode 2); Eileen Hespen (eliminated in Episode 2); Julielinh Parker (eliminated in Episode 3); Matt Sarracco (eliminated in Episode 2); Matthew Turner (eliminated in Episode 2); Melissa Panzio (eliminated in Episode 2); Reggie Austin (eliminated in Episode 2); Scott Herrera (eliminated in Episode 2)

PRODUCTION COMPANIES Silver Pictures Television; Brass Ring Entertainment; GRB Entertainment, Inc.

EXECUTIVE PRODUCERS Cris Abrego; Gary R. Benz; Joel Silver; Rick Telles; Steve Richards

PRODUCERS Chris Brewster; Fernando Mills
DIRECTOR Omid Kahangi

Next Action Star began with a nationwide casting search for action movie actors, which resulted in thirty men and women heading to Hollywood for a series of semifinals. The thirty contestants were narrowed to fourteen (seven men and seven women), who competed in a series of acting, stunt, underwater, and combat challenges to win the male and female lead roles in the NBC movie *Bet Your Life*. The winners were Corinne Van Ryck de Groot and Sean Carrigan.

THE NEXT BEST THING

GENRE	Competition (Talent)
FIRST TELECAST	5/30/2007
LAST TELECAST	7/24/2007
NETWORK	ABC
AIR TIME	Wednesday, 8:00 p.m.
EPISODE STYLE	Story Arc
CAST	Michele Merkin (Host); Elon Gold (Judge); Lisa Ann Walter (Host); Jeff Ross (Judge)
PRODUCTION COMPANIES	New Wave Entertainment, Peter Engel Productions
EXECUTIVE PRODUCERS	Fax Bahr, Barry Katz, Peter Engel
PRODUCER	Jonathan Bourne

In this celebrity impersonator competition, the winner was awarded a grand prize of $100,000. The show featured contestants impersonating Little Richard, Howard Stern, Jack Nicholson, George W. Bush, Bono, Angelina Jolie, Celine Dion, and Lucille Ball, to name a few. The winner was Trent Carlini, who billed himself as the "Heartbreak Elvis."

THE NEXT FOOD NETWORK STAR

GENRE Competition

FIRST TELECAST 6/5/2005

NETWORK Food Network

EPISODE STYLE Story Arc

TALENT Marc Summers (Host—Seasons 1 and 2); Gordon Elliott (Judge); Bob Tuschman (Judge); Susie Fogelson (Judge); Bobby Flay (Guest Judge—Season 3); Robert Irvine (Guest Judge—Season 3); Cat Cora (Guest Judge—Season 3); Alton Brown (Guest Judge—Season 3); Giada De Laurentis (Guest Judge—Season 3); Duff Goldman (Guest Judge—Season 3); Guy Fieri (Guest Judge—Season 3); Paula Deen (Guest Judge—Season 3); Rachael Ray (Guest Judge—Season 3);

CAST

Season 1 Dan Smith and Steve McDonagh (Winners); Deborah Fewell; Brook Harlan; Susannah Locketti; Harmony Marceau; Hans Rueffert; Michael Thomas; Eric Warren

Season 2 Guy Fieri (Winner): Reggie Southerland; Carissa Seward; Nathan Lyon; Andrew Schumacher; Evette Rodriguez; Elizabeth Raynor; Jess Dang

Season 3 Amy Finley (Winner); Rory Schepisi (Runner-up); Paul McCullough (eliminated in week 6); Adrien Sharp (eliminated in week 5); Michael Salmon (eliminated in week 4); Colombe Jacobsen Derstine (eliminated in week 3); Thomas Grella, Jr. (eliminated in week 3); Nikki Shaw (eliminated in week 2); Viven Cunha (eliminated in week 1); Patrick Rolfe (eliminated in week 1) and Joshua Adam Garcia (resigned)

PRODUCTION COMPANY	Food Network
EXECUTIVE PRODUCER	Bob Kirsh
PRODUCERS	Neil Regan; Beth Paholak
DIRECTOR	Michael Pearlman

On *The Next Food Network Star,* eight chefs—some professional, some amateur—competed for the opportunity to star on their own Food Network cooking show. Judged by Food Network executives and television host/producer Gordon Elliot, competitors were challenged to prepare food while looking good on camera. One by one, the cooks were eliminated until the winner was determined by viewer votes online at www.food network.com. Dan Smith and Steve McDonagh, a catering duo, won the competition. Their series, *Party Line with the Hearty Boys,* premiered in September 2005. In the second season, Guy Fieri won and went on to star in *Guy's Big Bite.* Season 3 winner, Amy Finley, went on to host *The Gourmet Next Door.*

THE NEXT GREAT CHAMP

GENRE	Competition
FIRST TELECAST	9/7/2004
LAST TELECAST	12/3/2004
NETWORKS	FOX; Fox Sports
AIR TIME	Tuesday, 9:00 p.m.
EPISODE STYLE	Story Arc
TALENT	Oscar De La Hoya (Host); Lou Duva (Trainer); Tommy Brooks (Trainer)
CAST	Otis "Triple O.G." Griffin (Winner); Mohamad "The Monarch" Elmahmoud; Luis "The Body Snatcher" Corps; James "Marvelous" Mince; Rene "Lone Star" Armijo, Jr.; Paul "The Perfect Storm" Scianna; David "Danger" Pareja; Fred "Boom Boom" Bachmann; Gilbert "The General"

	Zaragoza; Lawrence "Lights Out" Alonzo; Mike "Pit Bull" Vallejo; Arsenio "R.C. Rey" Reyes
PRODUCTION COMPANIES	Endemol USA; Oscar de La Hoya and his Golden Boy Promotions; Lock & Key Productions
EXECUTIVE PRODUCERS	Paul Buccieri; Joe Livecchi; Oscar De La Hoya; Richard Schaefer
DIRECTOR	Brian Smith

Twelve aspiring boxers competed for a professional contract with Oscar De La Hoya's Golden Boy Promotions and a title fight within the World Boxing Organization (WBO) in this competition series. *The Next Great Champ* producers shot several versions of the final bout, to avoid having the results leak to the press. After the fourth episode, the show moved to Fox Sports. Otis Griffin was crowned "The Next Great Champ."

NICE PACKAGE

GENRE	Competition (Makeover)
FIRST TELECAST	4/16/2004
NETWORK	Oxygen
EPISODE STYLE	Self-contained
TALENT	Leila Sbitani (Host); Ryan Burnham (Handyman); Nicole Facciuto (Designer); Jeff Mark (Handyman); Helen Maalik (Designer); Elfya Van Muylem (Designer)
PRODUCTION COMPANY	Banyan Productions
EXECUTIVE PRODUCERS	John Bertholon; Susan Cohen-Dickler; Jan Dickler; Ray Murray
PRODUCER	Ronnie Krensel

Relationships were tested as a couple, using only the contents of a custom-designed "Nice Package," had to make over a room in their home. Along the way, the couple was given a chance to win exciting prizes tailored to their personal desires.

NO BOUNDARIES

GENRE	Competition
FIRST TELECAST	3/3/2002
NETWORKS	The WB; OLN
AIR TIME	Sunday, 7:00 p.m. (WB run)
EPISODE STYLE	Story Arc
TALENT	Troy Hartman (Host);
	Melanie McLaren (Co-Host)
CAST	Allen Chen; Rob Oddi; Eli Swanson; Kirsten Jonzon; John Hodges; Ina Kerckhoff; Matt Springer; Sharon Hicks; Jill Pellerin; Stephanie Etherington; Todd Bershad; Kelly Breidenstein; Dustin Dumas; Rosie Dossett; Jesse Garcia
PRODUCTION COMPANY	Lions Gate Entertainment
CREATED BY	Brady Connell; James A. Jusko
EXECUTIVE PRODUCERS	Brady Connell; James A. Jusko
DIRECTOR	Marc Lawrence VII

Based on the European show *71 Degrees North, No Boundaries* followed fifteen contestants as they endured grueling challenges in a trek across North America. The tasks encouraged teamwork, but in the end, the group leader had to vote somebody off. The last remaining player won $100,000 and a Ford Explorer.

NO OPPORTUNITY WASTED

GENRE	Docudrama
FIRST TELECAST	10/3/2004
NETWORK	Discovery Channel; FitTV
EPISODE STYLE	Self-contained
TALENT	Phil Keoghan (Host)

PRODUCTION COMPANY   No Opportunity Wasted Television, Inc.
EXECUTIVE PRODUCERS   Phil Keoghan; Louise Keoghan; Peter Pistor

Phil Keoghan (*The Amazing Race*) served as executive producer and host of this dream-making series in which lucky participants were surprised by camera crews at home or work and given $3,000 and seventy-two hours to fulfill a once-in-a-lifetime fantasy adventure. Stories included a DJ getting a chance at broadcasting from New York City, a rocket scientist who wanted to start a rock band, and a kickboxing champ who wanted to build a boxing ring for inner-city kids.

OFF THE LEASH

GENRE	Docusoap
FIRST TELECAST	10/9/2006
LAST TELECAST	11/13/2006
NETWORK	Lifetime
EPISODE STYLE	Self-contained
CAST	Michelle Zahn; Stuart Kinzey; Addison Witt; Zack Grey
EXECUTIVE PRODUCERS	Mechelle Collins; Kevin Dill
DIRECTOR	Kevin Dill

On *Off the Leash*, Le Paws, a pet talent agency, searched for the next big four-legged superstar to hit the entertainment industry.

ON THE LOT

GENRE	Competition
FIRST TELECAST	5/22/2007
LAST TELECAST	8/21/2007
NETWORK	FOX
AIR TIMES	Tuesday, 9:00 p.m. (5/2007); Thursday, 9:00 p.m. (5/2007); Monday, 8:00 p.m. (6/2007); Tuesday, 8:00 p.m. (6/2007–8/2007)
EPISODE STYLE	Story Arc
TALENT	Adrianna Costa (Host); Carrie Fisher (Judge); Garry Marshall (Judge)
CAST	Will Bigham (Winner); Jason Epperson; Adam Stein; Sam Friedlander; Zach Lipovsky; Andrew Hunt; Mateen Kemet; Kenny Luby; Hilary Graham; Shalini Kantayya; Shira-Lee Shalit; David May; Jessica Brillhart; Marty Martin; Trever James; Phil Hawkins; Claudia La Bianca; Carolina Zorilla de San Martin
PRODUCTION COMPANIES	Amblin Television; Dream Works Television; Mark Burnett Productions
EXECUTIVE PRODUCERS	Steven Spielberg; Mark Burnett; David Goffin
CO-EXECUTIVE PRODUCERS	Justin Falvey; Darryl Frank; Conrad Riggs
PRODUCERS	Simon Lythgoe; Lee Metzger; Sam Gollestani; Dana Buning; Benjamin Beatie
DIRECTOR	Michael Simons

Helmed by Academy Award–winning filmmaker Steven Spielberg and reality television powerhouse producer Mark Burnett, *On the Lot* followed eighteen filmmakers as they wrote, produced, and directed original short films each week using a cast supplied by the show. Carrie Fisher, Garry Marshall, and a weekly guest celebrity judged the films, while home viewers voted to determine who would be eliminated each week.

Will Bigham won the grand prize, a $1 million development deal with Dream Works film studio.

THE ONE:
THE MAKING OF A MUSIC STAR

GENRE	Competition (Talent)
FIRST TELECAST	7/18/2006
LAST TELECAST	7/27/2006
NETWORK	ABC
AIR TIMES	Tuesday, 9:00 p.m., Wednesday, 8:00 p.m.
EPISODE STYLE	Story Arc
TALENT	George Stroumboulopoulos (Host); Kara DioGuardi (Judge); Mark Hudson (Judge); Andre Harrell (Judge)
CAST	Nick Brownell; Austin Carroll; Michael Cole; Caitlin Evanson; Scotty Granger; Adam McInnis; Jackie Mendez; Syesha Mercado; Jeremiah Richey; Aubrey Collins (2nd eliminated) Jadyn Maria (1st eliminated)
PRODUCTION COMPANIES	Endemol USA; Pulse Creative
EXECUTIVE PRODUCERS	Matt Kunitz; Michael Dempsey; Rick Ringbakk
PRODUCERS	Trice Barto; Curtis Colden; Joe Coleman
DIRECTORS	Alan Carter; J. Rupert Thompson

Based on the hit Spanish Endemol show *Operación Triunfo,* this talent competition was a combination of *American Idol* and *Big Brother.* Contestants were trained by the show's "music academy," competed in a weekly talent competition, and lived together. Airing twice a week, the series chronicled the activities of the challengers in the house and featured live performances along with clips of each performer. The audience was encouraged to vote not only on talent but also on the contestants' behavior. Unlike versions in other countries, *The One* was short-lived, as it was canceled after just two weeks.

ONE BAD TRIP

GENRE	Docucomedy (Hoax)
FIRST TELECAST	11/2003
NETWORK	MTV
EPISODE STYLE	Self-contained
PRODUCTION COMPANY	Brad Kuhlman Productions
EXECUTIVE PRODUCER	Brad Kuhlman
PRODUCER	Natalia Garcia
CO-PRODUCER	Robert Taylor
DIRECTOR	Evan B. Stone

On *One Bad Trip*, young men and women win an all-expenses-paid trip, but there's a catch: their families and significant others are following them. Occasionally, the family members and friends drop in on the party in disguise.

ONE OCEAN VIEW

GENRE	Docusoap
FIRST TELECAST	7/31/2006
LAST TELECAST	8/7/2006
NETWORK	ABC
AIR TIME	Monday, 10:00 p.m.
EPISODE STYLE	Story Arc
CAST	Anelka; Heather; John, K.J.; Lauren; Lisa; Mary; Miki; Radha; Usman; Zack
PRODUCTION COMPANY	Bunim-Murray Productions
EXECUTIVE PRODUCERS	Jonathan Murray; Joey Carson
PRODUCERS	Jonathan Murray; Joey Carson
DIRECTORS	Jonathan Murray; Joey Carson

Eleven single, successful twentysomethings left New York City to look for love while weekending at a beach house on Long Island's Fire Island on *One Ocean View*. The career-driven individuals had their share of issues and baggage, but did they manage to leave it all behind for forty-eight hours to enjoy themselves? Viewers never found out, as the show, which was billed as a more "adult" version of MTV's *The Real World*, was canceled after just two episodes.

OPEN BAR

GENRE	Docusoap
FIRST TELECAST	8/22/2005
LAST TELECAST	9/26/2005
NETWORK	LOGO
EPISODE STYLE	Story Arc
CAST	Tyler Robuck; Yawar Charlie; Tyrone Jackson; Adam; Gary; Richard; Benjamin
PRODUCTION COMPANY	Real Trio
EXECUTIVE PRODUCERS	Annie Hanlon; Dave Mace; Adam McGinnes; Eileen Opatut; James E. Tooley
PRODUCERS	Tyler Robuck; Paul Taylor
DIRECTOR	James E. Tooley

Open Bar followed Tyler Robuck's personal decision to reveal his homosexuality to his family and friends, a story told against the backdrop of i-Candy, a new gay bar Robuck was opening in West Hollywood. From the groundbreaking to the grand opening, the series followed the entrepreneur as he balanced his new personal and professional endeavors.

ORDINARY/EXTRAORDINARY

GENRE	Docudrama
FIRST TELECAST	8/1/1997

LAST TELECAST	9/5/1997
NETWORK	CBS
AIR TIME	Friday, 8:00 p.m.
EPISODE STYLE	Self-contained
TALENT	John Schneider (Host); Leanza Cornett (Host)
PRODUCTION COMPANY	LMNO Productions
PRODUCER	Scott Coburn
DIRECTOR	Chris Pechin

Ordinary/Extraordinary featured stories about amazing accomplishments by everyday people. Highlights included a man who could lick stamps while blindfolded and identify their country of origin, a man who could scale a four hundred-foot cliff in just five minutes, and a scuba-diving dog.

THE OSBOURNES
(Season 1)

GENRE	Docudrama (Celebrity)
FIRST TELECAST	3/5/2002
LAST TELECAST	5/7/2002
NETWORK	MTV
AIR TIME	Tuesday, 10:30 p.m.
EPISODE STYLE	Self-contained
CAST	Ozzy Osbourne; Sharon Osbourne; Jack Osbourne; Kelly Osbourne
PRODUCTION COMPANIES	iCandy Productions; Big Head; MTV Music Development
EXECUTIVE PRODUCERS	R. Greg Johnson; Jeff Stilson; Lois Curren; Sharon Osbourne
CO-EXECUTIVE PRODUCER	Jonathan J. T. Taylor
DIRECTORS	Sarah K. Pillsbury; C.B. Harding; Donald Bull; Todd Stevens; Brendon Carter; Katherine Brooks; Darren Ewing; Rob Fox; Kelly Welsh

The Osbournes followed the real-life exploits of legendary Black Sabbath frontman Ozzy Osbourne and his dysfunctional family.

In Episode 1, Ozzy and his family moved into a Beverly Hills mansion. Ozzy became frustrated when he couldn't operate the new satellite TV system. His daughter Kelly constantly bickered with her brother, Jack. Ozzy's wife and manager, Sharon, talked him into performing on *The Tonight Show*.

The family's dog population overran the house in Episode 2. Sharon hired a pet therapist to calm the animals down, but it didn't work. Ozzy and Sharon contemplated getting rid of the biggest offender, Jack's bulldog, Lola, but decided to keep her. Meanwhile, Kelly brought home a second cat, and later got a ticket for running a stop sign.

In Episode 3, Sharon and Kelly accompanied Ozzy as he promoted his new album, *Down to Earth*. Meanwhile, Jack had a miserable time on a school camping trip. When the family returned, they threw Kelly a huge seventeenth birthday party. Afterward, Kelly got a tattoo, which she unsuccessfully tried to hide from her mother.

Ozzy freaked out in Episode 4 when he learned that Kelly was scheduled to see a gynecologist, fearing she'd been sexually active. Upset at their noisy neighbors, Sharon tossed a ham over the fence, and Ozzy threw a log through their window.

In Episode 5, Ozzy rehearsed and worked out to prepare for an upcoming tour. He became upset after Sharon and Kelly used his credit cards to go on a shopping spree. He also worried that his exhausting tour schedule would make him lose his voice, but Sharon reassured him that he'd be okay.

In Episode 6, Ozzy broke his leg and had to take a few weeks off from touring. Coincidentally, back at the house, Kelly broke her foot. Sharon was upset to learn that Kelly had a fake ID. Meanwhile, Ozzy encouraged Jack to stop his drug use. After the kids threw several late-night parties, Ozzy and Sharon finally put their foot down.

In Episode 7, Ozzy got stoned after mixing alcohol with pain medication, and Jack had to bring him back from a walk with Lola. There was more drama from Kelly, as she became jealous of the attention Jack was getting from helping a band get noticed in the industry. Ozzy decided to return to the tour by himself, and the family surprised him in Chicago for his birthday.

In Episode 8, Jack invited his slacker/drinker friend Dill to stay with them, much to the family's chagrin. Kelly talked Sharon out of urinating in Dill's empty whiskey bottle to teach him a lesson. The family finally got Jack to ask Dill to leave. They also gave away Jack's dog, Lola, but they eventually let him keep her, as long as he promised to take care of her.

In Episode 9, the Osbournes' security guard, Mike, was arrested for robbing a neighbor's house, but he insisted he was innocent. The extended family gathered for Christmas dinner.

In the Episode 10 finale, Ozzy reflected on his life, wondering what a "normal" family was really like. He emphasized the need for honesty and hard work, and talked about coping with ADD and dyslexia. He was excited to receive a star on the Hollywood Walk of Fame.

THE OSBOURNES
(Season 2)

GENRE	Docudrama (Celebrity)
FIRST TELECAST	11/5/2002
LAST TELECAST	8/12/2003
NETWORK	MTV
AIR TIME	Tuesday, 10:30 p.m.
EPISODE STYLE	Self-contained
CAST	Ozzy Osbourne; Sharon Osbourne; Jack Osbourne; Kelly Osbourne
PRODUCTION COMPANIES	iCandy Productions; Big Head; MTV Music Development
EXECUTIVE PRODUCERS	R. Greg Johnson; Jeff Stilson; Lois Curren; Sharon Osbourne
CO-EXECUTIVE PRODUCER	Jonathan J. T. Taylor
DIRECTORS	Sarah K. Pillsbury; C.B. Harding; Donald Bull; Todd Stevens; Katherine Brooks; Darren Ewing; Rob Fox; Kelly Welsh

The Osbournes returned for an expanded twenty-two episode second season.

In Episode 1, Sharon talked about the effect the show had had on the family. The

Osbournes met the queen at Buckingham Palace, and Sharon got into a fight with Bill Cosby over his comments about the show.

Jack used sprinklers to deter the tourists swarming the house in Episode 2. Ozzy and Sharon attended a dinner with the president in Washington. Kelly performed "Papa Don't Preach" at the MTV Movie Awards, and Jack got to sit on actress Natalie Portman's lap.

In Episode 3, Sharon was diagnosed with colon cancer, while Ozzy battled his addictions on tour. Jack broke his elbow surfing.

In Episode 4, Kelly flew to Europe for a press tour, and performed "Papa Don't Preach" on *Top of the Pops*. Jack guest-starred on *Dawson's Creek*. Ozzy made Sharon laugh when he fell in the ocean trying to catch a fish.

In Episode 5, Sharon worried when Kelly started dating Bert, the lead singer of The Used. Kelly threatened to run off to Vegas to elope. Ozzy got upset when the television became stuck on a cooking show channel.

In Episode 6, Sharon patched things up with her father, whom she hadn't spoken with in more than twenty years. She punished Kelly for underage drinking by talking about disgusting foods while Kelly was trying to get over a hangover. Jack was also turning into a party animal, and started hanging out with actress/singer Mandy Moore. Ozzy's oldest daughter, Jessica, had a baby girl, making Ozzy a grandfather. Ozzy developed a burrito habit.

In Episode 7, Kelly's friend Sarah played drums in Kelly's band, but Kelly had Sharon fire her after Sarah proved to be a lousy drummer. Dill returned to stay with Jack, which the family wasn't too happy about.

The stress of public appearances got to Kelly in Episode 8, as she threw a series of tantrums. P. Diddy invited her to a party as his guest, prompting Sharon to joke about becoming P. Diddy's mother-in-law. Jack encountered difficulty while trying to sign a band.

Ozzy went on a cleaning binge in Episode 9, worried that the dogs' eliminations were carrying germs that might affect Sharon's weakened immune system. The family took in Robert, a friend of Aimee's and Kelly's whose mom had died from colon cancer. Sharon announced that her cancer was in remission.

In Episode 10, the family went to Las Vegas for Kelly's eighteenth birthday, while Ozzy played a show. Kelly got in a fight with some girls who were hanging around

Jack, and accused Jack of ruining her birthday. Ozzy won a small jackpot while playing the slots.

In Episode 11, Sharon became upset when she found Jack in bed with his best friend's ex-girlfriend. Sharon and Ozzy renewed their wedding vows in a Jewish ceremony, since Sharon's father was Jewish. At the reception, Sharon asked Justin Timberlake to marry Kelly. Ozzy drank too much and passed out, ruining Sharon's plans for an intimate night.

Kelly got mad at Jack in Episode 12 for hanging out with her enemy, Christina Aguilera. Ozzy inhaled too much nitrous at the dentist. The family took Jack to a medieval restaurant for his birthday and bought him a sword, which he later used in a street duel with his friend.

In Episode 13, the house became infested with fleas, thanks to the dogs. Ozzy was bewildered by the results of their home's redecoration. Sharon drove Robert and Jack crazy when she couldn't settle on a location in the garden for a heavy statue. Kelly flew to Philadelphia to visit Bert and got a nose ring, upsetting Sharon.

It was Ozzy's fifty-fourth birthday in Episode 14, and his trainer had him run five miles. Robert and Jack put on a fireworks display at Ozzy's party. Ozzy got frustrated when the voice-recognition system in his car couldn't understand him.

Ozzy and Sharon headed to Hawaii for a vacation in Episode 15. While they were gone, Kelly hit Jack in the face, as punishment for throwing a late-night house party.

In Episode 16, Sharon and the kids traveled to New York, while, back home, Robert annoyed Ozzy with his music. Nanny Melinda announced that she was pregnant, and irritated Kelly by constantly talking about it.

In Episode 17, the family became annoyed by their neighbors who were always playing tennis. After blasting loud music failed to get them to stop, Jack shot at them with a paintball gun, which resulted in a visit from the cops. When three cats disappeared, the family wondered if the neighbors had had something to do with it.

In Episode 18, Jack went to Courtney Love's house, where he met and started dating Kurt Cobain's sister, Brieann. Ozzy gave the two lovebirds a preview of his new song.

Ozzy took Jack fishing in Episode 19, where they got busted for throwing firecrackers at pelicans.

Jack went to London with Robert in Episode 20, and Kelly went on tour, causing

Sharon to miss her children. Ozzy, meanwhile, was obsessed with getting an old keyboard to work and eating carrot cake.

In Episode 21, Bert broke up with Kelly on Valentine's Day, and she demonstrated her anger by biting Jack's arm. Meanwhile, Jack started having violent fits in his sleep, and accidentally killed their dog Minnie during one of them, leaving Sharon distraught. Just then, the director yelled, "Cut!" and it was revealed that the episode was fake, leaving some viewers to wonder whether the entire series had been faked.

In a special Christmas episode, a variety of guest stars coerced the Osbournes into participating in a series of holiday-themed skits.

THE OSBOURNES
(Season 3)

GENRE	Docudrama (Celebrity)
FIRST TELECAST	1/27/2004
LAST TELECAST	5/4/2004
NETWORK	MTV
AIR TIME	Tuesday, 10:30 p.m.
EPISODE STYLE	Self-contained
CAST	Ozzy Osbourne; Sharon Osbourne; Jack Osbourne; Kelly Osbourne
PRODUCTION COMPANIES	iCandy Productions; Big Head; MTV Music Development
EXECUTIVE PRODUCERS	R. Greg Johnson; Jeff Stilson; Lois Curren; Sharon Osbourne
CO-EXECUTIVE PRODUCER	Jonathan J. T. Taylor
DIRECTORS	C. B. Harding; Katherine Brooks; Darren Ewing; Rob Fox; Kelly Welsh

Thanks to the success of *The Osbournes*, Sharon got her own talk show, which she hosted while the reality show taped Season 3.

Episode 1 found Sharon balking at her producers' suggestions that she improve her show. Kelly and Jack turned down her offers to co-host the show, and Ozzy was upset when his guest appearance on Halloween turned into a co-hosting job.

In Episode 2, Jack got a car for his eighteenth birthday. Despite crashing it during practice, he passed the driving test and got his license. Meanwhile, Kelly headed to the MTV Europe Music Awards and worried about squaring off with Christina Aguilera again.

Rapper DMX threatened to be a no-show at Sharon's talk show in Episode 4. Meanwhile, Ozzy had fun watching porn on their high-tech television. He also bought a motorcycle, but couldn't figure out how to start it.

In Episode 4, Ozzy desperately searched for his missing $100,000 pinkie ring, while Sharon went out and bought Bentleys for each of them. The family decided to neuter their dog Colin, whose hormones were raging out of control.

In Episode 5, Ozzy begrudgingly joined Kelly on a trip to England to sing a duet of her song "Changes" on *Top of the Pops*. He later predicted that the song would be a number one hit. Meanwhile, Kelly's relationship with her new boyfriend, Rob, was on the rocks. Ozzy got in an accident while riding an ATV and was knocked unconscious.

In Episode 6, Ozzy developed a craving for éclairs while recovering from his accident in a British hospital. Meanwhile, Sharon got frustrated with the constant tweaking by producers to her talk show and quit. Jack finally got a haircut after two years. Ozzy returned home to Los Angeles, to the delight of the family.

In Episode 7, Kelly didn't shower for several days, repulsing everyone with her stench. Someone played a prank on Ozzy, pretending to be the Canadian prime minister and inviting Ozzy to his country to receive an award. Ozzy suspected something was fishy when the supposed prime minister sang to him on the phone.

Ozzy became stir-crazy while recuperating from his ATV accident in Episode 8. Jack got a new tattoo and showed it to Ozzy.

Ozzy felt he was being ignored in Episode 9, as Kelly spurned his request that she dress less revealingly and Jack refused to give away the increasingly violent Colin.

In Episode 10, Kelly told Rob on Valentine's Day that she was too young for a serious relationship. Meanwhile, Sharon tried to redecorate Ozzy's studio, against his wishes. The kids headed to Las Vegas, leaving Ozzy and Sharon to spend Valentine's Day together.

THE OSBOURNES
(Season 4)

GENRE	Docudrama (Celebrity)
FIRST TELECAST	1/17/2005
LAST TELECAST	3/21/2005
NETWORK	MTV
EPISODE STYLE	Self-contained
CAST	Ozzy Osbourne; Sharon Osbourne; Jack Osbourne; Kelly Osbourne
PRODUCTION COMPANIES	iCandy Productions; Big Head; MTV Music Development
EXECUTIVE PRODUCERS	R. Greg Johnson; Jeff Stilson; Lois Curren; Sharon Osbourne
CO-EXECUTIVE PRODUCER	Jonathan J. T. Taylor
DIRECTORS	C.B. Harding; Katherine Brooks; Darren Ewing; Rob Fox; Kelly Welsh

In Episode 1 of the new season, Ozzy went to a specialist to seek help for his insomnia. Ozzy and Sharon disapproved of Jack's getting a huge cross tattooed on his chest.

In Episode 2, Kelly had to miss a family trip to Hawaii after she was cast in a TV pilot.

In Episode 3, Ozzy was having a terrible time in Hawaii until a private luau lifted his spirits. Jack went diving in a shark cage, and later was embarrassed when his friends invited strippers to the luau. The Osbournes ended up leaving Jack's friends behind when they showed up late for the flight to Hawaii.

Ozzy and Sharon suspected that Kelly was using drugs, after she got a lip ring and started exhibiting unusual behavior in Episode 4. Kelly eventually confessed and entered rehab.

Kelly returned from a month in rehab in Episode 5, and fought Sharon over the strict rules she was forced to follow. Meanwhile, Jack celebrated a year of sobriety.

In Episode 6, Sharon and Kelly considered taking a charity trip to Kenya, but Ozzy worried about diseases and their safety. Sharon received an award at a charity auction for the Covenant House. Elton John dropped by the house and embarrassed Ozzy by giving him a pricey necklace.

In Episode 7, a young woman won an auction to spend the day with Sharon, and was invited to spend the night at the family's home. Jack got a ticket for speeding and enrolled in online traffic school.

In Episode 8, the Osbournes headed to Japan, where Kelly made personal appearances and Ozzy received the Legend award at the Video Music Awards.

Sharon left her talk show again in Episode 9, as she fought with producers and deliberately showed up late to tapings. She took out her frustrations by criticizing Kelly's wardrobe, hurting Kelly's feelings.

Dr. Phil dropped by in Episode 10, to talk about drugs and other serious issues affecting the family.

OUTBACK JACK

GENRE	Competition (Dating/Endurance)
FIRST TELECAST	6/22/2004
LAST TELECAST	8/10/2004
NETWORK	TBS
EPISODE STYLE	Story Arc
TALENT	JD Roberto (Host)
CAST	Vadim Dale (Outback Jack); Natalie Franzman (Winner); Adrienne Roberts; Cortney Owen; Harmonie Krieger; Jillian Carman; Laura Croft; Maria Kanellis; Marissa Clark; Maru Iaconelli; Natasha Maldanado; Shannon Emerson; Summer Posey
PRODUCTION COMPANY	Nash Entertainment
CREATED BY	Bruce Nash; Mike DiMaggio
EXECUTIVE PRODUCERS	Brady Connell; Scott Satin; Michael Canter

PRODUCERS Bruce Nash; Andrew Jebb; Kevin Greene
DIRECTOR Tony Croll

Twelve single women parachuted into the Australian Outback and engaged in survival-style competitions while competing for the affection of Vadim Dale, the show's "Outback Jack." The winner was Natalie Franzman, who married Vadim on September 22, 2005.

PARADISE HOTEL

GENRE	Competition (Dating)
FIRST TELECAST	6/18/2003
NETWORK	FOX
AIR TIMES	Monday, 9:00 p.m.; Wednesday, 9:00 p.m.
EPISODE STYLE	Story Arc
TALENT	Amanda Byram (Host/Narrator)
CAST	Charla Philstrom (Winner); Keith Cuda (Winner); Tara Gerard (Winner); Dave Kerpen (Runner-up); Scott Hanson (eliminated in Episode 29); Holly Pastor (eliminated in Episode 29); Amy Toliver (eliminated in Episode 27); Beau Wolf (eliminated in Episodes 16 and 26); Tom Rodriguez (eliminated in Episode 26); Melanie Barger (eliminated in Episodes 2 and 25); Desiree Boyd (eliminated in Episode 25); Alex Van Kamp (eliminated in Episode 20); Kristin Ellis

(eliminated in Episode 18); Toni Ferrari
(eliminated in Episode 14); Zack Stewart
(eliminated in Episode 12); Amanda Dominguez
(eliminated in Episode 10); Matthew Cehi
(eliminated in Episode 8); Kavita Channe
(eliminated in Episode 6); Andon Guenther
(eliminated in Episode 4)

PRODUCTION COMPANIES	Mentorn; A. Smith and Co.
CREATED BY	Howard Davidson; Phil Roberts
EXECUTIVE PRODUCERS	Tom Gutteridge; Charles Thompson; Arthur Smith; Kent Weed; Larry Barron
PRODUCERS	Jarratt Carson; Mechelle Collins; Billy Cooper; Cyndi Hubach; Omid Kahangi; Jennifer Orme; Jack Poorman; Bill Pruitt; Evan Weinstein; Mara B. Waldman; Bruce Toms; Andrew Scheer; Rick Ringbakk; Andrea Richter; John Moffet
DIRECTORS	Brad Kreisberg; Kent Weed

This eight-week elimination competition featured eleven contestants (either six women and five men, or six men and five women) living in a luxurious hotel. The goal was to pair up with a roommate or risk being eliminated, losing the chance to win the mysterious "ultimate prize." As the hotel guests were eliminated, they were replaced by television viewers. The remaining guests chose from two candidates who were in a studio in Los Angeles. Under the rules, if the replacement guest was a woman, then the male guests decided who would enter the hotel; if the replacement was a man, the women decided. The show featured many twists and turns designed to keep the guests on their toes. The biggest twist occurred in Episode 21, when all of the previously eliminated guests were brought back—with the advantage of having seen what had transpired since their departure. In the end, two couples remained: Charla and Dave, and Keith and Tara. A second-to-last twist was thrown in, as the couples were forced to switch partners.

The ultimate prize of $500,000 was split between the winning couple, Charla and Keith. However, in one final twist, Charla and Keith were given the opportunity to split their share of their winnings with their original partners, Dave and Tara. After deliberation, Keith decided to split his $250,000 with Tara, while Charla decided to keep the $250,000 for herself.

PARENTAL CONTROL

GENRE	Competition (Dating)
FIRST TELECAST	2/6/2006
NETWORK	MTV
EPISODE STYLE	Self-contained
PRODUCTION COMPANY	MTV Productions
EXECUTIVE PRODUCER	Michael Canter
PRODUCERS	Liz Givens; Craig Brooks; Ben Hatta; Frank Murgia; Cat Rodriguez
DIRECTORS	Glenn Taylor; Brendon Carter; Bruce Klassen; Brad Kreisberg

In this dating show with a twist a mother and father choose candidates to date their teenage child, in order to replace their kid's current, unacceptable love interest. The show begins with the mom and dad each picking a candidate, then planning and carrying out their child's date. The teen then has to choose the mom's pick, the dad's, or stay with the current significant other.

PARTY AT THE PALMS

GENRE	Docucomedy
FIRST TELECAST	6/15/2005
NETWORK	E!
EPISODE STYLE	Self-contained
TALENT	Jenny McCarthy (Host)
PRODUCTION COMPANY	E! Entertainment Television

EXECUTIVE PRODUCERS	Sean Olsen; Brent Zacky
PRODUCER	Dave Schapiro
DIRECTOR	Michael McNamara

On *Party at the Palms,* host Jenny McCarthy gave viewers an inside look at Las Vegas hot spot the Palms Casino Resort. Various areas of the hotel, such as the rooftop Ghost Bar and the nightclub Rain, were featured on the series.

PARTY PARTY

GENRE	Docudrama
FIRST TELECAST	12/6/2005
NETWORK	Bravo
EPISODES	Self-contained
PRODUCTION COMPANY	World of Wonder
EXECUTIVE PRODUCERS	Fenton Bailey; Randy Barbato

Families organizing and throwing parties were the focus of this docudrama on Bravo. The series featured parties of all kinds including bar mitzvahs, weddings, graduations, and kids' birthdays.

PERFECT MATCH: NEW YORK

GENRE	Docudrama (Romance)
FIRST TELECAST	7/27/2003
NETWORK	ABC Family
EPISODE STYLE	Self-contained
TALENT	Harriette Cole (Host)
PRODUCTION COMPANY	RDF Media
CREATED BY	Stephen Lambert
EXECUTIVE PRODUCERS	Michael Davies; Stephen Lambert
DIRECTOR	Anna Davies

Based on a British series, *Perfect Match: New York* followed relationship expert and author Harriette Cole as she found three perfect dates for a single man or woman from a pool of thirty suitors. Each suitor lived with the potential love match for one week. Following a three-week courtship period, the suitor was presented with three choices: continue seeing the match, agree to meet a new love match, or keep looking for love on his or her own.

PERFORMING AS . . .

GENRE	Competition (Talent)
FIRST TELECAST	8/26/2003
LAST TELECAST	9/24/2003
NETWORK	FOX
AIR TIMES	Tuesday, 8:00 p.m. (8/2003–9/2003); Monday, 9:00 p.m. (9/2003); Wednesday, 8:00 p.m. (9/2003)
EPISODE STYLE	Story Arc
TALENT	Todd Newton (Host); Steven Ivory (Judge); Brigitte Barr (Judge)
CAST	Sharon Youngblood (Winner—Aretha Franklin); Kelia Collins (Christina Aguilera); Conchita Leeflang (Tina Turner); Darren Tolliver (Meatloaf); Arlis Alfred (Annie Lennox); Lenny Hirsh (Garth Brooks); Jessica Keehan (Madonna); Carmel Helene (Toni Braxton); Jasmine Chadwick (Cyndi Lauper); Tiffany Baldwin (Faith Hill); Nikki Loiero (Shania Twain); Steve Bermudo (Ricky Martin); Sara Bruni (Alanis Morissette); Jason Ebs (Jon Bon Jovi); Brian Duprey (Frank Sinatra); Cooper Cambell (Justin Timberlake); Ferras Algaisi (Elton John); Lawrence Faljean (Freddie Mercury); Sharon Owens (Barbra Streisand); Ron Knight

(James Brown); Lisa Jamie Cash (Cher);
Michael John (Billy Joel); Pamela Newlands
(Celine Dion); Buck McCoy (Tim McGraw);
Kyah Combs (Britney Spears)

PRODUCTION COMPANY	Endemol
EXECUTIVE PRODUCERS	David Goldberg; John De Mol; Paul Buccieri
PRODUCER	Melissa Butts

A popular show previously produced in ten countries, *Performing As...* featured five everyday people who dressed and sang like major recording artists. The competitors learned special choreography, and wore makeup and costumes, to enhance their performances. Each week, a winner was selected to go to the finals. Sharon Youngblood won the $200,000 grand prize for her Aretha Franklin–inspired performance.

PET STAR

GENRE	Competition (Talent)
FIRST TELECAST	1/31/2003
NETWORK	Animal Planet
AIR TIME	Friday, 8:00 p.m.
EPISODE STYLE	Self-contained
TALENT	Mario Lopez (Host)
PRODUCTION COMPANY	Brad Lachman Productions
EXECUTIVES PRODUCERS	Brad Lachman; Ann King
PRODUCER	Richard Crystal
CO-PRODUCER	William Longworthy
DIRECTORS	Charlie Foley; Ann King; Barrett Moore; Debbie Placio; Eric Tang; Dave Thomas; Adam West; Billy West; Bob Widmer

In this pet talent competition, three celebrity judges using a one-to-ten-point scoring system, selected the three most talented animal performers per show. A subsequent audience vote determined the most talented pet, whose owner was awarded a $2,500 prize. Each episode-winning owner was eligible for a chance to return with his or her pet to compete for $25,000 on the season finale.

THE PICK UP ARTIST

GENRE	Competition
FIRST TELECAST	8/6/2007
NETWORK	VH1
EPISODE STYLE	Story Arc
CAST	Mystery; Matador; J Dog; Erik Von Markovik; Alvaro; Brady; Fred; Joe; Joseph; Pradeep; Scott; Stephen
PRODUCTION COMPANY	3 Ball Entertainment
EXECUTIVE PRODUCERS	Adam Greener; J.D. Roth; Todd A. Nelson
CO-EXECUTIVE PRODUCER	Doug Wilson
PRODUCER	Angela Malloy

Shot in Austin, Texas, this dating show followed bestselling author and entertainer Mystery as he guided eight dating-challenged men in the art of seducing single women. Those who didn't learn the lingo or master the art of kissing were eliminated each week until one remained to claim the title of "Master Pick-Up Artist." Alvaro, who changed his name to Kosmo in Episode 2, was the winner.

PIMP MY RIDE

GENRE	Docudrama (Makeover)
FIRST TELECAST	3/4/2004
NETWORK	MTV
EPISODE STYLE	Self-contained

TALENT	Xzibit (Host); Danny (Suspension and Body); Aren (Paint and Body—Season 1); Shay (Paint and Body—Season 2); Buck (Paint and Body—Season 3), Ish (Interiors); Ryan Friedlinghaus (Owner/West Coast Customs); Alex (Wheels and Tires); Big Dane (Accessories); Mad Mike (Electronics); Beau Boeckmann (Owner—Season 5); Gyasi (Wheels and Tires Specialist—Season 5); Luis (Paint and Body—Season 5); Diggity Dave (Accessories); Rick (Interiors—Season 5); Cabe (Fabricator—Season 5)
CREATED BY	Bruce Beresford-Redman; Rick Hurvitz
EXECUTIVE PRODUCERS	Bruce Beresford-Redman; Rick Hurvitz
CO-EXECUTIVE PRODUCER	Larry Hochberg
PRODUCERS	Jennifer Colbert; Tess Gamboa; Joel Ratz; Mark A. Ryan; Ari Shoflet

Pimp My Ride surprises car owners with makeovers for their run-down vehicles. A team of experts transforms the jalopies into unique masterpieces, complete with amenities such as MP3 players, lounge seats, and television screens. In the fifth season, the show moved from West Coast Customs to another garage, Galpin Auto Sports (GAS).

PIRATE MASTER

GENRE	Competition
FIRST TELECAST	5/31/2007
LAST TELECAST	7/17/2007
NETWORK	CBS
AIR TIME	Thursday, 8:00 p.m. (5/2007–7/2007); Tuesday, 10:00 p.m. (7/2007)
EPISODE STYLE	Story Arc

TALENT	Cameron Daddo (Host)
CAST	Ben Fagan (Winner); Christa DeAngelo (Runner-up); Jay Hatkow (14th eliminated); Louie "Rufus" Frase (13th eliminated); Laurel Schmidt (12th eliminated); Kendra Guffey (11th eliminated); Nessa Nemir (10th eliminated); Azmyth Kaminski (9th eliminated); Elicia "Jupiter" Mendoza (8th eliminated); Joe Don "J.D." Morton (7th eliminated); Jocelyn "Joy" McElveen (6th eliminated); Sean Twomey (5th eliminated); Cheryl Kosewicz (4th eliminated); Alexis Shubin (3rd eliminated); Christian Okoye (2nd eliminated); John Lakness (1st eliminated)
PRODUCTION COMPANY	Mark Burnett Productions
EXECUTIVE PRODUCER	Mark Burnett

Sixteen modern-day pirates participated in a high-seas adventure around the Caribbean island of Dominica in search of hidden treasure totaling $1 million on *Pirate Master*. Over the course of 33 days, the pirates lived aboard a massive 179-foot pirate ship, while embarking on extraordinary expeditions and deciphering clues along the way. Gold coins—real money the pirates were able to take with them after the show—were awarded after each treasure hunt. The show last aired on July 17, 2007, several weeks before the finale was set to air. The rest of the series was offered online. Ben Fagan won the grand prize of $500,000, plus the money he won during the course of the series, for a total of $587,624.

THE PLAYER

GENRE	Competition (Dating)
FIRST TELECAST	8/3/2004
LAST TELECAST	9/15/2004
NETWORK	UPN
AIR TIMES	Tuesday, 9:00 p.m.; Wednesday, 9:00 p.m.

EPISODE STYLE	Story Arc
TALENT	Rob Mariano (Voice of the Player Operator/Host)
CAST	Dawn (The Chooser); Ananda (The Chooser's Friend); Jinelle (The Chooser's Friend); Acie (Winner); Alex (Player); Ben (Player); Bryan (Player); Byron (Player); Chyno (Player); Eian (Player); Federico (Player); Jason (Player); J.J. (Player); Kyle (Player); Marvin (Player); Trever (Player)
PRODUCTION COMPANY	Unreal Productions, Inc.
EXECUTIVE PRODUCERS	Don Weiner; Happy Walters; Teri Kennedy
DIRECTORS	Chris Donovan; Kenny Hull

The Player followed thirteen single men, who boasted of great dating skills, during their quest to win the affection of a single woman, Dawn. The men received instructions via phone from the Player Operator, an unseen host who was later revealed to be *Survivor*'s Rob Mariano. The men were given challenges testing their courting abilities, and two of Dawn's friends assisted her in selecting the winner, Acie.

RATINGS: UPN brought in four million viewers a week with *The Player.*

PLAYING IT STRAIGHT

GENRE	Competition (Dating/Hoax)
FIRST TELECAST	3/12/2004
LAST TELECAST	3/26/2004
NETWORK	FOX
AIR TIME	Friday, 8:00 p.m.
EPISODE STYLE	Story Arc
TALENT	Daphne Brogdon (Host)
CAST	Jackie (The Bachelorette); Banks (Winner—straight); Gust (straight); Louis (straight); Ryan (straight); Sharif (straight); Alex (gay); Bill (gay);

Bradley (gay); Chad (gay); Chris (gay); Eddie (gay); John (gay); Lee (gay); Luciano (gay)

PRODUCTION COMPANIES Lion Television; Paddenswick Pictures

EXECUTIVE PRODUCERS Ciara Byrne; Jeremy Mills

PRODUCERS Priya Balachandran; Elayne Cillic

DIRECTOR Lauren Alvarez

On *Playing It Straight,* one single woman dated fourteen bachelors, some of whom were gay. If she selected a straight guy as her final choice, both she and the guy each received $500,000. If she selected a gay man, the guy would win $1,000,000. Jackie picked Banks, a straight guy, and they continued their relationship after the series ended.

POPSTARS

GENRE Competition (Talent)

FIRST TELECAST 1/12/2001

LAST TELECAST 1/3/2002

NETWORK The WB

AIR TIMES Friday, 8:30 p.m. (Season 1); Thursday, 8:00 p.m. (Season 2)

EPISODE STYLE Story Arc

TALENT Jaymes Foster-Levy (Music Executive—judge); Travis Payne (Choreographer—Season 1 Judge); Jennifer Greig-Costin (Manager—Judge); David Foster (Music producer—L.A. Judge); Roger Love (Vocal Coach); Tony Michaels (Choreographer—Season 2 Judge); Brad Daymond (Producer/Songwriter—Season 2 judge)

CAST

Season 1 Nicole Scherzinger (Eden's crush); Ivette Sosa (Eden's crush); Ana Maria Lombo (Eden's Crush);

Rosanna Taverez (Eden's Crush); Maile Misajon (Eden's Crush); Cheaza Figueroa (Final 26); Keitha Lind Brown (Final 26); Ciamar Hernandez (Final 26); Kerrie Roberts (Final 26—quit); Margaux Yap (Final 26—quit); Alexandria Bachelier (Final 26); Molly Zimpfer (Final 26); Nikki McKibbin (Final 26); Shaunda Johnston (Final 26); T. V. Carpio (Final 26); Garland Gerber (Final 26); Baby Norman (Final 26); Camille Guaty (Final 26); Curtisha Johnson (Final 26); Alexis Brown (Final 26); Isadelle Mercedes (Final 26); Jean Perlman (Final 26); Jessica Robinson (Final 26); Christina Petty (Final 26); Katie Morris (Final 26); Crystal Donahue (Final 26); Petagay Rowe (Final 26)

Season 2   Donavan Green (Scene 23); Dorothy Szamborska (Scene 23); Moi Juarez (Scene 23—kicked out of band); Josh Henderson (Scene 23); Laurie Gidosh (Scene 23); Monika Christian (Scene 23); Michael Washington; Jackie Salvucci (Final 26); Jahzeel Mumford (Final 26); Tom Tusler (Final 26); Corey Clark (Final 26); Greg Treco (Final 26); Ejay Day (Final 26); Jillion Schulz (Final 26); Vanessa Salvucci (Final 26); Lian Ellis (Final 26); Angela Peel (Final 26); Katie Webber (Final 26); Sharra Dade (Final 26); Shannon Yoesle (Final 26); Kimberly Caldwell (Final 26); Angel Ortiz (Final 26); Miredys Peguero (Final 26); Shariana Suliafu (Final 26); Tenia Taylor (Final 26); Shana Montanez (Final 26)

PRODUCTION COMPANIES   Stone-Stanley Productions; Screentime; Target Entertainment

EXECUTIVE PRODUCERS   David Perler; David G. Stanley; Scott A. Stone

PRODUCERS   Ed Singer; Jamie Hammons; Gina Meyers

Based on an Australian series, *Popstars* followed the formation of a pop group, beginning with auditions and culminating in the group's first live concert. In Season 1, music industry professionals, including music producer/*Princes of Malibu* dad David Foster chose five women to create the band Eden's Crush. The show followed the girls as they lived together, recorded their album, and made their first music video.

Season 2 featured a new group, with three men and three women, called Scene 23. Controversy brewed as Moi Juarez was forced to leave the show after he brought outsiders into the group's house and went out to see his friends after being told it was forbidden.

THE PRINCES OF MALIBU

GENRE	Docudrama (Celebrity)
FIRST TELECAST	7/10/2005
NETWORK	FOX (Episodes 1 and 2); Fox Reality Channel
AIR TIME	Sunday, 8:30 p.m. (Fox Run)
EPISODE STYLE	Self-contained
CAST	Brody Jenner; Brandon Jenner; David Foster; Linda Thompson-Foster
PRODUCTION COMPANY	GRB Entertainment
EXECUTIVE PRODUCERS	Gary R. Benz; Brant Pinvidic; Spencer Pratt; Sean Travis
PRODUCERS	Andra Duke; David Foster; Joel Zimmer

In a format inspired by possible real-life events, camera crews followed the antics of Brandon and Brody Jenner, the sons of Olympic gold medalist Bruce Jenner and songwriter and former beauty queen Linda Thompson-Foster. During the show, Brandon and Brody lived at the twenty-two-acre mansion of their stepfather, music producer David Foster. Wife Linda spoiled her sons, to the frustration of David, who wanted the kids to start earning their own money and pay him rent. The moneymaking schemes the boys devised included organizing a car wash run by bikini-clad girls and creating a drive-in movie theater on the mansion's front lawn. The Fosters publicly announced their intention to file for divorce while the show was still airing.

PROJECT GREENLIGHT

GENRE	Docusoap
FIRST TELECAST	12/2/2001
NETWORKS	HBO (Seasons 1 and 2); Bravo (Season 3)
EPISODE STYLE	Story Arc
CAST	Ben Affleck; Matt Damon; Pete Jones (Screenwriter—Season 1); Erica Beeney (Screenwriter—Season 2); Efram Poetelle (Director—Season 2); Kyle Ranki (Director—Season 2); Wes Craven (Executive Producer—Season 3); Joel Soisson (Producer—Season 3); Mike Leahy (Producer—Season 3); John Gulager (Director—Season 3); Marcu Dunstan (Screenwriter—Season 3); Patrick Melton (Screenwriter—Season 3)
PRODUCTION COMPANIES	Miramax Film and Television; HBO; LivePlanet
CREATED BY	Alex Keledjian
EXECUTIVE PRODUCERS	Matt Damon; Ben Affleck; Chris Moore; Sean Bailey (Seasons 1 and 2); Harvey Weinstein; Bob Weinstein; Billy Campbell (Season 1); Dan Cutforth (Seasons 2 and 3); Jane Lipsitz (Season 2); Bob Osher (Season 2); Jane Lipsitz (Season 3)
CO-EXECUTIVE PRODUCERS	Elizabeth Bronstein (Season 1); Tony Yates (Season 2)
PRODUCERS	Eli Holzman; Tina Gazzaro (Season 1); Tony Yates (Season 1); Kevin Morra (Season 2); Jennifer Berman (Season 3); Marc Joubert (Season 3); Larry Tanz (Season 3)
CO-PRODUCERS	Alex Keledjian (Season 1); Kent Kubena (Season 1); Sheila McLaughlin (Season 1); Marc Joubert (Season 2); Larry Tanz (Season 2); Amy Wruble (Season 2)

This documentary series took viewers behind the scenes in the making of a feature film. The show was executive-produced by Academy Award winners Ben Affleck and Matt Damon. Filmmakers were given a $1 million budget to direct their screenplays with a professional cast and crew. The earnings from the first two films, *Stolen Summer* ($134,736) and *Shaker Heights* ($280,351) were underwhelming. The series moved to Bravo in Season 3 and focused on *Feast,* a horror film written by Marcus Dunstan and Patrick Melton. Legendary director Wes Craven was brought in to serve as an executive producer on the film.

PROJECT RUNWAY
(Season 1)

GENRE	Competition (Job)
FIRST TELECAST	12/1/2004
LAST TELECAST	2/23/2005
NETWORK	Bravo
AIR TIME	Wednesday, 10:00 p.m.
EPISODE STYLE	Story Arc
TALENT	Heidi Klum (Host/Judge), Michael Kors (Judge) Tim Gunn (Fashion Consultant)
CAST	Jay McCarroll (Winner); Kara Saun (Runner-up), Wendy Pepper (Runner-up); Austin Scarlett (9th eliminated); Robert Plotkin (8th eliminated); Kevin Johnn (7th eliminated), Alexandra Vidal (6th eliminated); Nora Calguri (5th eliminated); Vanessa Riley (4th eliminated); Starr Ilzhoefer (3rd eliminated); Mario Cadenas (2nd eliminated); Daniel Franco (1st eliminated)
PRODUCTION COMPANIES	Bravo Cable; Magical Elves; Full Picture; Miramax Television; The Weinstein Company
CREATED BY	Eli Holzman

EXECUTIVE PRODUCERS   Andy Cohen; Heidi Klum; Bob Weinstein; Harvey Weinstein; Frances Berwick

On *Project Runway,* supermodel Heidi Klum gave twelve aspiring designers the opportunity to become a part of the fashion industry by competing in challenges until one was declared the winner. Contestants were eliminated each week, and the top three designers showed their work at New York's Fashion Week. Klum led a panel of fashion industry notables, including top designer Michael Kors and *Elle* magazine fashion director Nina Garcia, who were the show's judges. Tim Gunn, chair of fashion at Parsons School of Design, mentored the designers. Each week, guest judges tailored to the specific challenges joined the panel.

In Episode 1, the twelve designers were challenged to design a sexy, glamorous outfit for a night on the town. The designers had to purchase materials at a popular Manhattan supermarket. Austin won the challenge with his cornhusk gown, saving himself from being cut. Daniel's garbage bag/butcher paper/tinfoil "masterpiece" didn't impress the judges, including guest Patricia Field, and he was the first designer eliminated.

In Episode 2, the contestants designed dresses representing "Envy." Their wares were privately auctioned. Since Kara's military-inspired gown, which connected the dots between envy and war, received the most bids, she won the challenge. Guest judges Constance White and Paul Berman were not impressed by Mario's simple white gown with a red splash, so he was eliminated.

Each designer created a party dress that would appeal to Banana Republic's customers in Episode 3. Wendy won the challenge, and her dress was sold at Banana Republic stores. The judges, including guest Deborah Lloyd, voted to eliminate Starr.

The remaining designers were challenged to design a new look for singer Sarah Hudson in Episode 4. Jay, Kevin, and Austin led three teams. Sarah picked Kevin's design as her favorite, and he was granted immunity on the next challenge, while Vanessa was eliminated.

In Episode 5, the designers selected models, then worked with them to design the wedding gown of their dreams. All of the gowns were stunning, but the judges picked Kara's design as the winner. Nora's inability to please her model/client was her downfall, and she was cut.

In Episode 6, the designers created swimsuits that doubled as evening wear. After completing their designs, the contestants and their models attended a magazine party where, to gain immunity, they had to make an impression on guest judge Richard Johnson, and be mentioned in his column. Jay and Austin won the challenge. Alexandra's swimsuit/gown failed to impress the judges, including guest Constance White, and she was sent packing.

The designers created a collection in Episode 7. One designer served as a leader, while each of the others created one outfit for the line. In the workroom, Tim Gunn added that their collection had to carry the theme "the year 2055." The designers had to build their collection from used vintage store items, rather than shopping at a fabric store. By lottery, Kevin was chosen to be the leader. Kara won the challenge, and immunity from the next week's elimination. Kevin's lack of leadership was noticed by guest judges Constance White, Anne Slowey, and and Betsey Johnson, and he was eliminated.

In Episode 8, the five remaining challengers had to redesign the U.S. Postal Service uniform. After spending the morning walking postal routes with actual mail carriers, Kara decided to concentrate on function, and her pocket-emphasized uniform earned her immunity. With the help of guest judge U.S. postal worker Becky Negich, the judges eliminated Robert.

In Episode 9, guest judge Nancy O'Dell challenged the final four to design a gown for her to wear on the Grammy Awards red carpet. Despite ex-contestant Robert's "help," Wendy won her first challenge, while fan favorite Austin was eliminated. Jay, Wendy, and Kara earned an opportunity to showcase their designs at New York's Fashion Week.

On the eve of Fashion Week, all the designers were brought back for a reunion show.

In the finale, Tim Gunn visited the final three at their homes, where they showed him the progress they'd made on their collections. Each designer created a twelve-piece collection for Fashion Week. The judges, including guest Parker Posey, voted Jay McCarroll the Season 1 winner. He won $100,000 and a mentorship with Banana Republic, which he turned down. He did display his work in *Elle* magazine.

PROJECT RUNWAY

(Season 2)

GENRE	Competition (Job)
FIRST TELECAST	12/7/2005
LAST TELECAST	3/8/2006
NETWORK	Bravo
AIR TIME	Wednesday, 10:00 p.m.
EPISODE STYLE	Story Arc
TALENT	Heidi Klum (Host/Judge); Michael Kors (Judge); Nina Garcia (Judge); Tim Gunn (Fashion Consultant)
CAST	Chloe Dao (Winner); Daniel Vosovic (Runner-up); Santino Rice (3rd place); Kara Janx (11th eliminated); Nick Verreos (10th eliminated); Andrae Gonzalo (9th eliminated); Zulema Griffin (8th eliminated); Emmett McCarthy (7th eliminated); Diana Eng (6th eliminated); Marla Duran (6th eliminated); Guadalupe Vidal (5th eliminated); Daniel Franco (4th eliminated); Raymundo Baltazar (3rd eliminated); Kirsten Ehrig (2nd eliminated); John Wade (1st eliminated); Heidi Standridge (1st eliminated)
PRODUCTION COMPANIES	Bravo Cable; Magical Elves; Full Picture; Miramax Television; The Weinstein Company
CREATED BY	Eli Holzman
EXECUTIVE PRODUCERS	Andy Cohen; Heidi Klum; Bob Weinstein; Harvey Weinstein; Frances Berwick

Unlike in the previous season, the sixteen Season 2 challenge winners were not always granted immunity from elimination at the next week's challenge, but they did have the option to switch models.

In Episode 1, Season 1 contestants Kara, Wendy, Austin, Jay, and Robert returned for the Season 2 auditions. Daniel F. also returned, determined to prove that the judges had made a mistake in Season 1. Designers were given six yards of plain white fabric, twenty dollars, and one week to create an outfit that best represented who they were as fashion designers. Santino was declared the winner of the first competition, while John Wade and Heidi Stanridge were eliminated.

In Episode 2, Heidi Klum invited the designers to a party, where they were given their next challenge: to design an outfit using only the clothes off their backs. Guest judge Diane Von Furstenberg helped choose the week's winner, Chloe. Kirsten was the next eliminated.

In Episode 3, the designers had to create a look for one of fashion's most important and stylish icons, Barbie. Nick's design was chosen as the winner by guest judge Lily Martinez, while Raymundo was eliminated.

In Episode 4, the designers sketched a lingerie line with three looks, which they pitched to Heidi. She chose four designers to pick teams and continue creating their lines. Guest judges Cynthia Rowley and Alessandra Ambrosio helped choose Daniel V., Zulema, and Andrae as the winners. Daniel F. was eliminated.

In Episode 5, the designers created a party dress for fashion maven, designer, and socialite Nicky Hilton. She chose Santino's dress as the winner, while Guadalupe had to go.

In Episode 6, the designers paired up to create a day-to-evening ensemble for Banana Republic. Andrae and Daniel V. were the winning duo. Guest judge Deborah Lloyd helped declare Diana and Marla's outfit the loser, and they were eliminated.

The designers created ice-skating outfits for Olympic figure skater Sasha Cohen in Episode 7. Zulema won the challenge, while Emmet's poor performance forced guest judges Sasha and Anne Slowey to give him the boot.

In Episode 8, the designers visited Michael Kors's showroom, where he gave them digital cameras and told them to take photographs of the things that inspired them. Then each designer chose one picture to inspire a garment. Daniel V. impressed the judges, including Season 1 winner Jay McCarroll. Zulema was eliminated.

In Episode 9, each contestant designed a garden party dress using plants and flowers. Guest judges Mark Badgley and James Mischka liked all of the designs, but only Daniel V. won. Andrae was eliminated.

The designers gave each other head-to-toe makeovers in Episode 10. Celebrity stylist Freddie Leiba helped pick Chloe as the challenge winner, while Nick was eliminated.

In Episode 11, each designer created a red-carpet dress representing the collection he or she planned to show at Olympus Fashion Week. Competition became fierce when the designers discovered that fashion icon Iman was the guest judge and would wear the winning dress to a red-carpet event. Daniel V. won the challenge, while Kara was eliminated.

As in Season 1, on the eve of Fashion Week, all the designers were brought back for a reunion show.

In the first part of the Season 2 finale, Tim Gunn visited the homes of the final three designers, Daniel V., Santino, and Chloe, to check on their progress. Later, the finalists returned to New York City to prepare their collections for Fashion Week. They were surprised with one final challenge: they each had to design an additional garment with the help of one eliminated designer of their choice. Nick, Andrae, and Diana returned to help Daniel, Santino, and Chloe, respectively.

In the second part of the finale, the three finalists presented their lines at Fashion Week, and with the help of guest judge Debra Messing, Chloe Dao was named the winner. She won $100,000 to help launch her line, a 2007 Saturn Sky Roadster, a spread in *Elle* magazine, and a mentorship with Banana Republic.

PROJECT RUNWAY
(Season 3)

GENRE	Competition (Job)
FIRST TELECAST	7/12/2006
LAST TELECAST	10/18/2006
NETWORK	Bravo
AIR TIME	Wednesday, 10:00 p.m.
EPISODE STYLE	Story Arc
TALENT	Heidi Klum (Host/Judge); Michael Kors (Judge); Nina Garcia (Judge); Tim Gunn (Fashion Consultant)

CAST   Jeffrey Sebelia (Winner); Uli Herzner (Runner-up);
Laura Bennett (3rd place); Michael Knight
(4th place); Kayne Gillaspie (10th eliminated);
Vincent Libretti (9th and 10th eliminated);
Angela Keslar (8th and 10th eliminated);
Robert Best (7th eliminated); Alison Kelly
(6th eliminated); Bradley Baumkirchner
(5th eliminated); Bonnie Dominguez (4th eliminated),
Keith Michael (disqualified); Katherine Gerdes
(3rd eliminated); Malan Breton (2nd eliminated);
Stacey Estrella (1st eliminated)

PRODUCTION COMPANIES   Bravo Cable; Magical Elves; Full Picture;
Miramax Television; The Weinstein Company

CREATED BY   Eli Holzman

EXECUTIVE PRODUCERS   Andy Cohen; Heidi Klum; Bob Weinstein; Harvey
Weinstein; Frances Berwick

In a casting special, Tim Gunn hosted a behind-the-scenes look at how the third season designers were chosen, including videos of the contestants. The show also updated viewers on the Season 2 designers.

In Episode 1, the fifteen designers were given fifteen minutes to raid their own living quarters and fill only one with personal items they would use to create a design. Guest judge Kate Spade helped choose Keith as the winner, and he thus gained immunity from the next week's cut. Stacy was the first designer sent home.

In Episode 2, the designers paired up to design and create a gown for Miss USA Tara Conner to wear to the Miss Universe pageant. Guest judges Connor and Vera Wang chose Kanye and Robert as the winners, granting Kanye immunity from the next elimination. Malan was eliminated.

In Episode 3, the designers went to Central Park, where they were instructed to pick a dog and design an outfit for the owner they imagined it would have, as well as one for the dog. Uli's design was picked as the most pet-friendly by guest judge Ivanka Trump, while Katherine was sent home.

Working in teams of three, the designers created an ensemble look for Macy's in

Episode 4. In a show first, Keith was sent home after it was discovered that he had broken the rules. Vera Wang returned to guest-judge with Mehmet Tangoren, and they picked Angela as the winner of the competition. In addition to Keith's disqualification, Bonnie was eliminated.

Episode 5 began with a twist: the models chose their designers. Then each model picked a fashion icon for the designer to base a creation on. Diane von Furstenberg helped the judges decide that Michael's Pam Grier–inspired outfit was the best, while Bradley, with his tribute to Cher, had to go.

In Episode 6, the remaining designers were asked to create an outfit in just one day using only materials found at a waste management center in New Jersey. Once again, Michael won the challenge, but Alison's outfit failed to impress guest judge Rachel Zoe, and she was eliminated.

In Episode 7, Heidi told the designers they had to create a look for an "everyday woman." The designers were shocked to discover that the models would be their own mothers and sisters. For a twist, each designer had to choose another contestant's family member as model. Vincent won the week's challenge. Robert's poor performance forced guest judge Joan Kors (Michael Kors's mother) to give him the boot.

In Episode 8, the designers were the models. After a review on the runway, Heidi informed them that the final test would be to see how their creations traveled. Once at the airport, their destination was revealed. In Paris, the ensembles were reviewed by guest judge Catherine Malandrino. Jeffrey impressed the judges, while Angela was eliminated.

In Episode 9, the designers had to make a couture gown that was judged by Catherine Malandrino and Richard Tyler. The judges named Jeffrey as their favorite, while Vincent was eliminated.

In Episode 10, the designers were told they'd have two surprise guests: previously cut designers Angela and Vincent, who could earn entry back into the competition if they won the challenge. The competitors were asked to design a cocktail dress in a black-and-white palette. Designer Zac Posen helped the judges decide that Laura had done the best. That week, three designers were eliminated: Angela, Vincent, and Kanye.

In Episode 11, the remaining designers created an outfit that expressed "their specific point of view as a designer." The winner of this challenge had their look and model featured in *Elle* magazine's "First Look" page, photographed by Gilles Bensimon. The final four were shocked to discover that there would be no elimination for this challenge, and that all of them would show their work at the Olympus Spring Fashion Week. The guest judge for this episode was Teri Agins.

On the eve of Fashion Week, all of the designers returned for a reunion show. Keith addressed his disqualification, and Michael won $10,000 in the "Bravotv.com Fan Favorite" contest.

In part one of the finale, Tim Gunn visited the homes of the final four designers—Uli, Laura, Michael, and Jeffrey—to check in on their progress. Later, the finalists returned to New York to prepare their collections for Fashion Week.

In part two of the finale, the four finalists presented their lines at Fashion Week. With the help of guest judge Fern Mallis, Jeffrey Sebelia was named the winner. He won a spread in *Elle* magazine, a mentorship with INC Design, a year of representation by Designers Management Agency, a 2007 Saturn Sky Roadster, and $100,000 from TRESemmé hair care to help start a clothing line.

PROS VS. JOES

GENRE	Competition
FIRST TELECAST	3/6/2006
LAST TELECAST	5/16/2006
NETWORK	Spike
AIR TIME	Tuesday, 10:00 p.m.
EPISODE STYLE	Self-contained
CAST	Petros Papadakis (Host)
PRODUCTION COMPANY	Mess Media
EXECUTIVE PRODUCER	Scott Messick
PRODUCERS	Trevor Baierl; Steve Burke; Heath Luman; D. Max Poris; Ismael Soto
DIRECTOR	Tim Warren

On *Pros vs. Joes,* three everyday men—the "Joes"—competed against one another for a chance to win season tickets to their favorite sports team. The Joes had to go up against five of the world's best athletes in various challenges. The "Pros" included Clyde Drexler, Jerry Rice, Rebecca Lobo, Dennis Rodman, and Bill Goldberg.

THE PUSSYCAT DOLLS PRESENT: THE SEARCH FOR THE NEXT DOLL

GENRE	Competition (Job)
FIRST TELECAST	3/6/2007
LAST TELECAST	4/24/2007
NETWORK	The CW
AIR TIME	Tuesday, 9:00 p.m.
EPISODE STYLE	Story Arc
TALENT	Mark McGrath (Host); Robin Antin (Judge); Li'l Kim (Judge); Ron Fair (Judge)
CAST	Asia Nitollano (Winner); Melissa Reyes (Runner-up); Chelsea Korka (2nd Runner-up); Melissa Smith (6th eliminated); Anastacia Rose (5th eliminated), Mariela Arteaga (4th eliminated), Sisely Treasure (3rd eliminated), Jaime Benjamin (2nd eliminated), Brittany Diiorio (1st eliminated)
PRODUCTION COMPANIES	10 x 10 Entertainment; Warner Horizon Television
EXECUTIVE PRODUCERS	Ken Mok; Robin Antin; Steve Antin; Laura Fuest
PRODUCERS	Anna Mastro; McG
DIRECTORS	Brad Kreisberg; Kevin Tancharoen

On this competition series, young women auditioned to be a part of The Pussycat Dolls musical group. Nine girls sang and danced in front of a panel of judges, including PCD founder Robin Antin. The winner, Asia Nitollano, earned a chance to join the Dolls, but for unconfirmed reasons she left the group.

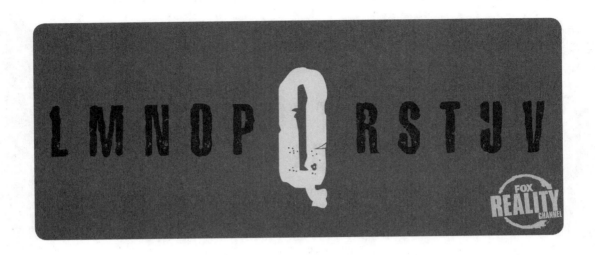

QUEER EYE FOR THE STRAIGHT GIRL

GENRE	Docucomedy (Makeover)
FIRST TELECAST	1/11/2005
LAST TELECAST	2/23/2005
NETWORK	Bravo
EPISODE STYLE	Self-contained
TALENT	Danny Teeson (The Life); Damon Pease (The Locale); Robbie Laughlin (The Look); Honey Labrador (The Lady)
PRODUCTION COMPANY	Scout Productions
CREATED BY	David Collins
EXECUTIVE PRODUCERS	Dave Metzler
PRODUCERS	David Collins; Gerrit V. Folsom; James O'Donnell; Michael Williams
DIRECTORS	Glenn Gaylord; Shanda Sawyer

In this short-lived spin-off of *Queer Eye for the Straight Guy*, a team of gay stylists, dubbed the "Gal Pals," coached women in the Los Angeles area with beauty tips, recipes, and product suggestions, giving what they called "make-better" makeovers designed to impress and inspire.

QUEER EYE FOR THE STRAIGHT GUY

GENRE	Docucomedy (Makeover)
FIRST TELECAST	7/15/2003
NETWORK	Bravo
EPISODE STYLE	Self-contained
TALENT	Kyan Douglas (Grooming); Ted Allen (Food and Wine); Carson Kressley (Fashion); Jai Rodriguez (Culture); Thom Filicia (Design)
PRODUCTION COMPANY	Scout Productions
CREATED BY	David Collins
EXECUTIVE PRODUCERS	Dorothy Aufiero; Christian Barcellos; Frances Berwick; David Collins; Amy Introcaso; David Metzler; Michael Williams; Lynn Sadofsky
PRODUCERS	Jeff Hasler; Michael Kaufman; Jerry Kolber; Jill Lopez Danton; Kathleen Murtha; Craig H. Shepherd
DIRECTORS	Brendon Carter; Stephan Kijak; Max Makowski; Joshua Seftel; Michael Selditch; Becky Smith, Jörg Fockele

This makeover show became a cultural phenomenon as it centered on the makeover magic of "The Fab Five," five gay men with expertise in life and style topics who mentored a heterosexual man in need of a change. After a little training and a makeover, the straight man was left on his own at an event that served as a test of his new look and attitude. The Fab Five observed the event from their loft, critiqued the straight man, and determined if he really had changed his ways. Each episode often featured the man's spouse, girlfriend, friends, or family being surprised with his transformation in manner, food preparation, personal grooming, and dress.

R U THE GIRL
WITH T-BOZ AND CHILLI

GENRE	Competition (Talent)
FIRST TELECAST	7/27/2005
LAST TELECAST	9/20/2005
NETWORK	UPN
AIR TIME	Wednesday, 9:00 p.m.
EPISODE STYLE	Story Arc
TALENT	Tionne "T-Boz" Watkins (Host); Chilli
CAST	O'So Krispie (Winner); Mirrah (Runner-up); Meah (7th eliminated); Alju (6th eliminated); Crystal (5th eliminated); Arielle (4th eliminated); Nazanin (3rd eliminated); Lauren (2nd eliminated); Lesli (1st eliminated)
EXECUTIVE PRODUCERS	Jay Blumenfield; Anthony Marsh; Chilli; Tionne "T-Boz" Watkins

CO-EXECUTIVE PRODUCERS   Bill Diggins; Laurie Girion
DIRECTOR   Tony Sacco

TLC's T-Boz and Chilli went on a cross-country search to find a new member for their group in this talent competition. The series began with T-Boz and Chilli going through audition tapes and making surprise visits to several semifinalists. The contestants sang for T-Boz and Chilli to help them determine which eight would make their way to the Atlanta finals. The finalists moved into an Atlanta mansion, and were presented with a number of challenges, including choreographing a number and designing a CD cover. In the live finale, T-Boz and Chilli announced that O'So Krispie would be the new member of TLC. The new group concluded the series by performing their new single, "I'll Bet."

RACE TO THE ALTAR

GENRE	Competition (Talent)
FIRST TELECAST	7/30/2003
LAST TELECAST	9/13/2003
NETWORK	NBC
AIR TIMES	Wednesday, 8:00 p.m. (7/2003–8/2003); Saturday, 9:00 p.m. (8/2003–9/2003)
EPISODE STYLE	Story Arc
TALENT	Lisa Dergan (Host); Colin Cowie (Wedding Planner)
CAST	Susan and Coyt (Winners); Tonya and Andree (Runners-up); Grace and Robert; Carolyn and Ethan; Becca and Andy; Jessica and Scott; Cindy and Chris; April and Vinny
PRODUCTION COMPANIES	NBC Studios; TWI; LMNO Productions
CREATED BY	Liz Ostow
EXECUTIVE PRODUCERS	Robert Horowitz; Eric Schotz; Bill Paolantonio
PRODUCERS	Michael Bailey; Joe Coleman; Brady Connell;

Bechera Gholam; Jenna Hovland; Jorgiana Jake;
Steve Mayer; Brian Richardson; Sheryl Zohn

DIRECTOR   Brady Connell

On *Race to the Altar,* eight engaged couples competed in *Fear Factor*–like stunts to win the wedding of their dreams. Each episode's winning couple voted out another team of competitors. In the final episode, Susan and Coyt were declared the winners and were married. They were surprised with a honeymoon prize.

RAISING THE ROOFS

GENRE	Docucomedy
FIRST TELECAST	7/6/2006
NETWORK	Spike
EPISODES	Self-contained
CAST	Michael Roof, Jr.; Steve "Uncle Stevie" Roof; Michael "Papa" Roof, Sr.
PRODUCTION COMPANY	The Jay & Tony Show
EXECUTIVE PRODUCERS	Jay Blumenfield; Anthony Marsh
CO-EXECUTIVE PRODUCER	Trevor Baierl
DIRECTOR	Patrick Fraser

In this *Beverly Hillbillies*–type comedy, comedian Michael Roof, Jr.'s new Hollywood life gets some unexpected visitors as his family from rural Florida moves in to live with him. The series centered around his country-raised relatives blending in with Michael's new city life.

THE REAL GILLIGAN'S ISLAND

GENRE	Competition
FIRST TELECAST	11/3/2004

LAST TELECAST 7/29/2005
NETWORK TBS
EPISODE STYLE Story Arc
TALENT Scott Lasky

CAST

Season 1 Glenn Stears (Winner—The Millionaire); Mark "Gooner" Groesbeck (Gilligan); Chris O'Malley (Gilligan); Bob Fahey (Skipper); Jim Murray (Skipper); Bill Beavens (The Millionaire); Donna Beavens (The Millionaire's Wife); Mindy Burbano (The Millionaire's Wife); Rachel Hunter (The Movie Star); Nicole Eggert (The Movie Star); Pat Abbott (The Professor); Eric Anderson (The Professor); Amanda Dodson (Mary Ann); Kate Koth (Mary Ann)

Season 2 **Green Team** Charlie Albert (Winner—The Skipper); Zac Turney (Gilligan); Howard Schur (The Millionaire); Melissa Jones (The Millionaire's Wife); Erika Eleniak (The Movie Star); Andrew Schuler (The Professor); Mandy Weaver (Mary Ann)
Orange Team: Shawn Manning (Gilligan); Ken Callen (The Skipper); Jim Bounce (The Millionaire); Donna Bounce (The Millionaire's Wife); Angie Everhart (The Movie Star); Tiy-e Muhammad (The Professor); Randy Silvers (Mary Ann)

PRODUCTION COMPANIES Next Entertainment, in association with Telepictures Productions
CREATED BY Mike Fleiss; Sherwood Schwartz
EXECUTIVE PRODUCERS Mike Fleiss; Sherwood Schwartz; Lloyd Schwartz; Lisa Levenson; Scott Jeffress
PRODUCERS Joel Zimmer; Nelson Soler; Tiffany McLinn Lore; Michael Bailey

Castaways participated in *The Real Gilligan's Island* while playing characters established on the sixties sitcom *Gilligan's Island*. Two sets of characters competed in challenges to determine one final winner for each season. "The Millionaire character Glenn received $250,000 and a car for winning Season 1. Season 2 awarded $250,000 to "Skipper" Charlie.

REAL HOUSEWIVES OF ORANGE COUNTY

GENRE	Docusoap
FIRST TELECAST	3/21/2006
NETWORK	Bravo
EPISODE STYLE	Self-contained
CAST	Kimberly Bryant (The Trophy Wife); Jeana Keough (Former Playmate); Vicki Gunvalson (The Working Woman); Lauri Waring (The Divorcee); Johanna De La Rosa (The New Girl); Tamra Barney; Quinn Fry; Tammy Knickerbocker
PRODUCTION COMPANIES	Kaufman Films; Dunlop Entertainment
EXECUTIVE PRODUCERS	Scott Dunlop; Kevin Kaufman; Patrick Moses; Dave Rupel
PRODUCER	Brad Isenberg
DIRECTORS	Stephen W. Alvarez; Brenda Coston; Amy Elkins

This docusoap features real-life housewives living in a wealthy gated community in Southern California. The women's lives are full of drama, excitement, and extravagance. They attend Botox parties and buy fancy cars and jewelry, while taking care of their families and furthering their careers. While the women are rich, life isn't always peachy behind the gates. *Real Housewives* was one of the more successful reality shows inspired by *Desperate Housewives*. A spin-off show, *The Real Housewives of New York City*, premiered in March 2008 on Bravo.

THE REAL ROSEANNE SHOW

GENRE	Docucomedy (Celebrity)
FIRST TELECAST	8/6/2003
LAST TELECAST	8/13/2003
NETWORK	ABC
AIR TIME	Wednesday, 9:00 p.m.
EPISODE STYLE	Story Arc
CAST	Roseanne; Bill Pentland; Becky Pentland; Jacob Pentland; Drew Ogier
PRODUCTION COMPANIES	Actual Reality Pictures, in association with Full Moon & Half Tide Productions
EXECUTIVE PRODUCERS	R. J. Cutler; Roseanne
DIRECTOR	Robert Swope

Comedian and actress Roseanne Barr attempted to make a comeback with *The Real Roseanne Show*. The series featured Roseanne's real family in their natural habitat, at home and in the office, as she tried to launch her cooking show, *Domestic Goddess*. The show was pulled after the second episode, due to low ratings and Roseanne's health problems. *Domestic Goddess* never filmed an episode.

REAL STORIES OF THE HIGHWAY PATROL

GENRE	Docudrama
FIRST TELECAST	4/1993
LAST TELECAST	9/1996
NETWORK	Syndicated
EPISODE STYLE	Self-contained
TALENT	Maury Hannigan (Host)

PRODUCTION COMPANIES	Leap Off Productions; Genesis Entertainment; New World Pictures
EXECUTIVE PRODUCER	Mark Massari
SENIOR PRODUCERS	Hilary Heath; Mark Phillips; Craig Piligian
PRODUCERS	Tony Lawrence; Tom Logan; Stephen Messer; Victory Tischler-Blue; Julie Volpe
DIRECTORS	Mark Cole; George Elanjian, Jr.; Jerry P. Jacobs; Tom Logan; Gerald Massimei; Joe Menendez; Star Price; Victory Tischler-Blue; Josh Becker; Brady Connell; Rupert Hitzig

Real Stories of the Highway Patrol followed the exploits of patrolmen, featuring a mix of crime reenactments, interviews, and recollections, as well as real-life coverage of police beats. California Highway Patrol commissioner Maury Hannigan hosted the series.

THE REAL WORLD

(Season 1—New York)

GENRE	Docusoap
FIRST TELECAST	5/21/1992
LAST TELECAST	8/13/1992
NETWORK	MTV
EPISODE STYLE	Story Arc
CAST	Heather B.; Becky Blasband; Andre Comeau; Julie Gentry; Norman Korpi; Eric Nies; Kevin Powell
PRODUCTION COMPANY	Bunim-Murray Productions
CREATED BY	Mary-Ellis Bunim; Jonathan Murray
EXECUTIVE PRODUCERS	Mary-Ellis Bunim; Jonathan Murray

The Real World introduced American audiences to reality television by sticking seven strangers in a house together for three months and filming the results.

Season 1 cast members included folk singer Becky, socially conscious musician

Andrew, hip-hop artist Heather, gay free spirit Norman, troubled model Eric, and African American poet and educator Kevin.

In Episode 1, the roommates moved into a loft in the SoHo neighborhood of Manhattan. Julie, a country girl from Birmingham, Alabama, stood out the most. While exploring the house, the roommates found a love and sex book, which prompted a discussion. Julie confessed to being a virgin. Later that night, Kevin was impressed with Julie's open-mindedness during a dinner discussion about racism and prejudice.

In Episode 2, Eric appeared in a cologne commercial, sparking a household conversation about nudity, and whether Eric was "selling out" his good looks. Heather was recording an album, and invited Julie and Eric to the studio. Meanwhile, something was brewing between Julie and Eric. Julie became jealous when Eric mentioned his girlfriend, Missy, and Eric was unhappy when Becky tried to set up Julie on a blind date. Eric showed up at Julie's hip-hop class and tried to impress her. He even claimed that Julie had been in his bed one morning.

Sexual tensions increased in Episode 3 when Eric began dating a model, Taryn, after they starred in a sexy photo shoot together. But after a few strange dates trying on leather chaps and sequins, Eric was confused about where things stood. Meanwhile, Andre's band, Reigndance, had its rehearsal shut down by the cops. Thanks to Julie's encouragement, everyone in the house attended the band's performance, and Andre dedicated a song to his new housemates.

In Episode 4, Becky tried to get friendly with the producer helping her record a song. She later stuffed her bra with Dixie cups before going to a party, and got more out of control as the night wore on. Her behavior started to bother Heather, and after the party a house meeting was called. Meanwhile, the roommates ganged up on Eric while his sister was visiting, making him feel uncomfortable. Later, he blasted Kevin for circulating a letter around the house that detailed complaints about him.

After a long discussion about stereotypes and basic differences, Kevin and Eric patched things up in Episode 5. Later, Kevin went to dinner and an art show with Morris, a teenager he was mentoring. As part of his probation requirement, Eric did community service work in a basketball program for troubled kids. He was worried about the impending arrival of his girlfriend, Missy. He invited Kevin to a Knicks game, where they met Isaiah Thomas, and Kevin learned that Eric's dad was an NBA referee.

In Episode 6, Julie and Kevin developed a brother-sister relationship, and candidly discussed sex. Concerned that Kevin was spending too much time outside the loft, the roommates played a prank on him by adopting drastically different personalities, including Julie, who pretended to be more promiscuous. Unnerved by their behavior, Kevin fled the house, leaving the others to wonder if he'd come back.

Kevin returned in Episode 7, and the roommates apologized for their prank. Kevin admitted that their behavior had made him consider quitting the show. Later, Julie and Heather attended a Knicks–Hornets game, and Heather confessed her infatuation with Hornets star Larry Johnson. She flirted with Johnson, but nothing came of it. Next, Becky and Kevin had a heated discussion about racism in America. The household tensions eased after a package arrived in the mail informing the women in the house that they'd be going on a week's vacation to Jamaica.

The girls had fun in Jamaica in Episode 8, while back in New York, Andre and Kevin bonded for the first time during a night on the town. Norman also got cozy with a guy named Charles, who he thought might be "the one." Becky returned from vacation with a boyfriend, but he was not from Jamaica—he was a *Real World* director!

In Episode 9, Norman was falling for Charles, although Charles didn't seem as willing to make the same commitment. Meanwhile, the rest of the roommates traveled to Washington, D.C., for a pro-choice rally. During the trip, Julie was profoundly affected by a woman she met at a homeless shelter, and she decided to spend the night there herself.

The roommates' moms showed up in Episode 10. Andre's mother watched his band perform, while Julie and her mother had a more contentious visit. Meanwhile, the housemates found a stray dog and named it Yoda. They discussed keeping it, but instead decided to look for its owner.

Tensions were on rise in Episode 11, when Julie accused Kevin of throwing a candleholder at her while she was on the phone. Kevin denied it, claiming that Julie had started the fight by being rude to him on the phone, possibly costing him a job. Kevin let off steam by going back to Jersey City to hang out with his girlfriend. He finally returned, and after another heated argument with Julie, the two reconciled. Kevin threw a birthday party for Eric, where Heather got in a fight with one of the guests, and the police showed up.

Heather was arrested in Episode 12 for fighting at the party, then stubbornly warned the other loftmates not to start in with her. She and Eric continually clashed over little things, which escalated into a wrestling match in the loft.

In Episode 13, the roommates expressed how much they had learned while being on the show and from one another. Before they left the loft, they visited the control room to see what it was like to be on the other side of the camera.

THE REAL WORLD
(Season 2—Los Angeles)

GENRE	Docusoap
FIRST TELECAST	6/26/1993
LAST TELECAST	11/11/1993
NETWORK	MTV
EPISODE STYLE	Story Arc
CAST	Tami Akbar; Beth Anthony; Aaron Bailey; Irene Berrera-Kearns; Jon Brennan; David Edwards; Dominic Griffin; Glen Naessens; Beth Stolarvzyk
PRODUCTION COMPANY	Bunim-Murray Productions
CREATED BY	Mary-Ellis Bunim; Jonathan Murray
EXECUTIVE PRODUCERS	Mary-Ellis Bunim; Jonathan Murray

Thanks to the success of the first season, *The Real World* expanded to twenty-two episodes for Season 2. Over the course of the season, nine housemates moved into a Venice, California, loft. The roommates included AIDS care specialist and R&B singer Tami, film school grad Beth S., Republican business student Aaron, deputy marshall Irene, country singer Jon, comedian David, Irish bartender Dominic, band frontman Glen, and lesbian craft services worker Beth A.

Episode 1 featured a reunion of the Season 1 cast to discuss their lives since being on the show. Eric's modeling success seemed to have gone to his head, as Julie complained he never returned her pages. Norman had managed to stay close to Becky, and had also been involved in a car commercial with Andre, Heather, and Julie. Everyone discussed their newfound fame, surprised that some people thought the show had been scripted.

Tami and Dominic traveled to the loft in Episode 2, stopping to pick up country boy Jon, who had trouble accepting Dom's hard-drinking, clubbing lifestyle. He confessed he didn't believe in sex before marriage, and he offended Tami and Dom by telling them what his parents thought of them.

Jon continued to be the odd man out in Episode 3, as Tami and Dom criticized his religious beliefs. Jon retaliated by calling Tami trash, which didn't sit well with her. Once they arrived at the loft, they decided to leave behind what was said on the drive and move forward.

Beth S. got off on the wrong foot in Episode 4 by bringing her cat into the house without asking permission, angering Dominic. She later invited her loftmates to a party she hadn't even been invited to. After they get kicked out, Dominic blamed Beth S. for humiliating everyone. Later, David and Jon's discussion about their differences escalated into fisticuffs, causing Aaron to step in and break up the fight.

In Episode 5, David and Tami's potential romance ended when David invited two of his buddies to join them on a group outing. Tami called off their date, then went on the dating game show *Studs.* Later, David flew into a rage when the group went bowling without him; he went to the alley with Tami and her date to chew them out. After Dominic and David got into it, Irene stormed off, unable to take it anymore. David was singled out during a house meeting for having a bad attitude.

Tami and her TV show date Kenya unsuccessfully tried to cheat on the game show *Studs,* and they ultimately lost the game in Episode 6. Meanwhile, Aaron and Dominic became friends and dished about Beth S. and Jon. Irene took pity on Jon and invited him home with her for the weekend, causing them to grow closer.

There was plenty of drama in Episode 7, as David's practical joke of pulling the blankets off Tami's bed prompted Beth S. to accuse him of rape. Tami opted to leave the house for the night, as David tried to convince the other housemates of his innocence. Irene called a house meeting without David to discuss the situation, as David looked on from a television monitor upstairs.

In Episode 8, the housemates brought David into the meeting and asked him to leave the loft. After unsuccessfully pleading his case, he ultimately agreed to leave.

The housemates interviewed three potential replacement housemates in Episode 9, ultimately settling on Glen. Jon took Glen aside and filled him in on the house politics. Glen managed to get into trouble right away, arguing with Dominic after a concert.

Episode 10's camping trip to Joshua Tree turned into a disaster after their tour guides got lost and it rained. However, their frustration with the guides brought everyone closer together. Tami shocked everyone during the trip when she revealed she was pregnant. After a rigorous rock climb, she exploded at Aaron, whom she accused of having a huge ego.

In Episode 11, Tami decided to have an abortion, prompting much debate among the housemates. Despite his conservative upbringing, Jon supported Tami's decision. Later, Aaron's girlfriend, Erin, visited him at the loft. Then, Aaron argued with Dominic for flirting with Erin.

In Episode 12, Irene prepared to leave the house, as she was about to be married. Beth S. and Tami speculated that Jon had fallen in love with Irene, making her departure really hard on him. Beth S. decided to play a joke on Aaron by plastering the walls with his photo from a "Men of UCLA" calendar, prompting him jokingly to accuse her of rape.

Beth A. was chosen to replace Irene in Episode 13, and her lesbian lifestyle rubbed Tami the wrong way. Glen's bandmates traveled from Philadelphia to L.A., and moved into the house, which upset the roommates. Dom was angry after Glen, Jon, and Aaron played an April Fool's joke on him, making him think his car had been towed.

In Episode 14, Dominic flew to Ireland to visit his sick father. Back in L.A., Jon advanced to the second round of a country music competition.

Actress Beth and musician Tami commiserated about their struggling careers in Episode 15. Tami ran an HIV seminar for her loftmates while she battled depression over having to deal with AIDS patients every day. In an effort to lose weight, she had her jaw wired shut. She concluded the episode by quitting her job at the clinic.

In Episode 16, a producer pursued Jon for a lead movie role. After meeting about the role, he flew home to Owensboro, Kentucky, where he was welcomed by family and several fans. He returned to California and decided not to take the role. In the meantime, Dominic and Aaron became closer friends, with Dom taking an interest in Aaron's passion for studying and surfing.

Glen was the target in Episode 17, as the roommates claimed that his bandmates had taken over the house. Glen accused everyone of not wanting to get to know one another, so the house played a question-and-answer game. After some very personal questions, Tami realized that she and Beth A. had more in common than she'd thought.

The game seemed to bring the housemates together, as they wound up feeding the homeless together, then cheering Jon to victory in his country singing competition.

Romance almost blossomed in Episode 18, as Beth S. was pursued by two guys, but she decided not to date either of them, despite accusations that she had sex in the closet with one of them. Tami's beau, Tootie, and Aaron's date, Heather, were introduced to the house. (Neither relationship worked out.) Meanwhile, Dominic played the field, dating three women at once, and Glen and Beth A.'s relationship grew closer.

In Episode 19, what started as a potential bonding trip to Cozumel, Mexico, broke the group apart. Dom and Aaron seemed happy to hang out on their own, while Glen and Beth A. formed their own little clique. Beth S. injured her arm, and the roommates wondered if Dom had an alcohol problem after finding him passed out in the sand. Later, at a group dinner, Glen, Beth A., Aaron, and Dom got into a heated fight with Jon and Beth S.

Episode 20 shed some light on Beth S.'s life when her mom visited, and voluntarily cleaned and cooked a traditional Polish meal for the loftmates. Feeling somewhat like an outcast, Beth S. conversed with Glen and Aaron about improving her relationships with them. She later raised her standing in the house by winning a game of paintball.

Episode 21 featured a musical showcase, as the housemates performed with their respective groups. Tami and Glen had a little competitive rivalry, but overall the night brought the roommates together.

In Episode 22, the roommates prepared to part ways, musing how their newfound fame would affect their lives. Everyone predicted where they thought they'd be in five years. Arguing surfaced during a group confessional, but the roommates eventually said tearful goodbyes.

THE REAL WORLD
(Season 3—San Francisco)

GENRE Docusoap
FIRST TELECAST 6/23/1994
LAST TELECAST 11/4/1994

NETWORK	MTV
EPISODE STYLE	Story Arc
CAST	Mohammed Bilal; Rachel Campos; Pam Ling; Cory Murphy; David "Puck" Rainey; Joanna Rhodes; Judd Winick; Pedro Zamora
PRODUCTION COMPANY	Bunim-Murray Productions
CREATED BY	Mary-Ellis Bunim; Jonathan Murray
EXECUTIVE PRODUCERS	Mary-Ellis Bunim; Jonathan Murray

The expulsion of a housemate, plus the spotlight on AIDS, made *The Real World: San Francisco* perhaps the most memorable season in the show's history. During Season 3, eight housemates lived together in the Bay Area, including band frontman Mohammed, Catholic Republican Rachel, star medical student Pam, undecided college student Cory, bike messenger and soapbox racer Puck, extreme sportswoman Jo, struggling cartoonist Judd, and HIV-positive AIDS spokesman Pedro.

In Episode 1, Pedro and Cory headed to San Francisco by train, where Pedro confessed that he was HIV-positive. Rachel and Judd shared a shuttle to the loft, while Pam and Mohammed arrived later. Puck showed up late, having just gotten out of jail. Pam ended up the proud recipient of the single bedroom because of her need to get up very early. After dinner, the roommates discovered that Pedro had full-blown AIDS. Rachel worried about how it would affect the house.

In Episode 2, Puck flirted with Rachel, although he rejected her offer to be a replacement for his double date on Valentine's Day. Instead, all loftmates except Mohammed spent February 14 at the Stinking Rose restaurant. Puck resented being harassed for his poor hygiene habits, after Pedro criticized him for eating peanut butter from the jar with his fingers, and Rachel unsuccessfully tried to create separate men's and women's bathrooms. She also voiced her concerns to Pedro about his AIDS.

The housemates attended Mohammed's poetry reading in Episode 3, which inspired him to hold another poetry night in the house. The group went to a Jack Kemp rally, instigating an argument between Mohammed and conservative Rachel. Later, Mo took issue with Cory's implication that his girlfriend looked half-white. Meanwhile, Pedro started dating a guy named Sean.

In Episode 4, Puck was bummed when Rachel was the only one who showed up at a screening of his soapbox racing video. In response, he didn't go to Pedro's birthday breakfast. Puck's outcast status was later confirmed when a thinly veiled conversation about *Beverly Hills, 90210* actually seemed to be about him. Everyone's opinion of Puck lightened after he brought his pit bull into the house. Meanwhile, Judd had an unsuccessful date with a girl named Jeannie.

Judd got his big break in Episode 5, as the *San Francisco Examiner* hired him as a cartoonist. The roommates went to the "Bammies"—the Bay Area version of the Grammys—where Mo tried to promote his band, and later performed with them.

Conflict surfaced in Episode 6 as Pedro overheard Rachel and Puck making gay jokes. Pedro's relationship with Sean was moving along quickly. Puck and Rachel's strange relationship took a combative turn, as Puck interfered with Rachel's date with another guy, and Rachel became annoyed when Puck flirted with her visiting friend Heather. Meanwhile, Judd had a brief romance with Rachel's other friend, Francis.

The women struggled to get by in Episode 7, as Cory couldn't find a job, Rachel stressed over grad school applications, and Pam was buried in med school projects. Puck showed his softer side when he found a stray dog and searched for its owner.

In Episode 8, AIDS began to take its toll on Pedro, but he continued giving seminars on living with HIV. Puck criticized Pedro about the way he lived his life. Later, Cory and Rachel went with Puck to meet his mother, and Pedro, Judd, and Pam enjoyed a day in the park.

Tension built between Puck and Pedro in Episode 9, to the point where Pedro started withdrawing from the group whenever Puck was around. Later, Pedro went home to visit his family, while Puck boasted that people needed to prove themselves to earn his respect. One of those people appeared to be Cory, who had been spending a lot of time with Puck lately.

The house grew tired of Puck's attitude in Episode 10. Things came to a head when he skipped Mohammed's birthday celebration. After he responded defensively to their criticism, the housemates discussed if they wanted him to remain in the house.

By Episode 11, the loftmates had finally had enough of Puck, and decided to kick him out of the house. Many *Real World* fans considered this to be the seminal moment in the series. *TV Guide* and TV Land later listed it as one of their "100 Most Memorable TV Moments."

With Puck out of the picture in Episode 12, the housemates seemed to enjoy one another's company much more. Rachel invited Pedro to come home with her to Arizona, where her religious mother was horrified to discover that Rachel had had her belly button pierced. Pedro gave an HIV seminar at the junior high school where Rachel's dad worked. Back at the house, Pam's boyfriend, Christopher, was secretly flown in for her birthday. After performing a *This Is Your Life*-style skit, the loftmates took Pam skiing in Tahoe to celebrate.

In Episode 13, Pedro returned to Miami to reflect on his shaky relationship with Sean. Much to the concern of his friends and family, he became increasingly sick, and decided to see a doctor. Meanwhile, Cory was spending a lot of time with the recently exiled Puck.

In Episode 14, Puck tried to ingratiate himself with the housemates by inviting them to a party, but no one went. A drunk Rachel called Puck a few days later to invite him to join her at a bar, where they ended up arguing. The house officially replaced Puck with a British woman named Jo.

Jo took her new housemates rock-climbing in Episode 15, immediately impressing everyone with her upbeat personality. Her energy was contagious; Rachel climbed to the top of the rocks. Later, Jo showed signs of weakness when she learned that her ex-husband had appealed the restraining order she'd placed on him. Fortunately, Cory was there to support her, and they grew closer. Later on, Judd and Rachel pretended they were a couple in public, hoping to appear more attractive to members of the opposite sex.

In Episode 16, the housemates went horseback riding to try to take their minds off Pedro, who was becoming sicker. He'd gone to the emergency room with a temperature of 104 degrees. Meanwhile, Mohammed was having relationship troubles. After breaking up with his girlfriend, Stephanie, and having a fling with a friend from San Diego, he had second thoughts and called Stephanie in tears to apologize.

In Episode 17, the cast went to Hawaii, where the women proved to be better surfers than the men, and Rachel survived a scary slip while cliff-diving. At a luau, vegan Jo took offense to the pig roast. Later, Jo and Rachel looked for guys, while Pedro spent his free time parasailing.

Rachel was the center of attention in Episode 18, as she joined a staunch Republican group, yet contradicted her conservatism by getting a tattoo on her back. Meanwhile, Cory became jealous of Rachel's relationship with Jo, while Jo rebuffed her friend Steve's advances to be more than friends.

In Episode 19, Pedro's relationship with Sean vastly improved, and the two were married at the house. They briefly considered relocating to Miami, but opted to stay in San Francisco. Meanwhile, Puck harassed the house with phone calls. He was involved with a woman named Toni, who he thought might be "the one."

Before parting ways in Episode 20, Rachel and Jo hung out in San Francisco, while Pedro, Cory, Pam, and Judd spent the day in Monterey. Mohammed was off in his own world, working on his band. Pedro and Rachel ate lunch and agreed to accept each other's differences. Puck eventually got his driver's license, and picked up items he'd left at the house. The housemates had one last question-and-answer game before making their tearful goodbyes.

THE REAL WORLD
(Season 4—London)

GENRE	Docusoap
FIRST TELECAST	6/28/1995
LAST TELECAST	11/15/1995
NETWORK	MTV
EPISODE STYLE	Story Arc
CAST	Jacinda Barrett; Neil Forrester; Jay Frank; Sharon Gitau; Mike Johnson; Kat Ogden; Lars Schilchting
PRODUCTION COMPANY	Bunim-Murray Productions
CREATED BY	Mary-Ellis Bunim; Jonathan Murray
EXECUTIVE PRODUCERS	Mary-Ellis Bunim; Jonathan Murray

The Real World went international in Season 4 as seven young adults from three continents lived together in England's capital city. This season's cast included Paris-based model Jacinda, "noise" musician Neil, playwright Jay, singer/songwriter Sharon, race-car driver Mike, anthropology student and fencer Kat, and disk jockey/aspiring event marketer Lars.

In Episode 1, everyone met at the Notting Hill flat, where they figured out the roommate situation. Mike paired off with Jay, Lars went with Neil, Kate shared with Jacinda, and Sharon got a room to herself, partly because she slept with the lights on.

The housemates struggled to adapt to their new surroundings in Episode 2. Mike was surprised to discover that local supermarkets didn't carry ranch dressing. Meanwhile, Neil and Kat developed an attraction to each other, which was a problem, since Neil was already dating a girl named Chrys.

Neil took issue with Americans in Episode 3, much to Yankee Mike's chagrin. Jealous Chrys sent Neil a shocking Valentine's Day gift: a pig's heart with a nail through it. Since Neil still loved Chrys, he decided not to pursue his attraction for Kat. Meanwhile, Jacinda received more conventional Valentine's Day gifts from her boyfriend in New York.

Sharon had surgery to remove a growth in her throat in Episode 4. Despite being told not to talk for a week, she spoke by the end of the day. Meanwhile, disc jockey Lars was offered a job by a commercial station, but it turned out not to be what he wanted.

Episode 5 had a sports theme, as Mike's frustration at not being able to find a sponsor for his racing team forced him to turn to his father, who said he'd sponsor Mike only if he returned to the States. Meanwhile, Kat flew to San Jose, California, and bombed at the junior Olympic fencing trials. She returned to London.

Employment was the theme of Episode 6, as Jacinda begrudgingly took modeling jobs, though she didn't particularly care for them. Mike, who was chastised by his housemates for being lazy, went out and found a job as a rollerblading instructor. After a failed stint as a waitress, Sharon discovered her calling as a technology fair salesperson.

While performing a concert in Episode 7, a drunk fan bit off a chunk of Neil's tongue, and he was rushed to the hospital. He could not talk, eat, or drink for a while. Meanwhile, Jay had trouble finding a theater to perform his play, *The Bedroom*. After sending an e-mail to Blues Traveler, Jay was surprised when the band dedicated a song to him at their London concert, and invited him to hang out with them after the show.

In Episode 8, Mike envied the way Lars was able to meet women, and later he received a visit from his German exchange student friend, Mia. Jacinda's boyfriend, Paul, also visited. They bought a puppy together, which didn't sit well with the other housemates. Jacinda also started to take flying lessons.

Mike's family visited in Episode 9, and his dad talked Lola racecars into sponsoring his son, helping improve their father-son relationship. Jay's girlfriend, Marisa, also arrived. They had a great time hanging out, but ultimately decided to take things easy.

Tensions rose in Episode 10, as the house phone line was disconnected, requiring £530 to be reactivated. Sharon became the black sheep of the household, despite everyone's unhappiness with the messes left everywhere by Jacinda's dog, Legend. Lars later had his bike stolen, and the girls lost all of their wallets.

In Episode 11, the cast was sent on a mystery getaway in Northern England. The group participated in a series of bonding tasks, such as wall-climbing, raft-building, and a ropes course. Sharon's fear of heights triggered an argument with Jacinda, who didn't respect Sharon's needs. Throughout the episode, the housemates realized how much they ostracized Sharon, and they made amends, especially Lars, who got down on his knees to apologize to her.

In Episode 12, Mike finally got a taste of auto racing. His housemates attended the race, but technical difficulties with his car prevented him from winning. The cast was supportive nonetheless, and the whole experience brought the group closer.

Unable to find a theater for his play, Jay performed his piece, *The Bedroom,* in the flat in Episode 13. The rest of the housemates helped out by running lights and cheering him on. The play was about his true experience dealing with his estranged father, and the court battle he had had to fight to be adopted by his stepfather. The housemates were moved and impressed by Jay's acting and writing talents.

Following the play in Episode 14, the housemates transformed their house into a club, with rocker Neil and disc jockey Lars as the entertainment. Everyone had a few drinks, and Jacinda rebuffed Mike's romantic overtures, so he hooked up with a woman named Hannah. Kat also had a brief exchange with a motorcycle-driving guy named Sebastian.

In Episode 15, Kat seemed to be enjoying her acting classes, but she choked while delivering her monologue, sending her into a depression. The cast visited Sharon while she was working at a home show convention, but she still felt that they didn't really understand or appreciate her. Later, when she got sick, the roommates showed their support by bringing flowers and gifts to the hospital.

Jacinda showed her wild side in Episode 16 by getting her tongue pierced, and persuading Kat to run naked through the streets. A homesick Jay went home to Portland, Oregon, to see his girlfriend, Alicia, then returned to London reinvigorated.

It was confession time in Episode 17, as Jacinda shared her belief in the Bible, and Mike admitted that he didn't know himself very well. But the confessionals soon devolved into silliness. The girls went sightseeing, and Lars proved he was a hard partyer.

Romance blossomed in Episode 18 as Mike met a woman named Nina, who seemed to change his womanizing ways. Kat fell for Sharon's British friend Spencer, who invited her to a wedding. Lars met a special woman. His plans to rent a convertible were curtailed when he got a flat tire, so the two took a romantic train ride instead.

Music was the focus of Episode 19, as disc jockey Lars tried to meet more promoters, and rocker Neil was forced to look for a real job. Sharon was also part of a band, but her chronic tardiness cost her when she arrived very late to a rehearsal.

Convinced he could achieve greater success racing in the States, Mike returned to America in Episode 20. He quickly realized that he missed London and his flatmates, and he came back "home." Meanwhile, Jacinda tried to further her modeling career by going to Italy, where she participated in photo shoots.

Episode 21 featured the most exotic *Real World* excursion yet, as the seven castmates went to Kenya for a week. They went on safari, watched an African sunset, visited a native village, and met Masai warriors. Sharon was appalled when the Masai slaughtered a goat for dinner.

In Episode 22, the Masai drank the slaughtered goat's blood, and a curious Neil tasted it. A disgusted Sharon eventually came to terms with the slaughter after talking it over with a Masai warrior, and went on a fast as her way of protesting the event. The week concluded with a balloon ride, and the trip proved to be a bonding experience for everyone.

The season ended with a special reunion episode, where the casts from the first four seasons discussed their experiences on the show and answered questions from a studio audience.

THE REAL WORLD

(Season 5—Miami)

GENRE Docusoap
FIRST TELECAST 6/28/1995

LAST TELECAST	11/15/1995
NETWORK	MTV
EPISODE STYLE	Story Arc
CAST	Flora Alekseyeun; Sarah Becker; Mike Lambert; Melissa Padrón; Joe Patane; Dan Renzi; Cynthia Roberts
PRODUCTION COMPANY	Bunim-Murray Productions
CREATED BY	Mary-Ellis Bunim; Jonathan Murray
EXECUTIVE PRODUCERS	Mary-Ellis Bunim; Jonathan Murray

It was back to the United States in Season 5 of *The Real World*, as the castmates moved into a waterfront house in Miami, Florida's South Beach. The cast included the uninhibited Flora, comic book editor Sarah, restaurant manager Mike, Cuban Melissa, business owner Joe, gay model Dan, and innocent waitress Cynthia.

In Episode 1, the future housemates said goodbye to their friends and families at home. Upon arrival at the house, the roomates met and the girls fought over the upstairs bedroom. Sarah and Joe showed their impulsive sides by jumping in the pool with their clothes on.

Employment was the theme of Episode 2, as the housemates talked about going into business together. They turned down Flora's suggestion of opening a hip coffee shop. Meanwhile, Dan landed a magazine job after getting rejected at a restaurant, and Flora flirted her way into a bartending gig, as well as a date with her boss, Louis. Flora's flirtation didn't sit well with her housemates, who felt she was acting like a "ho."

Joe was the focal point of Episode 3, after he stayed home while the others went dancing. He claimed he wanted to stay loyal to his girlfriend, Nicki, yet Mike said he'd seen Joe flirt with a waitress. Joe's photo album betrayed his sordid history with women.

Frustrations arose in Episode 4 as Cynthia was unsatisfied with her love life. Dan felt he couldn't talk about problems with his roommates but he got a boost after he was discovered by a modeling agency and was invited to appear in an Armani show, which the housemates attended.

In Episode 5, it was revealed that flirtatious Flora had a boyfriend when Mitchell visited from Boston. He had no idea about Flora's fling with Louis. Meanwhile, Joe returned to New York to clean out his apartment and officially relocate to Miami.

More relationships were revealed in Episode 6, as Melissa introduced her extremely possessive boyfriend, Cesar, to the house. Dan also had a boyfriend named Arnie, who hadn't come out to his parents yet. The idea of the housemates' going into business together was revisited, but they couldn't settle on which business to start.

The housemates started a fashion line in Episode 7. Sarah wasn't sold on the idea, so she started her own restaurant-supply delivery business.

In Episode 8, Joe's relationship with Nicki was tested when he met a flirtatious girl named Leah at a fashion show. Meanwhile, Flora's fling with Louis seemed nearly over after he refused to take her to the hospital for a spider bite, thinking she was acting childish.

The cast met Nicki in Episode 9, and secretly made fun of her huge size, and how she always complained about Joe. Meanwhile, Mike questioned everyone's commitment to the fashion line, threatening to back out unless they all became serious.

Joe worked out his problems with Nicki in Episode 10, after mysteriously disappearing for a while. Meanwhile, Dan had difficulty with Arnie's refusal to come out of the closet, and he offered to help.

In Episode 11, Sarah annoyed Flora by allowing three inner-city kids to visit the house, who turned the place upside down. The two women made peace. Meanwhile, Cynthia grew increasingly unhappy at her lack of independence in the house.

Melissa caused trouble in Episode 12 as she insulted Sarah's friend, and read one of Dan's personal letters out loud to the whole house. She and Dan argued, but they made up the following morning.

The spotlight was back on relationships in Episode 13, as Mike returned to Boston and decided he was not ready to commit to his on-again, off-again girlfriend, Heather. Dan's parents visited and were surprisingly accepting of Arnie and their lifestyle. Sarah's puppy, Leroy, was introduced.

The business was falling apart in Episode 14, as Flora and Joe complained that they were doing all the work. Sarah talked them into starting a dessert-delivery business.

In Episode 15, Joe was in danger of failing a class, something that would prevent him from graduating from Fordham University. In desperation, he flew to New York to give a presentation on his failed business efforts, and he eventually was allowed to pass. Meanwhile, the others hammered out the details of their new company, Delicious Deliveries.

Leroy the puppy took center stage in Episode 16 by biting Cynthia, which triggered an argument between her and Flora. Joe raised eyebrows by handing over his share in the business to the dog. Meanwhile, homesick Cynthia flew to Atlanta, and Dan returned to Kansas to be with his family. Later, Dan blindsided Arnie by going on a date with a guy named Johnny, claiming that he and Arnie were never exclusive.

The signature moment of the season occurred in Episode 17, when Mike, Melissa, and a waitress had a threesome in the bathroom. Flora accidentally broke the bathroom window while trying to get a peek at the action, which Mike and Melissa later denied happened.

In Episode 18, Flora and Sarah accused Dan of being a liar after he backed out of his commitment to the business. Joe returned to New York for his graduation, then shocked everyone by proposing to Nicki during the commencement ceremony. He announced the news to the house at a surprise birthday party that Mike threw for him.

In Episode 19, all of the cast members except Flora and Melissa went on a nature retreat to the Bahamas, where they camped, snorkeled, sailed, and enjoyed the beauty of their surroundings.

In Episode 20, Sarah's friend Hank showed everyone a video he'd shot during his last visit, but Flora and Melissa disliked the way they were portrayed in it. Sarah got into a heated argument with Melissa, which resulted in Melissa packing up and leaving the house.

Unwilling to give up on her idea, Flora pursued a coffee shop business with Mark in Episode 21. Their investors backed out, leaving them without a business. Meanwhile Dan broke the news to his new boyfriend, Johnny, that he was moving to Italy to model.

The castmates said their goodbyes in Episode 22, with Cynthia taking a job in Miami, Dan heading to Milan to model, Sarah returning to San Diego, Mike going back to Jacksonville, Joe getting ready to settle down with Nicki, and Flora deciding to stay with Mitchell in Miami.

THE REAL WORLD

(Season 6—Boston)

GENRE	Docusoap
FIRST TELECAST	7/15/1997
LAST TELECAST	12/10/1997
NETWORK	MTV
EPISODE STYLE	Story Arc
CAST	Jason Cornwell; Sean Duffy; Montana McGlynn; Genesis Moss; Kameelah Philips; Elka Walker; Syrus Yarbrough
PRODUCTION COMPANY	Bunim-Murray Productions
CREATED BY	Mary-Ellis Bunim; Jonathan Murray
EXECUTIVE PRODUCERS	Mary-Ellis Bunim; Jonathan Murray

Beantown was the site of Season 6, as MTV introduced America to poet and philosopher Jason, lumberjack Sean, aspiring archaeologist Montana, lesbian Southern belle Genesis, outspoken African American Kameelah, Spanish-speaking Elka, and basketballer Syrus.

In Episode 1, the cast moved into an old converted firehouse. Jason roomed with Genesis and Syrus, while Elka and Montana paired up, leaving Kameelah and Sean. The housemates got to know one another by going out to dinner and then to a club. Upon learning that Elka was staunchly religious, Genesis decided to hold off revealing that she was a lesbian.

Conflicts surfaced in Episode 2, as Kameelah proved to have an overly domineering personality. Elka and Montana argued over Montana's atheism. Elka got shut out while trying to join her housemates at a bar, and Genesis admitted to Elka that she was gay.

Sean and Jason got off on the wrong foot, but later reconciled in Episode 3. Kameelah took issue with the fact that Syrus dated only white women. Genesis had an identity crisis when the guys tried to convince her to go back to being straight.

In Episode 4, the housemates began working at an after-school program for kids. They also started to open up to one another, as Genesis admitted that she'd had a rough childhood. Syrus confessed that he was once accused of rape, prompting Montana to argue with Syrus. On the way back to the house, Sean and Kameelah had a nasty argument, which they never fully resolved.

In Episode 5, the housemates danced naked on the pool table, in an effort to cheer up Elka on the anniversary of her mom's death. Later, Elka, Jason, and Montana formed a band called Scotch Tape. Genesis found a gay bookstore where she could meet other gays and lesbians. She also went on a website for transsexuals, and met a nice cross-dressing guy.

Dating was the hot topic in Episode 6, as Kameelah revealed the two hundred requirements a guy had to meet before she'd go out with him. She made an exception when she agreed to go on a second date with a "substandard" guy named Aaron. Montana's budding chemistry with Sean was nullified when her boyfriend, Vai, came to visit.

In Episode 7, Jason's girlfriend, Timber, came to the house for a visit. They enjoyed a few days of a passionate reunion, then argued and broke up after she accused him of being jealous of Syrus. Syrus got into a discussion with Sean about the history of African American oppression.

Despite Montana and Vai's consensual open relationship, Montana felt guilty in Episode 8 when she started having feelings for a new guy named Matt. Genesis went to a gay bar with Sean and Kameelah, and met a cross-dresser named Adam (or Eve). She also made out with a girl at a bar, which eventually led to her breaking up with her girlfriend, Tammy.

In Episode 9, Syrus considered dating Louetta, the mother of one of his after-school kids. The roommates weren't happy, and threatened to kick him out of the loft if the relationship caused him to get fired.

In Episode 10, Montana got upset at Syrus over his late-night phone calls and constant visitors. Things come to a head when Kameelah found one of Syrus's friends making out with a girl in their bathroom. Facing possible termination, Syrus agreed to stop seeing Louetta, but continued the relationship anyway. Meanwhile, Genesis's struggle with her sexuality was preventing her from being an effective contributor to the after-school program.

After falling for her drag queen friend, Adam/Eve, in Episode 11, Genesis wondered if she might be bisexual. Kameelah tried to come to terms with dating Doug, despite the fact that she didn't date guys with kids. Sean was hospitalized after coming down with a bad case of hives.

In Episode 12, Montana decided to spend Valentine's Day with Matt since Vai was busy working, then found she was not excited to see Vai when he finally visited. Elka also had dating woes, with her struggling musician boyfriend, Walter, who eventually came up with the money to visit her.

In Episode 13, Anthony from the after-school program sent the roommates to start a computer and pen-pal program in Puerto Rico. While there, Montana went out with a guy named Rafael. During a fun day on the beach, she flashed Sean's video camera. Later, Montana confessed to the group that her real dad had once rebuffed her attempt to contact him when she was younger. On their last night in Puerto Rico, the roommates had a stirring dinner conversation about affirmative action, although Genesis still felt uncomfortable sharing with her roommates.

Two-timing was the order of the day in Episode 14, as Jason learned that Timber had been involved with another guy during their separation. Jason kissed another girl at a party, and eventually forgave Timber. Montana dumped Matt for Vai, but Vai dumped her when he found out that she had been seeing Matt. Montana continued to pursue the relationship with Vai by flying to New York, where they reunited.

Elka's father and brother visited in Episode 15, and had trouble explaining her recent eyebrow piercing and gay bar visits to her dad. Later, at the after-school program, she accused Kameelah of having sex with Doug. Anthony scolded them for making a scene in front of the kids, and sent them home.

After cleaning up the house in Episode 16, Sean, Syrus, and Montana put Jason's dirty dishes on his bed while he was sleeping, with a sign that read "Pig of the Day." They joined their roommates on an after-school program ski trip, where Anthony criticized Sean after he and Jason abandoned the kids to ski on their own. Sean and Genesis got in a tiff and stopped talking to each other. Genesis started posting "Genesis-isms" around the house, which Syrus ripped down, causing controversy in the rapidly dividing household.

Mother's Day led to drama in Episode 17, as Elka flew home to Brownsville, Texas, to pay her respects to her late mom. She offered to take over her mom's duties, but her dad insisted that he had it covered. Genesis was distraught to learn that her alcoholic mother was drinking again. Later, she confessed that she had contemplated suicide when she was younger, while living with her mom.

In Episode 18, kids at the after-school program gave their mentors an unfavorable evaluation, which upset Montana. Elka said that her relationship with Walter would probably end if his visit didn't go well. Everyone but Elka and Jason went to Philadelphia with the after-school program to attend President Clinton's summit. Sean slept through the speech, and the morning after he and Syrus went AWOL following a night of wild partying. The group left for the day without them.

The housemates met LL Cool J at a presidential rally in Episode 19, then attended the "Taste of Philly," where Sean and Montana broke the rules by drinking alcohol in front of the kids. When they returned to Boston, Anthony suspended Syrus, Sean, and Montana from the program. He eventually lifted the suspension on the first two, but fired Montana for allowing the kids to try alcohol.

In Episode 20, to repent for their transgressions, Montana got a volunteer job with Shelter, Inc., while Sean and Syrus tried to start a log-rolling program, and Syrus started a basketball program. The housemates considered evicting Montana from the house because she'd been fired, but they dismissed the idea.

An Episode 21, a vacation to Martha's Vineyard brought high drama as Jason, Kameelah, and Genesis played a disrobing game, and Sean ripped into Kameelah after finding a nasty note she'd written about Montana. Sean accused Kameelah of racism, which prompted Kameelah to level the same charges at Sean.

Eager to redeem themselves in Episode 22, the housemates put on a play at the after-school program for Parents' Night, which was a big success. Anthony repaid the housemates by waking them up with a surprise rendition of "Put a Little Love in your Heart," as sung by the kids. Meanwhile, tension built between Montana, Elka, and Kameelah.

All was forgiven in the Episode 23 finale, as the housemates attended a final group dinner and resolved their differences. At the airport, they said emotional goodbyes to one another and to the after-school kids, then headed their separate ways.

THE REAL WORLD
(Season 7—Seattle)

GENRE Docusoap
FIRST TELECAST 6/10/1998
LAST TELECAST 11/3/1998

NETWORK	MTV
EPISODE STYLE	Story Arc
CAST	Nathan Blackburn; Lindsay Brien; David Burns; Janet Choi; Rebecca Lord; Irene McGee; Stephen Williams IV
PRODUCTION COMPANY	Bunim-Murray Productions
CREATED BY	Mary-Ellis Bunim; Jonathan Murray
EXECUTIVE PRODUCERS	Mary-Ellis Bunim; Jonathan Murray

For Season 7, *The Real World* headed to Seattle. For the first time, two of the housemates knew each other ahead of time: former military men Nathan and David. The other housemates included peppy radio host Lindsay, aspiring reporter Janet, old-fashioned romantic Rebecca, star student Irene, and Jewish African American Stephen.

Episode 1 was a casting special, which offered a look at the selection process for Season 7.

In Episode 2, the castmates moved in to the Pier 70 house on Elliott Bay and met one another. Nathan revealed that he had raised himself since age fifteen, after his dad died, and David said he'd overcome a tough neighborhood and drug addiction. Nathan and Janet developed an attraction, even though he had a long-term girlfriend, Stephanie. Nathan predicted that Lindsay and David would hook up.

In Episode 3, Stephanie wanted to join Nathan in Seattle, while he was thinking more along the lines of their breaking up. Later, he gave Janet a hand massage in the hot tub. Everyone wondered who wrote the diary page on the table complaining about the lack of diversity in the house. (The author was David.) Nathan and David went to a club and picked up women, while Stephen and Rebecca were carded and went home. At the end of the episode, Janet and Lindsay were ready to play, so they burst into the guys' room while they were in bed.

In Episode 4, Rebecca and David appeared to be starting a romance, while a stressed-out Irene sought chiropractic help. The housemates became "modulators" at Seattle's top alternative radio station, and were told they'd eventually get their own show. The band Cornershop performed in the studio, then came back to the house and jumped into the hot tub with the girls. The following night, Rebecca attended a basketball game with another band member, prompting a jealous David to call her a heart-breaker.

The housemates were forced to do roadie work at the radio station in Episode 5. After destroying a door frame while hauling a speaker, the girls were forced to fix it themselves. Meanwhile, Irene and Nathan started flirting, as he tried to reconcile his shaky relationship with Stephanie.

It was Valentine's Day in Episode 6, and Janet accompanied Nathan to buy gifts for Stephanie. Irene got a stuffed gorilla from her grandmother, and a lonely Stephen called his ex, Natasha. Janet felt better about her parents' not supporting her decision to go on the show, after they surprised her by sending flowers. The group went out drinking to commiserate spending Valentine's Day dateless.

David and Stephen were in a sexual identity crisis in Episode 7. After kissing a drag queen at a gay club, David started hanging out with another guy from the gym, whom he later discovered was gay. He freaked out when he learned that the others assumed he was gay, and he immediately dropped his gym buddy. To confirm his straightness, he exposed himself to an impressed Lindsay and Irene. Meanwhile, Stephen was hanging out with a gay friend, and later mentioned in a teary secret confession that he enjoyed spending time with him.

In Episode 8, David was seeing a mystery woman, who turned out to be Kira, the *Real World* casting director. During Irene's birthday party, Nathan vented his frustration with Stephanie to Irene, but later apologized.

Kira quit her job in Episode 9, so she could fly to Seattle to be with David. She second-guessed whether she had made the right decision and left, but David tracked her down. David skipped out on the others, who had to do a promo gig for the radio station on the snowboard slope. He also arrived late to his new job throwing fish at Pike's Place.

Lindsay's brother visited in Episode 10, and they talked about their father's death from colon cancer. The housemates found out that the radio station was sending them to Nepal. Upon arrival, they were overcome by Nepal's beauty, but the high altitude caused Janet to pass out.

In Episode 11, Stephen led the housemates when they recorded six commercials for a sporting and outdoor adventure store. However, he alienated Janet when she overheard him criticizing her for wearing excessive makeup. He also falsely accused someone of stealing his money, which turned out to be on his seat. Group experiences, such as hiking and washing elephants, had a bonding effect on the housemates.

The radio station finally gave the housemates a radio show in Episode 12, but only three of them could be DJs. After plenty of practice and auditions, Lindsay, Irene, and Janet were selected, while Rebecca was the producer and the guys were relegated to field-reporting roles, which upset Stephen. Meanwhile, Nathan was ecstatic when Stephanie visited, and they had several passionate encounters.

In Episode 13, the guys resented Rebecca for overproducing the radio show, titled *Dead Air*. Janet went on a date with a guy named Justin, who was immediately smitten, but she was turned off by his overeagerness.

David's troubled history was explored in Episode 14, as he discussed how he had dodged jail. He fought with his visiting friend Shannon, was called a "BS-er" by his housemates, then was scolded by the radio station for doing a poor job editing an interview. He finally redeemed himself by conducting a good interview. Meanwhile, Stephen's mom had a baby, and he met his uncle for the first time.

Irene had a breakdown in Episode 15, a result of discovering she had Lyme disease. Meanwhile, the other housemates struggled to produce the commercials they'd shot in Nepal.

In Episode 16, an exhausted Irene left the radio show. After fighting with Stephen, she left the house, too. During their final conversation, Irene called Stephen a homosexual, and Stephen called her a bitch. Then he slapped her in the face.

After the slapping incident, the producers intervened in Episode 17, giving the cast an ultimatum: either kick Stephen out of the house or make him undergo anger-management therapy. The housemates let him stay, and he apologized for his actions.

The dark cloud continued to hover in Episode 18, as Lindsay found out that her close friend Bill had committed suicide. She canceled her skydiving trip with Janet to try to come to terms with Bill's death. David received a visit from his friend Anthony, who was in remission from cancer. Later, David complained of chest pains and was taken to the hospital.

In Episode 19, Nathan was excited when he was picked to replace Irene as the third DJ on *Dead Air*. However, when Nathan didn't hear from Stephanie on their two-year anniversary, he got drunk at a bar and hooked up with a girl named Lisa. Later, he tearfully regretted his actions, and chose not to mention Lisa during Stephanie's next visit. Meanwhile, Rebecca recorded an original song for Sir Mix-a-Lot, which was incredibly well received.

Episode 20 was a *Real World/Road Rules* challenge. Nathan led his housemates to victory in a series of water games during a rainy day at Lake Washington.

Episode 21 was the season finale. Stephen revealed that the therapy sessions were working. Later, he talked on the phone with his new woman, Oruba. Nathan was excited to return to Stephanie, and David spent his last day at the fish market engaging in some "fishy" behavior with his male co-workers. Lindsay was pleasantly surprised to receive phone calls from listeners who said they would miss the radio show. Everyone went to the airport for an emotional farewell.

Episodes 22 and 23 were highlight shows from Season 7.

THE REAL WORLD
(Season 8—Hawaii)

GENRE	Docusoap
FIRST TELECAST	6/8/1999
LAST TELECAST	11/9/1999
NETWORK	MTV
EPISODE STYLE	Story Arc
CAST	Ruthie Alcaide; Kaia Beck; Amaya Brecher; Justin Deabler; Teck Holmes; Colin Mortensen; Matt Simon
PRODUCTION COMPANY	Bunim-Murray Productions
CREATED BY	Mary-Ellis Bunim; Jonathan Murray
EXECUTIVE PRODUCERS	Mary-Ellis Bunim; Jonathan Murray

The eighth season of *The Real World* was set in Honolulu. The cast members included bisexual triplet and native Hawaiian Ruthie, strong-minded Kaia, former bulimic Amaya, gay activist Justin, aspiring entertainer Teck, good-looking Colin, and outspoken writer Matt.

Episode 1 kicked off with a splash, as Ruthie and Teck christened the house by going skinny-dipping. Kaia took off her shirt and joined them. Amaya was single and looking, and Matt was bummed to learn that Ruthie wasn't single. Teck got Justin to admit he was gay. Former *Real World* reject Colin showed up with the house key. After choosing roommates, the group went to a club, where Ruthie drank until she passed out.

In Episode 2, the cast confronted Ruthie about her alcohol problem, but she was unwilling to join a twelve-step program. Amaya criticized Teck for not helping out with the Ruthie situation.

In Episode 3, it was revealed that Teck was not very accepting of gay men. The housemates were hired to book talent at a surf shop and café called Local Motion, and their boss, Calvin, gave them a car. Local girl Ruthie hired a band she knew, and they drew one hundred people to the show, earning the house a bonus.

In Episode 4, an inebriated Kaia made out with Ruthie, which she regretted the next day. The house rejected Amaya's suggestion that they promote their club at frats and sororities, but she felt better when she and Colin grew closer.

In Episode 5, Amaya and Colin started sleeping in the same bed, although supposedly nothing happened. After a silly fight, they shared their first kiss, on the beach. Meanwhile, a guy asked Kaia on a date to a Janet Janet Jackson concert.

Ruthie showed off her rapping skills at a barbecue in Episode 6, then overstepped her bounds by giving Calvin's girlfriend a lap dance at her birthday party. The roommates were concerned over changes in Ruthie's personality after she drank. Meanwhile, Amaya vented her sexual frustration at a kickboxing class, as she discovered that her feelings for Colin were stronger than his for her.

Romance was in the air in Episode 7, as Teck brought back a suggestively dressed woman to the house, and later met a more impressive woman, named Andrea. Colin came to terms with his intimacy issues and asked Amaya out on an actual date.

In Episode 8, Justin was offended by a Local Motion comic's anti-gay jokes. Later, Matt accused Justin of being "heterophobic," after Justin took issue with Matt's female-related banter while promoting their club on a local radio station. Justin took his anger out on Amaya, kicking her out of his room for being too sexually involved with Colin. During Justin's seven-day fast with Kaia, he opened up and admitted that he had once almost been arrested for "turning" his first boyfriend gay at age sixteen.

After a drunk-driving incident in Episode 9, the producers stepped in, demanding that Ruthie start seeing an alcohol-addiction counselor. Justin and Ruthie grew closer and went on a hike together, while Colin blamed Justin for encouraging Ruthie's drinking on the night she drove while intoxicated.

Amaya was dealt a double whammy in Episode 10, as she learned her father might have cancer, and Colin asked her for space. After a week apart, Colin and Amaya were sharing a bed again. Matt was psyched when he got an on-air job at the local radio station.

In Episode 11, Kaia met and grew close to rapper Trey, from The Pharcyde. She came to terms with some intimacy issues of her own, which she attributed to having lost her father to AIDS. She and Justin took a getaway trip to the Big Island, while the cast learned they'd be going to India.

Ruthie had another drinking incident in Episode 12, which led her to contemplate suicide from the balcony of her twin sister Sara's hotel room. The other housemates planned an intervention, but Ruthie didn't show up, after Matt spilled the beans. She finally scheduled a meeting of her own, where she prepared to make a shocking confession.

In Episode 13, Ruthie admitted that alcohol had taken over her life. The housemates gave her an ultimatum: check into rehab or leave the house. Unable to compromise, Ruthie chose to leave.

The cast showed concern for Ruthie in Episode 14. She met Matt for dinner and told him she felt betrayed by the housemates. Meanwhile, Matt became closer with Sara. The rest of the house put on a talent show to draw publicity for Local Motion.

The housemates flew to India in Episode 15, and discovered they'd be traveling throughout the country on the fanciest of trains. Justin conspired to split up Colin and Amaya by playing them against each other. During a stop, Teck entertained the locals by beat-boxing.

In Episode 16, Amaya and Colin learned of Justin's plot against them. After hearing about the scheme, Kaia distanced herself from Justin. Later, Justin discovered that his great-aunt was dying of cancer, and he decided to leave the show.

Back in Hawaii, and with Justin gone, Colin had a bedroom to himself, until Amaya showed up, trying to hit on him again. Colin attempted to distance himself from her, which caused her pain. She felt better after skydiving with Matt and Teck. Teck's wild ways came back to haunt him, as the housemates found out through a woman he was dating that he'd called one of the housemates a bitch. Meanwhile, Matt found out that Ruthie was coming back to the house.

Relationship troubles ruled Episode 18, as Ruthie returned and found out that she and Teck were dating the same girl, Malo. Meanwhile, Amaya's anguish over Colin caused her to stop eating.

In Episode 19, Local Motion sponsored a charity boat cruise. Ruthie and Colin silk-screened T-shirts for the cause, and Amaya and Colin toured the children's hospital that would receive the charity donation. The cruise was a huge success, and the roommates presented a large check to the hospital. Colin welcomed two friends to the house, while Amaya still had it out for Ruthie.

Amaya met a new guy, Michael, in Episode 20, and they went on a romantic first date. After Matt found an open magazine article about sexually transmitted diseases and overheard Amaya talking on the phone about a medical problem, he wrongly suspected that she had one.

Amaya stirred the pot again in Episode 21 by spending the night with Colin's friend Tony, though she assured Colin that nothing happened. With the rest of the house disgusted with her, Amaya made an ill-fated attempt to clear the air, only causing tensions to escalate.

In Episode 22, Ruthie speculated that Amaya's household rejection might force her to become a better person. The housemates put on their own talent show at Local Motion, and a stage kiss between Kaia and Matt resulted in her inviting him to sleep in her bed that night. Matt admitted he was torn between his feelings for Kaia and Sara.

In the Episode 23 finale, Amaya talked to Kaia to clear the air. The housemates went to the airport for a final chance to reminisce, then said their goodbyes.

THE REAL WORLD
(Season 9—New Orleans)

GENRE Docusoap
FIRST TELECAST 6/8/2000
LAST TELEECAST 11/16/2000

NETWORK	MTV
EPISODE STYLE	Story Arc
CAST	David Broom; Melissa Howard; Kelley Limp; Jamie Murray; Danny Roberts; Matt Smith; Julie Stoffer
PRODUCTION COMPANY	Bunim-Murray Productions
CREATED BY	Mary-Ellis Bunim; Jonathan Murray
EXECUTIVE PRODUCERS	Mary-Ellis Bunim; Jonathan Murray

Season 9 in the Crescent City featured the African American overachiever David, manic Filipina Melissa, gorgeous straight-shooter Kelley, objectivist entrepreneur Jamie, gay hunk Danny, Catholic hipster Matt, and innocent Mormon Julie.

The season unofficially premiered with a casting special, which documented the search for *Real World* and *Road Rules* contestants.

The housemates moved in to the Belfort Mansion and met in Episode 1. They discovered they had a pet dog named Shorty. During a traditional Cajun dinner, Julie told everyone she was a Mormon, and Danny gradually revealed that he was gay and dating a military man.

In Episode 3, Julie told Danny that she supported his sexual orientation, even if she didn't agree with it. David and Melissa began flirting with each other, but David became upset when Melissa drank too much, embarrassing herself at a strip club. They eventually made up.

In Episode 4, the cast got a job producing a public-access television show, with Kelley producing and Danny directing. They were chewed out by their boss, Elton, for arriving late on their first day. Melissa went on a few dates with a frat guy, Matt, but later broke things off when she suspected he was dating her because of *The Real World*.

In Episode 5, Melissa and Kelley were attracted to Jamie, but Kelley later set her sights on a med student, Peter. She invited him to a Chinese New Year drag performance by her, Julie, and Melissa. Meanwhile, Melissa and Jamie became closer, eventually taking a bubble bath together.

David wasn't pulling his weight at the television station in Episode 6, drawing complaints from Kelley and Melissa. Later, he gave Melissa a striptease for her birthday, upsetting Melissa's ex, Ryan, who was visiting.

Valentine's Day caused controversy in Episode 7, as Danny contemplated cheating on his boyfriend, Paul, with a guy named Wes. Paul surprised Danny with a visit, and all was right in their world again. Meanwhile, Peter left his girlfriend for Kelley. The two had a romantic dinner and spent the night at his place. Julie was distracted from her unrequited flirtation with Matt when her brother, Alan, visited.

The cast pulled off their first live television show with flying colors in Episode 8, although Kelley complained to Elton about her difficulty managing the staff, particularly David.

Race was the hot topic in Episode 9, as Melissa and David gave Julie a crash course in racial terminology. During a boating excursion with Jamie's four visiting friends, Melissa became upset when the tour guide described a bird using a racial term.

In Episode 10, David produced their next public-access show. After communication problems with the staff, they flaked out on an important meeting. The housemates eventually resolved their problems, producing their best show yet. Also, David sang the national anthem at a hockey game.

Matt invited a different Kelley to the house in Episode 11, but wanted to get to know her better before asking her on a date. After Julie accused Melissa of not respecting her Mormonism, Melissa saw a therapist to help her deal with the issues that were making her consider leaving the house.

Mardi Gras was featured in Episode 12. The cast was invited to author Anne Rice's house, and later took a ride on a float. Drunk Danny cheated on Paul during a party, but Paul forgave him. Julie surprisingly enjoyed the sinful celebration.

The cast headed to South Africa in Episode 13. The trip brought everyone together, except David, who seemed intent on isolating himself from the others. Still, the group helped him break down his barriers so he could enjoy the rest of his time with them.

In Episode 14, David opened up to the group through their experiences bungee-jumping and visiting needy locals. They returned to New Orleans, and Melissa congratulated David on his improved attitude.

Danny's parents met Paul for the first time in Episode 15, but his dad didn't realize that Paul was Danny's boyfriend. Danny took issue with Matt's Catholic belief that homosexuality was wrong. Jamie produced the next television show on African music, and the others criticized him for working hard only when he was in charge.

In Episode 16, Julie hit on a guy named Matt at a coffeehouse, but found that he was gay. Then she approached a waiter, Baxter, but decided she didn't like his crowd. Kelley and Jamie had a heated discussion about their differences.

Julie produced the show in Episode 17, and it was a big hit, but she had trouble justifying her recent behavior in New Orleans to her visiting family. Danny took offense at Julie's brother's anti-gay beliefs. Matt went on a "Mullet Hunt" as a piece for their next show.

In Episode 18, Julie had an emotional blowup at her father because of their strained relationship. Meanwhile, Kelley stayed in New Orleans to continue her relationship with Peter.

Tired of partying in Episode 19, Jamie focused more on his spirituality. He mud-wrestled and kissed Julie, who appealed to his new spiritual side. Melissa began painting as a way of helping her cope with the craziness in the house.

David produced a "Stripper Fashion Show" in Episode 20, though Kelley and Matt salvaged the show, and David was upset when he didn't get credit. Matt met a girl, Brandi, and invited her to sign his website guest book. Julie forged Brandi's signature, causing Matt to call Brandi, discovering she already had a boyfriend.

In Episode 21, Julie became upset with Matt after he made a rude comment to her visiting friend Jacob. Meanwhile, the house called a meeting to discuss David's behavior after he planned a stripper hot tub party and ditched Matt before a recording studio session.

In Episode 22, David explained that his recent behavior was a result of his mother being sick, and he made amends with the housemates. Julie started a game of Spin the Bottle, and Matt refused to kiss her when it was his turn. Later, they cuddled during a slumber party.

Before leaving in Episode 23, Julie got Matt to kiss her on the lips. He returned to Georgia Tech and she to BYU, although her experience in New Orleans made her reconsider some of her religious beliefs. David went home to tend to his mom, Kelley stayed in New Orleans with Peter, Danny returned to be with Paul, and Melissa moved to Los Angeles.

The cast reappeared in a reunion special more than a week later. They talked about their experiences on the show and what they were up to since it finished taping.

THE REAL WORLD
(Season 10—Back to New York)

GENRE	Docusoap
FIRST TELECAST	6/8/2000
LAST TELECAST	11/16/2000
NETWORK	MTV
EPISODE STYLE	Story Arc
CAST	Rachel Braband; Malik Cooper; Kevin Dunn; Nicole Jackson; Mike Mizanin; Coral Smith; Lori Trespicio
PRODUCTION COMPANY	Bunim-Murray Productions
CREATED BY	Mary-Ellis Bunim; Jonathan Murray
EXECUTIVE PRODUCERS	Mary-Ellis Bunim; Jonathan Murray

To celebrate its tenth season, *The Real World* returned to the Big Apple, the city where it all began. The anniversary cast included music fanatic Rachel, biracial DJ Malik, cancer survivor Kevin, star African American student Nicole, all-American frat guy Mike, beautiful and outspoken Coral, and singing superstar Lori.

Before the new season began, VJ John Norris emceed a tenth-anniversary special, revisiting some of the controversial characters and topics from previous seasons.

Then, there was another *Real World* and *Road Rules* casting special, showing how the current season's cast had been selected.

The cast arrived in New York in Episode 1. They met and settled in at their loft on Hudson Street.

Kevin and Lori immediately started flirting in Episode 2. Mike made a racially insensitive comment. Later, he apologized to Malik and Coral.

Black History Month was highlighted in Episode 3. Coral hadn't accepted Mike's apology for his comment, prompting the others to feel she was being unreasonable. Malik's friend Namane visited, and sided with Mike, angering Coral. Insecure Nicole went out with a guy, Rene, but dumped him when she found out he had voted for George W. Bush.

In Episode 4, underage Rachel faked her way into a club, where she was put off by a guy who came on too strong. Meanwhile, Kevin kissed Lori on the dance floor, but told her he didn't want them to get together, humiliating her.

It was Valentine's Day in Episode 5. Mike invited sketchy women to the house, and ended up dating one of them, Becky. Disgusted, the women of the house insulted the visiting women and went out on their own. Mike apologized for his behavior by sending flowers to each of his female housemates, prompting Coral to give Mike a surprise hug. Lori started flirting with British bartender Stevie B., and Kevin sent flowers to a girl named Emily, from back home.

Mike felt like the outcast in Episode 6, until the housemates were offered a job as a street team to promote bands for Arista Records. It turned out he'd share a desk with Coral.

In Episode 7, Nicole accused Malik of being a hypocrite, for projecting a pro-black image while being open to dating white women. Kevin tried to defend him, but Nicole would hear none of it.

In Episode 8, Lori became upset when her housemates asked her to stop singing all the time. She ended up meeting a band through her work with Arista and became their new singer. Meanwhile, Rachel, Malik, Nicole, and Kevin didn't take their work assignment seriously, screwing it up.

Coral and Nicole fell out of favor in Episode 9 after they yelled at Rachel, which made her cry. In what could be considered karmic payback, Coral and Nicole skipped a voluntary workday and missed out on tickets to see Outkast. They yelled at their roommates for not getting extra tickets for them, and had the nerve to ask their boss if they could still get tickets, immediately after he chewed them out for having a poor work ethic.

In Episode 10, the cast went to Morocco, where they discovered the *Road Rules* cast had been sent to join them. Coral met her match in Adam, who refused to put up with her attitude. Rachel and Blair seemed to strike up a romance.

Back in New York in Episode 11, Mike invited his friend Sarah to visit. The girls were disgusted when Mike boasted that he was the first in the house to have sex. Rachel planned to hang out with a cute guy, Gabe, who was in town with his band, but he called and broke the news that he had a girlfriend. Rachel and Lori wondered why they were the only ones who weren't getting any action.

In Episode 12, Lori wasn't happy with the direction of her new band, and submitted her demo CD to a music supervisor at Arista. He was impressed and wanted to use her on a track. Meanwhile, Nicole and Coral improved their work ethic, which made them easier to be around.

Nicole and Malik were still fighting in Episode 13, and she did not go to his birthday party. Mike's separated parents visited, and his dad embarrassed him with a racially insensitive comment. Malik met his father's family for the first time, since his dad had walked out on him when he was six months old. The meeting went well, and the family embraced him.

In Episode 14, the girls made a pact to get dates by the end of the month. Lori flirted with a jewelry store doorman, and he invited her to try on jewels, but she found out he had a serious girlfriend. The housemates met Run-D.M.C. at Arista and had Adidas shoes signed. The girls pranked Mike by hanging a poster over his bed that read, "Arista Kiss-Ass and Proud."

The housemates competed in a window display contest for Arista in Episode 15. Kevin, Lori, and Coral's display for Outkast beat Rachel, Nicole, Mike, and Malik's display for Dido. Mike developed a professional wrestling alter ego called "The Miz." Nicole surprised everyone by organizing a house meeting to apologize for her attitude, which brought the house together.

There was finally peace in the house in Episode 16. Nicole's efforts to hook up with a guy named Bobby were thwarted when she drank too much and kept vomiting.

In Episode 17, Kevin started dating a model, Beth, and they hit it off, although he wondered if he wanted to start something serious during his last month in New York City. Lori stressed over planning a house trip to Boston, where they would watch her final performance with her a capella group. They got lost on the way there, but it was worth it after Lori and her group gave a spectacular performance.

Rachel was chastised for not pulling her weight in the housecleaning in Episode 18. The *Road Rules* cast visited New York, and Malik and Jisela hit it off. They all went to a party, which resulted in lots of drinking, lap-dancing, and girl-on-girl kissing. Rachel opened up by giving her best attempt at a pole dance in the subway.

The housemates went to the Hamptons in Episode 19, and each brought one guest from the casting finals. After a wild, sexually charged party, Jisela ended up naked with Blair in the confessional room, which deeply hurt Malik. Meanwhile, Nicole became close to the guy she'd brought, Bobby.

In Episode 20, the cast marveled at how Nicole's obsession with Bobby had softened her normally assertive edge. On their last night in the Hamptons, he gave in and slept with Nicole. It was the first time she'd had sex in four years. Meanwhile, Malik was disappointed with Jisela, who shot a video in which she made fun of the guys.

It was their last week at Arista in Episode 21, and their task was to get K-Rock to add a song by the Arista band Adema to their playlist. Thanks to the cast's underprepared pitch and a lukewarm reaction to the band's music, K-Rock passed on Adema. Regrouping with better preparation, they got a second chance to pitch, and ultimately convinced Arista to put Adema on their playlist. Arista threw a going-away party for the housemates.

In Episode 22, Coral and Mike patched things up, while Mike got back at Rachel for making fun of "The Miz" by soaking her in the shower. The two bonded during a final dinner together, and left with good feelings.

THE REAL WORLD
(Season 11—Chicago)

GENRE	Docusoap
FIRST TELECAST	1/8/2002
LAST TELECAST	7/16/2002
NETWORK	MTV
EPISODE STYLE	Story Arc
CAST	Chris Beckman; Kyle Brandt; Tonya Cooley; Keri Evans; Aneesa Ferreira; Theo Gantt III; Cara Nussbaum
PRODUCTION COMPANY	Bunim-Murray Productions
CREATED BY	Mary-Ellis Bunim; Jonathan Murray
EXECUTIVE PRODUCERS	Mary-Ellis Bunim; Jonathan Murray

The Real World kicked off its second decade in the Windy City, housing seven strangers in a converted warehouse in the Bucktown/Wicker Park area. Season 11's housemates included gay recovering alcoholic Chris, "recovering" footballer Kyle, beautiful former foster child Tonya, aspiring FBI agent Keri, interracial lesbian Aneesa, church and ladies' man Theo, and Jewish and recently single Cara.

As usual, the season kicked off with a special casting episode.

The housemates moved in and met one another in Episode 1. Small-town Tonya had trouble adjusting to being around a black man like Theo. Theo had his eyes on Aneesa, who liked to walk around naked and revealed that she was a lesbian. During a house gathering in the hot tub, Chris said he was a recovering alcoholic, but he didn't disclose his homosexuality.

In Episode 2, Chris responded to accusations that he was a virgin by claiming that his babysitter deflowered him at age twelve. Aneesa figured out the truth and reassured him that it was okay. She told Theo she just wanted to be friends, yet joined him in the shower and slept naked with him in bed.

The gang went to the beach in Episode 3, where boy-hungry Cara, who was conflicted by feelings for her ex, Jared, met a guy named Jason. Theo said he was surprised there weren't any gay guys in the house, then learned that Chris was gay. He seemed to accept Chris and his boyfriend, Kurt, while Tonya had trouble reconciling Chris's homosexuality with her idea of sin.

By Episode 4, Tonya preferred to talk to her boyfriend, Justin, on the phone, instead of hanging out with the housemates. The cast found out they'd work as lifeguards, but only Chris, Keri, and Kyle passed certification. Tonya developed a kidney problem and returned home to Washington state, but the others thought she was simply homesick.

In Episode 5, Kyle and Keri developed an attraction, but Kyle had a girlfriend back home. Whenever they were out with friends, Kyle disregarded Keri, which frustrated her. Back in Washington, Tonya realized how homesick she really was.

Keri was fed up with Kyle in Episode 6, and went on a date with a guy named Tyler. Kyle became jealous, and Keri decided she'd rather continue pursuing him. The housemates criticized Theo for constantly inviting over his rowdy friends, but he refused to apologize. Later, he disconnected the phone while Tonya was talking to Justin, and she threw a glass, nearly hitting him. After the girls met to talk about Theo's behavior, he agreed to tone things down.

Episode 7 highlighted the first day of work. Since Theo, Tonya, Cara, and Aneesa didn't pass the lifeguard test, they helped children design a mural for the Chicago Parks program. Kurt visited Chris. He wanted more of a commitment than Chris was ready to give. Everyone went to a human rights dinner, except Theo, whose dad convinced him that supporting homosexuality was a sin. Kurt slept over with Chris, so Keri suggested Kyle sleep with her.

In Episode 8, Aneesa's mom tried to convince her over the phone not to be gay. Later, Aneesa hooked up with a girl named Veronica, but after a huge argument, Veronica came over with her ex to pick up her belongings. Meanwhile, the mural team met the kids they'd work with, and realized the impact they could make on their lives.

Aneesa still missed Veronica in Episode 9. They reconciled briefly, then had another highly dramatic split. Cara's dad visited and took the cast to dinner. Later, Cara had a fling with Kyle's friend Djordje, and was upset by the way it ended.

Tonya became sick again in Episode 10 and went to the hospital, although Theo still thought she'd skipped work for other reasons. Kyle invited the group to his dad's lake house. He tried to get Theo and Aneesa to come, but they backed out when they realized he just wanted some non-couples to go so he and Keri would look less conspicuous. Kyle's girlfriend, Nicole, broke up with him, freeing him to date Keri.

The cast had a fun visit to the lake house in Episode 11. Even though he was single, Kyle still wasn't ready to hook up with Keri, so she broke things off. When they returned to the house, Chris broke up with Kurt because he wanted more out of their relationship than Chris wanted to give.

In Episode 12, Theo overslept and arrived late to the mural project, leaving the kids with Tonya, whom they felt was too strict. While Keri returned home for the weekend, Kyle became closer with Cara.

In Episode 13, Tonya took issue with Aneesa's constant nudity, but they reached a compromise. Cara had a fling with her ex-boyfriend, Ali, giving her closure. Chris sensed that Cara had an eating disorder and talked to her about it.

In Episode 14, Aneesa annoyed the house by not doing her chores on time. She even neglected to visit Tonya, who had gone to the hospital after passing a kidney stone. Aneesa eventually came around and pulled her weight, while Tonya returned to the house with a pile of hospital bills to pay.

The housemates wrapped up their jobs in Episode 15, and celebrated by going out drinking. Chris didn't go with them, due to his alcohol recovery, and later, Kyle joined Chris at an AA meeting for support. The cast got a new job as storytellers on Halloween, which upset Theo because he didn't like celebrating a demonic holiday. He became more upset when Keri's story involved a hanging, because it reminded him too much of black slavery.

Episode 16 occurred on September 10, 2001, the day before Aneesa's birthday. Tonya refused to give up the phone so Aneesa could get early birthday greetings from her friends. The following day was September 11, and everyone tried to get in touch with their friends and family. When Tonya wanted to use the phone, Aneesa wouldn't let her, as punishment for the night before. The housemates reconciled after attending a prayer service and lighting candles, which brought them together. This episode received critical acclaim for the way MTV handled the September 11 terrorist attacks.

In Episode 17, Kyle was affected by September 11, and wanted to get back together with Nicole. While Kyle continued to hook up with Keri, he became jealous after Keri went out with Cara's friend. The two eventually had an argument and things appeared to be over. Meanwhile, Aneesa had a breakdown after losing the keys to the minivan.

In Episode 18, the cast drove to St. Louis with Cara so she could have closure with her ex, Jared. Chris had a family emergency and couldn't go, while Tonya chose to stay behind and complain about her roommates on the phone to Justin. The others, in turn, spent the car ride dissing her.

In Episode 19, the cast went to New England, without Tonya, whom Theo had called out as being antisocial. Justin defended Tonya, and they eventually settled things. Later, Justin became jealous of Tonya's friend Darren, who was sending her money and writing "I love you" at the end of his e-mails. In New England, Theo had a breakthrough by attending a gay party with Chris, and was now proud to say he had a gay friend.

The gang visited haunted houses in Episode 20, then returned to Chicago to prepare for their Halloween storytelling performance. Tonya accused Cara of telling everyone she'd had a boob job, and tried to retaliate by divulging Cara's fear of getting an eating disorder, but Cara wouldn't let her.

In Episode 21, Cara and Kyle accused Keri of underpreparing her skit, so Keri agreed to cut it. When Cara lied and told their boss they were cutting the skit because Tonya was having surgery, Tonya flew off the handle and made Cara confess the true reason. They performed all of the skits anyway, and each was well received.

In Episode 22, Aneesa was ready to tell her father she was gay, but her mom refused to facilitate the conversation. She turned to Chris, who reassured her that his parents had eventually come to accept his orientation. Aneesa was also torn between dating two women, and broke up with both of them. Meanwhile, cash-strapped Tonya applied for patient financial assistance so she could undergo her next surgery.

Kyle invited his younger brother, Austin, to visit in Episode 23, but Tonya and Keri thought he was just doing it to appear sensitive on camera. Later, Kyle later modeled in a charity fashion show, but worried it would make him appear gay. He refused to drive Keri to the parks manager to drop off time sheets. Later, she flirted with other guys in front of him, which led to a huge blowup and a falling-out.

In Episode 24, everyone was emotional about leaving, except Tonya, who couldn't wait to go. She and Chris blew off a night of singing at a coffeehouse organized by Cara. Chris later apologized for missing it. The housemates shared one last conversation in the hot tub before leaving.

A week later, the cast starred in a reunion special. They talked about their experiences in Chicago, and what they had been doing since the show finished taping.

THE REAL WORLD
(Season 12—Las Vegas)

GENRE	Docusoap
FIRST TELECAST	9/8/2002
LAST TELECAST	3/25/2002
NETWORK	MTV
EPISODE STYLE	Story Arc
CAST	Trishelle Cannatella; Arissa Hill; Steven Hill; Frank Roessler; Brynn Smith; Alton Williams II; Irulan Wilson
PRODUCTION COMPANY	Bunim-Murray Productions
CREATED BY	Mary-Ellis Bunim; Jonathan Murray
EXECUTIVE PRODUCERS	Mary-Ellis Bunim; Jonathan Murray

A penthouse suite at the Palms Casino and Resort, Las Vegas, was home for the cast of *The Real World* Season 12. The show starred pretty and athletic Trishelle, feisty Arissa, recently separated Steven, small-town boy Frank, gorgeous heartbreaker Brynn, former navy brat Alton, and artist Irulan.

The season began with a one-hour casting special.

In Episode 1, the castmates met and explored their three-story, high-roller suite. While hanging out at a bar, Frank took an interest in Trishelle, and Steven predicted they'd end up together.

The love quadrangle was in effect in Episode 2: Frank liked Trishelle, and Brynn liked Steven, but Trishelle and Steven made out at a nightclub, upsetting Brynn and Frank.

In Episode 3, former good girl Trishelle called home and apologized for behaving sinfully so soon after moving in. Her dad chastised her, especially for having kissed another girl. Alton got a scare when his ex thought she was pregnant with his child, but it turned out to be a false alarm.

The cast was hired to book entertainment for the Palms nightclub, Rain, in Episode 4. After a rough previous night, Brynn threw up during orientation. Arissa missed her boyfriend, and resisted a strong urge to hook up with Steven.

In Episode 5, Irulan's boss, Marc, hit on her, and the housemates suggested she talk to him about it before he got a bad reputation. Frank jokingly called Arissa "the black bitch of the house," which she did not find funny because of the comment's racial overtones.

Brynn was jealous of Trishelle's relationship with Steven in Episode 6, and the other housemates objected to their sexual activity. Brynn threw a fork at Steven, prompting him to ask the producers to kick her out of the house. The producers left the decision up to him, and he decided to let her stay.

In Episode 7, the housemates dressed as angels and devils for Rain's "Good to Be Bad" night. Trishelle failed to promote the event, then backed out of a group performance to flirt with the bartender, drawing criticism from her housemates. She agreed to improve her work ethic.

In Episode 8, Alton admitted he still had feelings for his ex, yet he got naked with the winner of a bikini contest. When he confessed to his ex, she admitted she'd also cheated on him. They officially ended their relationship. Brynn filled in as a go-go dancer to make some extra money.

The girls suspected Trishelle had an eating disorder in Episode 9. Alton hooked up with Irulan.

Irulan's boyfriend, Gabe, visited in Episode 10, and Alton took his mind off it by spending time with his mother, who was also in town. Unfortunately, his mom was there on business: she needed Alton to sign papers for a case about the man who had abducted and murdered Alton's younger brother.

When Steven's gay best friend, John, visited, Alton confessed that his anti-gay instincts were based on a near-molestation incident that occurred when he was younger. He talked it over with Brynn, whose father was gay. Later, at the bar, Alton almost punched a guy who grabbed his crotch, but the two talked it out instead. Trishelle became upset when Steven flirted with a group of sorority girls. Alton had a dream that Trishelle was pregnant, which was freaky because she was "late" in real life.

Frank finally got some action in Episode 12 when he brought a girl, Melanie, to the confessional room. Thinking it was the perpetually naked Alton, Arissa yelled for them to come out. She apologized profusely when she realized it was Frank. At work, Marc was unhappy with the roommates' recent promotions and staged a team-building exercise.

A team-building seminar in Episode 13 helped everyone come to terms with his own personal issues, including Alton, whose brother had been killed, and Trishelle, who had lost her mom at age fourteen.

In Episode 14, Brynn chose between two guys, settling on Austin. Trishelle finally agreed to take a pregnancy test, which came back negative, even though Steven said he was willing to become a dad.

Arissa was thrilled when her boyfriend, Dario, visited in Episode 15. Later, she fought with a girl at Rain, and was given a stern warning by Marc. Irulan pitched a tent in the living room so Arissa and Dario could have the room to themselves, and Alton found it hard to resist hooking up with her in the tent.

In Episode 16, Irulan's friend Mikey visited for her birthday. That night, Alton and Irulan got kissy at her party, but drunk Alton shacked up with a girl named Carrie instead. Irulan found out about this from Brynn, and confronted Alton. She also called her boyfriend, Gabe, and confessed that she and Alton had had a thing. Gabe forgave her, making her appreciate him even more.

The cast found out in Episode 17 that they were going to Australia to promote the

Palms. Steven told Trishelle that he loved her, but after a discussion, they stopped dating. Trishelle sought comfort with Frank, and later, Steven accused her of hooking up with Frank.

The housemates lived it up in Australia in Episode 18. Arissa was invigorated, and Alton scored a threesome, much to Irulan's chagrin. Upon returning to Las Vegas, Irulan contemplated leaving the house.

In Episode 19, Arissa talked Irulan into staying. Irulan confronted Alton about the threesome, but he denied it, claiming it didn't matter because she had a boyfriend anyway. They started to reconcile after a night of drinking, but tensions remained.

In Episode 20, Arissa's mom called to say that the woman Arissa had filed a restraining order against had filed one back. Later, Arissa's uncle berated her for having her birthday dinner with her housemates instead of with him. Steven thought Arissa's family was trouble and that she should cut them off, but Alton urged her to work things out. Meanwhile, Frank's ex-girlfriend, Emily, visited, and they gave their relationship another shot.

In Episode 21, Trishelle, Steven, and Frank went to Los Angeles so Frank could interview for business school. When they returned to Vegas, Frank caved in to Trishelle's advances and kissed her. The next day, he called Emily to confess, expecting the worst, but Emily forgave him. After some thought, Frank realized that he didn't want a long-distance relationship, and he broke up with Emily. Meanwhile, the housemates got a new job working on a photo shoot for *Stuff* magazine.

In Episode 22, Alton and Irulan started dating other people to make each other jealous. They both broke up with their new flings, and suddenly were single again. Meanwhile, Arissa took time apart from Dario so she could discover who she really was.

In Episode 23, Trishelle was in a similar jealousy-inducing mood, as she hooked up with a new guy, Brian, to annoy Steven. Arissa and Irulan applied to be waitresses at the Palms new poolside bar, but discovered that it wouldn't open for a few days.

The jealous lovebirds came clean in Episode 24, as Irulan and Alton admitted their feelings for each other, and Trishelle and Steven hooked up on Steven's birthday. Earlier, Alton had an incident where he knocked over drinks and tried to blame it on someone else, which almost resulted in a fight.

After a phone argument with Dario in Episode 25, Arissa fell for a new guy, Alex, who had to leave to go back to Los Angeles. He planned to return to Las Vegas the following weekend, but he stood up Arissa. She called Dario and spilled her guts, claiming that it was a sign that they were meant to be together. In the meantime, Brynn thought she was going crazy, and her mom informed her that panic attacks were hereditary. Later, her mom checked into rehab, prompting Brynn to consider going home.

In Episode 26, Steven admitted to Trishelle that he was interested in her only for sex, and broke up with her. Later, when Steven and Frank brought two women back to the house, Trishelle grinded on Steven, causing the women to leave. Meanwhile, things got hot and heavy with Irulan and Alton, but he still got a dancer's phone number . . . using Irulan's pen!

Arissa learned in Episode 26 that Dario had slept with another woman and gotten her pregnant. To get back at him, Arissa lied and said she'd slept with someone, too. She eventually called back and admitted to her lie. They resumed being friendly, but realized that their romantic relationship was over. Meanwhile, Steven helped Trishelle find a new guy—a model, Tyler, whom she immediately fell for. While it was hard on Steven, he wanted Trishelle to be happy and for them to remain friends.

The season concluded with a reunion show hosted by MTV VJ Hilarie Burton.

THE REAL WORLD
(Season 13—Paris)

GENRE	Docusoap
FIRST TELECAST	6/3/2003
LAST TELECAST	11/11/2003
NETWORK	MTV
EPISODE STYLE	Story Arc
CAST	Ace Amerson; Adam King; Leah Gillingwater; Simon Sherry-Wood; Mallory Snyder; Chris "CT" Tamburello; Christina Trainor
PRODUCTION COMPANY	Bunim-Murray Productions
CREATED BY	Mary-Ellis Bunim; Jonathan Murray
EXECUTIVE PRODUCERS	Mary-Ellis Bunim; Jonathan Murray

Season 13 was lucky for the Paris-bound cast, which consisted of bar owner and sixth-year college student Ace, aspiring lyricist Adam, fashionista Leah, gay Irish model Simon, soccer-playing virgin Mallory, nightclub bartender CT, and biracial bartender Christina.

In Episode 1, the cast met and moved into their French château. Most of the guys were hot for Mallory, while CT ogled Christina, and Simon revealed he was gay. The housemates went out at night, marveling that they were in Paris.

In Episode 2, Leah flirted with Ace while at a club, but he told her he didn't date smokers because his mom had died of cancer. Later, she bit his butt in the hot tub, but then overheard him telling a girl named Kate on the phone that he loved her. Meanwhile, Adam didn't have a chance with Mallory, and vented his bitterness by telling Leah she didn't have a chance with Ace, causing her to cry.

Christina and CT flirted in Episode 3, while Ace had trouble adapting to French life. The cast found out they'd be working for Frommer's guidebooks, which would require them to learn French.

In Episode 4, Ace and Mallory started to flirt, but Mallory said she wouldn't act on it. After a night of drinking, Mallory invited Ace to sleep in her bed. In her drunken state, she lost her purse, which contained Leah's passport. Mallory was worried about being on camera, and acted much more freely when she thought she wasn't being watched. Ace, on the other hand, worried what Kate would think. Meanwhile, Adam apologized to Leah for his earlier hurtful comments, which she begrudgingly accepted.

In Episode 5, CT alienated his roommates with his lack of consideration, although he promised to try harder. Meanwhile, Ace's friend convinced him not to worry about kissing Mallory.

The cast got their first Frommer's assignment in Episode 6, reviewing Parisian stores and shopping districts. Leah was in charge of submitting everyone's reviews by the 6:00 p.m. deadline, but sent only hers and Adam's on time, since the others' reviews all needed reformatting. After a short lecture, their boss, Brice, said that Leah and Adam would get a bonus. Adam hooked up with a "blurry woman," someone he was too drunk to see clearly, who stayed the night and overslept a presentation she was supposed to give.

It was Valentine's Day in Episode 7, and after a big argument between CT and

Leah, huge bouquets arrived for Leah and Christina, signed by "Christopher." CT took credit for them, but it turned out they were from Leah's friend Christopher, from home—which landed CT back in the dog house.

In Episode 8, girl-crazy Adam started seeing Talayeh, then went out and kissed another girl, Anna. He later told Talayeh that he couldn't be tied down to one woman. Meanwhile, after Christina's boss criticized her writing, she submitted her next assignment early, directly to the Frommer's office. Her housemates disapproved of her renegade act, and her boss insisted that all future assignments be turned in together.

In Episode 9, Leah cleaned the house for her brother Pascual's visit and criticized Mallory for being messy. Later, Mallory came on to Pascual during his last night in town. Mallory and Leah apologized to each other for their actions.

In Episode 10, Christina complained that the roommates really didn't know one another personally. Then she and Ace fooled around after a ketchup fight. Leah tattled on CT when he didn't go to a Frommer's meeting, and CT was hurt that everyone was talking about him behind his back. Christina was furious when someone stole her eggs, but laughed when Ace confessed by replacing the eggs in the carton with smiley-faced lemons. Her anger resurfaced later when CT and Ace played late-night pool above her room.

In Episode 11, CT submitted everyone's assignments on time, but they were incomplete. Leah was irate, but relented when CT apologized. Meanwhile, Christina and Ace resolved their pool-table issues from the previous night.

The cast found out in Episode 12 that they wouldn't get their bonus because their submission had been incomplete. Despite a pep talk from the Frommer's advisor, David, Leah stormed out of the room. Later, CT went to lunch with the advisor and excitedly pitched a really bad idea for a book called *Women 101*. CT ordered flowers for Leah and Christina, but the two women were still upset. CT finally opened up and admitted to having had problems at home, which changed the way the girls thought about him. Meanwhile, Adam went to a gay bar with Simon and Mallory, danced onstage, then reacted uncomfortably when a gay man gave him sunglasses and kissed him on the cheek. Simon received a visit from his boyfriend, Tkisco, which went extremely well.

Kate visited Ace in Episode 13, though her reluctance to snuggle or call him her boyfriend made for an awkward stay. On her last night in town, they had a bizarre altercation with a cabdriver, which prompted Ace to shove him and Kate. After she left, Ace concluded that their relationship was over. Meanwhile, CT helped a drunken Christina return to the house. He made her a fruit plate the next morning, impressing her with this "new CT."

In Episode 14, the girls persuaded Mallory to get hotter shoes, while Adam blew a ton of money on a girl named Stephanie, who liked him only as a friend.

The cast learned they were going on a European vacation in Episode 15, so Christina feverishly worked to make sure they finished their assignment before they left. The first stop on the trip was Nice, but CT missed the train because he'd forgotten his ticket at the château. He arrived the next day, only to find that Mallory's cousin and aunt happened to be staying at the same hotel. Ace was excited to celebrate his twenty-fourth birthday in the French Riviera.

In Episode 16, the gang traveled to Italy, where Leah fell for a waiter, Giuseppe. The two went on a few dates, but he broke her heart by confessing he already had a girlfriend.

In Rome in Episode 17, Leah loudly announced to her friend, Matt, that CT was dumb. On the train to Switzerland, Christina criticized Leah for always being loud, but Leah said she was proud of it. Mallory joined in the Leah-bashing at dinner that night, starting an argument that had the group thrown out of the restaurant. Upset that everyone hated her, Leah turned for support to CT, who surprisingly was there for her. The trip ended on a sour note, with Leah very upset.

In Episode 18, Ace's good intentions backfired as he accidentally hung up Christina's dirty clothes in her closet, and shrank Leah's clothes in the dryer. Upset over their reaction, he skipped the Frommer's meeting and was docked a week's pay. He contemplated leaving the house, but instead made the girls' beds and left apology notes, winning them over. Meanwhile, the American housemates expressed concern over how the French would view them in light of the impending Iraq war.

In Episode 19, CT returned to his brutish ways, punching a guy in a bar, then threatening to hit Adam for not defending him. He turned sensitive again when his ex-girlfriend, Jamie, visited for her birthday, decorating the house with balloons. Although when CT asked her if he was a nice guy, she couldn't answer him with conviction.

Ill-advised romances were featured in Episode 20, as Leah accepted Giuseppe's invitation to return to Italy for some action, and CT tried to get back together with Jamie. This didn't look likely, thanks in part to poor advice from his cousin Mike.

In Episode 21, CT found out that Leah and Christina had tattled on him regarding his conversations with Mike. Meanwhile, Leah had a fling with Adam's friend Samir, but she still had feelings for Giuseppe.

In Episode 22, Adam wrote a song after learning his dad had split with his mom and moved into his own apartment. Leah's friend Stephanie visited, bringing a note from Leah's doctor that said she might have cervical cancer. Leah confessed to Mallory that she'd felt rejected by her mom and stepfather as a child, which helped Mallory understand her better.

Adam was back in action in Episode 23, as he met a German girl, Lamyae, but his fear of commitment led him to hook up with another girl, Ashley. He confessed the hookup to Lamyae, who called him a jerk. During their latest assignment reviewing hotels, the housemates invited Brice and David to dinner at the house.

An e-mail from Kate in Episode 24 confirmed to Ace that they were over, so he went out and blew $1,000 at a strip club. The housemates were burnt out on travel writing for Frommer's, so they cheated, looking online for information for their Château Versailles submission. Ace invited the housemates to go back to a strip club. After lots of alcohol, he and Mallory hooked up that night.

In Episode 25, Brice interrogated each housemate individually about whether they'd actually gone to Château Versailles. He promised not to bust them, so CT admitted that he and his partner hadn't gone. Later, Ace, Adam, Leah, and Christina got naked in the hot tub for one last frolic. CT felt excluded and withdrew from the final group bonding activities.

The season concluded with a reunion special, hosted by MTV VJ La La.

THE REAL WORLD
(Season 14—San Diego)

GENRE	Docusoap
FIRST TELECAST	1/6/2004
LAST TELECAST	7/13/2004
NETWORK	MTV
EPISODE STYLE	Story Arc

CAST	Frankie Abernathy; Randy Barry; Jamie Chung;
	Charlie Dordevich; Cameran Eubanks;
	Brad Fiorenza; Robin Hibbard; Jacquese Smith
PRODUCTION COMPANY	Bunim-Murray Productions
CREATED BY	Mary-Ellis Bunim; Jonathan Murray
EXECUTIVE PRODUCER	Jonathan Murray

Southern California was the setting for Season 14, which featured masseuse Frankie, industrial artist and nightclub security manager Randy, second-generation Korean American Jamie, free-spirited Charlie, southern belle Cameran, motorcycle daredevil Brad, nightclub dancer Robin, and the Steve Urkel–esque Jacquese.

The housemates moved into their Driscoll's Wharf pad in Episode 1. Despite her aversion to bike-riding "Yankees," southern girl Cameran was attracted to Brad. Frankie revealed that she had cystic fibrosis. She hit on Brad, but he had a long-term girlfriend. Frankie drank too much and vomited. Randy and Robin bonded because they both worked at nightclubs.

In Episode 2, Frankie called her boyfriend, David, admitting she had flirted with Brad the night before. Worried about abstaining from sex for five months, Brad called his girlfriend, Andrea, and suggested they be friends, clearing a path for Cameran to act on her attraction to him.

Jacquese felt left out in Episode 3. He and Robin argued after she called a black man "the *N* word" at a club, but they made up and played basketball.

Robin and Randy got cozy in Episode 4. Randy got naked in front of her, and the housemates overheard him saying, "Boom! Bazooka Joe," although the two later claimed nothing happened. The cast found out that their job had something to do with a boat and water. Frankie freaked out because she was afraid of boats, and Jacquese was concerned because he couldn't swim.

In Episode 5, the roommates learned to sail. They were given a test, which Cameran and Brad initially failed. They retook the test and passed, and everyone earned their $200 salary. Frankie and Robin kissed, and coerced Cameran and Jamie to exchange a peck. Later, Cameran kissed Robin, and Brad showed them his large penis in exchange.

In Episode 6, Robin was arrested for punching a guy in a nightclub who had teased her about being on *The Real World*. Brad was arrested for public drunkenness. While Randy dealt with the situation, Frankie got touchy-feely with him.

In Episode 7, Brad was freed from jail after he sobered up, while Randy drove fifty miles to bail out Robin, who was moved by the gesture. Frankie called David again, worried that she'd done something bad with Randy the night before. An unhappy David threatened to dump her if she cheated on him, so Cameran encouraged Frankie to stop calling him.

In Episode 8, the IDs of underage Jacquese and Cameran were confiscated at a bar. Frankie was in trouble again when she met a guy named Adam. Back at the house, a drunken Robin ran around naked, and was seen urinating in the shower. She crawled into Randy's bed and tried to fool around with him, but he denied her.

Fidelity was on the ropes in Episode 9, as Frankie kissed Adam, but he prevented it from going any further. The roommates were put off by Frankie's liberal attitude about what constituted "cheating." Later, Cameran pulled Brad into the bathroom, but changed her mind when he tried to kiss her.

In Episode 10, Brad chewed out Robin for reneging on her promise to look out for Cameran, who'd met a sketchy guy named Ryan at a club. Robin hit Brad several times, but they talked it out. Frankie admitted that her fear of dying from cystic fibrosis was affecting her decisions in life.

Robin gave up on Randy in Episode 11 and started dating a Marine named Mike. Ryan invited Cameran and the girls to a Playboy-type party, sending a limo to pick them up. The party got too wild for their taste, and ended when someone crashed the owner's Mercedes-Benz. Cameran decided that Ryan was too shady, and she didn't want to see him anymore.

Brad's girlfriend, Andrea, visited in Episode 12, although Brad was late picking her up at the airport because he'd spent the night in jail again for public intoxication. Cameran had stomach problems that day, which Jacquese thought were due to jealousy. That night, Andrea got into a fight with Brad after he flirted with other girls. The next morning they amicably agreed to give each other some space.

In Episode 13, everyone hated their boat job and their boss, Brian. When he made an insensitive comment about Frankie's struggles with work, Jamie told him about Frankie's cystic fibrosis, and Brian approached Frankie to talk to her about it. Randy went out with a girl who had a fake front tooth, but he tired of her and stopped returning her calls.

In Episode 14, Frankie brought home a pet python, which refused to eat a live mouse, so Robin got Frankie to let her keep the mouse as a pet. When Robin pointed out the snake/mouse symbolism between them, Frankie threatened to feed her mouse to the snake again. Meanwhile, Brad's parents informed him that they were kicking him out of the house, and that he had to pay off a lot of bills after a recent motorcycle wreck.

In Episode 15, Frankie's problems with Adam and Dave led her to cut herself with a knife. A concerned Jamie got the girls to take Frankie to dinner, and she then sought help from a therapist.

Brad hooked up with a ditzy blonde, Jackie, in Episode 16. At an amusement park the next day with the girls, Cameran claimed she'd lost respect for Brad and was no longer interested in him.

Dave visited Frankie in Episode 17, forcing her to keep Adam at bay. When Jamie revealed to Adam that Dave was in town, Adam wanted to meet him. After a successful visit with Dave, Frankie cut ties with Adam.

In Episode 18, Brad regretted his hookup with Jackie, yet he kissed Cameran during a group camping trip. The housemates learned they'd be going to Greece.

While in Greece in Episode 19, a bitter feud erupted among Frankie, Robin, and Cameran. Jacquese crashed his moped, but was not hurt.

In Episode 20, an intoxicated Robin told Mike she loved him. Mike drunkenly asked her to marry him. When Robin became an angry drunk, Mike left in disgust, although they made up the next day. Meanwhile, Randy hooked up with his friend Jessica.

Frankie's family visited in Episode 21 to help her deal with her problems. She told the producers she needed to go home, either temporarily or permanently. Meanwhile, Jamie had a great conversation with her mom when she visited, which motivated her to learn Korean.

In Episode 22, the producers told Frankie that if she went home she couldn't come back, but she decided to leave anyway. Jacquese took this hard, because he thought they'd made a connection. Frankie finally called and told everyone that she was happier now that she was with Dave.

In Episode 23, Cameran called Brad to the hot tub while he was on the phone with Andrea, causing Andrea to suspect that something was up. Later, she called Brad and admitted she'd hooked up with another guy, so they split up for good. The roommates interviewed replacements for Frankie, selecting free-spirited Charlie.

In Episode 24, Jacquese was upset over his estranged father, a man he hadn't met until he was in second or third grade. Jacquese's mom visited and had him call his dad. The conversation went surprisingly well. After being docked fifty dollars for not showing up to work on time, Cameran and Robin "accidentally" fell overboard so they could be sent home. Jamie was upset when she found out it wasn't an accident.

Charlie skipped work in Episode 25 to fool around with his girlfriend, Laura, causing the housemates to get docked another fifty dollars each. Charlie claimed he'd cleared the absence with their boss, Troy, but when this turned out to be a lie, Cameran broke Charlie's guitar. Later, she apologized, and found out it would cost $800 to fix it. Troy punished Charlie by making him scrape off the boat's name with his fingernails and a heat gun.

In the Episode 26 finale, after a bouncer realized Cameran's ID was a fake, Brad grabbed it and fled. He was apprehended, but talked his way out of being arrested. The group reminisced about their stay in San Diego. Robin planned to have a long-distance relationship with Mike, while the others went their separate ways.

Vanessa Minnillo hosted a reunion episode a week later. Footage was shown from a previously unseen trip to Mexico with Charlie.

The following week, a special episode aired, highlighting more of the season's unseen footage.

THE REAL WORLD
(Season 15—Philadelphia)

GENRE	Docusoap
FIRST TELECAST	9/7/2004
LAST TELECAST	3/15/2004
NETWORK	MTV
EPISODE STYLE	Story Arc
CAST	Shavonda Billingslea; Karamo Brown; Sarah Burke; MJ Garrett; William Hernandez; Landon Lueck; Melanie Silcott
PRODUCTION COMPANY	Bunim-Murray Productions

CREATED BY Mary-Ellis Bunim;

Jonathan Murray

EXECUTIVE PRODUCER Jonathan Murray

Season 15 of *The Real World* was set in the City of Brotherly Love. The tenants of the turn-of-the-century Philadelphia home were African American homecoming queen Shavonda, non-profit worker Karamo, sexy Sarah, former football star MJ, gay Puerto Rican Willie, super-athlete Landon, and aspiring English teacher Melanie.

The roomies moved in and met in Episode 1. Sarah said she liked to walk around naked, and invited everyone to touch her fake breasts. Karamo revealed to Shavonda that he was gay.

In Episode 2, Karamo told the guys he was gay, which blew MJ's mind. Sarah claimed she "thinks like a guy," and was looking for sex with no strings attached.

Things heated up in Episode 3, as Sarah and MJ hooked up, and Shavonda shacked up with Landon, despite having a boyfriend at home. Sarah became jealous when MJ later gave his number to a girl at a club. He didn't know what to make of Sarah's "purely sexual" intentions.

In Episode 4, Sarah revealed that she had an eating disorder, while Melanie disapproved of Sarah's boob job. Melanie told the others how much Sarah spent on her jeans, and later apologized when Sarah became upset. Willie brought his old flame, Daniel, to the house to fool around, making MJ and Landon uncomfortable. Willie bemoaned to Daniel that his mom still didn't accept his orientation.

Race issues surfaced in Episode 5, as Karamo took offense when Landon admitted he used to use "the *N* word" when he was younger. Later at a club, Karamo became upset after being accosted by cops, who were told he had a gun. MJ tried to calm him down, which upset Karamo further, and he later refused to accept MJ's apology. Meanwhile, Shavonda was angry at her dad for not depositing money in her account as promised, and for not protecting her when her mom used to hit her.

The Philly locals were an unwelcoming crowd, as they threw things at the cast members in Episode 6. MJ wanted to patch things up with Karamo, but Karamo was still angry. The cast got invited to a Philadelphia Soul arena football game and met Jon Bon Jovi. It upset MJ to watch the game because his own NFL dreams had recently been dashed. Bon Jovi informed the cast that their job would be to build a city playground.

In Episode 7, Sarah told Melanie that she was once raped, which helped explain her risqué behavior. Shavonda earned free drinks for everyone at a bar after licking whipped cream off a banana. She was upset that her boyfriend, Shaun, wouldn't allow her to fool around with Landon. MJ told his girlfriend, Ashley, about Sarah, then spent the night with Sarah. MJ's feelings for Ashley made him decide to stop sleeping with Sarah.

Karamo went out with a guy named Dorian in Episode 8, and grew more comfortable expressing his sexuality while the cameras were rolling. Willie was excited when Dan visited. The housemates bickered about ideas for the new playground.

In Episode 9, Shavonda turned Landon on by reading erotic literature, but after Landon got hammered at a club, she told him that his drinking was a turn-off. Needing space, Melanie went to a tavern instead of joining her housemates at the club, and annoyed them when she wouldn't reveal the tavern's name. Later, Mel talked about her adoption experience, and insensitively reacted to Sarah's bulimia by saying that she could never do that to herself.

In Episode 10 Shavonda logged on to Shaun's e-mail account to see if he'd received the e-card she'd sent. She discovered he was seeing someone else. She called him and cursed him out. Meanwhile, lonely Landon's ex, Becky, visited, and he was disappointed that she was happy with her new boyfriend, Jason, and wouldn't consider getting back together.

It was MJ's birthday in Episode 11, so Sarah brought him breakfast in bed, and the cast took him out to Dave & Buster's. Landon made Shavonda jealous by hooking up with a Coyote Ugly girl at the house. Shaun sent Shavonda flowers to apologize, and they got back together.

In Episode 12, Landon was upset when Willie accused him of not cleaning up. Sarah was angry when Landon and MJ woke her up at 3:00 a.m. Rather than apologize, Landon blamed Willie for keeping *him* awake until 5:00 a.m. the previous day. The cast completed their first assignment for the Soul, although they were scolded for arriving late and for excluding some of the castmates from the assignment altogether.

In Episode 13, horny Sarah tried to hook up with a gay guy, Jason, which was an unsatisfying experience. MJ had a one-night stand with a girl named Nicole, then did not call her back because he cared about Ashley.

Landon dated a Philadelphia Soul employee, Gina, in Episode 14, despite a "no fraternization" rule. After a meeting about the issue the next day, Landon cut things off with Gina. Shavonda tried to overcome her discomfort around disabled people, after the group was assigned to participate in an Easter Seals Walk-a-Thon.

In Episode 15, Karamo grew tired of Dorian, wanting someone more in touch with hip-hop culture. Sarah's mom and sister visited, and it was discovered that Sarah's eating disorder had been brought on by her mom's battle with cancer.

In Episode 16, MJ's rejection of Sarah's opinion that the film *The Passion of the Christ* was anti-Semitic led her to believe MJ couldn't deal with strong women. MJ started to hit on an old friend, Kim, but admirably resisted. He and Shavonda fought over phone use, which upset Shavonda because it reminded her of her angry ex-boyfriend. The cast was angry at Willie for skipping work because he was hung over.

In Episode 17, Melanie was mad at Landon and MJ for invading "her" special tavern, and the housemates were bothered that she felt the need to escape from them. After another incident of Landon drinking too much, he threatened to fight Mel's friends from the tavern. He apologized the next day, and tried to curtail his drinking. Meanwhile, Karamo attempted to get to know Shavonda better.

Melanie developed scabies in Episode 18, forcing the roommates to wash all the sheets and clothing in the house and to apply preventative lotion. Mel's behavior continued to annoy her housemates. The cast stepped up and gave a stellar presentation of their playground plans. Bon Jovi rewarded them with a trip to Fiji.

In Episode 19, sexual frustration ran rampant in Fiji, as Sarah tried unsuccessfully to sleep with three different British guys. Landon hit on Shavonda, but all he got was a makeout session.

The cast jumped off waterfalls and enjoyed the beach in Episode 20. Sarah went topless, and Landon exposed his butt. This drew Shavonda's interest, and she went topless, too. A game of truth-or-dare resulted in Shavonda's kissing Sarah and Landon, and Landon dropped his pants. Later, Shavonda kissed Landon in the rain, and they wound up in bed together, presumably having sex for the first time. Karamo suspected that Shavonda was trying to get back at Shaun.

In Episode 21, the cast returned to Philly, where Shavonda broke the Landon hookup news to Shaun, effectively ending their relationship. Meanwhile, she and Landon contemplated starting something serious. Karamo brought a Puerto Rican guy, Ed, to the house, and admitted that it was his first time dating outside his race.

In Episode 22, Shavonda blew up at Melanie for being so isolated, and a teary Mel contemplated going home. ING Direct announced they'd donate $5,000 to the playground project. After Landon, Mel, and Karamo blew off work one day, ING offered a $1,000 savings account to each cast member as an incentive for them to get it together and complete the project successfully.

In Episode 23, Willie was tempted to cheat on Dan with a guy named Neil, but he canceled the date at the last minute. Karamo confessed he liked "mentally harming people," but tensions eased after a house game of dodge ball.

MJ's girlfriend, Ashley, and buddy David visited in Episode 24, and Ashley complained MJ was spending more time with David than with her. After MJ confessed that he'd hooked up with someone else in Philly, Ashley decided she wanted to date other people. Meanwhile, Landon found out from David that MJ was a much different person back home than he was in the house.

In Episode 25, Sarah's weight issues caused her to get in a fight with her mom. The cast finished the playground, and Karamo gave special plaques to Landon and their bosses for their exceptionally hard work.

As the cast prepared to leave in Episode 26, Willie opened up to MJ and Landon, so they thought of him as more than just a character. Landon invited a girl, Mackenzie, to the hot tub as punishment to Shavonda, who refused to have a relationship with him. He apologized to her the next day, and she realized how much she really cared for him. Everyone shared a tearful good-bye, then parted ways at 30th Street train station.

The series concluded with a reunion episode featuring the seven Philly residents.

THE REAL WORLD
(Season 16—Austin)

GENRE	Docusoap
FIRST TELECAST	6/21/2005
LAST TELECAST	11/22/2005
EPISODE STYLE	Story Arc
NETWORK	MTV
CAST	Wes Bergmann; Johanna Botta; Lacey Buehler;

	Nehemiah Clark; Danny Jamieson; Rachel Moyal; Melinda Stolp
PRODUCTION COMPANY	Bunim-Murray Productions
CREATED BY	Mary-Ellis Bunim; Jonathan Murray
EXECUTIVE PRODUCER	Jonathan Murray

Austin, Texas, was the setting for Season 16 of *The Real World*. The seven strangers who moved in together were aspiring businessman Wes, opinionated Peruvian Johanna, sheltered Lacey, son-of-a-rehab-mom Nehemiah, sensitive future lawyer Danny, Iraq war vet Rachel, and former ugly duckling Melinda.

In Episode 1, the cast moved in to an Austin warehouse. Sexual tension sparked as Wes was interested in Johanna, Johanna liked Danny, and Danny had a thing for Melinda (who already had a boyfriend). After a night of drinking, Melinda and Rachel made out, and everyone ended up in the shower together. Danny and Wes asked Rachel and Melinda to marry them.

Johanna regretted kissing Danny in Episode 2. Danny fractured his skull in a street fight with Wes.

In Episode 3, Melissa's upsetting phone call with her boyfriend caused her to grow closer to Danny, as she comforted him while he recovered from his injury. The cast found out their job was to shoot a documentary on the South by Southwest Festival.

Danny had surgery in Episode 4, and his dad and Melissa accompanied him. Meanwhile, the housemates continued to have unrequited crushes on one another.

The housemates learned film production to prepare for their documentary project in Episode 5. Nehemiah argued about war with veteran Rachel. Danny was turned off by Melinda after learning she'd made out with Wes.

In Episode 6, Rachel went out with a new guy, Colin, while on a break with her boyfriend, but was bummed to learn that he already had a girlfriend. Meanwhile, Nehemiah and Wes considered hooking up with *Real World* groupies.

Melinda and Danny got together in Episode 7, as their housemates went out for a night on the town.

In Episode 8, Danny canceled his Valentine's Day date with Melinda after his mom passed away. Meanwhile, Johanna was excited when the guy she liked, Leo, surprised her with flowers.

In a sobering Episode 9, Danny returned home for his mom's funeral, and Melinda wondered if he'd stay in the house. Meanwhile, Nehemiah feared his mom wouldn't make it out of rehab. Lacey got a visit from her wheelchair-bound boyfriend, Ryan.

Johanna and Leo finally went out in Episode 10. She continued to flirt with him even after deciding she was not that crazy about him, and Leo wasn't thrilled that she'd led him on.

Danny returned in Episode 11, but chose to hang out with the guys instead of with Melinda. After Melinda drank too much to help cope with this, Danny helped her recover. The housemates' next film assignment was to pair up and shoot individual profiles of one another.

In Episode 12, Wes fell for a gorgeous girl named Wren, but Johanna became jealous and later made out with him. Nehemiah was mad because he wanted Johanna, too. Danny and Rachel went on a walk, and she opened up about her experience in Iraq.

Episode 13 was unlucky for Nehemiah, after his film about Wes was criticized. Later, a drink was spilled on him, causing him to almost get into a fight. He told his mom that he couldn't stand Lacey. Meanwhile, Wes and Wren were back together.

The gang went bar-hopping in Episode 14. Wes was kissed by a "mystery girl," and he panicked as he explained to Wren that he didn't know who the woman was. Slightly hung over, the housemates arrived at a dude ranch, where Mel demonstrated her horseback-riding skills. Danny and Mel cuddled by the campfire following the "poo war" they had while mucking stalls. Danny told Wes they needed to get away from the girls so they could date the ladies in Austin.

Johanna's drunken behavior had Rachel and Mel concerned in Episode 15. Danny confessed his love for Mel in a letter, but then Mel caught him getting another girl's phone number. Johanna stole a rose from a homeless man and was arrested for public intoxication. The charges were dismissed when she paid a fine and agreed to perform community service.

In Episode 16, Johanna and Leo grew closer even though Leo was also seeing another girl. Wes threw a chair into the pool during a tantrum. Leo started to pull away from Johanna, just as she was letting her guard down. After a confrontation at a bar, tears started to flow.

By Episode 17, South by Southwest boss, Paul, told the cast they needed to finish a rough cut of their documentary by the next week or they wouldn't get a vacation.

Danny asked Mel to be his girlfriend, and she accepted. Nehemiah confronted the gang about getting drunk and not completing the documentary. Johanna developed serious feelings for Leo, who wasn't as interested in being in a relationship with her.

In Episode 18, the band Halifax was the subject of the housemates' documentary. A drunken Rachel was smitten with lead singer Mike. She accidentally broke the house's basketball hoop, and cried when Nehemiah yelled at her. Danny, Wes, and Rachel went on location to film the band Hellogoodbye, but couldn't find them. Danny and Melinda hooked up the next day and joyfully leaped off a cliff. Rachel confronted Lacey when she discovered footage of her trash-talking Rachel.

Rachel's boyfriend, Erik, arrived with her dog, Reese, in Episode 19. Rachel told Erik she didn't want to have sex with him. She became upset when Erik talked to her nemesis, Lacey, and the two broke up. A warrant was issued for the guy who'd sucker-punched Danny.

In Episode 20, the roommates asked experienced editor Nehimiah to edit their film. Their boss, Paul, wasn't very happy with the results, and asked the housemates to continue working on their film. Melinda and Rachel worked on it as Nehimiah went to a freestyle rap club. Nehimiah finished the film, but their computer locked up, and with one minute to spare before the screening, Lacey and Rachel managed to deliver the final product. The gang earned their trip to Costa Rica.

While in Costa Rica in Episode 21, the housemates went on a canopy tour through the trees on a zip-line. They also took surfing and white-water-rafting lessons. Wes pretended to be Prince Harry, while Nehemiah and Danny acted like bodyguards while meeting girls at a club. Danny heard Mel say she would hook up with Wes, which made him angry. He apologized the next morning as they returned to Austin.

In Episode 22, the housemates were offered suggestions and a pep talk from documentary director Ondi Timoner. Wes and Danny didn't participate in the discussion. Nehemiah was unable to get the film done, which upset Rachel and Lacey. Johanna and Wes got a little hot and heavy in front of Wren, which made her jealous. Later, Wren and Wes got together. Instead of finishing the film, Nehemiah wound up in jail.

Danny organized everyone to finish the film in Episode 23. Nehemiah's bail for hitting someone was $200, but Wes told him he could face another $4,000 and a year in jail. Nehemiah was released and continued to edit the film while the others partied. A drunken Wes slapped Rachel. Nehemiah finished the film in time for the screening.

In Episode 24, the roomates packed up to go home and reminisced about the time they'd spent together. Mel told Danny she would go to Boston with him. Wren slapped Wes for spreading rumors about their relationship. Wes confronted Rachel about spreading rumors, and as they argued, she cried. Rachel left without saying good-bye to Wes or Nehemiah. Nehemiah stayed in Austin until his court date. Lacey's boyfriend took her home. A tearful Johanna left, followed by the remaining roommates.

THE REAL WORLD
(Season 17—Key West)

GENRE	Docusoap
FIRST TELECAST	2/28/2006
LAST TELECAST	8/15/2006
NETWORK	MTV
AIR TIME	Wednesday, 10:00 p.m.
EPISODE STYLE	Story Arc
CAST	Janelle Casanave; John Devenanzio; Tyler Duckworth; Zach Mann; Paula Meronek; Svetlana Shusterman; Jose Tapia
PRODUCTION COMPANY	Bunim-Murray Productions
CREATED BY	Mary-Ellis Bunim; Jonathan Murray
EXECUTIVE PRODUCER	Jonathan Murray

Season 17 of *The Real World* was set in the Key Haven neighborhood of Key West. The housemates were biracial San Jose State graduate Janelle, recent Penn State grad John, Puerto Rican rental property owner Jose, corporate party girl Paula, Ukranian-born Svetlana, gay athlete Tyler, and energetic Zach, who was once overweight. The cast's job was to open a Mystic Tan franchise. The season was taped during late summer and fall of 2005, the busiest Atlantic hurricane season on record.

Prior to the season premiere, Coral of *The Real World: Back to New York* hosted a *Key West* casting special. Coral and past *Real World* castmembers discussed the *Key West* cast.

In Episode 1, the roommates waited for Hurricane Katrina to pass, then moved in and met at their new house. John and Zach liked Svetlana, but she had a boyfriend at home. Paula admitted she thought all of the male roommates were hot.

The roommates thought Paula had an eating disorder in Episode 2. She confided in Zach about her insecurities, then had an anxiety attack, which Janelle and Svetlana helped her through. Later, the roommates talked about Paula's attack.

In Episode 3, Paula felt bad she'd lost control. The cast went to a gay club, but John persuaded everyone to leave. The group split up, and an argument erupted when they arrived home. Janelle showed Tyler a new angle on John's behavior that night, and approached Paula about seeking professional help.

In Episode 4, Svetlana researched eating disorders to educate the roommates. They went on a ghost tour, and later the guys scared the girls with their own ghost. The cast found out about their Mystic Tan job, and met their partner at the "Pineapple Gallery." Svetlana tried to approach Tyler at work to address the animosity in their relationship.

Svetlana was unhappy in her relationship in Episode 5, and she started to notice John more. Zach made a new friend.

Things became stressful in Episode 6, when, among other problems, the group couldn't decide on a manager, and they were scheduled to open the tanning salon in a few hours.

The deadline for the store opening casued everyone's personalities to clash in Episode 7. As the opening credits predicted, the roommates actually stopped being nice.

In Episode 8, the cast went to a bar, where Paula shared intense secrets with Svetlana.

In Episode 9, John and Paula fought about what had happened at a club the night before. The roommates tried to plan for the approaching Hurricane Rita.

As Hurricane Rita touched down in Episode 10, the roommates were forced to evacuate to Fort Lauderdale.

In Episode 11, the hurricane passed and the weather cooled down, and Zach and Crystal's relationship heated up.

Tyler and Svetlana conversed about homosexuality in a deep Episode 12. The roommates spent the day putting the finishing touches on their opening-day bonanza at Mystic Tan.

In Episode 13, Janelle took Jose to task for being an ineffectual assistant manager, which, to no one's surprise, caused a good amount of friction.

Svetlana told John that Tyler had talked trash behind his back in Episode 14. John and Tyler eventually made up and crafted a burn book against Svetlana.

Zach's hands were full in Episode 15, as he was torn between three women.

In Episode 16, the roommates prepared for Fantasy Fest, and another fight broke out, this time between John and Janelle.

In Episode 17, the housemates were displaced again, when they were evacuated to Orlando to prepare for Hurricane Wilma; their previous refuge in Fort Lauderdale had been destroyed.

In Episode 18, the roommates met their boss at Mystic Tan. They decided three hurricanes were enough, and the salon was permanently closed. At home, sparks flew when Svetlana found Tyler's burn book.

The cast was invited to go on vacation in Episode 19. Everyone was giddy with excitement as they prepared to travel to Spain.

Tensions ran high in Spain as John and Tyler immediately fought in Episode 20. Tyler's behavior also rubbed Jose the wrong way. Zach's parents and sister arrived, and were visiting the house when Zach announced he'd invited seven-time Olympic medalist Amanda Beard to a tanning salon to promote the debut of Speedo's Axceleration swimwear line.

In Episode 21, Janelle's ex visited Key West. After they got into a fight, she kicked him out, leaving him with nowhere to go. While at a bar, Jose tried to get to know Jessica. Zach told Jose it was time to go home, and they left. The two talked about how Jose had feelings for Jessica, but Jose said he wasn't rushing things.

In Episode 22, Tyler decided to run a marathon, but wanted only Jose, Paula, and Zach there to support him, which offended the other housemates.

In Episode 23, Martin made plans to visit for Svetlana's birthday, which she looked forward to. As she finished therapy, Paula looked back on how she had changed.

In the Episode 24 finale, after being postponed by Hurricane Wilma, the roommates finally went to Fantasy Fest, where they entered costume contests. John encountered trouble with the gang's parade float.

THE REAL WORLD

(Season 18—Denver)

GENRE	Docusoap
FIRST TELECAST	11/22/2006
LAST TELECAST	5/16/2007
NETWORK	MTV
AIR TIME	Wednesday, 10:00 p.m.
EPISODE STYLE	Story Arc
CAST	Davis Mallory; Alex Smith; Tyrie Ballard; Stephen Nichols; Jenn Grijalva; Colie Edison; Brooke LaBarbera
PRODUCTION COMPANY	Bunim-Murray Productions
CREATED BY	Mary-Ellis Bunim; Jonathan Murray
EXECUTIVE PRODUCER	Jonathan Murray

Season 18 of *The Real World* was set in Denver, the Mile High City. The cast included confident party boy Alex, flirty Southern belle Brooke; attention-hungry sorority girl Colie, Southern conservative Christian gay guy Davis, Oakland Raiderette cheerleader and party girl Jenn, religious conservative Howard University student Stephen, and funny guy and former gang member Tyrie.

In Episode 1, the party got started quickly, as the roommates vowed to make their four and a half months in Denver wild ones. Stephen and Davis found camaraderie in their Baptist roots; party girls Jenn and Colie became friends; and Tyrie developed a crush on Brooke. Wild Jenn suggested a nude pool party, and she and Brooke kissed in the hot tub. Colie wound up in Alex's bed on the first night.

In Episode 2, Colie revealed to the girls that she'd hooked up with Alex. Davis revealed that he was gay, which troubled religious Stephen. Alex had a three-way kiss with friends Colie and Jenn, then worried that Colie was becoming too emotionally attached. He drank all night and had sex with Jenn.

Jenn's post-romp hickey was discovered, so she was forced to admit she'd had sex with Alex. Colie and Jenn decided that their friendship wasn't worth ruining over any guy, but Colie stayed mad at Alex. Colie went out that night and brought guys home with her in an attempt to make Alex jealous. But not long after, she talked to Alex and spent the night with him. The next morning, Alex said that he'd been drunk and didn't remember their heartfelt conversation.

In Episode 4, Davis didn't hear a bartender call Stephen the *N* word, which upset Stephen, who complained to Tyrie. Tyrie confronted Davis, who violently pushed Tyrie and taunted him to fight. Tyrie threatened to beat up Davis after the show finished taping, which caused Davis to become so scared that the producers let him spend the night in a hotel. Then, drunken Davis used the *N* word, which angered Stephen again. The next day, Davis returned to the house to apologize to Tyrie and Stephen, told the roommates he was leaving the show because of his drinking problem, but ended up sticking it out after the others urged him to stay.

In Episode 5, Tyrie complained he was sexually frustrated, but he got phone numbers from two women, Ashley and Jazalle, and the latter visited him at the house. Davis, Stephen, and Alex woke up early to go skiing. To celebrate the date 6/6/06, the roommates dressed up for a "Sin Party." Tyrie ran into Jazalle at the bar, and they had their first argument, but talked it out at the house later.

In Episode 6, a drunken Jenn told Tyrie that she had a tough time distinguishing him from a bad ex-boyfriend. She drank too much on a party bus and argued with Tyrie. The next day, everyone expressed concern over her attitude change from drinking. She admitted she drank every day and said that alcoholism ran in her family. Then she apologized to Tyrie for their party bus fight.

Colie came down with mononucleosis in Epsiode 7. Brooke was afraid she'd get sick, so she left the house and Colie's germs to search Denver for hours, looking for a manicure. She later told Colie and Tyrie that she'd walked through the "ghetto," a term that upset Tyrie. Brooke called her mother and cried that she was "in hell."

In Episode 8, the cast got a special delivery—two Jeep Compasses—and learned they'd work for Outward Bound. Jenn became close frinds with bar security guy John. Alex proposed another romp with Jenn, which caused her to explode at him, saying she'd never spend the night with him again. Still sick with mono, Colie missed her first day of work at Outward Bound, where the housemates met their boss, Chris. Their job would be to create two wilderness courses for teenagers displaced by Hurricane Katrina, which Brooke was not looking forward to.

The housemates met their boss's co-instructor, Raleigh, in Episode 9. Sick Colie tried to work, but had to skip the 6:00 a.m. wake-up routine of stretching, running, and swimming, a task Brooke disliked. The cast rock-climbed and rappelled, which Brooke pushed through, thanks to the others' encouragement.

In Episode 10, Tyrie had an emotional moment after scaling a cliff, a task Brooke skipped. Then Brooke flipped out when Alex asked her to help clean up camp. Colie, still sick with mono, missed an overnight excursion, but hung out with Outward Bound outdoorsman Adam, who'd caught her attention. While hiking, Brooke stripped to short shorts, but Chris made her put her long pants back on. Later that night, he also caught her with her pants down in the middle of camp, which he said was unprofessional.

Davis and Brooke flirted in Episode 11, but she turned down his advances because he had a boyfriend. Then Jenn called out Stephen for kissing a girl in the hot tub, which turned into a heated argument. Alex told Stephen that Jenn was being irrational, and Davis informed Jenn of this. Jenn confronted Alex, and he apologized. Then she apologized to Stephen.

Brooke sprained her ankle in Episode 12, which got her an excuse note from her doctor. Adam quit his Outward Bound job, which meant that he and Colie could date. Davis and Stephen became sick on their way to work. Chris sent all of the sick and injured housemates to the doctor, and Stephen, Davis, and Brooke returned to Denver, while Colie went to work at Outward Bound. The healthy housemates hiked for hours, and said that Brooke and Stephen's attempts to skip work were weak ones. Meanwhile the two relaxed at home in the hot tub.

Team morale weakened in Episode 13, until the group found a patch of snow while hiking. Meanwhile, Brooke, Davis, and Stephen recuperated by eating and drinking in Denver. Tyrie suffered an asthma attack while hiking, and skipped the next day's activities. Davis returned to Outward Bound, and Chris said that the four roommates who completed training would become lead interns, while the other would just be assistants.

In Episode 14, Alex cozied up to a woman at the bar, Stacy, and brought her home, which was awkward for Colie and Brooke, especially when Stacy's visit with Alex grew loud. Colie went on a dinner date with Adam. Later, Alex brought Stacy home again, this time asking permission from Colie if she could stay. Alex admitted he had feelings for Colie, but he still spent alone time with Stacy.

Davis, Jenn, and Colie went to a gay pride festival in Episode 15, and Davis finally felt he was in his element, in a gay-friendly city. The next Sunday, Stephen accompanied Davis to a gay-friendly church service. Davis admitted he was an outcast in his family because of his sexual orientation, and Stephen offered support. The next day, Davis's boyfriend, P.J., visited, and Davis tried to make Stephen more comfortable around them. Then Stephen's girlfriend, Mercii, arrived, and the four went on a double date, which made Stephen more accepting of homosexuality.

In Episode 16, Jenn helped a drunken Alex get to bed, but he eventually spent the night with Colie. The next day, Tyrie warned Alex not to give in to temptation with Colie. Brooke and Colie argued about dirty dishes, and Brooke told Tyrie she hated Colie. Alex's friend Brett visited and told Colie that Alex didn't want a relationship with her. The housemates went to a water park, all except Colie, who picked up her visiting boyfriend, Corey, at the airport. She later witnessed Jenn and Alex kissing at the bar, making their love triangle even more uncomfortable.

Colie and Corey spent a lot of time together in Episode 17. The other housemates were jealous, especially Brooke, who generally felt left out.

In Episode 18, Outward Bound boss Chris told Davis, Stephen, and Brooke they had to make up work at the gym and on the mountain. Davis suggested a threesome with P.J. and Brooke, but Brooke kissed Tyrie at the bar instead. Later, Davis apologized to P.J. for the Brooke drama, and promised he wouldn't hook up with her. Then he complained to Brooke that she had caused awkwardness with P.J. Their argument lasted for days, and Brooke threw water in his face, while he said she couldn't treat her housemates so poorly.

In Episode 19, Jenn was excited that her boyfriend, Jared, would soon visit. Feeling guilty, she confessed about her hookup with Alex, which made Jared upset. Jenn talked to her sister, who told her that Jared was reportedly kissing other girls back home, which made Jenn feel betrayed. Stephen's best friend, Darnell, visited, and Jenn was attracted to him and didn't feel guilty, since she thought Jared had cheated on her. At the bar, the Tyrie-Jazalle-Ashley love triangle escalated, causing Jazalle to leave. At home, Tyrie called Jazalle and said he loved her. She came to the house, they argued, and she retreated to the bathroom to cry. Their argument became even more heated when he yanked her arm and she screamed.

In Episode 20, Tyrie relieved himself on the side of the house and was arrested for public drunkenness. Jazalle bailed him out of the Denver Detox Center. Tyrie broke down crying that he'd be seen as a woman beater after yanking Jazalle's arm the night before. Eventually they talked out their problems and shared the blame for the blowout. Meanwhile, Jenn and Jared talked on the phone, and he said he couldn't hold her back. Jenn was eager to return to her wild ways, and brought Darnell back to her bed.

Jenn hooked up with Darnell in Episode 21. Meanwhile, the displaced Hurricane Katrina kids arrived for the group's Outward Bound training, but Stephen left for his sister's wedding instead.

Episode 22 featured day three of the Outward Bound excursion. Alex and Davis led the steepest hike, while Colie, Tyrie, and Jenn headed the boys' peak climb. The housemates encouraged the children when they became tired, and everyone reached the peak for a breathtaking view and an emotional moment. Stephen returned from his sister's wedding, and Chris held one-on-one meetings with the housemates. Chris told Stephen he wasn't prepared for the trip, which upset him. Davis told Stephen that Tyrie had referred to him as "integrated." Stephen asked Tyrie if he was "white-washed," while Tyrie pointed out that Stephen had referred to him as "hood."

In Episode 23, Davis vented to Jenn about their housemates. He said he wanted a male friend in the house, and he thought he could be pals with Tyrie if it weren't for his homosexuality. He also told Jenn that Colie was not very pretty and that Brooke had a double chin. Then he said to Jenn that she was pretty but should lose some weight. Jenn told the other housemates about Davis's comments, and Brooke was furious. Jazalle and Tyrie talked on the phone, but hung up on each other, and later broke things off. The guys told Davis the girls were upset about his comments, but Davis said he didn't care. Brooke confronted Davis, and later trashed his room and left him a nasty note.

In Episode 24, Jared called Jenn to say he still wanted to visit, and she agreed to it. Later, the girls went out for sushi. Brooke spotted her dream man and she slipped him her number. Later, sushi guy Kyle called her and asked her to go bowling, much to her dismay. Later, at the bar, Davis told Jared about Jenn's hookups. Jenn confessed, and Jared stormed out to talk to Tyrie, who said that Jenn had slept with Darnell. Jared left, but the next morning, he seemed over it. Then Jenn revealed another one-night stand, but Jared was okay, since the truth was out.

It was the housemates' final week at Outward Bound in Episode 25. Brooke bravely and proudly completed a rappel down a cliff. Colie became sick again and returned to

Denver. Brooke and Stephen led the girls on a course, and, for the kids' sake, Brooke hid her fear when a lightning storm struck. Camper Ashley couldn't breathe and needed medical attention, and Chris had to evacuate with her, leaving Stephen and Brooke alone and in charge. Once the campers completed their adventure and returned home, the housemates discussed their Outward Bound experience. Brooke cried and said it had changed her life and she could stop living in fear.

In Episode 26, the roommates returned to Denver, where Colie was sick with strep throat, but happy after "Hot Justin," the model, called her. Davis was surprised to hear that his mother and sister would visit on his birthday weekend. Despite Justin, Colie went on a date with Adam and asked him to sleep over, but he declined, making her realize that their relationship wasn't going in the right direction. Alex returned home from a night of drinking, and Colie jumped in his bed, promising to show him her talents. They woke up together, but Alex pieced together that they hadn't gone all the way. The housemates found out they had earned a trip to Thailand, which made sheltered Brooke nervous. Later, Colie made out with Justin at the bar and brought him back to the house, where she kissed him in front of Alex. Davis's family visited, but he woke up late and hung over, missing brunch, which upset his mother.

The group traveled to Thailand in Episode 27. Still nervous about traveling abroad, Brooke was stung by a sea urchin. Excited to reenact a *Friends* moment, the housemates peed on Brooke's stung foot. Stephen and Jenn flirted, while Alex and Colie argued over bad manners. Colie and Davis had a few too many drinks, and Colie fell and cut her toe, while Brooke took a tumble on her rear end. Colie and Alex argued again, and she tried to make a "friendship pact," but he turned her down.

In the Episode 28 finale, Davis and his new friend Josh went out on the town, but ended up back at the house. Despite boyfriend P.J., Davis admitted he wanted to hook up with Josh. Davis left and Josh told Colie he had made out with Davis. The guys got into bed, as Jenn and Colie peeked in on the cheating action. Davis denied that anything happened, saying he and Josh had only kissed. P.J. called the next day to tell Davis that he'd read on MySpace about his hookup with Josh. Davis felt regret, and cried to Jenn. Meanwhile, Jenn and Stephen continued to flirt, and admitted they would have hooked up if they'd been single. They cozied up in bed, and the next morning she called her boyfriend while Stephen went to church. On their final night in Denver, the housemates partied together.

THE REAL WORLD/ROAD RULES CHALLENGE

GENRE	Competition
FIRST TELECAST	9/28/1997
NETWORK	MTV
EPISODE STYLE	Story Arc
TALENT	Eric Nies (Host); Mark Long (Host); Jonny Moseley (Host); Dave Mirra (Host); T. J. Lavin (Host)

CAST

Season 1 **The Real World** *(Winners)*
Jason Cornwell; Sean Duffy; Montana McGlynn; Genesis Moss; Kameelah Phillips; Elka Walker; Syrus Yarbrough
Road Rules
Erika Ruen; Jake Bronstein; Kalle Dedolph; Oscar Hernandez; Vince Forcier

Season 2 **The Real World**
Beth Stolarczyk; Janet Choi; Jason Cornwell; Montana McGlynn; Nathan Blackburn; Neil Forrester
Road Rules *(Winners)*
Anne Wharton; Kalle Dedolph; Kefla Hare; Mark Long; Noah Rickun; Roni Martin

Season 3 **The Real World**
Amaya Brecher; David Burns; Heather B.; Kat Ogden; Mike Lambert; Teck Holmes
Road Rules *(Winners)*
Dan Setzler; Holly Shand; Carlos Jackson; Piggy Thomas; Veronica Portillo; Yes Duffy

Season 4—"Extreme"   **The Real World** *(Winners)*

Dan Renzi; Jamie Murray; Julie Stoffer; Kameelah Phillips; Rebecca Lord; Syrus Yarbrough

Road Rules

Ayanna Mackins; Christian Breivik; Emily Bailey; James Orlando; Laterrian Wallace; Michelle Parma; Susie Meister

Season 5—"Battle of the Seasons"   **The Real World** *(Winners)*

Norman Korpi; Rebecca Blasband; Jon Brennan; Beth Stolarczyk; Mike Johnson; Sharon Gitau; Mike Lambert; Flora Alekseyeun; Sean Duffy; Elka Walker; Stephen Williams IV; Lindsay Brien; Danny Roberts; Kelley Limp; Mike Mizanin; Coral Smith

Road Rules

Tim Beggy; Emily Bailey; Chris Melling; Belou Den Tex; Dan Setzler; Tara McDaniel; Chadwick Pelletier; Piggy Thomas; Joshua Florence; Holly Shand; Yes Duffy; Veronica Portillo; Theo Vonkurnatowski; Holly Brenston; Adam Larson; Jisela Delgado

Season 6—"Battle of the Sexes"   **The Men** *(Winners)*

David Edwards (*Real World*); Puck Rainey (*Real World*); Dan Renzi (*Real World*); Syrus Yarbrough (*Real World*); Colin Mortensen (*Real World*); David Broom (*Real World*); Jamie Murray (*Real World*); Theo Gantt III (*Real World*); Mark Long (*Road Rules*); Antoine de Bouverie (*Road Rules*); Jake Bronstein (*Road Rules*); Yes Duffy (*Road Rules*); James Orlando (*Road Rules*); Laterrian Wallace (*Road Rules*); Blair Herter (*Road Rules*); Eric Jones (*Road Rules*); Shane Landrum (*Road Rules*)

The Women

Beth Stolarczyk (*Real World*); Genesis Moss (*Real World*); Amaya Brecher (*Real World*); Ruthie

Alcaide (*Real World*); Julie Stoffer (*Real World*); Melissa Howard (*Real World*); Lori Trespicio (*Real World*); Aneesa Ferreira (*Real World*); Tonya Cooley (*Real World*); Emily Bailey (*Road Rules*); Anne Wharton (*Road Rules*); Christina Pazsitzky (*Road Rules*); Gladys Sanabria (*Road Rules*); Ayanna Mackins (*Road Rules*); Veronica Portillo (*Road Rules*); Ellen Cho (*Road Rules*); Jisela Delgado (*Road Rules*); Rachel Robinson (*Road Rules*)

Season 7—"The Gauntlet" **The Real World**

Norman Korpi; Elka Walker; Montana McGlynn; Nathan Blackburn; Matt Smith; David Broom; Mike Mizanin; Coral Smith; Rachel Braband; Tonya Cooley; Theo Gant III; Alton Williams; Trishelle Cannatella; Irulan Wilson

Road Rules *(Winners)*

Roni Martin; Veronica Portillo; Laterrian Wallace; Theo Vonkurnatowski; Steve Meinke; Adam Larson; Katie Doyle; Darrell Taylor; Sarah Greyson; Rachel Robinson; Dave Giuntoli; Abram Boise; Cara Zavaleta; Tina Barta

Season 8—"The Inferno" **The Real World**

Syrus Yarbrough; David Burns; Julie Stoffer; Coral Smith; Mike Mizanin; Trishelle Cannatella; Ace Amerson; Chris Tamburello; Leah Gillingwater; Mallory Snyder

Road Rules (Winners) Tim Beggy; Holly Shand; Veronica Portillo; Katie Doyle; Darrell Taylor; Kendal Sheppard; Shane Landrum; Abram Boise; Christena Pyle; Jeremy Blossom

Season 9—Battle of the Sexes 2 **The Men** *(Winners)*

Mike Mizanin (*Real World*); Frank Roessler (*Real World*); Steven Hill (*Real World*); Ace Amerson (*Real World*); Adam King (*Real World*); Brad

Fiorenza (*Real World*); Jacquese Smith (*Real World*); Randy Barry (*Real World*); Mark Long (*Road Rules*); Dan Setzler (*Road Rules*); Shawn Sealy (*Road Rules*); Theo Vonkurnatowski (*Road Rules*); Shane Landrum (*Road Rules*); Abram Boise (*Road Rules*); Chris Graebe (*Road Rules*); Derrick Kosinski (*Road Rules*); Nick Haggart (*Road Rules*)

The Women Cynthia Roberts (*Real World*); Genesis Moss (*Real World*); Ruthie Alcaide (*RealWorld*); Coral Smith (*Real World*); Aneesa Ferreira (*Real World*); Tonya Cooley (*Real World*); Arissa Hill (*Real World*); Cameran Eubanks (*Real World*): Robin Hibbard (*Real World*); Ayanna Mackins (*Road Rules*); Veronica Portillo (*Road Rules*); Sophia Pasquis (*Road Rules*); Katie Doyle (*Road Rules*); Rachel Robinson (*Road Rules*); Tina Barta (*Road Rules*); Ibis Nieves (*Road Rules*); Kina Dean (*Road Rules*); Angela Trimbur (*Road Rules*)

Season 10—"The Inferno 2" **The Good Guys** (The Winners)

Jon Brennan; Mike Mizanin; Brad Fiorenza; Darrell Taylor; Shavonda Billingslea; Landon Lueck; Jamie Chung; Robin Hibbard; Julie Stoffer; Jodi Weatherton

The Bad Asses

Abram Boise; Dan Renzi; Chris Tamburello; Derrick Kosinski; Karamo Brown; Beth Stolarczyk; Veronica Portillo; Tonya Cooley; Rachel Robinson; Tina Barta

Season 11—"The Gauntlet 2" **Rookies** (The Winners)

Adam King; Alton Williams; Cameran Eubanks; Cara Zavaleta; Danny Dias; Ibis Nieves; Jamie Murray; Jeremy Blossom; Jo Rhodes; Jodi Weatherton; Jillian Zoboroski; Kina Dean; Landon Lueck; MJ Garrett; Randy Barry; Susie Meister

Veterans
Ace Amerson; Adam Larson; Aneesa Ferreira; Beth Stolarcyzk; Brad Fiorenza; David Burns Derrick Kosinski; Jisela Delgado; Julie Stoffer; Katie Doyle; Mark Long; Montana McGlynn; Robin Hibbard; Ruthie Alcaide; Syrus Yarbrough; Tim Beggy

Season 12—"Fresh Meat" Aviv Melmed and Darrell Taylor (Winners); Kenny Santucci and Tina Barta (2nd place); Casey Cooper and Wes Bergmann (3rd place); Diem Brown and Derrick Kosinski; Chanda and Theo Vonkurnatowski; Linette and Shane Landrum; Evan Starkman and Coral Smith; Eric Banks and Katie Doyle; Johnnie and Tonya Cooley; Jesse and Johanna Botta; Ryan and Melinda Stolp; Evelyn Smith and Danny Jamieson

Season 13—"The Duel" Wes Bergmann (Winner); Jodi Weatherton (Winner); Brad Fiorenza (2nd place); Svetlana Shusterman (2nd place); Chris "CT" Tamburello; Aneesa Ferreira; Derrick Kosinski; Beth Stolarczyk; Eric Banks; Casey Cooper; Evan Starkman; Diem Brown; John Devenanzio; Kina Dean; Kenny Santucci; Paula Meronek; Nehemiah Clark; Robin Hibbard; Tyler Duckworth; Tina Barta

Season 14—"The Inferno 3" **The Good Guys**
Colie Edison; Davis Mallory; John Devenanzio; Paula Meronek; Rachel Moyal; Susie Meister; Tim Beggy; Ace Amerson; Cara Zavaleta; Alton Williams

The Bad Asses
Danny Jamieson; Ev Smith; Janelle Casanave; Jenn Grijalva; Kenny Santucci; Tonya Cooley; Chris "CT" Tamburello (replaced); Abram Boise; Aneesa Ferreira; Tyrie Ballard

PRODUCTION COMPANY	Bunim-Murray Productions
CREATED BY	Mary Ellis-Bunim; Jon Murray
EXECUTIVE PRODUCERS	Julie Pizzi; Jonathan Murray; Marry-Ellis Bunim
PRODUCER	Rick de Oliveira
DIRECTORS	Jeff Fisher; Craig Borders; Matt Kunitz

On the first *The Real World/Road Rules Challenge,* eight players from both *The Real World* and *Road Rules* battled for $300,000 to split.

Later seasons offered various twists. In *Battle of the Sexes,* the competition featured cast members, some who didn't get along, from *Real World* and *Road Rules* as they competed, girls versus guys, in physical challenges to determine which team would win $60,000. The guys won the first season, which was filmed in Jamaica. They also won Season 2, which was filmed in New Mexico.

In *Battle of the Seasons,* the competition featured former cast members from *The Real World* and *Road Rules* as they challenged each other in two-person teams. When the three winning teams remained from each side, they took turns eliminating one opposing player. The final player standing won $300,000, which he or she could share with fellow team members.

The Inferno was shot on location in Mexico, and featured audience favorite cast members from *The Real World* and *Road Rules* in fifteen survival challenges for cash and prizes. Competitors schemed and fought to avoid elimination in head-to-head Inferno competitions. *The Inferno 2*'s teams were determined by an audience vote. In *Fresh Meat,* a *Real World* and *Road Rules* alum paired with a team of "Challenge" newcomers.

THE REALITY SHOW

GENRE	Competition
FIRST TELECAST	9/13/2005
LAST TELECAST	10/11/2005
NETWORK	MTV
EPISODE STYLE	Story Arc

TALENT	Dan Levy (Host); Andy Dick (Lead Critic); Trishelle Canatella (Critic); Keenyah Hill (Critic); Stephen "Steve-O" Glover (Critic); Veronica Portillo (Critic); Austin Scarlett (Critic); Bam Margera (Critic); Omarosa Manigult-Stallworth (Critic); Corey Clark (Critic)
CAST	Shelley (*After the Reign*); Andy (*Life with Uncle Bobby*); Niki Kirby (*Love You to Death*); Kipchoge (*Out of the Woods*); Nick Roses (*Nick Roses: 10% Teen*); Karishma and Bansri (*Karma Chameleons*); Jude and Jacob (*Nearly Identical*); Heather (3rd cancelled—*Ramona: The Real San Diego County*); Kaitlin (2nd cancelled—*There's Something Funny with Kaitlin*); Cyndee and Toi (1st cancelled—*Almost Fabulous*)
PRODUCTION COMPANIES	Super Delicious Productions; MTV Productions
CREATED BY	Jerry Mahoney; Adam Cohen; Cara Tapper; Joanna Vernetti
EXECUTIVE PRODUCERS	Adam Cohen; Cara Tapper; Joanna Vernett; Andy Dick
SENIOR PRODUCER	Jennifer Rowland
PRODUCERS	Jerry Mahoney; Paul Greenberg; Molly O'Rourke;
CO-PRODUCERS	Sara Campos; Claudia Frank; Jeff Fisher; Troy Vander Heyden

On *The Reality Show,* contestants competed to star in their own six-episode reality show on MTV. There were ten series in total, ranging from *Out of the Woods,* about a young man named Kipchoge who lived in the forest in a place with no electricity; to *Nick Roses: 10% Teen,* about a talent manager who happened to be sixteen years old. Each week a panel of critics, including comedian Andy Dick and two reality stars, judged mini-episodes of each series and picked three to be put up for "cancellation." Home viewers voted to determine which of those three would be canceled. *The Reality Show* itself was canceled after the third episode, leaving the remaining shows to air on MTV's website.

THE REBEL BILLIONAIRE

GENRE Competition (Job)

FIRST TELECAST 11/9/2004

LAST TELECAST 1/11/2005

NETWORK FOX

AIR TIME Tuesday, 8:00 p.m.

EPISODE STYLE Story Arc

TALENT Richard Branson (Host)

CAST Shawn Nelson (Winner); Sarah Blakely (Runner-up); Gabriel Baldinucci (3rd place); Heather MacLean (4th place); Erica Vilardi (5th place); Nicole Harvat (6th place); Candida Tolentino (7th place); Steve Berke (8th place), Michael Zindell (9th place); Jessica McCann (10th place); Sam (11th place); Jermaine Jamieson (12th place); Jennifer (13th place); Tim Hudson (14th place); Aisha Krump (15th place); Spencer (16th place)

PRODUCTION COMPANY Bunim-Murray Productions

CREATED BY Lori Levin-Hyams; Laura Fuest, Tod Dahlke

EXECUTIVE PRODUCERS Lori Levin-Hyams; Laura Fuest; Tod Dahlke

Adventure-seeking tycoon Sir Richard Branson took a group of young, promising entrepreneurs around the world on *The Rebel Billionaire*. Along the way, Branson tested the mettle of each person, eliminating the weakest until he decided who would win the grand prize of $1 million plus, the twist, an opportunity to follow in his footsteps. Shawn Nelson won the competition.

REDHANDED

GENRE	Docucomedy
FIRST TELECAST	3/8/1999
LAST TELECAST	9/28/1999
NETWORK	UPN
AIR TIMES	Monday, 8:00 p.m. (3/1999–4/1999); Monday, 9:00 p.m. (6/1999–7/1999); Tuesday, 8:30 p.m. (9/1999)
EPISODE STYLE	Self-contained
TALENT	Adam Carolla (Host)
PRODUCTION COMPANY	Lion's Gate Films, Inc.; Termite Art Productions
EXECUTIVE PRODUCER	Erik Nelson
PRODUCER	Michael Caleo
DIRECTORS	Edward Barbini; Tom Kramer; John Tindall

This hidden-camera prank show put people in often humiliating situations. Victims of these stings were often set up by close revenge-seeking friends.

REGENCY HOUSE PARTY

GENRE	Docudrama
FIRST TELECAST	11/3/2004
LAST TELECAST	11/24/2004
NETWORK	PBS
EPISODE STYLE	Story Arc
TALENT	Chris Gorell Barnes (Master/Host)
CAST	Lisa Braund (Lady); Victoria Hopkins (Lady); Hayley Conick (Lady); Tanya Samuel (Lady); Larushka Ivan-Zadeh Griaznov (Countess); Zebedee Helm (Estate Hermit); Francesca Martin (Lady's Companion); Paul Robinson (Army Officer);

John Everett (Gentleman); Jeremy Glover (Royal
Naval Captain); James Carrington (Gentleman
Composer)

PRODUCTION COMPANIES Wall to Wall Television Ltd., in association with
Thirteen/WNET New York

EXECUTIVE PRODUCERS Jody Sheff; Alex Graham; Helen Hawken;
Emma Willis

PRODUCERS Caroline Ross Pirie; Cate Hall

DIRECTORS Tim Carter; Carl Hindmarch; Sam Kingsley;
Caroline Ross Pirie

Inspired by PBS's *The 1900s House* and *Manor House,* this docudrama followed ten men and women who gave up the conveniences of modern life to adopt the lifestyle of the residents of the Regency mansion circa 1805. For more than two months, the house guests lived with no electricity, telephones, or indoor plumbing. The men engaged in shooting, drinking, and bare-knuckle wrestling, while the women, who wore constricting corsets, spent time on calmer activities, such as needlepoint and dance classes.

RENOVATE MY FAMILY

GENRE Docudrama (Makeover)

FIRST TELECAST 9/1/2004

LAST TELECAST 8/22/2005

NETWORK FOX

AIR TIMES Wednesday, 8:00 p.m. (9/2004); Monday,
9:00 p.m. (9/2004–10/2004); Friday, 9:00 p.m.
(10/2004–11/2004); Monday, 8:00 p.m. (8/2005)

EPISODE STYLE Self-contained

TALENT Jay McGraw (Host); Kahh Lee (Interior Designer);
Jaclyn Dahm (Construction Worker);
Scott McCray (Construction Foreman);
Erica Dahm (Construction Worker); Nicole Dahm
(Construction Worker)

PRODUCTION COMPANY Rocket Science Laboratories
EXECUTIVE PRODUCERS Jean-Michel Michenaud; Chris Cowan;
Ray Giuliani
CO-EXECUTIVE PRODUCER Janelle Fiorito
DIRECTORS Craig Borders; Cord Keller

Best-selling author Jay McGraw, son of Dr. Phil, hosted this makeover/home improvement show, in which professional stylists and construction workers worked together to
transform families struggling with psychological issues. The team remodeled homes,
restored cars, and worked to rebuild the troubled family unit.

RESIDENT LIFE

GENRE Docudrama
FIRST TELECAST 9/8/2003
LAST TELECAST 12/1/2003
NETWORK TLC
AIR TIME Monday, 8:00 p.m.
EPISODE STYLE Story Arc
CAST Frank Scholl (10th-year Cardiothoracic Chief
Surgical Fellow); Jim Bob Faulk (4th-year Surgical
Resident); Rachel LaMar (1st-year OB/GYN
Resident); Spencer Greene (2nd-year Emergency
Medicine Resident); Richie White (1st-year
Pediatric Resident); Chuck Stevenson (2nd-year
Neurosurgery Resident); Pilar Levy (2nd-year
Pediatric Resident); Victor Levy (1st-year Pediatric
Cardiology Fellow); Jason Shipman (2nd-year
Surgical Resident); Joel Maier (1st-year Burn
Fellow and Plastic Surgery Resident); Tarek Absi
(1st-year Cardiothoracic Surgery Fellow);
Kristina Storck (2nd-year OB/GYN Resident);
John Spooner (2nd-year Neurosurgery Resident);

Adele Maurer (1st-year Pathology Resident); Justin Johnsen (4th-year Ophthalmology Resident); Fred Starr (1st-year Pediatric and Adolescent Psychiatry Fellow)

PRODUCTION COMPANY	New York Times Television
SENIOR PRODUCER	Wendy Greene
PRODUCER	Xackery Irving

For more than five and a half months, thirteen videographers followed twenty-six young doctors-in-training at Nashville's Vanderbilt University Medical Center as they lived the real-life drama of performing surgery, making the rounds, and practicing clinic research on *Resident Life*. Rock band They Might Be Giants wrote the theme to the show, "Am I Awake?"

THE RESTAURANT

GENRE	Docusoap
FIRST TELECAST	7/20/2003
LAST TELECAST	6/5/2004
NETWORK	NBC
AIR TIMES	Sunday, 10:00 p.m. (7/2003–8/2003); Monday, 10:00 p.m. (4/2004–5/2004); Saturday, 10:00 p.m. (5/2004–6/2004)
EPISODE STYLE	Story Arc
CAST	Rocco DiSpirito (Restaurant Owner); Pete Giovin (Waiter); Brian Petruzzell (Food Runner); Lola Belle (Bartender); Caroline Matler (Waitress—Season 1); Colleen Fitzgerald (Captain); Susanna Hari (Kitchen Staff); John Charlesworth (Kitchen Staff); Matt DiBarro (Bartender—Season 2); Perry Pollaci (Kitchen Staff); Laurent Saillard (General Manager); Carrie Keranen (Waitress);

Tony Acinapura (Chef); Emily Shaw (Captain); Topher Goodman (Waiter—Season 1); Natalie Norman (Waitress); Alex Corrado (Maître D'); Nicolina Dispirito (Executive Chef); David Miller (Sous-Chef); Uzay Tumer (Captain); Heather Snell (Bartender); Gideon Horowitz (Waiter); Lonn Coward (Waiter); Jeffrey Chodorow (Financier)

PRODUCTION COMPANIES Mark Burnett Productions; Reveille; Magna Global Entertainment

EXECUTIVE PRODUCERS Mark Burnett; Ben Silverman; Robert Riesenberg; Jamie Bruce; Henrietta Conrad; Sebastian Scott

PRODUCER Saskia Rifkin

The Restaurant featured Chef Rocco DiSpirito's launch of his Manhattan restaurant Rocco's. The first season revolved around the construction of the restaurant, the hiring of the staff, and the struggle to open the restaurant on deadline. The second season focused on the restaurant's struggle to stay afloat amid pressure from the establishment's financier, Jeffrey Chodorow. The show went off the air in June 2004, and soon after the restaurant closed its doors, too.

RICH GIRLS

GENRE Docudrama (Celebrity)

FIRST TELECAST 10/28/2003

LAST TELECAST 12/30/2003

NETWORK MTV

EPISODE STYLE Self-contained

CAST Jaime Gleicher; Ally Hilfiger

PRODUCTION COMPANY MTV

PRODUCERS Jaime Gleicher; Alex Hilfiger; Ally Hilfiger; Matthew Swanson

DIRECTORS Matt Anderson; Kelly Welsh

Rich Girls followed the lifestyles of Ally Hilfiger (daughter of designer Tommy Hilfiger) and Jaime Gleicher, as they went to their prom, shopped, and spent lots of money. Alex and Jamie also served as coproducers of the series.

RIDE WITH FUNKMASTER FLEX

GENRE	Docudrama (Makeover)
FIRST TELECAST	6/6/2003
NETWORK	Spike TV
EPISODE STYLE	Self-contained
HOST	Funkmaster Flex
PRODUCER	Heather Pullman
DIRECTORS	Lashan Browning; Monica Taylor

Ride with Funkmaster Flex features rapper FunkMaster Flex as he travels the country helping customize cars and showcasing the best vehicle customizers today. Episode highlights have included Flex helping Lil' Kim customize her car, and joining the Orange County Choppers to customize a Ford Excursion.

ROAD RULES

GENRE	Competition
FIRST TELECAST	7/19/1995
NETWORK	MTV
EPISODE STYLE	Story Arc

CAST

Season 1	Allison Jones; Kit Hoover; Carlos Jackson; Mark Long; Shelly Spottedhorse
Season 2	Christian Breivik; Devin Elston; Effie Perez; Emily Bailey; Tim Beggy

Season 3 (Europe)	Antonie de Bouverie; Belou Den Tex; Chris Melling; Michelle Parma; Patrice Boudibela
Season 4 (Islands)	Erika Ruen; Jake Bronstein; Kalle Dedolph; Oscar Hernandez; Vince Forcier
Season 5 (Northern Trail)	Anne Wharton; Dan Setzler; Jon Holmes; Noah Rickun; Roni Martin; Tara McDaniel
Season 6 (Down Under)	Chadwick Pelletier; Christina Pazsitzky; Kefla Hare; Piggy Thomas; Shayne McBride; Susie Mesiter
Season 7 (Latin America)	Abe Ingersoll; Brian Lancaster; Gladys Sanabria; Holly Shand; Joshua Florence; Sarah Martinez;
Season 8 (Semester at Sea)	Ayanna Mackins; Pawel Litwinski; Pua Medieros; Shawn Sealy; Veronica Portillo; Yes Duffy
Season 9 (Maximum Velocity Tour)	Holly Brenston; James Orlando; Kathryn; Laterrian Wallace; Msaada Nia; Theo Vonkurnatowski
Season 10 (The Quest)	Adam Larson; Blair Herter; Ellen Cho; Jisela Delgado; Sophia Pasquis; Steve Meinke; Katie Doyle
Season 11 (Campus Crawl)	Darrell Taylor; Eric Jones; Kendal Sheppard; Rachel Robinson; Sarah Greyson; Shane Landrum; Raquel Duran
Season 12 (South Pacific)	Abram Boise; Cara Zavaleta; Christena Pyle; Dave Giuntoli; Donell Langham; Mary-Beth Decker; Chris Graebe; Tina Barta; Jeremy Blossom
Season 13 (X-Treme)	Danny Dias; Derrick Kosinski; Ibis Nieves; Jodi Weatherton; Kina Dean; Patrick Maloney; Nick Haggart; Angela Trimbur; Jillian Zoboroski
PRODUCTION COMPANY	Bunim-Murray Productions; MTV
CREATED BY	Mary-Ellis Bunim; Jonathan Murray
PRODUCERS	Rick de Oliveira; Jonathan Murray; Mary-Ellis Bunim
DIRECTORS	Donald Bull; Sean Rankine; Robert Sizemore; Craig Spirko

On *Road Rules,* teams of "Roadies" drive an RV on the highways of the world during a ten-week adventure. Three girls and three guys begin their mission with no money or credit cards. With a small budget, the teams have challenges to complete on the route. Beginning with Season 10, if the group couldn't complete two missions, the "Roadies" had to vote a teammate off the trip, to be replaced by a new one. At the end of the journey when the mission concluded, the surviving "Roadies" receive a generous reward.

ROAD TO STARDOM WITH MISSY ELLIOTT

GENRE	Competition (Talent)
FIRST TELECAST	1/5/2005
LAST TELECAST	3/2/2005
NETWORK	UPN
AIR TIME	Wednesday, 8:00 p.m.
EPISODE STYLE	Story Arc
TALENT	Missy Elliott (Host/Judge); Teena Marie (Judge); Dallas Austin (Judge); Mona Scott (Judge)
CAST	Jessica (Winner); Akil; Cori; Deltrice; Eddie; Frank; Heather; Marcus; Matthew; Melissa; Nic; Nilyne; Yelawolf
PRODUCTION COMPANIES	Arnold Shapiro and Alison Grodner Productions, in association with Monami, Inc.
EXECUTIVE PRODUCERS	Arnold Shapiro; Allison Grodner; Mona Scott; Jay Blumenfield; Anthony Marsh
CO-EXECUTIVE PRODUCER	Missy Elliott

Thirteen singers and rappers hopped on a tour bus with Missy Elliott in a ten-week competition to see who would be the next big hip-hop/R&B star in *Road to Stardom with Missy Elliott.* In each episode, the aspiring artists participated in a number of challenges, which included presenting an original song, singing for donations on the streets of New York, and giving a performance amid distractions at a club, such as ringing cell phones and technical problems. Each week, a panel of judges determined which two contestants would be put up for elimination. Eliott made the final decision as to who would be sent home. The winner was Jennifer, who received the $100,000 grand prize and a recording contact with Elliott's label.

ROB & AMBER: AGAINST THE ODDS

GENRE	Docusoap
FIRST TELECAST	1/11/2007
NETWORK	Fox Reality Channel
EPISODE STYLE	Story Arc
TALENT	Rob Mariano, Amber Mariano; Daniel Negranu
PRODUCTION COMPANY	Ellman Entertainment
EXECUTIVE PRODUCERS	Linda Ellman; Rob George; Christopher Meindl; Rob Mariano; Bob Boden
DIRECTORS	Linda Ellman; Rob George

This Fox Reality Channel original followed reality television's most famous couple to their new life in Las Vegas. The series began with Rob's decision to use their reality show winnings to fund his dream of becoming a professional poker player. Amber, while often supporting Rob, had her doubts. In the premiere, they had a heated argument about the risks of leaving their Pensacola, Florida, home for the glitz of Vegas. Eventually Amber agreed, telling Rob that he had three months to prove to her that he had what it took to be a professional poker player.

Poker star Daniel Negranu was Rob's coach. Daniel tried to get the sometimes uncontrollable Rob focused with a series of rules, which included not drinking before a game and playing in lower-level tournaments before going into the big leagues.

The show offered an insider's look at life with the Marianos, outside of the confines of a *Survivor* island and in surroundings a bit more domestic than their globe-trotting journeys on *The Amazing Race*.

While Rob was learning poker and trying to earn some cash from table to table, Amber apartment-hunted in Sin City, and traveled back east to attend her high-school reunion. The latter proved to be a source of drama, as Rob was scheduled to meet her there but missed his flight, leaving Amber alone on the other side of the country.

Rob tried to stay true to Daniel's rules, competing in poker tournaments such as the Mansionpoker.net Poker Dome tournament in Las Vegas, and a World Series of Poker tournament at Caesars in Indiana. While Rob was a master manipulator in the realm of reality, this wasn't true at the poker table, as he had much to learn. The stress of trying to translate his success within reality to the world of cards proved to be a strain on his and Amber's relationship, but the couple stayed strong and stuck by each other.

In the finale, Amber agreed to let Rob follow his dream; however, it would have to wait as a small wrinkle presented itself: an invitation to be participants in *The Amazing Race: All-Stars*.

ROCK OF LOVE

GENRE	Competition (Dating)
FIRST TELECAST	7/15/2007
NETWORK	VH1
EPISODES	Story Arc
TALENT	Bret Michaels
CAST	Jessica Rickleff (Winner); Heather Chadwell (Runner-up); Bonnie; Brandi Cunningham; Brandi Maron; Cindy "Rodeo" Steedle; Dallas Harrison; Erin Shattuck; Faith Rorrer; Jessica Kinni; Kelly; Kimberly; Krista; Kristia Krueger; Lacey Connor; Lauren; Magdalena Widz; Meredith; Mia Tidwell; Pam Raven; Rodeo; Samantha Weisberg; Tamara Witnzer; Tawny Amber; Tiffany Carmona
PRODUCTION COMPANIES	51 Minds Entertainment; Mindless Entertainment
EXECUTIVE PRODUCERS	Leah Horwitz; Cris Abrego; Mark Cronin; Ben Samek
COEXECUTIVE PRODUCERS	Walt Moiecinski; Courtland Cox
DIRECTORS	Zach Kozek; Robert Sizemore; Mike L. Taylor

Following the success of *Flavor of Love,* VH1 ventured into the world of rock for this celebrity dating show. At the center of it all was Poison lead singer Bret Michaels.

Twenty-five women vied for Bret's affection and in each episode he put the girls through challenges to test their love. Bret eliminated girls at the end of each show and moved others forward by giving them a backstage pass.

The show's first season ended with Bret selecting Jes over Heather but it was revealed in the reunion show after the finale that their love did not last long. Soon after, VH1 went into production of a second season of the series.

ROCK STAR: INXS

GENRE	Competition (Talent)
FIRST TELECAST	7/11/2005
LAST TELECAST	9/20/2005
NETWORK	CBS; VH1
AIR TIMES	Monday, 9:30 p.m.; Tuesday, 10:00 p.m.; Wednesday, 9:30 p.m.; Wednesday, 9:00 p.m. (moved 7/2005)
EPISODE STYLE	Story Arc
TALENT	Brooke Burke (Host); Dave Navarro (Host/Judge); Kirk Pengilly (Judge/INXS); Garry Beers (Judge/INXS); Tim Farriss (Judge/INXS); Andrew Farriss (Judge/INXS); Jon Farriss (Judge/INXS)
CAST	J. D. Fortune (Winner); Marty Casey (Runner-up); Mig Ayesa (12th eliminated); Suzie McNeil (11th eliminated); Jordis Unga (10th eliminated); Ty Taylor (9th eliminated); Deanna Johnston (8th eliminated); Jessica Robinson (7th eliminated); Brandon Calhoon (6th eliminated); Tara Slone (5th eliminated); Heather Luttrell (4th eliminated— with Daphna); Daphna Dove (4th eliminated— with Heather); Neal Carlson (3rd eliminated);

Wil Seabrook (2nd eliminated); Dana Robbins (1st eliminated)

PRODUCTION COMPANY	Mark Burnett Productions, in conjunction with INXS
CREATED BY	Mark Burnett
EXECUTIVE PRODUCERS	Mark Burnett; David Goffin; Lisa Hennessey; David Edwards; Michael Murchison; Conrad Riggs; Al Berman
DIRECTOR	Michael Simon

Rock Star: INXS featured the search for a lead singer for the band INXS. Fifteen men and women auditioned before a live audience, performing rock 'n' roll classics, original songs, and INXS tunes. Viewer votes determined the three least popular singers on each show, who were given one more chance to impress the band by singing a specific song requested by INXS. Each episode ended with the band eliminating one or more of the contenders. J. D. Fortune won, and performed as part of the new INXS during the show's final musical number.

ROCK STAR: SUPERNOVA

GENRE	Competition (Talent)
FIRST TELECAST	7/5/2006
LAST TELECAST	9/13/2006
NETWORK	CBS
AIR TIMES	Tuesday, 9:00 p.m.; Wednesday, 8:00 p.m.
EPISODE STYLE	Story Arc
CAST	Dave Navarro (Host); Brooke Burke (Host); Tommy Lee (Judge); Gilby Clarke (Judge); Jason Newsted (Judge)
TALENT	Lukas Rossi (Winner); Dilana Robichaux (2nd place); Toby Rand (3rd place); Magni Ásgeirsson (4th place); Storm Large (10th eliminated); Ryan Star (9th eliminated);

Patrice Pike (8th eliminated); Zayra Alvarez (7th eliminated); Jill Gioia (6th eliminated—tie); Josh Logan (6th eliminated—tie); Dana Andrews (5th eliminated); Phil Ritchie (4th eliminated); Jenny Galt (3rd eliminated); Chris Pierson (2nd eliminated); Matt Hoffer (1st eliminated)

PRODUCTION COMPANY Mark Burnett Productions

EXECUTIVE PRODUCERS Mark Burnett; David Goffin; Lisa Hennessy; Tommy Lee; Dave Navarro

PRODUCERS Benjamin Beatie; Curtis Colden; Lee Metzger; Matt Van Wagenen

DIRECTOR Michael Simon

In this search for a lead singer for the band Supernova, fifteen performers lived together in Hollywood Hills, facing tough competitions and a weekly elimination. The grand prize for the last singer standing was the coveted lead singer spot of a new rock supergroup featuring Mötley Crüe's Tommy Lee, Guns and Roses' Gilby Clarke, and Metallica's Jason Newsted. Lukas Rossi was the winner.

ROLLERGIRLS

GENRE Docusoap

FIRST TELECAST 1/2/2006

LAST TELECAST 4/2/2006

NETWORK A&E

EPISODE STYLE Self-contained

CAST Lux (The Rhinestone Cowgirls); Sister Mary Jane (The Holy Rollers); Punky Bruiser (The Holy Rollers); Miss Conduct (The Holy Rollers); Venis Envy (PDF); Cha Cha (PDF); Chola (PDF); Witch Baby (The Rhinestone Cowgirls); Jail Bait (The Holy Rollers); Lunatic (Hellcats); Catalac (Hellcats)

PRODUCTION COMPANY	Go Go Luckey Productions
EXECUTIVE PRODUCERS	Karen Jacobs; Julie Auerbach; Gary Auerbach
PRODUCERS	Dan Brown; George Sledge; Alycia Rossiter
DIRECTORS	Bradley Beesley; Dan Brown; Mark Miks; Tina Gazzerro

Rollergirls followed the lives of a diverse group of women who competed in the physically demanding sport of roller derby. The series followed the ladies as they raised kids, attended school, dated men, and went about their daily lives, while at night they strapped on helmets and pads for tough competition in the roller rink.

ROOM 401

GENRE	Docudrama (Hoax)
FIRST TELECAST	7/17/2007
NETWORK	MTV
EPISODES	Self-contained
TALENT	Jared Padalecki (Host)
PRODUCTION COMPANIES	Katalyst Films; Proud Mary Entertainment
EXECUTIVE PRODUCERS	Jason Goldberg; Ashton Kutcher; Mary L. Aloe; Billy Rainey
CO-EXECUTIVE PRODUCERS	Chris Gongora; Rico de la Vega

This hidden-camera show named after the room in which Harry Houdini died featured people being the victims of hoaxes inspired by horror movies. These pranks saw victims witnessing an ice sculptor still living after being cut in half by a chainsaw, crabs crawling out of a man's opened chest, and somebody walking on water.

ROOM RAIDERS

GENRE	Competition (Dating)
FIRST TELECAST	2/17/2004
NETWORK	MTV
EPISODE STYLE	Self-contained
PRODUCTION COMPANIES	Granada Television; MTV Productions
EXECUTIVE PRODUCERS	Charles Tremayne
PRODUCERS	Yessica Garcia; Zosimo Maximo; Brian Prowse-Gainy; Tripp Swanhaus
DIRECTORS	Irad Eyal; Yessica Garcia; Eli Kabillio; Miles Kahn; Zosimo Maximo; Farrell Roth; Michael Swanhaus; Tripp Swanhaus; Lorna Thomas

Three young men or women competed for a date with another young man or woman in *Room Raiders*. In a twist, contestants based their choice on a surprise inspection of each of the suitors' homes. Before the inspection, the suitors were kidnapped by the *Room Raiders* crew and put in a van, where they watched the inspections as they happened. After all three rooms were inspected, the man or woman chose which room was the best. The suitor whose room was chosen got to go on a date.

RUN'S HOUSE

GENRE	Docusoap
FIRST TELECAST	10/13/2005
NETWORK	MTV
EPISODE STYLE	Story Arc
CAST	Joseph (Rev. Run) Simmons; Justine Simmons; Vanessa Simmons; Angela Simmons; Diggy Simmons; JoJo Simmons; Russy Simmons

PRODUCTION COMPANIES	Bad Boy Worldwide Entertainment Group;
	Carbone Entertainment Inc.;
	Russell Simmons Television
EXECUTIVE PRODUCERS	Jason A. Carbone; Tony DiSanto; Liz Gateley
PRODUCER	Gary Shaffer

Run's House features Rev. Run, former Run-DMC member turned reverend. The series is set in his mansion, and highlights the daily lives of Run, wife Justine, and his two daughters and three sons.

SCARE TACTICS

GENRE	Docudrama (Hoax)
FIRST TELECAST	4/4/2003
LAST TELECAST	12/15/2004
NETWORK	Sci-Fi Channel
EPISODE STYLE	Self-contained
TALENT	Shannen Doherty (Host—Seasons 1 and 2); Stephen Baldwin (Season 2)
PRODUCTION COMPANIES	Hallock Healey Entertainment; The Sci-Fi Channel
CREATED BY	Scott Hallock; Kevin Healey
PRODUCER	Scott Hallock
DIRECTOR	Mike Harney

Played for laughs, this hidden camera show followed friends as they set up their friends. The series featured horror film–inspired pranks, including an alien invasion, an attack by a Bigfoot-like creature, and the reawakening of a terrifying mummy. The show was the subject of a lawsuit in 2003, in which a woman claimed physical and psychological injury from one of the show's pranks.

SCAREDY CAMP

GENRE Competition
FIRST TELECAST 10/2002
NETWORK Nickelodeon
EPISODE STYLE Story Arc
TALENT Emma Wilson (Host)

Two teams of three kids solved mysteries at the "haunted" Camp Lindenwood in this competition. The first season dealt with the disappearance of David Williams, while the second centered around the legend of Sally, a camp counselor. In the course of the series, the kids performed challenges, including doing an apache relay and swinging on a trapeze. The host was Emma Wilson, the daughter of Anne Robinson, the host of *The Weakest Link*.

THE SCHOLAR

GENRE Competition
FIRST TELECAST 6/6/2005
LAST TELECAST 7/18/2005
NETWORK ABC
AIR TIME Monday, 8:00 p.m.
EPISODE STYLE Story Arc
TALENT Rob Nelson (Host); Marquesa Lawrence (Scholarship Committee); Peter Johnson (Scholarship Committee); Shawn Abbott (Scholarship Committee)
CAST Melissa (Winner); Amari; Alyssa; Davis; Elizabeth; Jeremy; Milana; Scot; Gerald; Max
PRODUCTION COMPANIES Bunim-Murray Productions; Martin/Stein; Carsey-Werner

CREATED BY	Jaye Pace; Shannon Meairs and Waxman Williams Entertainment
EXECUTIVE PRODUCERS	Steve Martin; Joan Stein; Jon Murray; Marcy Carsey; Tom Werner
DIRECTOR	Robert Sizemore

The Scholar featured ten high-school seniors, some of whom might not otherwise have had the opportunity to attend a top university, competing for a college scholarship. Contestants were tested in academics, leadership, creativity, and community service. Each of the preliminary episodes began with a captain's quiz to determine which two students would lead the two teams. A team challenge was presented, and the winning team's captain advanced to the weekly showdown at the end of the episode. The scholarship committee then chose two other students to advance to the weekly showdown. The winner of the weekly showdown earned a $50,000 scholarship and advanced to the finals for the grand-prize scholarship. The Ivy League scholarship committee judged the final oral examination and declared Melissa the winner of the full-ride scholarship. The show was recorded in and around the University of Southern California's campus.

SCOTT BAIO IS 45 . . . AND SINGLE

GENRE	Docudrama
FIRST TELECAST	7/15/2007
NETWORK	VH1
EPISODE STYLE	Story Arc
CAST	Scott Baio; Alison "Doc Ali" Arnold; (Therapist); Johnny "Johnny V" Venokur (Friend); Steve Cuccio (Friend); Jason Hervey (Friend)
PRODUCTION COMPANIES	Bischoff Hervey Entertainment; 3Ball Productions
EXECUTIVE PRODUCERS	Claire McCabe; Michael Hirschorn; Jeff Olde; J. D. Roth; Todd A. Nelson; Jason Hervey; Eric Bischoff; Scott Baio; Adam Greener;

CO-EXECUTIVE PRODUCER	Matt Assmus
PRODUCERS	Angela Molloy; Caleb Nelson; Haylee Vance; Juliana Kim; Shannon Horan; Julie Singer; Steve Youel

Former child actor Scott Baio, best remembered for his starring roles on *Happy Days* and *Charles in Charge,* sought the services of a life coach to help him figure out why he hadn't been able to commit to marriage in *Scott Baio Is 45 . . . and Single.* With the coach's guidance and the support of his friends, Scott revisited women he had dated in the past to understand how to proceed with his future. At the end of Season 1, he committed to marrying his longtime girlfriend, who announced that she was pregnant with his first child.

SCREAM PLAY

GENRE	Competition
FIRST TELECAST	6/13/2004
NETWORK	E!
EPISODE STYLE	Self-contained
TALENT	Matt Iseman (Host)
PRODUCTION COMPANIES	E! Entertainment Television; Reveille Productions
EXECUTIVE PRODUCERS	David Hurwitz; Joel Klein; Mark Koops; Ben Silverman
CO-EXECUTIVE PRODUCER	H. T. Owens
PRODUCERS	David Basinski; Jennifer Clayton
DIRECTOR	David Basinski

Scream Play featured contestants performing stunts based on scenes from popular movies and television shows. Stunts included drinking raw eggs like Sylvester Stallone did in *Rocky,* managing a zip line at the top of a clock tower the way Doc Brown did in *Back to the Future,* and doing a water rescue like the lifeguards on *Baywatch.*

SEASON OF THE TIGER

GENRE	Docusoap
FIRST TELECAST	4/27/2006
LAST TELECAST	5/25/2007
NETWORK	BET
EPISODE STYLE	Self-contained
CAST	Bruce Eugene; Blue; Eva; Mancel; Shunnie
PRODUCTION COMPANY	DAFT Films
EXECUTIVE PRODUCERS	Adam Hall; Jimmy Higgins; Jesse Scaccia; David Schewel
PRODUCERS	Jairus Cobb; Ben Faulks
DIRECTOR	Jairus Cobb

Season of the Tiger followed members of the Grambling State University marching band and football team during the 2005–2006 football season. The show focused on the lives of three band members and two football players as they tried to fulfill their potential, despite setbacks encountered along the way.

SHALOM IN THE HOME

GENRE	Makeover
FIRST TELECAST	4/9/2006
NETWORK	TLC
EPISODE STYLE	Self-contained
TALENT	Rabbi Shmuley Boteach
PRODUCTION COMPANY	Diverse USA
EXECUTIVE PRODUCERS	Roy Ackerman; Andrew Harrison; Ronnie Krensel; Bernadette McDaid; Deborah Adler Myers
DIRECTORS	Marcus Boyle; Beth Paholak

Shalom in the Home features Rabbi Shmuley's insight into relationships, marriage, and parenting as he goes from home to home repairing family dysfunction. In each episode, he takes one family on an intensive ten-day journey, and, through a series of exercises, helps them come to terms with their problems and find the skills and resolve needed to improve their situation.

SHEAR GENIUS

GENRE	Competition (Job)
FIRST TELECAST	4/11/2007
LAST TELECAST	5/24/2007
NETWORK	Bravo
EPISODE STYLE	Story Arc
CAST	Jaclyn Smith (Host); Sally Hershberger (Judge); Michael Carl (Judge); Rene Fris (Mentor)
TALENT	Anthony (Winner); Ben (Runner-up); Daisy (10th eliminated); Dr. Boogie (9th eliminated); Tabatha (8th eliminated); Tyson (7th eliminated); Danna (6th eliminated); Evangelin (5th eliminated); Theodore (4th eliminated); Lacey (3rd eliminated); Jim (2nd eliminated); Paul-Jean (1st eliminated)
PRODUCTION COMPANY	Reveille Productions
PRODUCER	Adam Kaloustian
CO-EXECUTIVE PRODUCER	Mark Koops

Following the formats of *Project Runway* and *Top Chef,* this hairstyle competition series follows contestants as they are given two challenges in each episode: a Shortcut Challenge and an Elimination Challenge. The judges discussed the results of the Elimination Challenge, and, each week, the poorest-performing stylist was eliminated. Anthony was the winner, receiving $100,000 from Nexxus Salon Hair Care.

SHEER DALLAS

GENRE	Docusoap
FIRST TELECAST	4/15/2005
LAST TELECAST	5/20/2005
NETWORK	TLC
EPISODE STYLE	Story Arc
TALENT	Larry Hagman (Narrator)
CAST	Deanne Dipizio (Salon Owner); Carolyn Shamis (Real Estate Agent); Lance Hooper (Stylist); Billy Scoggins (Stylist); Dee Simmons (Author); D'Andra Simmons Manges (Dee's daughter)
PRODUCTION COMPANIES	Lion Television; TLC
EXECUTIVE PRODUCERS	Ciara Byrne; Michael Klein
PRODUCER	Fred Grinstein
SUPERVISING PRODUCER	Fred Grinstein

Narrated by *Dallas* star Larry Hagman, this docusoap profiled rich and famous Dallas residents, revealing their "everything's bigger in Texas" lavish lifestyles. The show's centerpiece was Salon Pompeo, where many wealthy personalities converged to be groomed and pampered. One story line focused on the wedding of D'andra Simmons, an elaborate affair that was described as "Sultan meets Queen Elizabeth."

SHE'S MOVING IN

GENRE	Docusoap
FIRST TELECAST	7/21/2007
NETWORK	WE
EPISODE STYLE	Self-contained
CAST	Peggy Bunker (Host); Nicole Facciuto (Designer); Mark Montano (Designer); Cat Wei (Desgner)

PRODUCTION COMPANY   New Harbor
EXECUTIVE PRODUCERS   Linda Benya; Steve Schwartz

Professional designers helped couples combine two opposite tastes to create one compatible space in this home makeover show.

SHIPMATES

GENRE	Docudrama (Dating)
FIRST TELECAST	8/27/2001
NETWORK	Syndicated
EPISODE STYLE	Self-contained
TALENT	Chris Hardwick (Host)
PRODUCTION COMPANIES	Columbia TriStar Domestic Television; Avoca Productions
CREATED BY	Robert Buchalter; Manny Rashid; Betsy Schechter; John Tomlin; Bob Young
EXECUTIVE PRODUCERS	John Tomlin; Bob Young
SENIOR PRODUCERS	Jim Duphinee; Dennis O'Brien
PRODUCERS	Robert Buchalter; Chris Rantamaki; Manny Rashid; Gabriel Roth; Mike Stafford

Shipmates followed a man and woman as they met for the first time on a cruise ship. Over three days and two nights on the ship and at the couple's Caribbean destination, the series observed the two to see if sparks flew.

SHOOTING SIZEMORE

GENRE	Docudrama
FIRST TELECAST	1/7/2007
NETWORK	VH1

EPISODES	Self-contained
CAST	Tom Sizemore; Byron de Mares; Luree Thomas
PRODUCTION COMPANY	Tijuana Entertainment
EXECUTIVE PRODUCERS	Terence Michael; Gordon Gilbertson; John Foy; Troy Searer
CO-EXECUTIVE PRODUCERS	Bill Hochhauser; Shye Sutherland

This gritty docudrama followed the life of notorious actor Tom Sizemore. Episodes showed Sizemore struggling to fight addiction and rebuild his career after bankruptcy, and a bad reputation surrounding Heidi Fleiss's battery charges against him. Helping him through this journey were his friend Byron and personal assistant Luree.

THE SHOP

GENRE	Docudrama
FIRST TELECAST	3/2/2006
NETWORK	MTV
EPISODES	Self-contained
CAST	Pop Agbayani; Van Alexander; Deb Hammon; Teddy Jones; Bobby McLean; Tim Smith
PRODUCTION COMPANIES	The Mottola Company; Varsity Entertainment
EXECUTIVE PRODUCERS	Jeb Brien; Tony DiSanto; Liz Gateley; David Kaufman; Rushion McDonald; Matt Morchower; Tommy Mottola; Corey Rooney
DIRECTOR	Kenny Hull

A local Queens barbershop owned by music producer Cory Rooney was the setting for this MTV docusoap. The shop was often visited by celebrities in the hip-hop world and many of the shop's employees were aspiring musicians.

SHOWBIZ MOMS AND DADS

GENRE	Docusoap
FIRST TELECAST	4/13/2004
LAST TELECAST	5/18/2004
NETWORK	Bravo
EPISODE STYLE	Story Arc

CAST

The Nutters	Duncan (dad); Cynthia (mom); Duncan, Jr. (son, 17); Grace (daughter, 16); Aaron (son, 13); Ellie (daughter, 12); Emma (daughter, 10); Isaiah (son, 9); Forrest (son, 7)
The Barrons	Tiffany (mom); Jordan (daughter, 14); Samantha (daughter, 9); Dave (Tiffany's husband)
The Klingesmiths	Debra (mom); Jim (dad); Shane (son, 13)
The Moseley-Stephens	Kim (mom); Jordan (daughter, 8)
The Tyes	Deborah (mom); David (dad); Emily (daughter, 4); Susan (grandma); Brenden (son, 9)
PRODUCTION COMPANY	World of Wonder
EXECUTIVE PRODUCERS	Fenton Bailey; Randy Barbato; David Perler; Frances Berwick; Amy Introcaso-Davis; Shari Levine
SUPERVISING PRODUCER	Todd Radnitz

Showbiz Moms and Dads followed five families seeking fame and fortune for their talented children, as the youngsters rehearsed, auditioned, and struggled to win beauty pageants and roles in feature films, sometimes under extreme pressure.

Duncan Nutter moved his nine-member family of actors into a two-bedroom apartment in New York City. The Barrons' daughter Jordan tried to make it in the film world after scoring parts in music videos. The Klingesmiths' story centered on son Shane, as he pursued a career in acting, singing, and modeling. The Moseley-Stephens consisted of mom Kim, who had had a career in show business singing backup for M.C.

Hammer, and daughter Jordan, who had appeared in *The Parkers* and *That's So Raven*. Deborah, the mother in the Tyes family, wanted her daughter, Emily, to make it big in the pageant circuit.

SHOWDOG MOMS AND DADS

GENRE	Docudrama
FIRST TELECAST	3/30/2005
LAST TELECAST	5/18/2005
NETWORK	Bravo
AIR TIME	Wednesday, 10:00 p.m.
EPISODE STYLE	Story Arc
CAST	George and Connie Boulton (Pepe and Oolala); Ryan Pacchiano and Brandon Kindle (Daisy and Liberace); Moira and Adam Cornell (Riot, Tooter, Scooter and Roxy); Lourdes and Peter Cofino (Max, Katie and Duke); Kyra Sundance (Chalcy)
PRODUCTION COMPANY	World of Wonder
EXECUTIVE PRODUCERS	Fenton Bailey; Randy Barbato; Shari Levine, Andrew Cohen
PRODUCERS	Todd Radnitz; Angela Rae Berg; Thomas Jaeger; Robin Nelson; Chris May; Skylar Smith; Nicole Solomon

Showdog Moms and Dads featured five sets of dog owners as they navigated through the competitive and often tumultuous world of the dog show circuit, culminating at the National Dog Show in Philadelphia. The series highlighted the extremes to which show dog owners will go for their pets. Episodes featured Ryan and Brandon taking their dogs to a dentist for teeth whitening, George and Connie spreading their deceased pet's ashes along a favorite desert trail, and Moira holding a puppy party to find a new dog for her niece and nephew.

THE SIMPLE LIFE
(Season 1)

GENRE	Docusoap (Celebrity)
FIRST TELECAST	12/2/2003
LAST TELECAST	1/26/2004
NETWORK	FOX
AIR TIMES	Tuesday, 8:30 p.m.; Wednesday, 8:30 p.m.; Thursday, 9:00 p.m.
EPISODE STYLE	Story Arc
TALENT	John Gary (Narrator); David Richards (Narrator)
CAST	Paris Hilton; Nicole Richie; Albert Leding; Braxton Leding; Cayne Leding; Curly Leding; Janet Leding; Justin Leding; Richard Leding; Tinkerbell the Dog; Trae Lindley
PRODUCTION COMPANIES	By George Prods Inc.; 20th Century Fox Television; Bunim-Murray Productions
EXECUTIVE PRODUCERS	Mary-Ellis Bunim; Jonathan Murray
CO-EXECUTIVE PRODUCER	Patty Ivins Specht

The Simple Life featured wealthy celebutantes Paris Hilton and Nicole Richie as they attempted to live in rural Arkansas for one month.

In Episode 1, the girls traveled to Altus, Arkansas, and met their host family, the Ledings. The family was immediately shocked at how skimpily they were dressed. They sent the girls to buy groceries, including pigs' feet. When the girls returned, they refused to help pluck a chicken. Upon seeing their bedroom, Paris and Nicole were upset at how many insects also resided in their room. The night concluded with the girls chatting up fifteen-year-old Cayne, teasing him that they were going to offer him a threesome.

Paris and Nicole went to a dairy farm early in the morning to help milk cows in Episode 2. The girls did shoddy work, and were fired after they were caught napping on the job. That afternoon, they met Justin's friends at a barbecue. Later, they dressed up and sneaked out past curfew for a night on the town.

Episode 3 picked up at the local dance club, where the girls drank too much and Nicole made out with a local. Just a few hours later, they were awakened for their first day of work at a fast food restaurant. After they rearranged an outdoor sign to spell something filthy, the manager made them wear giant milkshake costumes. That night, they blew their paychecks on a trip out on the town.

The mayor asked Paris and Nicole to be honorary co-chairs at the Springtime Gala in Episode 4. Nicole campaigned for their host family's infant son Braxton to become "prince" by having his name painted across her breasts. While drinking at a pub at 8:00 a.m., Paris got two guys to kiss each other, then Nicole let another guy kiss her butt. Then the girls tried to make Justin's ex-girlfriend jealous by claiming they had both kissed him.

In Episode 5, the girls went to work for a cattle auctioneer, although they spent most of their time flirting with the farmhands. They got in trouble after using their boss's account to buy a birdhouse as a Mother's Day gift for their host mother. As punishment, they had to check the cows to see if they were pregnant by sticking their arms inside the cows.

In Episode 6, Paris and Nicole began working at a gas station, where they met two guys named Anthony and Trae. Against Albert's wishes, they went out with the boys, got drunk, and made a scene at a local bar.

A reunion special hosted by Leeza Gibbons aired between Episodes 6 and 7.

In Episode 7, Paris and Nicole had to settle the debts they had run up all over town. Albert and the boys dumped the girls in the pool. But that night everyone bonded at a family get-together. The next morning, the girls said their good-byes and headed home.

Episode 8 was a "lost episode," cobbled together from previously unaired footage. Paris and Nicole spoiled a country dance by getting the DJ to switch to rock music. They experienced their first tornado in the family's shelter. Then they got a job cleaning and transporting animals for a taxidermist. Paris surprised everyone by cooking a lasagna dinner.

THE SIMPLE LIFE 2: ROAD TRIP

GENRE	Docusoap (Celebrity)
FIRST TELECAST	6/16/2004
LAST TELECAST	8/4/2004
NETWORK	FOX
AIR TIME	Wednesday, 9:00 p.m.
EPISODE STYLE	Story Arc
TALENT	John Gary (Narrator); David Richards (Narrator)
CAST	Paris Hilton; Nicole Richie; Tinkerbell the Dog
PRODUCTION COMPANIES	By George Prods Inc.; 20th Century Fox Television; Bunim-Murray Productions
EXECUTIVE PRODUCER	Jonathan Murray
CO-EXECUTIVE PRODUCER	Patty Ivins Specht

Season 2 of *The Simple Life* followed Paris and Nicole as they trekked from Miami to Beverly Hills without money, credit cards, or cell phones.

In Episode 1, Paris and Nicole were offered a ride in a pickup truck with a trailer. They were forced to beg for money to pay a road toll and to refill their gas tank. While working at a rodeo, Paris fell off a horse and was airlifted to an emergency room. Once she was released, the sympathetic head rancher got duped into picking up the girls' tab at a gift store, which totalled more than $100.

In Episode 2, Paris was pulled over by the police and didn't have her driver's license, but she got off with just a warning. While trying to cook at a trailer park, Paris stuck a metal pot in the microwave. A couple let the girls babysit their daughter for ten dollars, and they taught the child to curse and dress like them. Paris and Nicole dressed like a mermaid and a turtle, but failed to be hired by a water park for a live mermaid show. They drowned their sorrows by dancing on the bar at Coyote Ugly.

The girls blocked a fast food drive-thru line while begging for money from customers in Episode 3. They were then hired as chambermaids at a nudist colony, where they used a guest's cell phone to call room service, and ordered another maid to clean the room. They attended a body-acceptance class, where they wrote poems about their feelings. That night, the girls went to a nude disco.

Paris and Nicole stayed with the Skinner family in Mississippi in Episode 4. Nicole helped dad, Jimmy, cook a deer. Jimmy invited local firemen to pose with the girls for a calendar. The girls skipped dinner to go out to a club. The next day, they got a job at a sausage factory. When they bungled the sausage making, they were forced to try to sell the defective sausages to passing motorists. The girls brought home sausages for the Skinners, including a special one made of dog food for James, as payback for when he earlier called them "Dumb and Dumber."

In Episode 5, the girls went to Louisiana, where they helped the Mequet family's daughter, Jenny, prepare for her date. After they charged almost $500 on the family credit card, the girls were forced to return what they'd bought. The next morning, they worked as crawfish catchers. After coming up short of their catch quota, Paris stole cooked crustaceans from a crawfish boil to make up the difference, and they were paid $78. That night, the girls got Jenny dressed up for her date with Matthew.

In Episode 6, Nicole discovered a truck's CB radio and sent dirty messages to truckers. The girls alternated working as farmhands at the Lutz-Carillo farm, where they sneaked the sons away to a spray-tan salon. They introduced the boys to girls, and made them exchange phone numbers. The girls did farmhand work in the morning, then hit the road.

In Episode 7, Paris and Nicole stayed with the devoutly Christian African American Cash family, where they disgusted their hosts by cursing. Nicole attempted to cook for the first time in her life. The next day, the girls got jobs shagging balls and massaging players for a minor league baseball team. They made a scene during the game, and were thrown out of the stadium.

The girls stayed with the Bahm family in Episode 8. Paris said biker son Denny was "hot." The next morning, the girls were hired at a hair salon, where they waxed a guy's back and gave an older woman a platinum dye job. Despite their poor work, they earned $100.

Paris and Nicole slept at the Click Ranch in Episode 9. Bob gave the girls driving lessons, and they gave him love lessons before he and his wife went on a romantic date. The girls were then hired as deputies, but they abused their privileges while doing a poor job. Nicole left handcuffs for Bob before his date.

The girls ran out of gas in Episode 10, and were rescued by a ranch family. They were hired to brand and rustle cows, and Paris faced her fear, getting back on a horse. They used the money they'd earned to buy a bull to protect it from slaughter. The girls bummed gas money to get back to Los Angeles, where a giant party awaited them. During the party, a delivery man showed up with their bull.

Three months later, a special episode aired, featuring previously unseen footage.

THE SIMPLE LIFE: INTERNS
(Season 3)

GENRE	Docusoap (Celebrity)
FIRST TELECAST	1/26/2005
LAST TELECAST	5/12/2005
NETWORK	FOX
AIR TIMES	Wednesday, 8:30 p.m.; Thursday, 9:00 p.m.
EPISODE STYLE	Story Arc
TALENT	John Gary (Narrator); David Richards (Narrator)
CAST	Paris Hilton; Nicole Richie; Tinkerbell the Dog
PRODUCTION COMPANIES	By George Prods Inc.; 20th Century Fox Television; Bunim-Murray Productions
EXECUTIVE PRODUCER	Jonathan Murray
CO-EXECUTIVE PRODUCER	Patty Ivins Specht

In Season 3, Paris and Nicole worked a series of jobs across the country.

In Episode 1, the girls and their three dogs—Tinkerbell, Honey Child, and Foxy Cleopatra—hit the road together. Their first stop was the home of the Brower family, in New Jersey. They were hired at an auto center as mechanics and as customer-service representatives, and managed to bungle both jobs. The girls surprised Joyce Brower with great danes from a breeder, who angrily demanded the dogs be returned when they weren't paid for. The next stop was Staten Island, where they stayed with Lou and Phyllis Zuccaro. Lou taught the girls jujitsu. They screwed up another job as secretaries at a New York ad agency, but were paid $200 anyway.

Paris and Nicole stayed with the Ritchey family in Pennsylvania in Episode 2. They were hired at an airport to wave in airplanes, unload baggage, empty waste, and work in customer service. Later, Nicole tried to get the Ritchey's son, Jason, back together with his ex, Kayla.

In Episode 3, the girls crashed with the Hirrel family in New Jersey. They were hired at a mortuary to drive caskets to a cemetery, help a couple make funeral plans, and load ashes into urns. Nicole accidentally dumped an urn on the floor, and she and Paris vacuumed up the ashes. Later, they hired a hypnotist from California to help the Hirrels stop smoking.

In Episode 4, the girls returned to Pennsylvania, where they stayed with the Sclafani family. They were hired to work for a plastic surgeon, where Nicole made more money because Paris kept throwing up. After work, the girls accompanied the Sclafani brothers to a gym, and later brought the whole family to a drag strip club, where Paris took a turn onstage.

In Episode 5, Paris and Nicole lived with the Eisner family in Baltimore. They got an internship at a news station, where they demonstrated their ineptitude at writing a script, scrolling a TelePrompTer, running a camera, and creating weather graphics. On day two, they were put on camera. Their boss paid them $100. While with the Eisners, they made over the sons, piercing Cody's ear and offering to get Josh's nose pierced.

In Episode 6, Paris and Nicole stayed with the McGivneys in Delaware. The girls botched a job at a daycare center, but were paid anyway. They bought a bed for the McGivney's son, Liam.

The girls returned to Baltimore to stay with the Sawczenkos in Episode 7. They worked a variety of odd jobs at the Baltimore Zoo, including measuring a sixteen-foot python. Later, they bought alcohol and sex toys for dad Steve, to celebrate his birthday. Nicole's fiancé, Adam, made a surprise visit, and they went on a romantic date. Meanwhile, Paris went out with Nicole Sawczenko and danced on a bar.

In Episode 8, the girls stayed with the Foote family in Ellicott City, Maryland. They were hired to make a variety of desserts at a bakery and earned $80, despite their numerous mistakes. Paris cooked lasagna in exchange for massages from the masseuse mom. It turned out to be an engagement dinner, as Adam proposed to Nicole.

Before leaving Ellicott City in Episode 9, the girls set up their elderly widow neighbor on a date. They were sent to a spa to give psychic readings, but were fired after taking a manicure break.

In Episode 10, the girls were the house guests of the Doughertys in New Jersey. They worked at an assisted-living center, where they gave the old folks makeovers. Paris put antlers on Chuck Doughtery, and shot him with a paintball gun to teach him a lesson about hunting.

Paris and Nicole then stayed in Miami with Linda Jacobs, her son, and two orang-utans in Episode 11. They were hired at an ad agency, where they competed against two other interns to come up with ideas for the Burger King account. After a bad first presentation, they were sent to do research at Burger King. Later, they dressed up the orangutans as part of their second presentation.

In Episode 12, the girls returned to New Jersey, where they stayed with the Graeff family. They interned at a fire station, where they demonstrated their ineptitude in mastering a wide array of firefighting skills. During an actual call, Nicole freed a man's arm from a toilet, after he was fishing for his car keys. In their off time, the girls found friends for the lonely daughter, Jee.

Paris and Nicole then spent time with the Dempseys in Timonium, Maryland, in Episode 13. They took a boring job at a circuit board manufacturer. At night, they sneaked the Dempsey boys out to a bowling alley, where they persuaded Andrew to hit on women.

Paris and Nicole were off to Nashville in Episode 14, where they stayed with single mom Pebe Sebert, whom they later set up with a prospective boyfriend. Mean-while, they worked as wedding planners.

In Episode 15, the girls took an internship at a dentist's office in Nashville. Paris entered the Miss Belle Rive beauty pageant and won. They took a bus back to New York City on a high note.

THE SIMPLE LIFE: 'TIL DEATH DO US PART

(Season 4)

GENRE	Docusoap (Celebrity)
FIRST TELECAST	6/4/2006
LAST TELECAST	7/23/2006
NETWORK	E!
AIR TIME	Sunday, 10:00 p.m.
EPISODE STYLE	Story Arc
TALENT	James DuMont (narrator)
CAST	Paris Hilton; Nicole Richie; Tinkerbell the Dog
PRODUCTION COMPANIES	George Prods Inc.; 20th Century Fox Television; Bunim-Murray Productions
CREATED BY	Jonathan Murray
EXECUTIVE PRODUCERS	Jonathan Murray; Patty Ivins Spech
CO-EXECUTIVE PRODUCERS	Tim Atzinger; Ross Breitenbach; Rich Buhrman; Adam Cohen; Claudia Frank

On each episode of *The Simple Life: 'Til Death Do Us Part,* Paris and Nicole took over the housewife/mother role in the household, but at different times, as the girls were no longer best friends.

In Episode 1, Paris and Nicole donned thirty-five-pound pregnancy suits to replace the nine-months-pregnant stay-at-home wife in the Nolan family. The girls had a tough time keeping the house clean, taking care of a three-year-old, and going to Lamaze class. Bad girl Nicole took Mr. Nolan to a strip club. Paris was chosen as the top housewife.

Paris and Nicole swapped designer duds for Pakistani saris in Episode 2, as they joined the Ghauri family. The girls tried to speak, dress, and dance like traditional Pakistani housewives under the guidance of Mr. Ghauri and an Americanized fifteen-year-old son. Paris and Nicole taught the Ghauris how to party like Americans.

The girls' mission was to rekindle the Weekes' love life in Episode 3. Paris and Nicole's new "husband" showed them how life was with his wife. To rekindle their love life, Paris got wet 'n' wild on the golf links. Nicole held an erotic photo shoot in the bedroom, complete with blindfolds and tequila. The husband chose Nicole as the best fill-in wife.

Paris and Nicole took care of four rowdy children when they joined the Padilla family in Episode 4. The out-of-control kids had lots of questions for their fill-in mothers, and Paris and Nicole were so overwhelmed they resorted to out-of-the-ordinary parenting techniques.

In Episode 5, Paris and Nicole tackled raising the two teenage daughters of a lesbian couple. When the girls learned that the moms had never married, they went into wedding planner mode. A surprise commitment ceremony was in the works, thanks to Nicole, while Paris planned an even grander party, which was chosen by the moms.

In Episode 6, Paris and Nicole filled in as mom for the Murrie boys. Liam, five, helped Paris plan a birthday bash for Sean, who was turning one. Nicole was to play host at the party, and the former friends had to awkwardly work together to pull off the bash.

Paris and Nicole joined the Contreras family on a camping trip in Episode 7. Paris turned a hotel room into a forest, complete with live bears, to impress the single dad and his two kids. But she left a mess for hotel housekeeping. Nicole couldn't cook hot dogs, so her friend flew in a pizza, and then she took the family on an airplane ride.

In Episode 8, Paris and Nicole had to clean the Beggs family's messy house, but the girls weren't exactly model maids. Nicole took the family for makeovers, while Paris whipped up a dinner party. The husband said Paris would make the best housewife and mom.

Paris and Nicole delved into the art world with the Burton family. Nicole created an R-rated rap video, while Paris directed a cross-dressing video. Both made the Burtons think about censorship.

In the Episode 10 finale, Paris sent an impersonator in her place to the Siegals, a couple married for sixty-four years. Nicole was already at the Siegals' house when the fake Paris arrived, and she set up a press conference to embarrass the real Paris, who eventually showed up for a final confrontation.

THE SIMPLE LIFE GOES TO CAMP
(Season 5)

GENRE	Doucsoap (Celebrity)
FIRST TELECAST	5/28/2007
LAST TELECAST	8/5/2007
NETWORK	E!
AIR TIME	Sunday, 10:00 p.m.
EPISODE STYLE	Story Arc
CAST	Paris Hilton; Nicole Richie
PRODUCTION COMPANIES	George Prods Inc.; 20th Century Fox Television; Bunim-Murray Productions
CREATED BY	Jonathan Murray
EXECUTIVE PRODUCERS	Jonathan Murray; Patty Ivins Spech
CO-EXECUTIVE PRODUCERS	Tim Atzinger, Ross Breitenbach, Rich Buhrman, Adam Cohen, Claudia Frank

The fifth and final season of *The Simple Life* found Paris and Nicole reunited as friends. This time, the girls served as counselors at Camp Shawnee, a camp created specifically for the series that served as host to camps for couples, the elderly, overweight people, aspiring actors, and beauty-pageant hopefuls. The camp was set at the location of a real camp, Camp JCA Shalom, located in Malibu, California.

Each episode dealt with a different camp with episodes 1 and 2 showing the girls counseling overweight people. Weight-loss guru and infomerical legend Susan Powter was a guest in this episode. Susan got the girls to round up the fat campers' junk food and lock it in a refrigerator. This is all for naught as, by the end of the episode, the girls got one of the campers to help them break open the refrigerator, much to the chagrin of the leaders of the camp.

In the second half of their fat camp saga, Paris and Nicole led the campers through a hike. The girls and boys in the camp were separated, with Paris and Nicole left in charge of the girls. Paris and Nicole gave the girls their unique take on losing weight and told them to flirt and dance their way to a thinner body. This episode also introduced a potential new love interest for Paris: Hunter, one of the other counselors at Camp Shawnee.

Episodes 3 and 4 moved the girls to the camp's beauty pageant training program. Paris and Nicole counseled mothers and their pageant-aspiring daughters. This program was headed up by pageant expert Kyle Haggerty. As a means of bonding with the latest set of campers, Paris and Nicole participated in a three-legged race with their fellow counselors and campers. Never one to avoid stirring things up, Nicole taught the aspiring pageant girls how to flip off Kyle. Paris and Nicole also taught Joey, the son of Ed (the camp's leader), how to date by having him speed date with the pageant girls.

The pageant camp ends with a pageant, but, in a twist, it's not for the daughters. The moms were the contestants, and the daughters had to prepare them for the "Beautiful Moms Pageant." *Project Runway*'s Nick Verreos guest starred as the judge for the pageant.

Episodes 5 and 6 had the girls counseling at a love camp at Shawnee. The attendees of the love camp were couples looking to find that lost spark from their relationships. To help the couples, Paris and Nicole put together a romantic dinner. Porn star Jenna Jameson also made an appearance at a ceremony where the couples redeclare their love for each other.

Episodes 7 and 8 had the girls working for Shawnee's survival camp. This camp was led by survival expert Myke Hawke. Paris and Nicole did not hesitate to call Myke by his full name as much as they could, leading to a string of double-entendres. Paris and Nicole learned about and taught the campers the art of insect eating and fish cleaning. Their stint in the world of survival ended with the girls going on an overnight camping trip, where they get so lost a helicopter needed to be flown in to take them to a local hotel.

The final two episodes centered around the girls teaching at an acting camp at Shawnee. Award-winning actress Sally Kirkland made a guest appearance to help out Paris and Nicole. The drama program and *The Simple Life* series culminated with a play produced and performed by the actors called *Paris and Nicole: The Musical*, a production all about the personal lives of the *Simple Life* stars. The girls go out with a bang by painting the camp leader's house pink.

SITUATION: COMEDY

GENRE	Competition (Job)
FIRST TELECAST	7/26/2005
NETWORK	Bravo
EPISODE STYLE	Story Arc
TALENT	Sean Hayes (Host); Todd Milliner (Host); Stan Zimmerman (Judge); Maxine Lapiduss (Judge); Greg Proops (Narrator)
CAST	Mark Treitel and Jason "Shoe" Schuster (*The Sperm Donor*—Writers); Andrew Leeds and David Lampson (*Stephen's Life*—Writers)
PRODUCTION COMPANIES	Arnold Shapiro and Alison Grodner Productions; HazyMills Productions
EXECUTIVE PRODUCERS	Arnold Shapiro; Stan Zimmermanl; Rich Meehan; Todd Milliner; Allison Grodner; Sean Hayes

In *Situation: Comedy,* producer/actor Sean Hayes (*Will and Grace*) and producer Todd Milliner received more than ten thousand original scripts to be considered for production. The series followed the behind-the-scenes decision-making surrounding casting, set design, rewrites, rehearsals, taping, and post-production of a network sitcom throughout six weeks.

Two fifteen-minute scripts (*The Sperm Donor* and *Stephen's Life*) were given the go-ahead to be taped and directed by actors Fred Savage and Amanda Bearse. The winning writing team received $25,000 and a deal with a major talent agency to help their writing careers. Andrew Leed and David Lampson were the winners with *Stephen's Life.*

SKATING WITH CELEBRITIES

GENRE	Competition (Talent)
FIRST TELECAST	1/18/2006
LAST TELECAST	3/2/2006
NETWORK	FOX
AIR TIMES	Wednesday, 9:00 p.m. (1/2006); Monday, 8:00 p.m. (1/2006–2/2006); Thursday, 9:00 p.m. (2/2006–3/2006)
EPISODE STYLE	Story Arc
CAST	Summer Sanders (Host); Scott Hamilton (Host); Dorothy Hamill (Judge); John Nicks (Judge); Mark Lund (Judge)
TALENT	Lloyd Eisler and Kristy Swanson (Winners); Jillian Barberie and John Zimmerman (2nd place); Bruce Jenner and Tai Babilonia (3rd place); Dave Coulier and Nancy Kerrigan (4th place); Deborah Gibson and Kurt Browning (5th place); Todd Bridges and Jenni Meno (6th place)
PRODUCTION COMPANIES	Fox Television; A. Smith and Co.
EXECUTIVE PRODUCERS	Arthur Smith; Kent Weed
PRODUCERS	Jordan Beck; Terry Coyle
DIRECTOR	Kent Weed

Six mixed pairs of celebrities and professional skaters performed figure skating routines and were judged by a panel of experts in *Skating with Celebrities*. One pair was eliminated each week. Actress Kristy Swanson and Lloyd Eisler won the competition.

SKUNKED TV

GENRE	Docudrama (Hoax)
FIRST TELECAST	7/10/2004
NETWORK	NBC/Discovery Kids
EPISODE STYLE	Self-contained
TALENT	Madai Zaldivar (Host); Chuck Cureau (Co-Host)
PRODUCTION COMPANY	Spectrum Productions, Inc.
EXECUTIVE PRODUCERS	Guy Nickerson; Jim Rapsas
ASSOCIATE PRODUCER	Lauryn Cole

On this family-friendly hidden-camera show, shot on location at famous animal parks, kids and adults are set up by the hosts, and the stunts, played for laughs, all involve unexpected situations featuring animals.

SLEDGEHAMMER

GENRE	Docudrama (Hoax)
FIRST TELECAST	9/13/2001
NETWORK	VH1
AIR TIME	Thursday, 10:00 p.m.
EPISODE STYLE	Self-contained
TALENT	Phoebe Jonas; Jonathan Blitt; Robert Leaver; Rob Huebel; Billy Merritt; Danielle Schneider
PRODUCTION COMPANY	Fractured Hip Productions
CREATED BY	Adam Dolgins, Frank Gregory
EXECUTIVE PRODUCERS	Fred Graver; Adam Dolgins; Frank Gregory

On *Sledgehammer,* hidden cameras caught unsuspecting rock 'n' roll fans in silly situations at concerts, in shopping malls, and elsewhere. Pranks included someone posing as Bono's grandfather to get into a sold-out U2 concert, and cast members acting as salespeople for a new line of rock star fragrances.

S.O.B.
(SOCIALLY OFFENSIVE BEHAVIOR)

GENRE	Docucomedy (Hoax)
FIRST TELECAST	7/25/2007
NETWORK	BET
EPISODE STYLE	Self-contained
TALENT	D. L. Hughley (Host); Vince Morris; Sydney Castillo
PRODUCTION COMPANY	Peter M. Cohen Productions
EXECUTIVE PRODUCERS	David Franzke; Reginald Hudlin; Byron Phillips; Mark Schulman

On *S.O.B.,* hidden cameras captured a comedic look at stereotypes, racism, classism, religion, sexuality, and more. Unsuspecting participants' habits, values, and preconceived notions about society were challenged by a cast of comedic actors.

SO YOU THINK YOU CAN DANCE

GENRE	Competition (Talent)
FIRST TELECAST	7/20/2005
NETWORK	FOX
AIR TIMES	Wednesday, 8:00 p.m. (Season 1), Wednesday, 8:00 p.m.; Thursday, 9:00 p.m. (Seasons 2 and 3)
EPISODE STYLE	Story Arc
TALENT	Lauren Sanchez (Host—Season 1); Cat Deely (Host—Seasons 2 and 3), Nigel Lythgoe (Judge); Alex De Silva (Judge/Choreographer); Mia Michels (Judge/Choreographer); Brian Friedman (Judge/Choreographer); Mary Murphy (Judge/

Choreographer); Dan Karaty (Judge/
Choreographer); Shane Sparks (Judge/
Choreographer)

CAST

Season 1   Nick Lazzarini (Winner); Melody Lacayanga
(Runner-up); Ashle Dawson; Jamile McGee;
Blake McGrath (eliminated in Episode 11);
Kamilah Barrett (eliminated in Episode 11);
Artem Chigvinsev (eliminated in Episode 10);
Melissa Vella (eliminated in Episode 10);
Ryan Conferido (eliminated in Episode 9);
Destini Rogers (eliminated in Episode 9);
Allan Frias (eliminated in Episode 8);
Snejana "Snow" Urbin (eliminated in Episode 8);
Craig DeRosa (eliminated in Episode 7);
Michelle Brooke (eliminated in Episode 7); Jonnis
(eliminated in Episode 6); Sandra Colton
(eliminated in Episode 6)

Season 2   Benji Schwimmer (Winner); Travis Wall (Runner-up);
Heidi Groskreutz (Runner-up); Donyelle Jones
(Runner-up); Ivan Koumaev (8th eliminated);
Natalie Fotopoulos (8th eliminated); Ryan Rankine
(7th eliminated); Allison Holker (7th eliminated);
Dmitry Chaplin (6th eliminated); Martha Nichols
(6th eliminated); Musa Cooper (5th eliminated);
Ashlee Nino (5th eliminated); Jaymz Tuaileva
(4th eliminated); Jessica Fernandez
(4th eliminated); Ben Susak (3rd eliminated);
Aleksandra Wojda (3rd eliminated);
Jason Williams (2nd eliminated); Joy Spears
(2nd eliminated); Stanislav Savich
(1st eliminated); Erin Ellis (1st eliminated)

Season 3   Sabra Johnson (Winner); Danny Tidwell (Runner-up); Neil Haskell (2nd Runner-up); Lacey Schwimmer (3rd Runner-up); Pasha Kovalev (8th eliminated); Lauren Gottlieb (8th eliminated); Dominic Sandoval (7th eliminated); Sara Von Gillern (7th eliminated); Kameron Bink (6th eliminated); Jaimie Goodwin (6th eliminated); Hokuto "Hok" Konishi (5th eliminated); Anya Garnis (5th eliminated); Cedric Gardner (4th eliminated); Shauna Noland (4th eliminated); Jess Solorio (3rd eliminated); Jessi Peralta (3rd eliminated); Jimmy Arguello (2nd eliminated); Faina Savich (2nd eliminated); Ricky Palomino (1st eliminated); Ashlee Langas (1st eliminated)

PRODUCTION COMPANIES   19 TV Ltd.; Dick Clark Productions

CREATED BY   Simon Fuller; Nigel Lythgoe

EXECUTIVE PRODUCERS   Nigel Lythgoe; Simon Fuller; Allen Shapiro

PRODUCERS   Nicola Gaha; Bonnie Lythgoe; James Breen; Jeff Thacker; Simon Lythgoe

DIRECTORS   Don Weiner; Bruce Gowers

From the creators of *American Idol* and *American Bandstand, So You Think You Can Dance* featured the search for the best dancer in the United States. The series began with cross-country auditions. Fifty of the best contestants went to Hollywood, where they were narrowed down to the top sixteen. Each week, the remaining dancers were randomly paired up and given up to two dances to perform. Dance styles for the pairs were randomly chosen, and the judges then determined the weakest two couples. Each contestant got one chance to dance solo at the end of the show, and the home audience voted for the dancer they wanted to be saved. The competitor receiving the fewest votes was eliminated the following week. The winner, Nick Lazzarini, received $100,000 and the opportunity to pursue his dream of becoming a professional dancer in New York City. In the second season, the contestant pool was expanded to twenty, and the grand prize included a contract with Celine Dion's Las Vegas show. In Season 3, the grand prize rose to $250,000, and was won by Sabra Johnson.

SOLITARY

GENRE	Competition
FIRST TELECAST	6/5/2006
NETWORK	Fox Reality Channel
EPISODE STYLE	Story Arc

CAST

Season 1 Steven G. (Winner—aka Number 7); Mark C. (Runner-up—aka Number 5); Taralee D. (7th to leave—aka Number 3); Pamela C. (6th to leave—aka Number 1); Florin N. (5th to leave—aka Number 4); Cliff H. (4th to leave—aka Number 6); Danielle M. (3rd to leave—aka Number 8); Michelle R. (2nd to leave—aka Number 2); David D. (1st to leave—aka Number 9)

Season 2 Phu Pham (Winner—aka Number 8); Tyler Tongate (Runner-up—aka Number 7); Nikki Epel (7th to leave—aka Number 3); J. P. Playok (6th to leave—aka Number 9); Michelle Sims (5th to leave—aka Number 6); Deena Holland (4th to leave—aka Number 2); Leroy Patterson (3rd to leave—aka Number 5); Stephen Sutton (2nd to leave—aka Number 1); Kimberly Shields (1st to leave—aka Number 4)

PRODUCTION COMPANIES	Hiattmedia; A. Golder Production
CREATED BY	Lincoln Hiatt; Andrew Golder
EXECUTIVE PRODUCERS	Andrew J. Golder; Lincoln Hiatt; Bob Boden
DIRECTOR	Rob George

Fox Reality Channel's first original reality series pitted nine people against each other in the ultimate battle of endurance. Unlike other reality series, there was no voting off, nor were there judges to tell the contestants they had been eliminated. The only way to leave *Solitary* was by being the first to quit during elimination challenges (known as "treatments") or of one's own volition.

The contestants, or "guests," were isolated from the rest of the world and from one another. They were subjects in a series of strange and taxing experiments conducted by Val, a female computer entity who was both their only companion and their taskmaster through the series. Val controlled everything—when the guests ate, drank, relieved themselves, and slept. She controlled the temperature and what the guests heard and saw.

Each episode had a "test" and a "treatment." A test was a challenge that granted the winner immunity from the treatment. The first guest to quit each treatment had to leave the show. The tests and treatments that guests endured involved hunger, pain, sleep deprivation, and mind control. Some treatments from Season 1 included having guests drinking shots of increasingly spicy liquids until they couldn't take it, and having them lie on bed of nails for as long as possible.

Solitary was the ultimate test of will and strength in the world of reality television. The series pushed people to their physical and mental limits so much that some guests left even when they weren't undergoing a challenge. This was the case with Season 1 guest Cliff, who left after a tantrum centering on his not being able to receive lip balm from Val.

The last person standing was declared the winner and received the coveted $50,000 prize. Season 1's winner was teacher Stephen Gee, aka No. 7.

Season 2 brought an interesting wrinkle in the cast. J. P. Palyok, a reality veteran best known for his stint on *Survivor*, inhabited Pod No. 9. J.P. quickly became a marked man by the rest of the guests despite nobody being able to see or talk to him during the course of the series. The treatments were even tougher and darker. In one, the guests drank concoctions consisting of their favorite foods blended together. In the final treatment, the two remaining guests struggled to stay above ground while balancing on a hammock made of two metal chains. The winner of Season 2's $50,000 grand prize was photographer Phu Pham, aka No. 8.

The reunion shows for *Solitary,* hosted by Todd Newton, also proved to be quite unique, as the guests met one another in person for the first time. Because of this, the reunion shows were referred to as "union" shows. During these shows, the guests reminisced about their experiences, and often discovered that while they'd never seen one another, they'd all shared the same feelings and frustrations from their pod experience.

SONS OF HOLLYWOOD

GENRE	Docudrama
FIRST TELECAST	4/1/2007
NETWORK	A&E
EPISODE STYLE	Story Arc
CAST	Randy Spelling; Sean Stewart; David Weintraub
EXECUTIVE PRODUCER	Jonathan Taylor
PRODUCERS	Randy Spelling; Sean Stewart; David Weintraub; Jason Lakeshore

Friends since attending boarding school together, Randy Spelling, Aaron Spelling's son; Sean Stewart, Rod Stewart's son; and their talent-manager friend David Weintraub tried to forge their own identities while living in the Los Angeles area. The series theme song, "The In Crowd," was written and performed by series star Sean Stewart.

SORORITY LIFE

GENRE	Docusoap
FIRST TELECAST	6/24/2002
NETWORK	MTV
AIR TIME	Wednesday, 10:00 p.m.
EPISODE STYLE	Story Arc

CAST

Season 1 (Sigma)	Rachel (Rush Chair); Leah (President); Leslie (Vice President); Becca (Pledge Master); Pauli (Asst. Rush Chair); Stacey (Treasurer); Amanda

(Pledge); Jessica (Pledge); DeDe (Pledge); Candace (Pledge); Mara (Pledge); Jordan (Pledge); Mara (Pledge)

Season 2 (Delta Xi Omega) Talia (President); Bridgette (Pledge Assistant); Colleen (Rush Chair); Tiffany C. (Risk Management); Lafonya (Sister); Tiffany L. (Sister); Loren (Historian); Janel (Social Chair); Dara (Recording Secretary); Darci (Publicity Chair); Laura (Pledge Assistant); Amy (Vice President); Courtney (Treasurer); Stacey (Pledge Mom); Nikki (Corresponding Secretary); Karissa (Pledge); Maggie (Pledge); Brittany (Pledge); Brooke (Pledge); MacKenzie (Pledge); Julia (Pledge); Nicole (Pledge); Melissa (Pledge); Amy (Rushee); Erin (Rushee); Maggie (Rushee); Rachel (Rushee); Sarah (Rushee)

Season 3 (Zeta Sigma Phi) Jennifer (President); Krisha (Vice President); Valancie (Pledge Educator); Melissa (Rush Chair); Kathryn (Secretary); Rana (Philanthropy); Sayuri (Sisterhood); Jenifer (Family Chair); Cat (Historian); Audrey (Alumni Chair); Danielle (Co-Historian); Katina (SCN Director); Natasha (International social); Vanessa (Treasurer); Kristine (Co-Historian); Amber (Academic Chair); Erin (Sister); Toya (Sister); Marquita (Sister); Sheryl (Sister); Lynnise (Sister); Casey (Sister); Stacie (Sister); Suyoung (Sister); Mamie (Sister); Michelle (Pledge); Salina (Pledge); Sharifa (Pledge); Janelle (Pledge); Bola (Pledge); Francia (Pledge); Imee (Pledge); Linda (Pledge); Misa (Pledge); Monica (Pledge); Sharae (Pledge); Shoko (Pledge); Veniesha (Pledge); Sacha (Pledge); Meena (Depledged); Carmen (Depledged)

CREATED BY Sergio Myers

EXECUTIVE PRODUCERS Catherine Finn; Russell Heldt; J. J. Jamieson; Sergio Myers

PRODUCERS Joey Castillo; Kevin Greene; Shannon Owen; Jennifer Lange

DIRECTORS Robin Fienberg; Jeff Fisher; Lilla Fiuma; Ethan Prochnik; Bill Pruitt; Michelle Brando; Shannon Fitzgerald; Robert Sizemore; Billie Speer; Veena Cabreros Sud; Rollen Torres; Heather Urban; Shannon Vandermark

Camera crews document the inner workings of a sorority house on *Sorority Life*. The first season featured the girls from UC Davis and rush week for Sigma. The second season followed the activities at Delta Xi Omega in Buffalo, New York. The third season was about Zeta Sigma Phi, a multicultural sorority in Los Angeles.

SPEED DATING

GENRE Competition (Dating)

FIRST TELECAST 3/2004

NETWORK PAX

EPISODE STYLE Self-contained

TALENT Michael Corbett (Host)

PRODUCTION COMPANY En Pea Productions

EXECUTIVE PRODUCERS Michael Mandt; Neil Mandt

CO-EXECUTIVE PRODUCERS Jonathan Bomser; Neil Gallow

PRODUCERS Gary Jarjoura; Beth Humphreys; Aristea Galusha

DIRECTOR Neil Mandt

Shot at the Terence Ballroom of the Argyle Hotel Los Angeles, *Speed Dating* featured sixteen single men and women who met prospective suitors through fast-paced dates. In the first round, the singles had eight minutes to get to know one another, and ranked the people they met according to looks, personality, and compatibility. The four highest-scoring men and the four highest-scoring women advanced to the next round, where the singles had an additional four minutes to learn about one another. The top two men and top two women advanced to the final round. Their final scores determined who made up the most compatible couple. The winning man and woman won a date at a five-star restaurant.

SPORTS ILLUSTRATED SWIMSUIT MODEL SEARCH

GENRE	Competition
FIRST TELECAST	1/5/2005
LAST TELECAST	2/9/2005
NETWORK	NBC
AIR TIME	Wednesday, 8:00 p.m.
EPISODE STYLE	Story Arc
TALENT	Cheryl Tiegs (Host); Roshumba Williams (Judge); Joe Wilkenfled (Judge); Jule Campbell (Judge); Jason Henson (Narrator)
CAST	Alicia (Winner); Shannon (Runner-up); Stacy (eliminated in Episode 5); Jenna (eliminated in Episode 4); Betti (eliminated in Episode 3); Krisi (eliminated in Episode 3); Adoara (eliminated in Episode 2); Stella (eliminated in Episode 2); Nancy (eliminated in Episode 1); Shantal (eliminated in Episode 1); Marcela (eliminated in Episode 1); Sabrina (eliminated in Episode 1)
PRODUCTION COMPANIES	PB & J Television; Sports Illustrated
EXECUTIVE PRODUCERS	Gavin Polone; Patty Ivins; Julie Pizzi; Terry McDonell; Roy S. Johnson

PRODUCERS Jessika Borsiczky; Jonathan K. Frank

DIRECTORS Luis Barreto; Kasey Barrett; Jeanne Begley; Eric Monsky

On this competition series, twelve women competed for a $1 million NEXT Model Management contract and the opportunity to be in the *Sports Illustrated* swimsuit issue. The models lived together in New York, and on each show they competed in challenges to win the Supermodel Pass, which gave its winner a specific power, such as the chance to determine the order in which the contestants were photographed at a shoot. A panel judged the models' photo shoots and challenges to determine who would "make the cut" or be "dropped." NBC viewers chose the winner, Alicia, from the final two contestants.

SPORTS KIDS MOMS & DADS

GENRE Docudrama

FIRST TELECAST 6/1/2005

NETWORK Bravo

EPISODE STYLE Self-contained

TALENT Tracy Austin (Narrator)

CAST Kim (mom) and Bryce (figure skating); Sharon (mom) and Sarah (cheerleading); Craig (dad) and Trenton (football); Karen (mom) and Karli (equestrian); T.J. (mom & coach) and Lindsay (basketball)

PRODUCTION COMPANY World of Wonder

EXECUTIVE PRODUCERS Fenton Bailey; Randy Barbato; David Perler

This spinoff of *Showbiz Moms and Dads* followed five child athletes and their parents on the road to sports superstardom. The series featured training, conflicts, competition, and the impact this pursuit had on the child and the family.

THE SPRINGER HUSTLE

GENRE	Docusoap
FIRST TELECAST	4/15/2007
LAST TELECAST	6/5/2007
NETWORK	VH1
EPISODE STYLE	Self-contained
CAST	Jerry Springer; Annette Grundy; Nicole Hall; Selina Santos; Kerry Smith; Toby Yoshimura; Steve Wilkos; Richard Dominick; Todd Schultz
PRODUCTION COMPANY	Universal TV
EXECUTIVE PRODUCER	Richard Dominick
PRODUCER	Toby Yoshimura

The Springer Hustle offered a behind-the-scenes look at one of television's most controversial series, *The Jerry Springer Show*. This VH1 docusoap followed the *Springer Show* production team and revealed what it took each day to create an episode of the popular long-running talk show.

SPY TV

GENRE	Docucomedy
FIRST TELECAST	6/21/2001
LAST TELECAST	8/6/2002
NETWORK	NBC
AIR TIMES	Thursday, 8:30 p.m. (6/2001–8/2001); Tuesday, 8:00 p.m. (6/2001–9/2001); Saturday, 8:00 p.m. (10/2001); Tuesday, 8:00 p.m. (6/2002–8/2002)
EPISODE STYLE	Self-contained
TALENT	Michael Ian Black (Host—Season 1); Ali Landry (Host—Season 2)

CAST	Tiffany Bolton; Jasper Cole; Travis Draft; Tom Konkle; George M. Kostuch; Jeff Norman; Eliza Schneider
PRODUCTION COMPANIES	Endemol Entertainment USA; Lock and Key Productions; Next Entertainment, Inc.
EXECUTIVE PRODUCERS	John De Mol; Jeff Boggs; Scott Hallock
PRODUCER	Lisa A. Higgins
DIRECTORS	Jeff Boggs; R. Brian DiPirro; Wesley Eure

Spy TV brought the hidden camera concept to the twenty-first century, and featured a group of improvisational comedy actors playing pranks on unsuspecting people.

STAR DATES

GENRE	Docucomedy (Dating)
FIRST TELECAST	12/15/2002
NETWORK	E!
EPISODE STYLE	Self-contained
TALENT	Jordan Black (Chauffeur—Season 1); Reggie Gaskins (Chauffeur—Season 2)
PRODUCTION COMPANIES	E! Entertainment Television
CREATED BY	George Verschoor
EXECUTIVE PRODUCERS	George Verschoor; Dave Pullano
CO-EXECUTIVE PRODUCER	David Parks
PRODUCERS	Doug Chernack; Chad Gajadhar; Gerg Normart; Daniel Shriver; Jeff Singer

Ordinary people were set up with celebrities on *Star Dates*. Season 1 featured dates with Phyllis Diller, Butch Patrick, Gary Coleman, Dustin Diamond, Kim Coles, and Jill Whelan. Season 2 included dates with Debra Wilson, Judy Tenuta, Marsha Warfield, Robbie Rist, Richard Hatch (the *Battlestar Galactica* star, not the *Survivor* winner), E. G. Daily, Leif Garrett, Jimmie Walker, Tiffany, Mary McDonough, Deney Terrio, and

Fred Berry. The dates were chaperoned by a chauffeur in a "kickin' Cadillac," Jordan Black in Season 1 and Reggie Gaskins in Season 2.

STAR SEARCH

GENRE	Competition (Talent)
FIRST TELECAST	1/8/2003
LAST TELECAST	3/13/2004
NETWORK	CBS
AIR TIMES	Wednesday, 8:00 p.m.; Thursday, 8:00 p.m. (Season 1); Wednesday, 8:00 p.m.; Friday, 8:00 p.m. (Season 2); Saturday, 8:00 p.m. (Season 3)
EPISODE STYLE	Story Arc
TALENT	Arsenio Hall (Host); Naomi Judd (Judge—Seasons 1–4); Ben Stein (Judge—Seasons 1–3); Ahmet Zappa (Judge—Seasons 2–3); Matti Leshem (Judge—Season 4); Carol Leifer (Judge—Season 1) *Guest Judges* Jack Osbourne; Lance Bass; Jessica Simpson; LeAnn Rimes; Donny Osmond; Kathy Griffin

CAST

Tournament One Winners	Porschla Coleman (Model); Jake Simpson (Adult Singer); Tiffany Evans (Junior Singer); John Roy (Comedian)
Tournament Two Winners	Chantele Doucette (Adult Singer); David Archuleta (Junior Singer); Jon Cruz (Young Dancer); Horace H. B. (Comedian—Winner)
Tournament Three Winners	Vickie Natale (Adult Singer); Mark Mejia (Junior Singer); Brandon Bryant and Candace Rodriguez (Young Dancers); Tracey MacDonald (Comedian)

Tournament Four Winners	Jake Simpson (Adult Singer); Mark Mejia (Junior Singer); Jon Cruz (Young Dancer)
PRODUCTION COMPANY	2929 Productions
EXECUTIVE PRODUCERS	Andrew Golder; Dan Funk
SUPERVISING PRODUCER	Meredith Fox
DIRECTOR	Glenn Weiss

An updated version of the career-launching mid-eighties series *Star Search,* this talent competition was broken down into four categories: Adult Singer, Junior Singer, Comedian, and Model. (In Season 1, the modeling category was replaced by dancing). Three celebrity judges and home viewers voted for their favorite entertainer in each category. The individual stage winners advanced to the final round of competition, where the overall winners from each talent arena were awarded $100,000. The adult singer also won a recording contact, while the comedy champions won development deals with CBS. The fourth round of shows dropped the comedy competition, and featured the "Winner's Circle," in which new contestants challenged champions from previous seasons.

THE STARLET

GENRE	Competition (Talent)
FIRST TELECAST	3/6/2005
LAST TELECAST	4/5/2005
NETWORK	The WB
AIR TIMES	Sunday, 8:00 p.m. (3/2005); Tuesday, 9:00 p.m. (3/2005–4/2005)
EPISODE STYLE	Story Arc
TALENT	Katie Wagner (Host); Faye Dunaway (Judge); Joseph Middleton (Judge); Vivica A. Fox (Judge)
CAST	Michelynne (Winner); Lauren; Mercedes; Katie; Donna; Courtney; Cecile; Andria; Andie; Neva

PRODUCTION COMPANIES	Next Entertainment Studios, in association with Telepictures Productions
EXECUTIVE PRODUCERS	Mike Fleiss; Jamie Kennedy
CO-EXECUTIVE PRODUCERS	Ellen Rapoport; Josh Etting; Scott Einziger

On *The Starlet,* ten aspiring actresses from around the country lived together in Hollywood as they participated in a showbiz boot camp, complete with acting classes, career advice, and brutally honest critiques of their performances. Eliminated contestants were dismissed when judge Faye Dunaway said, "Don't call us, we'll call you." The winner, Michelynn, received a management contract, a talent contract, and a part on the WB series *One Tree Hill.*

STARTING OVER

GENRE	Docusoap (Makeover)
FIRST TELECAST	9/8/2003
LAST TELECAST	9/2006
NETWORK	Syndicated
EPISODE STYLE	Story Arc
TALENT	Rana Walker (Life Coach—Season 1); Rhonda Britten (Life Coach—Season 1); Iyanla Vanzant (Life Coach—Season 2); Dr. Stan J. Katz (Psychologist—Season 2)

CAST

Season 1	Rain Adams; Amy Harkin Goodrich; Hailey Murray; Lynnell Stage; Jennifer P. J. Anbey; Maureen Goodman; Andy Paige; Nyanza Davis; Audrey Tucker; Erika Jackson; Brenda Starr-Wilson; Tereson Crone; Cassie Romanelli; Susan Santa Cruz; Hannah Buchanan; Karen Knoxcox

Season 2	Sommer White; Towanda Braxton; Jennifer Bernhard; Vanessa Atler; Kim Bookout
Season 3	Jodi Isaacs; Allison Stanley; Jill Tracy; Jessica Holland; Christie Duran
PRODUCTION COMPANY	Bunim-Murray Productions
CREATED BY	Mary-Ellis Bunim; Jonathan Murray
EXECUTIVE PRODUCERS	Jonathan Murray; Mary Ellis-Bunim; Millee Taggart-Ratcliffe; Bonnie Bogard Maier
PRODUCERS	Susan Baronoff; James Gavin Bedford; Lisa DiGiovine; Jule Gilfillan; Jules Hoffman; Guido Verweyen; Lisa Weiss; Brandon L. Wilson
DIRECTORS	Petra Costner, Sarah K. Pillsbury; Guido Verweyen

Airing on weekdays, *Starting Over* featured women from different walks of life living together in the Starting Over House. Each woman set out to rebuild her life, relationship, or career. Life coaches helped the women through the process of breaking down the barriers that prevented them from moving on with their lives. From the producers of *The Real World* and *Road Rules,* this daytime docusoap was the first reality show to win a Daytime Emmy Award for Best Series in 2004–2005.

STEVE HARVEY'S BIG TIME CHALLENGE

GENRE	Competition (Talent)
FIRST TELECAST	9/11/2003
LAST TELECAST	6/26/2005
NETWORK	The WB
AIR TIMES	Thursday, 8:00 p.m. (9/2003–5/2004); Thursday, 8:30 p.m. (12/2003–1/2004); Thursday, 9:30 p.m. (5/2004–6/2004); Sunday, 7:00 p.m. (6/2004–1/2005); Sunday, 9:00 p.m. (1/2005–6/2005)

EPISODE STYLE	Self-contained
TALENT	Steve Harvey (Host)
EXECUTIVE PRODUCERS	Madeleine Smithberg; Steve Harvey; Rushion McDonald
DIRECTORS	Morris Abraham; Don Weiner

This competition/variety show featured contestants with unusual skills or talents. Acts included a ninety-year-old rapper, a child James Brown impersonator, and a snake wrangler. Celebrity judges awarded the best act a $10,000 grand prize based on "originality, skill, and stupidity."

STRAIGHT PLAN FOR THE GAY MAN

GENRE	Docudrama (Makeover)
FIRST TELECAST	2/23/2004
LAST TELECAST	3/8/2004
NETWORK	Comedy Central
AIR TIME	Monday, 10:00 p.m.
EPISODE STYLE	Self-contained
TALENT	Kyle Grooms (Information Guy); Curtis Gwinn (Environment Guy); Billy Merritt (Appearance Guy); Rob Riggle (Culture Guy); Jackie Clarke (Dating Coach)
PRODUCTION COMPANY	Borderline
EXECUTIVE PRODUCERS	Mala Chapple; Dave Hamilton; Nick McKinney
DIRECTOR	Nick McKinney

This comedy makeover show parodied *Queer Eye for the Straight Guy*'s lifestyle coaches, the "Fab Five." The "Flab 4" were a team of straight men who coached a gay man on the art of being heterosexual. They then accompanied their makeover subject to see if he could pass for a straight man in bars and in the workplace.

STRANGE LOVE

GENRE	Docusoap (Celebrity)
FIRST TELECAST	1/9/2005
LAST TELECAST	4/24/2005
NETWORK	VH1
EPISODE STYLE	Self-contained
CAST	Bridgette Nielsen; Flavor Flav
PRODUCTION COMPANIES	Mindless Entertainment; 51 Minds; VH1
EXECUTIVE PRODUCERS	Mark Cronin; Cris Abrego
CO-EXECUTIVE PRODUCER	Ben Samek
PRODUCERS	Joe Coleman; Kevin Thomas
DIRECTOR	Robert Sizemore

This spinoff of the third season of *The Surreal Life,* chronicled the unlikely courtship of Danish actress Brigette Nielsen and Public Enemy rapper Flavor Flav as they traveled through Italy, New York, and Las Vegas. At the conclusion of the series, there was no marriage, but the couple remained good friends.

STREET MATCH

GENRE	Docudrama (Dating)
FIRST TELECAST	7/28/1993
LAST TELECAST	8/25/1993
NETWORK	ABC
AIR TIME	Wednesday, 8:30 p.m.
EPISODE STYLE	Self-contained
TALENT	Ricky Paull Goldin (Host)
PRODUCERS	Gabe Sachs; Noel Trisch
DIRECTOR	Gabe Sachs

Soap star Ricky Paull Goldin literally pulled people off the street and paired them up for a date on *Street Match*.

STRIP SEARCH

GENRE	Competition (Talent)
FIRST TELECAST	5/28/2005
LAST TELECAST	7/14/2005
NETWORK	VH1
AIR TIME	Monday, 10:00 p.m.
EPISODE STYLE	Story Arc
TALENT	Rachel Perry: (Host); Billy Cross (Host)
CAST	Ryan Westerburg (Winner); Rick Dejesus (Winner); Tony Cress (Winner); Adam Wynne (Winner); Terry Cress (Winner); Sean Cassidy (Winner); Josh Hall (Winner); Marco Iglesia (Contestant); David Nieves (Contestant); Blake Sandifer (Contestant); Johnny Constantin (Contestant); Steve Logan (Contestant); Brian Riggs (Contestant); Chris Mylonas (Contestant); Bryce Taylor (Contestant)
PRODUCTION COMPANIES	Pilgrim Films and Television; Screentime Pty Ltd; Distraction Formats
EXECUTIVE PRODUCERS	Craig Piligian; Matt Hanna; Michael Hirschorn; Jim Ackerman

An American version of an Australian reality show *Strip Search* followed fifteen men as they left their day jobs to compete for six-figure contracts and positions with a traveling male strip revue led by Billy Cross, creator of the *Thunder Down Under*. After putting them through tests, such as posing for a calendar or creating choreography set to popular music artists such as Britney Spears, Cross eliminated the men one by one. The show culminated with a final performance in Las Vegas for an all-female audience.

At the end of the show, the seven remaining men formed the new all-male revue, The American Storm.

STUDIO 7

GENRE	Competition
FIRST TELECAST	7/22/2004
LAST TELECAST	9/2/2004
NETWORK	The WB
AIR TIME	Thursday, 9:00 p.m.
EPISODE STYLE	Story Arc
TALENT	Pat Kiernan (Host)
CAST	Craig Phillips (Winner); Cassie Lilly; Sheila Shaigany; Drew Leary; J. C. Cary; Gregg; CK; Leslie Knott; Saira "Pepper" Weeks; Jong "Tom" Kim; Alice; Katie Madden; Rosie Hunter; Sean Patrick Taylor; Stephanie Chu; Francesca List; Sarah Baker
PRODUCTION COMPANY	Diplomatic Productions
EXECUTIVE PRODUCERS	Michael Davies; Jennifer Kelly
PRODUCER	Tiffany Faigus

Shot on location in New York City, this competition followed seven bright people as they lived together for four days. The contestants memorized and studied news, pop culture, sports, and politics in the hopes of defeating their fellow competitors while being quizzed in a television studio. The winner received $77,000. Once seven shows were produced, the seven winners were invited back for the finale to compete for $777,000. The winner was Craig Phillips.

STUPID BEHAVIOR CAUGHT ON TAPE

GENRE	Docudrama
FIRST TELECAST	5/29/2003
LAST TELECAST	9/4/2003
NETWORK	FOX
AIR TIMES	Thursday, 8:00 p.m. (5/2003–7/2003); Monday, 8:30 p.m. (7/2003–8/2003); Thursday, 8:00 p.m. (9/2003)
EPISODE STYLE	Self-contained
TALENT	Stacy Keach (Narrator)
PRODUCTION COMPANY	Nash Entertainment
EXECUTIVE PRODUCERS	Bruce Nash; Robyn Nash
CO-EXECUTIVE PRODUCER	Matt Harris
PRODUCERS	Gregory Carroll; Michael J. Miller; Dan Signer
DIRECTORS	Mike Miller; Don Weiner

Stupid Behavior Caught on Tape featured surveillance footage and other videos highlighting embarrassing and ridiculous moments caught on tape.

STYLE ME

GENRE	Competition (Job)
FIRST TELECAST	2/11/2006
NETWORK	WE
EPISODES	Story Arc
TALENT	Rachel Hunter (Host); Phillip Bloch (Judge); Millica Kastner (Judge)
CAST	Buick Audra (Winner); Phillip Guererro; Franco Lacosta; Pascale Lemaire; Airic Lewis;

John McNulty; Britnie Romain; Laura Siebold; Stacey Stevens; Remeka Sullivan; Chris Watts; Rachel Waymire

PRODUCTION COMPANIES Rainbow Media, in association with Spooky Truth Productions

DIRECTORS Michael Pearlman; Samantha Fogel; Lea Sheloush; Mike Stafford

Rachel Hunter hosted this show in which a group of aspiring fashionistas vied for the position of being her stylist for the red carpet at the People's Choice Awards. Each episode put the participants through challenges and they were evaluated and eliminated by Rachel Hunter and panel of judges. In the end, Buick Audra was declared the winner.

SUNSET TAN

GENRE Docudrama

FIRST TELECAST 5/28/2007

NETWORK E!

EPISODES Self-contained

CAST Devin Haman; Jeff Bozz; Heidi Cortez; Nick D'Anna; Holly Huddleston; Ania Migdal; Janelle Perry; Molly Shea; Erin Tietsort; Keely Williams

PRODUCTION COMPANY E! Entertainment Television in association with Intuitive Enteratinment

EXECUTIVE PRODUCERS Mechelle Collins; Kevin Dill; Carl Buehl

The lives of the employees and clientele at a trendy Los Angeles tanning salon are chronicled in this E! series. Characters include owners Devin and Jeff and bubbly staffers Holly and Molly (aka The Olly Girls). Celebrities that dropped by the salon and appeared in the series included Britney Spears, Kato Kaelin, and Chris Kattan.

SUPER AGENT

GENRE	Competition (Job)
FIRST TELECAST	7/22/2005
NETWORK	Spike
EPISODE STYLE	Story Arc
TALENT	Tony Gonzalez (Host); Shaun Cody (USC Football Player)
CAST	John Bermudez; Justin Breece; Scott Casterline; Jeff Guerriero; Harold Lewis; Tim McIlwain; Marlon Tucker; Lisa Van Wagner; Don West
PRODUCTION COMPANY	NBC Universal
EXECUTIVE PRODUCERS	Rick DeOliveira; James DuBose; Jack Bechta; Josh Ripple; Tami Holzman
CO-EXECUTIVE PRODUCER	Brian Keith Etheridge
DIRECTOR	Brendon Carter

In *Super Agent,* nine sports agents competed to be the agent of USC All-American defensive lineman Shaun Cody. On each episode, the agent who didn't live up to Cody's expectations was eliminated. The series finale occurred on NFL draft day, when Cody was drafted by the Detroit Lions.

SUPERGROUP

GENRE	Docusoap
FIRST TELECAST	5/21/2006
NETWORK	VH1
EPISODES	Story Arc
CAST	Sebastian Bach; Jason Bonham; Scott Ian; Doc McGhee; Ted Nugent; Evan Seinfeld
PRODUCTION COMPANIES	3Ball Productions

EXECUTIVE PRODUCERS   John Foy; Peter Jaysen; Todd A. Nelson; J.D. Roth; Troy Searer

Five hard-rock legends came together to form a supergroup called Damnocracy in this VH1 docusoap. The group included members of Anthrax (Scott Ian) and Skid Row (Sebastian Bach). Almost immediately, egos clashed among the rock veterans. One notable fight was sparked by a playful wrestling match between Evan Seinfeld and Sebastian that quickly turned serious. Things got so heated that by the series finale Evan quit the group temporarily before Damnocracy's big performance

SUPERNANNY

GENRE	Docudrama
FIRST TELECAST	1/17/2005
NETWORK	ABC
AIR TIMES	Monday, 8:00 p.m. (1/2005–5/2005); Wednesday, 8:00 p.m. (6/2005–8/2005); Friday, 8:00 p.m. (8/2005–12/2005); Monday, 9:00 p.m. (3/2006–8/2006); Monday, 10:00 p.m. (8/2006–9/2006); Monday, 9:00 p.m. (12/2006–3/2007); Monday, 10:00 p.m. (3/2007–present)
EPISODE STYLE	Self-contained
TALENT	Jo Frost (Supernanny)
PRODUCTION COMPANY	Richochet, Ltd.
EXECUTIVE PRODUCERS	Nick Powell; Craig Armstrong; Carl Buehl; Amanda Murphy; Tony Yates
PRODUCER	Tracey Finley
DIRECTOR	Casey Brumels

Based on a hit show in England, *Supernanny* features Jo Frost, a professional nanny with fifteen years' experience who gives her no-nonsense advice to parents and their out-of-control children. Once she assesses the situation, the Supernanny uses her proven methods to bring tranquility to the household. The show's theme song is Men at Work's "Be Good Johnny."

SUPERSTAR USA

GENRE	Competition (Hoax/Talent)
FIRST TELECAST	5/17/2004
LAST TELECAST	6/14/2004
NETWORK	The WB
AIR TIME	Monday, 9:00 p.m.
EPISODE STYLE	Story Arc
TALENT	Brian McFayden (Host); Tone Loc (Judge), Vitamin C (Judge), Chris Briggs (Judge)
CAST	"The Final Eight"—Jamie Foss (Winner); Omar; Jo Jo; Mario Roger; Tamara; John Michael; Rosa; Nina Diva
PRODUCTION COMPANIES	Next Entertainment, in association with Telepictures
CREATED BY	Mike Fleiss
EXECUTIVE PRODUCERS	Mike Fleiss; Chris Briggs; Jason A. Carbone; Mike Nichols
DIRECTOR	Ken Fuchs

This *American Idol*–like show featured the search for the worst singer in the United States, but with a twist: the contestants didn't know the competition was a joke. One by one, the unsuspecting talent was eliminated until there was a winner, who would receive a talent and recording deal worth $100,000. The winner was Jamie Foss.

THE SURREAL LIFE

GENRE	Docusoap (Celebrity)
FIRST TELECAST	1/9/2003

NETWORK	The WB (Seasons 1 and 2); VH1 (Season 3—present)
AIR TIMES	Thursday, 9:00 p.m. (Season 1); Sunday, 9:00 p.m. (Season 2)
EPISODE STYLE	Story Arc

CAST

Season 1	Gabrielle Carteris; Corey Feldman; M. C. Hammer; Emmanuel Lewis; Jerri Manthey; Vince Neil; Brande Roderick
Season 2	Tammy Faye Messner; Traci Bingham; Trishelle Cannatella; Erik Estrada; Vanilla Ice; Ron Jeremy
Season 3	Charo; Dave Coulier; Flavor Flav; Jordan Knight; Brigitte Nielsen; Ryan Starr
Season 4	Da Brat; Adrianne Curry; Christopher Knight; Joanie Laurer (aka Chyna); Marcus Schenkenberg; Verne Troyer; Jane Wiedlin
Season 5	Jose Canseco; Caprice Bourret; Sandra "Pepa" Denton; Janice Dickinson; Carey Hart; Omarosa Manigault-Stallworth; Bronson Pinchot
Season 6	Alexis Arquette; C. C. DeVille; Steve Harwell; Sherman Hemsley; Maven Huffman; Tawny Kitaen; Andrea Lowell; Florence Henderson (Therapist)
Season 7 ("Fame Games")	Traci Bingham (Winner); Ron Jeremy (Runner-up); Brigitte Nielsen; Rob Van Winkle; C. C. DeVille; Chyna; Andrew Lowell; Emmanuel Lewis; Pepa; Verne Troyer; Jordan Knight; Robin Leach (Host)
PRODUCTION COMPANIES	Brass Ring Productions; Mindless Entertainment; Renegade Productions, 51 Minds Entertainment; Go Sick Productions
CREATED BY	Cris Abrego; Mark Cronin; Rick Telles
EXECUTIVE PRODUCERS	Cris Abrego; Mark Cronin; David Garfinkle; Jay Renfroe; Rick Telles
CO-EXECUTIVE PRODUCERS	James Rowley; Ben Samek, Jacquie Dincauze

PRODUCERS Billy Cooper; Lamar Damon; Jason Elrich;
Cris Graves; Donny Jackson; J. Holland Moore;
John Platt; Julia Silverton; David Story;
Deboriah Dupree

DIRECTORS Lauren Alvarez; Ross Breitenbach; Tony Croll;
Erik Fleming; Julie Hemlin; Omid Kahangi;
Zach Kozek; Robert Sizemore

Celebrities from the sports, music, and entertainment worlds came together to live in one house for ten days on *The Surreal Life*. The housemates shared bedrooms, performed household chores, and went on adventures outside the house. At times, tensions ran high and some unlikely friendships were forged. Highlights from the show's five seasons include Season 2's cast making a visit to a nudist colony, Season 3's cast recording a song, Season 4's cast filming a Kung Fu movie, plus a notorious "knife incident" between former *Apprentice* contestant Omarosa and model Janice Dickinson during a photo shoot. During Season 6, *The Brady Bunch*'s Florence Henderson acted as *The Surreal Life* home's therapist.

Season 7 was an all-star edition dubbed the *Fame Games*. The celebrities lived in a Las Vegas home while competing in challenges dealing with celebrity and being famous. Competitions ranged from seeing who could get the most autographs to staying on guard while under the watchful eye of the paparazzi. Each week, the results of the competition determined who would live in the A-list side of the house and who would be relegated to the lesser trappings of the B-list side. Episodes culminated with a "Back to Reality" game show–style challenge that determined who would stay and who would be eliminated. Model/actress Traci Bingham was the grand-prize winner, earning $100,000.

SURVIVAL OF THE RICHEST

GENRE Competition
FIRST TELECAST 3/31/2006
LAST TELECAST 5/5/2006

NETWORK	The WB
AIR TIME	Friday, 8:00 p.m.
EPISODE STYLE	Story Arc
TALENT	Hal Sparks (host)

CAST

Rich Kids	T. R. Youngblood (Winner); Hunter Maats; Nick Movs; Kat Moon; Liz Rubin; Sam Durrani; Esmeralda Nunez
Poor Kids	Jim Perkins (Winner); Jacob LeBlanc; Michael Keck; Johanna Allio; Marcus Foy; Elizabeth Lewis; Tracy Huffstetler,
PRODUCTION COMPANY	RDF Media
EXECUTIVE PRODUCERS	Joe Houlihan; Stuart Krasnow; Zad Rogers; Kevin Williams
PRODUCER	Shana Kemp

On *Survival of the Richest* seven young rich people, worth a combined $3 billion, were paired with seven poor young contestants who carried a collective debt of $150,000. For six weeks, they lived together and competed in challenges, such as horse race betting and charity house building. Each week a team was voted off. Rich tire company heir T. R. Youngblood and his poor teammate, Jim Perkins, won the $200,000 grand prize.

SURVIVING NUGENT

GENRE	Competition (Endurance)
FIRST TELECAST	10/5/2003
LAST TELECAST	5/12/2004
NETWORK	VH1
EPISODE STYLE	Story Arc
TALENT	Ted Nugent; Big Jim (Ted's Ranch Hand); Josh Silberman ("The Bookworm")

	CAST
Season 1	Darren (DJ—Winner); Tila Nyguen (Model); Jack (Talent Manager); Sarah (Campaign Coordinator); Kara (Jersey Girl); Joe (Student); Adam (Student)
Season 2	Dawn (Winner—Bartender); Bob (final two—Hippie); Ariel (Vegan); Erik (Jock); Lin (Mama's boy); Riyak (5th eliminated—Strict Muslim); Nakia (4th eliminated—Diva); Josh (3rd eliminated—Bookworm); Danielle (2nd eliminated—Party Girl); Sajen (1st eliminated)
PRODUCTION COMPANIES	The Jay and Tony Show; VH1 Television
EXECUTIVE PRODUCERS	Jay Blumenfield; Anthony Marsh
PRODUCERS	Erin Comerford; Kim Kanter

Shot on location at Ted Nugent's ranch in Michigan, Season 1 of *Surviving Nugent* was an unconventional elimination competition. Seven contestants lived in a survivalist-like boot camp while trying to adhere to the rules established and enforced by "Motor City Madman" Ted Nugent. The winner, Darren, was awarded $25,000 and a Dodge truck. During Season 2, shot in Waco, Texas, ten "city slickers" hunted with Ted, went manure tossing, and learned about taxidermy. Dawn won $100,000 and a red, custom-made 1936 sedan resembling the ZZ Top music video car.

SURVIVOR: BORNEO
(Season 1)

GENRE	Competition
FIRST TELECAST	5/31/2000
LAST TELECAST	8/23/2000
NETWORK	CBS
AIR TIME	Wednesday, 8:00 p.m.
EPISODE STYLE	Story Arc
TALENT	Jeff Probst (Host)

CAST	Richard Hatch (Winner/Rattana/Pagong); Kelly Wiglesworth (Runner-up—Rattana/Tagi); Rudy Boesch (14th eliminated—Rattana/Tagi); Susan Hawk (13th eliminated—Rattana/Tagi); Sean Kenniff (12th eliminated—Rattana/Tagi); Colleen Haskell (11th eliminated—Rattana/Pagong); Gervase Peterson (10th eliminated—Rattana/Pagong); Jenna Lewis (9th eliminated—Rattana/Pagong); Greg Buis (8th eliminated—Rattana/Pagong); Gretchen Cordy (7th eliminated—Rattana/Pagong); Joel Klug (6th eliminated—Pagong); Dirk Been (5th eliminated—Tagi); Ramona Gray (4th eliminated—Pagong); Stacey Stillman (3rd eliminated—Tagi); B. B. Andersen (2nd eliminated—Pagong); Sonja Christopher (1st eliminated—Tagi)
PRODUCTION COMPANIES	CBS Television; Castaway Television Productions, Inc.; Survivor Entertainment Group; Survivor Productions LLC
CREATED BY	Charlie Parsons
EXECUTIVE PRODUCERS	Mark Burnett; Charlie Parsons
CO-EXECUTIVE PRODUCER	Craig Piligian

Based on the Swedish show *Expedition: Robinson, Survivor* strands sixteen Americans split into two "tribes" (teams) in a remote location for thirty-nine days. In each episode, the tribes face reward challenges in which the winning tribe earns prizes such as food, fire, and tools, to help them with the rest of their stay on the island. The contestants must survive both the environment and their peers, who vote one person out of the game every three days at Tribal Council, where host Jeff Probst popularized the catch phrase "The tribe has spoken." Only those with "immunity," which is won in an Immunity Challenge, are exempt from this vote. The sole survivor at the end of the game wins $1 million

In Episode 1 of the inaugural season the castaways were marooned on the deserted island of Pulau Tiga, in the South China Sea. They were divided into two tribes—Tagi: Dirk, Kelly, Richard, Rudy, Sean, Sonja, Stacey, and Susan; and Pagong: B.B., Colleen, Gervase, Greg, Gretchen, Jenna, Joel, and Ramona. For the first Immunity Challenge, each tribe rafted out to sea, lit a series of torches, and returned to land to ignite a "Fire Spirit" statue. Pagong won the challenge, sending Tagi to the first Tribal Council, where Sonja was voted off because she'd proved to be a physical liability in the challenge.

Thanks to Stacey's clutch performance against Gervase in a bug-eating Immunity Challenge, Tagi defeated Pagong in Episode 2. At Pagong's first Tribal Council, they voted off outspoken patriarch B.B., whose domineering personality grated on the tribe, especially after he used their clean water supply to wash his clothes.

Romance blossomed between Pagong's Greg and Colleen in Episode 3. During the first Reward Challenge, tribes swam to retrieve a submerged treasure chest and dragged it back to shore. Tagi completed the task quickest and won the contents of the chest: a snorkel, mask, fins, and a fishing spear. Without fishing supplies and running out of food, Pagong was forced to eat rats. The Immunity Challenge was to run into the jungle, "rescue" a tribe member, and haul him or her on a stretcher back to the beach. Pagong won the challenge, forcing Tagi to go to Tribal Council, where a stunned Stacey was sent packing.

Episode 4 featured a Reward Challenge to build the most eye-catching distress signal. Tagi won the challenge, earning a knife, spices, and a hammock for their tribe. Rudi, age seventy-two, led Tagi to victory in the Immunity Challenge, a buried treasure hunt–meets–obstacle course. At Pagong's Tribal Council, Ramona was the next victim, since she'd been sick almost since her arrival at camp.

In Episode 5, Pagong emerged victorious in the Reward Challenge, which involved blow darts, slingshots, and spears, and received much-needed fruit and three egg-laying chickens. Pagong also won the Immunity Challenge, by rescuing bobbing teammates from the ocean. Tagi voted off Dirk, whose strong religious beliefs were making some of his tribe members uncomfortable.

Pagong donned night goggles and sought items in snake- and scorpion-infested barracks to win the Reward Challenge in Episode 6. The tribe earned canned goods and chocolate. Tagi blamed their loss on a crucial mistake by Richard, but later won a half-mile obstacle course race to receive immunity. At Tribal Council, Pagong shockingly voted off athletic Joel, in part because he was perceived as being sexist.

In Episode 7, Tagi and Pagong merged into a new tribe called Rattana. Tribe ambassadors Jenna and Sean met to discuss the guidelines of the merger and were given a lobster and wine dinner, while their tribemates went hungry. Sean and Jenna shared a tent, although they claimed nothing sexual happened. Greg earned individual immunity for winning an underwater swim race. Later, he started flirting with gay Richard to earn his favor, but Richard saw through his scheme. At Tribal Council, Gretchen was seen as too much of a threat and got voted off.

In Episode 8, each survivor, except Jenna, was shown a one-minute clip of a home video sent by a loved one. Jenna was distraught to learn her video hadn't arrived. Greg won an archery Reward Challenge and saw the rest of his five-minute video. Meanwhile, Richard established himself as a strong player by forming the Tagi Alliance and by being the only one who knew how to fish. Also, Colleen established herself as the object of several guys' affection. Gervase earned immunity by racing from one end of a rope to the other across treacherous terrain. Thanks to Sean's alphabetical voting strategy to avoid partiality, Greg was the tribe's next victim.

Episode 9 featured an elevated jungle rope course as the Reward Challenge. Colleen won, and invited Jenna for a barbecue dinner, where they formed an alliance to oust Richard. Rudy won immunity in a chessboard game. Meanwhile, Richard's birthday fell on the day of Tribal Council, and he celebrated by spending most of the day naked. He barely survived elimination at Tribal Council, as Jenna was voted off instead.

Gervase earned pizza and a phone call home after winning a tightrope race across bamboo poles in Episode 10. Later, Richard was chastised for attempting to bribe his island mates with a shell necklace, and a rift developed between Susan and Kelly. Gervase's luck ran out as Richard won a fire-starting Immunity Challenge, leaving Gervase as the castaway voted out during Tribal Council.

In Episode 11, Sean beat everyone in a trivia contest about Borneo life and won a night on a luxury yacht, where he was surprised to be greeted by his father. Kelly won immunity by being the last one standing on a plank over water without losing her balance. The popular Colleen finally met her fate, as she was voted out at Tribal Council. Meanwhile, Richard and Rudy revealed an alliance, which was surprising because of Rudy's vocal aversion to homosexuals.

In Episode 12, Kelly won her second straight challenge by triumphing in a mud-packing competition, earning a night at a bar. Then she made it three in a row by winning the Immunity Challenge, finding five masks in the jungle, and correctly answering the questions written on them. However, her attempts to ally herself with Richard were unsuccessful. Sean was the next tribe member voted off.

Kelly kicked off Episode 13's two-hour finale by winning her fourth straight competition, a trivia contest about the voted-off castaways. At the first Tribal Council, she turned on former friend Sue and voted her off. Kelly continued her improbable winning streak by keeping her hand on an idol for the longest time. As the lone voter at the second Tribal Council, she ousted Rudy from the game. The third and final Tribal Council featured a jury of voted-off castaways, who evaluated Kelly and Richard's behavior on the island. Sue delivered a memorable speech, calling Richard a snake and Kelly a rat, and concluded that the snake should eat the rat. True to her prophecy, Richard beat Kelly by one vote and became the first $1 million *Survivor* winner.

SURVIVOR: THE AUSTRALIAN OUTBACK
(Season 2)

GENRE	Competition
FIRST TELECAST	1/28/2001
LAST TELECAST	5/10/2001
NETWORK	CBS
AIR TIME	Thursday, 8:00 p.m.
EPISODE STYLE	Story Arc
TALENT	Jeff Probst (Host)
CAST	Tina Wesson (Winner—Barramundi/Ogakor); Colby Donaldson (Runner-up—Barramundi/Ogakor); Keith Famie (14th eliminated—Barramundi/Ogakor); Elisabeth Hasselback (13th eliminated—Barramundi/Kucha); Rodger Bingham (12th eliminated—Barramundi/Kucha); Amber Brkich (11th eliminated—

Barramundi/Ogakor); Nick Brown
(10th eliminated—Barramundi/Kucha);
Jerri Manthey (9th eliminated—Barramundi/
Ogakor); Alicia Calaway (8th eliminated—
Barramundi/Kucha); Jeff Varner (7th eliminated—
Barramundi/Kucha); Michael Skupin
(6th eliminated—Kucha); Kimmi Kappenberg
(5th eliminated—Kucha); Mitchell Olson,
(4th eliminated—Ogakor); Maralyn Hershey
(3rd eliminated—Ogakor); Kel Gleason
(2nd eliminated—Ogakor); Debb Eaton
(1st eliminated—Kucha)

PRODUCTION COMPANIES	Castaway Television Productions, Inc.; Survivor Productions LLC
CREATED BY	Charlie Parsons
EXECUTIVE PRODUCERS	Mark Burnett; Charlie Parsons
CO-EXECUTIVE PRODUCER	Craig Piligian

In Episode 1, the sixteen castaways were dropped off in the Outback by an Australian military plane and forbidden to speak to one another until the plane left. They were divided into two tribes, Kucha and Ogakor. The tribes were allowed to take as many supplies from the plane as they could carry before embarking on a five-mile trek to their camps. With both teams desperate for fire, waterproof matches were thrown in as a prize for the Immunity Challenge. Ogakor earned immunity for navigating an obstacle course while keeping their torch lit. At Kucha's Tribal Council, Debb's lie about Jeff being too sick to compete was exposed, so the tribe eliminated her by a seven-to-one vote.

There was a terrifying Reward Challenge in Episode 2. The castaways had to dive off a cliff to retrieve a crate of supplies, then bring it back to the beach. Ogakor won and received warm blankets. Back at camp, chef Keith fell out of favor with Ogakor after overcooking rice twice. Kucha won the Immunity Challenge of eating disgusting aboriginal foods, and Ogakor voted Kel out by a seven-to-one count.

Ogakor defeated Kucha in a challenge while carrying buckets of water across a plank without losing their balance in Episode 3. As a reward, Ogakor received fishing tackle. Meanwhile, Kucha's Rodger and Elisabeth began to bond, Jeff and Alicia formed their own alliance, and romance sparked between Colby and Jerri. Kucha earned immunity by winning an obstacle course race while tied together. After much plotting, Ogakor voted off "Mad Dog" Maralyn, since her stumbles had cost them the race.

In Episode 4, Jerri's difficult personality began to wear on her Ogakor tribemates. Nevertheless, she was allowed to join the alliance of Colby, Amber, and Mitchell, while Keith and Tina formed one of their own. Kucha was the first to unscramble a map puzzle and find their reward: three live chickens. Vegetarian Kimmi was horrified as Kucha decided to kill the rooster and eat it. She was further horrified when Michael managed to kill a pig. Kucha received immunity after winning a trivia competition about their environment. At a tense Tribal Council, Ogakor voted out Mitchell, a vote that came down to a tiebreaker of total votes received at previous Tribal Councils.

In Episode 5, a heavy storm hit the Outback, followed by wildfires. Colby cut ties with Jerri, as Ogakor's lack of food heightened tension in the group. Meanwhile in Kucha, Kimmi's staunch vegetarianism led to a shouting match with Alicia. Ogakor blew an opportunity to earn food and hygiene products when they lost the "Triage" Rescue Challenge to Kucha. Ogakor finally won immunity in a maze competition, and Kucha voted Kimmi out of the game.

Disaster struck in Episode 6, when Michael passed out from smoke inhalation and sustained burns on his hands. He was airlifted out and removed from the competition. Meanwhile, a storm forced Kucha to suffer through a damp, miserable night. In Ogakor's camp, tensions between Jerri and Keith escalated. The Reward Challenge required every member in each tribe to be blindfolded except one, who guided the tribe through a series of tasks. Kucha won the challenge and received Mountain Dew and Doritos. With Michael's departure, there was no Tribal Council. Instead, the two tribes were informed they would merge with five members each.

In Episode 7, the newly merged tribe of Barramundi hiked for two hours to their new camp, where they discovered and devoured a crate of food. In the first individual Immunity Challenge, Keith outlasted everyone else standing on pillars in the middle of the river, thanks to Tina, who bowed out to protect her former Ogakor tribemate from certain elimination. Instead, Jeff barely edged out Colby to become the first member voted out of the Barramundi tribe.

In Episode 8, Jerri won a boomerang-throwing Reward Challenge and invited Amber for a gourmet dinner. Meanwhile, Colby prepared to double-cross Jerri for being an unscrupulous player. The Immunity Challenge was a life-size version of the game Dots, which Keith won by completing seventeen boxes in a row. Alicia was voted out at Tribal Council, because the others perceived her as a threat.

In Episode 9, Barramundi had little rice left and their fire was extinguished, thanks to the previous night's storm. Colby and Jerri won a team Reward Challenge and spent the day snorkeling and feasting at the Great Barrier Reef. Nick won immunity after a three-stage challenge, which included two water-based tug-of-war games and a boat-rocking contest. Jerri Manthey finally met her end, as she was voted off at Tribal Council.

Episode 10 featured an auction as the Reward Challenge, where each Survivor was given five hundred Australian dollars to bid on various food items. Unfortunately, the adjustment to eating real food was hard on some castaways' stomachs, and they ended up regurgitating their prizes. Meanwhile, the river began to rise significantly, raising concerns. Colby won the Immunity Challenge, which involved using a bucket of water as a counterweight to raise a flaming pan up to a fuse to ignite it. Host Jeff Probst offered rice to the food-depleted Barramundi in exchange for their shelter, which they accepted. The weakened Nick was the next casualty of the Tribal Council.

In Episode 11, Colby won a ranch retreat with food after conquering a rope course Reward Challenge. Meanwhile, a torrential storm destroyed the Barramundi camp, leaving everyone in dire straits. For the Immunity Challenge, everyone had to break plates with a slingshot. Colby made it two for two with a victory. At Tribal Council, Amber's attempts to fly under the radar were thwarted, as she was voted out.

The castaways had a chance to say hello to their loved ones by e-mail in Episode 12. Then Tina's loved ones answered the most questions correctly, so she earned a thirty-minute online chat with them, plus a $500 Internet shopping spree. During their good-byes to their loved ones, Keith surprisingly proposed to his girlfriend, and she accepted. Colby was fed up with Keith wasting their rice. During the Immunity Challenge, the castaways answered questions to earn keys that unlocked their shackles. Colby edged out Keith to win. In a moving gesture, Rodger persuaded the others to vote him out instead of Elisabeth, who needed the money more than he did.

Episode 13 featured a Pentathlon Reward Challenge, which combined elements from previous challenges. Colby beat Elisabeth to win a hot meal, a shower, a brand-new Pontiac Aztek, and a surprise visit from his mother, who gave each Survivor a care package from their loved ones. The castaways discovered a scale and weighed themselves, discovering that they had all lost a tremendous amount of weight. Challenge master Colby emerged victorious in the Immunity Challenge, a version of *Concentration* in which the Survivors had to match images of items from the Outback. At Tribal Council, Elisabeth was the first of the final four to be voted out.

In Episode 14, the three remaining Survivors—Colby, Keith, and Tina—carved idols and threw them over a waterfall, as a gesture of "giving back" to the land. Colby won an impressive fifth straight Immunity Challenge, correctly answering the most questions about their fallen tribemates. Colby and Tina kept their previous pact and voted Keith out of the game. A jury of their former tribemates gathered to cast their final votes, but host Jeff Probst announced that the results would not be revealed until they returned to Los Angeles.

In a live two-hour finale, Tina was crowned champion and won $1 million.

SURVIVOR: AFRICA
(Season 3)

GENRE	Competition
FIRST TELECAST	10/4/2001
LAST TELECAST	1/17/2002
NETWORK	CBS
AIR TIME	Thursday, 8:00 p.m.
EPISODE STYLE	Story Arc
TALENT	Jeff Probst (Host)
CAST	Ethan Zohn (Winner—Moto Maji/Boran); Kim Johnson (Runner-up—Moto Maji/Boran); Lex van den Berghe (14th eliminated—Moto Maji/Samburu/Boran); Tom Buchanan (13th eliminated—Moto Maji/Samburu/Boran); Teresa Cooper (12th eliminated—Moto Maji/

Boran/Samburu); Kim Powers (11th eliminated—Moto Maji/Samburu); Frank Garrison (10th eliminated—Mot Maji/Boran/Samburu); Brandon Quinton (9th eliminated—Moto Maji/Samburu); Kelly Goldsmith (8th eliminated—Moto Maji/Samburu/Boran); Clarence Black (7th eliminated—Moto Maji/Boran); Lindsey Richter (6th eliminated—Samburu); Silas Gaither (5th eliminated—Boran/Samburu); Linda Spencer (4th eliminated—Samburu); Carl Bilancione (3rd eliminated—Boran); Jessie Camacho (2nd eliminated—Boran); Diane Ogden (1st eliminated—Boran)

PRODUCTION COMPANY	Castaway Television Productions, Inc.
CREATED BY	Charlie Parsons
EXECUTIVE PRODUCER	Mark Burnett
CO-EXECUTIVE PRODUCER	Craig Piligian

Sixteen castaways were stranded in the middle of Kenya for Season 3 of *Survivor*. They were separated into two tribes, Samburu and Boran. During the four-hour hike to camp, ex-Army man Frank managed to annoy his Samburu tribemates with his military demeanor, while Diane's faulty navigation started her off on the wrong foot with Boran. Samburu won the first Immunity Challenge, dragging a fire cauldron across the beach and lighting a series of torches. After Diane ratted out Clarence for opening a can of beans without the others' permission, she was voted out at the first Tribal Council.

In Episode 2, Clarence was shaken after he received two Tribal Council votes because of his renegade act. Samburu won blankets, water containers, and food in the Reward Challenge, which entailed dragging logs to a tower, building a staircase, and climbing to the top. Boran's fifty-six-year-old Kim Johnson feared the worst, after her stumble gave Samburu the victory. Meanwhile, Boran's Lex, Tom, and Ethan formed an early alliance. It was Kelly's turn to falter in the Immunity Challenge, as Boran lost a cow's blood–drinking contest to Samburu. At their second Tribal Council, Boran voted off Jessie, who was weakened by dehydration.

Boran got a scare in Episode 3 when lions entered their camp at night. Meanwhile, a division formed between Samburu's older and younger members. Boran won immunity in a distress signal competition, during which Samburu's Lindsey collapsed from dehydration. Lindsey survived Samburu's first Tribal Council when she won a tie-breaker against Carl.

The rift between Samburu's older and younger members grew wider during Episode 4. Samburu won a Reward Challenge by retrieving twelve baskets from a rope web, earning the food-related contents of the baskets. Boran's loss was compounded when their water-boiling pots cracked. They also had a scare when they encountered a buffalo. But Boran was vindicated in the Immunity Challenge, when they relocated replicas of African homes two hundred yards away before Samburu did. At Tribal Council, Samburu voted Linda out of the game.

In Episode 5, host Jeff Probst told each tribe to send their "best" members to meet him. Boran chose Kelly, Tom, and Lex, while Samburu sent Frank, Teresa, and Silas. In a shocking twist, the six Survivors were instructed to switch tribes. Tom and Lex were dismayed to join Samburu. Boran won a goat herding Reward Challenge, and received three egg-laying chickens and a rooster. The intolerable Lindsey was temporarily spared as Samburu won a puzzle-building Immunity Challenge. Viewers saw that Boran threw the challenge to vote out their recent addition, Silas.

In Episode 6, Boran ate one of their egg-laying chickens. Samburu ate even better, after winning a feast in the Reward Challenge for answering the most Africa-related questions correctly. Ethan led Boran to immunity in an archery competition. At Samburu's Tribal Council, Lindsey lost a tiebreaker and was eliminated from the game.

The two tribes merged into a new tribe, Moto Maji, in Episode 7. During the first individual Immunity Challenge, the castaways stood under a water bucket with a rope attached to their wrists. Any movement caused the rope to pull the bucket and drench that player, eliminating him or her from the game. Teresa defeated Clarence in a tiebreaking game of Rock, Paper, Scissors, and at Tribal Council, Clarence was voted out for being too much of a physical threat.

In Episode 8, a furious Lex sought in vain to find out who had voted for him at the previous Tribal Council. (It was Teresa.) Ethan won the Reward Challenge by catapulting objects into a basket on a tower. He received two goats to barter at an African village. Ethan brought Lex with him, and they sold the goats and bought lunch, as well as some treats to bring back to the tribe. Ethan also won immunity after memorizing the contents of a barrel and re-creating them. Kelly was the next player voted out at Tribal Council, thanks in part to Brandon betraying his former Samburu tribemate.

Tom developed a nasty boil on his neck in Episode 9. Random pairs were chosen for an obstacle course Reward Challenge, and Brandon and Frank's victory earned them a trip to the movies to watch the ominously titled *Out of Africa*. Lex won immunity in a fire-building competition, and the traitorous Brandon was voted out at Tribal Council.

In Episode 10, the weary castaways were offered relief at the Reward Challenge, which was a food auction. Lex won the Immunity Challenge, a trivia contest about African folklore. The outspoken Frank was sent home at Tribal Council.

Videograms from the Survivors' loved ones arrived in Episode 11. The Reward Challenge involved a contest to see who could correctly predict the answers their loved one gave to a series of questions. Lex won the challenge, and invited Tom to join him on a safari trip and feast. Later, Tom won immunity in a spear-throwing challenge by shattering pots labeled with his tribemates' names. At Tribal Council, Kim P. fell victim to the old Boran alliance and was voted out of the game.

The tribe was dealt a setback in Episode 12, when they found elephant dung in their watering hole. Kim opted to bathe there anyway. Meanwhile, the stench of Tom's feet was even more off-putting to Ethan. Lex won a Swahili word search Reward Challenge, and earned a brand-new Chevy Avalanche, which he used to transport medical supplies to a local AIDS hospital. Lex doubled his pleasure by winning immunity in an obstacle course, which combined elements of previous challenges. In an act of desperation, Teresa admitted to Lex that she was the one who'd voted for him in the previous Tribal Council. Her confession was not enough to save her, as the Boran alliance conspired to vote her out of the game.

The pressure was on for the final four in Episode 13. Kim won her first Immunity Challenge by answering the most questions correctly about the eliminated castaways. Tom was voted out at the first Tribal Council. The three remaining Survivors underwent an emotional Samburu ritual, walking past staffs with the names of all thirteen of their fallen comrades. Kim, the fifty-six-year-old grandmother, surprisingly won immunity by keeping her hand on a hard idol for the longest time. At the second Tribal Council, Lex was sent packing, leaving only Kim and Ethan. The jury of former castaways convened for the final Tribal Council, and Ethan was proclaimed the winner of $1 million.

SURVIVOR: MARQUESAS
(Season 4)

GENRE	Competition
FIRST TELECAST	2/28/2002
LAST TELECAST	5/19/2002
NETWORK	CBS
AIR TIME	Thursday, 8:00 p.m.
EPISODE STYLE	Story Arc
TALENT	Jeff Probst (Host)
CAST	Vecepia Towery (Winner—Soliantu/Rotu/ Maraamu); Neleh Dennis (Runner-up— Soliantu/Maraamu/Rotu); Kathy Vavrick-O'Brie (14th eliminated—Soliantu/Maraamu/Rotu); Paschal English (13th eliminated—Soliantu/ Maraamu/Rotu); Sean Rector (12th eliminated— Soliantu/Rotu/Maraamu); Robert DeCanio (11th eliminated—Soliantu/Rotu); Tammy Leitner (10th eliminated—Soliantu/Rotu); Zoe Zanidakis (9th eliminated—Soliantu/Rotu); John Carroll (8th eliminated—Soliantu/Rotu); Rob Mariano (7th eliminated—Soliantu/Rotu/Maraamu); Gina Crews (6th eliminated—Maraamu); Gabriel Cade (5th eliminated—Rotu); Sarah Jones (4th eliminated—Maraamu); Hunter Ellis (3rd eliminated—Maraamu); Patricia Jackson (2nd eliminated—Maraamu); Peter Harkey (1st eliminated—Maraamu)
PRODUCTION COMPANIES	Castaway Television Productions, Inc.; Survivor Productions LLC

CREATED BY Charlie Parsons
EXECUTIVE PRODUCERS Mark Burnett; Craig Armstrong

The sixteen castaways were immediately put to the test, as they were stranded without food or water on a South Pacific island in the Marquesas Islands. After swimming to shore on life rafts, the castaways were split into two tribes, Maraamu and Rotu. Kathy irritated her Rotu tribemates by barking orders, while Hunter's leadership skills in Maraamu earned everyone's respect, especially Gina's, who claimed she was "already in love" with him. Also, Maraamu tribemate Sarah began flirting with construction worker Rob. Rotu won a fire-lighting canoe race to gain immunity. At Tribal Council, Peter's poorly concealed strategy to vote out the weak players backfired, as Maraamu made him the first casualty of Season 4.

In Episode 2, Rotu tribe members bonded, except for Kathy, who was clearly an outsider. She found some edible sea creatures and fruit, but didn't receive the credit she hoped for. Similarly, Maraamu's Sarah resented Hunter's receiving credit for her idea to make a palm roof for their shelter. Meanwhile, Maraamu's Vecepia and Sean started to bond, although Sean's laziness rubbed his tribemates the wrong way. Rotu won fishing gear in the Reward Challenge, which involved salvaging a sunken ship, bailing out the water, and sailing the ship out to the finish line. Rotu also won immunity in an eating competition, where the castaways had to swallow disgusting Marquesan "delicacies." Maraamu's second victim was Patricia, whose alpha personality didn't sit well with the others.

Maraamu accused Hunter of poor leadership and communication skills in Episode 3. Also, everyone awoke covered with bites from "No No" bugs. Meanwhile, Rotu's Paschal and Neleh formed a father/daughter-type relationship. Injuries piled up for Rotu, as Robert sliced his foot on a rock, while John was bitten by an eel and stung by a sea urchin. Kathy urinated on John's wound to prevent infection. Rotu earned pillows, blankets, and lanterns in the Reward Challenge after winning a raft race. Rotu also received immunity for navigating a coconut through a maze, using a system of pulleys to tilt the maze. At their third straight Tribal Council, a demoralized Maraamu followed Rob's strategy and voted out Hunter.

Episode 4 started with a twist, as the tribe members were shuffled, upsetting the group dynamics. Maraamu's new members were excited to find fruit at their new camp, while Rotu's new tribemates were put off by the worker bee environment. Rotu kept their winning streak intact in the Immunity Challenge, by unscrambling a Polynesian tapestry puzzle. Maraamu chose to vote off the difficult Sarah at Tribal Council.

In Episode 5, Rob lamented leaving Maraamu, where he was in control. Rotu's John struck up alliances with Robert, Zoe, and Tammy, but remained cautious of Gabe. Maraamu finally broke their losing streak in the Reward Challenge, in which a "caller" directed blindfolded tribemates to find pieces of tikis and assemble them. Their prize was two minutes to raid Rotu's camp of whatever supplies they wanted. Maraamu also won the Immunity Challenge after building a better distress signal, and Rotu voted out Gabe.

Episode 6 featured some controversy, as host Jeff Probst originally named Rotu the winners of a jungle relay Reward Challenge, but then had to disqualify them because Robert had broken the rules. Maraamu earned a picnic for their victory. Rotu vindicated itself in the Immunity Challenge, gathering rungs in a maze, building a ladder, and climbing to the finish platform. Despite Kathy's shaky status, Gina was the one eliminated at Tribal Council, as the former Rotu members conspired against her.

In Episode 7, Rob and Kathy were sent as representatives to discuss the tribal merger. They agreed to form an alliance, although Rob admitted he had been lying to everyone throughout the game. The new tribe, Soliantu, competed in an Immunity Challenge in which each member remained standing on a floating platform in the choppy sea. Kathy won the challenge, and declined Jeff's offer to assign immunity to someone else. After a heated discussion, the scheming Rob was voted out of the tribe.

Kathy's winning ways continued in Episode 8, as she emerged victorious in a kite-flying contest, earning a coral reef excursion and a Snickers bar, which she split with the tribe. Tammy won the Immunity Challenge, answering questions about the Marquesas and knocking the others out by chopping down their bundle of coconuts. At Tribal Council, John discovered that his leader status had made him a target, as he was voted out.

Episode 9's Reward Challenge required the Survivors to split into pairs and fill a three-foot bamboo shoot with coconut juice, either by using individual coconuts scattered on the beach or by retrieving a bundle of coconuts anchored out at sea. Sean and Paschal were the winners. They bonded over a helicopter and horseback ride, and a Marquesan feast, from which they smuggled food back to their tribe. Tammy won a stilt-walking Immunity Challenge, sealing the fate of Zoe, whose tribemates were unimpressed by her attempt to bribe them with jewelry.

In Episode 10, Paschal invited Neleh on a one-day cruise after winning the Reward Challenge, a musical chairs–like contest that required them to retrieve sunken shells, then drag a forty-pound rock to shore. Robert won the Immunity Challenge by building a fire, popping popcorn, and igniting a pyre in the fastest time. Tammy was finally ousted at Tribal Council.

In Episode 11, the Survivors were thrilled to learn their loved ones had been flown in and would compete in the Reward Challenge. Kathy's son, Patrick, spent the night with the tribe, after winning a competition in which players moved one step at a time on a giant chessboard, eliminating the square they'd just stepped off. Vecepia earned immunity by winning a slingshot competition, and the tribe voted off Robert.

In Episode 12, Sean received a new Saturn SUV for winning the Reward Challenge, a combination of tasks from previous challenges. Kathy won a memory-retention Immunity Challenge, in which the Survivors answered questions about an ancient Marquesan tale Jeff read to them. Kathy found herself carrying the swing vote between the two alliances of Sean and Vecipia and Paschal and Neleh. Despite Vecepia's warnings not to "play the race card," Kathy cast her vote for Sean and eliminated him from the game.

In Episode 13, Vecepia earned immunity by answering the most questions correctly about the fallen castaways. The first Tribal Council vote resulted in a deadlocked tie between Neleh and Kathy, so Jeff had everyone draw colored rocks from a bag. Paschal drew the unlucky purple stone, and was sent packing. Neleh won the next Immunity Challenge, an endurance contest to keep one hand on a hard idol, after Vecepia agreed to step down in exchange for Neleh's taking her to the final two. True to their word, they voted out Kathy at the second Tribal Council. After the jury convened to make their final vote, Jeff took the jar back to New York and revealed the results before a crowd in Central Park. By a slim four-to-three margin, Vecepia was the sole Survivor, winning $1 million. The finale was followed by a reunion special hosted by Rosie O'Donnell.

SURVIVOR: THAILAND

(Season 5)

GENRE Competition
FIRST TELECAST 9/19/2002

LAST TELECAST	12/19/2002
NETWORK	CBS
AIR TIME	Thursday, 8:00 p.m.
EPISODE STYLE	Story Arc
TALENT	Jeff Probst (Host)
CAST	Brian Heidik (Winner—Chuay Jai); Clay Jordan (Runner-up—Chuay Jai); Jan Gentry (14th eliminated—Chuay Jai); Helen Glover (13th eliminated—Chuay Jai); Ted Rogers, Jr., (12th eliminated—Chuay Jai); Jake Billingsley (11th eliminated—Chuay Jai); Penny Ramsey (10th eliminated—Chuay Jai); Ken Stafford (9th eliminated—Chuay Jai); Erin Collins (8th eliminated—Sook Jai); Shii Ann Huang (7th eliminated—Sook Jai); Robb Zbacnik (6th eliminated—Sook Jai); Stephanie Dill (5th eliminated—Sook Jai); Ghandia Johnson (4th eliminated—Chuay Gahn); Jed Hildebrand (3rd eliminated—Sook Jai); Tanya Vance (2nd eliminated—Chuay Gahn); John Raymond (1st eliminated—Chuay Gahn)
PRODUCTION COMPANIES	Castaway Television Productions, Inc.; Living Films, Survivor Productions LLC
CREATED BY	Charlie Parsons
EXECUTIVE PRODUCER	Mark Burnett

Season 5's sixteen castaways were divided by gender on *Survivor: Thailand*. But in the Thai spirit of respecting the elders, host Jeff Probst appointed fifty-three-year-old Jan and sixty-one-year-old Jake as tribe leaders, and allowed them to alternate selecting their own tribemates. Jan's tribe was given the name Chuay Gahn, while Jake's was called Sook Jai. Sook Jai won a boat race Immunity Challenge, in which tribe members completed individual challenges to receive tribal flags. At Chuay Gahn's first Tribal Council, sick Tanya and incompetent puzzle-solver Ghandia feared the worst, but it was John who was voted out, six to two.

The Chuay Gahn members struggled to locate drinking water in Episode 2. Sook Jai's Jed and Stephanie resented being the main providers of food and water, while the others took a long time to build a shelter. Cold rain and an insufficient shelter took its toll on Stephanie, who woke up sick the next morning. Sook Jai won fishing gear in a Reward Challenge in which the members of each tribe were blindfolded and directed through a course by a guide on a palanquin chair. Sook Jai won the Immunity Challenge, a water race to retrieve floating puzzle pieces to form a giant lotus. The ailing Tanya was Chuay Gahn's next victim at Tribal Council.

In Episode 3, Chuay Gahn's Ted mistook Ghandia for his wife in his sleep, and later apologized for groping her. Not content with the apology, Ghandia tried to rally the tribe's women to vote him out. Chuay Gahn won the Reward Challenge, in which tribe members tried to cross a narrow course and steal ten of the opposing tribe's baskets, without getting knocked into the water. The reward was the services of two Thai Red Beret soldiers, who retrieved food that afternoon, which Chuay Gahn feasted on that night. Later, Chuay Gahn won immunity in a challenge in which they transferred a temple from one platform to another, piece by piece. At Sook Jai's first Tribal Council, the tribe turned against their contrary leader and voted Jed out of the game.

In Episode 4, Sook Jai earned a bunch of bananas, and a surprise reward of four chickens, after winning a race around the island while transporting a 250-pound dummy. Meanwhile, divisions started forming within Sook Jai—Stephanie complained that she was doing all the work in the challenge, while the tribe women claimed the men weren't pitching in back at camp. Sook Jai won the Immunity Challenge by solving a Thai puzzle. At Chuay Gahn's Tribal Council, Ghandia's attempt to rally the women to vote together backfired, as swing voter Helen made her the tribe's third victim.

In Episode 5, Chuay Gahn's Brian and Ted formed an alliance during a fishing trip. Sook Jai's Robb stepped on a stingray and injured his foot. Ted was blamed for allowing Chuay Gahn's canoe to drift away during the night. During the Reward Challenge, both tribes bid on various food items in an auction. Prior to the challenge, Jeff gave everyone the option to switch tribes, but no one accepted. Later, Chuay Gahn won a fish-sorting Immunity Challenge, and Sook Jai voted disgruntled rebel Stephanie out of the game.

In Episode 6, Robb fell into disfavor with Sook Jai after he angrily defended his right to eat a banana without the tribe's permission. Sook Jai earned a Thai feast in the

Reward Challenge by catching wicker balls launched by their tribe, while preventing the opposing tribe from catching them. Jan led Chuay Gahn in a funeral for a dead baby bat, leading her tribemates to wonder if she was "losing it." During the Immunity Challenge, the tribes alternately took one, two, or three of the twenty-one Thai flags, with Chuay Gahn winning by taking the last flag. Robb's early brazenness cost him, as Sook Jai voted him out at Tribal Council.

In Episode 7, host Jeff Probst twice teased the tribes with the trappings of a tribal merger. First, he had every tribe member paint his or her body a different color, and paired them up for the afternoon with their color-coded counterpart from the opposing tribe. Next, he arranged for both tribes to live together on the Chuay Gahn beach. The united tribes decided to call themselves Chuay Jai, however Jeff later told them that the tribes had *not* merged—they were just living together on the same beach. Chuay Gahn won the Immunity Challenge by escaping from a makeshift cell. At Tribal Council, Shii Ann became the victim of assuming she was safe, when her double-dealings with Chuay Gahn's tribe prompted Sook Jai to vote her out.

In Episode 8, Sook Jai's Penny tried to ingratiate herself with Chuay Gahn's Ted and Clay, but they weren't buying it. Helen constantly boasted about her famous recipes, which got on Jake's nerves. Chuay Gahn won immunity in a snorkeling competition by holding their breath underwater the longest, but their spirits were dampened when they discovered a monkey had stolen their bananas. Sook Jai held an emotional Tribal Council, in which Erin was voted off.

The tribes finally merged in Episode 9. Jeff showed everyone a preview of videos sent from their loved ones. Brian was allowed to watch his entire video after winning a wicker ball relay race and building a wicker ball pyramid puzzle. Jake tried to stir up an alliance against the demanding Ted. Clay won the Immunity Challenge, which involved memorizing the numbers one through ten in Thai, then using the Thai language to collect buried discs. At the first merged Tribal Council, the former Chuay Gahn members allied against Ken and voted him off.

In Episode 10, Ted was upset about having received three votes at the previous Tribal Council. Brian invited Clay to join him for an elephant ride and Thai lunch, after winning a team Reward Challenge featuring obstacles that required a two-person team. Jake, who did not pair up in a team, was eliminated before the challenge began. Helen won immunity in a Thai culture quiz, in which a correct answer allowed a castaway to eliminate a tribemate from the competition. Penny's overeager elimination of Jake during the Immunity Challenge came back to haunt her, as she was voted out at Tribal Council.

Episode 11's Reward Challenge featured a surprise visit from the castaways' family members and loved ones, who, in a twist, were invited to compete in a creature-eating contest. Helen's husband, Jim, won by eating a tarantula and scorpion, and was able to spend twenty-four hours at camp with her. The loved ones also participated in the Immunity Challenge—won by Ted and his brother, Alwan, when they were the first to form of cube from a pile of puzzle pieces. After the loved ones left, Jake's status as the lone surviving member of Sook Jai proved a liability, as the Chuay Gahn alumni voted him out of the game.

In Episode 12, Ted won a word puzzle-solving Reward Challenge, forming the words *road trip* from the eight letters he'd gathered at stations along the way. He won a Chevy Trailblazer, and invited Helen to join him on a spa retreat. Brian won the Immunity Challenge by successfully fitting puzzle pieces into staircase steps, then climbing to the top. Ted was the next victim of Tribal Council, as the other Survivors viewed him as too much of a threat.

The final four castaways honored their fallen predecessors by sending thirteen custom-made *krathongs*, or rafts, out to sea in Episode 13. Brian won the first Immunity Challenge, which was a combination of tasks from previous competitions. A stunned Helen was voted out in the first of two Tribal Councils. Then Brian won the second Immunity Challenge—his third in a row—by outlasting the others in a traditional Thai stance, called a *kahn,* while holding three large coins between the fingers of each hand. Jan was the victim of the second Tribal Council. Having reached the final two, Brian and Clay were then cross-examined by a jury of their ex-tribemates, and their votes secured a four-to-three victory for the sole Survivor, Brian Heidik, who won $1 million.

SURVIVOR: THE AMAZON

(Season 6)

GENRE Competition
FIRST TELECAST 2/13/2003

LAST TELECAST	5/11/2003
NETWORK	CBS
AIR TIME	Thursday, 8:00 p.m.
EPISODE STYLE	Story Arc
TALENT	Jeff Probst (Host)
CAST	Jenna Morasca (Winner—Jacare); Matthew von Ertfelda (Runner-up); Rob Cesternino (14th eliminated—Jacare); Butch Lockley (13th eliminated—Jacare); Heidi Strobel (12th eliminated—Jacare); Christy Smith (11th eliminated—Jacare); Alex Bell (10th eliminated—Jacare); Deena Bennett (9th eliminated—Jacare); Dave Johnson (8th eliminated—Jacare); Roger Sexton (7th eliminated—Jacare); Shawna Mitchell (6th eliminated—Jamburu); Jeanne Hebert (5th eliminated—Jamburu); JoAnna Ward (4th eliminated—Jamburu); Daniel Lue (3rd eliminated—Tambaqui); Janet Koth (2nd eliminated—Jamburu); Ryan Aiken (1st eliminated—Tambaqui)
PRODUCTION COMPANIES	Castaway Television Productions, Inc.; Survivor Entertainment Group; Survivor Productions LLC
CREATED BY	Charlie Parsons
EXECUTIVE PRODUCER	Mark Burnett

Survivor finally made good on the threat to stage a battle of the sexes by dividing the Season 6 castaways into male (Tambaqui) and female (Jamburu) tribes in *Survivor: The Amazon*. After settling in at their camps in Episode 1, Christy told her tribemates that she was deaf, and expressed her concern that she'd miss at lot of information after dark, when she couldn't read lips. Meanwhile, Roger established himself as the bossy leader of Tambaqui. Rob confessed to having a crush on Heidi. The women shocked the men with a come-from-behind victory in the Immunity Challenge, which required tribemates to run an obstacle course while chained to each other, then unlock sections of chain with keys they'd earned at different stations. Ryan's struggles in the challenge led him to be the first Tambaqui victim of Tribal Council.

In Episode 2, the Jamburu women desperately lacked leadership, which kept them from building sufficient shelter before the rains came. The women pulled it together to win fishing bait in the Reward Challenge, which required a "caller" to direct blindfolded tribemates to pick up puzzle pieces in a field and then assemble them into a giant Amazonian puzzle. Back at the camps, Alex and Roger argued about homosexuality, while Christy was fed up with JoAnna's strict religious beliefs. The men won a memory-based Immunity Challenge that required the tribes to answer questions about a traditional Amazonian dwelling they recently visited. At Jamburu's first Tribal Council, Janet was ousted because she was struggling to adapt to the survivalist conditions.

Jamburu strategically picked Deena to be their leader in Episode 3, figuring her temper would cause her own downfall. During the Reward Challenge, the players asked opposing tribe members if they had a matching hygiene item in their possession. The women won by obtaining eighteen pairs of matching items, and, for their reward, they kept the collection of hygiene items. Jamburu won the Immunity Challenge by escaping a makeshift jail cell. The men decided to vote out lazy Daniel at Tribal Council.

In Episode 4, Deena joined an alliance with the younger women Jenna, Heidi, and Shawna. Each tribe's morale was boosted after both successfully caught fish. The men won a refrigerator full of Coca-Cola in the Reward Challenge by starting a fire tall enough to burn through four ropes and release their tribal banner. Later, Tambaqui won immunity in a fish-catching competition, sending the women to Tribal Council, where the young alliance voted off JoAnna, despite sick Shawna's pleas to vote her off instead.

Alex accidentally slashed his eyebrow while using a machete at the start of Episode 5. Host Jeff Probst had the youngest tribe representatives, Jenna and Dave, reform their tribes by selecting new members. At the end, Jamburu consisted of Jenna, Deena, Shawna, Rob, Alex, and Matthew; Tambaqui's members were Dave, Butch, Roger, Heidi, Christy, and Jeanne. The diversification of gender seemed to energize both tribes. The new Jamburu tribe won the Immunity Challenge by finding five words in a word-search puzzle, then paddling out to sea and retrieving the five flags labeled with those words. At Tambaqui's Tribal Council, Heidi abandoned her all-female alliance, conspiring with the men to vote off Jeanne.

The Reward Challenge in Episode 6 consisted of a one-on-one test of who could remain standing on a revolving log the longest before falling into the mud. Tambaqui won the challenge, earning fruit and spices for the tribe. In Jamburu's camp, Rob struck up separate alliances with Deena and Matthew, and Alex, Matthew, and Rob each took turns flirting with Shawna by telling her where they'd take her on a fantasy date. At the Immunity Challenge, Tambaqui defeated Jamburu by using their mouths to tear off the most meat from a slab. At Tribal Council, Rob's swing vote was cast against Shawna, expelling her from the tribe.

The two tribes merged to form Jacaré in Episode 7. Deena, Heidi, and Jenna formed an alliance against the headstrong Roger. In the Immunity Challenge, the tribe members tried to outlast one another while standing on perches in the water. Jenna and Heidi agreed to strip naked in exchange for a reward of peanut butter and chocolate. Matthew and Dave were bribed off their perches by buffalo wings. Deena eventually defeated Christy in a tiebreaker game of Rock, Paper, Scissors, earning immunity. Overconfident Roger was blindsided when he was voted out at Tribal Council.

Dave became paranoid over losing his ally, Roger, while Jamburu was disturbed by Matthew's obsession with sharpening his machete in Episode 8. For the Reward Challenge, the tribe members retrieved flags in a mud pit while attached to each other with bungee cords. Dave won the challenge, and invited Deena to join him for a cold bath and dessert. The Immunity Challenge tested their knowledge of Amazon culture and survival. A correct answer let the contestant send a log smashing through a tribemate's mask, eliminating that member from the competition. Jenna emerged victorious, and Dave was the next victim at Tribal Council.

In Episode 9, Alex won a target-shooting Reward Challenge, using blow darts, spears, and a bow and arrow. He invited Jenna to join him at an Amazon coffee bar, from which they brought back two chocolate cookies for each tribemate. Back at camp, Butch suffered a piranha bite while fishing, and a spider bit Heidi. Matthew won immunity by eating disgusting Amazonian "delicacies." At Tribal Council, Deena's double-crossing ways secured her elimination.

Episode 10 was a recap, showing highlights from previous episodes.

In Episode 11, a strong alliance formed between Heidi, Jenna, Alex, and Rob. At the Reward Challenge auction, everyone earned food, and Christy and Jenna outbid the others for a right to read letters sent from their loved ones back home. Rob won the Immunity Challenge, which asked them to predict the most popular answers to a previous questionnaire about their fellow tribemates. At Tribal Council, a stunned Alex was eliminated after Rob secretly recruited Matthew in an alliance against him.

In Episode 12, Heidi and Jenna were furious with Rob's scheme that went against the alliance's plan to vote out Matthew. Meanwhile, Matthew earned a visit from his mother after winning a Reward Challenge, which involved unearthing paddles, rowing a canoe out to a floating box, answering a survival-related question, bringing a bag of puzzle pieces to shore, and forming the pieces into a snake. Later, Matthew gave up his mother's visit in exchange for allowing five other tribemates to meet with their loved ones. His selflessness was later rewarded when he was allowed to join his mother for a feast and a night together at an Amazonian village. Jenna won immunity in a sling-shot and shuffleboard challenge, and Rob persuaded Heidi and Jenna to vote out Christy at Tribal Council.

Matthew earned a Saturn Ion in Episode 13, when he won a Reward Challenge featuring tasks from previous competitions. While the tribe was at the Reward Challenge, sparks jumped from their fire pit to the wood supply under the shelter, starting a blaze that burned the camp to the ground. Matthew won the Immunity Challenge, an obstacle course race in which the contestants had to gather five feathers. Despite speculation that Jenna would be voted out following her emotional breakdown, the alliance decided to make Heidi the next player to go.

In Episode 14, the contestants read Braille in order to navigate a maze to retrieve four necklaces representing the elements at the first Immunity Challenge. Jenna won critical immunity, as her status as the only woman in the final four made her a target. Instead, Butch was the next one voted out at Tribal Council. The final Immunity Challenge was a test of endurance that challenged the tribemates to stand on a perch the longest while holding a headdress above their heads. Matthew was the first to drop out. Jenna rejected Rob's offer to step down in exchange for taking her to the final two. She won immunity and voted Rob out of the game. The jury of eliminated castaways convened to cross-examine Jenna and Matthew. After the votes were cast, Jeff Probst decided to withhold the results until he was back in New York, at the Ed Sullivan Theater. By a surprising six-to-one vote, the sole Survivor and winner of the $1 million was Jenna Morasca.

SURVIVOR: PEARL ISLANDS
(Season 7)

GENRE	Competition
FIRST TELECAST	9/18/2003
LAST TELECAST	12/14/2003
NETWORK	CBS
AIR TIME	Thursday, 8:00 p.m.
EPISODE STYLE	Story Arc
TALENT	Jeff Probst (Host)
CAST	Sandra Diaz-Twine (Winner—Balboa Tribe); Lillian Morris (Runner-up—Balboa/3rd eliminated—Morgan); Jon Dalton (16th eliminated—Balboa); Darrah Johnson (15th eliminated—Balboa); Burton Roberts (14th eliminated—Balboa/4th eliminated—Drake); Christa Hastie (13th eliminated—Balboa); Tijuana Bradley (12th eliminated—Balboa); Rupert Boneham (11th eliminated—Balboa); Ryan Opray (10th eliminated—Balboa); Andrew M. Savage (9th eliminated—Balboa); Osten Taylor (8th eliminated—Morgan); Shawn Cohen (7th eliminated—Drake); Trish Dunn (6th eliminated—Drake); Michelle Tesauro (5th eliminated—Drake); Ryan Shoulders (2nd eliminated—Morgan); Nicole Delma (1st eliminated—Morgan)
PRODUCTION COMPANIES	Castaway Television Productions, Inc.; Survivor Entertainment Group; Survivor Productions LLC
CREATED BY	Charlie Parsons
EXECUTIVE PRODUCERS	Mark Burnett; Charlie Parsons
CO-EXECUTIVE PRODUCER	Tom Shelly

For Season 7, *Survivor: Pearl Islands* featured a pirate theme, as the castaways were stranded in the Pearl Islands, off the coast of Panama. En route to their location in Episode 1, host Jeff Probst dumped the Survivors' shoes overboard, then gave them currency to buy necessities from the locals. While the Morgan tribe was out bartering, the Drake tribe stole their shoes. Morgan tribe members Ryan and Lillian struck up a bond, while Drake's Burton and Rupert competed for alpha-male supremacy. Drake won an Immunity Challenge by carrying a heavy cannon around the island. Nicole's dishonesty caused Morgan to vote her off.

In Episode 2, Drake's Rupert proved to be an excellent fisherman. Drake won the Reward Challenge by filling a sunken treasure chest and dragging it to shore. Their prize was the first piece of a map to buried treasure. Drake was additionally rewarded with the opportunity to pillage one item from Morgan's camp, so Sandra took their tarp. Drake won the Immunity Challenge by freeing their three captive prisoners, crossing an obstacle course, digging up their buried flag, and raising it. At Morgan's Tribal Council, a demoralized Osten asked to be ousted, but they voted off Ryan S. instead.

Drake won the Reward Challenge in Episode 3 by using hooks to pull corks out of Morgan's boats, thereby sinking them. As their reward, Drake received bedding, the second piece of the treasure map, and the opportunity to loot Morgan's water pot. Drake also won the Immunity Challenge by being able to use a pulley system to suspend their weakest member above water the longest. Morgan deemed Lillian the least valuable member, and voted her off.

In Episode 4, Morgan's losing streak continued when Drake won a puzzle-solving Reward Challenge. Their reward was a sewing kit, the third and final piece of the treasure map, and the opportunity to steal Morgan's lantern. Using the map, Drake dug up the treasure chest and found a bounty of food and luxury items. Morgan finally tasted victory during the Immunity Challenge, winning a human checkerboard game played above the water. Inexplicably, Drake's Rupert and Burton sat out the competition. Morgan was also rewarded with the surprise opportunity to kidnap one member of Drake's tribe until the next Immunity Challenge. They chose Rupert. Burton's plan to deliberately lose the Immunity Challenge so they could finally vote a woman off the Drake tribe backfired when he was the one ousted at Tribal Council.

In Episode 5, Drake's Rupert taught Morgan's Ryan O. how to fish, earning everyone's respect. Morgan won the Reward Challenge by retrieving rungs from the water and building a ladder, so they could place an idol at the top of a platform. For their victory, Morgan earned hygiene supplies, their first piece of the treasure map, and the right to steal a bag of rice from Drake. Morgan's next victory came during the Immunity Challenge, a contest based on drinking two different foods blended together. Michelle's failure to strategically feign weakness at the Immunity Challenge prompted Drake to vote her off in retaliation.

In Episode 6, Drake accused Shawn of having a lousy work ethic. Drake's prizes for winning a cannon-firing Reward Challenge included a grill, lobsters, steaks, and cooking spices. Morgan rebounded and won the Immunity Challenge by astutely assigning Drake competitor Rupert to shoulder all of the weight in a pole-balancing competition. Drake member Trish's attempt to form an alliance against Rupert backfired when Rupert found out about it, and organized a counteralliance to vote her out.

Episode 7 began with a twist, as the exiled castaways returned to form the Outcast tribe, which competed against Drake and Morgan in a three-way jailbreak Reward Challenge. The Outcasts won the challenge, sending *both* Drake and Morgan to Tribal Council, where Drake jettisoned Shawn. Morgan's Osten also quit the game, becoming the first contestant on *Survivor* to leave of his own accord.

Episode 8 began with the Outcast tribe conducting its own Tribal Council. Exiled Burton was voted back *into* the game with former tribe Drake, and Lill returned to compete as a renewed member of Morgan. Instead of a Reward Challenge, there was a member merger, as Drake and Morgan united to form the Balboa tribe. Burton won a breath-holding Immunity Challenge, and Andrew fell victim to an alliance and was voted out at Balboa's first Tribal Council.

Burton caught a stingray, providing food for the tribe in Episode 9. Rupert won a slingshot Reward Challenge, but passed his breakfast reward to Burton, who invited Lill to join him. While breakfasting together, Burton and Lill conspired against Rupert, biting the hand that had fed them. Rupert won a pirate trivia Immunity Challenge, and Ryan was the next Balboa tribe member voted out.

In Episode 10, Burton and Lill won the Reward Challenge, an obstacle course set on a pirate ship. They earned a luxury day at sea, although Burton chose to re-gift his reward to Jon. Next, Burton won a blowgun-shooting Immunity Challenge. Rupert was stunned to learn that he was the next castaway voted out of the game.

In Episode 11, Sandra framed Christa for having spilled the tribe's bucket of fish, when in fact Sandra was the one who'd done it. In a twist, the Reward Challenge incorporated the contestants' loved ones in the contest, with each standing on a plank. Every time a tribe member's answer to Jeff Probst's question matched their loved one's, that contestant could select *any other* member's loved one to take a step forward on the plank. The last loved one standing would get to spend the night with the winning castaway. Jon's bogus story about his grandmother's death caused Burton to let Jon's loved one win, thus earning Jon (aka Jonny Fairplay) a place in *Survivor* infamy. Darrah won a word-puzzle Immunity Challenge, and Jon's "dead grandmother" strategy paid off again, as he was spared, leaving Tijuana to be voted out at Tribal Council.

Darrah, Lill, and Jon won a water obstacle course Reward Challenge, earning a spa retreat in Episode 12. Darrah also won her second consecutive Immunity Challenge, in a musket-shooting competition. Christa was betrayed by Jon, and voted out.

In Episode 13, Burton won the Reward Challenge, which was a combination of previous competitions, and he invited Jon to join him for a feast and a night in Panama City. Burton's surprise reward was a GMC truck. Darrah won her third straight Immunity Challenge in a competition to release planks by using corks and keys. At Tribal Council, the women turned against the men, and Burton was voted out.

Episode 14's Immunity Challenge was a pirate and survival trivia contest, in which the jury competed together as one team. The jury won, meaning *none* of the Survivors had immunity at the next Tribal Council. Darrah's strength proved to be her undoing, as her threatened tribemates voted her out at the first of two Tribal Councils. After an emotional ceremony for the eliminated castaways, Lillian won the Immunity Challenge by balancing on a raft at sea the longest, and Jonny Fairplay was voted out at the second Tribal Council. The jury reconvened to weigh the merits of finalists Lillian and Sandra, and by six-to-one vote, they chose Sandra Diaz-Twine as the sole Survivor and winner of $1 million.

SURVIVOR: ALL-STARS

(Season 8)

GENRE Competition

FIRST TELECAST 2/1/2004

LAST TELECAST	5/13/2004
NETWORK	CBS
AIR TIME	Thursday, 8:00 p.m.
EPISODE STYLE	Story Arc
TALENT	Jeff Probst (Host)
CAST	Amber Brkich (Winner—Chaboga Mogo); Rob Mariano (Runner-up—Chaboga Mogo); Rupert Boneham (Winner—America's Tribal Council, 14th eliminated—Chaboga Mogo); Jenna Lewis (13 eliminated—Chaboga Mogo); Tom Buchanan (12th eliminated—Chaboga Mogo); Shii Ann Huang (11th eliminated—Chaboga Mogo); Alicia Calaway (10th eliminated—Chaboga Mogo); Kathy Vavrick-O'Brien (9th eliminated—Chaboga Mogo); Lex van den Berghe (8th eliminated—Chaboga Mogo); Jerri Manthey (7th eliminated—Chapera); Ethan Zohn (6th eliminated—Mogo Mogo); Colby Donaldson (5th eliminated—Mogo Mogo); Sue Hawk (quit); Richard Hatch (4th eliminated—Mogo Mogo); Rob Cesternino (3rd eliminated—Chapera); Jenna Morasca (quit); Rudy Boesch (2nd eliminated—Saboga); Tina Wesson (1st eliminated—Saboga)
PRODUCTION COMPANIES	Mark Burnett Productions; Castaway Television Productions, Inc.; Survivor Productions LLC
CREATED BY	Charlie Parsons
EXECUTIVE PRODUCERS	Mark Burnett; Charlie Parsons
CO-EXECUTIVE PRODUCER	Tom Shelly

The best and most popular castaways from the first seven seasons of *Survivor* reconvened in a remote area near Panama to compete in *Survivor: All-Stars*. With eighteen competitors, the group was divided into three tribes—Saboga, Mogo Mogo, and Chapera—

in Episode 1. Sue distanced herself from her Chapera tribemates by refusing to help start a fire, while Saboga's Rudy and Rupert forged an early alliance. The first Immunity Challenge was identical to the one that kicked off Season 1: a water race to retrieve fire, bring it back to land, and light torches. Mogo Mogo's Richard "let it all hang out" again as he competed naked. Saboga finished in third place, and Tina was the first victim.

In Episode 2, each tribe received a mysterious box sealed with three padlocks. Saboga earned blankets for winning the Reward Challenge, in which five logs retrieved from the sea were used as ladder rungs to reach a final platform. Saboga agreed to trade their blankets for flint, a cooking pot, and a clue to help find the key to the first padlock on the lockbox, which they later learned contained rice. This trading exchange enabled all three tribes to receive the same reward. Saboga wasn't so lucky in the Immunity Challenge. They finished last in a competition to free a boat from the ocean floor, bail the water out, and paddle it to shore. At Tribal Council, Saboga voted Rudy out due to his advanced age and limited physical abilities.

Ethan tried to rival Rupert as Saboga's top fisherman in Episode 3. Mogo Mogo's Richard was bitten by a shark—and retaliated by biting it back. Chapera won the Reward Challenge by building the best shelter, thus earning mats, blankets, wine, and a clue to a lockbox key. For finishing second, Mogo Mogo received a key clue. During the challenge, Rob Mariano caught Amber's fancy. Later, Jenna Morasca shocked the contestants by opting out of the game, so she could tend to her ailing mother. The Immunity Challenge and Tribal Council were canceled.

During a storm in Episode 4, romance bloomed between Chapera's Rob M. and Amber, while Saboga's faulty shelter caused them to endure the worst of it. Chapera received a "Survival Bathroom" for winning a Reward Challenge matching game. Later, Chapera lost the Immunity Challenge, a contest in which one tribe member guided the other blindfolded tribemates to find and assemble pieces to a cube puzzle. Chapera's Rob Cesternino was voted out at Tribal Council.

Mogo Mogo won a Reward Challenge raft rescue, earning themselves fishing equipment and a clue to a lockbox key in Episode 5. As a consequence of losing the Reward Challenge, remaining members of Saboga merged into the Mogo Mogo and Chapera tribes. Chapera won the Immunity Challenge by crossing balance beams over water and stealing twenty flags from the opposing tribe's stash. At the Mogo Mogo's Tribal Council, the tribe voted off Richard.

In Episode 6, Chapera lovebirds Rob M. and Amber approached newcomers Rupert and Jenna Lewis about forming an alliance. Prior to the Reward Challenge, Sue complained about being inappropriately grazed by a naked Richard during the previous challenge, and abruptly quit the game. Mogo Mogo earned a food basket for winning a catapult Reward Challenge. Given Sue's unexpected departure, the Immunity Challenge and Tribal Council were canceled.

Jerri's poor attitude began to wear on her Mogo Mogo tribemates in Episode 7. Thanks to Rupert's motivational speech, Chapera won the boat-based Reward Challenge, earning them a one-day yacht excursion. Chapera was given the opportunity to invite Mogo Mogo's Kathy into their tribe, thus sparing her from elimination. At Tribal Council, Mogo Mogo blindsided Colby, voting him off because he was perceived as too much of a threat.

In Episode 8, Chapera was awarded Mogo Mogo's grill, fishing sling, and a bag of rice for winning a log-rolling Reward Challenge. Back at camp, Chapera's Rob and Amber shared their first kiss, and Rupert and Rob showed the value of their new sling by each snaring a slew of fish. Chapera won immunity in a target-shooting challenge, using a combination of blowgun, spear, and bow and arrow. Ethan was voted out by Mogo Mogo, eliminating the game's last reigning sole Survivor.

Episode 9 was a recap of highlights from the season's previous episodes.

Instead of participating in a Reward Challenge in Episode 10, the two tribes gathered for a picnic, after which the members were randomly realigned to one of two tribes, and the tribes switched camps. The new Mogo Mogo tribe later triumphed in an Immunity Challenge based on *Survivor* history, and Chapera ousted lazy Jerri at Tribal Council.

In Episode 11, Rupert invited Jenna and Amber on a helicopter excursion after winning an underwater, "musical chairs" Reward Challenge using colored pots. Upon their return, the two tribes merged to form Chaboga Mogo. Kathy and Rob won joint immunity in an underwater breath-holding challenge. At Tribal Council, Rob helped vote Lex out of the game, despite having earnestly told him, "I won't stick a knife in your back."

In Episode 12, Alicia, Amber, Rob, and Shii Ann conquered a difficult obstacle course to earn the right to see videos from their loved ones back home. Rob defeated his teammates in a puzzle-solving challenge, earning immunity. He traded the right to watch a video from his loved ones in exchange for allowing his teammates to read letters from their loved ones. Kathy tried in vain to cobble together a new alliance, but she got voted out at Tribal Council.

Rupert won the Reward Challenge in Episode 13 by best predicting the tribe's answers to questions about his fellow castaways. For his reward, he took his tribe to a restaurant and selected each member's meal. He chose the steak for himself and, in a snub, cold rice for Shii Ann. Shii Ann staved off certain elimination by winning the water bucket Immunity Challenge. Alicia, who had rejected Shii's earlier overtures to form an alliance, became the next victim at Tribal Council.

Episode 14 featured a visit from the castaways' loved ones. Tom's son earned the right to spend time with his father by winning a disgusting food–eating competition. As an additional reward, Tom invited Rob and Rob's brother to join them. He later won the Immunity Challenge, which involved lighting a fuse using a teeter-totter with a water bucket as a counterweight. Fate finally caught up with Shii Ann at Tribal Council, as she was eliminated from the game.

Rob won the Reward Challenge, which was a combination of previous challenges, earning him a Chevy Colorado in Episode 15. He was also rewarded with the opportunity to invite his sweetheart, Amber, to join him at a drive-in movie. Later, he narrowly defeated Amber in the Immunity Challenge, a word puzzle based on the seventeen tribe names from previous *Survivor* seasons. At Tribal Council, Rob and Amber broke their promise to Tom, and helped vote him out of the game.

Episode 16 featured a surprise celebratory breakfast for the final four All-Star castaways, who appeared locked into teams of two: Rupert and Jenna versus Amber and Rob. Amber won the first Immunity Challenge by finding rungs within a maze, then building a ladder to climb to the top of a tower. Jenna turned on her teammate at the first of two Tribal Councils, and Rupert was voted off. Rob won the final Immunity Challenge, an endurance test to keep his hand on an idol for the longest time. He and Amber conspired to vote Jenna out of the game. The jury assembled to cross-examine Amber and Rob, and by a narrow four-to-three vote, named Amber the sole All-Star Survivor and the winner of $1 million. Before the vote was read, Rob proposed marriage to Amber, and she accepted. Also during the finale, host Jeff Probst announced that the home audience had played "America's Tribal Council," and voted to give one of the All-Stars another $1 million. Viewers declared Rupert Boneham their favorite Survivor, and he also won a check for $1 million.

SURVIVOR: VANUATU— ISLANDS OF FIRE

(Season 9)

GENRE	Competition
FIRST TELECAST	9/16/2004
FIRST TELECAST	12/12/2004
NETWORK	CBS
AIR TIME	Thursday, 8:00 p.m.
EPISODE STYLE	Story Arc
TALENT	Jeff Probst (Host)
CAST	Chris Daugherty (Winner); Twila Tanner (Runner-up—Alinta); Scott Cloud Lee (16th eliminated—Alinta); Eliza Orlins (15th eliminated—Alinta); Julie Berry (14th eliminated—Alinta); Ami Cusack (13th eliminated—Alinta); Leann Slaby (12th eliminated—Alinta); Chad Crittenden (11th eliminated—Alinta); Lea Masters (10th eliminated—Alinta); Rory Freeman (9th eliminated—Alinta); John Kenney (8th eliminated—Lopevi); Lisa Keiffer (7th eliminated—Yasur); Travis Sampson (6th eliminated—Yasur); Brady Finta (5th eliminated—Lopevi); Mia Galeotalanza (4th eliminated—Yasur); John Palyok (3rd eliminated—Lopevi); Dolly Neely (2nd eliminated—Yasur); Brook Geraghty (1st eliminated—Lopevi)
PRODUCTION COMPANIES	Mark Burnett Productions; Castaway Television Productions, Inc.; Survivor Productions LLC
CREATED BY	Charlie Parsons

EXECUTIVE PRODUCERS   Mark Burnett; Charlie Parsons
CO-EXECUTIVE PRODUCER   Tom Shelly

Upon arriving at the volcanic island of Vanuatu, the eighteen castaways were met by native warriors, who slaughtered a pig and smeared its blood on the men's faces. Brady successfully retrieved a spiritual stone from atop a pole smeared with pig fat, which supposedly would bring him good luck. Then the warriors divided the castaways into tribes by gender: Lopevi for the men, and Yasur for the women. At the Lopevi camp, Chad revealed that he had a prosthetic foot. Yasur received flint and the first immunity by completing an obstacle course and igniting a wok. Despite losing the challenge for his tribe, Chris got a shocking reprieve when an alliance voted off Brook instead.

In Episode 2, Yasur earned pillows, blankets, and a hammock for winning a Reward Challenge, in which the tribe members had to cross over one another on a narrow beam suspended above water and leading to a final platform. Back at camp, Twila and Dolly formed an alliance, bucking the older-versus-younger trend that had been developing. Lopevi finally tasted victory, and received flint, in the Immunity Challenge, which involved a guide leading blindfolded tribemates to find and piece together a puzzle, then climb to the top of an observation deck. At Tribal Council, Yasur decided that Dolly was too much of a threat, and voted her out of the game.

Lopevi won fishing gear after escaping locked cages in Episode 3's Reward Challenge. John K. won an Immunity Challenge by digging up puzzle-like rungs in the sand, forming them into a ladder, and climbing to freedom. Host Jeff Probst announced that both tribes would have a Tribal Council, and that John's victory allowed him to grant immunity to one of the Yasur women. John K. gave immunity to Ami, and John P. and Mia were the next two players voted off.

In Episode 4, the Yasur women accused Lisa of breaking her alliance to vote for Mia, while the Lopevi elders were pleased that their plan to vote off the younger players was working so far. For winning a matching Reward Challenge, Yasur received twenty-four hours of services from a Vanuatu tribesman, who taught them several survivalist tips. Yasur also won the Immunity Challenge, a brainteaser puzzle involving tile patterns. Brady became the latest Lopevi youngster ousted.

In Episode 5, the tribes appointed Lea (aka "Sarge") and Scout as their respective tribal leaders. These two became the team captains for a tribe reshuffling; ultimately only Rory, Travis, Julie, and Twila swapped tribes. The new Lopevi tribe earned a waterfall excursion for winning an ocean relay race Reward Challenge. The new additions to both tribes found it difficult to ingratiate themselves with their opposing-gender tribemates. Lopevi won the Immunity Challenge by retrieving canoe parts from the jungle, assembling them, and paddling the canoe out to retrieve a flag. At Tribal Council, the mostly female Yasur chose to vote off Travis, particularly after he tried to maintain communication with opposing tribesman Chris.

Lopevi won steak and eggs in Episode 6's Reward Challenge by successfully corralling ten pigs into their tribe's pen. Back at the Lopevi camp, Julie raised eyebrows by sunbathing bottomless. Lopevi also won the Immunity Challenge by transporting pieces of a tiki through a water obstacle course and reassembling it back on shore. Rory managed to dodge elimination at Yasur's Tribal Council, as untrustworthy Lisa was sent home.

In Episode 7, Yasur earned a trip to the Vanuatu Home Café by winning the Reward Challenge, which involved transporting coconut juice through an obstacle course. Yasur narrowly won a slingshot Immunity Challenge. Lopevi elected to vote out dangerous but lazy John K.

In Episode 8, Julie tried to flirt her way into good standing with Lopevi, while Rory resented getting saddled with most of the labor in female-heavy Yasur. Lopevi won a water-relay Reward Challenge and received cookies, cake, and milk. Then the two tribes merged into a new tribe called Alinta. Lea won immunity in a flag-retrieval swimming competition, leaving everyone at camp uncertain about their alliances. The all-female Yasur alliance ultimately conspired to vote out Rory.

Leann won a Vanuatu culture and history question-and-answer Reward Challenge in Episode 9. As her reward, she invited Julie for chicken wings and Champagne at the base of a volcano. Ami won the Immunity Challenge, a test to replicate a mosaic pattern using tiles. Lea was the next victim of the female voting bloc.

Episode 10 began with Scout approaching Chad and Chris about forming an alliance. For the Reward Challenge, the contestants divided into teams for the purpose of navigating one of their members—the "Sacrificial Lamb"—through a tricky obstacle course. For winning the challenge, the team of Ami, Chad, Chris, and Eliza earned a trip to another island, where a fancy meal awaited them. Twila won a pole-holding Immunity Challenge. Chad was voted out at Tribal Council.

Episode 11 began as the castaways communicated for one minute with their loved ones via the Internet. By winning a memory-based Reward Challenge, which tested their knowledge of the results of the previous season's challenges, Eliza communicated with her mother for a full hour. Later, host Jeff Probst revealed that the contestants' loved ones were already on the island, and he brought them out for a reunion. Then the loved ones joined the Survivors for a blindfolded puzzle-solving Immunity Challenge, which was won by Ami and her girlfriend. Chris's fear of elimination was never realized, as the women altered their strategy and voted off Leann instead of another man.

In Episode 12, a furious Ami accused Twila of breaking rank to vote off a woman, even though Twila had sworn that she wouldn't. Eliza won a water obstacle course Reward Challenge and received a Pontiac G6. For finishing second and third, Ami and Chris joined Eliza at a resort with showers, food, and real beds. Chris earned immunity by winning a customized shuffleboard competition, landing metal discs as close as possible to drawings of islands. Ami became the next Tribal Council victim, largely due to her powerful status as the head of the former female alliance.

Julie won Episode 13's Reward Challenge, which was a combination of competitions from previous challenges. She chose Chris to join her for a horseback trek and picnic, during which she tried to talk him out of his alliance with Scout and Twila. Eliza won the Immunity Challenge by completing a series of tasks based on a story host Jeff had told about legendary Vanuatu chief Roy Matta. Chris found himself the swing vote between Twila, Scout, Eliza, and Julie; he cast the deciding ballot to eliminate Julie.

The first Immunity Challenge in Episode 14 was an eight-level vertical maze, which Chris completed while gathering tiles to spell out the words *final three*. The first of two Tribal Councils was Eliza's last, as she was voted out. Chris proceeded to win the final Immunity Challenge endurance test by maintaining a warrior pose while holding a bow and arrow. Realizing he stood a better chance in the jury vote against the unlikable Twila, Chris cast his deciding vote to eliminate Scout. The jury convened for the final deliberation between Chris and Twila, and named Chris the sole Survivor and the winner of $1 million.

SURVIVOR: PALAU

(Season 10)

GENRE	Competition
FIRST TELECAST	2/17/2005
LAST TELECAST	5/15/2005
NETWORK	CBS
AIR TIME	Thursday, 8:00 p.m.
EPISODE STYLE	Story Arc
TALENT	Jeff Probst (Host)
CAST	Tom Westman (Winner—Koror); Katie Gallagher (Runner-up—Koror); Ian Rosenberger (16th eliminated—Koror); Jennifer Lyon (15th eliminated—Koror); Caryn Groedel (14th eliminated—Koror); Gregg Carey (13th eliminated—Koror); Stephenie LaGrossa (12th eliminated—Ulong/Koror); Janu Tornell (11th eliminated—Koror); Coby Archa (10th eliminated—Koror); Bobby Jon Drinkard (9th eliminated—Ulong); Ibrehem Rahman (8th eliminated—Ulong); James Miller (7th eliminated—Ulong); Angie Jakusz (6th eliminated—Ulong); Willard Smith (5th eliminated—Koror); Kimberly Mullen (4th eliminated—Ulong); Jeff Wilson (3rd eliminated—Ulong); Ashlee Ashby (2nd eliminated—Ulong); Jolanda Jones (1st eliminated—Ulong); Wanda Shirk (unpicked); Jonathan Libby (unpicked)
PRODUCTION COMPANIES	Mark Burnett Productions; Castaway Television Productions, Inc.; Survivor Productions LLC
CREATED BY	Charlie Parsons

EXECUTIVE PRODUCERS	Mark Burnett; Charlie Parsons, Tom Shelly
CO-EXECUTIVE PRODUCERS	Vittoria Cacciatore; Kevin Greene,
	Douglas McCallie, Conrad Riggs; Holly M. Wofford
DIRECTOR	Mark Burnett

To kick off Season 10, twenty castaways were sent to the island nation Palau. The first male and female castaways to reach the beach from the boat—Jolanda and Ian—became tribe leaders of Ulong and Koror. They each selected one remaining castaway to join their tribe, who in turn chose someone else, who chose someone else, and so on, until only two castaways remained—Jonathan Libby and Wanda Shirk—who were eliminated. The Immunity/Reward Challenge was a land and water obstacle course filled with supplies, which would slow the tribes down if they stopped to pick them up. Koror won the race and immunity, but capsized their canoe and lost all of their fire-making supplies. Meanwhile, Ulong chose tribe leader Jolanda as the first castaway to be voted off.

In Episode 2, Koror found their campground infested with rats, then was drenched by a storm after failing to build ample shelter. Ulong's Kimberly and Jeff got romantic, as did Koror's Gregg and Jennifer. Ulong won fins, a mask, and a fishing sling in the Reward Challenge, a water gauntlet where tribe members had to cross over floating objects to retrieve ten flags, while the opposing tribe tried to knock them off with swinging sandbags. In the Immunity Challenge, the tribes dragged foot lockers across the ocean floor and opened them, releasing mess kits containing letters written in Morse code. Koror won the challenge by translating the code into the word *immunity*. At Tribal Council, Ulong voted off Ashlee, whose heart didn't seem to be in the game.

Tensions flared between Koror's Caryn and Katie in Episode 3, while Ulong blamed their challenge failures on Jeff and Kimberly's distracting relationship. The Reward Challenge featured one-on-one and two-on-two battles to retrieve floating safety rings and bring them back to the tribe's buoy. Ulong snagged three rings to win the challenge, which earned them a sewing kit. In the Immunity Challenge, the tribes had to walk around a large oval course in shallow water, while each member carried a twenty-pound backpack. If anyone dropped out, they had to hand their backpack to a fellow tribe member. Koror won their third straight challenge by catching up to the other tribe and "tagging" them. Ulong mercifully ousted Jeff, who had asked to be voted off after injuring his ankle.

In Episode 4, Tree Mail informed each tribe to pick one member as a representative. Koror chose Ian, while the unraveling Ulong eventually settled on James. Koror won the Reward Challenge by building the best bathroom, and received a custom shelter built by the *Survivor* production team. In the Immunity Challenge, individual tribe members faced off "sumo style," using duffel bags to knock each other into the water. Koror won immunity by knocking down six Ulong members, sending Ulong to their fourth straight Tribal Council, where Kim was voted off because of her poor work ethic.

Episode 5 featured two Tribal Councils, one for each tribe. For winning the sunken sake bottle salvage Reward Challenge, Koror witnessed Ulong's council, where Angie was voted off after Ibrehem surprisingly was given immunity, despite single-handedly losing the challenge. At Koror's first Tribal Council, an alliance between Gregg, Jennifer, and Coby conspired to vote off fifty-seven-year-old Willard, whose age made him a physical liability.

In Episode 6, Ulong won the target-shooting Reward Challenge and received a jellyfish snorkeling excursion, along with Pringles potato chips and mai tais. Meanwhile, Koror's Janu suffered an emotional breakdown during a vicious storm. During the Immunity Challenge, the tribes were given twenty minutes to build a fortress and hide the opposing team's flag somewhere inside it. Koror amazingly won their fifth straight Immunity Challenge by being the first to storm the other tribe's fortress, find their flag, and hoist it up a flagpole. Ulong's James got the boot at Tribal Council for repeatedly letting his tribe down during challenges.

By Episode 7, Ulong was down to three members. Meanwhile, Koror had a feast after Ian retrieved a giant clam, and Tom speared a shark. Koror also won an airdrop of supplies during the Reward Challenge by building the best distress signal, which read "Got Food?" Koror won yet another Immunity Challenge for completing an underwater puzzle, sending Ulong to Tribal Council, where Ibrehem fell victim to Bobby Jon and Stephenie's alliance.

In Episode 8, Coby complained he was being ignored by Koror, despite doing all the work. The Reward Challenge was an eating competition of the Palauan delicacy *balut,* or partially formed duckling eggs. Koror won the challenge, receiving water and personal hygiene supplies. The Immunity Challenge was a word puzzle, and the pieces had to be retrieved from the ocean. Koror continued its winning streak by spelling out "Victory at Sea." Since Ulong had only two members left, their Tribal Council was an individual Immunity Challenge, where Stephenie ousted Bobby Jon by being the first to start a fire.

In Episode 9, Stephenie received a Tree Mail inviting her to join Koror's tribe. Upon her arrival, Coby took her aside and secretly revealed all of the alliances. Stephenie divulged Coby's information to the women in the tribe. The Immunity Challenge tested how long each castaway could stand on a perch under the hot sun while being tempted with sweet treats. Tom won the challenge, and the tribe voted troublesome Coby off the island.

Two new teams formed for Episode 10's Reward Challenge, which required building a tower in the water to retrieve a flag and bring it back to the beach. The winning team was Tom, Caryn, Gregg, and Janu, who enjoyed a Palauan feast. In a show of solidarity, Gregg smuggled some of the food to the losing team. The Immunity Challenge tested who could stay inside a steel cage in the water the longest as the tide rolled in. Tom won the challenge, and debated with the other castaways whether to vote off Janu or Stephenie. Janu shocked everyone at Tribal Council by setting down her torch before anyone could vote, thus eliminating herself from the game.

Episode 11 featured a mystery auction for the Reward Challenge, where each Survivor received $500 to bid on items without knowing what they were beforehand. For the Immunity Challenge, the Survivors hurled coconuts at ceramic tiles, which were color-coded to represent each castaway. Ian won the challenge by being the first to shatter all five of his tiles. At Tribal Council, Stephenie was the twelfth castaway voted off the island.

The Episode 12 Reward Challenge was a question-and-answer contest about Palauan history and culture. Gregg won the challenge, and selected Katie and Jennifer to join him for a feast, hot showers, and massages aboard a luxury yacht, where they were greeted by Gregg's best friend, Katie's brother-in-law, and Jennifer's sister. Later, the six of them swam with dolphins. The Immunity Challenge was a combination of previous challenges, won by Ian in a last-second shootout with Tom. Caryn fully expected to be voted off, but Ian's secret realignment of alliances caused a stunned Gregg to get the heave-ho.

As Episode 13 began, Ian and Tom feared that a female alliance would spell doom for one of them. The Reward Challenge required the Survivors to paddle rafts to gather mileage markers and place them under signs of cities whose distance from Palau matched the number on the marker. Ian was the first to correctly match the mileage to the cities, winning a brand-new Chevrolet Corvette. In the Immunity Challenge, the castaways traversed a watercourse and noted the arrangement of various icons, which they then had to replicate on a blank grid back on the beach. Tom was the first to arrange his grid correctly, earning immunity. Ian was granted a reprieve as the female alliance turned on Caryn, voting her off the island.

Episode 14 started with three of the final four castaways agreeing to vote Tom off as soon as he lost a challenge. The first Immunity Challenge had the Survivors scale a tower and hoist a flag, retrieve and crack a combination box, then hoist the second flag. Tom won the challenge, and Jennifer was eliminated after a tiebreaking fire-starting challenge at Tribal Council. The second and final Immunity Challenge required the three remaining Survivors to hold on to a bobbing buoy in the ocean. After several excruciating hours, Katie let go of her buoy, then Ian agreed to let go if Tom took *Katie* to the final two. Tom agreed, and Ian was the sixteenth castaway eliminated. At the final Tribal Council, the jury grilled Tom and Katie on their strategies and integrity. They ultimately selected Tom as the sole Survivor and winner of $1 million.

RATINGS An astounding 23.66 million viewers tuned in for the premiere episode. Roughly more than 3.6 million viewers tuned in to the premiere of the previous season, *Survivor: Vanuatu*.

SURVIVOR: GUATEMALA— THE MAYAN EMPIRE
(Season 11)

GENRE	Competition
FIRST TELECAST	9/15/2005
LAST TELECAST	12/11/2005
NETWORK	CBS
AIR TIME	Thursday, 8:00 p.m.

EPISODE STYLE	Story Arc
TALENT	Jeff Probst (Host)
CAST	Danni Boatwright (Winner—Nakum, Yaxha, Xhakum); Stephenie LaGrossa (Runner-up—Yaxha, Nakum, Xhakum); Rafe Judkins (16th eliminated—Yaxha, Nakum, Xhakum); Lydia Morales (15th eliminated—Yaxha, Nakum, Xhakum); Cindy Hall (14th eliminated—Nakum, Xhakum); Judd Sergeant IV (13th eliminated—Nakum, Xhakum); Gary Hogeboom (12th eliminated—Yaxha, Xhakum); Jamie Newton (11th eliminated—Yaxha, Nakum, Xhakum); Bobby Jon Drinkard (10th eliminated—Nakum, Yaxha, Xhakum); Brandon Bellinger (9th eliminated—Nakum, Yaxha, Xhakum); Amy O'Hara (8th eliminated—Yaxha); Brian Corridan (7th eliminated—Yaxha); Margaret Bobonich (6th eliminated—Nakum); Blake Towsley (5th eliminated—Nakum, Yaxha); Brooke Struck (4th eliminated—Nakum); Brianna Varela (3rd eliminated—Yaxha); Morgan McDevitt (2nd eliminated—Yaxha); Jim Lynch (1st eliminated—Nakum)
PRODUCTION COMPANIES	Mark Burnett Productions; Castaway Television Productions, Inc.; Survivor Productions LLC
CREATED BY	Charlie Parsons
EXECUTIVE PRODUCERS	Mark Burnett; Charlie Parsons; Tom Shelly

Season 11 placed eighteen castaways in the Guatemalan jungle for the toughest version of the show yet. *Survivor: Palau* contestants Stephenie LaGrossa and Bobby Jon Drinkard returned and were given a second chance to play the game.

In Episode 1, the castaways were split into two tribes, Nakum and Yaxha. The contestants were surprised to learn that two former Survivors had returned to play the game again: Bobby Jon and Stephenie from *Survivor Palau,* who joined the Nakum and Yaxha tribes, respectively. The tribes competed in an eleven-mile jungle hike, which Nakum won, earning the better campsite and flint. Then many of the Nakum tribe members fell ill, which gave Yaxha an advantage in the Immunity Challenge, which involved paddling boats, hauling them up a hill, and lighting a "victory cauldron." Nakum lost and went to the season's first Tribal Council, where Jim was the first voted out of the tribe.

In Episode 2, Nakum won the Reward Challenge, a tag-team race consisting of gathering bags while hanging from a giant web over a pool of water. The tribe picked up fishing gear, while Blake earned the title of hero. Nakum won the Immunity Challenge, where Danni exposed Gary's secret of being an ex-NFL quarterback, which he denied. At Tribal Council, Yaxha eliminated Morgan.

During the Episode 3 Reward Challenge, blindfolded tribe members followed voice commands from a sighted caller, searching the area for the tent pieces. Once all of the pieces were obtained, the blindfolds were removed and the tribes assembled the tents. Nakum won the challenge, earning blankets and other luxuries. The Immunity Challenge was based on the ancient Mayan game of court ball. The first tribe to throw a ball through a hoop scored. After losing the challenge, Yaxha went to Tribal Council, where they unanimously voted out Brianna.

Instead of a Reward Challenge in Episode 4, tribe members answered questions in an attempt to get to know one another. The castaway whose name appeared the most on the parchment received a gift. Danni and Jamie were most in need of nourishment, and were given an apple. Smelly Gary and Bobby Jon earned a bush shower to clean up. Judd, Margaret, Gary, and Amy were elected to leave the challenge area for a picnic. Jeff shuffled the tribes while they were away. Stephenie, Jamie, Rafe, Lydia, Brooke, Cindy, Margaret, and Judd comprised the new Nakum. The new Yaxha included Bobby Jon, Blake, Brandon, Danni, Brian, Gary, and Amy. During the Immunity Challenge, the tribes paddled out to retrieve three bags filled with Mayan war clubs, then raced to shore to toss the clubs at targets. Yaxha was the first tribe to break all three targets. At Tribal Council, Nakum eliminated Brooke from the game.

Nakum suffered a humiliating loss in Episode 5, as Jamie couldn't get the complicated challenge started. Yaxha took a crocodile-proof cage back to camp, which allowed them to swim safely. The tribes reconvened for the Immunity Challenge, and Jeff explained that working together as a unit, each tribe would be divided into two groups of three holding a catch net. The remaining tribe member acted as a ball launcher from a catapult. The castaways had to catch the balls in the net, and the first tribe to catch five won immunity. Yaxha's loss signaled the end for "golden boy" Blake, as he was eliminated.

The tribes split up into pairs to push a giant ball across a playing field in the Episode 6 Reward Challenge. A point was scored when a tribe pushed the ball across their opponent's end zone. Before the challenge began, host Jeff Probst said both tribes would go to Tribal Council, and one person from each tribe would be sent home. Also, the Reward Challenge winners would face off in an individual Immunity Challenge. Having won the barbecue Reward Challenge, Nakum competed for individual immunity. The tribe members collected three bags of letter tiles, emptied them on a table to spell out the two-word phrase "ancient ruin." Rafe won immunity. At the double-elimination ceremony, Yaxha voted off Brian, while Nakum sent Margaret home.

During the Episode 7 Reward Challenge, the castaways spooled fabric from a pole onto their bodies. At each pole, another contestant joined them as they also got wrapped in the fabric. Yaxha crossed the finish line first, and won a zip-line trip through the jungle ending with a chocolate feast. For Danni's birthday, Yaxha invited Nakum to their camp for a pool party. At the Immunity Challenge, the tribes raced to uncover puzzle pieces. Nakum won the close competition. With Amy and Bobby Jon at risk, Yaxha voted out the weaker Amy. After the elimination, Yaxha was surprised to learn that the two tribes were merging.

In Episode 8, the newly merged Xhakum tribe discovered that somewhere in the jungle was a hidden immunity doll that could secure a player's safety until the final four. The Immunity Challenge featured a feast with a twist. Castaways had to balance a clay pot on their heads while standing on a podium, or they could skip the challenge to enjoy the feast. Jamie, Stephenie, Rafe, and Lydia opted for the feast, while all of the former members of the old Yaxha tribe, plus Judd and Cindy, participated in the challenge, which Gary won. While eating, Jamie revealed Nakum's plan to vote as one, picking off each of the four former Yaxha members. At tribal Council, Jamie's words rang true, as Brandon was eliminated.

Episode 9 issued a Reward Challenge, in which the castaways used an ancient Mayan weapon called an *atlatl* to sling an arrow at a huge target on the ground. Each castaway had only one throw. The contestant whose arrow landed closest to the target's center won a feast and a clue to the location of the hidden immunity idol. The unusual feast had diminishing returns. From first to last place, the meals decreased in size. Judd won first place: a steak and lobster dinner. He also picked two people—Stephenie and Bobby Jon—to join him at the open bar. While the clue indicated that the immunity idol was in a tree, Judd told his tribemates that it was on the ground. For the Immunity Challenge, the castaways had to untie wooden planks attached to a balance beam, then use them to move across a rope bridge. The final round required navigating across a knotted rope bridge. Jamie reached the finish line first, and earned immunity. Before Tribal Council, Gary caught Judd looking for the hidden idol in the trees and restructured his own hunt. Later, he surprised everyone by revealing the hidden idol, forcing the tribe to rethink their voting strategy. Bobby Jon was eliminated.

Everyone congratulated Gary on his newfound immunity in Episode 10. Danni, Judd, Gary, and Stephenie won the mud pit obstacle course Reward Challenge, earning a helicopter ride to a coffee banquet, plus videotaped messages from their loved ones. Gary tried his best to navigate the complicated tethered maze at the Immunity Challenge, but Rafe was victorious, and therefore safe from elimination. At Tribal Council, Jamie's constant paranoia convinced the majority to eliminate him instead of Gary.

For the Episode 11 Reward Challenge, each castaway had three hanging pots filled with corn, which were smashed by the contestants who correctly answered questions about Mayan culture and Guatemala. The castaway whose pot was the last one hanging won a natural hot-water waterfall retreat with a tropical feast and a full-body massage. Cindy won, and took Rafe along for her reward. For the Immunity Challenge, the castaways had to pay attention while a Mayan folklore story was read. A puzzle revealed a question about the story. A correct answer revealed a flag to be hung on the starting platform; while a wrong answer revealed a stick that had to be put into a fire. The competition between Gary and Rafe was close, but Rafe was the first castaway to hang all seven flags, winning individual immunity for the third time. At Tribal Council, Gary's luck finally ran out, and he was eliminated from the game.

The Survivor auction was featured in the Episode 12 Reward Challenge. Danni successfully bid on an envelope containing an advantage for the next Immunity Challenge. The castaways could also bid on a visit from their loved ones. Escalating prices forced tribemates to pool their money. Cindy's money helped Judd outbid Stephenie to earn an overnight reward with his wife. Judd was able to choose two other Survivors' loved ones to join them, while the three castaways without a loved one were exiled to the old Yaxha camp. Judd quickly picked Cindy and Stephenie. During the strategic Immunity Challenge, the castaways made moves, one at a time, on a giant multilevel playing board. Danni's envelope allowed her to switch places with any player, which helped her outmaneuver Stephenie to win the immunity necklace. At Tribal Council, Judd called the remaining castaways "scumbags," as he was blindsided and eliminated.

Episode 13 featured the much-awaited car reward challenge. Combining past challenges, players raced across a balance beam and untied three sets of macanas. The first three players moved on to the second round. At the second stage, the players tossed the macana to break a clay tile. The first two to break the tile moved on to the final stage. The third stage was a small Mayan calendar puzzle. After solving the puzzle, the players jumped into the primitive wooden cart, chopped the rope, and raced to the finish. Cindy won the challenge, but before she got her new car, she was given the option to give it up in order to award the other four players with a new car instead. After a moment's thought, she decided she could have it all, and took the car. She and Stephenie then drove to a barbecue feast at an archeological dig. During the Immunity Challenge, the castaways' hands and feet were bound in metal shackles while they had to unwind rope attached to poles. For the first time in two seasons, Stephenie won individual immunity. At Tribal Council, karma came knocking on Cindy's door, and she was forced to drive her new car home.

On the season finale, the castaways were visited by a group of native Mayans who performed a traditional blessing. For the first Immunity Challenge, the players faced the largest Survivor maze ever. Inside, they raced to collect colored puzzle pieces from six stations, then returned through the elaborate maze to the puzzle board, where they had to assemble the pieces to form one of three images. Rafe won the challenge. Back at camp, Stephenie convinced everyone but Rafe to eat the chicken from the earlier ceremony. Shortly afterward, they were bombarded by a torrential downpour. Lydia was eliminated at Tribal Council.

The next morning, the final three paid homage to the eliminated castaways, and headed to the final Immunity Challenge. They had to hold on to two ropes and balance on a wobbly platform for one hour. After the first hour, they each had to release one rope. After thirty more minutes, they released the other rope. The last person standing would win a spot in the final two. After ninety minutes, Danni emerged victorious. She cast the one and only vote to eliminate Rafe, who confessed Stephenie would get his vote. Rafe was in the minority at the end of the finale. The jury chose Danni as the winner in a six-to-one vote. She was the sole Survivor of Season 11, and the winner of $1 million.

SURVIVOR: PANAMA—EXILE ISLAND

(Season 12)

GENRE	Competition
FIRST TELECAST	2/2/2006
LAST TELECAST	5/14/2006
NETWORK	CBS
AIR TIME	Thursday, 8:00 p.m.
EPISODE STYLE	Story Arc
TALENT	Jeff Probst (Host)
CAST	Aras Baskauskas (Winner—Viveros, Casaya, Gitanos); Danielle DiLorenzo (Runner-up—Bayoneta, Casaya, Gitanos); Terry Dietz (14th eliminated—La Mina, Gitanos); Cirie Fields (13th eliminated—Casaya, Gitanos); Shane Powers (12th eliminated—La Mina, Casaya, Gitanos); Courtney Marit (11th eliminated—Bayoneta, Casaya, Gitanos); Bruce Kanegai (10th eliminated—La Mina, Casaya, Gitanos); Sally Schumann (9th eliminated—Bayoneta, La Mina, Gitanos); Austin Carty (8th eliminated—Viveros, La Mina, Gitanos); Nick Stanbury (7th eliminated—Viveros, La Mina, Gitanos); Dan Barry (6th eliminated—La Mina); Bobby Mason (5th eliminated—Viveros, Casaya); Ruth Marie Milliman (4th eliminated—Casaya, La Mina); Misty Giles (3rd eliminated—Bayoneta,

	La Mina); Melinda Hyder (2nd eliminated— Casaya); Tina Scheer (1st eliminated—Casaya)
PRODUCTION COMPANIES	Mark Burnett Productions; Castaway Television Productions, Inc.; Survivor Productions LLC
CREATED BY	Charlie Parsons
EXECUTIVE PRODUCERS	Mark Burnett; Charlie Parsons; Tom Shelly

A new set of castaways traveled to a previous show location, Panama, for Season 12's *Survivor: Panama—Exile Island.* This version of the game featured a twist; in every cycle, one or more players were sent to Exile Island, where they lived alone, without shelter or food, for days at a time. Hidden on Exile Island was a small immunity idol that its finder could use anytime up through the final four Tribal Council, to keep himself or another player safe from elimination. The game also started in a completely different way, with four tribes divided by gender and age.

In Episode 1, the first Reward Challenge occurred before the castaways could talk to one another. One member from each of the four tribes ran into the Exile Island jungle in search of an amulet hidden in a skull. The Bayoneta young women's tribe runner came up empty-handed, and after a game of Rock, Paper, Scissors, Misty was selected to go to Exile Island until the next morning's Immunity Challenge. There, the tribes raced over a wall, dove into the ocean, swam to a raft, and paddled to shore, where they solved a brainteaser puzzle, leading to immunity. The first three tribes to complete the task won immunity, but the older women of Casaya lost, and voted out Tina, the lumberjack, at the first Tribal Council.

In Episode 2, the four tribes became two. The new Casaya tribe comprised Danielle, Courtney, Aras, Shane, Cirie, Bobby, and Melinda. The new La Mina tribe was made up of Dan, Terry, Austin, Nick, Ruth Marie, Sally, and Misty. Bruce was not selected, and was sent to Exile Island, but would be immune at the next Tribal Council, where he'd replace whoever was eliminated. During the Reward Challenge, the tribes raced an obstacle course, and La Mina won fishing gear. At the Immunity Challenge, the teams transported a giant zombie head from the ocean to the beach on a boat that was filling with water and sinking. La Mina won again, and at Casaya's Tribal Council, Melinda was voted out.

In Episode 3, Bruce joined Casaya and taught them how to filter their water. At the Reward Challenge, three members of each tribe used slingshots to launch balls at four teammates perched on balance beams over the water. La Mina was the first tribe to catch five balls, winning a kerosene lantern, water canisters, blankets, pillows, rope, and a tarp. They also sent Bruce back to Exile Island until the Immunity Challenge. Casaya won the sand-digging Immunity Challenge. La Mina went to Tribal Council, where Misty was eliminated for being too smart.

In Episode 4, the tribes dove underwater to unclip puzzle pieces, which they brought back to shore to assemble into a picture for the Reward Challenge. Casaya won, earning a bathroom. They also sent La Mina's Terry to Exile Island, where he found the hidden immunity idol. For the Immunity Challenge, the castaways raced across a balance beam while carrying buckets to fill a drum with water until one team member could reach and release a flag. Casaya won the challenge. At Tribal Council, La Mina eliminated Ruth Marie.

For the Episode 5 Reward Challenge, each team picked one player to transport rice, beans, and fish from a boat to the shore. The food items, plus fish, were passed along until the final castaway put all of the goods in the correct bins. Casaya won the food, and sent Terry from La Mina to Exile Island. For the Immunity Challenge, the castaways rowed out into the water and gathered skull puzzle pieces from four coffins on the ocean floor. They brought the pieces back to shore, where they built a skull pyramid. La Mina won immunity, and the Casaya ladies voted off Bobby at Tribal Council.

The challenge in Episode 6 was both for a reward and immunity. Three castaways from each team raced into a field to pick up four puzzle pieces, which the other tribe members used to solve a spinning puzzle. La Mina's Dan couldn't complete the puzzle, so Casaya won immunity and a feast in a Panamanian fishing village. Casaya also banished Sally to Exile Island, but she didn't go to Tribal Council and also had immunity. The La Mina guys had to vote off one of their own, and Dan was eliminated.

The contestants merged to form the Gitano tribe in Episode 7, as La Mina arrived at Casaya's camp with firewood, food, and new buffs. Nick accidentally cut Bruce with the machete, causing him to fear he'd be the next to go. For the Immunity Challenge, the castaways had to wrap themselves around a pole and hang upside down for as long as possible. Terry won the challenge, while Nick was correct to assume he'd be voted off.

The castaways were divided into three teams of three for the Episode 8 Reward Challenge. Each team had a boat and one hundred coconuts. The teams raced to put coconuts in the other teams' boats, then paddle to a tribe flag to pick up a fishing net, which they used to carry their coconuts to a bin once back on shore. Aras, Sally, and Bruce won breakfast in bed, and sent Danielle and Austin to Exile Island. Before they went to the four-part immunity challenge, Sally was excited to hear that Terry had already found the hidden immunity idol. He also won immunity from that night's vote. The former Casaya members worked together to vote out Austin at Tribal Council.

Courtney, Bruce, Sally, and Terry won the flag-grabbing Reward Challenge in Episode 9. They sent Aras to Exile Island. They also ate peanut butter and jelly sandwiches, drank milk, and watched videos from their loved ones. Nurse Cirie had to check out Shane's rash, which had been caused by wetness. Hoping for relief, he took off his pants to air himself out. At the Immunity Challenge, the castaways were given the option to sit out and eat hamburgers, fries, and soda instead of competing. Only Aras, Sally, and Terry chose to compete in the strenuous memorization challenge. Terry, once again, won immunity. The Casaya alliance had to vote out Sally.

Bruce complained of severe abdominal pains caused by constipation in Episode 10. The castaways were quizzed on one another's questionnaires for the Reward Challenge. Cirie won, and invited Aras and Danielle along for her spa reward. She also picked Terry to go to Exile Island. Meanwhile, Bruce was taken away by a medical team, and Courtney was upset that the others had voted her "Most Annoying." The next morning, host Jeff Probst told the tribe that Bruce had been hospitalized and would serve as that day's elimination.

The tribe worried about Shane when he imagined that a small piece of wood was his BlackBerry in Episode 11. The castaways divided into two teams of three for the obstacle course Reward Challenge. Terry, Courtney, and Danielle sent Aras to Exile Island. They also earned a barbecue feast, plus the chance to take home a car at a slingshot competition. Terry won the new car. For the endurance Immunity Challenge, the castaways had to kneel on a plank over water while holding on to ropes connected to increasing weights. Terry won his fourth straight Immunity Challenge. Courtney was voted out at Tribal Council.

The Episode 12 Reward Challenge featured different elements of past challenges. Terry won, and earned a visit from a loved one. His wife, Trish, and Shane's son, Boston, accompanied him and Shane to a villa overnight. Terry sent Cirie's husband, H.B., back to camp, and Aras got a hug from his mom. Danielle had just a few seconds to talk to her mom, Denise, before going to Exile Island. Terry won the flag-raising Immunity Challenge, his fifth consecutive victory. At Tribal Council, the castaways were forced to vote out Shane.

The castaways argued in Episode 13, and the tension continued during the maze and memory competition Reward Challenge. Aras won a luxury yacht tour, and asked Cirie to join him. He picked Terry and Danielle to go to Exile Island. When Cirie returned to camp, she made her first fire, a feat for a castaway who was once afraid of leaves. Aras won the three-part Immunity Challenge. Danielle and Cirie each received two votes at Tribal Council, and were forced to compete in a fire-making competition to determine who would be eliminated. The challenge was the cliffhanger leading into the season finale.

On the season finale, Cirie's fire began strong, but Danielle's burned brighter, so she was saved. Aras, Danielle, and Terry comprised the final three. Terry won a tough race, earning a cot and a high-protein meal at the Reward Challenge. The next morning, the final three honored the eliminated castaways, then went to the final Immunity Challenge, where they had to balance on floating platforms that decreased in size every fifteen minutes. Terry fell off his platform first, and Aras and Danielle made a deal to bring each other to the final two. Aras jumped down, and Danielle kept her word, eliminating Terry. The jury voted Aras the $1 million winner.

SURVIVOR: COOK ISLANDS
(Season 13)

GENRE	Competition
FIRST TELECAST	9/14/2006
LAST TELECAST	12/17/2006
NETWORK	CBS
AIR TIME	Thursday, 8:00 p.m.
EPISODE STYLE	Story Arc
TALENT	Jeff Probst (Host)

CAST Yul Kwon (Winner—Puka Puka, Aitutaki, Aitutonga); Oscar "Ozzy" Lusth (Runner-up—Aitutaki, Aitutonga); Becky Lee (2nd Runner-up—Puka Puka, Aitutaki, Aitutonga); Sundra Oakley (17th eliminated—Manihiki, Aitutaki, Aitutonga); Adam Gentry (16th eliminated—Rarotonga, Aitutonga); Parvati Shallow (15th eliminated—Rarotonga, Aitutonga); Jonathan Penner (14th eliminated—Rarotonga, Aitutaki, Aitutonga); Candice Woodcock (13th eliminated—Rarotonga, Aitutaki, Aitutonga); Nathan "Nate" Gonzalez (12th eliminated—Manihiki, Rarotonga, Aitutonga); Jenny Guzon-Bae (11th eliminated—Puka Puka, Rarotonga); Rebecca Borman (10th eliminated—Manihiki, Rarotonga); Brad Virata (9th eliminated—Puka Puka, Rarotonga); Jessica "Flicka" Smith (8th eliminated—Rarotonga, Aitutaki); Cristina Coria (7th eliminated—Aitutaki, Rarotonga); Anh-Tuan "Cao Boi" Bui (6th eliminated—Puka Puka, Aitutaki); Stephannie Favor (5th eliminated—Manihiki, Rarotonga); J. P. Calderon (4th eliminated—Aitutaki, Rarotonga); Cecilia Mansilla (3rd eliminated—Aitutaki); Billy Garcia (2nd eliminated—Aitutaki); Sekou Bunch (1st eliminated—Manihiki)

PRODUCTION COMPANIES Mark Burnett Productions; Castaway Television Productions, Inc.; Survivor Productions LLC

CREATED BY Charlie Parsons

EXECUTIVE PRODUCERS Mark Burnett; Charlie Parsons; Tom Shelly

Season 13 was set in the Cook Islands and again featured Exile Island. Every cycle, one or more players were sent to an island to live alone without shelter or food for days at a time. Hidden somewhere on Exile Island was a small immunity idol which its finder could use anytime up through the final-four Tribal Council to stay safe from elimination. *Survivor: Cook Islands* featured a controversial new twist—the game began with four tribes divided by race: Hispanic, Asian, African American, and Caucasian.

In Episode 1, each tribe took little time identifying its weakest link. For example, in Rarotonga, Flicka accidentally freed the tribe's chickens. The inaugural Reward/Immunity Challenge featured a mental and physical test, which Puka won, earning a fire kit, kindling, waterproof matches, and kerosene, plus immunity. Aitu and Raro finished second and third, also earning immunity and a flint. The Hiki tribe finished last, but was able to send another castaway to Exile Island. They chose Raro's Jonathan, because he'd earlier stolen Yul's chicken when they were gathering supplies. Sekou was the first castaway voted off island.

The Aitu tribe plotted to throw the next challenge in Episode 2, because they wanted to vote off the ineffective Billy. The Reward/Immunity Challenge tested each tribe's strength, memory, and their ability to work together. Puka won two large tarps and immunity. Aitu threw the challenge, and sent Yul to Exile Island. At the end of the challenge, Billy looked at Raro's Candice and whispered, "I'm next." Candice tried to lift his spirits by saying, "Well, we love you." Billy responded, "I love you." Meanwhile, Yul found the hidden immunity idol on Exile Island. Billy was eliminated at Tribal Council.

Each castaway was assigned to one of two new teams in Episode 3. The new Raro tribe was Nate, Rebecca, and Stephannie from the old Hiki tribe; Brad and Jenny from Puka; J.P. and Cristina from the Aitu tribe; and Adam and Parvati from Raro. The new Aitu comprised Yul, Becky, and Cao Boi, from the old Puka tribe; Sundra from Hiki; Jonathan, Candice, and Flicka from the old Raro tribe; and Ozzy and Cecilia of Aitu. Later, Yul told Becky he'd discovered the hidden immunity idol. At the Immunity Challenge, each tribe was connected by a rope while each member carried 15 pound sand bags. They raced through knee-deep water trying not to be tackled by an opposing tribe member. Raro won, and sent Candice to Exile Island, where she was safe from elimination. At Tribal Council, Cecilia was voted off by Aitu.

In the Episode 4 Reward Challenge, the teams navigated two tribe members, who were attached to a rope, through an obstacle course. Then one castaway from each tribe swam to retrieve a decoding wheel, which they used to decipher a phrase. Aitu won the comfort of three blankets, two pillows, and one hammock, and sent Adam to Exile Island. The Immunity Challenge involved stretchers and puzzles and ended in a race to build a fire. Aitu won immunity. At Tribal Council, overconfident J.P. was blindsided by Raro.

The tribes split into three pairs for the weight-holding endurance Reward Challenge in Episode 5. Raro won fishing supplies, spices, and bottles of wine, and sent Jonathan to Exile Island. While looking for coconuts, the Aitu tribe accidentally found Raro's camp. They begged for spices, but Raro gave up nothing. At the Immunity Challenge, the tribes had to assemble stepping poles to transport castaways from one platform to another, then swim out to a tower. Aitu won for the second consecutive time. At Tribal Council, Raro chose to eliminate Stephannie, because she'd expressed desire to go home and eat some "chicken and mashed potatoes."

At the Episode 6 challenge, each tribe stationed three castaways at a post, while two opposing tribe members tried to drag them through the sand and over the finish line. The prize was a feast of lamb shanks, bread, and apple cider. There was a catch, as the winners indulged by having the feast at Tribal Council, where both tribes voted out one castaway. Aitu won the Tribal Council feast. Cao Boi thought Jonathan had the hidden immunity idol. He told Yul about his "Plan Voodoo," which would create a tie: three votes each against Jonathan and Candice would force Jonathan to use the idol to eliminate Candice. At the night's first Tribal Council, Cao Boi's Plan Voodoo failed, and his seemingly loyal tribemates eliminated him. Before Raro voted someone out, Aitu was able to kidnap one of its members, who could feast with them and then return to Raro's camp and remain a member of the tribe through the next Reward Challenge. Aitu kidnapped Nate and looked on as the depleted Raro kicked out Cristina.

For the Episode 7 Reward Challenge, teams were split into three swimmers and three puzzlers. Aitu won peanut butter and potatoes, and sent Adam to Exile Island. At the Immunity Challenge, the castaways used logs to build a set of stairs to reach the top of a tower, then zip-lined into the water to get a bag of puzzle pieces, which they gave to the remaining teammates to solve a puzzle. Raro finally won immunity, while Aitu voted out Flicka at Tribal Council.

In Episode 8, the castaways were given the chance to mutiny against their tribe to join the other. With mere seconds remaining, Candice chose to mutiny, and Jonathan wasn't far behind her, with both joining Raro. At the Reward Challenge, two castaways squeezed into a barrel while the others rolled it through an obstacle course while picking up four buoys. They floated the barrel and collected underwater flags, paddled back to shore, hung the flags, recovered a buried axe, chopped a rope, and hoisted the flags. The four members of Aitu won coffee, muffins, danishes, and letters from home, and they were equally happy to banish Candice to Exile Island. At the Immunity Challenge, four castaways from each tribe paddled glass-bottom boats to look for three targets on the ocean floor to release six buoys, which they collected and brought back to shore. Aitu won the challenge, and Raro voted off Brad at Tribal Council.

Candice and Adam grew closer in Episode 9. At the Reward Challenge, the castaways located buried treasure chests that contained nautical flags that spelled out a specific word. Aitu won the chance to join a local feast and celebration, and again banished Candice to Exile Island. The unbeatable Aitu was the first to identify all the islands on their map at the Immunity Challenge. Raro voted off Rebecca, then opened a bottle they were given earlier. A note inside instructed them to vote out another player, which ended up being Jenny.

The tribes merged in Episode 10, and they chose to live on Raro's beach, where the coconuts were plentiful and there were no rats. At the Immunity Challenge, the new Aitutonga tribe members had to hang onto poles for as long as possible. Candice gave her all, but Ozzy won his first of many Immunity Challenges. Nate was voted off at that evening's Tribal Council.

In Episode 11, the castaways arrived at the Survivor auction. Biddable items included bubble bath, chocolate cake, pizza, beer, and ice cream, but the most valuable item was a note, purchased by Becky, that entitled her to send someone to Exile Island immediately. Without hesitation, she exiled Candice, and to add insult to injury, Yul revealed he had the immunity idol. After a complicated mathematical- and memory-oriented Immunity Challenge, Adam won the immunity necklace, fueling his confidence in the game. Back at camp, Adam, Parvati, and Candice cuddled in the tent, while the rest of the tribe ate without them. An argument ensued, which carried over to Tribal Council. Candice and Adam shared a passionate good-bye kiss before she was sent to the jury.

In Episode 12, Parvati suffered the season's worst injury, gouging her thumb with a machete, but was still able to compete in the Reward Challenge. The castaways were joined by their loved ones for the water-transporting Reward Challenge. Parvati and her father, Mike, won the challenge, and invited Sundra and her mom, Jeanette, and Adam and his dad, George, to accompany them to another island, where locals escorted them to a sacred cave for a ritual. They also enjoyed a picnic of fried chicken, meat loaf, and apple pie. Parvati sent Jonathan to Exile Island, while the other castaways returned to camp with their three loved ones. Ozzy, Becky, and Yul plotted to hide food from Adam, Parvati, and Jonathan to keep them weak. But Sundra, Parvati, and Adam returned with plenty of leftover food, and Becky threw the food-hiding idea out the window. Ozzy out-swam his tribe mates to win the Immunity Challenge. Jonathan's luck finally ran out at Tribal Council, and he was eliminated.

Episode 13 offered the castaways a reward of "eating and sleeping in splendor." The castaways dove into a mudpit, covered themselves with mud, then scraped it into a bucket in the Reward Challenge. Ozzy won the challenge, and earned a luxury spa reward with a massage, pool, plenty of food, plus beer, wine, and Champagne. He invited Parvati and Yul to join him, and sent Adam to Exile Island for the final time. Parvati tried to win over Ozzy and Yul at the spa, hoping to stay safe in the game. At the Immunity Challenge, the castaways used puzzle pieces to create a table maze to maneuver one cannonball into two corner pockets. Ozzy won again, and voted with his alliance to eliminate Parvati.

On the season finale, the final five faced another puzzling Immunity Challenge. They used pieces to create an eight-point compass rose puzzle to raise a flag. Ozzy won again, securing Adam's elimination. The final "Aitu four" reflected on the eliminated castaways by lighting their torches on an altar. For the final Immunity Challenge, the castaways had to stand on a small steel perch that became smaller every fifteen minutes, when each Survivor removed a section until the perch was less than half the size of a postcard. Host Jeff Probst also revealed that the final three would be part of the final Tribal Council. Sundra fell into the water, leaving Ozzy with immunity. As the final four talked about elimination, it was discussed that Becky and Sundra should face off in a tiebreaker. Yul offered his Immunity Idol to Becky to save herself. At Tribal Council, Becky and Sundra both received one vote, forcing the long fire-making tiebreaker, which Becky won. The jury asked the final three questions at the final Tribal Council. Yul said he had influenced the entire game; Becky said she had played a social game; while Ozzy said he was the hardworking underdog. In vote, Yul edged out Ozzy 5 votes to 4 and was named the winner. Becky got zero votes.

SURVIVOR: FIJI

(Season 14)

GENRE Competition

FIRST TELECAST 2/28/2007

LAST TELECAST 5/13/2007

NETWORK CBS

AIR TIME Thursday, 8:00 p.m.

EPISODE STYLE Story Arc

TALENT Jeff Probst (Host)

CAST Earl Cole (Winner—Ravu, Moto, Bula Bula); Cassandra Franklin (Runner-up—Moto, Bula Bula); Andria "Dre" (aka Dreamz); Herd (Runner Up—Moto, Ravu, Bula Bula); Yau-Man Chan (15th eliminated—Ravu, Moto, Bula Bula); Kenward "Boo" Bernis (14th eliminated—Moto, Bula Bula); Stacy Kimball (13th eliminated—Moto, Bula Bula); Alex Angarita (12th eliminated—Moto, Ravu, Bula Bula); Mookie Lee (11th eliminated—Ravu, Bula Bula); Edgardo Rivera (10th eliminated—Moto, Ravu, Bula Bula); Michelle Yi (9th eliminated—Ravu, Moto, Bula Bula); Lisette "Lisi" Linares (8th eliminated—Moto, Ravu); James "Rocky" Reid (7th eliminated—Ravu); Anthony Robinson (6th eliminated—Ravu); Rita Verreos (5th eliminated—Ravu); Liliana Gomez (4th eliminated—Moto); Gary Stritesky (left—Moto); Sylvia Kwan (3rd eliminated—Ravu); Erica Durosseau (2nd eliminated—Ravu); Jessica deBen (1st eliminated—Ravu)

PRODUCTION COMPANIES Mark Burnett Productions; Castaway Television Productions, Inc.; Survivor Productions LLC
CREATED BY Charlie Parsons
EXECUTIVE PRODUCERS Mark Burnett; Charlie Parsons; Tom Shelly

Nineteen new castaways were stranded on an island in Season 14. In Episode 1, the twentieth castaway, Melissa McNulty, quit before the contest started. On the island, a crate containing shelter-building instructions was opened thanks to Yau-Man, who discovered that dropping it on its weak spot would crack it open. For the first challenge, Sylvia divided the remaining eighteen castaways into two tribes—Ravu and Moto. Sylvia was sent to Exile Island and didn't join a tribe until after the first Tribal Council. There she was informed that there was a hidden idol at her camp. Meanwhile, Moto won the more comfortable camp and new supplies, while Ravu went to Tribal Council, where Jessica was the first voted off.

In Episode 2, Moto was living a life of luxury, while Ravu licked water off leaves for hydration. Sylvia left Exile Island to join Ravu. Flagpole-building skills were tested at the Reward/Immunity Challenge, and Moto won for the second time. Erica panicked at the challenge, so Ravu eliminated her at Tribal Council.

Moto won the Episode 3 Reward Challenge, and picked Sylvia to go to Exile Island from Ravu. Moto's Gary had trouble breathing, but the medics said it wasn't serious. Later, he beat Anthony in the food-eating Immunity Challenge, as Moto won their third straight challenge. Sylvia couldn't find the hidden idol at Ravu, and she was the third castaway voted out at Tribal Council.

A king-size bed was the prize at the Episode 4 Reward Challenge. Moto remained undefeated, but the team suffered a loss when Gary informed the medics he wanted to leave the game. Once again, Moto won the Immunity Challenge, but the had to eliminate a team member or move to Ravu's shoddy camp. They gave up immunity to Ravu, and at Tribal Council, Liliana was the first Moto member to leave.

In Episode 5, Yau-Man and Earl searched for the hidden immunity idol while Ravu slept. At the Reward Challenge, Moto won again, and picked their prize from a catalog. Ravu's loss sent them to Tribal Council, where Rita was voted out.

The tribes were switched around in Episode 6. After a schoolyard-style pick, Lisi was left out and was sent to Exile Island. Despite the shuffle, Moto won another Immunity Challenge. Ravu's Rocky and Anthony argued at Tribal Council, and Anthony was the first man eliminated.

In Episode 7, Lisi went from Exile Island to Ravu. Earl pointed out that the new Moto consisted of three former Ravus and three former Motos, and he plotted to get a former Moto in his alliance. Ravu finally caught a break and won the Reward Challenge. Yau-Man found the hidden immunity idol at Ravu and replaced it with a fake. Ravu's short-lived luck ran out, as Moto won another Immunity Challenge. Ravu voted out Rocky, who was named the first castaway on the jury.

Alex, Edgardo, and Mookie found Moto's hidden immunity idol, while Dreamz and Lisi slept in Episode 8. Both tribes learned a traditional Fijian dance, *meke,* before they went to the Reward Challenge, which Moto won, and celebrated by dancing. They also sent Lisi to Exile Island again. Moto used three weapons—a spear, a blow dart, and a bow and arrow—to win the Immunity Challenge. Ravu voted out Lisi.

In Episode 9, Mookie said that the idol was for him but he would still use it with Alex and Edgardo if he needed to.

Tree Mail informed the castaways to paddle to Exile Island with their personal belongings in Episode 9. There, they merged and called themselves Bula Bula. They moved to Moto's camp, but all luxuries were eliminated. Mookie accidentally slipped to Dreamz that he had the hidden idol while Alex was nearby. The castaways competed as teams at the Immunity Challenge. Cassandra, Earl, Boo, Edgardo, and Yau-Man were the orange team; while Alex, Dreamz, Michelle, Stacy, and Mookie were green. It was a tight puzzle race, but thanks to Yau-Man, orange won. Green immediately went to Tribal Council, where Michelle was eliminated, as the orange team enjoyed a prize back at camp: a steak, vegetable, and wine dinner.

Mookie was mad because he thought Dreamz had screwed the team in Episode 10. Earl thought Boo would be a good candidate to join his alliance. Cassandra scored perfectly in the question-and-answer Reward Challenge, inviting Boo, Dreamz, and Yau-Man for drinks, food, and fireworks on the yacht. She also sent Mookie to Exile Island. Earl told Cassandra and Dreamz that Mookie had the Ravu's hidden idol, while Yau-Man said he was nervous about the other idol. Yau-Man won the endurance Immunity Challenge. Mookie gave Alex the idol prior to Tribal Council, where Edgardo was eliminated.

Alex and Mookie confronted Dreamz about the betrayal in Episode 11. Two teams formed at the Reward Challenge. Boo sustained an injury, sending the opposing team to a victory. Four green team Bula Bula castaways enjoyed showers, food, and an overnight stay. Mookie and Alex tried to blackmail Yau-Man into revealing that he had the immunity idol. Stacy won the Immunity Challenge. At Tribal Council, Mookie was voted off the island.

Boo won Episode 12's Reward Challenge, and invited Yau-Man and Dreamz on a river-rafting trip, plus lunch and letters from home. At the immunity challenge, Boo's advantage let him skip to the final round of the Immunity Challenge, which he won. Alex was eliminated at Tribal Council.

Boo eavesdropped on conservations in Episode 13. Yau-Man won a car at the Reward Challenge, but he gave it to Dreamz in exchange for a promise not to be voted off, then exiled himself. Dreamz, Stacy, and Cassandra delivered supplies to a local school, where they ate lunch with the children for their reward. Then Dreamz expressed his frustration about the deal he had made with Yau-Man. Boo won the Immunity Challenge. Yau-Man used his hidden immunity idol at Tribal Council. His four votes were not counted against him, so Stacy was eliminated.

In the season finale, Yau-Man and Earl were upset that their allies had tried to blindside Yau-Man at Tribal Council. Earl questioned Cassandra's loyalty to their alliance. Yau-Man realized his deal with Dreamz had made him a target, so he vowed to win the Immunity Challenge, which was a maze. He was successful, earning a final four spot. Yau-Man, Cassandra, and Dreamz targeted Boo at Tribal Council, and he was eliminated by a four-to-one vote. The final four—Earl, Dreamz, Cassandra, and Yau-Man—honored the eliminated castaways before the final Immunity Challenge. Dreamz won individual immunity, holding up his deal with Yau-Man, but Dreamz was tormented by it. At Tribal Council, a teary-eyed Dreamz broke his promise, keeping immunity for himself so he'd make the final three. Because of this, Yau-Man was voted out, being the last to join the jury. Dreamz tried to defend his decision to Earl and Cassandra back at camp, but Earl could only mourn the loss of his friend Yau-Man. The next morning, the final three celebrated their last day in Fiji with a surprise feast. On their final day, they ceremoniously burned the cave and tools they'd used for thirty-nine days. The jury grilled Earl, Cassandra, and Dreamz with questions, and cast their votes for Earl to win. He was awarded $1 million and title of sole Survivor.

SWITCHED

GENRE	Docudrama
FIRST TELECAST	5/26/2003
LAST TELECAST	10/11/2003
NETWORK	ABC Family
EPISODE STYLE	Self-contained
PRODUCTION COMPANY	Evolution Tape and Film
EXECUTIVE PRODUCERS	Charles Cook; Kathleen French; Dean Minerd; Douglas Ross; Greg Stewart
CO-EXECUTIVE PRODUCER	Jared Tobman
PRODUCER	Jack Walworth
SEGEMENT PRODUCERS	Steve Czarnecki; Christine Ecklund; Ben Hatta; Camie Holmes; David de Vos
DIRECTORS	Amy Brooks; Erik Fleming; Larry Grimaldi; Brian Krinsky; Babette Pepaj; Sean Rankine; Lenid Rolov; Mykelle Sabin; Suju Vijayan; Amy Woods; David de Vos; Ondi Timoner

Switched featured two participants willing to trade places for four days to experience the other person's friends, family, and lifestyle. To add to the drama, each participant gave the other a challenge to accept or deny.

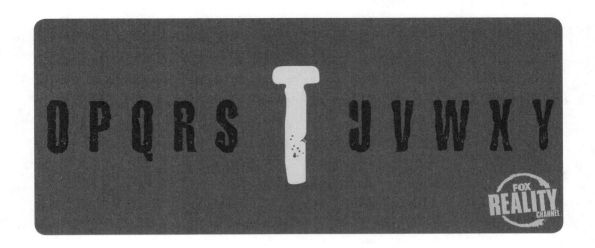

TAILDATERS

GENRE	Competition (Dating)
FIRST TELECAST	4/6/2002
LAST TELECAST	9/2/2003
NETWORK	MTV
EPISODE STYLE	Self-contained
PRODUCTION COMPANIES	Chameleon Entertainment; SokoLobl, Inc.
EXECUTIVE PRODUCERS	Damon Harman; John J. Hermansen; Rob Rollins Lobl; Sam Sokolow; Jeffrey Ullman
DIRECTORS	Ryan Nielsen Craig; Damon Harman

Dating met backseat driving in *Taildaters*. While on a blind date, a couple was followed by four friends in an RV, otherwise known as the "Backseat Daters." They secretly listened to and watched the date in progress. When the observers had advice or encouragement for the couple, they paged them.

TAQUITA AND KAUI

GENRE	Docudrama
FIRST TELECAST	4/2/2007
LAST TELECAST	4/23/2007
NETWORK	MTV
EPISODES	Self-contained
CAST	Kaui; Taquita
PRODUCTION COMPANY	Ted & Perry Company
EXECUTIVE PRODUCERS	Sean "P Diddy" Combs; Perry Dance; Ted Iredell

This spinoff of *Making the Band 3* featured Taquita and Kaui moving to Las Vegas as they tried to pursue a career in the entertainment world.

TEMPTATION ISLAND
(Season 1)

GENRE	Docusoap (Romance)
FIRST TELECAST	1/10/2001
LAST TELECAST	2/28/2001
NETWORK	Fox
AIR TIME	Wednesday, 9:00 p.m.
EPISODE STYLE	Story Arc
TALENT	Mark L. Walberg (Host)

CAST

Couples Billy Cleary and Mandy Lauderdale; Andy Lukei and Shannon Roghair; Kaya Wittenburg and Valerie Penso; Taheed Watson and Ytossie Patterson

Singles Ace; Carla Betz; Britt; Yvonne Brown; Charlie; Lola Corwin; Megan Denton; Alison Dietrich;

Patti Dunn; Greg; Lisa Heath; Jim; Johnny; Jon;
Elizabeth Kee; Keith; LaWonna; Dano Legere;
Maceo; Matt; Vanessa Norris; Heather Perry;
Venus Ramos; Evan Reynolds; Tom Ritchie; Sean

PRODUCTION COMPANY Rocket Science Laboratories
EXECUTIVE PRODUCERS Chris Cowan; Jean-Michel Michenaud;
Michael Shevloff

On *Temptation Island,* four unmarried couples traveled to a remote island, where a series of temptations tested the strength of their relationships. Season 1's couples were Andy and Shannon, Billy and Mandy, Kaya and Valerie, and Taheed and Ytossie.

In Episode 1, the couples arrived in Belize and were promptly separated. The men spent the night at Captain Morgan's Retreat, while the women headed to Mata Chica. In the morning, the contestant couples reunited and were introduced to a group of singles, who would tempt the significant others throughout the course of the show. Each gender collectively voted off the one tempter they viewed as the biggest threat. The men voted off Ace, while the women picked Yvonne. Each male contestant got to block one of the remaining single guys from dating his girlfriend, and vice versa for the females. The couples reunited at Mata Chica at the end of the day.

In Episode 2, host Mark Walberg met with the men and women separately to discuss their feelings. The first blind dates with the singles began. Kaya had a good date with Alison, while a jealous Valerie couldn't enjoy her date with Charlie. Taheed had the best date of his life with LaWonna, while Ytossie thought Sean was too self-involved. Andy hit it off with Megan, while Shannon was charmed that Matt had bought her wine. Billy was captivated with Lisa, while Mandy didn't enjoy her scuba-diving date with single Keith as much as he did. After the dates, the men and women separately discussed their experiences. In the morning, each contestant group voted off a single person of the *opposite* gender. The women dispatched Maceo, while the men sent Lola packing. That night, at a ritual bonfire, host Mark Walberg let each guy watch a video of his significant other's date, in exchange for allowing her watch a clip from *his* date. Billy and Taheed accepted the offer, while Kaya and Andy refused. Every contestant was allowed to leave a video message for his or her significant other; all but Taheed and Ytossie accepted.

Episode 3 began with everyone's reaction to the bonfires. Then it was time for

"Power Dating," in which each of the contestants interviewed a single tempter for two minutes each. Based on their interviews, they selected a date. Tempter Tom was picked by three contestants, and chose Ytossie. Matt was picked by two contestants, and chose Valerie. Single Johnny escorted Mandy; Charlie joined Shannon; Carla escorted Andy; Heather joined Kaya; Lisa was selected by Taheed; and Vanessa wound up with Billy. Each pair went on an exotic date. The next day, the men sent single Keith home, while the women didn't get a choice, because Heather had left voluntarily. At that evening's bonfire, the female contestants were given the same reciprocal option to watch video from their boyfriends' second dates. Ytossie and Mandy chose to see the videos, while Valerie and Shannon declined. Every woman contestant opted to leave a video message for her boyfriend. At the men's bonfire, Billy refuseed to watch the complete clip of Mandy doing body shots with Johnny. Every male contestant except Taheed left a video message for his girlfriend.

In Episode 4, Billy acted on his disappointment with Mandy by doing a faux striptease for Vanessa. Upset that Taheed hadn't left her a message, Ytossie confessed to Greg that she and Taheed had an eighteen-month-old baby together—something they hadn't disclosed before coming on the show. Upon learning this, executive producer Chris Cowan forced Taheed and Ytossie to withdraw from the show, letting them spend time together at a different Belize resort. The couples were reunited, and Mark introduced the rules of Peer Dating. Each woman picked the perfect single guy for each of their fellow women, and vice versa. Valerie was paired with Jon, Mandy went with Tom, Shannon got Dano, Kaya hooked up with LaWonna, Billy joined Megan, and Andy ended up with Venus. At the bonfire, the men unanimously accepted host Mark Walberg's offer to remove the dating "blocks" they'd put on their girlfriends. Each man was allowed to watch video of one woman's after-hours activities—but with no guarantee that the video would be of his *own* girlfriend. At the women's bonfire, they matched the men's decision by removing the dating "blocks" on their boyfriends. The women were likewise allowed to watch video of the men's after-hours activities, which they found upsetting. Mandy broke down crying, thinking her relationship with Billy might be over.

In Episode 5, everyone talked about the videos viewed at the last bonfire. In the morning, the single guys nominated the female contestants they liked the most: Johnny and Sean picked Mandy, while Jon and Jim liked Valerie. Charlie, Dano, Matt, Evan, Greg, and an emotional Tom expressed their affection for Shannon. The women contestants voted off single Sean. The single girls picked the male contestants they liked the most: Elizabeth, Lisa, Vanessa, Britt, Venus, and Carla nominated Billy. LaWonna and Patti picked Kaya. Megan was noncommittal, leaving Andy without a vote. The male contestants voted off single Patti. Next, it was time to pick "DayLong Dates." Andy escorted Elizabeth, Billy took Vanessa again, and Kaya settled for Megan. Separately, all the women contestants wanted to date single Tom, but they deferred to fellow contestant Shannon, who seemed to have clicked with him. Mandy escorted Matt, while Valerie took Evan. On their date, single Vanessa told Billy she was willing to do anything he wanted. Andy escorted Megan, and was upset because his girlfriend was hitting it off with her date. That night, host Mark Walberg stated that all the singles who weren't chosen for the fourth "Dream Date" would be sent home. At the "Final Date" selection in the morning, contestant Kaya picked Alison, Andy chose Elizabeth, and Billy selected Vanessa, sealing the fate of a stunned Megan. The episode ended with the women contestants deliberating over whom they would choose for their final date.

In Episode 6, Shannon picked Tom, Vanessa chose Dano, and Mandy opted for John, leaving Matt out in the cold. The new couples picked their final date locations and headed off together. Separately, viewers caught up with the exited Taheed and Ytossie, who had decided to work through their problems and stay together.

Episode 7 followed the conclusions of the final dates. The three contestant couples gathered at a bonfire to make their final decisions. After emotional speeches, all three decided to stay with their significant others. In an epilogue, we learned that Kaya and Valerie spent a week locked in their condo to get "reconnected," Billy and Mandy maintained a long-distance relationship from Los Angeles and Atlanta, and Shannon accepted Andy's wedding proposal immediately after the final bonfire.

A special wedding episode aired on November 7, 2001. Andy and Shannon invited the other couples, who talked about their relationships since being on the island.

TEMPTATION ISLAND

(Season 2)

GENRE Docusoap (Romance)
FIRST TELECAST 11/7/2001

LAST TELECAST	2/14/2002
NETWORK	FOX
AIR TIME	Thursday, 9:00 p.m.
EPISODE STYLE	Story Arc
TALENT	Mark L. Walberg (host)

CAST

Couples   Catherine Chiarelli and Edmundo Cruz;
Genevieve Deittrick and Tony Schmitt;
Shannon Rutledge and John Dolan;
Nikkole Palmatier and Thomas McGuan;
Mark Detrio and Kelley Sutphin

Singles   Oscar Acosta; Tom Adams; Nayla Akrawi;
Kishi Anderson; Ali Azarvan; Caneel Carsell;
Tommy Caruso; Chad; Amanda Cole; Brian DiCinti;
Debbie Entin; Kaine Fisher; Anna Maria Gentiluomo;
Kristin Gerbert; Katie Heeran; Juleby Hirsch;
Jocelyn; Jeff Kunard; Ruben Lopez; Magalie;
Hilary Mills; Rossi Morreale; Omar Payne;
Kevin Pritchard; Aaron S.; Donna Shepherd;
Meredith Spira; Kristen Stout; Aaron T.;
Tony Vanchieri; Tiffani Webb; Linda Wojcio

PRODUCTION COMPANY   Rocket Science Laboratories

EXECUTIVE PRODUCERS   Chris Cowan; Jean-Michel Michenaud;
Michael Shevloff

For Season 2, the locale shifted to Playa Tambor, in Costa Rica. Initially, four couples competed—Shannon and John, Genevieve and Tony, Nikkole and Thomas, and Catherine and Edmundo—but a fifth couple, Mark and Kelley, joined them later.

In Episode 1, the couples were introduced, and they explained their reasons for coming on the show. Then they flew to the island, where they met the singles. The men decided that tempter Brian posed the biggest threat, and they voted him out, while the women opted to get rid of tempter Caneel. The contestants gave "blocking" bracelets to the people they didn't want their significant other dating. Shannon gave hers to Linda, John to Tony, Nikkole to Katie, Tommy to Rossi, Catherine to Katie, Genevieve to Amanda, Edmundo to Juleby, and Tony to Kaine. The contestant couples were given one last moment in private before being paired off for their first dates.

In Episode 2, first date selection began. John was paired with Anna Maria, Tony with Donna, Edmundo with Hilary, Tommie with Kristen, Shannon with Kaine, Genevieve with Kevin, Catherine with Oscar, and Nikkole with Jeff. A twist called "Date Sabotage" was introduced, as each contestant gender group got to pick one of their significant other's *dates* to vote off. The men ousted Oscar, while the women eliminated Anna Maria. Suddenly dateless, Catherine and John stayed behind with the singles, while the other pairs went on their first dates. Afterward, at the women's bonfire, all four women chose to see videos of their boyfriends' dates, thus allowing their boyfriends to watch tapes of *their* dates, as well. Expressions of jealousy ensued.

"Power Dating" was introduced in Episode 3, as contestant Genevieve picked Tom, Catherine picked Jeff, Nikkole picked Ali, Shannon picked Rossi, Tommy picked Kishi, Edmundo picked Tiffani, Tony picked Linda, and John wound up with Nayla. Everyone except contestant Tom and single Jeff enjoyed their dates. Then, singles Hilary and Amanda fought over Edmundo. At the bonfire, the male contestants were given the option of watching a video of their girlfriends' secret admirers. Tony found out Genevieve's admirer was Ali; Tom learned that Nikkole's was Tommy, and Edmundo discovered that Catherine's was Tom. John declined the offer to learn who was Shannon's admirer. Everyone but Tommy elected to send a video message to his girlfriend. The women contestants learned that Tommy's admirer was Kristen, Tony's was Donna, and Edmundo's was Tiffani. All of the women sent video messages to their boyfriends.

In Episode 4, the women voted off singles Juleby and Omar, while the men sent Meredith and Kristin home. For the third date, male contestant John escorted Linda, Tony took Katie, Tommy brought Amanda, and Edmundo went with Donna. Female contestant Catherine escorted Thomas, Genevieve took Ruben, Nikkole brought Tommy, and Shannon went with Jeff. Afterward, the single women dressed the male contestants in drag, and they all ended up in the swimming pool. Much later that night, Edmundo and Hilary kissed. Meanwhile, the single guys set up a massage parlor to fawn over the female contestants.

It was revealed that Edmundo and Hilary spent a sexless night together in Episode 5. The contestant couples viewed their significant others' video messages. Tony was told he could not see Genevieve's message, which upset him. At the women's bonfire, all three chose to see video of their men in action; Catherine and Nikkole were upset at Edmundo and Tommy's exploits. At the men's bonfire, Tommy and Edmundo saw their girlfriends' videos and were unfazed; John declined to see Shannon's video; and, belatedly, Tony viewed Genevieve's message, in which she proposed to him. Tony accepted host Mark Walberg's offer to see Genevieve in person, and he said yes to her marriage proposal. They left the island together.

In Episode 6, everyone learned that Tony and Genevieve were gone, and Mark informed them that a new couple, Mark and Kelley, were being flown in to replace them. Hilary and Edmundo became a couple and hooked up in the bathroom. The next date selection was free choice, and Edmundo shockingly picked Linda instead of Hilary. Mark chose Donna, Tommy picked Tiffani, John elected to go on a second date with Nayla, Shannon chose Ruben, Nikkole picked Tommy, Catherine chose Tony, and Kelley opted for Thomas. While no one was watching, Tommy and Kristen sneaked down to the beach to make out.

In Episode 7, the new pairs went on their dates and generally had a good time. At the vote-off, host Mark Walberg revealed that single Jeff had left for family reasons. Each female contestant chose one single guy to stay, and the unselected Ruben, Kaine, and Tony had to leave the island. Similarly, each male contestant chose one single woman to stay, and the unselected Donna, Hilary, Tiffani, and Kishi were sent home, officially ending the Hilary-Edmundo coupling. After a game of tug-of-war, the men's and women's groups were sent on different one-day trips. At the end of the day, host Mark Walberg surprised everyone by inviting back the first two singles voted off, Brian and Caneel, as well as six new singles.

In Episode 8, it was revealed that single Brian was specifically selected to romance contestant Catherine, Aaron S. for Nicole, Aaron T. for Shannon, Chad for Kelley, Caneel for John, Magalie for Mark, Debbie for Edmundo, and Jocelyn for Tommy. The new pairings went on a first date, with varying romantic success. Later, at the men's bonfire, John and Tommy opted to watch their girlfriends' videos, while Mark and Edmundo declined.

Every woman but Kelley watched videos of their boyfriends in Episode 9. Catherine was upset to see Edmundo and Hilary hooking up. Shannon was confronted for breaking the rules by stashing notes for John—which were intercepted. For the second-to-last date, Mark joined Debbie, Kelley went with Ali, John joined Kristen, Shannon coupled with Kevin, Edmundo joined Amanda, Catherine went with Rossi, Thomas joined Linda, while Nikkole took her recent beau, Tommy. After the dates, both Edmundo and Linda, and Catherine and Brian made out. At the men's bonfire, everyone watched footage of his girlfriend, who was unaware of the filming. Thomas was disturbed to see Tommy and Nikkole passionately making out.

Episode 10 started with the women's bonfire, as everyone watched secret videos of their boyfriends. Nikkole accepted watching Thomas about to hook up with someone, since she had been fooling around with Tommy. Later, Brian tried but failed to persuade Catherine to leave Edmundo. At the women's resort, Tommy got naked and jumped in the pool. The "Final Date" selections were made, as Edmundo picked Linda, Mark chose Debbie, Thomas went with Debbie out of pity, and John picked Nayla. The women's "Final Date" selections would be revealed in the next episode.

In Episode 11, Catherine picked Brian for her final date, Shannon chose Kevin, Nikkole picked Tommy again, and Kelley went with Ali. All of the unselected singles were sent home. Following the final dates, the remaining singles were sent home.

At Episode 12's final bonfire, late contestant Mark announced he wanted to stay with Kelley, but Kelley's connection with Ali made her realize her feelings weren't mutual. Shannon and John chose to stay together. Edmundo and Catherine said they'd try to work things out, but broke up by the end of the night. Knowing her feelings for Tommy, Thomas gave Nikkole the chance to back out, and she took it.

TEMPTATION ISLAND

(Season 3)

GENRE	Docusoap (Romance)
FIRST TELECAST	7/28/2003
LAST TELECAST	9/9/2003
NETWORK	FOX
AIR TIME	Thursday, 9:00 p.m.

EPISODE STYLE	Story Arc
TALENT	Mark L. Walberg (Host)

CAST

Couples	Stephanie Cantu and Anthony Hernandez; Kara Ludlin and Jason; Kristin Cobb and Eric Hurt; Melissa Huggins and Michael Pulice
Singles	Amy; Kelly Anne; Chris; Corie; Ian Dallimore; Derrick; Erryn; Eve; Giulio; Ida; Jeff; Jerome; John; Ryan J.; Kaileen; Kristin; Michael; Ryan M.; Sandra Petko; Maria Santos; Scott; Ashley Smith; Ryan Sopo; Melanie Specht; Sterling; Tanaya; Tiffany
PRODUCTION COMPANY	Rocket Science Laboratories
EXECUTIVE PRODUCERS	Chris Cowan; Jean-Michel Michenaud; Michael Shevloff

Season 3 was set in the Bay Islands off the coast of Honduras. The four couples were Anthony and Stephanie, Eric and Kristin, Jason and Kara, and Michael and Melissa.

The contestant couples and singles were introduced in Episode 1. Host Mark Walberg instructed the single men to inform the contestant men whom they were most interested in. Similarly, the single women informed the contestant women whom they liked the most. The contestant couples were given some private time alone before they were split up into two camps, and the competition began. The next morning, the contestant men and women were each asked to pick one single they considered the biggest threat to their significant other. In a twist, host Mark Walberg directed eight singles to be immediately sent home: Jeff, Derrick, Ryan M., Ian, Tiffany, Amy, Maria, and Tanaya. Later, at camp, he revealed a second twist to the contestant men: the four single men seemingly sent home would actually be the first dates for their girlfriends.

In Episode 2, the contestant men learned that the single women they thought their girlfriends had voted out were in fact their first dates, which resulted in mixed results. At the women's bonfire, everyone but Kristin decided to watch the boyfriends' videos. At the men's bonfire, Mark showed the girlfriends' tapes. The men concluded that the women had been more active than they, so they decided to change that.

In Episode 3, Anthony got upset after watching Stephanie get cozy with Derrick, and Jason was unhappy after seeing Kara with Jeff. The contestant men were allowed to choose their second date: Michael picked Sandra, Anthony chose Ida, Eric selected Amy, and Jason picked Erryn. After the men's first dates, the single women put on a sexy lingerie show for the contestant men. Sandra and Tiffany fought over Michael, but he seemed to like Tiffany more. Meanwhile, tensions rose at the contestant women's camp as singles Jeff and Jerome began to fight. Order was restored quickly when the women threatened to vote both singles out. The next day, the women voted out singles John and Ryan M. Back at the men's camp, they voted off singles Corie, Tanaya, and Kelly Anne. Later, at the women's bonfire, everyone but Kristin watched video of their boyfriends getting close to one particular single temptress. After the bonfire, Melissa and Jerome got close, while Kara and Jeff both ended up in her room.

The contestant women finally chose their first dates in Episode 4. Stephanie took single Jeff, Kristin picked Derrick, Melissa chose Sterling, and Kara gave Giulio a try. Stephanie and Jeff were the only new couple who seemed to hit it off. Back at the men's camp, Anthony and Ashley got cozy. In the morning, the contestant men voted out singles Melanie and Kristin, while the contestant women made the difficult decision to vote out Chris. At the men's bonfire, host Mark Walberg informed them that the women would have to watch their boyfriends' tapes, but he gave the men the option of not watching. Anthony and Michael chose to watch, while Eric and Jason declined.

In Episode 5, contestant Jason yelled at single Sandra over dinner for saying things on the video that weren't true, causing silence for the remainder of the meal. Host Mark Walberg summoned the contestant men together for what they thought would be a vote out, but turned out to be their second date selection. Jason chose Eve out of pity, Eric picked Kaileen, Michael chose Ida, and Anthony went with Ashley. Michael and Anthony both had successful dates. Later that night, Mark told the men that one of the single women had to be voted out, so they chose Sandra. At the women's camp, Melissa threatened to strangle Kristin after she tried to interfere with hers and Jerome's budding romance. The next day, the women were told to vote off a single man, so they ousted Derrick. Next, they picked their second dates: Stephanie selected Michael, Kristin chose Giulio, Kara selected Ian, and Melissa went with Jerome, over Kristin's objections. The women seemed to enjoy themselves. At the men's bonfire,

Mark informed the contestants that he had to play every girlfriend's video. At the women's bonfire, he likewise played every boyfriend's video. Stephanie was upset to see Anthony getting close to Ashley, and Melissa was disturbed after privately watching footage of Michael with Tiffany, which Mark deemed "unsuitable for TV."

Episode 6 began with the contestant women's reactions to the videos of their boyfriends. The next day, Mark announced that the final dates would take place overnight. In a twist, the contestants learned that the singles could choose to decline a contestant's date offer. At the men's camp, Eric picked first and went with single Ida, but she vetoed him. His being snubbed put him at the end of the selection line. Jason picked Amy, and she accepted. Anthony chose his squeeze, Ashley, who accepted. Michael opted for still-available Ida, who said yes. Eric finally got to pick again, and settled for Kaileen. Meanwhile, at the women's camp, Kara took single Ian, Melissa picked Jerome, Stephanie chose Jeff, and Kristin selected Ryan. The pairs embarked on their incredible final dates. Afterward, at the final bonfire, Kara said she still wanted to be with single Jeff, but needed a break. Michael was ready to propose to his girlfriend, Melissa, but she upstaged him by saying she wanted to dump him. Couple Kristin and Eric decided to stay together. In an emotional epiphany, couple Anthony and Stephanie realized that they should break up. After they left the island, contestant Kara and single Jeff became a couple.

THERE & BACK: ASHLEY PARKER ANGEL

GENRE	Doucsoap (Celebrity)
FIRST TELECAST	1/4/2006
NETWORK	MTV
EPISODE STYLE	Story Arc
CAST	Ashley Parker Angel;
	Tiffany Lynn Rowe
EXECUTIVE PRODUCER	Matt Anderson
CO-EXECUTIVE PRODUCER	Larry Rudolph
DIRECTORS	Katherine Brooks; Jennifer Morton

Making the Band and O-Town veteran Ashley Parker Angel tried to make a comeback with this series that chronicled his life as a husband-to-be and a new dad. The show also centered on his attempt to launch his post–boy band solo career.

THINGS I HATE ABOUT YOU

GENRE	Competition (Relationship)
FIRST TELECAST	7/20/2004
NETWORK	Bravo
EPISODE STYLE	Self-contained
TALENT	Mo Rocca (Host); Jacqui Malouf (Relationship Expert)
PRODUCTION COMPANY	Wall to Wall Media

Each episode of *Things I Hate About You* featured a couple with one partner who had a habit that annoyed the other. The competition required each couple to do a role reversal. The partner deemed the most annoying faced a special punishment designed by his or her significant other, with a special gift awarded.

THREE WISHES

GENRE	Docudrama (Makeover)
FIRST TELECAST	9/23/2005
LAST TELECAST	12/9/2005
NETWORK	NBC
AIR TIME	Friday, 9:00 p.m.
EPISODE STYLE	Self-contained
TALENT	Amy Grant (Host); Carter Oosterhouse (Carpenter); Amanda Miller (Architect); Diane Mizota (Designer); Eric Stromer (Contractor)
PRODUCTION COMPANIES	Glassman Media; June Road Productions; NBC Universal Television

EXECUTIVE PRODUCERS	Andrew Glassman; Jason Raff
PRODUCERS	Nate Harrington; Mike Aho; Tim Gaydos; Mike Hazan; Emily Sinclair
DIRECTORS	Tony Croll; Andrew Glassman; Jason Raff

On each episode of *Three Wishes,* singer Amy Grant and the show's team granted wishes to a town's most deserving people. The show took over the town square, where they were given wishes at the "Wish Tent." Then the wishes were granted as the show was filmed over the following days. Many times, the town was given a free concert, often featuring a performance by Grant.

TIARA GIRLS

GENRE	Docudrama
FIRST TELECAST	4/10/2006
NETWORK	MTV
EPISODES	Self-contained
EXECUTIVE PRODUCERS	Marshall Eisen; Dave Sirulnick

Each episode of this docudrama focused on a different pageant and one of the contestants in that featured contest. Viewers followed the girls as they rehearsed and did whatever it took to win the pageant crown.

'TIL DEATH DO US PART: CARMEN AND DAVE

GENRE	Docusoap (Celebrity)
FIRST TELECAST	1/21/2004
NETWORK	MTV
AIR TIME	Wednesday, 10:30 p.m.

EPISODE STYLE	Story Arc
CAST	Carmen Electra; Dave Navarro
EXECUTIVE PRODUCERS	Fernando Hernández; Lois Curren
PRODUCERS	Rod Aissa; Heather Parry
DIRECTORS	Matt Anderson; Fernando Hernández

'Til Death Do Us Part chronicled the build-up to the wedding of *Playboy* actress/model/dancer Carmen Electra and her rock star fiancé, Dave Navarro. Scenes included the couple's risqué bachelor/bachelorette parties, Carmen selecting her $9,000 gown, and the wedding ceremony, which featured an unconventional cake-cutting and bouquet toss.

TIM GUNN'S GUIDE TO STYLE

GENRE	Docudrama
FIRST TELECAST	9/6/2007
NETWORK	Bravo
EPISODE STYLE	Self-contained
CAST	Tim Gunn (Host); Veronica Webb (Host, Fashion Accomplice)
PRODUCTION COMPANY	Stone and Company
EXECUTIVE PRODUCERS	Scott Stone; Sarah-Jane Cohen
DIRECTORS	Michael Z. Wechsler

On each episode of *Tim Gunn's Guide to Style,* stylist, author, and *Project Runway* advisor Tim Gunn and model Veronica Webb raided the closets of women in need of a makeover. They applied a tough-love approach to their fashion guidance. Along the way, Tim built an "essential shopping list" of ten basic pieces of clothing each woman should own.

TODD TV

GENRE	Docusoap
FIRST TELECAST	1/21/2004
LAST TELECAST	3/3/2004
NETWORK	FX
AIR TIMES	Wednesday, 10:00 p.m.
EPISODE STYLE	Story Arc
TALENT	George Gray (Host)
CAST	Todd Santos
PRODUCTION COMPANIES	Endemol; Lock and Key Productions
EXECUTIVE PRODUCERS	John De Mol; Tom Forman
CO-EXECUTIVE PRODUCERS	Leslie Radakovich; Jeff Kaufman
PRODUCERS	Daniel Soiseth; Carlos Ortiz; Cynthia Stockhamm

In this Americanized version of Endemol's *Masterplan,* viewers helped directionless Todd, age thirty, make life decisions through phone, computer, or text-message suggestions. They helped him do everything from deciding whether to have an enema to selecting a job.

TOMMY LEE GOES TO COLLEGE

GENRE	Docucomedy (Celebrity)
FIRST TELECAST	8/16/2005
LAST TELECAST	9/13/2005
NETWORK	NBC
AIR TIME	Tuesday, 9:00 p.m.
EPISODE STYLE	Story Arc
CAST	Tommy Lee; Natalie Riedmann (The Tutor); Matt Ellis (The Roommate)
PRODUCTION COMPANIES	Eddie October Productions and B Cubed
CREATED BY	Brad Wyman and BT

EXECUTIVE PRODUCERS	Eddie October; Richard Bishop; Brad Wyman and BT
CO-EXECUTIVE PRODUCER	Mike Nichols
PRODUCERS	Carl Stubner; Tommy Lee
DIRECTOR	Eddie October

On *Tommy Lee Goes to College,* Mötley Crüe's drummer badboy Tommy Lee went back to college, enrolling at the University of Nebraska at Lincoln. He tried out for the school marching band, worked with a lab partner to dissect a frog, and attempted to figure out the nuances of rads in physics class. The cast of characters he encountered included his beautiful tutor, Natalie, and his geeky roommate, Matt. The series concluded with Tommy passing English and horticulture, but failing chemistry. He capped things off by giving the college a free concert.

TOP CHEF

GENRE	Competition (Job)
FIRST TELECAST	3/8/2006
NETWORK	Bravo
EPISODE STYLE	Story Arc
TALENT	Katie Lee Joel (Host—Season 1); Padma Lakshmi (Host—Seasons 2 and 3); Tom Colicchio (Head Judge); Gail Simmons (Judge); Ted Allen (Judge—Season 3)

CAST

Season 1 Harold Dieterle (Winner); Tiffani Faison (Runner-up); Dave Martin (10th eliminated); Lee Anne Wong (9th eliminated); Stephen Asprinio (8th eliminated); Miguel Morales (7th eliminated); Lisa Parks (5th eliminated); Candice Kumai (4th eliminated); Brian Hill (3rd eliminated); Andrea Beaman

(2nd & 6th eliminated); Kenneth Lee
(1st eliminated)

Season 2   Ilan Hall (Winner); Marcel Vigneron (Runner-up);
Sam Talbot (12th eliminated); Elia Aboumrad
(eliminated in Episode 12); Cliff Crooks
(11th eliminated); Michael Midgley
(10th eliminated); Betty Fraser (9th eliminated);
Mia Gaines-Alt (8th eliminated); Frank Terzoli
(7th eliminated); Carlos Frenandez (6th eliminated);
Josie Smith-Malave (5th eliminated);
Marisa Churchill (4th eliminated); Emily Sprissler
(3rd eliminated); Otto Borsich (2nd eliminated);
Suyai Steinhauer (1st eliminated)

Season 3   Casey Thompson (Final 3); Dale Levitski (Final 3);
Hung Hyunh (Final 3); Brian Malarkey
(12th eliminated); Sara Mair (11th eliminated);
Chris Jacobsen (10th eliminated); Howie Kleinberg
(9th eliminated); Tre Wilcox (8th eliminated);
Sara Nguyen (7th eliminated); Joey Paulino
(6th eliminated); Lia Bardeen (5th eliminated);
Camille Becerra (4th eliminated); Micah Edelstein
(3rd eliminated); Sandee Birdson (2nd eliminated);
Clay Bowen (1st eliminated)

PRODUCTION COMPANY   Magical Elves Productions
EXECUTIVE PRODUCERS   Dan Cutforth; Jane Lipsitz; Shauna Minoprio
PRODUCER   Kathey Leverton
DIRECTOR   Kent Weed

Fifteen top up-and-coming chefs from around the country show off their culinary skills as they compete for a grand prize on *Top Chef*. Harold Dieterle, Season 1's winning chef, received $100,000 in seed money to encourage his culinary career, a feature in *Food & Wine* magazine, and an appearance at the Food and Wine Classic in Aspen, Colorado. He was also awarded a suite of Sears Kenmore kitchen appliances.

Padma Lakshmi took over as host in Season 2, which was marked by the emergence of Marcel as a target of the other contestants' ire. Ilan Hall, twenty-four, a chef from New York, was declared the winner, defeating Marcel in the final challenge, set in Hawaii.

Season 3 added *Queer Eye*'s culinary expert, Ted Allen, to the judging panel. This season shifted locales to Miami. Season 3 guest judges included Anthony Bourdain and The *Restaurant's* Rocco DiSpirito.

TOP DESIGN

GENRE	Competition (Job)
FIRST TELECAST	1/31/2007
LAST TELECAST	4/11/2007
NETWORK	Bravo
EPISODE STYLE	Story Arc
TALENT	Todd Oldham (Host); Jonathan Adler (Judge); Kelly Wearstler (Judge); Margaret Russell (Judge)
CAST	Matt Lorenz (Winner); Carisa Perez-Fuentes (Runner-up); Andrea Keller (9th eliminated); Goil Amornvivat (8th eliminated); Michael Adams (7th eliminated); Erik Kolacz (6th eliminated); Ryan Humphrey (5th eliminated); Felicia Bushman (4th eliminated); Elizabeth Moore (3rd eliminated); John Gray (2nd eliminated); Lisa Turner and Heather Ashton (1st eliminated)
PRODUCTION COMPANY	Stone and Company Entertainment
EXECUTIVE PRODUCERS	Cori Abraham; Andrew Cohen; Clay Newbill; Dave Serwatka; Scott A. Stone
DIRECTOR	Glenn Lazzaro

Twelve aspiring interior designers competed against one another on *Top Design*. The contestants lived together in a Los Angeles loft while enduring a series of design challenges. A panel of judges eliminated contestants each week until the final winner, Matt Lorenz, was chosen. Lorenz won $100,000 and a spread in *Elle Décor* magazine.

TORI & DEAN: INN LOVE

GENRE	Docusoap
FIRST TELECAST	3/20/2007
NETWORK	Oxygen
EPISODE STYLE	Self-contained
CAST	Tori Spelling; Dean McDermott
PRODUCTION COMPANY	World of Wonder
EXECUTIVE PRODUCERS	Fenton Bailey; Randy Barbato; Dean McDermott; Tori Spelling
PRODUCER	Michael Call

In *Tori & Dean: Inn Love,* actress Tori Spelling and new husband, Dean McDermott, headed past the Hollywood Hills to make a new start. They opened a bed and breakfast while Tori was eight months pregnant.

TOTALLY OUTRAGEOUS BEHAVIOR

GENRE	Docucomedy
FIRST TELECAST	1/9/2004
LAST TELECAST	11/5/2004
NETWORK	FOX
AIR TIME	Friday, 8:00 p.m.
EPISODE STYLE	Self-contained
TALENT	Lisa Dergan (Host)
PRODUCTION COMPANY	Nash Entertainment
EXECUTIVE PRODUCERS	Bruce Nash; Robyn Nash

Totally Outrageous Behavior spotlighted outrageous, unbelievable moments caught on tape, some of which were funny, while others were shocking or even frightening. Videos were taken from submissions by home viewers.

TOWN HAUL

GENRE	Docudrama (Makeover)
FIRST TELECAST	1/22/2005
LAST TELECAST	4/13/2006
NETWORK	TLC
AIR TIME	Saturday, 8:00 p.m.
EPISODE STYLE	Story Arc
TALENT	Genevieve Gorder (Host); Ray Romano (Contractor—Season 1); Patrick Brown (Contractor); Jimmy Little (Designer); Jimmy Moss (Landscape Architect)
EXECUTIVE PRODUCERS	Lauren Brady; Glenda Hersh; Craig H. Shepherd
CO-PRODUCER	Todd Broder
DIRECTOR	Katherine Brooks

Trading Spaces designer Genevieve Gorder and a team of designers made over an entire town in this renovation show. In just four weeks, the *Town Haul* team not only fixed up the town, they also helped the townspeople by assisting them with their businesses, careers, and homes. Each season focused on a specific town. Season 1 featured Jeffersonville, New York. Season 2 centered on makeover projects in Laurens, South Carolina. Season 3 took Genevieve and her team to Washington, Missouri.

TRADING SPACES

GENRE	Docudrama (Makeover)
FIRST TELECAST	9/1/2000

NETWORK	TLC
EPISODE STYLE	Self-contained
TALENT	Alex McCloud (Host—2000–2001); Paige Davis (Host—2001–2005); Ty Pennington (Carpenter—2000–2004); Amy Wyn Pastor (Carpenter); Carter Oosterhouse (Carpenter—2003–present); Faber Dewar (Carpenter—2004–present); Dez Ryan (Designer—2000–2001); Hilda Santo-Tomas (Designer); Frank Bielec (Designer); Vern Yip (Designer—2001–2004); Douglas Wilson (Designer); Laurie Hickson-Smith (Designer); Genevieve Gorder (Designer); Edward Walker (Designer—2002–present); Kia Steave-Dickerson (Designer—2002–present); Christi Proctor (Designer—2003–present); Richard Whiteford II (Designer—2003–present); Barry Wood (Designer—2003–present); Laura Day (2004–present); Jon Laymon (2004–present); Rick Rifle; Jimmy Little (Carpenter); Andrew Dan-Jumbo (Carpenter)
PRODUCTION COMPANY	Banyan Productions; Ross Television Productions
EXECUTIVE PRODUCERS	Denise Cramsey; Susan Cohen-Dickler; Jan Dickler; Ray Murray; Stephen H. Schwartz
PRODUCERS	Alyssa Kaufman; Brian Schmidt; Larry Blasé; Aimee Kramer; Laura C. Swalm; Patrick Denzer; Jivey Rivas; Laura Swalm; Amy Van Vessem

Based on the BBC series *Changing Rooms,* this home makeover series has neighbors agree to swap homes for a forty-eight-hour redesign. Guided by a designer and operating on a budget of $1,000, each group of neighbors tries to fulfill the expectations of the makeover recipients. As the renovations are completed, the host interviews the designers to check on their progress and gives tips to viewers on building, painting, and sewing projects. The host leads the recipient neighbors—who kept their eyes closed—into their newly made-over room for their reactions. While most recipients are happy with the results, not all room makeovers are well received. Beginning in March 2005, *Trading Spaces* moved to a "no host" format, eliminating the host in favor of allowing each team its own carpenter. The success of the show led to two spinoffs: *Trading Spaces: Family* and *Trading Spaces: Boys vs. Girls*.

TRADING SPACES: BOYS VS. GIRLS

GENRE	Docudrama (Makeover)
FIRST TELECAST	5/17/2003
NETWORK	Discovery Kids; NBC
EPISODE STYLE	Self-contained
TALENT	Diane Mizota (Host); Jordin Ruderman (Designer); Scott Sicari (Designer); Ginene Licata (Carpenter); Barte Shadlow (Carpenter)
PRODUCTION COMPANY	Banyan Productions
EXECUTIVE PRODUCERS	Karen Stein-Solomon; Susan Cohen-Dickler; Jan Dickler; Ray Murray; Jim Rapsas
PRODUCERS	Annie Bennett; Gabrielle Mahler; Brian Schmidt; Marianne Vogel

This spinoff of the show *Trading Spaces* features two friends who use power tools and paint brushes to redecorate each other's room on a $5,000 budget. Each is guided by a designer, but uses his or her own knowledge of the other's favorite hobbies and interests in this two-day "boys vs. girls" decorating challenge.

TRADING SPACES: FAMILY

GENRE	Docudrama (Makeover)
FIRST TELECAST	7/6/2003
NETWORK	TLC

EPISODE STYLE Self-contained

TALENT Joe Farrell (Host): Kia Steave-Dickerson (Designer); Frank Bielec (Designer); Christi Proctor (Designer); Jon Laymon (Designer); Laura Day (Designer); Barry Wood (Designer); Edward Walker (Designer); Amy Wynn Pastor (Carpenter); Genevieve Gorder (Designer); Douglas Wilson (Designer); Laurie Smith (Designer); Vern Yip (Designer); Richard Whiteford II (Designer); Cat Wei (Designer); Carter Oosterhouse (Carpenter); Faber Dewar (Carpenter); Hilda Santo-Tomas (Designer)

PRODUCTION COMPANY Banyan Productions

EXECUTIVE PRODUCER Shawn Visco

DIRECTORS Kathleen Blake; Suzy Garra; Shari Poland; Jivey Rivas

On each episode of *Trading Spaces: Family,* under the guidance of a design expert, a family redecorates a room in another family's home on a budget of only $1,000. Host Joe Farrell leads each family—who keeps their eyes closed—into their newly made-over room for their reveal reactions.

TRADING SPOUSES: MEET YOUR NEW MOMMY

GENRE Docudrama

FIRST TELECAST 7/1/2004

NETWORK FOX

AIR TIMES Tuesday, 8:00 p.m. (7/2004–9/2004); Monday, 8:00 p.m. (10/2004–2/2005); Tuesday, 8:00 p.m. (5/2005–8/2005); Wednesday, 9:00 p.m.

	(11/2005–12/2005); Friday, 9:00 p.m.
	(1/2006–4/2006) (10/2006–2/2007); Thursday,
	9:00 p.m. (4/2007–5/2007)
EPISODES	Self-contained
PRODUCTION COMPANY	Rocket Science Laboratories
EXECUTIVE PRODUCERS	Jean-Michel Michenaud; Chris Cowan
CO-EXECUTIVE PRODUCER	Jeff Cvengros
CO-PRODUCER	Megan Estrada
DIRECTOR	Allan Palmer

Moms and dads agreed to switch spouses with another family for one week on *Trading Spouses: Meet Your New Mommy*. When later reunited with their own families, the contestants decided how the other family would spend a $50,000 prize. The show was the subject of a lawsuit by ABC, claiming FOX stole the idea for this show from *Wife Swap*.

Marguerite Perrin of Ponchatoula, Louisiana, was a memorable *Trading Spouse*s participant who appeared in the two-part, 2005 season premiere. Perrin, who professed to be a fundamentalist Christian, traded homes with a New Age humanist from Boxborough, Massachusetts. Viewers were shocked by Perrin's erratic behavior, yelling, and attempt to convert her host family to Christians. She initially refused the "tainted" $50,000 prize and ripped up the other family's instructions on how to spend the money. Later, it was revealed that Perrin accepted the money.

TRAILER FABULOUS

GENRE	Docucomedy (Makeover)
FIRST TELECAST	8/03/2005
NETWORK	MTV
EPISODE STYLE	Story Arc
TALENT	Brooks Buford (Host); Johnny Hardesty (Designer);
	Gino Panaro (Landscaper); Erika Martin (Stylist)
PRODUCTION COMPANIES	One Louder Productions; MTV Productions

CREATED BY	Bob Kusbit; Angie Day
EXECUTIVE PRODUCERS	Bob Kusbit; Tony DiSanto; Liz Gateley; Angie Day
CO-EXECUTIVE PRODUCER	George Plamondon

Rapper Brooks Buford hosted this series, a comic twist on the home makeover genre. In it, Brooks and his team of designers gave a lucky teen a makeover for their personal style, their family, and their mobile home.

TREASURE HUNTERS

GENRE	Competition
FIRST TELECAST	6/18/2006
LAST TELECAST	8/21/2006
NETWORK	NBC
AIR TIMES	Sunday, 8:00 p.m. (6/2006); Monday, 8:00 p.m. (6/2006–7/2006); Monday, 9:00 p.m. (7/2006–8/2006)
EPISODE STYLE	Story Arc
TALENT	Laird Macintosh (Host)
CAST	Geniuses (Winners—Sam Khurana, Charles Taylor, Francis Goldshmid); Air Force (Runners-up—Brooke Rillos, Matt Rillos, Matt Zitzlsperger); Southie Boys (Runners-up—John Collins, Matthew Mullen, Martin Mullen); Ex-CIA (7th eliminated—Jacob Porter, Mark West, Todd Moore); Miss USA (6th eliminated—Melissa Witek, Kaitlyn Christopher, Kristen Johnson); Fogal Family (5th eliminated—Margie Fogal, Kayte Andersen, Brad Fogal); Brown Family (4th eliminated—Keith Brown, Tonny Brown, Terrance Brown); Wild Hanlons (3rd eliminated—Josh Hanlon,

Patrick "Pat" Hanlon, Ben Hanlon);
Grad Students (2nd eliminated—
Jessica Schilling, Melissa Schilling,
Kathleen Krapfl); Young Professionals
(1st eliminated—Taryn Brown, Drew Brown,
Chandra Lewis)

PRODUCTION COMPANY	Magical Elves Productions
EXECUTIVE PRODUCER	Rick Ringbakk
PRODUCERS	Tony Sacco; Joe Coleman; Al Edgington; Dan Cutforth; Brian Grazer; Fred Pichel; Devon Platte; Joy Rillo
DIRECTOR	Tony Sacco

Teams of three tried to stay a step ahead of one another in their quest for hidden treasure on *Treasure Hunters*. The teams had to avoid elimination as they traveled to historically significant locations where they deciphered cryptic codes and puzzles, each with a clue leading them closer to solving the ultimate puzzle and the grand prize, a treasure valued at $3 million.

Home viewers competed in an online version of the show and could guess the final location of the online treaure. Of the thirty-seven thousand people who correctly guessed the location, ten won $10,000 and went to Washington, D.C., for a "mini-hunt," where Scott Gray, an environmental scientist from Brandon, Mississippi, won an additional $100,000. This segment aired during the season finale, on August 21, 2006.

TRISTA AND RYAN'S WEDDING

GENRE	Docudrama
FIRST TELECAST	11/26/2003
LAST TELECAST	12/10/2003
NETWORK	ABC
AIR TIME	Wednesday, 9:00 p.m.

EPISODE STYLE	Story Arc
TALENT	Chris Harrison (Narrator)
CAST	Trista Rehn; Ryan Sutter
PRODUCTION COMPANY	Next Entertainment, in association with Telepictures.
EXECUTIVE PRODUCER	Mike Fleiss
CO-EXECUTIVE PRODUCERS	Scott Einziger; Scott Jeffress; Lisa Levenson; Sally Ann Salsano
PRODUCERS	Dan Goldberg; Nelson Soler
CO-PRODUCERS	Glen Freyer; Gary Lucy; David Pullano
DIRECTORS	Ross Breitenbach; Jason A. Carbone; Ken Fuchs

The Bachelorette Trista and her true-love contestant Ryan consulted with a wedding planner and searched for the perfect gown, wedding cake, and flowers on *Trista and Ryan's Wedding*. The couple's families were introduced, and Ryan's bachelor party and Trista's bachelorette party were featured. The two-hour final episode featured their lavish wedding. The show garnered an audience of 17.1 million viewers.

TUCKERVILLE

GENRE	Docudrama
FIRST TELECAST	10/22/2005
NETWORK	TLC
EPISODE STYLE	Self-contained
CAST	Tanya Tucker; Grayson Tucker; Presley Tucker; Layla Tucker; Annie Carroll
PRODUCTION COMPANIES	GRB Entertainment Inc; The Learning Channel (TLC)
EXECUTIVE PRODUCERS	Michael Branton; Elizabeth Browde; Tanya Tucker
PRODUCERS	Alex Eastbury; Peter Glowski; Ralph Greco; Jason Hunt; Paul Kolsby; Heather Urban
DIRECTOR	David Robertson

Country music icon Tanya Tucker is portrayed as a mother of three, living in a beautiful home in the Tennessee hills. The show follows the lives of Tanya, the kids, and their friends. The country legend invites the cameras to chronicle her struggles as she balances her role as a good mother, smart businesswoman, and country star.

TUESDAY NIGHT BOOK CLUB

GENRE	Docusoap
FIRST TELECAST	6/13/2006
LAST TELECAST	6/20/2006
NETWORK	CBS
AIR TIME	Tuesday, 10:00 p.m.
EPISODE STYLE	Story Arc
CAST	Cris (The Loyal Wife); Sara (The Party Girl); Jenn (The Trophy Wife); Jamie (The Conflicted Wife); Kirin (The Doctor's Wife); Lynn (The Newlywed); Tina (The Divorced Mom)
PRODUCTION COMPANIES	The Jay & Tony Show; Magic Molehill Productions
EXECUTIVE PRODUCERS	Jay Blumenfield; Anthony Marsh
PRODUCERS	Patrick Bachmann; Susie Delava; Dean Ollins; Melanie Switzer
DIRECTOR	Tony Sacco

This reality show, patterned after *Desperate Housewives*, followed the lives of a group of women as they dealt with the day-to-day pressures of family life. The series dissected life in suburbia, as seen through the eyes of the women who got together each Tuesday night to discuss everything in their lives, from sex, to spouses, to inner conflicts. The show was pulled off CBS's schedule after two episodes.

TWENTYFOURSEVEN

GENRE	Docudrama
FIRST TELECAST	12/6/2006
LAST TELECAST	12/20/2006
NETWORK	MTV
EPISODES	Self-Contained
CAST	Matt Barker; Chris Carney; Greg Carney; Greg Cipes; Frankie Delgado; Ty Hodges; Greg Whitman
PRODUCERS	Eric Salat; David Shaye
DIRECTOR	Kevin Tancharoen

An entourage of young friends were the central characters of this MTV docudrama set in Hollywood. They included actors, singers, club promoters and producers. The show was one of MTV's shortest-lived reality shows and was canceled after only three episodes.

TWO-A-DAYS

GENRE	Docusoap
FIRST TELECAST	8/23/2006
NETWORK	MTV
EPISODES	Story Arc
CAST	Alex Binder; Kristin Boyle; Jonathan "Goose" Dunham; Max Lerner; Bryan Morgan; Rush Propst; Jeremy Pruitt; Dwarn "Repete" Smith; Cornelius Williams; Ross Wilson
PRODUCTION COMPANIES	Humidity Entertainment
EXECUTIVE PRODUCERS	Amy Bailey; Dave Sirulnick
COEXECUTIVE PRODUCERS	Richard Calderon; Jesse James Dupree; Jason Sciavicco
DIRECTOR	Farrell Roth

The lives of the Hoover High football team in Alabama were chronicled in this docu-soap. One of the most notable characters was the team's tough coach Rush. Stories focused on the rocky relationship between team captain Alex and his cheerleader girl-friend Kristin. Each season followed that year's journey towards the state championship. The first season found the team victorious while the second saw the Hoover Buccaneers losing out on the championship title for the first time in four years.

THE TWO COREYS

GENRE	Docusoap
FIRST TELECAST	7/29/2007
LAST TELECAST	8/12/2007
NETWORK	A&E
EPISODE STYLE	Self-contained
CAST	Corey Haim; Corey Feldman; Susie Feldman
PRODUCTION COMPANY	Insight Film Studios
EXECUTIVE PRODUCERS	Corey Feldman; Corey Haim; Andrew Hoegl; Jonathan Singer
CO-EXECUTIVE PRODUCER	Shannon Fitzgerald
PRODUCERS	Wendy McKerman; Kirk Shaw
DIRECTOR	Jason Bourque

The Two Coreys featured former child stars Corey Feldman and Corey Haim, both grown up, but at very different stages of their lives. Determined to jump-start his acting career and find a stabilizing force, Haim moved in with Feldman and his wife to help get his life on course and to relaunch the "Two Coreys" brand.

TY MURRAY'S CELEBRITY BULL RIDING CHALLENGE

GENRE	Competition
FIRST TELECAST	8/10/2007
NETWORK	CMT
EPISODE STYLE	Story Arc
CAST	"Cowboy" Kenny Bartram; Denny Lee Clark; Jon Dalton; Josh Haynes; Vanilla Ice; Raghib Ismail; Ty Murray; Francesco Quinn; Stephen Baldwin; Leif Garrett; Cody Lambert
PRODUCTION COMPANY	Mess Media
EXECUTIVE PRODUCERS	Trevor Baierl; Scott Messick; Brian Richardson; Melanie Bluthe; Bob Kusbit
PRODUCERS	Tom Cline; Ty Roberts

Ten celebrities saddled-up for ten days of training before taking to the rodeo ring for the longest eight seconds of their lives as bull riders in this competition series. The stars went on to compete at the Professional Bull Riders event held in Nashville, Tennessee. Stephen Baldwin left the show with a broken shoulder and injured ribs. It was reported that Francesco Quinn broke three ribs when a bull stepped on his chest.

THE ULTIMATE COYOTE UGLY SEARCH

GENRE	Competition (Job)
FIRST TELECAST	4/10/2006
NETWORK	CMT
EPISODE STYLE	Story Arc
CAST	Liliana Lovell; Chantel (Mentor); Cyndi (Mentor); Jacqui (Choreographer)
PRODUCTION COMPANY	Touchstone Television
EXECUTIVE PRODUCER	Julie Christie
DIRECTOR	Tiff Winton

Coyote Ugly founder Liliana Lovell heads a nationwide search for the ultimate coyote—a woman who can sing, dance, flair, and bartend better than any other in this job competition. In the first season, women from five cities joined a road trip to New Orleans, the home of Lovell and the spot where the Coyote Ugly bar was having a grand reopening. On the way, the contestants learned Coyote skills, as Lovell eliminated five women. The other final five competed to win $25,000 on grand reopening night at New Orleans's Coyote Ugly.

THE ULTIMATE FIGHTER

GENRE Competition
FIRST TELECAST 1/17/2005
NETWORK Spike
EPISODE STYLE Story Arc
TALENT Willa Ford (Host); Dana White (UFC President—Host); Randy Couture (Coach—Season 1); Chuck Liddell (Coach—Season 1); Matt Hughes (Coach—Season 2); Rich Franklin (Coach—Season 2); Ken Shamrock (Coach—Season 3); Tito Ortiz (Coach—Season 3); Mark DellaGrotte (Season 4); Marc Laimon (Coach—Season 4); Jens Pulver (Coach—Season 5); B.J. Penn (Coach—Season 5); Matt Serra (Coach—Season 6); Matt Hughes (Coach—Season 6)

CAST

Season 1 Forrest Griffin (Winner—Light Heavyweight); Diego Sanchez (Winner—Middleweight); Stephan Bonnar; Kenny Florian; Sam Hoger; Alex Karalexis; Josh Koscheck; Chris Leben; Nate Quarry; Josh Rafferty; Christopher Sanford; Alex Schoenauer; Lodune Sincaid; Bobby Southworth; Mike Swick; Jason Thacker

Season 2 Rashad Evans (Winner—Heavyweight); Rob MacDonald (Heavyweight); Keith Jardine (Heavyweight); Kerry Schall (Heavyweight); Brad Imes (Heavyweight); Seth Petruzelli (Heavyweight); Mike Whitehead (Heavyweight); Tom Murphy (Heavyweight); Eli Joslin (Heavyweight); Joe Stevenson (Winner—

Welterweight); Jorge Gurgel (Welterweight);
Anthony Torres (Welterweight); Melvin Guillard
(Welterweight); Josh Burkman (Welterweight);
Marcus Davis (Welterweight); Sammy Morgan
(Welterweight); Kenny Stevens (Welterweight);
Luke Cummo (Welterweight)

Season 3   Kendall Grove (Winner—Middleweight); Mike Stine
(Middleweight); Rory Singer (Middleweight);
Danny Abbadi (Middleweight); Kalib Starnes
(Middleweight); Solomon Hutcherson
(Middleweight); Ed Herman (Middleweight);
Ross Pointon (Middleweight); Michael Bisping
(Winner—Light Heavyweight); Noah Inhofer (Light
Heavyweight); Josh Haynes (Light Heavyweight);
Matt Hamill (Light Heavyweight); Jesse Forbes
(Light Heavyweight); Kristian Rothaermel (Light
Heavyweight); Tait Fletcher (Light Heavyweight);
Mike Nickels (Light Heavyweight)

Season 4   Travis Lutter (Winner—Middleweight);
Charles McCarthy (Middleweight); Gideon Ray
(Middleweight); Jorge Rivera (Middleweight);
Pete Sell (Middleweight); Scott Smith
(Middleweight); Patrick Côté (Middleweight);
Edwin DeWees (Middleweight); Matt Serra
(Winner—Welterweight); Rich Clementi
(Welterweight); Mikey Burnett (Welterweight);
Jeremy Jackson (Welterweight); Pete Spratt
(Welterweight); Shonie Carter (Welterweight);
Chris Lytle (Welterweight); Din Thomas
(Welterweight)

Season 5   B.J. Penn (Winner over Jens Pulver);
Nate Diaz (Winner over Manvel Gambaryan);
Manvel Gambaryan; Gray Maynard; Matt Wiman;

	Gabe Ruediger; Joe Lauzon; Rob Emerson; Andy Wnag; Allen Berube; Noah Thomas; Corey Hill; Brandon Melendez; Marlon Sims; Cole Miller; Brian Geraghty; Wayne Weems
Season 6	(Winner—TBA), Matt Arroyo; Daniel Barrera; Blake Bowman; Mac Danzig; Paul Georgieff; Richie Hightower; John Kolsci; Troy Mandaloniz; Billy Miles; Roman Mitichyan; Dorian Price; Jared Rollins; Ben Saunders; Joe Scarola; George Sotiropoulos; Tommy Speer
PRODUCTION COMPANIES	Pilgrim Films and Television; Full Circle Entertainment
CREATED BY	Craig Piligian; Robert Riesenberg
EXECUTIVE PRODUCER	Robert Riesenberg
CO-EXECUTIVE PRODUCERS	Andrea Richter; Ralph Wikke
PRODUCERS	Angela Chiu; Rob Dorfman; Tom Greenhut; Mark Leonard; Eric Mazer; Dana White; Thomas Loureiro; Jamie Campione; Dax Dobbs; Amanda Ross; Zosimo Maximo

This competition series features eighteen martial arts fighters (representing different disciplines and weight classes) who live and train together, and battle against each other for more than thirty-eight days in pursuit of a contract with the Ultimate Fighting Championship organization. In Season 4, the format changed. Instead of featuring UFC hopefuls, the contestants were fighters who had fought in the UFC but hadn't won a title. In Season 5, all competitors were from the same weight division. The coaches also competed in the season finale.

ULTIMATE FUSE GIG: THE VJ SEARCH

GENRE	Competition
FIRST TELECAST	3/10/2005
NETWORK	Fuse

EPISODE STYLE	Story Arc
PRODUCTION COMPANY	Teale-Edwards Productions
CO-EXECUTIVE PRODUCER	Brian Wahlund

Ultimate Fuse Gig: The VJ Search chronicled the television music network's hunt for a new VJ. Both good and bad auditions were spotlighted, and the winners from casting calls in each city flew to New York to participate in the live finale, where viewers decided who would become Fuse's next VJ. That honor went to Adonis Thompson, from Memphis, Tennessee, a graduate of Arkansas State University. Thompson beat Los Angeles DJ Ronnie Ruelas, Jr.

THE ULTIMATE LOVE TEST

GENRE	Docudrama (Romance)
FIRST TELECAST	6/2/2004
LAST TELECAST	7/21/2004
NETWORK	ABC
AIR TIME	Wednesday, 10:00 p.m.
EPISODE STYLE	Story Arc
CAST	Frank Primorac; Carolyn; Jayre; Heather Ballentine; Diego Currier; Kenesha; Amber Rood; Brandon Showalter; Brooke Barlow (Brandon's Date); Amanda Boyce (Jayre's Date); C. R. Clatworthy (Heather's Ex-Boyfriend/Date); Eva (Jayre's Date); Teneisha (Jayre's Date); Roy Vongtama (Amber's Date)
PRODUCTION COMPANY	American Broadcasting Company (ABC); Renegade 83.6
CREATED BY	David Garfinkle; Jay Renfroe; Greg Goldman
EXECUTIVE PRODUCERS	David Garfinkle; Clay Newbill
PRODUCER	Greg Goldman
DIRECTORS	Jeff Fisher; Bryan O'Donnell; Sean Travis

The Ultimate Love Test gave couples an opportunity discover if their long-term dating relationships would evolve in to marriage or be dissolved. Couples were separated, and one partner went to Cabo San Lucas, Mexico, to meet with people whose lives represented everything they felt was missing from their current relationship. The stay-behind partner received video messages from his or her significant other, showing what was transpiring.

ULTIMATE REALITY

GENRE	Docudrama (Wish-Fulfillment)
FIRST TELECAST	10/11/2001
NETWORK	A&E
EPISODE STYLE	Self-contained
PRODUCTION COMPANY	A&E Television Networks, Inc.; Diplomatic Productions
EXECUTIVE PRODUCERS	Yann Debonne; Matti Leshem; Michael Davies
PRODUCERS	Patrick Doody; Chris Valenziano

Ten ordinary people were given the opportunity to live their dreams and fulfill their lifelong goals on action-packed adventures in *Ultimate Reality*. Experiences included swimming close to a great white shark, jousting, auto racing, flying an F-16, and joining the circus.

UNAN1MOUS

GENRE	Competition
FIRST TELECAST	3/22/2006
LAST TELECAST	5/10/2006
NETWORK	FOX
AIR TIME	Wednesday, 9:30 p.m.
EPISODE STYLE	Story Arc

TALENT	J. D. Roth (Host)
CAST	Tarah Smith (Winner); Richard; Jameson; Kelly; Jonathan; Jamie; Steve; Vanessa; Adam
PRODUCTION COMPANY	3 Ball Productions
EXECUTIVE PRODUCERS	John Foy; Lincoln D. Hiatt; Todd A. Nelson; J. D. Roth
PRODUCER	Adam Paul
DIRECTOR	Brian Smith

Nine *Unan1mous* contestants were locked in a bunker with no sunlight, no outside contact, and no clocks. Under these conditions, they had to unanimously decide which contestant would get $1.5 million, but for every second they failed to make a unanimous decision, the pot depleted by one dollar. Meanwhile, many twists and turns were thrown at the competitors. Tarah Smith won, earning the grand prize, which, by the end of the show, had dwindled to $382,193.

UNDER ONE ROOF

GENRE	Competition
FIRST TELECAST	3/22/2002
LAST TELECAST	7/16/2002
NETWORK	UPN
AIR TIMES	Friday, 8:00 p.m. (3/2002); Tuesday, 9:00 p.m. (7/2002)
EPISODE STYLE	Story Arc
TALENT	Rob Nelson (host)
CAST	The Skofields (Holly, Matt, Mike, and Brittany); The McRaes (Trent, Kristen, Shannon, Jeanelle and Larry); The Hatmakers (Jonathan, Michelle, and Daniel with Mark Anderson); The Paganis (Robin, Jorge, Giancarlo, Marchella, and

Bianca Paganis); The Distels (David, Lyn, Melissa, and Mike)

PRODUCTION COMPANY Endemol
CREATED BY Charlie Parsons
EXECUTIVE PRODUCER Bruce Toms
PRODUCER Monica Ramone

Five families competed against one another in this competition series set on the Fijian island of Koro. The families lived together in a house for three weeks and competed in a series of challenges. Each episode featured a Property Quest and a Family Face Off. The Face Off was a challenge for a reward, while the Property Quest challenge earned the winning family a ribbon that put them one step closer to winning the grand prize: a house in the Polynesian islands. At certain points in the series, the family that had the fewest number of ribbons from the Property Quest challenges was eliminated. Only three of the episodes aired, and the winner of the competition remained a mystery to viewers.

VEGAS SHOWGIRLS: NEARLY FAMOUS

GENRE Docusoap

FIRST TELECAST 1/21/2002

NETWORK E!

EPISODE STYLE Story Arc

CAST Ritchie Allen (Dancer—Season 2); Pudgy Cardella (Comedienne—Season 2); Tony D'Andrea (Comedian—Season 2); Shannon O'Keefe (Lead Dancer—Season 2); Nicole Paone (Dancer—Season 2); Darryl Ross (Lead Singer—Season 2); Greg Thompson (*Skintight* Producer—Season 2); Laine (Dancer—Season 1); Amelia Bruff (Dancer—Season 1); John Ortiz (Dancer—Season 1); Greta Corey (Dancer—Season 1); Tammi (Dancer—Season 1); Scott Lockwood (Quality Captain—Season 1); Fluff (Company Manager—Season 1)

PRODUCTION COMPANY	E! Entertainment Television
EXECUTIVE PRODUCERS	Brent Zacky (Season 2); Jeff Shore (Season 1)
PRODUCER	Carmen Mitcho (Season 2)

Vegas Showgirls: Nearly Famous followed the backstage drama of a real Vegas dance revue. Season 1 followed the behind-the-scenes action of Bally's *Jubilee!,* while the show's second season focused the Vegas Strip's sexiest show, Harrah's *Skintight.*

VEGAS WEDDINGS UNVEILED

GENRE	Docudrama
FIRST TELECAST	6/18/2004
NETWORK	GSN
EPISODE STYLE	Self-contained
TALENT	Darva Conger (Host)
PRODUCTION COMPANY	Sokolobl Entertainment
CREATED BY	Sam Sokolow; Rob Lobl
EXECUTIVE PRODUCERS	Sam Sokolow; Rob Lobl; John Hermansen
CO-EXECUTIVE PRODUCER	Matthew Gaven

Whether preplanned and elaborate or impromptu and themed, the weddings featured on *Vegas Weddings Unveiled* showed the time-honored tradition of getting hitched in Sin City. Through interviews, anecdotes, and hidden-camera footage, often bizarre Las Vegas nuptials were highlighted.

VENUS AND SERENA: FOR REAL

GENRE	Docudrama (Celebrity)
FIRST TELECAST	7/20/2005
NETWORK	ABC Family
EPISODE STYLE	Story Arc

CAST	Venus Williams; Serena Williams
PRODUCTION COMPANY	Repeat Offender
EXECUTIVE PRODUCERS	Fernando Hernandez; Bobby Pura
CO-EXECUTIVE PRODUCERS	Jill Dickerson
DIRECTOR	Jill Dickerson

This docudrama spotlighted the lives of professional tennis stars and sisters Venus and Serena Williams. In addition to featuring the sisters' preparations for tennis matches, the series showed Venus and Serena attending red-carpet events, posing for photo shoots, and spending time at home with their family.

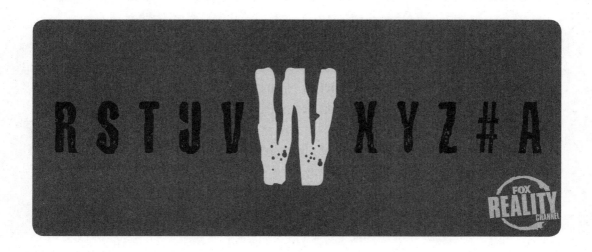

WANNA COME IN?

GENRE	Competition (Dating)
FIRST TELECAST	7/2/2004
NETWORK	MTV
EPISODE STYLE	Self-contained
TALENT	Evan Scott Golden (Coach); Colby Christopher (Coach)
PRODUCTION COMPANY	Nash Entertainment
EXECUTIVE PRODUCERS	Yann Debonne; Bruce Nash
PRODUCERS	Michelle Brando; Jason Cooper; Claudine Magre
CO-PRODUCERS	Glen Freyer; Gary Lucy; David Pullano
SEGMENT PRODUCERS	Aaron Ginsburg; Wade McIntyre
DIRECTORS	Katherine Brooks; Jen Friesen

On each episode of *Wanna Come In?*, a single guy goes out on a date. Unbeknownst to the woman, he is wearing an earpiece over which a self-professed stud transmits advice in an attempt to improve the guy's confidence in impressing the girl. If the escorted girl asks the guy to enter her house, the stud earns a monetary prize.

WANTED: TED OR ALIVE

GENRE	Competition
FIRST TELECAST	11/5/2005
NETWORK	OLN
TALENT	Ted Nugent (host)
PRODUCTION COMPANIES	Outdoor Life Network (OLN); The Jay & Tony Show
EXECUTIVE PRODUCERS	Jay Blumenfield; Anthony Marsh
PRODUCERS	Patrick Bachmann; Trevor Baierl; Susie Delava; Scott Hirsch; Erin Paullus; Ty Roberts; Marla Schwartz; Shelley Sinha; Brian Spoor
DIRECTOR	Jennifer Lane

In this competition series, five city slickers had to spend a week in the wilderness, competing against one another in challenges of survival and outdoor skill, while rock legend and hunting enthusiast Ted Nugent looked on. Participants won points by completing challenges. The contestant who earned the most points won $25,000.

A WEDDING STORY

GENRE	Docudrama
FIRST TELECAST	1996
NETWORK	TLC
EPISODE STYLE	Self-contained
PRODUCTION COMPANIES	Banyan Productions; Film Garden (2004–2005)
EXECUTIVE PRODUCERS	Charles DeBevoise (2004–2005); Mark Hickman (2004–2005)
PRODUCERS	Tatiana Fuster (2004–2005); Jennifer Holbach (2004–2005); Kelly Nathe (2004–2005)
DIRECTOR	Joe Dea

Each episode of *A Wedding Story* features one wedding seen through the eyes of the bride and groom. Shot over three days, and beginning with the pre-wedding preparations and moving through the reception, the series shows couples tying the knot, sometimes in unusual locations throughout the world.

WELCOME TO THE PARKER

GENRE	Docusoap
FIRST TELECAST	7/26/2007
NETWORK	Bravo
EPISODE STYLE	Self-contained
CAST	Thomas Meding; Samir Chraibi; Michael Crawford; John Federbusch; Lynne Dibley; Rocia Varela; Michael Twomey; Andrea Higgins; Nathan Lourn
PRODUCTION COMPANY	Snackaholic
EXECUTIVE PRODUCERS	Belisa Balaban; Ted Skillman
CO-EXECUTIVE PRODUCERS	Blake Levin; Michaline Babich
PRODUCERS	Jairus Cobb; Ben Faulks; Gregg Paine
DIRECTOR	Jairus Cobb

The luxurious Parker Palm Springs Hotel was the setting for *Welcome to the Parker,* which followed the dramatic, complicated, exhausting lives and relationships of the esteemed hotel staff and the demanding guests.

WHAT NOT TO WEAR

GENRE	Docudrama (Makeover)
FIRST TELECAST	5/10/2003
NETWORK	TLC
AIR TIMES	Friday, 9:00 p.m.
EPISODE STYLE	Self-contained

TALENT	Stacy London (Fashion Guru); Clinton Kelly (Fashion Guru); Nick Arrojo (Hair Stylist); Carmindy (Makeup Artist)
PRODUCTION COMPANY	BBC Productions
EXECUTIVE PRODUCER	Abigail Harvey
PRODUCER	Brooke Smiler

Inspired by the BBC series of the same name, *What Not to Wear* features a fashion-challenged person who was nominated by friends for a $5,000 makeover by the Fashion Police. While shopping in New York City for two days, the "fashion victim" is given wardrobe tips, while the old apparel is thrown away.

WHILE YOU WERE OUT

GENRE	Docudrama (Makeover)
FIRST TELECAST	7/6/2002
NETWORK	TLC
EPISODE STYLE	Self-contained
TALENT	Anna Bocci (Host—Episodes 1–10); Teresa Strasser (Host—Episodes 11–60); Evan Farmer (Host—Season 2–present); Ali Barone (Carpenter—Season 2–present); Mark Montano (Designer—Season 2–present); Nadia Geller (Designer); Stephen Saint-Onge (Designer); Leslie Segrete (Carpenter); Peter Bonsey (Garden Designer—Season 1); Mayita Dinos (Landscape Designer—Season 1); Chayse Dacoda (Designer); John Bruce (Designer); Jason Cameron (Carpenter—Season 2–present); Andrew Dan-Jumbo (Carpenter)
EXECUTIVE PRODUCER	Stephen Schwartz
DIRECTORS	Boaz Halaban; Dean Slotar; Todd Brodar; Virginia Somma

In *While You Were Out,* under the aid of a designer, two carpenters, and the host, a homeowner's close friend redecorates a room or landscapes the backyard of the homeowner in two days. When the makeover recipient returns to his or her home, the surprise is revealed.

WHO WANTS TO BE A SUPERHERO?

GENRE	Competition
FIRST TELECAST	7/27/2006
NETWORK	SCI FI
EPISODES	Story Arc

CAST:

Season 1 Matthew Atherton (Winner—aka Feedback); Nell Wilson (Runner-up—aka Fat Momma); Chris Watters (9th eliminated—aka Major Victory); Tonatzin Mondragon (8th eliminated—aka Lemuria); Tonya Kay (7th eliminated—aka Creature); E. Quincy Sloan (6th eliminated—aka Tyveculus); Mary Votava (5th eliminated—aka Monkey Woman) Steel Chambers (4th eliminated—aka The Iron Enforcer); Chelsea Weld (3rd eliminated—aka Cell Phone Girl); Darren Passarello (2nd eliminated—aka Nitro G); Tobias Trost (1st eliminated—aka Levity)

Season 2 Jarrett Crippen (Winner—aka The Defuser); John Stork (Runner-up—aka Hyper-Strike); Melody Mooney (Runner-up—aka Hygena); Dan Williams (7th eliminated—aka Parthenon); Paula Thomas (6th eliminated—aka Whip-Snap); Aja De Coudreaux (5th eliminated—aka Basura); Trisha Paytas (4th eliminated—aka Ms. Limelight); "Sir

Ivan" Wilzig (3rd eliminated—aka Mr. Mitzvah);
Phillip Allen (2nd eliminated—aka Mindset);
Crystal Clark (1st eliminated—aka Braid)

PRODUCTION COMPANIES	POW! Entertainment; Nash Entertainment
EXECUTIVE PRODUCERS	Stan Lee; Scott Satin; Gill Champion; Bruce Nash
CO-EXECUTIVE PRODUCERS	Yuka Kobayashi; Gabriel Grunfeld; Robert Kosberg; Rick Telles
DIRECTOR	Craig Borders; Rick Telles

This unique competition series hosted by comic book legend Stan Lee featured a group of aspiring superheroes fighting for the ultimate prize: immortality. This immortality came in the form of having their character appear in their very own comic book and in a SCI FI Channel movie.

Each episode put competitors through challenges that tested their superhero skills; often the competitors would be in the middle of a challenge without knowing it. These challenges included helping out a lost crying child in the middle of a park, walking through a yard of vicious guard dogs, and a hidden-camera task set in a café where servers tried to trick the aspiring heroes into revealing their hidden identities.

Season 1's winner was Matthew Atherton whose hero was Feedback, a character who took on the powers of the video game characters he played. Season 2's winner was Jarrett Crippen whose hero was The Defuser, a weapons expert whose skill was the ability to do everything 110%.

WHO WANTS TO MARRY MY DAD?

GENRE	Competition (Dating)
FIRST TELECAST	7/14/2003
LAST TELECAST	8/2/2004
NETWORK	NBC
AIR TIME	Monday, 10:00 p.m.
EPISODE STYLE	Story Arc

CAST

Season 1 **Family** Don Mueller (dad); Joe Mueller (son); Chris Mueller (son); Karla Barela (daughter); Christy Fichtner (daughter)

Bachelorettes Christena (Winner); Christy (Runner-up); Christie (eliminated in Episode 5); Cynthia (eliminated in Episode 4); Lori (eliminated in Episode 3); Kathy (quit in Episode 3); Joanne (eliminated in Episode 2); Patti (eliminated in Episode 2); Carol (eliminated in Episode 1)

Season 2 **Family** Marty Okland (dad); Brooke Okland (daughter); Jennifer Okland (daughter), Nicole Okland (daughter)

Bachelorettes Stacy (Winner); Suzanne (Runner-up); Marilyn (eliminated in Episode 5); Melanie (eliminated in Episode 4); Nicole (eliminated in Episode 4); Sharon (eliminated in Episode 3); Tammy (eliminated in Episode 3); Machel (eliminated in Episode 2); Sarah (eliminated in Episode 2); Lola (mole in Episodes 1 and 2); Layne (eliminated in Episode 1); Debbie (eliminated in Episode 1); Tina (eliminated in Episode 1)

PRODUCTION COMPANY Nash Entertainment; Satin Productions

CREATED BY Bruce Nash

EXECUTIVE PRODUCERS Bruce Nash; Scott Satin

CO-EXECUTIVE PRODUCER Andrew Jebb

PRODUCERS Ed Horwitz; Jeff Kopp; Eric Waddell (Season 2); Timothy Scott (Season 2)

DIRECTOR Chris Donovan

In *Who Wants to Marry My Dad?*, the adult children of a single father looking for love searched for a woman to be their father's next wife. Looks and personality mattered, but so did the lie-detector test administered to the prospective brides. Season 2 added a twist when the daughter's aunt acted as a mole in the first two episodes. At the conclusion of Season 1, single dad Don proposed to contestant Christena. At the end of Season 2, single dad Marty proposed to Stacy. Neither proposal resulted in marriage.

WHY CAN'T I BE YOU?

GENRE	Docudrama
FIRST TELECAST	6/4/2006
NETWORK	MTV
EPISODES	Self-contained
TALENT	Nick Zano (host)
PRODUCTION COMPANY	Axial Entertainment
EXECUTIVE PRODUCER	Riaz Patel
DIRECTORS	Larry Grimaldi; Jerry Carita; Esther Frank; Christopher Hutson; Riaz Patel; Michael Rotman

This makeover show featured young people stepping into the shoes of people in their lives whom they admired. The person whom they admired guided them through the makeover process in an effort to get them to live their new lives in a two-day period.

WICKEDLY PERFECT

GENRE	Competition (Job)
FIRST TELECAST	1/6/2005
LAST TELECAST	3/5/2005
NETWORK	CBS
AIR TIMES	Thursday, 8:00 p.m. (1/2005); Saturday, 8:00 p.m. (1/2005–3/2005)
EPISODE STYLE	Story Arc
TALENT	Joan Lunden (Host); Bobby Flay (Judge);

	David Evangelista (Judge); Candace Bushnell (Judge)
CAST	Kimberly Kennedy (Team Artisan—Winner); Mitchell Pennell (Crafty Beavers—Runner-up); Dawn Schedule (Team Artisan—9th eliminated); Amy Guglielmo (Crafty Beavers—8th eliminated); Darlene Cahill (Team Artisan—8th eliminated); Heather Shrake (Crafty Beavers—7th eliminated); Denise Crandall (Crafty Beavers—6th eliminated); Margo Leidigh (Team Artisan—5th eliminated); Tim Bell (Crafty Beavers—4th eliminated); Mychael Chang (Crafty Beavers—3rd eliminated); Michelle Cozens (Team Artisan—2nd eliminated); Tom Frank (Team Artisan—1st eliminated)
PRODUCTION COMPANY	LMNO Productions
EXECUTIVE PRODUCERS	Eric Schotz; Bill Paolantonio; Larry Bleidner; Laurie Girion; Marc Summers
PRODUCERS	Julie Bean; Jennifer L. Ehrman
DIRECTOR	Chris Donovan

Set on a palatial Connecticut estate, this thirty-day elimination competition searched for the next Martha Stewart. Twelve competitors divided into two teams—the Crafty Beavers and Team Artisan—competed in baking, cooking, crafts, gardening, party planning, and entertaining challenges. The winner, Kimberly Kennedy, earned numerous prizes, including six guest appearances on CBS's *The Early Show,* a book publishing deal, and a development deal for a lifestyle-oriented television show.

WIFE, MOM, BOUNTY HUNTER

GENRE	Docusoap
FIRST TELECAST	4/20/2007
LAST TELECAST	6/29/2007

NETWORK	WE
EPISODE STYLE	Self-contained
CAST	Sandra Scott; Ron Scott; Sabree Scott; David Rozen; J. D. Wall; Les Fjelstul; Dana Schnell; Darrell Roy
PRODUCTION COMPANIES	Rainbow Media; World of Wonder
EXECUTIVE PRODUCERS	Fenton Bailey; Randy Barbato
PRODUCER	Jill Williams

On *Wife, Mom, Bounty Hunter,* a woman juggled being a mom to two kids, acting as a loving wife and working as an adventurous bounty hunter, catching lawbreakers.

WIFE SWAP

GENRE	Docudrama
FIRST TELECAST	9/26/2004
NETWORK	ABC
AIR TIME	Sunday, 10:00 p.m. (9/2004); Wednesday, 10:00 p.m. (9/2004–3/2005); Monday, 8:00 p.m. (9/2005–3/2007); Friday, 9:00 p.m. (3/2007–4/2007); Monday, 8:00 p.m. (5/2007–present)
EPISODE STYLE	Self-contained
PRODUCTION COMPANY	RDF Media
EXECUTIVE PRODUCERS	Stephen Lambert; Michael Davies; Jenny Crowther; Wendy Roth
PRODUCER	Michael Kaufman
DIRECTORS	Adam Kassen; Sara Mast; Phillip Lott

Based on the award-winning show in the United Kingdom, American families with opposite lifestyles swapped wives for a week on *Wife Swap.* Each wife tried to take control of her new family by changing dietary, spending, and cleaning habits, sometimes encountering resistance, but often creating humorous situations as well. The original couples later met for the first time at the end of the week to exchange ideas and feelings about the experience. Season 1 featured two variations: one episode swapped bosses, while a second swapped vacations.

WILDBOYZ

GENRE	Docudrama
FIRST TELECAST	11/11/2004
LAST TELECAST	4/22/2005
NETWORK	MTV
EPISODE STYLE	Self-contained
CAST	Chris Pontius; Steve-O
EXECUTIVE PRODUCERS	Trip Taylor, Jeff Tremaine
PRODUCER	Derek Freda
DIRECTOR	Jeff Tremaine

Jackass alumni Chris Pontius and Steve-O took their show on the road in *Wildboyz*, touring the world and showing off their absurd antics while exploring animal life, sampling native cuisine and soaking up local culture.

THE WILL

GENRE	Competition
FIRST TELECAST	1/8/05
LAST TELECAST	1/8/05
NETWORK	CBS
AIR TIME	Saturday, 8:00 PM
EPISODES	Story Arc
CAST	Bill Long (The benefactor—Scottsdale, Arizona land developer); Penny Long (The wife); Bill Long

Jr. (The son); Bette Miller (The mother-in-law); Scott Miller (The brother-in-law); Ashley Mutrux (The stepson); Josh Magee (The surrogate son); Crystal Salas (The family friend); Danielle Pino (The trusted employee); Kristin Holinsworth (Ashley's ex-girlfriend—9th place); Mickey Nelson (Lifelong friend—10th place)

PRODUCTION COMPANY	Next Entertainment in association with Telepictures
CREATED BY	Mike Fleiss
EXECUTIVE PRODUCERS	Mike Fleiss

Produced by *The Bachelor* creator Mike Fleiss, ten friends and family of a wealthy Arizona land developer competed in the hope of inheriting a large ranch in Kansas. Despite being ordered for six episodes, the show was cancelled by CBS after only one airing because of low ratings (9.3 million viewers).

WING NUTS

GENRE	Docudrama
FIRST TELECAST	9/28/2004
NETWORK	Discovery Channel
AIR TIME	Tuesday, 10:00 p.m.
EPISODE STYLE	Self-contained
TALENT	Timothy Roberts (Host)
CAST	Donovan Fell (MotoArt Owner); Dave Hall (MotoArt Owner); Mark Morriss; Thomas Ramey
PRODUCTION COMPANY	Original Productions
CREATED BY	Donavan Fell; Dave Hall
EXECUTIVE PRODUCER	Thom Beers
PRODUCER	Dean Ollins

On *Wing Nuts,* the owners of MotoArt turned salvaged aircraft parts into furniture. The series came to an end when host Tim Robert died unexpectedly from a heart attack.

WORK OUT

GENRE	Docudrama
FIRST TELECAST	7/19/2006
NETWORK	Bravo
EPISODE STYLE	Self-contained
CAST	Jackie Warner; Jesse Brune; Brian Peeler; Erika Jacobson; Andre Riley; Doug Blasdell; Rebecca Cardon; Jennifer Gray
PRODUCTION COMPANY	Bravo TV
EXECUTIVE PRODUCERS	Cori Abraham; Lori Kaye; Amy Shpall; Bruce Toms

Work Out follows the professional and personal life of Jackie Warner, noted trainer, businesswoman, and owner of the successful Sky Sport and Spa in Beverly Hills. The show also features her team of trainers and their elite clientele.

THE WORLD'S CRAZIEST VIDEOS

GENRE	Docucomedy
FIRST TELECAST	1/9/2004
LAST TELECAST	11/5/2004
NETWORK	FOX
AIR TIME	Friday, 8:30 p.m.
EPISODE STYLE	Self-contained
TALENT	Brian Unger (Host)
PRODUCTION COMPANY	Brad Lachman
EXECUTIVE PRODUCER	Brad Lachman

The World's Craziest Videos featured hilarious videos from around the world, including TV bloopers and mishaps from weddings, vacations, and home videos.

WWE TOUGH ENOUGH

GENRE	Competition
FIRST TELECAST	6/21/2001
LAST TELECAST	12/9/2004
NETWORK	MTV; UPN
EPISODE STYLE	Story Arc
TALENT	Al Snow (Judge); Tazz (Judge); Tori (Judge); Jacqueline (Judge); William DeMott (Judge); Lisa Moretti (Judge); Bob Howard (Judge); Chavo Guerrero, Jr. (Judge); Raphael Verela (Judge)

CAST

Season 1 Nidia (Winner); Maven (Winner); Darryl; Bobbie Jo; Jason; Victoria; Shadrick; Greg; Chris Ni; Josh; Chris No; Taylor; Paulina

Season 2 Jackie Gayda (Winner); Linda Miles (Winner); Aaron; Danny Carney; Jake; Anni King; Kenny Layne; Matt Morgan; Pete Tornatore; Jessica Ward; Kenny Yates; Hawk Younkins

Season 3 Matt Cappotelli (Winner); John Hennigan (Winner); Jonah Adelman; Chad; Scott Chong; Kevin Dunn; Eric Markovcy; Rebekah

Season 4 Daniel Puder (Winner); Josh Matthews; Chris Nawrocki; Ryan Reeves; Justice Smith; Daniel Rodimer; John Meyer; Nick Mitchell; Mike Mizanin

EXECUTIVE PRODUCER Ken Mok
DIRECTORS Darren Ewing; Michael E. Polakow; C. B. Harding

This World Wrestling Entertainment–produced series followed aspiring male and female wrestlers as they competed for a contract with a professional wresting company. Two winners were chosen from first three seasons. The fourth season, which aired as part of UPN's *SmackDown*, produced only one winner, who captured the $1 million professional wrestling contract.

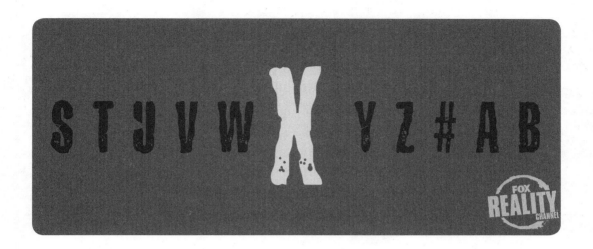

THE X EFFECT

GENRE	Competition (Dating)
FIRST TELECAST:	6/6/07
NETWORK	MTV
EPISODES	Self-contained
TALENT	Thomas Bridgegroom
PRODUCTION COMPANY	4th Row Films
EXECUTIVE PRODUCERS	Amy Wruble; Mike Powers; Douglas Tirola
CO-EXECUTIVE PRODUCER	Suzanna Pate

In this competition series, two exes who were currently seeing other people were brought to a resort. There the ex-boyfriend and ex-girlfriend were reunited and spent a weekend together while their current partners watched via hidden cameras. At the end of each episode, the exes had to choose whether they wanted to reconcile or stay with their current partners.

XTREME FAKEOVERS

GENRE	Docusoap (Hoax)
FIRST TELECAST	4/18/2005
NETWORK	i; PAX
EPISODE STYLE	Story Arc
TALENT	Samantha Phillips (Host)
PRODUCTION COMPANY	Woody Fraser Productions; Keller Productions
CREATED BY	Eytan Keller; Woody Fraser
EXECUTIVE PRODUCERS	Eytan Keller; Woody Fraser

This comedy reality series featured two people undergoing complete body makeovers from a crew of skilled Hollywood makeup artists. The participants donned body-sculpting suits and wore prosthetic appliances to fool their close friends and family. The resulting comedic moments were captured on hidden camera.

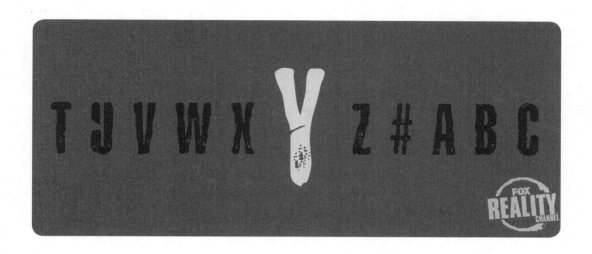

YOUR BIG BREAK

GENRE	Competition (Talent)
FIRST TELECAST	9/1999
LAST TELECAST	9/2000
NETWORK	Syndicated
EPISODE STYLE	Story Arc
TALENT	Christopher Reid (Host, 1999–2000); Alfonso Ribeiro (Host, 2000)
PRODUCTION COMPANY	Dick Clark Productions
EXECUTIVE PRODUCERS	Dick Clark; Larry Klein
PRODUCER	Sue Nadell
DIRECTOR	Barry Glazer

Talented amateur singers received makeovers to look like their favorite recording artists on *Your Big Break*. The hopefuls then performed before a studio audience that voted for the best lookalike and sound-alike contestant. The winners from each episode competed in the finals for a $25,000 grand prize.

THE ULTIMATE REALITY TV QUIZ

1. Which of these reality stars did *not* appear on E!'s *Kill Reality*?

a. Johnny Fairplay

b. Tonya Cooley

c. Trishelle Cannatella

d. Clay Jordon

2. Which of these has *not* been a nickname for one of the girls on *Flavor of Love*?

a. Somethin'

b. Sex-E

c. Spunkee

d. Smokey

3. *Gene Simmons: Family Jewels* star Gene Simmons has appeared on all but which of these reality series?

a. *Star Search*

b. *The Apprentice*

c. *Rock School*

d. *The Contender*

4. Which *NewsRadio* actor starred in the MTV reality series in which twelve talented young people groveled for the opportunity for the position of "the Assistant"?

a. Dave Foley

b. Joe Rogan

c. Andy Dick

d. Maura Tierney

5. What uniform did Lillian "Lill" Morris wear on *Survivor: Pearl Islands*?

a. Boy Scoutmaster

b. Nurse

c. Meter Maid

d. Lifeguard

6. Which TV celebrity did *not* compete on the Bravo series *Battle of the Network Reality Stars*?

a. Melissa Howard

b. Gervase Peterson

c. Kelly Wiglesworth

d. Adam Mesh

7. The reality series title *Deadliest Catch* refers to catching what?

a. a great white shark

b. a ball

c. a bunch of crabs

d. a disease

8. Melissa Rivers was a competitor on which reality series?

a. *Battle of the Network Reality Stars*

b. *Celebrity Mole: Yucatan*

c. *Celebrity Paranormal Project*

d. *I'm a Celebrity, Get Me Out of Here!*

9. The third season of which reality competition series awarded the prize of becoming head chef at the Green Valley Ranch Resort, Spa and Casino?

a. *Hell's Kitchen*

b. *Top Chef*

c. *The Restaurant*

d. *Dinner: Impossible*

10. Which former *Brady Bunch* star has *never* appeared on a reality series?

a. Florence Henderson

b. Barry Williams

c. Maureen McCormick

d. Eve Plumb

11. Before appearing on *Beauty and the Geek*, Richard Rubin appeared on what MTV reality show?

a. *Next*

b. *Punk'd*

c. *Room Raiders*

d. *One Bad Trip*

12. On *The Anna Nicole Show,* Sugar Pie was what?

a. Anna's personal assistant

b. Anna's dog

c. Anna's decorator

d. Anna's hairdresser

13. Which film director was never a judge on FOX's *On the Lot*?

a. Carrie Fisher

b. Penny Marshall

c. Garry Marshall

d. Steven Spielberg

14. Which of these former MTV VJs made a cameo on *The Surreal Life: Fame Games*?

a. Kennedy

b. Adam Curry

c. "Downtown" Julie Brown

d. Carson Daly

15. Which of these series did Mark Burnett *not* executive-produce?

a. *Eco-Challenge*

b. *The Contender*

c. *The Casino*

d. *Temptation Island*

16. Which of these pairs of *Big Brother* contestants are not related to each other?

a. Season 4's Justin and Allison

b. Season 5's Nakomis and Cowboy

c. Season 5's Natalie and Adria

d. Season 8's Dick and Daniele

17. *The Complex* was a show about restoring and redecorating a four-unit apartment in which resort town?

a. Malibu, California

b. South Beach, Miami, Florida

c. Oahu, Hawaii

d. San Diego, California

18. Which *Survivor* star has *not* posed for *Playboy* magazine?

a. Jerri Manthey

b. Jenna Morasca

c. Lisa Keiffer

d. Heidi Strobel

19. Who was the winner of the first and only *World Idol* competition?

a. Kelly Clarkson (USA)

b. Kurt Nilsen (Norway)

c. Peter Evrad (Belgium)

d. Heinz Winkler (South Africa)

20. Which of these cities has served as a location for a *Real World* house?

a. Dallas

b. Reno

c. Houston

d. New Orleans

21. Which of these reality stars is *not* a doctor in real life?

a. *Survivor*'s Dr. Sean Kenniff

b. *The Bachelor*'s Dr. Andrew Baldwin

c. *The Surreal Life*'s Dr. Flo

d. *Big Brother*'s Dr. Will Kirby

22. Which competitor on ABC's *Dancing with the Stars* hosted Animal Planet's *Pet Star*?

a. Mario Lopez

b. Leeza Gibbons

c. John O'Hurley

d. Lisa Rinna

23. Which of these celebrities has *not* had a motorcycle built for them by the Teutuls on *American Chopper*?

a. Billy Joel

b. Jay Leno

c. Lance Armstrong

d. Peter Fonda

24. Which *So You Think You Can Dance* alum had a dancing part in Christina Aguilera's video for "Candyman"?

a. Nick Lazzarini

b. Benji Schwimmer

c. Travis Wall

d. Blake McGrath

25. Introduced in Season 10, which *Amazing Race* feature forces teams to pair up and work together in a task?

a. Yield

b. Intersection

c. Crossroads

d. Merge

THE REALITY CATCHPHRASE QUIZ

Name the reality series that produced each of these catchphrases.

1. "You just don't fit in."
2. "You're out of style."
3. "Pack your knives and go."
4. "See ya later, decorator."
5. "You're fired!"
6. "The tribe has spoken."
7. "Auf wiedersehen."
8. "I know I'm funnier than . . ."
9. "Soul Patrol!"
10. "Party is over."
11. "Bus driver? Move that bus!"
12. "That's hot!"
13. "Fear is not a factor for you."
14. "Your time is up."
15. "Don't call us, we'll call you."
16. "I'm sorry to say you're the last to arrive."

ANSWERS

The Ultimate Reality TV Quiz

1. D: Clay Jordon (Season 5 *Survivor* Runner-up)
2. B: Sex-E
3. A: *Star Search*
4. C: Andy Dick
5. A: Boy Scoutmaster
6. C: Kelly Wiglesworth
7. C: a bunch of crabs
8. D: *I'm a Celebrity, Get Me Out of Here!*
9. A: *Hell's Kitchen*
10. D: Eve Plumb
11. B: *Punk'd*
12. B: Anna's dog
13. D: Steven Spielberg (He just opened the doors of Dreamworks to the winner, Will Bigham.)
14. A: Kennedy
15. D: *Temptation Island*
16. A: Justin and Allison
17. A: Malibu, California

18. C: Lisa Keiffer
19. B: Kurt Nilsen
20. D: New Orleans
21. C: Dr. Flo (Florence Henderson in *The Surreal Life*)
22. A: Mario Lopez
23. D: Peter Fonda
24. B: Benji Schwimmer
25. B: Intersection

The Reality Catchphrase Quiz

1. *The Apprentice: Martha Stewart*
2. *The Cut*
3. *Top Chef*
4. *Top Design*
5. *The Apprentice*
6. *Survivor*
7. *Project Runway*
8. *Last Comic Standing*
9. *American Idol*
10. *The Entertainer*
11. *Extreme Makeover: Home Edition*
12. *The Simple Life*
13. *Fear Factor*
14. *Flavor of Love*
15. *The Starlet*
16. *The Amazing Race*

TOP TEN NETWORK PRIMETIME REALITY SHOWS, BY SEASON

BASED ON VIEWERSHIP, 2000-2007

2006–2007 Season

1. *American Idol*: Wednesday (FOX)—30.0 million
2. *American Idol*: Tuesday (FOX)—29.5 million
3. *Dancing with the Stars 4*: Performance (ABC)—20.5 million
4. *Dancing with the Stars 3*: Performance (ABC)—19.6 million
5. *Dancing with the Stars 4*: Results (ABC)—19.3 million
6. *Dancing with the Stars 3*: Results (ABC)—18.1 million
7. *Survivor: Cook Islands* (CBS)—15.4 million
8. *Survivor: Fiji* (CBS)—14.2 million
9. *Extreme Makeover: Home Edition* (ABC)—13.8 million
10. *America's Got Talent* (NBC)—11.7 million

2005–2006 Season

1. *American Idol*: Tuesday (FOX)—31.0 million
2. *American Idol*: Wednesday (FOX)—30.0 million
3. *Dancing with the Stars*: Performance (ABC)—18.8 million
4. *Survivor: Guatemala* (CBS)—18.3 million
5. *Survivor Panama—Exile Island* (CBS)—16.6 million

6. *Dancing with the Stars*: Results (ABC)—14.8 million
7. *Unanimous* (FOX)—13.8 million
8. *Extreme Makeover: Home Edition* (ABC)—12.2 million
9. *Skating with Celebrities* (FOX)—11.4 million
10. *The Apprentice 4* (NBC)—11.0 million

2004–2005 Season

1. *American Idol*: Tuesday (FOX)—27.3 million
2. *American Idol*: Wednesday (FOX)—26.1 million
3. *Survivor: Palau* (CBS)—20.9 million
4. *Survivor: Vanuatu* (CBS)—19.6 million
5. *Dancing with the Stars* (ABC)—16.8 million
6. *The Apprentice 2* (NBC)—15.9 million
7. *The Apprentice 3* (NBC)—14.0 million
8. *The Amazing Race 7* (CBS)—13.0 million
9. *Extreme Makeover: Home Edition* (ABC)—12.9 million
10. *The Amazing Race 6* (CBS)—11.5 million

2003–2004 Season

1. *American Idol*: Tuesday (FOX)—25.7 million
2. *American Idol*: Wednesday (FOX)—24.3 million
3. *Survivor: All-Stars* (CBS)—21.5 million
4. *Survivor: Pearl Islands* (CBS)—20.7 million
5. *The Apprentice* (NBC)—20.7 million
6. *My Big Fat Obnoxious Fiancé* (FOX)—16.6 million
7. *Average Joe* (NBC)—12.6 million
8. *The Bachelor* (ABC)—12.5 million
9. *Fear Factor* (NBC)—12.4 million
10. *The Simple Life*: Wednesday (FOX)—11.6 million

2002–2003 Season

1. *Joe Millionaire* (FOX)—22.9 million
2. *American Idol*: Wednesday (FOX)—21.2 million

3. *American Idol*: Tuesday (FOX)—21.6 million
4. *Survivor: Thailand* (CBS)—21.2 million
5. *Survivor: Amazon* (CBS)—20.0 million
6. *The Bachelorette* (ABC)—16.7 million
7. *The Bachelor* (ABC)—14.5 million
8. *Fear Factor* (NBC)—11.6 million
9. *Celebrity Mole: Hawaii* (ABC)—11.0 million
10. *Star Search*: Wednesday (CBS)—10.8 million

2001–2002 Season

1. *Survivor: Marquesas* (CBS)—20.8 million
2. *Survivor: Africa* (CBS)—20.7 million
3. *American Idol*: Wednesday (FOX)—13.6 million
4. *American Idol*: Tuesday (FOX)—12.1 million
5. *Fear Factor* (NBC)—11.4 million
6. *The Bachelor* (ABC)—10.8 million
7. *Meet My Folks* (NBC)—10.7 million
8. *The Amazing Race 2* (CBS)—10.3 million
9. *Big Brother*: Wednesday (CBS)—9.7 million
10. *Big Brother*: Thursday (CBS)—9.6 million

2000–2001 Season

1. *Survivor: The Australian Outback* (CBS)—29.8 million
2. *Temptation Island* (FOX)—16.6 million
3. *The Mole* (ABC)—12.6 million
4. *Fear Factor* (NBC)—12.0 million
5. *Boot Camp* (FOX)—11.0 million
6. *Big Brother*: Thursday (CBS)—9.6 million
7. *Big Brother*: Tuesday (CBS)—9.2 million
8. *Spy TV* (NBC)—8.8 million
9. *World's Most Amazing Videos* (NBC)—8.8 million
10. *America's Most Wanted* (FOX)—8.4 million

The 59th Annual Emmy Awards (2007)

OUTSTANDING REALITY COMPETITION SERIES

The Amazing Race (Winner)

American Idol

Dancing with the Stars

Project Runway

Top Chef

OUTSTANDING REALITY PROGRAM

Kathy Griffin: My Life on the D-List (Winner)

Extreme Makeover: Home Edition

Antiques Roadshow

The Dog Whisperer

Penn & Teller: Bullshit!

The 58th Annual Emmy Awards (2006)

OUTSTANDING REALITY COMPETITION SERIES

The Amazing Race (Winner)

American Idol

Dancing with the Stars
Project Runway
Survivor

OUTSTANDING REALITY PROGRAM
Extreme Makeover: Home Edition (Winner)
Antiques Roadshow
The Dog Whisperer
Kathy Griffin: My Life on the D-List
Penn & Teller: Bullshit!

The 57th Annual Emmy Awards (2005)
OUTSTANDING REALITY COMPETITION SERIES
The Amazing Race (Winner)
American Idol
The Apprentice
Project Runway
Survivor

OUTSTANDING REALITY PROGRAM
Extreme Makeover: Home Edition (Winner)
Antiques Roadshow
Penn & Teller: Bullshit!
Project Greenlight
Queer Eye for the Straight Guy

OUTSTANDING DIRECTION FOR NONFICTION PROGRAMMING
Death in Gaza (Winner)
American Idol
The Apprentice
Extreme Makeover: Home Edition
Unforgivable Blackness: The Rise and Fall of Jack Johnson

The 56th Annual Emmy Awards (2004)
OUTSTANDING REALITY COMPETITION SERIES
The Amazing Race (Winner)

American Idol
The Apprentice
Last Comic Standing
Survivor

OUTSTANDING REALITY PROGRAM
Queer Eye for the Straight Guy (Winner)
Colonial House
Extreme Makeover: Home Edition
Penn & Teller: Bullshit!
Project Greenlight 2

The 55th Annual Emmy Awards (2003)
OUTSTANDING REALITY COMPETITION PROGRAM
The Amazing Race (Winner)
American Idol
Survivor
AFI's 100 Years . . . 100 Passions: America's Greatest Love Stories
100 Years of Hope And Humor

OUTSTANDING NONFICTION PROGRAM (ALTERNATIVE)
Cirque Du Soleil: Fire Within (Winner)
Antiques Roadshow
Da Ali G Show
The Osbournes
Trading Spaces

OUTSTANDING DIRECTING FOR NONFICTION PROGRAMMING
American Experience (Winner)
American Idol
Da Ali G Show
James Cameron's Expedition: Bismarck
Journeys with George
Unchained Memories: Readings from the Slave Narratives

The 54th Annual Emmy Awards (2002)
OUTSTANDING NONFICTION PROGRAM (REALITY)
The Osbournes (Winner)

American High

Frontier House

Project Greenlight

Taxicab Confessions

Trauma: Life in the ER

OUTSTANDING SPECIAL CLASS PROGRAM
The West Wing: Documentary Special (Winner)

AFI's 100 Years . . . 100 Thrills: America's Most Heart-Pounding Movies

I Love Lucy 50th Anniversary Special

Survivor

Trading Spaces

THE 53RD ANNUAL EMMY AWARDS (2001)
NONFICTION PROGRAM (REALITY)
American High (Winner)

The Awful Truth with Michael Moore (Bravo)

The E! True Hollywood Story (E!)

Taxicab Confessions (HBO)

Trauma: Life in the ER (TLC)

NONFICTION PROGRAM (SPECIAL CLASS)
Survivor (CBS) (Winner)

Bands on the Run (VH1)

Eco-Challenge: Borneo (USA)

Junkyard Wars (TLC)

Road Rules: Maximum Velocity Tour (MTV)

THE REALITY TIME LINE
PREMIERE DATES FOR MODERN REALITY SHOWS, BEGINNING MARCH 11, 1989

PREMIERE DATE	SHOW TITLE
March 11, 1989	COPS
January 14, 1990	America's Funniest Home Videos
September 1, 1990	America's Funniest People
May 21, 1992	The Real World (Season 1—New York)
August 16, 1992	I Witness Video
June 26, 1993	The Real World (Season 2—Los Angeles)
July 28, 1993	Street Match
June 23, 1994	The Real World (Season 3—San Francisco)
June 28, 1995	The Real World (Season 4—London)
July 19, 1995	Road Rules
June 18, 1996	Buzzkill
July 10, 1996	The Real World (Season 5—Miami)
July 15, 1997	The Real World (Season 6—Boston)
August 1, 1997	Ordinary/Extraordinary
September 28, 1997	The Real World/Road Rules Challenge
June 10, 1998	The Real World (Season 7—Seattle)
July 6, 1998	MTV's FANatic

PREMIERE DATE	SHOW TITLE
September 13, 1998	Junkyard Wars
October 1, 1998	Great Pretenders
March 8, 1999	Redhanded
June 8, 1999	The Real World (Season 8—Hawaii)
August 23, 1999	Destination Stardom
March 24, 2000	Making the Band
May 31, 2000	Survivor (Season 1)
June 8, 2000	The Real World (Season 9—New Orleans)
July 5, 2000	Big Brother (Season 1)
August 2, 2000	American High
January 9, 2001	The Mole
January 10, 2001	Temptation Island (Season 1)
January 12, 2001	Popstars
January 28, 2001	Survivor: The Australian Outback (Season 2)
February 18, 2001	Fear
March 23, 2001	Chains of Love
March 28, 2001	Boot Camp
April 1, 2001	Bands on the Run
June 11, 2001	Fear Factor
June 21, 2001	Spy TV
June 21, 2001	WWE Tough Enough
July 3, 2001	The Real World (Season 10—Back to New York)
July 5, 2001	Big Brother 2
July 24, 2001	Murder in Small Town X
August 3, 2001	Manhunt
August 6, 2001	Flipped
August 27, 2001	Shipmates
September 5, 2001	The Amazing Race (Season 1)
September 5, 2001	Lost
September 9, 2001	Ed McMahon's Next Big Star
September 13, 2001	Sledgehammer
September 25, 2001	Love Cruise

PREMIERE DATE	SHOW TITLE
October 4, 2001	Survivor: Africa (Season 3)
October 11, 2001	Ultimate Reality
November 7, 2001	Temptation Island (Season 2)
December 12, 2001	Project Greenlight
January 6, 2002	The It Factor
January 8, 2002	The Real World (Season 11—Chicago)
January 13, 2002	The Jamie Kennedy Experiment
January 16, 2002	Combat Missions
January 21, 2002	Vegas Showgirls: Nearly Famous
February 28, 2002	Survivor: Marquesas (Season 4)
March 3, 2002	No Boundaries
March 5, 2002	The Osbournes (Season 1)
March 11, 2002	The Amazing Race (Season 2)
March 22, 2002	Under One Roof
March 25, 2002	The Bachelor (Season 1)
April 6, 2002	Taildaters
April 29, 2002	Frontier House
June 2, 2002	Looking for Love: Bachelorettes in Alaska
June 11, 2002	American Idol (Season 1)
June 18, 2002	Houston Medical
June 23, 2002	Monster Garage
June 24, 2002	Sorority Life
July 6, 2002	While You Were Out
July 10, 2002	Big Brother 3
July 12, 2002	Invasion of the Hidden Cameras
July 17, 2002	30 Seconds to Fame
July 17, 2002	Meet the Marks
July 22, 2002	Meet My Folks
July 29, 2002	EXTreme Dating
August 3, 2002	Made
August 4, 2002	The Anna Nicole Show
August 11, 2002	The Last Resort

PREMIERE DATE	SHOW TITLE
September 8, 2002	The Real World (Season 12—Las Vegas)
September 9, 2002	Survivor: Thailand (Season 5)
September 17, 2002	Beg, Borrow, & Deal
September 25, 2002	The Bachelor (Season 2)
October 2, 2002	The Amazing Race (Season 3)
October 5, 2002	Endurance
October 18, 2002	Music Behind Bars
October 19, 2002	Making the Band 2
November 5, 2002	The Osbournes (Season 2)
December 15, 2002	Star Dates
January 5, 2003	High School Reunion
January 6, 2003	Joe Millionaire (Season 1)
January 8, 2003	The Bachelorette (Season 1)
January 8, 2003	Celebrity Mole
January 8, 2003	Star Search
January 9, 2003	The Surreal Life
January 20, 2003	My Life as a Sitcom
January 21, 2003	American Idol (Season 2)
January 27, 2003	Bridezillas
January 31, 2003	Pet Star
February 13, 2003	Are You Hot? The Search for America's Sexiest People
February 13, 2003	Survivor: Amazon (Season 6)
February 19, 2003	I'm a Celebrity, Get Me Out of Here!
February 21, 2003	Family Business
February 26, 2003	Fraternity Life
March 1, 2003	America's Most Talented Kid
March 3, 2003	Married by America
March 4, 2003	The Family
March 8, 2003	Nashville Star
March 12, 2003	All-American Girl
March 26, 2003	The Bachelor (Season 2)

PREMIERE DATE	SHOW TITLE
March 29, 2003	MTV's Burned
March 31, 2003	American Chopper
April 1, 2003	Mr. Personality
April 4, 2003	Scare Tactics
April 11, 2003	Love U
April 23, 2003	Extreme Makeover
April 28, 2003	Born to Diva
May 10, 2003	What Not to Wear
May 17, 2003	Trading Spaces: Boys vs. Girls
May 20, 2003	America's Next Top Model (Cycle 1)
May 22, 2003	Food Fight
May 24, 2003	For Better or for Worse
May 26, 2003	Switched
May 28, 2003	Fame
May 29, 2003	The Amazing Race (Season 4)
May 29, 2003	Stupid Behavior Caught on Tape
June 2, 2003	For Love or Money
June 2, 2003	Monster House
June 3, 2003	American Juniors
June 3, 2003	The Real World (Season 13—Paris)
June 6, 2003	Ride with Funkmaster Flex
June 10, 2003	Last Comic Standing
June 15, 2003	Chuck Woolery: Naturally Stoned
June 16, 2003	Anything for Love
June 18, 2003	Paradise Hotel
June 25, 2003	The Dating Experiment
June 27, 2003	Hitchhiker's Chronicles
July 6, 2003	Trading Spaces: Family
July 8, 2003	Big Brother 4
July 9, 2003	Cupid
July 13, 2003	Dance Fever
July 14, 2003	Who Wants to Marry My Dad?

PREMIERE DATE	SHOW TITLE
July 15, 2003	Queer Eye for the Straight Guy
July 20, 2003	The Restaurant
July 23, 2003	Blow Out (Season 1)
July 27, 2003	Perfect Match: New York
July 28, 2003	Temptation Island (Season 3)
July 29, 2003	Boy Meets Boy
July 30, 2003	Race to the Altar
August 6, 2003	Dog: The Bounty Hunter
August 6, 2003	The Real Roseanne Show
August 19, 2003	Newlyweds: Nick & Jessica
August 26, 2003	Performing As . . .
August 31, 2003	Freshman Diaries
September 2, 2003	The Joe Schmo Show
September 3, 2003	Starting Over
September 8, 2003	Resident Life
September 13, 2003	Steve Harvey's Big Time Challenge
September 13, 2003	Clean Sweep
September 18, 2003	Survivor: Pearl Islands (Season 7)
September 20, 2003	Date Patrol
September 23, 2003	Ambush Makeover
September 24, 2003	The Bachelor (Season 4)
October 3, 2003	Get Packing
October 3, 2003	Merge
October 5, 2003	Surviving Nugent
October 6, 2003	Knock First
October 10, 2003	House Rules
October 13, 2003	King of the Jungle
October 20, 2003	Joe Millionaire (Season 2)
October 28, 2003	Rich Girls
November 3, 2003	Average Joe
November 14, 2003	Interscope Presents: the Next Episode
December 2, 2003	The Simple Life (Season 1)

PREMIERE DATE	SHOW TITLE
January 3, 2004	America's Next Top Model (Cycle 2)
January 5, 2004	Airline
January 6, 2004	The Real World (Season 14—San Diego)
January 8, 2004	The Apprentice (Season 1)
January 9, 2004	Totally Outrageous Behavior
January 9, 2004	The World's Craziest Videos
January 14, 2004	The Bachelorette (Season 2)
January 16, 2004	Cowboy U
January 16, 2004	How Do I Look?
January 19, 2004	American Idol (Season 3)
January 19, 2004	Bands on the Run
January 19, 2004	My Big Fat Obnoxious Fiancé
January 21, 2004	'Til Death Do Us Part: Carmen & Dave
January 21, 2004	Todd TV
January 27, 2004	The Osbournes (Season 3)
January 28, 2004	College Hill
February 1, 2004	I Want a Famous Face
February 1, 2004	Survivor: All-Stars (Season 8)
February 2, 2004	In a Fix
February 14, 2004	Head 2 Toe
February 15, 2004	Extreme Makeover: Home Edition
February 17, 2004	Room Raiders
February 23, 2004	Straight Plan for the Gay Man
February 24, 2004	Crash Test
February 24, 2004	Dream Job
March 1, 2004	Forever Eden
March 4, 2004	Mad Mad House
March 4, 2004	Pimp My Ride
March 12, 2004	Playing It Straight
March 17, 2004	Fake-A-Date
March 17, 2004	Family Bonds
April 7, 2004	The Bachelor (Season 5)

PREMIERE DATE	SHOW TITLE
April 7, 2004	The Swan
April 13, 2004	Showbiz Moms and Dads
April 14, 2004	I'm Still Alive!
April 16, 2004	Nice Package
April 19, 2004	Family Plots
May 7, 2004	Colonial House
May 17, 2004	Superstar USA
May 24, 2004	Faking the Video
June 2, 2004	The Ultimate Love Test
June 8, 2004	Blow Out (Season 2)
June 13, 2004	Scream Play
June 14, 2004	Next Action Star
June 16, 2004	The Ashlee Simpson Show
June 16, 2004	The Simple Life 2: Road Trip
June 18, 2004	Vegas Weddings Unveiled
June 22, 2004	Live Like a Star
June 22, 2004	Outback Jack
July 2, 2004	Wanna Come In?
July 6, 2004	The Amazing Race (Season 5)
July 6, 2004	Big Brother 5
July 10, 2004	Skunked TV
July 11, 2004	Dr. 90210
July 12, 2004	The Assistant
July 20, 2004	Things I Hate About You
July 20, 2004	Trading Spouses: Meet Your New Mommy
July 22, 2004	Studio 7
July 23, 2004	Dr. G: Medical Examiner
July 28, 2004	Amish in the City
August 1, 2004	American Candidate
August 2, 2004	Growing Up Gotti
August 3, 2004	The Player
August 30, 2004	The Complex: Malibu

PREMIERE DATE	SHOW TITLE
September 1, 2004	Renovate My Family
September 5, 2004	In Search of the Partridge Family
September 6, 2004	How Clean Is Your House?
September 7, 2004	The Next Great Champ
September 7, 2004	The Real World (Season 15—Philadelphia)
September 9, 2004	The Apprentice (Season 2)
September 10, 2004	Film School
September 13, 2004	The Benefactor
September 13, 2004	The Dog Whisperer
September 13, 2004	Home Delivery
September 16, 2004	Survivor: Vanuatu—Islands of Fire (Season 9)
September 22, 2004	America's Next Top Model (Cycle 3)
September 22, 2004	The Bachelor (Season 6)
September 26, 2004	Wife Swap
September 28, 2004	I'd Do Anything
September 28, 2004	Laguna Beach: The Real O.C.
September 28, 2004	Wing Nuts
October 2, 2004	The Mansion
October 3, 2004	Cold Turkey
October 3, 2004	No Opportunity Wasted
October 4, 2004	Model Citizens
October 13, 2004	Manhunt: The Search for America's Most Gorgeous Male
October 16, 2004	I Wanna Be a Soap Star
October 19, 2004	The Biggest Loser
October 19, 2004	He's a Lady
October 25, 2004	Battle for Ozzfest
October 26, 2004	Motormouth
November 3, 2004	Nanny 911
November 3, 2004	The Real Gilligan's Island
November 3, 2004	Regency House Party
November 7, 2004	My Big Fat Obnoxious Boss

PREMIERE DATE	SHOW TITLE
November 9, 2004	I Hate My Job
November 9, 2004	The Rebel Billionaire
November 10, 2004	The Club
November 10, 2004	Film Fakers
November 11, 2004	Wildboyz
November 15, 2004	Date My Mom
November 16, 2004	The Amazing Race (Season 6)
November 22, 2004	The $25 Million Hoax
November 23, 2004	Trista and Ryan's Wedding
November 28, 2004	Love Is in the Heir
December 1, 2004	Project Runway (Season 1)
December 3, 2004	Best Friend's Date
December 15, 2004	Big Man on Campus
January 1, 2005	My Super Sweet 16
January 5, 2005	The Road to Stardom with Missy Elliott
January 5, 2005	Sports Illustrated Swimsuit Model Search
January 6, 2005	Wickedly Perfect
January 8, 2005	The Will
January 9, 2005	Celebrity Fit Club
January 9, 2005	Strange Love
January 10, 2005	American Dream Derby
January 10, 2005	The Bachelorette (Season 3)
January 10, 2005	Caesars 24/7
January 11, 2005	Queer Eye for the Straight Girl
January 16, 2005	Iron Chef America
January 17, 2005	The Osbournes (Season 4)
January 17, 2005	Supernanny
January 17, 2005	The Ultimate Fighter
January 18, 2005	American Idol (Season 4)
January 20, 2005	The Apprentice (Season 3)
January 22, 2005	Town Haul
January 23, 2005	The Entertainer

PREMIERE DATE	SHOW TITLE
January 26, 2005	The Simple Life: Interns (Season 3)
January 8, 2005	The Will
February 1, 2005	Gastineau Girls
February 17, 2005	Survivor: Palau (Season 10)
February 26, 2005	Carpocalypse
March 1, 2005	The Amazing Race (Season 7)
March 2, 2005	America's Next Top Model (Cycle 4)
March 3, 2005	Making the Band 3
March 6, 2005	Damage Control
March 6, 2005	Intervention
March 6, 2005	The Starlet
March 7, 2005	The Contender
March 8, 2005	Lie Detector
March 10, 2005	Ultimate Fuse Gig: The VJ Search
March 14, 2005	Mr. Romance
March 21, 2005	Las Vegas Garden of Love
March 23, 2005	Chasing Farrah
March 28, 2005	The Bachelor (Season 7)
March 29, 2005	Invasion Iowa
March 30, 2005	Showdogs Moms and Dads
April 1, 2005	I Married a Princess
April 5, 2005	Knievel's Wild Ride
April 6, 2005	Meet the Barkers
April 7, 2005	Forty Deuce
April 12, 2005	Deadliest Catch
April 15, 2005	Sheer Dallas
April 18, 2005	Xtreme Fakeovers
April 24, 2005	Making It Big
April 27, 2005	Cooking Under Fire
May 15, 2005	BSTV
May 17, 2005	Britney and Kevin: Chaotic
May 28, 2005	Strip Search

PREMIERE DATE	SHOW TITLE
May 29, 2005	Kept
May 30, 2005	Hell's Kitchen
June 1, 2005	Beauty and the Geek
June 1, 2005	Dancing with the Stars (Season 1)
June 1, 2005	Sports Kids Moms & Dads
June 2, 2005	Hit Me Baby One More Time
June 5, 2005	Fight for Fame
June 5, 2005	The Next Food Network Star
June 6, 2005	The Scholar
June 7, 2005	Fire Me, Please!
June 9, 2005	The Cut
June 10, 2005	30 Days
June 14, 2005	Filthy Rich: Cattle Drive
June 15, 2005	The Casino
June 15, 2005	Party at the Palms
June 21, 2005	I Want to Be a Hilton
June 21, 2005	The Real World (Season 16—Austin)
June 30, 2005	Being Bobby Brown
July 5, 2005	MTV's The 70s House
July 7, 2005	Big Brother 6
July 10, 2005	Hogan Knows Best
July 10, 2005	Minding the Store
July 10, 2005	The Princes of Malibu
July 11, 2005	Rock Star: INXS
July 13, 2005	Brat Camp
July 14, 2005	Hooking Up
July 19, 2005	Miami Ink
July 20, 2005	Inked
July 20, 2005	So You Think You Can Dance
July 20, 2005	Venus and Serena: For Real
July 20, 2005	Criss Angel: Mindfreak
July 22, 2005	Super Agent

PREMIERE DATE	SHOW TITLE
July 25, 2005	Kill Reality
July 26, 2005	Situation: Comedy
July 27, 2005	R U the Girl with T-Boz and Chilli
July 28, 2005	The Law Firm
August 2, 2005	Meet Mister Mom
August 3, 2005	Kathy Griffin: My Life on the D-List
August 3, 2005	Trailer Fabulous
August 7, 2005	American Princess
August 7, 2005	The Girls Next Door
August 12, 2005	Hi-Jinks
August 16, 2005	Tommy Lee Goes to College
August 17, 2005	Battle of the Network Reality Stars
August 18, 2005	Hidden Howie
August 19, 2005	Gene Simmons' Rock School
August 22, 2005	Open Bar
September 1, 2005	My Own
September 6, 2005	Kicked Out
September 11, 2005	Breaking Bonaduce
September 11, 2005	My Fair Brady
September 13, 2005	The Reality Show
September 14, 2005	Made in the USA
September 15, 2005	Survivor: Guatemala (Season 11)
September 21, 2005	America's Next Top Model (Cycle 5)
September 22, 2005	The Apprentice (Season 4)
September 23, 2005	Three Wishes
September 27, 2005	The Amazing Race: Family Edition (Season 8)
October 13, 2005	Run's House
October 17, 2005	Miss Seventeen
October 22, 2005	Tuckerville
October 30, 2005	But Can They Sing?
October 30, 2005	Homewrecker

PREMIERE DATE	SHOW TITLE
November 5, 2005	Wanted: Ted or Alive
December 6, 2005	Daisy Does America
December 6, 2005	Party Party
December 7, 2005	Project Runway (Season 2)
January 2, 2006	Rollergirls
January 4, 2006	There & Back: Ashley Parker Angel
January 5, 2006	Dancing with the Stars (Season 2)
January 5, 2006	Dallas: SWAT
January 9, 2006	The Bachelor: Paris (Season 8)
January 17, 2006	American Idol (Season 5)
January 18, 2006	Skating with Celebrities
January 22, 2006	#1 Single
February 2, 2006	Survivor: Panama—Exile Island (Season 12)
February 6, 2006	Parental Control
February 7, 2006	Get This Party Started
February 11, 2006	Style Me
February 27, 2006	The Apprentice (Season 5)
February 28, 2006	The Amazing Race (Season 9)
February 28, 2006	The Real World (Season 17—Key West)
March 1, 2006	America's Next Top Model (Cycle 6)
March 2, 2006	The Shop
March 4, 2006	Little People, Big World
March 6, 2006	Miracle Workers
March 7, 2006	8th & Ocean
March 8, 2006	Top Chef
March 12, 2006	Face the Family
March 16, 2006	American Inventor
March 21, 2006	Real Housewives of Orange County
March 22, 2006	Unan1mous
March 31, 2006	Survival of the Richest
April 4, 2006	King of Cars
April 7, 2006	Can't Get a Date

PREMIERE DATE	SHOW TITLE
April 9, 2006	Shalom in the Home
April 10, 2006	Tiara Girls
April 16, 2006	God or the Girl
April 17, 2006	Celebrity Cooking Showdown
April 27, 2006	Season of the Tiger
May 6, 2006	Pros vs. Joes
May 21, 2006	Cheyenne
May 21, 2006	Supergroup
May 31, 2006	The Hills
June 4, 2006	The Simple Life: 'Til Death Do Us Part (Season 4)
June 4, 2006	Why Can't I Be You?
June 5, 2006	Fast, Inc.
June 5, 2006	Solitary
June 6, 2006	The Dudesons
June 6, 2006	The Janice Dickinson Modeling Agency
June 12, 2006	How to Get the Guy
June 13, 2006	Tuesday Night Book Club
June 16, 2006	Blowin' Up
June 18, 2006	Treasure Hunters
June 21, 2006	America's Got Talent
June 21, 2006	Big Brother: All-Stars (Season 7)
June 21, 2006	America's Got Talent
June 22, 2006	Master of Champions
July 5, 2006	Rock Star: Supernova
July 6, 2006	Raising the Roofs
July 12, 2006	Project Runway (Season 3)
July 17, 2006	Driving Force
July 18, 2006	The One: The Making of a Music Star
July 19, 2006	Work Out
July 23, 2006	HGTV Design Star
July 23, 2006	The Messengers
July 27, 2006	Who Wants to be a Superhero?

PREMIERE DATE	SHOW TITLE
July 31, 2006	One Ocean View
August 6, 2006	Flavor of Love
August 7, 2006	Fight Girls
August 7, 2006	Gene Simmons Family Jewels
August 17, 2006	Ace of Cakes
August 22, 2006	Breaking Up with Shannen Doherty
August 23, 2006	Two-a-Days
August 28, 2006	Celebrity Duets
August 29, 2006	Million Dollar Listing
September 12, 2006	Dancing with the Stars (Season 3)
September 14, 2006	Survivor: Cook Islands (Season 13)
September 17, 2006	The Amazing Race (Season 10)
September 18, 2006	MTV's Little Talent Show
September 20, 2006	America's Next Top Model (Cycle 7)
September 26, 2006	Dallas Cowboy Cheerleaders: Making the Team
October 3, 2006	The Bachelor: Rome (Season 9)
October 9, 2006	Off the Leash
October 11, 2006	Hair Trauma
October 20, 2006	Ice-T's Rap School
October 22, 2006	Celebrity Paranormal Project
November 10, 2006	Man vs. Wild
November 22, 2006	The Real World (Season 18—Denver)
November 22, 2006	Corkscrewed: The Wrath of Grapes
December 3, 2006	Exposed
December 6, 2006	Bad Girls Club
December 6, 2006	Dirty Dancing; Living the Dream
December 6, 2006	Twentyfourseven
January 7, 2007	Grease: You're the One That I Want
January 7, 2007	I'm From Rolling Stone
January 7, 2007	Shooting Sizemore
January 8, 2007	Ego Trip's The (White) Rapper Show

PREMIERE DATE	SHOW TITLE
January 8, 2007	I Love New York
January 10, 2007	Armed and Famous
January 11, 2007	Rob & Amber: Against the Odds
January 15, 2007	Dancelife
January 16, 2007	American Idol (Season 6)
January 17, 2007	The Apprentice: Los Angeles (Season 6)
January 17, 2007	Maui Fever
January 24, 2007	Dinner: Impossible
January 30, 2007	Bam's Unholy Union
January 31, 2007	Top Design
February 1, 2007	Juvies
February 18, 2007	The Amazing Race: All-Stars (Season 11)
February 20, 2007	The Agency
February 28, 2007	America's Next Top Model (Cycle 8)
February 28, 2007	Survivor: Fiji (Season 14)
March 4, 2007	Dice: Undisputed
March 6, 2007	The Pussycat Dolls Present: The Search for the Next Doll
March 13, 2007	Bullrun
March 19, 2007	Dancing with the Stars (Season 4)
March 20, 2007	Tori & Dean: Inn Love
March 27, 2007	The Great American Dream Vote
April 1, 2007	Sons of Hollywood
April 2, 2007	The Bachelor: An Officer and a Gentleman (Season 10)
April 5, 2007	Adventures in Hollywood
April 7, 2007	America's Cutest Pup
April 7, 2007	Taquita and Kaui
April 11, 2007	Shear Genius
April 15, 2007	Flavor of Love Girls: Charm School
April 15, 2007	The Springer Hustle

PREMIERE DATE	SHOW TITLE
April 17, 2007	Living Lahaina
April 20, 2007	Wife, Mom, Bounty Hunter
April 21, 2007	Katie & Peter
May 22, 2007	On the Lot
May 23, 2007	America's Top Cowboy
May 24, 2007	The Academy
May 28, 2007	The Ex-Wives Club
May 28, 2007	The Simple Life Goes to Camp (Season 5)
May 28, 2007	Sunset Tan
May 30, 2007	The Next Best Thing
May 31, 2007	Pirate Master
June 6, 2007	The X Effect
June 11, 2007	Making News: Texas Style
June 17, 2007	Ice Road Truckers
June 18, 2007	Age of Love
June 28, 2007	Hey Paula
July 5, 2007	Big Brother 8
July 9, 2007	Hell Date
July 10, 2007	Baldwin Hills
July 13, 2007	A Model Life with Petra Nemcova
July 15, 2007	Rock of Love
July 17, 2007	Just for Laughs
July 17, 2007	Room 401
July 18, 2007	Back to the Grind
July 21, 2007	She's Moving In
July 25, 2007	S.O.B. (Socially Offensive Behavior)
July 26, 2007	Welcome to the Parker
July 29, 2007	The Two Coreys
July 31, 2007	Flipping Out
July 31, 2007	Murder
August 1, 2007	The Fashionista Diaries
August 6, 2007	Fat March

PREMIERE DATE	SHOW TITLE
August 6, 2007	Mission: Man Band
August 7, 2007	LA Ink
August 10, 2007	Celebrity Bull Riding
August 13, 2007	Newport Harbor
August 18, 2007	America's Next Top Producer
August 21, 2007	Anchorwoman